Living in the Light

Living in the Light

Byron Edwards

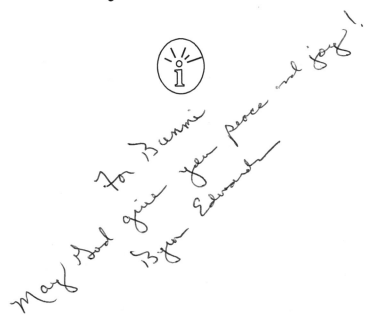

For Bunni

May God give you peace and joy!

Byron Edwards

Living in the Light

© Byron Edwards 2022
Front cover photo of sculpture -- Sandy Campbell
Back cover photo of author -- Dreama Stephenson
Book Trailer -- Steph Carse
Front cover design -- Mark Fleming
Front cover sculpture of the Holy Trinity -- Byron Edwards

This book is a work of fiction. Named locations are used fictitiously, and characters and incidents are the product of the author's imagination. Any resemblance to actual events or places or persons, living or dead, is entirely coincidental.

Scripture taken from the Holy Bible, New International Version ®, Copyright © 1973, 1978, 1984 by International Bible Society. Used by permission of Zondervan. All rights reserved.

Published by
Lighthouse Christian Publishing
SAN 257-4330
228 Freedom Parkway
Hoschton, GA 30548
United States of America

www.lighthousechristianpublishing.com

In Dedication and In Memory

Several of the conversations that take place in this story also took place between close friends and myself. Their souls have since left this earthly existence. These three people were special to me; and, I miss them and the deep discussions we had as we solved all the world's problems.
They were true friends.

I wish to dedicate this book to and in honor of the memories I have of:

Bruce Anderson Cannady – Died January 15, 2017 (68)
I had known Bruce since 1963 – 54 years.

Bruce Edward Clary – Died December 17, 2019   (89)
I had known Bruce since 1979 – 40 years.

James Earl Hayes – Died February 2, 2015   (71)
I had known Earl since 1993 – 22 years.

Byron Edwards 2020

THANK YOU!

It would be extremely difficult for any author today to be able to write a book in total isolation and without any help at all. Often, I've found that people will make a statement or ask a question and that, by itself, will trigger a thought in my mind that I will use in a book. The person didn't even realize that they were helping me. However, I appreciate it. Many people have simply been so encouraging. For this story, *Living in the Light,* I thank several people for their assistance.

First, I want to thank my best friend who is also my wife. Vivian, your love is the best. Without you even being aware, it often provides support and inspiration. I do love you. Always. KK, HH. Others I wish to alphabetically acknowledge for their supportive encouragement include Jean Chetley (deceased), Bob Clarke, Mike Finn, Bob Harper, Lt. Col. Timothy O'Leary (retired), Pastor Herb Mays, Jane Allen McKinney, Russell Melton, Dr. Roy Reynolds, Richard Salcido and Mary Ann Willis Wilson.

PROLOGUE

This is a story about the most powerful force in the universe – love. Iron spikes did not hold Jesus Christ on that Roman cross. Love did. (John 3:16)

This may seem a little strange to some but two of my favorite words in the Bible, repeated often, are "Fear not." For those with faith in Jesus, there is absolutely no reason to ever be afraid of anything. Psalm 23 states, "I will fear no evil." Why? Why will we fear no evil? The rest of the sentence answers that question – "For You are with me." That's it. God, who loves us, is always with us. If God is with us, why in the world would we have any fear?

Fear not.

CHAPTER ONE

"Make it your ambition to lead a quiet life, to mind your own business . . ."

– I Thessalonians 4:11

Mid 1ˢᵗ Century A.D.

From the back of the crowded elevator, Jake Fleming suddenly realized that he was a paradox. He was living a life that simply did not fit his perception of who he was. The elevator continued its graceful descent to the elaborate lobby of his office building. He recognized a couple of his fellow companions from previous trips up and down to and from the 48ᵗʰ floor. He had never met them – just nodded and shared the ride. As the elevator doors opened, everyone filed out and headed home. He was the last one off and, after a couple of steps; he paused and listened to the clicking sound of women's high-heeled shoes on the marble floor. He wondered why he had not previously noticed that sound. He walked out of the lobby into the stifling heat of a late New York City afternoon. The sidewalks were crowded with people – all in a rush. Jake Fleming saw his regular cab waiting on him. He got in and was soon on his way to his condominium. The traffic was thick. It always was. The condo is luxurious. He always described it as "comfortable" but it is much more than that. It has every computerized gadget that is on the market in 2005. It was extremely expensive; however, he could certainly afford it now. Much of the expense was due to the view – he could see saltwater from a large bay window and from a small balcony. He had told himself that it was an investment – he could always sell it for more than he had paid for it. Living alone, Jake turned the largest bedroom into a library. He has thousands of volumes lining the walls – from floor to ceiling. His library has an antique roll-top desk that sees much use. With his computer in his library, Jake spends most of his time there. When he isn't online, he is sitting in a large blue "easy" chair. This is the only piece of furniture that he kept when his divorce was final. His ex-wife didn't want it. She thought it was ugly. He liked it; used it often; and has kept it for many years. His friends say it is too worn – he should get rid of it and replace it with a new one. Jake replies that it is comfortable and it fits him. While sitting in this old chair, he likes to read and so he often does. He reminds himself that throughout the known history of civilization, it is books that transport the intellectual wealth of mankind.

Jake Fleming is tall and deeply tanned with brown fluffy hair. In college, his dates often said his hair felt like kitten fur. He has almost royal blue eyes that can pierce the facade of most people. Women love his eyes and men think he is wearing colored contact lenses. At 41, he wears the same size clothes he wore in college.

This is merely his outward appearance. Inside, as with everyone, is what is important. Jake Fleming is an intellectual. He is a thinker. Some of his friends call him "Dreamer." However, it is more than that. He likes contemplation. That is not to say that he sits around and thinks for hours at a time. No, his mind is quick, in every situation, to see several possibilities, analyze each and choose what he thinks best. It isn't an ability he developed; he was simply born this way. He recognized it as an asset and has often used it. It is one of the things that has made him so successful in his current work. Jake Fleming is a man with a sudden wit and an excellent sense of humor. He never tells "dirty" jokes but he laughs at one well told. He smiles often and people enjoy being around him. Truth be told, however, he doesn't much enjoy being around people. He likes solitude. He prefers being alone with his books.

About a year and a half ago, he was the guest speaker at a

Kiwanis Club event. He was actually shocked when the president of the club, during his introduction of Jake, referred to him as a 21st century Renaissance man. While the tag surprised him, it is appropriate. Jake's interests are extremely varied. He is a serious student of history, philosophy, archaeology and astronomy. He has a deep appreciation for music and the arts, particularly fine art and literature. He is an amateur sculptor who produces professional quality pieces. He loves to learn anything that is new to him. It is like a major discovery. However, Jake considers it much more important that he is a Christian.

For the past several years, Jake has felt an "uneasiness" concerning American culture and society as a whole. He thinks that it is deteriorating. He is a man who prefers to discuss ideas. Most people, he has found, would rather discuss other people. The idea that celebrities are people worth talking about is foreign to him. From his perspective, to spend any time talking about whom the latest starlet is dating is a complete and total waste of time. He could not possibly care who is in drug rehab, who is getting a divorce or who is involved in some sexual scandal. Jake agrees with Benjamin Franklin who said, "Do not waste time for that is the stuff life is made of." Celebrities have absolutely no impact on Jake's life. To him, they are meaningless people. He treats them with complete indifference.

Jake Fleming works for a large financial firm, Excalibur, Inc., in downtown New York City. Almost two years ago, he was promoted and rewarded with a large office on the 48th floor of a skyscraper in Manhattan. For the past three years, his compensation package has topped two million dollars and he is well on his way to his best year yet in 2005.

CHAPTER TWO

". . . Who do you say I am?"
" . . . You are the Christ, the Son of the Living God."

-- Matthew 16: 15-16

Late 1st Century A.D.

Jake Fleming, as the morning sun rose in the eastern sky, stood at his huge office window and looked across the view of skyscrapers. His heart still fluttered when he looked at the empty space where the Twin Towers had stood. It had been over three and a half years since they were destroyed; nonetheless, it still bothered him each time he looked where they had been. Nearly the entire Excalibur staff had watched both buildings crumble to the ground. There had been a call for everyone to evacuate the building. However, most people at Excalibur had gathered in the conference room and watched from the windows there. Jake had stayed in his office. Jake's office window was as much a wall as a window. It began at the floor and continued to the ceiling. He had spent many hours watching the wide view of downtown New York. The view had become somewhat monotonous. At first, he had been excited by it. Over time, however, Jake had seen the view in rainstorms, heat waves and snow showers. It changed little. As he gazed out the glass at dozens of other skyscrapers, he realized that there were probably several men and women looking out their windows in his direction. What were they thinking? What were they wondering? Were they also bored?

From the 48th story, Jake could see much of New York. And yet, there was little to see. The view was considered prestigious. He knew that. He realized that many people would do almost anything to have what this view represented. However, now that he had it, it meant nothing to him. He was a small town guy from a lower middle class family. He would rather be looking at the woods behind his parents' home in North Carolina. The plush office did nothing to increase his work efficiency or productivity. It did not hinder him but neither did it aid him. His productivity had increased – but it would have done as well had he remained in his old office. He was pretty much on autopilot now. With his contacts and previous successes, he was assured of additional success. As long as he played the game, his productivity would continue to increase. This office was, in reality, designed to impress his clients. It gave anyone who entered it for the first time an immediate awareness that this was the office of an extremely successful person. Of course, Jake was. The presumption was that the potential new client would want to be associated with the person who belonged to this office. The company had hired a professional designer to layout and furnish Jake's office. It was large. It contained a bar, a conference table, an office desk, a computer desk, lush carpet, a golf putting green with an automatic ball return and the huge window wall. Soon after moving into this office, Jake had removed all but one of the designer's wall hangings. In their place, he put up paintings, photographs, posters and plaques that meant something to him. A knock on his door interrupted his thoughts. Tom Jennings, the President of Excalibur, entered his office. Tom's dad, a big fan of the King Arthur legends, had founded Excalibur.

Jake nodded toward his bar and asked, "Coffee?"

"Believe I will," Jennings replied.

Jake walked over and poured two mugs of coffee. Tom Jennings was tall, gray, a little overweight and a pleasant man. He was religious about his workouts and tried to stay in shape. For a man in his sixties, he was in very good shape.

"So, how ya doing, Jake?"

Swallowing a sip of his coffee, Jake replied, "I'm hangin' in."

Tom laughed, "I bet you are."

"And how have you been?"

"Me? Oh, I'm good. You really ought to take advantage of the gym. Its got everything, you know."

"Yes, I know. I tried it out a couple of times."

Jake had tried to put together a workout routine with the trainer who worked at the gym. However, after about three weeks, he became bored with the whole thing and stopped going. He did practice yoga on his own and did a few pushups now and then.

Jennings said, "I think it has really helped me stay limber."

"That's good."

"Yes. Listen, Jake, the reason I stopped by this morning was I wanted to see if you need anything for your meeting this afternoon with Richard Drakes?"

"Thank you. No, I don't think so. I'm set."

"Good. Good. You know, he is a big golf fanatic. He likes to invest in developments along golf courses."

"Yes, I know. I have all that information. I have his complete investment portfolio."

"Of course. I was sure you would. I was thinking you might consider steering him towards that new Moonlight Valley development up in Connecticut."

"Good idea. I can see if he might have an interest in that."

"Good. Good . . . you all right, Jake? You seem a little pre-occupied."

"I've been thinking."

Jennings laughed. "You think too much."

"It seems to work for me. Most of the time."

"Well . . . as they say, whatever works."

After Jennings left, Jake got another mug of coffee and returned to his window. The view had not changed but he sipped his coffee and continued to think. He wondered if Tom Jennings had invested in the Moonlight Valley development.

About an hour later, after making sure he had everything lined up for his appointment with Richard Drakes, Jake got another mug of coffee and stood by his window. As he watched the people and traffic far below, he heard knocking on his wall. He walked over and knocked back in reply. This was a signal between Ted Perdue and himself. Ted had the office next to his and the two had developed a close friendship. If one wanted to visit the other's office, he first knocked on the wall. If there was no reply, it meant "don't come over now, I'm busy." If the other one knocked back, it meant it was okay to drop in and visit.

Ted Perdue was short with close-cropped red hair. He was 38 years old, married with two children and seemed to have an almost contrived sense of happiness. But it wasn't contrived; it was real. Ted was not stupid but his continual good-naturedness sometimes gave one that impression. Prior to getting to know him well, Jake too had suspected Ted of being a little slow-witted. But he was not. He was one of those people who liked everyone. Jake, on the other hand, had met a lot of people he did not like. Ted was doing well with Excalibur. He had not yet reached the million dollar mark but he was only a couple of hundred thousand away. This could be the year he made it to that milestone mark. A couple of minutes later, Ted walked into Jake's office and immediately walked over to the putting green.

"So how's it going?" Ted asked.

"Good. And you?"

With a serious tone, Ted whispered, "It all depends upon whether or not this little white ball decides to go into that little hole. Hush now. With deep concentration, the pro 'Redfire' strokes his club. The ball makes its approach to the hole and . . . and . . . it rolls away. Thousands of fans are disappointed but 'Redfire' will return."

"I, for one, certainly hope so. The entire golfing world would certainly miss the presence of 'Redfire' Perdue."

With a bow, Ted said, "I appreciate that support. What's up?"

"Not much. Been thinking."

"Uh-oh. You know you do way too much of that."

"So I've been told."

Jake looked out through the glass at the metropolis before him and asked Ted, "There are millions of people in this city and billions of people on this planet – do you believe that they are all different?"

Lining up his putt, Ted responded, "I guess so."

"Have you ever wondered why someone murders another person?" Ted shook his head. "When we start talking, I never ever know where you are headed." After a short pause, Ted said, "I'm not sure . . . I guess I probably have. You're wondering what makes people do as they do?"

"Exactly! Very perceptive of you. If you murder someone and totally get away with it . . ."

"I've lost my perceptiveness. I don't think I understand what you are getting at."

"Why do people commit crimes?"

"I dunno."

"Exactly. You are an upper middle class respectable family man. You have a wonderful wife and great children. You wouldn't murder anyone."

"Of course not."

"Yet, every day, somewhere, a respectable middle class family man murders his wife. Why?"

"I think sociologists suggest that poverty is the cause of most crimes."

"That, my friend, is total and complete bull crap. Most people living in poverty are honest and good people. I'm talking about people who earn their living – not people on government handouts. That's a different classification of people all together – especially those who are multi-generational welfare recipients. I'm a case in point. I was reared in poverty. We had a fairly large family, five of us, and there was never enough money to go around. My dad worked at his job. Neither he nor I ever committed any crimes. It never entered my head to steal something. When I was in high school, I probably went some places I shouldn't have gone, did some things I shouldn't have done and said some things I shouldn't have said. However, I can honestly say, and I could look God in the face and say it, I've never, in my whole life, ever intentionally hurt anyone. I think most people, living in poverty, can say the same thing. No, poverty is not the answer to the question why."

"What then?"

"We are all different – not just physically but also spiritually."

"You mean our souls?"

"Yes. Exactly. I think some of us have allowed our souls to develop spiritually and others have not."

"If that is so, then some people can go their entire lives without ever developing or growing."

"Certainly. If a person does not grow spiritually, would that person not be more inclined to commit crimes?"

"Uh, I . . . "

"I think so."

"I guess."

Looking at the place where the Twin Towers had stood, Jake asked, "Suppose you could kill Osama bin Laden and no one would ever know you did it, would you?"

"Back to murder, huh? Are you planning on killing someone? You could probably get away with it."

"No. Would you?"

"Kill bin Laden?" Ted thought about it.

"No, probably not. He deserves to die. But I wouldn't want to do it."

"Me either. I agree. He does deserve to die. Why do neither of us want to do it?"

"It's just not in our nature."

"Exactly. But why?" Pointing out the window, Jake said, "Right now, some guy, out there, is beating his wife – in front of his children. And no one will ever hear of it. And he thinks that makes him a real man. I worry about his wife. I worry about those children. You and I would never do such a thing. It's not, as you said, in our nature. But I wonder why some people are . . . just plain mean. Do you know? Do you know why some people are evil?"

Holding the putter in his right hand, Ted shrugged his shoulders.

"Right now, Ted, all across America, in little small towns, one or two people call the shots for those communities. They are like a little dictator of their community. They call all the shots to enrich themselves. Often they pretend to do good things for the community – but only if there is something positive in it for themselves, their families and their businesses. They get good publicity in the local paper. They get tax write-offs or some type of benefit from donating to a park, for example. They actually are corrupt and evil. But they have the money and the power to get their way and to advance their personal agendas. They own the mayor and the majority of the city council members. They get things to go their way. If a mayor happens to be elected who is not their man, that mayor will not be re-elected. It is weird that this still exists in America but it goes on all over the nation. Sociologists have documented this."

"Just small towns?"

"To some extent, it can happen in larger cities. However, it is much easier to gain absolute control in small towns. It makes me wonder why a person wants to have that kind of control and power. Why does a person, who has the wealth to control a small town, do so? Given such a situation, I don't think you or I would take advantage of the situation to further enrich ourselves. Once one has a certain amount of wealth, why would that person need more and more? Of course, this has been going on for centuries. Thousands of years ago, it was the same way."

"Amazing that mankind hasn't learned to be any kinder throughout the ages."

"Yes, Ted, you are right. It is incredible that we haven't progressed any."

"Any?" Ted didn't believe that.

"Yes. And we, you and I, and everyone . . . are a part of everyone else."

"What?" Ted was totally confused and lost now.

"Right now, as we speak, there are millions of people in Africa suffering from starvation, bondage and repression. The same is true of people in Tibet, North Korea and some Arab nations."

"Yes?"

"We, you and I, are a part of that."

Not understanding what Jake was getting at and, consequently, not knowing how to respond, Ted said nothing.

Turning to look across the New York skyline, Jake's heart hurt when he, once again, saw the vacant space. Not looking back at Ted, but still staring out the window, Jake said, "Humanity has changed so little over the centuries."

"What do you mean?" Ted asked.

"Almost five hundred years ago, Spanish conquistadors invaded what is now Mexico and Peru. They slaughtered millions of people. They brought diseases, such as smallpox, which killed millions more. They destroyed their homes, their books . . . their cultures. Almost four hundred years ago, the English began settling in North America. While perhaps not quite as harsh as the Spanish, the results were the same. The cultures of the indigenous peoples were destroyed – along with millions of people."

"But, like you said, that was hundreds of years ago."

"No, the same thing is still happening today."

"Now wait a minute. Okay, give me just one example where it is happening today."

"Okay. Today, it is happening in China. But less than two hundred years ago, one of the worst situations was the way the Cherokee, in the eighteen thirties were treated. The only reason to remove them was prejudice and greed. Even by U.S. law at the time, it was wrong. Yet Andrew Jackson ignored the law and forced the Cherokee to leave their own land. In nineteen-fifty, the communist Chinese government decided that Tibet was never an independent nation. No, this evil government determined that Tibet had always been a part of China. Consequently, with tanks and artillery, soldiers were sent into Tibet to explain this to the Tibetans. The Chinese military forces destroyed thousands of schools, hospitals, libraries and religious centers – not because they were bad places but because they were Tibetan places. They have replaced some of these Tibetan institutions with Chinese institutions. They murdered hundreds of thousands of innocent people; they imprisoned thousands more; and they still, to this day, in the twenty-first century, refuse to allow the Tibetan people to be Tibetans. The Tibetan leader, the Dali Lama, has been in exile since the invasion. Horrible atrocities have been committed and are still today being committed by the Chinese government. The goal of the Chinese government is the total elimination of Tibetan culture and the absorption of the nation of Tibet into China. Mankind has learned nothing in five hundred years. The Chinese are every bit as ruthless as the Spanish conquistadors were five hundred years ago."

"But . . ." Ted had no response.

"Religion, of course, was a big part of it all. Five hundred years ago, the Spanish forced Catholicism on the natives. Today, the Chinese are forcing their religion of communism on the people of Tibet. In both situations, in order to worship as they wished, the repressed people had to do so either in exile or in secret. So little has changed with the nature of man."

"I see what you mean."

"Sorry to get so serious with you."

"No, no. I enjoy these discussions. Forces me to think. And I never know where we will go with them."

Jake laughed. He said, "I could tell you some things about archaeology that would make your brain curl."

CHAPTER THREE

"O God, you are my God, . . . I will praise you as long as I live, and in your name I will lift up my hands . . . with singing lips my mouth will praise you."

– Psalm 63: 1, 4, 5

Mid 11th Century B. C.

The next morning, Jake was having his first mug of coffee when he heard Ted pounding on his wall. He walked over and knocked back. Ted appeared to bounce through Jake's doorway and into his office. He picked up a putter and said, "Redfire is hot today."

He putted three times and missed all three. He looked at Jake and said, "I'm so good, I could do the same thing all day.

"You've got a real talent. There's no denying it."

"Absolutely."

"Coffee?"

"Yeah. Thanks."

They both sat in chairs in front of the window wall. Ted has a similar window in his office and was used to the view. They were discussing their schedules for the day when Jake's intercom sounded.

"Yes?" Jake asked.

"Mr. Jennings on line two for you."

"Okay, thanks."

"Hello." Jake looked at Ted as he listened to Tom Jennings.

"Yes. It went well. Mr. Drakes is now a signed client of Excalibur, Incorporated. I put copies of the paperwork in your box."

Ted held up a thumb to Jake as Jennings continued to speak with Jake.

"All details to follow, Tom. He is ready to do business with us."

Jake continued to listen to Jennings and then said, "Right, right. Okay, good. Bye."

"So you got Drakes lined up. That's great. I figured you would."

"It makes sense for him. It should be another win-win."

"If you're not careful, Jake, you're gonna hit three million this year."

"The IRS would love that."

Ted laughed.

They got up, got another mug of coffee and returned to their chairs.

Ted said, "I've been meaning to ask and keep forgetting, how did your talk go last week with that community group?"

"Okay, I guess. I know Tom thinks it's good PR – giving back to the community and all – but I don't think I'm going to do those anymore. Say Ted, I'm wondering about something. Would you know if Jennings has invested in that Moonlight Valley development up in Connecticut?"

"No, I haven't heard anything about it. Why don't you just ask him?"

"I'm not sure I should. But I think I will."

Ted changed the subject by saying, "I read the editorial this morning and *The Times* is really down on Bush."

"No?"

Ted laughed. "I know. I was surprised too. No, really, I don't expect them to say anything good about a Republican. But this is so crazy – so off base."

Jake shrugged his shoulders. "You know I don't care much about politics. I don't like politicians – from either party. I guess that's why I don't like politics. Another reason I don't like it is because it's dirty. For example, the editorial you just mentioned that was negative about Bush . . . the reason it was negative is not due to whatever they said, but rather, because *The New York Times* does not want Bush to be viewed as doing well."

"You know, I follow politics like some people follow sports. I see the two parties becoming more and more polarized. That's probably not good for the country but it does make it easier to vote. I mean, for example, anyone who owns a business, is elderly, supports Israel, loves freedom and liberty would be nuts to vote Democrat."

Jake did not respond. That non-response irritated Ted. He asked, "Do you agree?"

Jake turned from looking out the window and replied, "Yes, of course. But for me, it's more about philosophical differences than specific issues."

"Meaning?"

"You know the old saying about teaching a man to fish or giving a man a fish?"

"Yes, of course."

"That sums up the main difference between the two parties for me. The Republicans would teach the man to fish . . . thus allowing him to feed himself and his family for the rest of his life. The Democrats would give the man a fish . . . thus making him dependent upon the Democrats and the government for the rest of his life. That's the primary difference I see in the two parties."

"I like that. It's simple but true. You mind if I use that?"

"Help yourself. I'm certainly not claiming that its original to me. I probably heard it somewhere or read it somewhere."

"I'll use it at the club."

"Of course, I also agree with TJ when he said . . ."

"TJ?"

"Thomas Jefferson. He said something to the effect that the government that governs least governs best."

"I like that too. It's true."

"Jefferson was a real genius."

"So, tell me, Jake, who's gonna win in two thousand eight?"

"My goodness, Ted. It's way too early to be talking about that. Ask me after the conventions in three years."

"The talking heads all say that Hillary has the Democratic nomination sewed up."

"The talking heads have extremely little credibility with me. I ignore them. She, like her husband, is a proven liar."

"Doesn't matter. The press seems to already be pushing for her to be the first female president."

"The press should be ashamed of themselves. They are no longer objective. Perhaps they never were but at least they pretended to be. Now, they no longer even try to make a pretense of being objective. They no longer do much actual reporting of information that they have themselves determined to be factual."

"What do you mean?"

"In last year's election, they just read press releases from the Democratic party as if it were news. You know, I noticed a big difference between two thousand and two thousand four. In two thousand, the media supported Gore. In two thousand four, the media not only supported Kerry but they defended and protected him. None of this is the role of a real press. The whole media should be ashamed that they have given up their traditional role of reporting facts and reporting both sides of a story. Instead, the media seems to be a propaganda arm of the Democratic Party."

"So, of all the possible candidates, who's the best on the Democratic side?"

"I don't know enough about any of them to say I like anybody. What I do know is, like you just said, what they stand for is not what any thinking American would support."

"What about Biden?"

"Ted, it really is too early to be speculating. Biden, to me is not an intellectual. The media tries to make Bush out to be a stupid man. That is because of the way he talks and because he is a Christian. Bush is not stupid. Biden, on the other hand, . . ."

"Clinton, you've already written off. Who else is there?"

"Pretty thin field."

"Yeah. What about the Republicans?"

"Ted, it's really too early. The media will push for McCain because he's the most liberal of all the Republicans. Then, in the general election, the media will support, defend and protect whomever the Democrat candidate is. I don't really think that McCain will get the nomination. I know who I'd like to see."

"Who?"

"Condi Rice. She could be the first black president and the first female President. I'd vote for her."

"Me too."

"But we won't get a chance to do so."

"Why not?"

"She's too intelligent."

"What do you mean?"

"People as intelligent as she is do not want to be president. She won't seek it. She won't run."

"I dunno. She'd have a good shot at winning."

"I know. But I don't think she wants the presidency. I think she has something more important to do."

"Like what?"

"Self-actualization."

"Okay, I don't even know what that means."

"Ted, I really don't like politics. I vote every election but I'm not interested in the game."

"You say that Rice is too intelligent. You just said that Jefferson was a genius and he was a president."

"That's true. However, he didn't really want it. He thought he owed it to the new nation to serve. He would have been much more content to stay at Monticello and study than to be president. His election was the first one to be nasty. It was horrible. The reason is that Jefferson was taking power away from those who had been in power with Washington and Adams. We can learn from that episode. We still see it happening today."

Ted got up and went over to the putting green. He picked up a putter and stroked a ball directly to the hole. It rimmed around the hole once and spun away.

CHAPTER FOUR

"I long to learn the things that are, and comprehend their nature, and know God."

– The Corpus Hermeticum

Late 1ˢᵗ Century A.D.

The next morning found a colleague, Ronald Cavendish, joining Ted and Jake in Jake's office for coffee. He was also an investment broker with Excalibur, Inc. Neither Ted nor Jake really knew Cavendish well. He was someone they "passed the time of day with" and spoke to in the halls and elevators. He was a nice enough person and, given a chance, the cordial working relationship could easily develop into a friendship. He was 46 years old and in the process of going through a divorce.

Ted was telling another joke. He said, "Stop me if you've heard this one. Really. A rabbi, a priest and a minister walk into a bar. The . . ."

Both Ronald and Jake said, "Stop!"

"No, no. You haven't heard this version. A rabbi, a priest and a minister walk into a bar. The bartender looks up, sees the three men of the cloth and says, 'What is this, a joke?'"

After the chuckles died down, Ronald said, "I'll tell you a joke. Women. Women are a joke. Does anyone understand women?"

Ted and Jake looked at each other and smiled. Jake said, "Ronald, you would be a customer for our book."

"Huh?"

"Yeah, Ted and I have talked about writing a book with the title *'What I Understand About Women.'*"

"I bet."

"No, really. Inside, all the pages would be blank."

Ted said, "No, you forgot. We were going to have a page in the middle that says, 'It has something to do with shoes.'"

Ronald laughed. He said, "At least it would be a book that made sense."

They all laughed.

Jake said, "I'm sure thousands of men have had the same idea."

"Imagine so," Ronald replied.

"Rough divorce?" Jake asked.

"Yeah, pretty bad. I'm just glad both our children are in college. You know, after twenty-one years of marriage, you'd think you would know a person. But you don't. She said she's never been happy. She said she has wanted a divorce for years. She was just waiting on the children to get grown. And now, she's saying bad things about me to our children – trying to turn them against me."

"I'm sorry, Ronald. That's a rotten situation," Jake gently said.

"Yeah, that's really tough," Ted added.

"You've been through a divorce, haven't you Jake?"

"Yes, years ago."

"Was it bad?"

"It got kind of nasty. But we were both right out of college. We were too young. Thought we were in love. There was more lust involved than love. I've always been glad there were no children. She thought that, if we had a child, the marriage might be saved. I didn't think that at all. She was furious with me, at the time, for wanting a divorce. However, she quickly remarried, and is, I hope happy."

"And you've never remarried?"

"No."

"Come close?"

"No."

"Jake's waiting to be swept off his feet." Ted laughed at

his comment.

Ronald was interested and concerned about Jake. He was sincere when he asked, "Why haven't you remarried?"

Jake sighed but smiled and said, "I guess I simply haven't found the right woman. I know I haven't fallen in love with anyone. For me, that is the number one reason to marry. I think everyone should marry their best friend. And that should be only after you've fallen in love with your best friend."

"That's a pretty high standard," Ronald observed.

"Marriage should be for the rest of one's life. You need high standards. But Ronald, you're asking the wrong person. Ask Ted. He's been married eleven years now. He's never been divorced."

"What about it, Ted? What does it take to have a happy marriage?"

Ted smiled. "I know one thing it takes. It takes two people. One person cannot carry a marriage. Both the man and the woman must be committed to the marriage. Both."

Ronald nodded in agreement. "That is so true. I tried. I tried to compromise. I tried to change. But she just doesn't want our marriage to continue."

Jake said, "You'll be all right, Ronald. It is rough right now. But, believe me, it gets much better. When the divorce is finalized, it's a wonderful feeling. At least, it was for me. But you'll be all right; you'll see."

"Sure, Ronald. Jake's right. A year from now, you'll have adjusted. Perhaps you'll even have found someone new."

"And let me give you a bit of a warning," Jake stated.

"Sure. Anything." Ronald replied.

"Women, some women, can be quite mercenary. Throughout our society today, what do most people most respect?"

"I don't know. I'm not sure." Ronald looked to Ted for help but Ted shrugged his shoulders.

"I am. The answer is money and fame."

"I suppose."

"It is. Now, I don't know why, but I have never been impressed with either. Even when I had no money, people with it neither impressed me nor intimidated me. The same has always been true regarding celebrities and fame. I have never found famous people to be impressive. But here's what I'm getting at – some women, because you earn a healthy income, will suddenly find you irresistible. I'm not kidding. I've had women half my age throw themselves at me. I've had mothers try to set me up with their daughters – not because I'm a wonderful person but rather because I've got money now. Back when I was single with very little money, not a single solitary mother tried to set me up with her daughter. It is a real problem. You'll soon see. Being single with money will make you adorable."

"I don't know that I'd mind being adorable and irresistible."

"Ahhh, but Ronald, it's not you that would be irresistible – it's your money. Your wealth is what would be attractive and adorable."

"Perhaps that won't be an issue. My wife is poised to get most of my wealth."

All three men knew that there was some truth to Cavendish's statement. They all smiled and nodded their heads.

"Tell me, Jake, how do you handle this problem?"

"Obviously, it's best if you meet someone new who has no idea that you have a large income. When they ask me what I do for a living, I reply that I'm in investments or that I work for a brokerage firm. Both answers are vague and both sound dull. Of course, Ronald, you can take the other perspective and only date wealthy women. That way, you'll know that they aren't after your money. But they may wonder if you are after theirs."

Ted laughed. He found that humorous. However, Ronald seemed to accept the idea of dating only wealthy women as something he had not previously thought about – and he liked it.

Jake noticed him deep in thought. He added, "Ronald, don't forget, you need to fall in love with your best friend and marry her."

"Right."

"Tell you what – I turn forty-two next month. I don't have a female best friend . . . so, no marriage prospects. But I do think that love will out. If it's meant to be, love will find a way. I've been single so long now, I'm not sure marriage will ever be in my future. If it's not, I'll be fine with that. If I find someone that I fall in love with and who falls in love with me, I'll be fine with that."

Ted laughed, "I told you. He's waiting for some woman to come along and sweep him off his feet."

All three men laughed.

Ronald said, "I haven't asked a woman out on a date since before I was married. I don't think I much like the idea of dating again."

Ted said, "My wife accuses me of marrying her so I could quit dating her."

Ronald and Jake laughed at Ted's statement.

"Ronald, you seem especially concerned about dating – almost too concerned for a man who isn't even officially divorced yet." Jake was teasing him.

"Yeah, Ronald," Ted was smiling. "Have you already got your sights on someone?"

They were kidding with Ronald but his face turned red.

"He does. Look at that blush. He does." Ted pointed at Ronald's face.

Jake smiled. "Ronald, I hope you don't go from the pan into the fire."

"Yeah, man, you'd better take it slow," Ted advised.

Jake nodded.

Ronald said, "Hey, I'm only in my mid-forties. I'm still interested in . . . female companionship."

Jake and Ted smiled.

Ronald continued, "My soon-to-be ex-wife has not been interested in sex – for a long time now. Or, at least, not with me. She's gonna get everything anyway. I don't see any reason to wait. I mean, to date until some judge says it's official. I might as well begin dating now."

"So, who's the lucky lady?" Ted asked.

"Actually, I've been talking a lot lately with April – over in accounting. Do you guys know her?"

Jake shook his head.

Ted said, "Me either. But Ronald, an office romance? Those can result in . . . problems."

Jake smiled.

Ronald seemed oblivious. "She's so nice. And I really enjoy our talks. This being the month of April, I thought it would be a perfect time to ask her out. I thought we could start with lunch."

Jake did not respond. Ted followed his lead.

"What do you guys think?"

"I think that any two people who work here and want to go to lunch together should be able to do so. Usually, it is three or four of us together. Sometimes, it's men only, sometimes it's women only and sometimes, it's mixed. I don't think it should matter. But knowing you are going through a divorce and . . . is April single?"

"Yes."

"Okay, a single woman goes to lunch with a guy about to be divorced to discuss a problem in the accounting department. It shouldn't be an issue."

Ted blurted, "But it will be one."

"Most likely. If it were two guys or two women – no. But, in your situation Ronald, it will cause talk."

"Absolutely," Ted added.

"So, what do you suggest?"

"Find someone else," Ted quickly stated.

"But I like her."

"Perhaps, Ronald, instead of lunch, you might want to ask her to dinner. That way, you need not tell anyone. Ted and I won't tell anyone. You and April can keep your dating between the two of you. If it develops into something serious, then you can let everyone know. If not, then no one in the office need ever know that you two have dated. April would not be embarrassed and there would be no talk."

"Eventually, someone somewhere will see you two out together." Ted was certain.

"Probably, but not necessarily," Jake said.

"Then the trick would be," Ronald responded, "to go public before that happened."

"When will your divorce be final?" Jake asked.

"Who knows? The blasted lawyers have to drag it out as long as they can. Every time they think about our case, they charge me more money. I hate lawyers."

"They've been called a necessary evil. I'm not so sure," Jake laughed.

"You seem to have adjusted to the idea of being divorced," Ted said.

"At first, I was flabbergasted," Ronald replied. "I didn't want a divorce. I wasn't happy with our marriage but I hadn't been thinking along those lines at all. But she made it clear that she had thought it all out and had been considering a divorce for some time. I don't know if she's got someone else lined up or not. I don't really care anymore. I have adjusted, as you say, and am looking forward to being a free man again."

"Good," Ted replied.

"I mean, divorce is so common in our society these days. There is no stigma attached to it like there was fifty or sixty years ago."

"And I think that's a good thing," Ted stated.

"I don't." Jake said.

"You don't what?" Ted questioned.

"I don't think it's a good thing that our society has embraced divorce so that there are no consequences. I have even heard of both men and women about to be married who say, 'If it doesn't work out, we can always get a divorce.' That seems a horrible attitude, to me, to have when you're about to get married. People, in our society today, don't seem to take marriage seriously. It is supposed to be a forever commitment. I think divorce is one of the reasons why people marry unwisely. People obviously make mistakes when they marry. They frequently marry the wrong person. I made such a mistake. Ronald made such a mistake. Divorce takes care of those mistakes. But I don't think that divorce should contribute to people making such mistakes."

"Okay, professor, how does one avoid making such mistakes?" Ted asked.

"Yeah," Ronald added, "If you can answer that, you may be able to write a book about women after all."

Jake smiled. He answered, "Love. One avoids making such mistakes by learning from such mistakes. In my case, we thought we loved each other. And, I suppose, to some degree, we did. But we were not friends. If you can't be friends, in the true sense of the word, with your own wife, then something is wrong with the relationship. If you have a genuine real friendship with a woman and that friendship develops into love, then you have a basis for considering marriage. Of course, it has to go both ways. Women think differently than us; they feel things differently than us; their logic is different from ours; but love bridges those differences. And, I think, those differences can actually make the marriage stronger. The union of our male traits with a female's way of seeing things can make for a strong couple. Rather than resist the differences, both should embrace and appreciate those differences. And love can be the catalyst to join the two different people into one couple."

"I think you can write that book," Ronald was impressed.

"So, if you know so much about it, how come, in all the years since your divorce, you haven't remarried?" Ted was truly interested.

"Like I said, I simply haven't found anyone with whom I have developed such a relationship. If I do, I'll ask her to marry me. If I don't, I'll still live a happy life."

"You really are a happy person, aren't you?" It was more of a statement than a question that Ronald asked.

"Yes, I am. I guess I choose to be. 'He that is of a merry heart hath a continual feast.' Proverbs."

CHAPTER FIVE

"And this is the testimony: God has given us eternal life, and this life is in his Son. He who has the Son has life; he who does not have the Son of God does not have life."

– 1 John 5: 11-12

Late 1st Century A.D.

After each ride down the elevator, Jake realized more and more that he was disconnected not only with people in general but also with his friends and relatives. It was something he sensed rather than knew. He couldn't quite explain it but felt it. He wasn't disconnected in that he couldn't relate and empathize with others; however, he was beginning to sense a real difference between the way he viewed things and the perspective that most people shared.

All his life, Jake had been an avid learner. Except for romance novels, he would read anything. He loved to learn something new. There was always something new to learn. He knew he would never run out of new things to learn.

However, this evening, as he sat in his old comfortable blue lounge chair in his library, he paused with the book he was reading and thought about Ronald and his pending divorce. Like himself, Ronald was soon to be a statistic – one of a growing number of people whose marriage ended in divorce. Divorce used to be extremely rare and, in less than fifty years, it had become extremely common. Why? What had also changed in fifty years that might be a factor, or the reason for divorce becoming so common? The first thing that came to Jake's mind was that there had been a corresponding decrease in church attendance. In

American society, religion was not as important in 2005 as it had been in 1955. If both husband and wife shared common religious beliefs, worshiped together, prayed together and looked to God for spiritual guidance, surely such a marriage had a better chance of being successful than one in which religion did not exist.

Jake thought about schools. He knew that, from the beginning of schools in the United States in the 1600s all the way through the 1960s, every classroom used to begin the day with a reading from the Bible and a prayer. Then, almost overnight, it was stopped. It was not considered "politically correct" anymore. Politically correct. What an absolutely stupid policy political correctness was. He laughed to himself at the thought. It was politically incorrect to use the word stupid anymore.

Born in 1963, Jake reflected on how much society had changed in his almost forty-two years. President Kennedy's assassination in November of his birth year had changed America. It altered television. Jake realized that, in almost forty-two years, the murder had not yet been solved. Jake thought that there were people who knew and documents "somewhere" which state the truth. The murderers were known but had not yet been revealed to the public. Jake had pretty clear memories of watching black and white television images of men walking on the moon in 1969. His parents had let him stay up and watch it – his sisters and his parents had fallen asleep. Jake had watched it all night long. It wasn't the events of his lifetime that bothered him, Jake reflected. The collapse of the Soviet Union under President Reagan's leadership had been a good thing. No, Jake thought, it was the decline of the culture in society that was the cause of so many problems today. There seemed to be no honor, no duty, no decency, no responsibility, no embarrassment or shame in today's culture.

Jake wondered about this. Was this a natural cycle? The ancient Greeks wrote, with disgust, over how the youth of their day had no respect for their elders. Did cultures rise and decline as did nations? Was America in the midst of a normal cultural decline? Would the pendulum swing back sometime in the future? It would probably get worse before that happened.

And why, Jake wondered, did he not participate in the decline? Why was he a person of high morals? Why didn't he spend evenings in bars trying to "score" with available women? Why didn't he spend hours every day in front of his television? How come he didn't care anything about celebrities, reality shows or politics? He followed sports to some degree but he could take it or leave it. Lately, he had been leaving it more often than not. Jake knew the answer to these questions. The answer was simply that he believed that Jesus was who he said he was – the Messiah, the Son of God.

Even with a strong belief in Jesus, Jake was aware that he felt something missing in his life. He sensed a void. He kept thinking that there was something major, something important, that he needed to learn. He could feel something pulling him. However, he couldn't grasp it; he couldn't make the feeling materialize. It was like trying to remember something that was on "the tip of your tongue" but you couldn't quite get it. Jake was sure that he would someday "get it." He felt confident that it would eventually come to him.

Jake was startled out of his thoughts by his phone ringing. He looked at the number and, although he hadn't called in several months, Jake recognized his nephew's number. This was Steve, his sister Lucy's son. He only called when he wanted something – usually advice. Jake relinquished his reverie and answered the call. Steve was in danger of flunking out of college and wanted some suggestions or options that he could do that would allow him to avoid being academically dismissed. Jake spent half an hour discussing options and was able to provide his nephew with some ideas that might help. He would probably be placed on academic probation and would need to have a good following semester to remove himself from probation.

Jake got up, went to his kitchen, got himself a glass of wine and walked out on his balcony. He looked down toward the water and could see the lights of moving ships. He decided, at that moment, that he would sell this condo. He was a little amazed to realize that he could get well over three million dollars for it, perhaps four. This view was one of the major reasons for that. He thought he would buy a small farm somewhere – perhaps Connecticut. Not an original idea, he thought. Like many others, this would force him to commute.

As Jake continued to think about a farm, he warmed to the idea. Maybe I'll even get a few chickens, he reflected. He liked the idea. A dog would be nice. A wife? A wife would be really nice. He would like to fall in love. None of the women he knew, none of the very few women he had dated in the past year had touched his heart. Perhaps he would meet some more compatible women in whatever small community he settled. That thought encouraged him even more. Jake was ready to move from New York. He finished his wine and felt content and happy about his decision to move.

CHAPTER SIX

"Let nothing trouble you, nothing frighten you. All things are passing; God never changes. Our goodness derives not from our capacity to think but to love."

– St. Teresa of Avila

Mid 16th Century A.D.

"A farm!? Are you crazy?" Ted was shocked that Jake might really move – and to a farm.

Standing at his glass wall, Jake simply nodded.

"Connecticut? Really, Jake. Be serious."

"A lot of people commute from Connecticut."

"That's true. But they don't have one of the best condos in the city."

Jake shrugged his shoulders. He said, "Maybe I can trade with one of 'em."

"Yeah, right. I can see the real estate ad now – will swap luxury condo for rustic farm."

"Why not?"

"I thought you liked your condo?"

"I do."

"And its got a great view."

"I'd rather have a view of some trees and some grass."

"Trees produce leaves. And grass has to be mowed."

"Trees also produce fruit and nuts. And cows and horses eat grass."

"Are you just toying with the idea or are you already leaning that way?"

"Leaning hard. I've decided to move to a small rural community and become a part of it. I want to be a patron of the local library. I want to have neighbors. I want to support the local festivals. I might join a local civic club. And I'll find a church I'd like to attend."

"You are serious."

"Why not?"

"You'll spend hours getting back and forth every day."

"It'll make me appreciate my weekends more."

"Well, as they say, you've always marched to the beat of your own drum."

Jake laughed. "That's true enough."

Later, Jake called a real estate agent he knew. The agent agreed to bring listing papers over to Jake's condo that evening.

After touring the condominium, making notes of the view and getting the square footage of each room, the agent told Jake he was certain he would walk away from the sale with a figure close to four million dollars, perhaps more.

After the papers had been signed and the agent had left, Jake got out an atlas and began looking at a map of Connecticut. He briefly thought of some upstate New York areas but decided that he didn't really want to live in New York any longer. Jake planned on spending Saturday driving around and getting familiar with the state of Connecticut.

His parents still lived in North Carolina and he thought about calling them and telling them of his plans. However, he decided he'd wait until he found a place "with his name on it" before he called. They always worry about everything. He didn't need to give them something else to worry about now.

Jake was excited. He was around ninety-five percent sure that this was the right thing for him to do. He still felt a little twinge in his being that this was wrong. That was common, he knew. Before many major decisions, most people felt that "twinge." Even prior to getting married, some people felt it. Jake realized that, once he was settled, he just might resign from

Excalibur. In fact, he knew that he probably would. He was financially secure. But what would he do with his life? He was almost forty-two. He knew he wouldn't be a real farmer – he wasn't qualified. He wasn't much of a handyman either. He would, he thought, have to buy a place in pretty good shape.

Jake had always known that his job at Excalibur was simply a means to making real money. He never intended to make a career of it. He didn't enjoy it. He knew he was good at it but it didn't bring him any real satisfaction. He didn't like most of his clients and had little respect for them. Their whole lives revolved around turning their wealth into more wealth. For most of them, their major accomplishment in life had been to be born into a family with wealth. Jake knew that, for him, there was more to life than accumulating wealth. As a Christian, it didn't interest him. It wasn't high on his list of things he wanted to do. In fact, it wasn't on his list at all. In reality, Jake didn't even have a list. He had been extremely successful at Excalibur but, he thought, it really was time to move on to something else. But what? That, he did not know.

CHAPTER SEVEN

"Therefore, if anyone is in Christ, he is a new creation; the old has gone, the new has come!"

– 2 Corinthians 5:17

Mid 1st Century A.D.

Standing at his window wall, Jake gazed out across the skyline of New York. He thought about the millions of people who lived and worked in this dynamic metropolis. What did they think of this huge city, he wondered? There were people from all nationalities, all income levels, all religious beliefs, all ethnic groups, all sexual orientations, all political leanings and all levels of spiritual development living their lives in this one relatively small area. While, in many ways, they differed greatly, most got along with all the others. There were murders every day but they were almost always committed by a member of one group against another member of the same group. They rarely crossed social boundaries. Of course, there was the occasional mugging that turned violent and, sometimes, deadly. However, those were not the normal murders.

There was a front page story in the morning paper that day about a prominent medical doctor who had been arrested for killing his wife. It made the front page because they were a well-known "high society" couple. Jake tried to determine in his mind what would cause someone to murder another. He never could seem to wrap his mind around the answer. And a spouse? Somewhere, it happened every day. Why? Had divorce not been considered? This doctor would lose everything and spend the rest of his life in prison because he thought killing his wife was preferable to divorcing her. Did he even take into consideration that he was taking another person's life? How could someone, anyone, be so soulless that he would consider murder? Jake simply did not understand. This was what he had just been discussing with Ted. It would seem such a person would have to be living an incredibly empty life. They would be existing as an animal in the wild. It didn't make any sense for a civilized person to be reacting at such a base level. Sometimes, Jake thought, a person murdered another person and got away with it. Another person may be unjustly convicted of the crime. Or no one was ever accused of the murder and the murderer escaped justice. That was rare but it happens. What would that be like? How would one live his life knowing that he had murdered another human being? That must be a terrible burden to carry around, Jake thought. Perhaps not. Perhaps, if one could murder, one had no conscience – no guilt. Such a person would be devoid of any degree of spirituality.

Jake looked in another direction. The skyscrapers continued as far as he could see. There are simply too many people here, he thought. Should humanity ever be gathered in such large numbers? He thought of other huge cities around the world like Mexico City, London, Tokyo and, well, there were dozens of such cities. Why had man congregated in such quantities? Was commerce enough of a reason to live like this? China and India were densely populated countries. Yet, both nations had large areas where hardly anyone lived.

People all over the globe had dreams and hopes for their futures and for that of their children. Some people, like him, were searching. Jake was always searching for answers. Why? What drove him to want to know? Most people seemed content to have a family, provide for that family, watch the children grow and have their own families. They would spoil their grandchildren, retire and die. Was that it? Was that what life was all about – procreation? Along the way, you would help your neighbors, you would volunteer in your community, you would pay your taxes, you would worship as you wished, you wouldn't hurt anyone and, when you died, people would say you were a nice guy. Was that it?

There was nothing wrong with such a life but Jake sensed that there was more to life than that. He didn't know exactly what but he knew that there was . . . something – out there. Something . . . he couldn't quite grasp it; but, it was there – somewhere. The answer was there. Why are we here? Once, while Jake was in a bookstore, he picked up a book entitled *The Meaning of Life*. He read the back jacket cover and the interior flaps. The conclusion of the author was that each person should leave the world in a better condition than he had found it. That was the meaning of life. It was a nice comfortable thought, Jake had realized. However, Jake also realized that it was total nonsense. That, he knew, was not the meaning of life. And it was, of course, completely subjective. One person's view of "better condition" may not be another person's perspective of "better" at all. No, the meaning of life was more than that – it would apply to each human being. But what? There should be a universal answer that would work for everyone.

Jake's thoughts were interrupted by Ted's pounding on the wall. Jake walked over and knocked back.

Ted burst through Jake's office door with a huge grin on his freckled face.

"Lunch is on me today, Farmer Jake. I just landed a huge new client."

"Congratulations."

"Old geezer with more money than he knows what to do with it."

"But you do?"

"Oh yeah. You bet'cha. You got that right."

"Is that any way to talk about a new client? Especially one that is going to make you a lot of money. I mean, really, calling him an "old geezer.""

"Just between us. Just between us."

Ted walked over to Jake's putting green, picked up the

putter and stroked a golf ball toward the hole. It passed by the hole on the left side.

"Rats," Ted complained. "I thought, after the morning I've been having, that I'd sink every single one."

"Ted, you know what they say about golf?"

"What?"

"It is one of life's mysteries."

"That's for sure. The mystery is why, after having played it once, anyone would play it again."

Jake laughed.

"So, Farmer Jake, what have you been doing this morning?"

"Thinking."

"Uh-oh. Do I dare ask what about?"

"Mysteries. Not golf mysteries but mysteries."

"Such as? Ted asked reluctantly."

Jake laughed. "A big mystery that, I think, proves the existence of God."

"Oh, is that all?" Ted hit another ball toward the hole and this one missed on the right.

"No, that's not all. But it's one mystery I've been thinking about this morning."

"Tell."

"Only a divine being could join spirit with matter. How it was done is still, of course, a major mystery."

Ted stopped "golfing," leaned on the putter and appeared interested.

Jake took that as his cue to continue.

"Our bodies are flesh, bone, liquids – matter. But we, our souls, inhabit those bodies. Only a universal power, God, could have joined spirit with matter."

"Okay. I'm convinced."

"So that means that every single human being – and there are millions of them right here in this city – every one of them, you and I included, have within us . . . a spark of the divine."

"Our souls."

Jake nodded. "Yes. We are spiritual beings living in a temporary human body."

"You know, Jake, when I come into your office, I never have any idea what we'll wind up discussing.'

"Nor I."

"So tell me. Have you got everything finalized for your vacation?"

"Yep. Pretty much."

"You're going camping or something, aren't you?"

"Yes."

"All by yourself?"

"That's right. And I'm really getting away. I don't think I've told you exactly where, have I?"

"No. A national park, I would guess. You've probably reserved a cabin by a lake. You'll do some fishing but wind up eating at the lodge restaurant. Right? How close am I?"

"Not at all close. Have you ever seen one of those maps of the United States taken from space at night?"

"Yeah. But . . .?"

"There is one area that doesn't have any lights at all. Northern Maine. That's where I'm going. I'm taking a tent, camping gear and a canoe. I don't even know exactly where I'll wind up – only that it will be wilderness. Kind of a back-to-nature trip."

"Northern Maine? They probably don't have lobsters way up there. Why there?"

"I'm not sure. I saw that space map and was attracted to the isolation. No lights means no towns, no people. It'll just be me and Mother Nature."

"Are you sure you don't want to take someone younger than Mother Nature with you? Maybe a soft cuddly woman?"

Jake smiled. "I'm sure. While a soft cuddly woman would be nice, I don't know one that I could ask to make this journey. Besides, for me, she would have to be my wife. Also, I really want to be alone with my thoughts."

"That ought to do it. But you'd better watch out."

"For what? He asked reluctantly."

Ted laughed. "For flying saucers. They always show up in places like that."

"Maybe they'd give me a ride."

Ted with much emphasis, shook his head and sighed. He asked, "You ready for lunch?"

"With you paying? Sure."

"Okay. But let's talk sports or something."

"Something."

CHAPTER EIGHT

"May the God of hope fill you with all joy and peace as you trust in him, so that you may overflow with hope by the power of the Holy Spirit."

– Romans 15:13

Mid 1ˢᵗ Century A.D.

Sitting in his comfortable old chair in his library, Jake lit a pipe and watched the smoke slowly permeate the room. Jake liked the smell of a pipe more than the taste.

As he sat puffing on his brier, he thought of his immediate future. He was excited about his upcoming journey into the wilds of northern Maine. He was excited about moving to a small town and owning a few acres of rural America.

He was not particularly excited about his soon-to-be 42ⁿᵈ birthday. He would be on his camping trip when it rolled around and would, consequently, avoid any "birthday hoopla." He preferred not to take notice of his birthdays. He often let them skip by without any fanfare at all. He had a sister who acted like she was the only person in the world with a birthday. She wanted to celebrate her birth every year with a big party. She was "put-out" with him because he didn't drop everything he was doing and travel down to North Carolina for her annual birthday bash. However, she always got over it.

Jake now knew that, once he had moved, he would not stay long at Excalibur. That made him think that he need not move to Connecticut. If he was not going to stay with his job in New York City, why live in Connecticut? He had no ties there.

He had neither family nor any friends there. He could move anywhere. He didn't have to limit himself to the New York area. He could even move back to North Carolina. He could move to Canada or the Caribbean. He could literally move almost anywhere.

If Jake was going to retire from Excalibur at the age of forty-two, what *was* he going to do with the rest of his life? He did not know.

Each year, Excalibur sponsors and hosts a fundraising formal ball for all its clients and potential clients. The Spring Ball takes place the first week of every April and always generates a check in the quarter of a million range for a children's orphanage. Jake is always delighted to purchase tickets. The only rule at the Spring Ball is that no business may be discussed. This year's Ball was over about a month ago and had been another success.

Jake blew smoke into his library as he recalled a comment that a man had made to him at this year's Spring Ball. The comment had been weighing on him ever since the man said it. Jake had only been introduced to the man about ten minutes earlier. They had been making the usual small talk that people who have just met make. This man mentioned that he had attended one of Jake's presentations a few months ago. Suddenly, out of nowhere, this man said to Jake, "You are a spiritual person, are you not?" How does one answer such a question? What reply is appropriate? Jake was genuinely taken aback by this man's question. He had not known what to say in response. He had smiled, shrugged his shoulders and said something silly like "I'm trying." The man patted him on the shoulder and said, with a big smile, "I know you are." The man left then and slipped into the crowd of people. That was it. However, Jake could not get rid of the uneasiness he felt by this man's simple question.

Was he spiritual? He had not considered himself to be a spiritual person. Jake always associated spirituality with religion. Need it be, he wondered?

What does it mean to be filled with the Holy Spirit? Who *can* be filled with the Holy Spirit? Can a person live a spiritual life without being filled with the Holy Spirit?

According to traditional Protestant faiths, when an individual asks Jesus Christ into his life, when this person accepts Christ as his personal savior, the Holy Spirit instantaneously enters that person's soul. That person becomes transformed – imbued with the presence of the Holy Spirit. The Holy Spirit is one aspect of God. This presence of the Holy Spirit is there, in the essence of each Christian, to give guidance in that Christian's daily life.

There are countless stories, Jake recalled, of individuals whose lives have dramatically changed in a single day. One day, they are living a life without direction or purpose. Perhaps they are abusing alcohol, abusing sexuality or abusing their fellow man. The next day, after accepting Christ and receiving the Holy Spirit, they are transformed. They are new persons. The Holy Spirit now dwells within. They stop abusing things. They see the world through fresh eyes. They follow the directions and guidance of the Holy Spirit. It is miraculous.

As Jake thought about this, he realized that, for some, it doesn't work quite so quickly. It takes longer to recognize or accept the presence of the Holy Spirit. People who have been living fairly normal lives prior to accepting Christ are not in a position to have the dramatic changes that an alcoholic may have. New Christians often strive to do what they perceive to be right. Rather than following the lead of the Holy Spirit, they try to think of what they should be doing. Sometimes, they falter. They can get discouraged. Frequently, however, these people continue forward, perhaps with small steps, until they too live a spiritual life under the direction of the Holy Spirit.

What about those people who have not accepted Christ and His teachings? Is it possible to learn and embrace a spiritual life without the presence of the Holy Spirit? Jake wondered. He re-filled his pipe and thought about it.

If every human has a soul, a "spark of the divine" within, could not this "spark" lead one to live a spiritual life? Jake remembered a Hindu word he had once read about – Namaste. It was used as a greeting and, more often, as a word of departure. It was similar to Americans saying "goodbye." It roughly translated, as best Jake could remember, as "I honor the divine within you." Then the word Namaste would be returned – "and I honor the divine within you." Jake thought that it was a nice custom. It was harmless and it would remind people that they were walking around, every single day, with a touch of Divinity within.

Jake puffed on his pipe and thought about this. It would seem that such awareness would have to lead one to live a more spiritual life. A constant reminder of one's tiny little spark of divinity would be like having a personal "Jiminy Cricket" in one's pocket. One's conscience would be at the forefront of one's existence. It would continually be telling one what to do and what not to do. Is that not the same as the Holy Spirit directing one's life, Jake wondered?

No, he concluded, it is not the same. Having the presence of the Holy Spirit in one's life adds a dimension to a person that just trying to think of what is right and wrong cannot accomplish. The Holy Spirit gives one comfort, strength, joy and peace. Just following one's conscience cannot do that. The Holy Spirit becomes a part of every Christian. The Holy Spirit is powerful and can direct a powerful prayer life for a Christian. The two are definitely not the same.

Recalling a recent poll of young people 20 – 30 years old, Jake was amazed that three-fourths of them considered themselves to be spiritual but not religious. Of course, Jake thought, considering one's self to be spiritual is not the same as living a spiritual life under the direction of the Holy Spirit.

Jake considered this poll and wondered, to what end? Why would 75 percent of these young adults think of themselves as spiritual beings? They said that they were embracing a somewhat generic secular spirituality. They seem to be adhering to a notion of spirituality – they borrow a little from Christianity, a little from Buddhism, a little from Hinduism and they blend it all into an idea of going about "doing good." Is that spirituality?

One woman who had responded to this poll said that she liked to burn candles and that was a sign that she was a spiritual person. *Really*, thought Jake.

What is the purpose of trying to live a spiritual life? To what end? What is the purpose of life? There has to be more than "we are born, we live and we die." Jake felt as if he were missing something obvious. He thought of Plato and the Seven Wise Men. They knew, he presumed, the meaning of life. Why had modern mankind forgotten . . . ?

With a sudden jolt, Jake woke up. He felt cramped from sleeping in his easy chair. When did he fall asleep? Was he thinking or was he dreaming? He needed to shave and shower and get to the office.

At about ten-thirty that morning, Jake was finishing with some paperwork when he heard Ted knocking on his wall. He got up and rapped on the wall. By the time Ted opened the door and walked in, Jake had sat back down and finished up with the last of the paperwork.

Jake smiled and said, "You're awfully fast this morning."

Ted responded by asking, "Have you read the paper?"

Jake put his paperwork in a folder, put that folder in his front desk drawer and shook his head. He pushed his chair back and said, "What?"

"I was just reading it. There's an article about mergers."

"There's always an article about mergers."

"I think Excalibur may be involved in this one."

"Did the article mention Excalibur?"

"No. No. But, reading between the lines, I think it's us."

"Have you asked Tom?"

"Jennings? No. I just now read it."

"You should ask him. I think he'd play it straight with us."

"I don't know."

"Until you ask, it's just a rumor. A rumor that you started."

Ted smiled. "Why don't you ask him?"

"Okay."

"Okay? Just like that?"

"Sure. Why not?"

Ted shrugged his shoulders and stepped over to the putting green.

Jake smiled and put a pen to his lips. In a whisper, he said, "And a hush falls over the crowd as Redfire approaches the eight-foot putt. If he sinks it, he will win the Open by one shot. If he misses, it could mean a playoff or even a second place finish."

Ted concentrated as he lined up his putt. Just as he swung, there was a knock on Jake's door.

"Come in," Jake responded to the knock.

The putt went wide.

Alice Hastings entered the room. Her presence surprised both Jake and Ted. Although she had the title of Executive Assistant, Alice was Tom Jennings' personal secretary. She was in her late twenties, tall, slim and pretty. She had shoulder length black hair, an impish face and big light blue eyes.

As she closed the door behind her, she said, "Oh, I'd forgotten what your office looked like, Jake."

"Guess it hasn't changed much."

She waved at Ted and said, "Oh, hi Ted."

With the putter in his hand, he waved back to her.

"So . . . how's it going, Alice?" Jake asked.

"That's what I wanted to talk to you about, if you've got a minute."

"Sure Alice. We were . . ." Jake turned to Ted.

Ted said, "I need to get back to my office. I just blew the Open championship and I need a cup of coffee. I'll see you guys."

Alice sighed. "I never understand what he's talking about."

"No one does. Don't worry about it, Alice. It's a joke . . . You kind of had to be there. What's up?"

Alice walked over to the large wall window and looked out across the city. Jake got up from his desk and went over to his coffee counter.

"Would you like a cup?"

Alice came over to the counter and sat down.

"Thank you."

Jake handed her a cup of coffee, got one for himself and sat down at the counter next to Alice. She seemed distracted. She took a small sip of coffee. Jake smiled at her. She smiled back.

Alice obviously had come to Jake's office with something on her mind. However, she was having a difficult time getting started. Jake didn't rush her.

Alice and Jake had a brief history. Three years ago, Jake had taken Alice to the Spring Ball. She was new at Excalibur; neither one had been seeing anyone at the time. They were mutual escorts for each other. They both enjoyed each other's company. However, Jake thought, and still thought, he was too much older than her for them to continue seeing each other.

She looked around Jake's office, took another tiny sip of coffee and said, "This is nice."

Jake smiled and said, "It's nice seeing you again. I don't see you executives too often."

Alice laughed. "I'm a glorified secretary and everyone knows it." She sounded bitter.

"What's wrong, Alice?"

She turned sharply, started to say something but did not. Instead, she drank a gulp of coffee. Finally, very softly, she said, "Roger broke up with me."

"I'm sorry, Alice." Jake almost whispered his response.

Alice and Roger had been dating for almost two years. It was assumed, by everyone in the office, that they would eventually get married.

Alice nodded her head. She drank some more coffee. Jake realized she was using the coffee cup as a crutch to help her overcome her awkwardness with the situation.

"May I freshen your cup?"

"Please."

Jake refilled her cup and his mug.

She turned to Jake and said, "I need some honest male advice."

"If I can help Alice, I'll be glad to give you my opinion."

"No, it's more than that. I don't know what to do. I don't know what I did wrong. I thought I was in love with Roger. I thought he was in love with me. And now . . . obviously, he is not in love with me. And . . . I'm not as bummed out about it as I thought I'd be. Maybe I never loved him either. I just don't know."

"Relationships can be confusing," Jake whispered.

"Yes, you got that right. This is all confusing to me. That's it. I am one confused woman right now. I mean, it hurts. It hurt real bad when it first happened. I was stunned. But now, it's been a week; I'm not hurting as much as I would have thought. In one sense, I'm even glad. I mean, if he doesn't truly love me, then I'm glad we're over. I certainly wouldn't want to be married to a man who wasn't in love with me."

In a low voice, again almost a whisper, Jake replied, "I understand that."

"Jake," Alice said, "you're one of the smartest people I've ever met. I thought you might be able to tell me how to live differently. What I could do. What I could have done differently. What I should . . ."

She started to say more, but didn't.

"Alice, I believe in love." Jake said those words softly.

Alice's face brightened. Her blue eyes sparkled and she gave Jake a radiant smile.

He continued, "I think we should all live our lives out of love. We should live with love towards all other people. This will give meaning to every day of our lives. With this approach, we cannot ever harbor hate, revenge or ill thoughts toward anyone. We will live with compassion and love for each other.

"At the same time, we cannot be naive or allow ourselves to be taken advantage of by those who will perceive our love as a sign of weakness. While we can and should live our lives from a foundation of love, we must be realistic and know that there is evil in this world.

"But I sincerely believe that love is the most powerful force in the universe. If we are living out of love, then when bad things happen – and they will – they don't have the impact and influence over us as they might for someone who is not living a life of love and compassion."

Alice smiled and the dimples on her face were prominent. Jake realized again what a truly pretty woman she was.

Alice said, "Jake, that is a beautiful philosophy of life. And I appreciate the sentiment. But that has nothing to do with what I am asking."

"Sorry."

"No. No. Look, Jake, I don't have a brother. There's just my little sister and me. She is married with one child and another on the way. What I want you to tell me is a male's point of view. What should I have done differently? What did I do, or not do, that turned Roger away from me?"

"Oh, I see what you're saying."

"Yes?"

"You want a 'trick' or a 'secret' to know how to not lose another man?"

"When you put it like that . . . I mean . . ."

"I think it is always best to be yourself. I know that sounds trite. But if you pretend to be someone you're not, it won't last. You wouldn't want to spend your entire life pretending to be someone other than yourself. There is someone 'out there' who is looking for someone exactly like you. And he will be exactly who you are looking for also."

"I thought that was Roger and me. But it wasn't." Alice sighed. "I can't figure out what I did wrong. That's what I want you to tell me. Whatever it was, I won't do it again."

"Alice, how in the world could I tell you something like that. I don't know where you went on dates, what you did, what you talked about or how you got along. I mean, how could I possibly know how to answer that question. Besides, I doubt that you did anything wrong. I think that's the wrong attitude to have.

Roger lost out on the opportunity to spend the rest of his life with a wonderful woman. Who says you did *anything* wrong?"

Alice smiled but said, "I must have. He left me and has gone looking elsewhere."

Jake looked into Alice's beautiful eyes and truly felt sorry for her. She is a sexy, attractive and intelligent woman, he thought. She should not feel as though she has done something wrong. However, she does feel that way. Maybe she did do something that turned Roger away.

Jake swallowed the last of his coffee and said, "What do *you* think you did that was so wrong?"

"That's just it. I don't know. I have no idea. Whatever it was, I want to avoid it in the future."

"I see. I'm beginning to understand now."

"Finally." Alice laughed.

"But Alice, in order to help, I need you to tell me more about your relationship with Roger."

"Hmmmm . . . well . . . he likes sports – all kinds of sports – and I don't like them at all. I tried to humor him. I mean, I tried to put up with all that sports nonsense . . . but, well . . . after a while, he just has, had, his 'sports times' and I wasn't involved with them. He spends way too much time with sports. Early in our relationship, he once had tickets to a Knicks game and he took me. That was the dumbest thing I've ever tried to watch."

"Did you tell him that?"

"Not at the time, no."

"But later?"

"Yes."

"What was his reaction?"

"Well, you see . . . this is when we were deciding that he would have his 'sports times' and he would just leave me out of it."

"And was that all right with you?"

"Yes. In fact, it was my idea. I guess I just decided that you males must have some time for sports." Nodding at the putting green, Alice said, "Like Ted with his golf thing."

"Now don't make the mistake of lumping all males in the same basket."

"Perhaps I did that with Roger."

"How?"

"Several ways, I suppose. I don't know. You know that old wives' tale about the way to a man's heart is through his stomach?"

"Yes."

"I have become quite an excellent cook. I even took classes with a gourmet chef. I have learned so much about cooking that I have amazed myself. I'll have to have you over one night. You'll see."

"I would love that. Thank you."

"Roger always praised the meals I prepared for him. And they were good. Honestly though, I think he would have been just as happy with hot dogs and a beer. For the last six months or so, he seemed to lose interest in my meals."

"Alice, can we talk frankly here?"

"Absolutely. Tell me what you think."

"Alice, I think that that old wives' tale was made up by old wives. You might want to listen to some old husbands' tales."

"What do you mean?"

"I think the way to a man's heart is not through his stomach. The way to a man's heart, in that sense, is located about six inches below his stomach."

Alice actually blushed.

"Now Alice, I'm not prying . . ."

"No. No. It's okay. I understand what you're saying. And I like sex. Roger and I had a good sex life. I mean, I think we did. I thought we did. But after all, we weren't married. I mean, we weren't really even engaged yet."

"Of course. I understand. But let me tell you something. I have heard from numerous . . . yes numerous is the right word . . . numerous married men who say that they had better sex with their wives before they were married than after they were married. In my personal case, that was certainly so. After we were married, sex seemed to drop off her list of priorities. And despite what they might say, men take it personally. They perceive it as if their wives don't truly love them anymore. Now, as for you and Roger, I can't accurately comment. But, if, for example, Roger thought that the sexual attention he was receiving from you was . . . mediocre – well then, he might have figured it would only get worse after you two were married. That thought may have scared him off."

Alice looked deep in thought.

"Then again, your sexual relationship may have been great and may have had nothing to do with Roger breaking up with you. It may have been something else entirely."

"You know something, Jake?"

"What?"

"You may have just found exactly what I was looking for."

"Only you can know that."

"I know. But what you said. You know, it is difficult for a single girl to know how far to go with a guy. I mean, if you're married – anything goes, right?"

"Yes, right."

"And perhaps, even if you're engaged. But if you're just dating, if, for example, a woman likes sex too much, she can be called a slut. If she doesn't like it enough, she's frigid."

"Yes, I understand the dilemma. That's why I think it's important for a couple to become real friends before they become lovers. Then both the male and the female can be themselves without worrying about what their partner is going to think of them."

In almost a whisper, Alice said softly, "I don't think Roger and I ever considered each other friends."

"I sincerely believe that everyone, both male and female, should marry their best friend."

"I like that," Alice smiled.

"I've already decided that, as a Christian, if I ever fall in love with my best friend, she and I will not have sex until we are married."

"Wow. How will that work?"

"Short engagement."

Alice laughed out loud.

CHAPTER NINE

"Know Thyself."

– Inscribed in the forecourt of the Temple of Apollo at Delphi, Greece. Plato, in *Protagorus*, ascribes this saying as the ultimate collected wisdom of the Seven Wise Men of ancient Greece.

Early 4th Century B. C.

On the next Friday evening, around nine-thirty, Jake Fleming was sitting in his big blue easy chair, in his library, smoking a pipe and reading a book. While he was engrossed with his novel, something unusual happened. His doorbell rang.

At first, he actually didn't realize what it was. It rang again and he remembered what that sound was. He got up and answered his door intercom. His condominium complex had an intercom system that kept visitors waiting in a room off of the lobby. He could press a button that signaled the doorman that it was all right to permit the visitors to enter the lobby and access the elevator. Jake was not expecting anyone so whoever this was would be a surprise to him. It turned out to be Ted and Jake was genuinely surprised.

When Jake opened the door, Ted was standing there looking sheepish and somewhat afraid. Jake had never known Ted to be sheepish about anything. Something was wrong.

Jake led Ted through the condo to his library. Ted refused a beer or anything else. He sat in the only place available – a small black wooden deacon's bench. Jake sat in his big old chair.

Ted looked around the room full of books. He had been to

Jake's condo once before about a year and half prior.

Ted said, "I'd forgotten you had a fireplace in here."

"Yeah. I actually use it in the winter."

After an uncomfortable pause, Ted asked, "Jake, what happens when a person dies?"

Softly, Jake asked, "Has someone died?"

Shaking his head, Ted replied, "No. But we just found out that my dad has been diagnosed with pancreatic cancer."

"Ted, I am so sorry. What's the prog...?"

"There's really nothing they can do. Oh, they can give him radiation treatment, chemo, whatever. But they never really work with this type of cancer. I've been on the Net looking at possible options and treatments and...for pancreatic cancer...there really isn't much that can be done. Earlier this evening, I called his doctor. He said my dad most likely has less than a year to live."

"I'm so sorry. Ted, I wish I could..."

"Tell me what happens when a person dies."

"Ted, I don't think *anyone* actually knows, with one hundred percent accuracy, exactly what happens during the dying process. It may even be different for different people."

Looking around the room full of books, Ted said, "But surely you've read books about it. You must know what..."

"There have probably been hundreds of books written about death and what happens when death occurs. But . . ."

"As they say down South, there ya go."

Jake smiled. "Not really. I have read several books on the subject. The problem is that each book seems to have a different perspective regarding what happens. The Buddhists seem to have the most detailed description of the death process. Whether it is accurate or not, who knows? And how can we know for sure unless someone were to die and then come back and tell us about it?"

"Haven't there been people who have done just that? What do they say about it? A clinical death. No. A..."

"A near-death experience."

"Yes. That's it. Have you read what those people say?"

"Yes. But . . ."

"And? What do they say?"

"They don't all say the same thing. But I can tell you this. Most say that they no longer fear death. Most say that the near-death experience was beautiful. Most say that they did not want to return to their bodies."

"So it was pleasant?"

"For most."

"What about the others?"

"Not so much. Some had very unpleasant experiences. Some went to a dark place."

"But for most, it was pleasant?"

"Yes. But Ted, there are many different religious beliefs about what happens when a person dies. To be up front about this Ted, it is not the dying process itself that is important. I mean, some people are killed instantaneously in a car wreck. There is no dying process. What is important Ted, is what happens after a person dies. What faith is your dad?"

"He's Methodist."

"I think that Methodists believe a person's soul travels instantly, upon death of the physical body, to either heaven or hell. But the Bible is extremely short on specifics regarding the process of dying. The Tibetans, who practice Buddhism, have entire books on the exact stages of the dying process. They have extremely detailed steps, or phases, that one's soul will encounter or go through as the body dies. I've never figured out how they know all this with such exactness."

"Have you ever known someone who had a near-death experience?"

"Actually, I have. Back when I was working over at Parkers. There was a man there from the marketing department. Nice guy. We were never close friends or anything. We ate lunch together a few times. We'd talk over a cup of coffee – you know."

"Yeah."

"Anyway, one day at lunch, he told me that he had had a

near-death experience. I don't know why he told me about it. He said he didn't tell many people because they tended not to believe him. He said it was like telling people you saw a flying saucer. But he said he wanted to tell me about it."

"What'd he say it was like?"

"He wouldn't tell me."

"What? What do you mean? You just said . . ."

"He never would tell me specifics. The only thing he told me was that I should definitely not fear death."

"Do you?"

"No. In some ways, I am actually looking forward to it. Death will answer a lot of questions."

"Like what happens when a person dies." Ted smiled.

Jake laughed. "Yes."

"But why would this guy not tell you any specifics about his near-death experience?"

"I don't know. When I asked him, he just shook his head and said that he didn't feel comfortable talking about what he had experienced. He just said it was a wonderful experience. He didn't remember actually dying. He said he floated up from the hospital and the next thing he knew he was in Heaven and felt the presence of Jesus. That's as much as he would say. He asked me not to question him about it or tell others about it. Since that was his wish, I respected that. You're the first person I've told about it."

"Is he still alive?"

"As far as I know. He left Parkers in nineteen ninety-nine. I haven't kept up with him."

"I'd like to talk with him."

"He wouldn't discuss it with you."

"Perhaps he would discuss it with my dad."

"Perhaps. I don't know. I can try to track him down. I've still got his phone number and address. Of course, they may both be changed by now."

"I'd appreciate it."

"Okay."

"So you think our souls survive death?"

"Naturally. Of course. You remember, about a month ago, we were talking about each human being having a teeny tiny spark of the Divine within them?"

"Yes."

"I think that spark, somehow, is connected to our souls, perhaps that spark is our souls – and they most certainly survive death. What would be the point of having a soul if it didn't survive death? I believe that Jesus and the Bible are very clear about our souls surviving death. There is absolutely no doubt in my mind that anyone who believes in Jesus – that He is the Christ, the Son of God – will, upon death, have his soul go to be with Jesus in Heaven."

Ted replied, "That's the way I have always heard it."

"Yes, of course. Listen, you know that saying 'from dust to dust?'"

Ted nodded. "Uh-huh."

"That actually comes from a verse in the Bible. And the second part of that verse says that our souls, when we die, go to be with God. Without looking it up, I'm pretty sure it is Ecclesiastes, chapter 12 . . . I think verse seven. It says the dust returns to the ground it came from *and* the soul returns to God. That's not exact but I think it is pretty close. Your dad may be interested in reading that verse – and the ones around it."

"Thanks. Let me write it down. Jake, why do people die when they die? I mean, I understand someone dying when they are in their nineties. But my dad is too young to die now. And what about little children?"

Jake felt a constriction, a lump, in his throat. He couldn't respond to Ted's question, "What about little children?" Instead, he stood up and said, "Can I get you anything?"

"No, I'm good."

"I think I'll make some tea."

Jake went to his kitchen and put a pot of water on the stove to boil. Ted had followed him. He sat at the kitchen table near a large window and looked at the night skyline. As Jake put some loose tea in a teapot, Ted could tell he was distracted and upset.

"You don't use teabags?"

"Nope. This is the real stuff."

Ted was trying to lighten the mood but it was strained. What was it about children that had upset his friend? Did he and his ex-wife lose a child? Was that why they divorced? Ted knew he couldn't understand the change in Jake without more information.

The water came to a boil. Jake poured it into his teapot and put the rest back on the stove.

"How long does it take?"

"It steeps for about five minutes."

"You're quite the cook in your spare time."

Jake smiled. "This really isn't cooking. Would you like some?"

"I'm not much of a tea drinker."

"This is straight from London. If you're gonna drink tea, get it from England. If you're gonna drink wine, get it from France."

"Yeah. And, if you're gonna drink beer, get if from the good ole USA."

"Or Mexico."

"Or Mexico. With lime."

"Sure you won't have a cup?"

"No thanks. But now that you brought it up, you wouldn't happen to have a lime in the place, would you?"

"Comin' right up."

"Thanks."

"Let's go out on the balcony and watch the ships."

Sitting there, with a small iron table between them, the two men both knew that their discussion wasn't finished. Ted held his bottle out to Jake in a salute, took a big swallow of the cold beer and said, "Man, I always love that first swallow."

"Yeah, I know what you mean."

Ted sat his bottle down on the table, looked at Jake and

asked, "Are you all right?"

Jake choked up, took a sip of his hot tea and answered, "I'm still searching. I'm still trying to get a handle, to understand...the death of little children."

Ted didn't respond. He knew Jake had more to say.

Jake looked into his cup of tea. Without looking at Ted, he asked, "Have I ever told you about Katherine?"

Ted shook his head and replied, "No."

Jake paused. He took another sip of tea. He stared at the tea in his cup.

Without looking up, he said, "I spent the first two weeks of June in the year two thousand with Katherine. My youngest sister, Lucy, and her husband were going on a two-week European cruise. Katherine was their youngest child and my youngest niece. She was seven years old that June. I was still at Parkers then. I had plenty of vacation time. I took the first two weeks of June off so that I could get to know my little niece. And I'm so glad I did." Jake smiled. He was still staring into his cup of tea. He continued, "Katherine was the smartest child I've ever known. She was so precocious. I had conversations with her and it was like I was talking with an adult. And she was only seven. Only seven. Anyway," Jake looked up at Ted briefly and then back down at his cup of tea. He was holding it between the fingers of both hands. He had not drunk much of the tea – just kept staring at it. "We went to all the places that visitors to New York want to see. We went to museums, art galleries, the observation decks at the Trade Towers and at the Empire State Building, the Statue of Liberty, a Broadway show, Rockefeller Center and she had her own list of things she wanted to see. We spent a week doing all that and then we drove upstate. We went to Niagara Falls. She was so excited to see that. We stayed one night in Canada. It was her first time outside the United States. We drove across Vermont, New Hampshire and into Maine. She thought that when she grew up, she might move to Maine. We both loved Camden and Mt. Battie. We spent a day in Boston and had to get back so she could meet her parents at the airport here in New York. They were to fly home together from there. Much more important than all the places we visited and the things we saw was the connection we developed between us. It is difficult to describe. I guess I came to love that little girl like my own daughter." A tear or two started rolling down Jake's cheeks. He shook his head and tried to smile. "I haven't told you much about her. She was naturally skinny. She was tall for a seven-year-old. She had long light blond hair. And her smile would just light up a room." The lump had returned to Jake's throat. Tears were now sliding down his face. Ted pretended not to notice. "You know," Jake continued, "Katherine had her own sense of humor. I was constantly surprised by it. I still remember one of her jokes. She asked me to guess who made the following remark: 'In this world, a woman's success pretty much depends upon the shoes she is wearing.' You know who said that?" Jake looked at Ted and smiled. Ted shook his head. "Dorothy." Ted laughed. "I still find that clever and funny. I remember once we had stopped at a fast food place and got some burgers. We took them to a park in New Hampshire. We were sitting at a picnic table. We had just finished eating when it started to rain. We just sat there looking across the table at each other. It started to rain even harder. We just smiled at each other. A lightning bolt cut across the sky. It thundered. We sat there getting completely and totally drenched. It *was* June. I got up and started to dance in the rainstorm. She joined me. We just laughed and laughed." A smile came across Jake's face. But Ted noticed that Jake's eyes were moist again. "One day we were sitting on the beach at Old Orchard Beach in Maine. I asked her what she wanted to be when she grew up. You know, at some point, I think there must be a law about it, but every adult has to ask every child that question. Like most children, she hadn't really decided. She said she was thinking about being a writer. And, she told me about a short story she had just written. It was about a caterpillar. This caterpillar was miserable. He was complaining about his lot in life. It seems he was just hanging around, feeling weird and accomplishing nothing. And then, when he thought things were getting worse and worse, he became a beautiful butterfly."

Jake had tears running down his face. He set his cup of cold tea on the little iron table and looked out at the harbor. He got up and went into the kitchen. He got a napkin, wiped his face and blew his nose. Ted didn't say anything. Jake came back out on the balcony and sat down. He picked up his cup of tea, stared out at a boat that was slowly moving out to sea and continued telling Ted about Katherine.

"I know we only spent two weeks together, but I really came to...I really loved that little girl. She was...special. So special. So precious. So..." The tears just flowed down Jake's face. He again began to choke up; he couldn't speak. He just shook his head and let the tears flow. Ted remained silent.

Finally, Jake got up and, using a paper towel, wiped his face and blew his nose.

Sitting back on the balcony, he turned to Ted and said, "I'm sorry. I just...uh, I'm sorry."

"No. No need to be sorry."

"I uh...I just can't seem to...I can't stop the tears."

Jake tried to smile.

Ted softly asked, "What happened?"

Jake shook his head. His throat was still tight. He picked up his cup of tea and thought of Alice doing the same thing with her cup of coffee. He took a deep breath.

He said, "Katherine went home with Lucy and her husband. A week later, while she was riding her bicycle on a sidewalk, in the afternoon...a drunk driver swerved onto the sidewalk, hit her with his car and killed her. I never...I never...I never got to tell her what she meant to me. I never got to say goodbye. I never saw her again."

Jake could not control his tears. As soon as he wiped them away, more returned. And now, Ted was wiping his eyes with a napkin.

Jake sat his cup of tea on the table again. He wiped his face, blew his nose and composed himself.

He turned to Ted and said, "I'm so sorry. It's been almost

five years now. I should not have told you about Katherine. I am...obviously still not over it yet."

"No, no, I'm glad you told me."

"No, it's not right. You came here asking for help and I burden you with a sad story. I'm sorry."

"I appreciate your sharing that with me. You know I have two little ones, Christy and Mark. If anything ever happened to one of them, I would be a total wreck."

Jake shook his head. "She would be twelve now. She would be turning into a butterfly."

The tears returned. Jake tried to wipe them away. He shook his head and said, "I'm sorry, Ted. I really loved that little girl. I'm uh . . . I'm sorry."

"No. It's all right."

"I just can't...I'm sorry. So senseless. I can't seem...I'm sorry."

"No, Jake. I understand. It's all right. You have no reason to apologize."

Jake smiled. "My nose won't seem to stop running." He grabbed another napkin and blew his nose. They had moved back into the kitchen and were sitting at the small breakfast table. Jake took another deep breath and said "Whoosh." He composed himself. He said, "I uh...I have forgotten what it was you had asked me."

"Me too."

Ted looked hard at Jake and said, "Jake, I'd really like to ask you something."

"Okay, shoot."

"No, it may not be okay. I'd like to know something in connection with...your niece."

"You can say her name. I'm not going to fall apart again. I'm good."

"Okay. What happened to that drunk guy?"

"He was given two years for involuntary manslaughter."

"Two years?"

"Yes. He was out in sixteen months."

"Sixteen months. I guess the family was pretty upset over that."

"Her dad was. The rest of the family – not so much. I forgave him."

"You forgave him? How is that…I mean, how can you forgive someone who has caused so much sorrow and pain?"

"Ted, when someone wrongs you…when someone goes out of their way to be mean to you…when someone intentionally plans to cause you harm, of whatever nature, the natural impulse is to strike back. But for a person traveling a spiritual path, this is not the first impulse. I learned this about myself as I went through my divorce. My ex-wife actually plotted ways to embarrass me and cause me grief. Rather than wanting to strike back at her, I found that I had compassion for her. I prayed for her. It is extremely difficult to be mad at someone for whom you are praying. Since then, whenever someone intentionally tries to harm me, I find myself forgiving them and praying for them. Forgiveness, I find, is healing."

"But this guy killed your niece."

"I know. My sister, Lucy, at first, wanted to hang him by his toes and slice little bits of his flesh from his body until he slowly died in great pain. It even got so bad, I thought that my sister and her husband might divorce over it. However, they have a son, Steve. He needed both his parents. Time, as they say, is a great healer."

"But Jake, I don't understand. I can tell, by what you have just said…I mean, I know how…deeply you loved Katherine. After five years, you haven't completely healed. How…?"

"When you forgive someone, it helps to heal your own heart. It doesn't matter if someone has committed an act of violence or an act of despicable behavior, like driving drunk – forgiving that person helps to put the act in the past. Forgiving them does not, in any way, mean that you condone or support their behavior – simply that you forgive them for it. And I do forgive him. Actually, I feel sorry for him."

"Now that I really do not understand."

"Think about it, Ted. He will have to live with the fact that he got himself drunk, got in a car, ran down and killed a little seven-year-old girl. It would be tough to shave your face every morning knowing who was looking back at you from the mirror. Yes, I feel sorry for him. And, I have prayed for him."

"It just seems such a shame that it happened. I mean, if the drunk had been a few seconds later, or earlier. If Katherine had been a few feet farther down the sidewalk, it seems so awful and meaningless. Why do little children have to die?"

"Ted, I have been down this road many, many times. It was an accident. It was a preventable accident. But most all accidents are preventable. I most certainly do blame the guy. There is no excuse for driving while you are so drunk that you can't even stay off of the sidewalks. And, as you have seen for yourself tonight, I am not over it. Enough."

Ted noticed a tear in the corner of Jake's left eye. He quickly changed the subject.

Ted asked, "So why do you think that guy you knew who had a near-death experience – what is his name?"

"Bill."

"Okay. Why wouldn't Bill talk with you about what he had experienced?"

"I don't know. He just said he did not want to discuss it. You ever see *Star Trek Four*?"

"Sure. The whale one. What's that got...?"

"When they are in the Klingon ship heading from Vulcan to Earth, McCoy asks Spock the question everyone would ask. He says you really have gone where no one has gone before. What was it like?"

"Yeah, I remember. He was talking about Spock dying and coming back."

"Right. And Spock says that it would be impossible to discuss it with Bones because Bones didn't have a point of reference. And Bones says, you mean I have to die first before we can discuss death?"

Ted smiled and said, "Still, it looks like, to me, that you'd want to tell everyone about the experience – that you'd want to share it."

"Yes, that does seem logical. However, have you ever told anyone that you've seen a UFO?"

"I haven't seen one."

"But if you had, would you go around telling people?"

"Perhaps not."

"Can't you understand that someone who has visited Heaven may not want the ridicule that would be sure to follow?"

"I guess."

"But now, some people have written books, in detail, about their near-death experience. They were sometimes criticized for making money from their experience. However, I'm sure that most of them genuinely wanted to share what they had learned."

"Sum it up for me."

"Hey, you know how to read. But okay. Basically, many of them say that death is really a rebirth. The soul that was attached to a particular body is now aware of previously unknown knowledge. Frequently, a tunnel, of some type, usually light, is described. When the soul emerges from the tunnel, that spirit entity, which is still identifying itself by its human earthly experience, encounters extreme and absolute love. Many talk of meeting Jesus Christ himself. They describe him as pure love. But they often say he showed a sense of humor. Most did not describe a physical place called Heaven. Instead, they talked of a place of great light, joy and love. One, I remember, described it as sitting in a beautiful blooming garden. They all said that being there was wonderful, joyful and a place they did not want to leave. Everyone there was a spiritual being. And every spiritual being had spent time on Earth living and learning in a human body. Now this isn't Biblical but many of these people who have these experiences say that the spiritual beings often get to choose the family that they would be born into so that they could experience and learn specific lessons. Sometimes the spiritual beings would choose to experience an earthly existence in order to provide a learning experience for one of their close friends. For example, perhaps a close friend has chosen to live an earthly life that included marriage and children. The close spiritual friend might choose to be a child of his friend – a child that would only live for a few days or a few years. This would be so that his friend could experience that utter sense of . . . senseless loss."

Jake had paused. Very softly, Ted said, "Like Katherine."

Jake nodded. Then he added, "That is not Biblical and may not have any reality to it. There may be some truth to it and there may not. I don't know."

"So tell me," Ted asked, "what do they say about life on earth? Are there any great revelations?"

"Not really. Each spiritual being is at a different level of spiritual development. As a consequence, they can only understand spiritual knowledge according to their level of development. One way of looking at it is that everyone on the planet Earth has a spiritual being within them."

"Their soul?"

"Yes. And each person is undergoing experiences that will help the spiritual being within to grow in spiritual development and spiritual knowledge."

"I actually followed that."

Jake smiled. "That would, of course, include you and me. And your dad. Now this spiritual being, this soul, is not to be confused with the Holy Spirit. The Holy Spirit lives within all real Christians. He is not a person's soul."

Ted replied, "I understand. What else do these people say?"

"Remember Ted, this is not presented in the Bible. These are individuals' descriptions of what they recall about their near-death experiences. Most are slightly different from each other. But you should read some of the books for yourself. Many don't remember a lot of specifics. A few do. But they all agree that we should love everyone as we love ourselves. They all say that there is no time for hate, jealousy, revenge, despair or negative thoughts. We are all on Earth going through our daily human lives, making mistakes, growing and, hopefully, learning. One thing these near-death experiencers seem to want everyone to know is that love is the absolute greatest thing in the world. And, there is a sequence of love: first, one is to love God; second, one is to love one's self; and third, one is to love others as one's self. They also seemed to say that they received the strong impression that it was important to learn about spiritual things while existing in a human body. Such knowledge that is obtained on Earth will enable the soul to progress more quickly when it is in Heaven."

"What about dying itself?"

"Ted, you really need to read some of these books yourself. From these people who have had this near-death experience, and please understand that I haven't read all the books written on this subject and am no expert on this matter, I think they primarily describe death as the soul slipping away from the human body. The soul then leaves for Heaven or Hell. However, sometimes, according to some of these people, the soul may remain near the dead human body for a while. Some mentioned that they went to view their human family one last time. Some even say that the soul may stay around until the body is buried. But I don't think that is likely."

"Ghosts?"

Jake shrugged his shoulders.

Ted asked, "What else?"

"Time in Heaven is not the same as time on Earth. Souls can travel long distances almost instantaneously. They can have long discussions. They can sit and experience joy and love for what may seem like hours. While doing all this, on Earth, maybe only a few minutes of time have passed."

"What else?"

"Ted, really. What else? What else?"

"Come on. One more thing."

"Okay. All of the people who have had a near-death experience say that we should never be judgmental of others. Now this refers to things like appearances – not acts of violence. This means not to be prejudiced because of someone's skin color or because someone is fat or skinny. However, if someone is a murderer, then something has gone terribly wrong and that person needs to be put away so that he cannot harm himself or any others. Oh, by the way, suicide and abortion are both considered horribly wrong. They both deny the soul within the human body the opportunity to learn the lessons for which they chose to enter the human plane of existence. The soul then has to start over again with new circumstances."

"Wow. This puts things in a new perspective for me."

"Listen, I've got some of these books right here. Let me loan you a few."

"That'd be great. Thanks."

Jake got up, walked over to a shelf and began removing some books. He brought them over to Ted and handed them to him. He pointed at the one on the top and said, "I think your dad would enjoy reading this one."

"This one?"

"Yes. It's probably the best of them all."

"Okay. Thanks."

"You're welcome."

"What about Buddhists?"

"What about them?"

"What do they believe about death?"

"Mercy. There are numerous books about this."

"I know. And you've probably read most of them. What do they say about death?"

"Ted, I've already told you that they have an explanation of the process of death that involves stages. But, I'm no expert on Buddhism."

"I know. But, basically, what do they think?"

"They believe that death is a rebirth. It is a transition. They believe the soul moves on. They also believe it is an opportunity for enlightenment. But that gets rather involved."

"What do they believe we should be doing while on Earth?"

"Actually, their beliefs are similar to those of Christianity.

They believe we should not have great attachment to things of this world. They believe in practicing, not just stating it, but practicing kindness toward all living beings. They believe that everyone should be loving and compassionate – regardless of what others do to you or say about you. They believe that if one is spiritually mature, that one will be aware that all humans are interdependent with everything and everyone else. To them, this means that our smallest insignificant word, action or even thought can have real consequences. They believe that everything is inextricably interrelated. As you probably know, Ted, they are big on meditation. But most people misunderstand meditation. Buddhists see meditation as a means for establishing a direct connection with the truth within themselves. It is a way to bring a person back to himself. Meditation can awaken the nature of one's mind so that a person can see who they really are. To sum things up, I think that Buddhists believe in compassion, kindness and love. But for it to be real, they believe it must be active. In other words, one can't simply say I feel compassion for that poor person over there. If one has compassion for that poor person over there, then one would do something to help alleviate the suffering of that poor person. See?"

"Yes, I understand."

"Now, of course, one of the biggest problems with Buddhism is that it does not recognize God as an entity. It does not accept the concept of sin – that it is not allowed in Heaven. Christianity shows that the only way for one's soul to dwell in Heaven with God is to lead either a sinless life, which is impossible for humans, or to accept the gift of Jesus who died for our sins, conquered death and by His grace and love, made a path for sinners to be received in Heaven. Buddhists believe that their souls can eventually be enlightened and exist in that enlightened state for all time. Buddhism has some nice beliefs but it certainly is not a philosophy that I would want to follow. I do have some books on the subject. Would you like some?"

Looking at the stack of books that Jake had already loaned him, Ted replied, "Maybe one or two."

"Okay."

Jake went over to another shelf and picked out one book for Ted.

Ted asked, "How do you know exactly where each book is located?"

"I put them all on the shelves. I know where they are."

"But there are thousands of books in this room."

"Yes, I know."

Shaking his head, Ted simply said, "Okay."

The two friends kept talking throughout the night, about death and different religious views of death. During a brief pause in their conversation, Jake had gotten up to go to the bathroom. On the way back, he called Ted into the kitchen. Jake pointed out toward the balcony. Ted turned to look. He saw the first rays of the morning sun as it broke on the horizon. They walked out onto the balcony.

"I always find this to be a beautiful sight," Jake whispered.

Ted asked, "Are you up this early every morning?"

"No, not every morning. But I do enjoy watching the sunrise. It's comforting and nice to know that, whether I'm watching it or not, the sun will rise every single morning."

CHAPTER TEN

"The authority of a thousand is not worth the humble reasoning of a single individual. I do not feel obligated to believe that the same God who has endowed us with sense, reason, and intellect has intended us to forgo their use."

– Galileo Galilei

Early 17th Century A.D.

Fortunately, for both Ted and Jake, the sun had risen on a Saturday morning. Ted, with his armload of borrowed books, had returned to his home. He had called his wife, Stacy, late the previous night and explained that he was talking with Jake. She understood. Jake was back in his easy chair, puffing his pipe and reading the novel he had started when Ted had arrived. However, he couldn't stay with it. His mind kept wandering. He kept returning to the conversation he had had with Ted. He kept thinking of things he should have said. He didn't think he was clear with Ted. He left so much unsaid. Perhaps, Jake thought, Ted will read the books and get a better understanding of what he was seeking. The Bible though, is sufficient to supply the answers and we know it is true. The stories from those people who claim near-death experiences could be totally false.

Jake's heart hurt when he thought of Katherine. But he was glad he had told Ted about her. He smiled as he remembered her cute smile and her inquisitive look. She was a remarkable little girl with a wonderful soul.

Jake forced himself to return to his novel. He had been up all night but was not at all sleepy. He went into the kitchen, got some tea from last night, heated it in the microwave, went out on the balcony and enjoyed the spring sun.

There was something about his discussion with Ted that was bothering him. There was something that didn't fit – something that didn't seem right. However, he couldn't place exactly what it was that was troubling him. It would come to him.

Jake looked out toward the water. He reflected, once again, that truly some of the best things in life are really free. He felt, briefly and suddenly, a pang of loneliness. It would be nice, he thought, to have a wife, sitting with him, sharing and enjoying this morning view. Nonetheless, the feeling of loneliness quickly passed. He finished his tea, got up and returned to his library and his book.

Jake's mind would just not focus on the novel. It wasn't a bad story; he simply could not stay with it. He thought he realized now what was bothering him regarding his talk with Ted. It seemed as if they were trying to reason their way or to think their way to an understanding of death and God. Jake knew that that wouldn't work. In the seventeenth century, a French genius, Blaine Pascal, noted that it is the human heart that perceives God and not human reasoning. Jake had not been clear about this with Ted. No, Jake told himself, this is not what was concerning him. It was something else.

Jake had planned to finish purchasing all his camping supplies for his vacation that Saturday afternoon. He wasn't going to let "no sleep" stop him. He decided to take a shower, shave and go. He'd grab something to eat before he started his shopping. He actually had very little left to buy. He wanted to get some freeze-dried meals – just in case the fish weren't biting. Jake wanted some more batteries. Where he was planning on being would keep him away from any source of electricity. It was a really isolated area that he was headed toward.

Monday morning was unusually busy. Jake worked through lunch. He ate an apple and drank some coffee. Ted must have been as busy. Jake didn't hear from him all day. They both spent hours on the phone with clients. Then they both spent hours emailing clients and finally writing up formal reports.

The next day, around ten-thirty, Jake heard Ted's familiar rap on the wall. He moved over and responded. Ted soon entered Jake's office.

With a big grin on his face, Ted announced, "Killer day yesterday."

"Yeah, I think everyone here was completely swamped."

"I love those days. Was hoping today would be the same."

"Rarely do we get two days in a row like that."

"I know. I know. But I was hoping."

Ted walked over to the wall window. As he gazed out over the skyscrapers, he said, "I gave my dad that book you suggested. I took it to him Sunday. He seemed anxious to read it."

"You know, Ted, I should mention that some behavioral scientists think that the near-death experience is all in the person's mind. They think that, due to the death experience, the lack of oxygen to the brain causes the person to have some type of visual dream. They say the "experiences" that these people have are not real. When they repeat things that were said in the hospital, after they were pronounced dead, the scientists say that they were not truly dead and that they subconsciously heard what was said."

"What do you think?"

"I think that some of them are real."

"Why?"

These people give very similar explanations of what happened to them. With some of them, the description of love is so absolutely wonderful and touching that I cannot imagine it wasn't a real experience. The connection with Jesus is so amazing with some of these people, that I certainly want the experience to be real. Also, there was one extremely accurate description of the outside roof of the hospital building . . . that the person who was pronounced dead, was in – and that description was later verified. And . . ."

"Wait! Explain that. What are you saying?"

"In one case, a person who claimed to have had a near-death experience said that he floated up above his body in the hospital. Then, he said, he floated up through the ceiling and out above the roof of the hospital. When he returned to his body in the hospital, he described objects that were on the roof. Later, when he repeated this story, people went up on the roof and saw the objects that he had described."

"Wow."

"Yeah. Also, there have been statements given by the person having the near-death experience in which the person quotes family members who were not in the same room as the body of the person having the experience. One case I remember, the family members were in a waiting room and the woman who died was not in a position to hear, even subconsciously, what her family members were saying. Her body was even on a different floor of the hospital. Yet, when she returns from her near-death experience, she can remember and quote what each family member said. This is, however, rare. Most scientists still don't buy it. I hope that your dad will find the books to be comforting."

"Thank you. So . . . are you counting down the days?"

"Yes. Not counting today, three to go. I'm leaving early Saturday morning."

"Man, I gotta tell ya. I really can't see you sleeping in a tent, cooking over a campfire, swatting mosquitoes, fishing and traveling by canoe."

"I'm looking forward to it all . . . well, except for the mosquitoes."

"I'd have thought you would go to Las Vegas or maybe a resort in the Caribbean. I can see you on the beach – sipping a Bahama Mama and watching all the bikinis walk by."

"While I've got nothing against watching bikinis, all the rest of that is just not my style. I have no interest in Las Vegas at all."

"Uh-huh."

Jake smiled. "Watching bikinis can be fun but I would much rather hold one in my arms."

"Now you're talking. So why are you going alone to the

middle of nowhere? The only thing you're going to see up there is a moose or two."

"I've told you – I want to try something different. And, for some strange reason, I really do feel almost an urge to travel up there."

"What do you mean 'an urge?'"

"I don't really know. It's a feeling like I'm supposed to go there."

"Right. If you say so. I still think you'd better watch out for UFOs. I'll be watching Fox news and there you'll be. You'll say, 'I'll tell ya what happened: I had just built up ma campfar; I just put a big ole log on it; the next thing I knew, this here bright light shown down on me; I was sucked up into this U-F-O; the next thing I knew, I was sitting by ma campfar and there was nothing but embers burnin'; three 'ours had done passed and I knew nothin'.'"

Jake laughed.

"Everyone who gets abducted winds up talking like that."

"You reckon? I didn't know that."

"Oh yeah. Proven scientific fact. Them aliens change your speech patterns. It must have something to do with the experiments they run on ya."

Jake nodded. "Okay, I promise. I'll be on the lookout for 'em."

"You remember that movie where all those folks had an 'urge' to go to Devil's Tower?"

"Yeah, I remember."

"Maybe that's what's happening to you. They have put an 'urge' on you to go to this out-of-the-world place so that they can take you away."

"Ted, that was a movie."

"Probably based on a real-life account."

Jake shook his head and laughed.

"You know, Jake, I really do hope you have a good time. I mean, I don't see how that's possible; but, I hope it works out for you."

"Thank you."

"How long you gonna be gone?"

"Today is the seventeenth. I'm leaving on the twenty-first. With two weeks of vacation time and three weekends, I'll be gone sixteen days and be back here on June sixth."

"Sixteen days in the middle of nowhere. I think, after three days of bugs, you'll turn around and find a nice hotel on the beach somewhere."

"It's possible. I don't think it'll happen but anything's possible, I suppose."

CHAPTER ELEVEN

"Though you have not seen him, you love him; and even though you do not see him now, you believe in him and are filled with an inexpressible and glorious joy, for you are receiving the goal of your faith, the salvation of your souls."

– 1 Peter 1:8-9

Mid 1st Century A.D.

Jake stayed busy all morning on Friday, May 20th. About 11:30, he finished getting everything ready for his upcoming absence. He was leaving early the next morning. He walked over to his bar, got a mug of coffee and stood by his wall window. After a few minutes, he looked over at his putting green. He walked over, picked up a putter and stroked a golf ball right in the hole. Ted would be so jealous, he thought.

Just then, he heard Ted knocking on the wall. He knocked back. He lined up another putt and just as he hit the ball, Ted opened his office door and watched the ball roll into the cup.

"I knew it!" Ted shouted. "That's all you do all day long, isn't it? I *thought* you played this all the time."

Jake smiled and handed him the club. "Try your luck, Redfire."

Inspired by Jake's putt, Ted lined up a shot. He spent quite a bit of time on it.

Jake said, "There's no break in the grass today and the wind is calm."

"Hush. I'm concentrating." Ted's ball slowly rolled a half inch past the cup on the left side. Ted looked dejected but said, "One of these days."

"That's the spirit."

"Tell me the truth – how often do you play with this?" Ted held up the putter.

Jake shrugged his shoulders. "Rarely."

"Uh-huh."

"Really. Maybe a couple of times once a month. Just to see if I still can."

"Anyone else, I'd tend to disbelieve them. But you're probably telling the truth."

"I am."

"I know. Listen, I came over to invite you to lunch. On me. A goodbye gesture."

"I'm ready. Let's go."

At the restaurant, the waitress had barely brought their orders when Ted said, "Don't stare, but look at the woman's hair over there." Ted nodded in the direction behind Jake's left shoulder.

Jake looked around the restaurant until he saw a woman with extremely short hair. It was like a man's crew-cut. He looked back at Ted.

"So?"

"So? That has got to be the ugliest hairdo I've ever seen on any woman. Don't you think so?"

"It's irrelevant."

"I will concede that. But it's only us two talking. Now don't give me any of that 'we are all connected by our souls stuff.' Just tell me what you think of that woman's hair."

"Okay. I agree with your assessment. It is ugly."

"Do you think she gets up in the morning, looks in the mirror and smiles as she brushes her hair?"

"She might."

"She might? You'd have to be blind not to see how bad that looks."

"Perhaps she is recovering from chemo treatments that caused all her hair to fall out. Now she is recovering and her hair is growing back. That would make her smile."

"You can take the fun out of everything."

Jake laughed. He said, "Or, she may actually have convinced herself that it looks really good and fits her face or something."

"I don't see how that is possible."

"People can convince themselves that things are true when facts show the opposite to be true."

"Such as?"

"Oh man, I could give you dozens."

"Gimme some."

"Okay. Let's see. Most people are completely convinced that Eve took a bite from an apple in the Garden of Eden. And suddenly, after she shared it with Adam, they knew things. The Bible clearly calls it the Tree of the Knowledge of Good and Evil – not an apple tree. I've eaten an apple. It didn't suddenly fill me with knowledge. But, if you went around and asked, most people would say it was an apple tree. They would be wrong, of course, but they believe it to be true."

"Give me an example not in the Bible."

"Okay. About ninety something percent of Black Americans vote for Democrat Party candidates. Why? They think Democrats like them and Republicans don't. The facts show the opposite to be true. During the Civil War, the Democrat Party opposed Lincoln and the Republicans issuing the Emancipation Proclamation. In 1864, the Democrats made it a campaign issue and ran on the idea of calling the Civil War a draw. They wanted to have peace immediately. The South could have their Confederacy and they could keep slavery. Thank God, the Republicans won. With the Civil Rights legislation in the nineteen sixties, a higher percentage of Republicans voted for it than Democrats. That is a historical fact. But the Democrats have much better press and PR than the Republicans. Of course, the media today are mostly all Democrats. They proved that in the two thousand and two thousand four elections. The major ploy that the Democrats use is to make minorities think that, in order to keep their welfare benefits, they need the Democrats. The

Democrats push and talk about federal handouts for minorities and poor people in general. We now have third and fourth generations of minorities living almost totally on welfare. It has resulted in a situation where eighty percent of black children have no father in their lives. In the nineteen fifties and sixties, the black family was the strongest family unit in the United States. Today, it is the weakest. Republicans have tried to pass legislation that would help people get an education so that they could get off welfare. This, according to the media and the Democrats, is mean-spirited. It is in the Democrats' interest to keep people on welfare – for the government to supply public housing, food stamps, medical care – all free. They want to keep people dependent upon them. That gives them power over minorities. But the facts show that, with all the government welfare, people are not better off; but rather, worse. If people would only look at the facts, they would see. But they won't. Consequently, they will remain wrong.

"I bet most people still believe the story of George Washington cutting down the cherry tree and owning up to it. A totally fictional story. But many people believe it to be true. And they are wrong."

Ted's mouth was full of his sub sandwich but he moved his fingers back and forth to indicate he wanted Jake to tell him more.

Jake took a bite of his sandwich. He then said, "Okay, how about science? Most people believe that global warming is caused by mankind. Scientific evidence says, 'no way.' The number one determining factor of what the temperature of the earth is . . . is the sun. The sun goes through cycles of relative brightness and relative dimness. Man has no control over the sun. This is an undisputed scientific fact. You might be interested to know that, in the past hundred years, the planets Mercury, Venus, Earth and Mars have all had a planet-wide increase in temperature. For people with critical thinking skills, that would be enough information to convince them that man-made global warming is not accurate. Of course, most adults in our society do not know how to think. Less than four percent of the carbon dioxide in the earth's atmosphere can be attributed to man. If we could magically make that percentage disappear . . . it would make no difference. The entire man-made global warming issue is nothing more than a scam. Carbon offsets is a hoax. The media reports on man-made global warming as if it is a proven scientific fact. By repetition, they try to convince others. I think they may have actually convinced themselves that man-made global warming is a fact. Most media people are not very intelligent. They have convinced themselves and believe it. But they are wrong. I truly think that twenty-five years from now, people will look back at today's newspapers and television news reporting and wonder how we *all* could have been so gullible."

"Okay, I'm convinced. No more."

"It really is amazing the little amount of critical thinking that actually takes place by adults in our society these days. If it's on TV, people assume it must be true. They don't know how to think for themselves."

"All right. All right. You made your point."

"You hear that guy who just ordered?"

"Yeah."

"I admire him."

"Why?"

"He is speaking English with an accent."

"So?"

"I admire anyone who can learn a second language. I've tried and just can't seem to grasp it."

Ted responded, "I took Spanish in high school."

"Remember any of it?"

"No, not really. A couple of words."

"And English. English has got to be one of the toughest languages to learn."

"You think so?"

"Definitely. Imagine someone from a country whose native language is not based on Latin."

"Latin?"

"Yeah. Spanish, French, German, Italian and English are all based on Latin. Imagine if you only read and spoke Hebrew. Hebrew is one of the oldest languages. It pre-dates the Roman Empire. It looks like symbols and is read from right to left. I can only guess at how hard it must be to try to learn English."

"I suppose."

"If I told you 'I before E," how would you respond?"

"'Except after C.'"

"Weird."

"What?"

"Weird."

"What's weird?"

"Spell it."

"W-E-I-R-D."

"'I before E except after C.'"

Ted smiled and said, "Weird."

"Their."

"There?"

"T-H-E-I-R. Neither and either."

"Eight." Ted said.

Jake nodded. He said, "reign."

"Rain? I don't get it."

"R-E-I-G-N. Reign."

Ted laughed. Okay. Heir. He was so-and-so's heir."

"Good one. Leisure."

"Yeah. Ummm . . . caffeine."

"I'm sure we could come up with more but imagine someone trying to learn English and being told 'I before E except after C.'"

"How's your sandwich?"

"Good. But only half-eaten. You talk and let me eat."

"You know, this conversation all started because I noticed a woman with ugly hair. I never have any idea, when I'm with you, what we are going to wind up talking about."

"Me either."

"So you're really going through with it, huh?"

"Yeah."

"You said something the other day. You said you had a feeling like you were supposed to go – you had an urge to go."

"Yes. I can't really explain it any more than that. It feels like something I should do."

"That's weird, Jake. That's really weird."

"I suppose so."

"But you're going to go anyway?"

"Yeah."

CHAPTER TWELVE

"Set your minds on things above, not on earthly things."

Colossians 3:2

Mid 1st Century A.D.

With an early start, Jake Fleming drove his rental car up Interstate 95 and, at around 7:30 AM, arrived at Bridgeport, Connecticut. He pulled off at an exit, got a fast food breakfast, got back on I-95 and ate as he drove toward Providence, Rhode Island. Due to a wreck that stalled traffic, he didn't arrive in Providence until 10:20 AM. It should have been a two-hour drive. He stayed on I-95 through Providence and continued north to Boston, arriving at 11:05 AM. Jake remained on I-95 and circled west of downtown Boston until the interstate took him north of the city. He stopped at an exit near Danvers and ate lunch. The restaurant was clean and the food was good. He got back on I-95 and headed north. At around 2:30 PM, Jake passed through Portsmouth, New Hampshire and, almost immediately, was in Maine. Staying on I-95, three hours later, Jake arrived in Bangor, Maine. After settling in at his motel, he found a nice local restaurant and ate an extremely good lobster dinner. He knew he had bypassed much of the scenic views in Boston, and Portland as well as along the coast. He had previously seen most of that, some with Katherine; and, he was determined to stay on his schedule.

Sunday morning, May 22nd, dawned bright and clear. Jake hoped for more such weather throughout his trip. After checking out of his motel, Jake stopped and had a leisurely breakfast at a local restaurant. He was only about two hundred miles from that night's destination, Fort Kent. He was in no hurry. He continued north on I-95 until he neared the small town of Sherman Hills. He exited near there onto Highway 11 and headed north. Jake noticed, on his map, that the large Baxter State Park was a few miles to his left. He was tempted to turn off at Patten and go over on Highway 159, however, he decided to stay on Route 11 which would take him all the way to Fort Kent. Jake arrived in Fort Kent in the early afternoon. He checked into his motel and got directions to a local steak house. Before going to sleep, Jake watched an old Alfred Hitchcock movie, *Suspicion*, and wondered why they couldn't make good movies like that anymore. As he dozed off, he realized that this would be the last time he would sleep in a bed for a couple weeks.

Early in the morning, Jake took what he knew would be his last shower for almost two weeks. As early as he could, Jake wanted to get in his canoe and be on his way to *wherever.* He stopped at another fast food place for coffee and biscuits that he ate as he drove west on Highway 161 to Allagash. Once there, he discovered that his canoe rental store was a mile or two west of town right on the St. John River.

Through the Internet and by phone, Jake had reserved a Kevler composite canoe. It was twelve feet and ten inches long and weighed only twenty-five pounds. The guy at the store, Rod, was the same guy he had talked with on the phone. He helped Jake get all his gear loaded, gave Jake some final instructions and wished him well. Jake left the car rental parked beside the store. Rod told Jake that it was somewhat early in the season and that he would probably not run into any other tourists. Maybe a few. Rod told him that there were several places where he could "beach" the canoe, take a bathroom break and rest his arms. Jake was pleased with the canoe and was eager to be on his way.

After getting in the canoe, Rod gave the stern a gentle push. Jake used his paddle and was on his way up the St. John River. In just a few minutes, Jake saw the town of Dickey on his left. Rod had told him that it would be the last sign of civilization he would see. The river turned left, then a horseshoe and Jake was completely isolated in the wilderness of upper northwest

Maine. It was just he, the canoe, the river and the forests on both sides of the river. Although the trees were all evergreens, the undergrowth on the hills had recently turned green with new spring growth. It was all simply and naturally beautiful. It had to be, Jake thought, some of Mother Nature's finest work.

The St. John River was fairly smooth flowing. The current was against him. The river flowed west to east and, for approximately eighty miles, was the border between Maine and Quebec and New Brunswick – and eventually flowed into the Bay of Fundy. There were numerous streams and brooks that flowed into the St. John. Several came from Jake's right or the Canadian side. They flowed from Quebec Province into Maine.

Jake truly didn't know where he was going or where he would wind up on his first day out in the Maine wilderness. He noticed several small ponds and knew, from maps, that there were lakes nearby. He also knew that, as the crow flies, he wasn't all that far from the St. Lawrence River or Québec City. However, it truly appeared as if he were in the middle of nowhere. There were a couple of privately owned and maintained dirt roads in the area. To use them, one had to obtain permission. They were, he understood, built by logging companies so that they could transport timber when it was being harvested. There was a rough gravel road that ran from Allagash to Escourt Station, the most northern community in Maine. It was exactly on the border with Quebec and the pleasant Canadian town of Pohenegamook. Pohenegamook extended along both shores of Pohenegamook Lake, a large lake that drew a sizable summer tourist crowd.

Jake felt comfortable slowly paddling on the river. It was peaceful. He kept telling himself, as he passed one stream after the other, that he would *know* or *sense* when it was time to leave the river. He munched on some trail mix bars and drank a bottle of orange juice from his small cooler. He took some photographs with his small pocket camera. Jake quickly noticed that, every time he quit paddling, even briefly, the canoe had a tendency to go broadside. He would quickly straightened the canoe and continued on his way. He thought, *I'll have to be a faster photographer or learn to take photos with one hand.*

By mid-afternoon, Jake noticed the river channel getting narrower. Then, the river split into two channels. The left channel, he thought, was the main one. However he, almost instinctively, took the right channel. He was still paddling against the current. After about two miles, the channel's source was reached – a larger stream or a small river. Again, Jake could turn left or right. As if he knew what he was doing, he turned right. He paddled upstream for about four miles and again had to decide on a left or right turn. He almost went right again, but, for some reason, at the last second, he turned and paddled up the left fork. He paddled for about three miles, noticed that the sun was beginning its descent and decided to camp for the night. He noticed a small curve to the left in the stream. On the right bank, there was a small rocky "beach" with a grassy clearing behind the bank. Jake decided to "land" on this beach. He knew the canoe had skid plates but he did not want to come into contact with a sharp rock. Jake eased the canoe over toward the right bank of the stream. He edged it up near the bank below the rocky beach area. Moving very slowly, the canoe touched bottom but Jake had to keep paddling to keep the canoe in place. The current wanted to move it downstream. He paddled up again until it touched bottom, removed his feet from the foot-brace, stepped into the cold water with his left foot, grabbed the gunwale with his left hand and the stern thwart with his right hand and, at the same time, lowered his right foot into the stream. He had a firm grip of the canoe. Now what? Holding onto the gunwale all the way, he worked his way to the bow of the canoe. He uncoiled a rope and dragged the canoe up onto the bank. He tied the rope to a tree and realized that his legs were extremely stiff. He'd been sitting in that canoe all day.

While there was still light, Jake wanted to gather firewood and set up his tent. He unloaded most of the canoe until he found a lightweight "overnight" bag that was full of clothes. He changed his shoes and socks and went to gather loose wood. Most of it was dead and rotten wood. It would burn easily but way too quickly without much heat. With a small hatchet, he cut some small green limbs and some small trees that were crowding larger trees. He would mix the green with the dead wood. As it began to get dark, Jake looked at his collected pile of wood and figured he had enough. With his hatchet, he dug out a small fire pit and surrounded it with stones from the rocky beach. It was really getting dark as Jake began to erect his tent. It was much larger than he really needed. It was a teepee style with one large room. The tent was made of lightweight, waterproofed polyester with a sewn-in polyethylene floor. It had covered mesh windows that were weatherproofed. There was a center aluminum pole for support. By the time Jake had used his handy hatchet head to pound the last stakes in the ground, it was totally dark. He was using a battery lantern and flashlight in order to see his stakes. The entire tent only weighed 20 pounds. It was eighteen feet across – both ways. He could easily fit all his gear including even the canoe, if he had wanted to do so, inside. Jake put his sleeping bag, clothes bag, food bag and gear bag inside. He lifted the now empty canoe completely out of the water and left it tied to a tree.

Jake used some small dry twigs to start the fire. He then put some dead wood on it and slowly added some fresh wood. Soon the fire was burning brightly. Jake looked at it and realized he didn't want to cook, or more accurately, heat anything over the fire. He retrieved some beef jerky, trail mix and a soft drink from his tent.

Returning from a brief visit behind a large tree, Jake was amazed at how clearly he could see stars in the sky. They almost seemed to glisten. He also noticed that it was getting quite cool. He put a jacket on and sat down by the fire. It was a beautiful night. Jake knew that he had to be close to the Canadian border. He also knew that this was not his final destination. He believed he would know it when he saw it. Jake thought he was close but didn't know how much more paddling he would need to do the following day.

Jake looked at the stream and wondered where it would take him. This was a Monday unlike any other Monday he had ever had. Tomorrow would be May 24, 2005. Tomorrow was his birthday. Jake would turn 42 years of age. He thought it would be fitting if he found his vacation "spot" on his birthday.

Dawn was beautiful as the sun slowly rose from among the trees. Jake, however, didn't witness it. He was sound asleep snuggled in his sleeping bag. When Jake finally stirred himself awake and went outside his tent, he immediately realized three things. He was sore; it was cold; and he needed to visit that big tree again. Jake got his campfire going – not to cook anything but for the warmth. As he began repacking supplies and taking down the tent, he munched on pre-packaged food. After several tries, he realized he would never get his tent back into the neat little bundle it had been. He folded it as best he could and managed to get it small enough to store in the canoe.

Jake made three trips from the stream with an orange juice container to make sure his campfire was thoroughly drenched. He then covered it with the soil he had originally dug to make his fire pit. Totally content that his campfire was completely extinguished, Jake now wondered how he was going to get his canoe back in the water without getting himself wet. He lifted the stern of the canoe and moved it over close to the edge of the stream. He then did the same with the bow. He stood up and stared at the canoe and at the water. He put the bow in the water and then eased the stern in – but quickly realized that the entire canoe was sitting on the bottom of the stream. If he got in now, he could do so without getting wet but he wasn't going to go anywhere. How to get the canoe into deeper water and still not get wet and not lose the canoe? This canoe did not come with an instruction manual. Lying down on the bank, he lifted, pushed and maneuvered the bow out into the stream until it was floating. He reasoned that he could do the same with the stern but then the canoe would float away and he would be left on the bank. He needed a large rock on which he could stand and lift the canoe into deeper water and then lower himself into the canoe. Looking around, he could see no such rock. Instead, he took off his shoes and socks and rolled up his jeans. He put his socks inside his shoes and put his shoes next to the foot-brace. He then walked into the cold stream, moved the stern into deeper water, climbed in and, with his oar, pushed off into the stream. His toes were freezing but he quickly got his socks and shoes on and headed upstream. Jake thought, *That's not the way a person who is experienced with canoes would have done it – but hey, there's more than one way to skin a cat. I am in the canoe. I am not wet. I am headed upstream. I am where I am supposed to be – right now.*

After an hour and a half of paddling against the current, Jake was tired. His arms were really sore. He reached into his collapsible cooler and retrieved his last container of orange juice. He drank that and ate some beef jerky strips. The scenery was beautiful. It soon warmed up to a nice spring temperature.

The stream's current wasn't all that strong and, despite his leisurely pace, Jake was making fairly good time. He looked at a compass and it confirmed what he had already known – he was traveling northwest. He had to be near the border between Maine and Quebec. He wondered if there would be signs stating that this was the border.

For some reason, for the first time that day, Jake realized that it was Tuesday, May 24th and his 42nd birthday. He smiled at the thought and was glad he was where he was.

He kept paddling upstream. At around 2:00 PM in the afternoon, Jake noticed what looked like a small beach up ahead on his right. He paddled over toward this area. He didn't see any "landing" rocks but went ahead and slowly "beached" the canoe. Jake stepped out on the right side of the canoe. The water was only a few inches deep and he didn't get wet. He lifted the bow out of the water and set it on the sandy area. Jake walked up on the bank and surveyed the surrounding woods. He caught a glimpse of something shining through the trees. He went back and moved the stern up on the sand. He then walked through the woods toward the shining object. After a short walk, he saw that the shining object was the sun reflecting off the surface water of a lake. He moved over to the edge of the woods where the shore of the lake came up to the trees. There was a small grassy area between the actual tree line and the shoreline. Over to his left, there was a sandy area. It was like a tiny beach curved like a horseshoe. Behind the beach was a small grassy area. Jake looked around and knew that this was his "spot." He would set up camp on this grassy slope. After he emptied the canoe, he could portage it over to the lake.

By evening, Jake had his camp all set up for an extended stay. He had gathered plenty of firewood, had his tent staked down, his supplies were all inside the tent and the canoe was tied down at the little beach.

Jake was camped in a little cove of the lake. The land extended away from him on both his left and his right. Straight across the lake, he could barely make out a tree line. Where the curve of the land bended back to the right, using binoculars and the last rays of the sun, Jake spotted a moose wading at the edge of the lake.

When it was too dark to see anything else, sitting next to his campfire, Jake opened a couple of tins of smoked oysters and a package of crackers. He ate those, sipped on a soft drink and enjoyed the night sky. He smiled as he thought of Ted's warnings. Right about now, according to Ted, an alien spaceship should hover over the lake and abduct him. Instead, the stars were bright and Jake enjoyed finding different constellations.

CHAPTER THIRTEEN

"In this life, there is only learning."

– Floyd "Looks for Buffalo" Hand
Elder of the Oglala Lakota

Late 20th Century A.D.

Jake added a couple of more pieces of wood to his campfire. He leaned back and relaxed. He still felt hungry. He got up, went to his tent and rummaged around in his food bag. Finding a package of chocolate cupcakes, he thought 'perfect' and took them out of the tent and headed back to his campfire. While walking back to the fire, Jake suddenly froze in his steps. On the left end of the lake, he saw a red dot. He stared at it for some time. It didn't appear to be moving. He thought it might be another camper's campfire. No, it wasn't fire. It was simply a red dot, perhaps a red light? He returned to his campfire and picked up his binoculars. Through them, it still looked like a shining red dot. It didn't make sense. Jake got up and walked over to the edge of the lake. He looked through the binoculars again. It was still a red light – small but a bright shining source of red light. It looked like a small red dot.

Returning to his campfire, Jake put another log on the fire. He sat down and stared at the red dot at the end of the lake. He could not imagine what it was. He even thought of Ted's UFO. This light was not flying. It didn't even appear to be an object, but rather, a light source. It was definitely unidentified.

Jake leaned back and took out his cupcakes. They were good. He thought, *I'm eating cake on my birthday. How appropriate. And, despite that red dot over there, this place is a true birthday present.*

The sky was illuminated only by the stars. It was a beautiful sight! Jake thought the silence was also beautiful. Suddenly, it was broken by the staccato calls of a loon. Jake jerked. He smiled to himself as it took a second or two for him to realize it was only a bird out on the lake. He remembered an old saying *Adonai li vlo Ira, God is with me, I fear not.* More loons joined this one and their calls actually had a calming effect on Jake. He was truly enjoying himself. He felt peaceful.

Before going inside his tent, Jake built the fire up with more wood. Just prior to opening his tent, he glanced over at the lake. The red dot was still there. He tried to place it by using large trees on the shore near the light but, even with binoculars, it was too dark.

Inside the tent, Jake stripped off his clothes and snuggled down into his sleeping bag. He felt contented. He never imagined that this would be the way he would be spending his 42nd birthday. With that thought he quickly went to sleep.

The next morning, Jake awoke to the sounds of Mother Nature. Birds were loudly singing and he felt good. Exiting his tent, Jake quickly looked over at the end of the lake. He could not see the red dot. He got his fire going again. Overnight, it had burned down to barely smoldering ashes. He went to the lake and filled a quart container of water. He filtered it through a .75 micron filter to get rid of any possible Giardia and/or Cryptosporidium. Using two forked green branches and placing them on either side of his campfire, he ran a straight green branch through a hanging metal pan and placed the branch in the fork of both upright branches. He then filled the pan with his water. Before trying his luck with the local fish, he would have some hot coffee. While his water was heating, he removed his fishing gear from his tent. He put more wood under the pan of water, leaned back and, with his binoculars, tried to determine exactly where that red dot had been.

It took a lot longer than he had thought it would take to

get his water hot. Finally, sipping his hot instant coffee, Jake sat back and admired the beautiful view. He felt extremely comfortable doing so. After enjoying the peace, he placed some more small logs on the fire, picked up his fishing gear and walked over to the right edge of the little cove. He quickly caught a small (but large enough to eat) fish. It looked like a brim but he wasn't at all sure. It took him another 20 minutes to land another one. He scaled and gutted them both. Setting a grill contraption (that had four legs which folded up to make a flat piece for traveling) over the fire, he placed his two fish in a frying pan and set the pan on the grill. As they cooked, he had another cup of coffee and enjoyed the view.

After his fresh fish breakfast, Jake put the canoe in the water. He left the stern up on the little sandy beach that had formed at the cove. Jake debated on whether or not to take his handgun, a .38 caliber revolver, with him. In the end, he decided to leave it in the tent. He stuffed a couple of beef jerky sticks in a pocket of his jeans, put his life jacket on, grabbed a bottle of water, put some more wood on the fire, placed his binoculars around his neck and shoved the canoe further into the water. He stepped in and, using the paddle, pushed away from the shoreline. The difference in the canoe was immediately obvious. It glided more smoothly through the water. Of course, the lake had no current.

It was a beautiful day and Jake leisurely paddled his way to the end of the lake. He was heading to the area where he had seen the red dot. Staying about 20 feet offshore, he slowly followed the shoreline. After traveling about 40 feet, something caught his eye. However, he had passed beyond it. He started paddling in reverse. The canoe stopped and slowly began to go backwards. It was awkward but Jake managed to reverse himself. Again, he went past the place he wanted to see. He was moving very slowly and began paddling forward. Barely moving now, he looked to his left and could just make out a path running back through the woods. Perhaps an animal trail down to the water? Yet, this was about where the red dot had appeared. Was there a connection? He turned the canoe around and slowly drifted back to that place. He was now only about 10 feet from the shore and, looking to his right, noticed that it was definitely a trail of some use. However, Jake could see nothing that would cause a red light to shine. He swung the canoe around again and drifted back. Using his binoculars, he tried to find a light bulb among the tree limbs on the shore. He could not. Turning around, once again, he paddled past the trail and headed back to his camp.

Jake spent the rest of the afternoon filtering water, gathering firewood and luxuriating in the beauty of Mother Nature's wilderness. The fish he had for breakfast were so good that he tried to catch more for supper. This time though, the only luck he had was bad. He couldn't even get a nibble. Instead, he warmed some soup, ate some canned smoked oysters and finished it off with a bag of trail mix.

As the sun sank behind him, Jake sipped some coffee and watched as darkness enveloped the lake. He was again amazed at how clear and bright the stars appeared against the sky. As he was looking up at the constellations, he noticed, with his peripheral vision, the red dot. It was back. Jake was neither startled nor surprised. He did look long through his binoculars at the red dot. It was clear. It just looked like a small red light. What was it doing there? He tried to turn his attention back to the heavens. He focused his binoculars on specific stars but the small red dot was a big distraction. It simply made no sense to him. Yet, there had to be a reason it was there. How was it powered? Rejecting several ideas, including some type of navigational aid for the lake, he had about decided that it was a boundary marker between Maine and Quebec. It was a way of letting people know that this was an international border. If so, however, why was there nothing obvious during daylight? It just didn't add up to any logical sense. It should not be there but, it was.

Jake's sleep did not come easily. He tried not to dwell on the red dot. However, his thoughts kept returning to it. Eventually, he dozed off and had a somewhat restful sleep.

After eating a reconstituted freeze-dried breakfast (the

fish still weren't biting), Jake set out on the lake again. Instead of heading toward the area of the red dot, he decided to explore the rest of the lake. He paddled out to the center and then turned right toward the major part of the lake. He stopped every now and then and took photographs. The thought occurred to him that he should have brought his fishing gear. Maybe they were biting out here, he optimistically hoped.

It was a larger lake than Jake had first guessed. He paddled toward the opposite end of the shoreline. With his binoculars and about 30 minutes of steady paddling, he could barely make out the trees of that shoreline. He scanned the entire rim of this portion of the lake and saw no structures – no human construction anywhere. The main length of the lake ran primarily north and south. The width of the lake was east and west. Jake's campsite was on a little western cove at the northern end. Jake let his binoculars fall back into place against his chest, picked up his paddle and started heading toward the southern shoreline. After a few strokes, he heard a distant rumble of thunder. Clouds had quickly moved in and covered the lake. Having heard the thunder, he turned around and headed back.

Jake paddled steadily and the canoe moved swiftly across the surface of the lake. He recalled a saying on a poster or a sweatshirt. It went something like "Don't run and hide from a rainstorm. Instead, learn to dance in the rain." Jake smiled at the recollection. He also recalled and cherished the memory of he and Katherine dancing in the rain. However, he preferred not to get caught in a thunderstorm while out in the middle of a lake. There would be no dancing in his canoe. Jake was returning much faster than his outward leisurely pace. After about 20 minutes of steady paddling, the sky got dark and a strong guest of wind blew across the lake. Jake kept paddling and steered for the western shore. If it got too bad too quickly, he might have to go ashore at the nearest place and walk through the woods to his camp. The wind was constant now and the sky had that look of impending rain. He could hear the thunder booming behind him. It looked like the bottom of the clouds could open at any second.

Jake figured he was going to get wet. He just kept paddling. The lightning and thunder were getting close. Finally, off in the distance, he could barely make out the beginning of the cove where he had his camp. He increased his speed. At the same time, a wall of water completely drenched him. It was amazing how quickly the rainstorm moved. There was no gradual sprinkling of rain. It was an immediate pouring of water over everything. Jake realized he had nothing in the canoe with which to bail water. The rain was so thick that he could no longer see the western shore or the little cove. He just kept paddling. The wind made the rain feel colder than it was. He noticed a couple of inches of water in the bottom of the canoe. He was paddling blind but figured he was headed in the right direction. The rain was just so heavy. He kept looking at the increasing amount of water in the canoe. He paddled as fast as he could. Suddenly, he passed by the jutting out right finger of his cove. That was where he had been when he was fishing. A few more strokes and the canoe slid up on the little sandy beach. With very tired "noddle-like" arms, Jake dragged the canoe up the grassy slope next to his tent. His fire was, of course, extinguished. His clothes were totally soaked. Jake quickly put the rain flaps over the tent windows and secured them. The peak of his tent had a rain-protected ventilation cap. He went inside and secured the entrance.

Jake stood in the large, mostly empty, tent and dripped water on the polyethylene floor. He stripped off all his clothes, rummaged through a knapsack, found a bar of soap and went back outside. He took a quick cold shower and washed his hair. After that, he turned the canoe upside down and went back inside the tent. He only had one small towel that was not much bigger than a washcloth. He used that to try to dry himself. He put on thick warm socks, briefs and long-sleeved t-shirt. He quickly covered that with a lined flannel shirt and jeans. Tying his boots on, he saw his "space-age" leather gloves. They had a thin lining but were supposed to be warmer than fur-lined gloves. He first put on his jacket and then the gloves. Jake slowly started to get warm.

Thunder was loud as it sounded across the lake. Jake, still wearing his jacket, boots and gloves, laid down on his sleeping bag. It felt warm and comfortable. He felt clean, tired and hungry. The rain got heavier and strongly pelted the tent. The wind seemed to be screaming as it blew against the tent. The thunder vibrations seemed to shake the ground.

It was almost like night inside the tent. Jake got off his sleeping bag and turned on a battery-operated lantern. He got a variety of "goodies" from his food knapsack, sat back on his sleeping bag and listened to the sounds of the thunderstorm. Jake actually liked thunderstorms – when he wasn't out in the middle of a lake in a canoe.

The storm continued all night. Jake had brought a total of three paperback books with him. He had two extra batteries for the lantern. He used a lot of the original battery that night as he read most of one of his books. He had been keeping his pipe smoking outdoors by the fire. However, as he read, he smoked his pipe.

He did not even try to see if the red dot was there or not. If it was, he didn't think he would be able to see it through the rain. He certainly didn't want to get wet again. During the night, occasionally the wind eased its force but the rain remained steady. Jake eventually quit reading, got undressed, crawled into his sleeping bag and slept through the rest of the night.

The next morning, Jake emerged from his tent to a beautiful day. The rain had completely stopped and the sky was a clear bright blue. He hung his wet clothes and shoes up on tree limbs to dry. It took Jake some time to get his fire going again. His campfire pit was a soggy mess of ashes and half-burned logs. Finally, with some warm water for instant coffee, Jake ate another reconstituted freeze-dried breakfast. After that storm, he didn't even consider trying to fish. As he sat there eating, he kept looking over at the area where he had seen both the red dot and the trail.

Jake suddenly decided that there must be a connection. He felt he had been drawn to come on this trip. He would be happy to stay right where he was for the next two weeks. Surely though, there was more of a reason, other than to commune with nature, for this compulsion to travel here. Perhaps the red dot was an invitation? That seemed far-fetched but Jake decided he would paddle over to the trail and see if it led anywhere.

Again, Jake was torn on whether to take his revolver with him or not. As before, he decided to leave it behind. Once he had his stuff in his pockets, he turned the canoe over and carried it to the little beach. He was soon paddling straight for that trail. However, with the first stroke, he could feel his arms were stiff. Despite the pain, he soon found the trail. He slowly ran the canoe right up to the spot where the trail ended at the water. He moved to the bow and stepped out onto the bank. He pulled the canoe up after him and tied it to a tree.

Slowly and cautiously, Jake began to walk down the trail.

CHAPTER FOURTEEN

"But when the kindness and love of God our Savior appeared, he saved us, not because of righteous things we had done, but because of his mercy. He saved us through the washing of rebirth and renewal by the Holy Spirit, whom he poured out on us generously through Jesus Christ our Savior, so that, having been justified by his grace, we might become heirs having the hope of eternal life."

– Titus 3:4-7

Mid 1st Century A.D.

After about 30 feet, the trail turned to the right. Jake stayed on it. It quickly veered to the left and ran straight for approximately 15 feet. As Jake was carefully walking down the trail, it occurred to him that, if he stepped off the trail and walked among the trees parallel to this trail, he would not be quite so noticeable. However, he reasoned, with his bright orange life jacket, he would still be easy to spot. Was there anyone to see him anyway? He stayed on the trail.

At the end of his supposed straight 15 feet, the trail gradually curved to the right. It went back toward the lake and then made a short quick turn to the left. Suddenly, it ended at the border of a huge Christmas tree farm!

Jake was amazed. What in the world was a Christmas tree farm doing out here in the middle of nowhere? His amazement continued as he saw how large this Christmas tree farm was. He had never seen so many Christmas trees. There were acres and acres of them. To his left, he could not see the end of the Christmas trees. Straight in front of him was a small rocky knoll rising from the ground. He walked toward it. As he drew near, he saw that one side of the mound consisted of bare rough rocks.

The other side of the little hill was covered with natural vegetation (weeds). Jake walked up to this side and plucked a small rock from the slope and turned it over in his hand.

Without warning, he suddenly heard someone walking! He turned to his left to look in the direction of the sound. From around the corner of the small knoll, a woman appeared. Jake was inwardly startled. The woman was tall, thin with shoulder length red hair. Her green eyes were set in an elegant face. He thought, she was in her late twenties. She was wearing a long white gown that fit her trim figure quite well.

She said, "So, you've finally come." It was a statement, not a question.

Jake replied, "Yes."

The woman smiled. She nodded and held out her hand, "I'm Laura. Laura Middleton."

Jake shook her hand and said, "Jake Fleming."

"Follow me."

Unknown, of course, to Jake, about 10 minutes earlier, Laura Middleton had been sitting in a mostly glass room with dozens of monitor screens. With her was Peggy Curtis. Peggy was a cute brunette with an enchanting smile. She was of medium height, about five - five, with a fully developed woman's figure. She was 22 years old.

When she had seen Jake on the monitor, she said, "He's cute. I'll greet him."

Laura had replied, "He's closer to my age. I'll go meet him."

Jake followed her around the rock corner of the small mound. Immediately past the corner was an opening. Laura stepped through and Jake, hiding his surprise, followed her through the opening. She stepped aside to let him pass, reached up and pressed a button on the wall. A door slid across the opening and it was completely sealed.

Laura said, "From the outside, one would never know it was there."

Jake, knowing that was true (as he had walked right by it),

simply stated, "I see."

A well-lit ramp descended to a bright hallway. Jake walked along beside Laura.

He asked, "Where are we?"

Laura stopped, looked at him and asked, "Have you read *Alice in Wonderland*?"

"Yes."

"*Peter Pan*?"

"Yes."

"*Lost Horizon*?"

Jake smiled and answered, "Yes."

"This place is sorta like a combination of Wonderland, Neverland and Shangri-La."

Jake laughed. He said, "Okay."

"But not quite," Laura quickly stated.

"Does it have a name?"

Laura answered, "Some people call it *The Refuge*. Others call it *The Sanctuary*. Still others call it *The Library*."

"What do you call it?"

"Home." With that, Laura resumed walking down the hall.

While Jake was totally amazed at this underground facility, he suppressed his surprise and tried to act as if things were progressing normally.

Laura led him to a door, knocked lightly, opened the door and said, "The man we have been expecting has arrived."

Jake masked his astonishment at that statement as a well-groomed, extremely neat man stood up and greeted him. The man was in his mid-fifties with graying hair, tall, slim, dark eyes and a pleasant smile. He was wearing a gray silk dress shirt with a pair of black slacks and well-polished black shoes. He had been sitting in a comfortable-looking recliner chair and reading a book. He leaned over and set the book on a small wooden table next to his chair. He stood and stepped toward Jake with his hand held out in order to shake hands.

Jake stepped forward, shook his hand and the man said,

"Welcome, Mr. Fleming."

"Thank you," replied Jake.

"My name is Jean Le Couteau."

As he heard the door close behind him, Jake turned. Laura had left the room.

"Sit down, Mr. Fleming. Sit down. Make yourself comfortable." Mr. Le Couteau waved Jake to a recliner chair opposite the one in which he had just been sitting. There was a glass coffee table between the two chairs.

Mr. Le Couteau asked, "Can I get you something to drink?"

"Coffee would be nice," Jake said.

"Certainly."

Mr. Le Couteau walked over to a sideboard and poured a cup of coffee into a large heavy white mug.

"Cream? Sugar?"

"No. Thanks. Black is fine."

Mr. Le Couteau set the mug on the glass coffee table. Jake took the mug and sipped the coffee. It was excellent. He glanced around the room. It appeared to be a lounge area. There was a sofa against one wall. There were paintings, mostly landscapes, on the walls. One wall was full of books. There was a television screen on another wall and several chairs around an oak table. He noticed a microwave next to the coffee maker and a small collection of alcoholic beverage bottles on a counter near a small refrigerator. For ice, he figured.

Jake sipped the coffee again and said, "Thank you. It's quite good."

Mr. Le Couteau smiled.

He said, "You may want to remove that life jacket you're wearing. Water is not a problem here."

Jake smiled, stood up and unzipped the life jacket. He placed it across the seat of a wooden chair and sat back down. He picked up the mug and took another sip.

As he nodded toward the book on the small wooden table next to Mr. Le Couteau's chair, Jake said, "I'm sorry if I interrupted your reading."

Mr. Le Couteau's eyebrows rose at Jake's unexpected statement. He replied, "Not at all. Not at all."

"What are you reading?"

"A biography. Thomas Jefferson."

"Really? He's my favorite American."

"Indeed? He was a fascinating man."

"Yes."

"You surprise me, Mr. Fleming."

Jake thought, *I surprise you? Good grief, man, do you not realize what an unbelievable and astonishing surprise I have had? An hour ago, I was at my rustic campsite in the wilderness of northwestern Maine and now I am drinking coffee in a modern underground lounge with a man who looks like he walked out of the pages of GQ magazine.*

Instead of saying what he thought, Jake replied, "Indeed, Mr. Le Couteau. How so?"

Mr. Le Couteau laughed and shook his head.

He said, "Please call me Jean. I am . . ."

"Jake," Jake said.

Mr. Le Couteau nodded. He said, "You have not asked a single one of the many obvious questions that, over the years, every guest of ours has always asked. That does truly surprise me . . . and, frankly, puzzles me."

Jake smiled. He said, "I figure that you will, in your own time and in your own way, supply the answers to those questions."

"That is, of course, true. What made you think that?"

"It seems logical. Also, Miss Middleton, just now, mentioned that you were expecting me. I don't mean to be presumptuous but it seems to be that, if you were expecting me, you intend to fill me in as to how and why."

Mr. Le Couteau nodded, smiled and said, "I see. Well then, I guess I'd better begin to fill you in. I think I'll have some of that coffee. Would you care for some more?"

"Yes. Thank you."

Mr. Le Couteau got up, picked up Jake's mug, refilled it, filled one for himself in the same white heavy mug style, sat them both on the glass table and sat back in his chair. Both men took sips of the hot coffee from their identical mugs. Jake held his but Mr. Le Couteau sat his over on the little wooden table next to his chair.

"Now then," he said, "where should I begin? What is this place? Exactly where are you? By air, in a straight line, we are currently sitting not too far from the St. Lawrence River and Québec City. We are in an extremely rural area. We are not too terribly near any town. The two nearest are Pohenegamook and St-Pamphile – both in Quebec. We are located between those two. Pohenegamook is to our north and St-Pamphile is to our south. We are located right on the border of Maine and Quebec. Most of the facility is in Quebec. We own that lake out there and it is mostly in Maine, if not all in Maine. We really don't know. I myself, as you may have already concluded, am a French Canadian. I am originally from Montreal, which is, of course, not all that far from here. My wife still works and lives in Montreal. I usually go home there on the weekends – but not always. Québec City is fairly close and many of our people who work here travel to Québec City for the weekend. From the air, this facility looks like a Christmas tree farm. This facility is, of course, a secret.

"Now what is this facility? It is many things. However, to understand that, you will need to understand how it came to be. What was its original purpose? This place was founded in eighteen sixty-five. An American, Robert Sinclair, founded it. He was a genius and had access to great wealth. The American Civil War had just ended. That was the catalyst that caused Sinclair to begin this effort. Originally, the land where the Christmas tree farm is now was cleared and buildings were constructed . . . above ground. The Native Americans had learned how to survive in this climate and, in the early stages, Sinclair borrowed from them. One major aspect of this project, as you will soon understand, was the need for secrecy. Sinclair soon realized that isolation alone was not going to be effective enough to maintain secrecy. Consequently, in eighteen eighty, he began to tunnel underground and built underground rooms and, eventually, an entire community.

"That required a lot of learning – a lot of trial and error took place. After some time, his architects figured out the water problem and the humidity problem and more. This was never designed nor intended to be a Utopian society. That was not its purpose at all. Sinclair was intelligent enough to realize that those never succeed. At about this same time, there was a group of English noblemen trying to establish a Utopian society in Tennessee. Sinclair knew it would not work. Of course, it didn't. Anyway, for some, throughout the years, it has been a utopia for them. However, that was because their personalities fit so perfectly with the goal of Sinclair's project. It was not . . . but I've gotten off track.

"Tell me something, Jake. Tell me what you know of the Knights Templar."

Jake's face showed the surprise he felt. If this guy was going to try to bring the Knights Templar into this, Jake was ready to get up and leave. He'd rather talk with Laura.

He replied, "You're not going to tell me that you have the cup of Christ hidden here somewhere, are you?"

Mr. Le Couteau laughed. He answered quickly, "No. No, of course not. You are jumping way ahead of the story. I see by that response that you are aware of some of the legends regarding the Templars. What do you know about them . . . other than legends?"

"All right. As I remember it, the Order of the Knights Templar was founded in Jerusalem in the early twelfth century – eleven nineteen, I think. Initially, their headquarters were located right beside Solomon's Temple – what is now called the Temple Mount. At first, they were organized to protect pilgrims traveling in Jerusalem and the area that is today the nation of Israel. It became . . . fashionable . . . to donate funds and land to the Order. They became extremely wealthy. They eventually amassed great amounts of money, land holdings, jewels and gold bullion. They organized chapters throughout Europe. With all this huge wealth, came power. Wealth and power, then as today, generates jealousy. People have often been surprised at how rapidly the Order grew. History, however, has uncovered its secret of success. Early on, the Order had a wealthy and influential patron – Bernard of Clairvaux. Now Bernard had used his influence to get Pope Innocent the Second declared Pope. In return, Pope Innocent the Second issued a papal bull, around twenty years after the Order was founded, that stated the Knights of the Order could travel freely throughout Europe, that the Order would owe no taxes to any nation and, and this is important, that the Knights Templar were not subject to any authority other than that of the Pope. They literally had free rein to go wherever they wanted, to do business without paying any taxes and were excluded from the regular rules and regulations of kings and governments. Knowing this, it is no wonder they did so well."

Jake smiled at his host. Mr. Le Couteau returned Jake's smile and nodded his head.

Jake continued, "About ten years after receiving all these favorable conditions from the Pope, the Order began issuing Letters of Credit to travelers in Jerusalem. This quickly became a system of banking and by the last quarter of the thirteenth century, say twelve seventy-five, they were the wealthiest organization in all of Europe. They had extreme financial power and control. They owned many buildings, fleets of ships, tens of thousands of acres of land and many prominent people, including kings and queens, were in their debt.

"King Phillip the Fourth, of France, was one such king. He was deeply in debt to the Order. Also, the Order had, by thirteen hundred, established headquarters in southeastern France. Phillip knew he would never be able to repay his debt to the Order and he was afraid that, with all their power and wealth, they might decide to replace him with one of their own on the throne of France. So what was a king to do? He couldn't attack them by force. They were stronger than his French army. He couldn't hurt them financially. From his point of view, what he did was extremely brilliant and successful. He accused them of committing crimes of blasphemy. Phillip trumped up people, most likely paid, who said that they had witnessed rituals of the Templars that included such things as urinating on crosses, of denying Christ and of acts of homosexuality. Others said that some of the rites conducted in Templar houses included sexual orgies. Phillip went public with his accusations and petitioned Pope Boniface the Eighth for help in addressing this serious problem of the Order having gone bad. Boniface didn't believe the accusations and delayed action. By thirteen twelve, Pope Clement the Fifth was in power and he convened a Council. Under pressure from King Phillip and others who were in debt to the Order, this Council, with Pope Clement's blessing, issued an edict, which dissolved the Order. The last known Grand Master of the Order, Jacques de Molay, and several other high-ranking Knights, were burned at the stake in thirteen fourteen.

"And, for historical purposes, that was the end of the Knights Templar. However, it seems that there is strong evidence that, in different forms, the Order survived. Apparently, and even quite openly, some Knights simply joined the Order of Hospitallers and continued on as they always had. They were quite active in Portugal. It seems several thousand moved to Switzerland. In England, Edward the Second was also in severe debt to the Templars. Now that the Pope had dissolved the Order, all that debt, all across Europe, was forfeited. Edward, to make sure and to increase his wealth and power, had dozens of the Knights killed and he seized all of their land holdings as his own. They were many survivors in England and, apparently, they moved to Scotland. Some of the Knights joined the Hospitallers and some continued to operate as the Order of Saint John and the Order of Christ, both in Portugal. There is a small stone fort that was built at the southern end of the island of Madagascar that some people say was built by Templars from Portugal. That has spread more rumors. Who really knows?

"Nonetheless, the Templars, as an official organization, were gone. Along with that, their banking business and land . . .

was gone. I think, primarily because they seemed to have vanished so quickly, many conspiracy theories have popped up to explain what *really* happened. No one seems to know, I mean historically, what happened to their fleets of ships. Where did they go? No one seems to know where all that physical wealth of gold bullion and jewels went. It is still unaccounted for to this day. The Order had plenty of time to plan for removing it. They could see what was coming. They had several years to prepare. This, I think, added to the numerous myths and legends about the Knights Templar but, as far as I know, none of them has any real historical evidence. I mean, for example, like the legend of the Holy Grail being buried under Rosslyn Chapel in Scotland."

Mr. Le Couteau spoke and asked, "You don't think that is possible?"

Jake replied, "I think it is nonsense."

"Why?"

"I think that, after Jesus and his disciples finished their meal, their last supper, whoever cleaned up afterwards simply gathered all the dirty cups and plates, washed them and put them away. The actual cup that Christ used would have been no different than any of the others. At that time, no one would have placed any significance on it. Only Jesus himself actually knew it was to be their last meal together until after the Resurrection. Certainly, the people serving the meal and cleaning up afterwards would not be aware of the significance of the meal. The cup itself would not have carried any meaning to anyone at the time."

"I see. I agree with you. I must admit, Jake, your knowledge of dates and names associated with the Knights Templar truly impresses me."

Jake smiled and said modestly, "Bit of a history buff."

Mr. Le Couteau smiled and nodded his head. He asked, "What do you think of the rumors regarding a link between the Knights and Freemasonry?"

"Not much, I'm afraid. Certainly, in the seventeen hundreds, several masonic lodges claimed to have received ritual instruction from Templars. While there is no historical evidence to support such claims, it has to be acknowledged that that is not something that would be recorded. It would be secret. And, of course, it is possible that someone pretending to be descended from the Templars could have given the lodges some rituals and claimed they were from the Templars. Some of the Templar connection probably comes from the active relationship between the Knights Hospitallers and Freemasonry. Since some of the Knights Templars did join the Knights Hospitallers, there could be a real thread of continuity there."

"Yes, I agree with what you have said. However, it wouldn't amount to much."

"No. Even if true, it wouldn't be much of an influence."

"Tell me this then, Jake, what is your opinion regarding all the treasure the Knights accumulated? I mean they supposedly had gold reserves, jewels and lots of silver. Where did it all go?"

Jake thought he sensed a different tone in Mr. Le Couteau's voice as he asked about the Knights Templars' wealth.

Jake answered, "Who really knows? History doesn't. I suppose it could have been dispersed among some of the survivors of the persecutions. Perhaps several wealthy European families got their start that way. Perhaps it was put on those ships of theirs and, as they sailed to escape, the ships ran into a severe storm and were lost at sea. I am aware of rumors that involve Oak Island, right off the coast of Nova Scotia, and Rosslyn Chapel. However, there is no proof or evidence of either. I obviously do not know what happened to it."

Mr. Le Couteau smiled and said, "Yes, who does?"

His tone disturbed Jake. Jake didn't change his tone or appearance. Instead, he said, "You asked me to tell you what I knew of the Templars. May I ask you why you asked that of me?" Jake thought that, if it were some type of test, he had passed.

Mr. Le Couteau responded by asking a question. "Have you ever heard of an early settlement on Cape Breton Island?"

Jake shook his head. He wondered if Jean was trying to imply that that colony consisted of former Templars.

Mr. Le Couteau said, "No reason you should have. There

are rumors . . . legends, particularly among the Mi'kmaq Native Americans that a rather extensive settlement, at Cape Dauphin on Cape Breton, was made in the very early fifteenth century…by the…Chinese."

"The Chinese?"

"Yes. You thought I was going to say Templars, didn't you?"

"I wondered."

He laughed. "The stone ruins are there today for anyone to see. The Mi'kmaq tribe has several things in common with Chinese culture. Their clothing, from photographs taken in the early twentieth century, looks very much like Chinese clothing. It's actually an amazing story."

"Sounds like. I'd like to look into it. What's it got to do with the Templars?"

"Oh, nothing. Nothing at all. It just shows that, sometimes, significant events have occurred that have been lost to history."

"You think something similar happened with the Templars?"

"It's possible. They were extremely wealthy. Of course, it could be as you say – that wealth was lost at sea. You know about Rosslyn Chapel?"

"Some. It was built in the mid-fourteen hundreds just south of Edinburgh. It is supposed to have hidden within it some of the treasure of the Knights Templar. I remember reading something about Rosslyn Chapel a few years ago. It seems that ground penetrating radar revealed the presence of a large subterranean chamber beneath the Chapel itself. The indications were that this structure was actually quite a bit larger than the Chapel above. If I remember right, the Chapel itself is privately owned. The owners would not allow any excavations to be done."

"Yes. You are correct about that. Do you know who built Rosslyn Chapel?"

"I think so. It was a Sinclair. He…"

"Sir William Sinclair."

"Yes. He actually claimed to be a Knights Templar."

Mr. Le Couteau nodded. He said, "Our Director, our Leader...of this organization . . . " At this point, Mr. Le Couteau extended his arms and hands out in an encompassing manner to include not only the room but also the entire underground facility. Jake understood what he meant.

"Actually," Mr. Le Couteau continued, "we don't really have a title for our...manager. But, his name is...William Sinclair."

CHAPTER FIFTEEN

"Know you not that you are the temple of God, and that the Spirit of God dwells in you?"

– 1 Corinthians 3:16

Mid 1st Century A.D.

Again, Jake showed no surprise. He was trying to figure out where all this was headed. What exactly was the purpose of all this Knights Templar stuff? It seemed as if Mr. Le Couteau was somehow testing him. And yet. And yet, what? He was missing something. A piece or two of the puzzle was definitely missing. What in the world was this place? Could he get up and leave?

Jake asked, "Are they related?"

Mr. Le Couteau smiled. He replied, "What do you know of the Sinclairs?"

Jake thought, *Another question. Why can't he just answer with a yes or a no?* Not saying what he thought, Jake responded to Mr. Le Couteau's question by saying, "Scottish clan, I believe. At one point, hundreds of years ago, it was St Clair, I think. The southern group kept the name St Clair and the northern group changed it to Sinclair. Something like that."

"Exactly right. The Scottish lowlanders remained St Clair and the highlanders became Sinclair. And yes, our Sinclair is a descendant of Sir William. Not a direct. He is descended from a brother of Sir William."

"Who built Rosslyn Chapel."

"Exactly."

"Therefore, all the discussion about the Knights Templar."

"Somewhat."

"The present Sinclair is, I presume, a descendant of the man who founded this place in eighteen sixty-five."

"Grandson."

"Indeed? He must be . . . rather elderly."

"No, not really. Mid-seventies. His mind is as sharp as ever."

"I really enjoy talking with elderly people."

"I don't know that I would refer to him as elderly. Most young people do not enjoy talking with older people."

"I don't know that I would refer to myself as 'young people.'"

Mr. Le Couteau laughed.

Jake continued, "I guess I listen more than talk. I find I can learn much from listening."

"Have you had the opportunity to talk, or listen, to many elderly people?"

"Not as much as I would like. I do remember, when I was nineteen, I met a lady – she was seventy-seven – whose father had fought in the battle of Gettysburg. That was in eighteen sixty-three. I said to her, 'Surely you mean your grandfather.' She said, 'No, my father married a young woman in nineteen oh two. I was born in nineteen oh five.' It was fascinating to hear her speak of Gettysburg when she was relating things that her own father had seen and done."

"I imagine so."

"Did the man who founded this place fight in the Civil War?"

"No. But the carnage of that war was part of the reason he decided to begin this."

"I understand."

Mr. Le Couteau stared at Jake for a moment and said, "I think that you are trying to figure out how our current Sinclair is the grandson of the founder. It really is simple. Robert Sinclair, the founder, was born in Scotland in eighteen thirty-five. As a very young man, he moved to America, became a naturalized citizen and married. They lived here all of their married life. However, they had no children. She died in eighteen eighty-six. He married his second wife, a younger woman, in eighteen ninety. They had a son, Hugh Sinclair, in eighteen ninety-five. Hugh married in nineteen twenty-five and had a son, William Charles, in nineteen thirty. It is now two thousand five. That makes William Charles Sinclair seventy-five. He goes by Charles."

"As you said, not really that old."

"No. Not elderly. Yet, getting on. Sadly, his physical health has been slowly but steadily deteriorating. His mind is still excellent."

"Does he have children?"

"He has a son, John. His daughter died about twenty years ago."

"Does John live here?"

"No. John is not much interested in his family's . . . heritage. He was born in nineteen sixty, was graduated from university and, since his graduation, has only visited here twice. He is a successful architect and has no interest in following his father here."

"I understand." Jake felt a twinge; a feeling he quite disliked. As he was trying to sort it out, Mr. Le Couteau interrupted his thoughts.

"It's a shame. However, at the same time, Charles himself is not convinced that John is the right person to lead us through the coming trials of the first half of the twenty-first century."

Jake didn't know what to say so he said nothing. He looked at a particularly nice watercolor landscape hanging on the nearby wall.

Mr. Le Couteau said, "Are you an artist?"

Jake smiled and quickly replied, "No. Yet I certainly appreciate art. This painting here..." Jake nodded toward the watercolor, "...is, I find, an excellent work of art."

"Thank you."

Jake stared at Mr. Le Couteau. He then got up and

examined the painting up close. In the lower right corner was the signature, *Jean Le Couteau.*

"It's yours?"

"Yes. I work primarily in watercolor."

"Jean, it's beautiful."

"Thank you."

"Are all the people here artists?"

"Oh no. Many are. Most are not. We do attract some excellent musicians. They are not professional musicians. They are just very good."

"I understand. What is it, exactly, that people do here?"

Jake went over to the coffee maker, poured himself another cup of coffee and held up the carafe as to question Mr. Le Couteau if he wanted another cup. He shook his head and Jake sat back down.

Mr. Le Couteau smiled and said, "That is usually one of the first questions someone new here will ask. You have showed great patience. The answer is quite simple. We study."

"Study what?"

"Whatever interests us. And we collect."

"Collect what?"

"Research primarily. We study subjects in which we have an interest; we research those subjects in as much detail as is possible; and, we maintain that research for others to use who come after us."

Jake felt like the rabbit who had been thrown in the briar patch. He said, "That is absolutely fascinating."

Mr. Le Couteau was staring at Jake. He smiled and nodded. "We find it so."

Jake sipped his coffee. "How wh . . . I mean, how is it financed?"

"We have, primarily thanks to Robert, a rather large endowment."

"That's nice."

"Yes, it is. Please don't get the wrong impression. We have regular jobs. Laura, for instance, teaches school. She does research on stone megaliths when she has time. All of us are pretty much in that same boat."

Before the two men could continue their conversation, Laura knocked, opened the door and announced, "Supper's ready."

Mr. Le Couteau said, "You will join us?"

Jake wasn't sure it was a question, and he was disappointed at the break in their discussion. It had been headed in a direction of which he was truly curious.

Jake replied, "My pleasure. Thank you."

They walked out of the room and continued down a long corridor. There were several doors along the corridor. They turned left and walked for about forty feet and then turned right. They walked for another fifty or sixty feet. There were numerous doors all along the way. Jake was amazed at the size of this underground structure. They turned left and Jake saw that a double door was open and inside was what looked like a nice informal restaurant. There were several tables with chairs for four. There were also long tables at which as many as twenty people could easily sit. He noticed one of those was full of laughing and smiling young people in their late teens and early twenties. Jake saw that some tables were occupied by families. Several couples with young children were already eating. It was a cafeteria-style place. Mr. Le Couteau led him through a buffet line, in which each person selected, from a variety of choices, whatever they wished and carried it back to their table. Mr. Le Couteau led Jake to a table for four.

They sat down across the table from each other. Just as they were scooting their chairs up closer to the table, Laura and Peggy walked over with their trays.

Laura said, "Mind if we join you?"

Mr. Le Couteau responded by saying, "Our pleasure."

Jake smiled at them. He looked at Peggy and nodded.

Laura noticed and said, "I'm sorry. Jake Fleming, this is Peggy Curtis. Peggy, Jake."

Jake said, "Hi, Peggy."

"Hi. Have you had a tour yet?"

"No. No, I haven't."

"Laura and I give tours. I'd be glad to show you around."

"Thank you. That would be nice."

Mr. Le Couteau spoke up. "That's all right, Peggy. As soon as we finish eating, I had planned on giving Jake a tour."

The conversation between the four of them was on conventional topics. Jake asked about the weather – how cold it got in the winter and did the building leak when it rained. They explained how things functioned.

Laura was sitting to Jake's left. Peggy was on his right. In a lull in the conversation, Jake turned to Laura and asked about her research of stone megaliths.

Laura's face lit up and she started telling Jake all about her research of Neolithic stone structures. Jake was surprised at her interest in this subject and, as he had a genuine fascination with them himself, was able to understand her enthusiasm and to comment with some degree of expertise.

Suddenly Laura asked, "How did you know of my research area?"

Jake answered, "Jean mentioned it as he explained that most people here have regular jobs and do research in their spare time."

Looking at Mr. Le Couteau, Laura replied, "Oh, I get it. Okay."

After an enjoyable meal, Mr. Le Couteau said, "If you ladies will excuse us, I will give Jake that tour now."

Jake turned to Laura and said, "When we get the chance, there's a dolman, a portal tomb, in Pembrokeshire, Wales, about which I'd like to ask your opinion."

Laura looked surprised and amazed. She said, "Do you mean Pentre Ifan in Brynberian?"

"Yes. Exactly."

"I'd be glad to talk about that with you."

"Thanks."

Peggy said, "I think they're talking in a foreign

language."

Mr. Le Couteau smiled and said, "This way."

Mr. Le Couteau led Jake out of the cafeteria, back through the double doors, and headed down the corridor.

After Jake and Mr. Le Couteau had left, Laura turned to Peggy and emphatically stated, "I cannot believe he is aware of Pentre Ifan. That is amazing."

Mr. Le Couteau and Jake continued walking. It was a bright and well-lit hallway. After several turns, Mr. Le Couteau opened a door that looked like all the others and motioned for Jake to enter ahead of him.

The room Jake entered was a vast library. It was huge! Jake immediately loved it. Despite its size, it felt comfortable, almost homey to Jake. There were a few people in the library, but Mr. Le Couteau explained that, in a few hours, there would be dozens more. One man was sitting at a wooden table with at least ten open books in front of him. He was apparently copying sections from each onto a legal pad. One woman was in the reading area absorbed in her book. Mr. Le Couteau explained that an unwritten rule was that there was absolutely no talking allowed in the reading alcove. To his knowledge, no one had ever broken that rule.

Jake wandered among the stacks. He noticed that they used the Library of Congress classification system. He thought that there must be close to a hundred thousand books in the room. At the opposite side of the library from the door they had entered, Jake saw a glass-walled room. Looking through the glass, he noticed that the volumes in this small room all appeared to be quite old. He guessed correctly that this was a special collection of ancient manuscripts and truly old and rare books. The room was climate controlled.

This library impressed Jake tremendously. He understood now why some people, as Laura had mentioned, called this place *The Library*. He walked back to where Mr. Le Couteau was waiting.

"Jean," he said, "this is one fantastic library. Truly

remarkable."

"Mr. Le Couteau smiled and replied, "I'm glad you like it. It is the heart of our organization. I can see that you appreciate places of learning."

He continued the tour. He showed Jake a fully equipped "health club" room. It had all the usual exercise machines, treadmills and weights. Next to it was a fairly large swimming pool. There was even a bowling alley with sixteen lanes. One of the biggest surprises for Jake was the "English pub." Not only was there a game of darts in progress but also several men were sitting in large leather chairs in a room with real wood paneling on the walls and they were all either smoking pipes or cigars. Jake thought, *It looks like a movie set. I bet they are all probably drinking brandy.*

Mr. Le Couteau pointed down a corridor and said, "This is the administrative offices."

They didn't walk down that way.

After more turns, Mr. Le Couteau pointed down another hallway and said, "Several of our living residences are down there. Those are for families. Single apartments are over this way."

The hallways all looked the same to Jake. It was a real maze to him. Eventually, Mr. Le Couteau stopped, turned to Jake and said, "You will stay the night?"

There was a question after the statement, but again, Jake wasn't sure he was being asked. What if he said no? Could he return to his campsite?

Jake's hesitation in responding prompted Mr. Le Couteau to say, "I'm sure your things at your camp will be fine."

"Yes, of course. I'd be glad to spend the night . . . if it's not a bother."

"No. No, not at all. In fact, this room here is a guest apartment and is available."

Mr. Le Couteau opened the door and motioned Jake inside. It was exactly like a one-bedroom apartment anywhere. It had a living room, a kitchen, a bedroom and a bathroom.

"I hope you will be comfortable here," Mr. Le Couteau said.

"I'm sure I will. Thank you."

"Good. There are some clothes in the closet. Please help yourself. Sleep well. Someone will call on you in the morning to lead you to the cafeteria for breakfast. I will see you tomorrow."

"Thank you. Goodnight."

"Goodnight."

CHAPTER SIXTEEN

"But if there is ignorance and learning does not exist in the soul of man, then the incurable passions persist in the soul. God sent to men knowledge and learning."

– Hermes Trismegistus

Mid 2nd Century A.D.

Jake lay in the bed and stared at the ceiling. The apartment was much like a hotel suite. The kitchen was more complete – more like an apartment with a full-size refrigerator and stove. The bedroom was simple but certainly satisfactory. There was a bookcase in both the bedroom and the living room – both full of books. While, prior to sleeping, Jake normally read for a while, tonight he didn't feel like reading. He felt like thinking.

What a day this has been. Foremost in his mind was the question of why he was here. *Was this place the draw?* The reason he had felt *drawn* to go camping in this isolated area of northwest Maine? How could that be? He had felt a strong impulse to getaway. To get away from what? To get to some place? To get here? Was he getting away from something or was he searching for something? And what about the odd conversation with Jean Le Couteau? *What was that all about?* There was something during their conversation that had caused him to sense something. He couldn't remember what. He couldn't bring that feeling back to the surface.

Jake smiled as he thought of Ted. Ted would be disappointed that he hadn't been abducted by aliens...but perhaps, he had.

How had Laura known his name? He thought that, when he had gone canoeing out on the lake and got caught in that rainstorm, someone could have slipped into his tent and gone through his things. His driver's license was in that tent. That would be a rational explanation for how she had known his name. However, as he thought about it, he wasn't convinced that that was the answer.

He thought, *All these people. For all these years. How had they kept it quiet?* This was a rather large secret. They had to have more than a Christmas tree farm as a cover. Or did they? There was much he had yet to learn.

Jake woke with a jerk. For half a second, he had no idea where he was. Then it all rushed in on him – Laura, Jean, Peggy – it was real; it was not a dream.

Barefooted, Jake walked across the navy-blue pile carpet to the bathroom. The carpet felt nice against his feet. A shower, he thought, would work wonders. It did. Jake luxuriated in the feel of the hot spray against his body. It felt good to his still very tired arms. He thought of his campsite and of the rental canoe. Jake quickly decided that his concern over them would serve no good purpose. It was, he thought, extremely unlikely that anyone would stumble across his campsite.

After shaving, Jake took a look in the bedroom closet. There were several new dress slacks and shirts, his size, on hangers. There was even a pair of black dress shoes, his size, on the closet floor. In the top drawer of the dresser, there were black socks and underwear still in their packages. Jake shook his head and dressed. He wore navy slacks with a crisp burgundy shirt.

With the morning news on the television, Jake sat down on the sofa, took his first sip of coffee and heard a knock on the door. Muting the TV, he answered the door to find Laura standing there smiling.

Jake was glad to see her. He smiled, stepped back and said, "Hi! Come in."

"Good morning." She walked a couple of steps into the

apartment. "Breakfast?"

Jake closed the door and walked toward the bedroom. Over his shoulder, he said, "Let me put some shoes on and I'll be ready for breakfast."

Laura followed him. She watched him work his feet into the shoes.

"Okay," he said, I'm ready."

"You forgot your belt," Laura pointed at his waist.

"Yeah, I know. I wasn't wearing one yesterday with my jeans."

"There should be one hanging up in your closet."

Laura walked over and quickly found a black leather belt hanging from a wire hanger with the shirts. She handed it to him.

"Thanks. I didn't see it."

Laura thought to herself, *He should be wearing gray slacks with that shirt.* She said nothing.

Jake slipped the belt through his pant loops and walked to the front door of the apartment. As Jake put his hand on the doorknob and started to open the door, Laura put her hand on his and said, "Wait."

Jake turned to look at her. Her intelligent beautiful green eyes seemed to be searching his face. She tossed her head in that way only women can do. Her red hair shifted from her face to behind her shoulder. This morning, she was dressed in tight jeans and a form-fitting hunter green sweater. Jake thought she looked absolutely wonderful.

Laura smiled at him. "Tell me something?"

"Sure." Jake nodded as he smiled in response.

"Really. How did you know about the Pentre Ifan dolmen in Wales?"

This was not anywhere near the question that Jake was expecting or hoping to receive. He answered, "It's not a secret or anything. I was recently reading a book about megalithic stones and was intrigued by several in Wales – including and especially Pentre Ifan."

"Oh, okay. I see." Laura sounded disappointed. However,

Jake had no idea what she had been expecting him to say.

"As I understand," Jake said, "the best guess of the 'experts' is that it was built around three thousand five hundred B. C."

"Yes, I think that's right."

"That makes it well over five thousand years old."

Laura smiled. "Yes," she replied.

"I can't visualize how they did it."

Laura's eyes brightened. As they left the room and headed toward the cafeteria, she said, "I've got some ideas about that."

"I'd love to hear them. You don't also happen to know why it was built, do you?"

Laura smiled, turned and looked at Jake, and said, "I've got some ideas about that."

Jake laughed. "I'd love to hear them."

Just as they were finishing breakfast, Mr. Le Couteau stopped at their table. After exchanging morning pleasantries, he said, "Jake, if you don't mind, I'd like to talk with you this morning."

Jake responded, "Sure, I'd be glad to."

Jake excused himself from Laura and followed Mr. Le Couteau out of the cafeteria and down a hallway. What might be behind each door they passed made Jake curious. Eventually, Mr. Le Couteau stopped, opened a door and, with a small hand gesture, indicated for Jake to proceed into the room. Jake immediately recognized it as the nice lounge room in which he and Mr. Le Couteau had talked the day before.

"Coffee?"

"Yes, thanks."

Mr. Le Couteau set a mug of black coffee on the glass table in front of Jake. He sat his own mug on the small wooden table next to his chair.

Mr. Le Couteau said, "I like this room."

Jake responded, "I do, too. If it had a fireplace, it'd be perfect."

Mr. Le Couteau laughed. He said, "I suspect you are right. Of course, the smoke might draw unwanted attention our way."

"Probably. How in the world have you managed to stay under the radar for so long?"

"We've just been careful not to do anything to draw attention to ourselves."

"Of course, I understand that but still – all these years. It seems as if someone – one of your people here, perhaps, would 'spill the beans.'"

Mr. Le Couteau laughed. "It's possible, of course. But, you see, we *are* a secret society . . . but not to do evil; not to overthrow any government; not to hurt anyone; but rather, to gather and store knowledge. To preserve knowledge. And to help people. This foundation has a charity side in which it, totally anonymously, helps people financially."

Jake started to say something but Mr. Le Couteau held up his hand. He said, "Let me finish. People who come through here, like yourself, for example . . . these people know that if our presence were known to the outside world, we would most likely no longer be able to operate. Knowing that, they don't reveal us to the outside world. Right now, I have every confidence that you, when you return to your home – that you will not tell anyone about us."

Jake was certainly glad to hear Mr. Le Couteau say that. He smiled and replied, "I suspect you are right about that."

Mr. Le Couteau smiled. "It appears we both have been right about everything this morning."

Jake took a sip of his coffee and wondered what it was Jean Le Couteau wanted to tell him. He also wondered what in the world he was doing there. He figured it would be a roundabout discussion before they got to the purpose of today's conversation.

"Jake, do you know much about the history of Maine?"

"I did read a little about it . . . prior to coming up here."

Mr. Le Couteau smiled. "Good. Good. Did anything about it surprise you?"

"Yes, Jean, something that surprised me was the amount of activity by the English, and others, before the settlements in Jamestown and Plymouth. I had not been aware of that."

"Most people are not."

"Yesterday, Jean, you mentioned a possible Chinese colony in Nova Scotia. Not many people are aware of that, I would think."

"You are right. That is a fascinating story. But there is more concrete evidence of earlier colonies in America – especially in New England. Are you aware of these?"

Jake nodded. "I am. You are referring to megalithic stones, dolmens and Ogham writings, are you not?"

Mr. Le Couteau smiled and also nodded. "Exactly," he replied. "But while Ogham is certainly definitive proof of a very early European presence, there are other writing examples that even indicate an Egyptian presence."

"You are referring to the Native American Micmac writing system."

Mr. Le Couteau was astonished by Jake's statement. His face showed his level of astonishment and amazement. He doubted if there were many more than a hundred people in the world who knew about the Micmac writing system – and here Jake was apparently one of them. Looking directly at Jake, he asked, "What do you know of the Micmac's ability to write?"

"Not much. I do know that the Micmacs lived in what is now the eastern provinces of Canada. They were a tribe of Algonquian Native Americans. One of the first French priests who was a missionary to the Micmacs related in his journals the story of children making symbols on pieces of tree bark. When he asked what they were doing, they replied that they were practicing putting their thoughts into writing. He could make no sense of the symbols. This was in the sixteen sixties. He witnessed a chief write a message on tree bark and the message was delivered to a chief of the Wabanaki, which by the way, translates as 'Men-of-the-East.' The Wabanaki Native Americans lived in what is now Maine and they were like first cousins of the

Micmacs. Anyway, as the priest recorded in his journals, about six weeks later, the Micmac chief received a reply from the Wabanaki chief, written with the same symbols, on a piece of tree bark. The priest recorded some of the symbols and their meanings in his journals. Those journals have survived to our time. The symbols that this priest recorded were found to be the same as ancient Egyptian hieroglyphics. He had only recorded a few symbols. In the seventeen hundreds, another French priest became fascinated with the Micmac symbols. He recorded over two hundred symbols. These also have survived to the present. Although there are some slight variations, those symbols are very close and, in some cases, identical to Egyptian hieroglyphics. An interesting point about all this is that Champollion didn't publish his first decipherment of Egyptian hieroglyphics until eighteen twenty-three. If Champollion had had access to the priests' journals, his work would have been a lot easier. Although, of course, the Rosetta stone made it rather easy for him."

Mr. Le Couteau didn't know what to say to Jake's response. He was quite awed by Jake and wondered just who he really was.

He paused and seemed unsure of what to say next. He asked, "What do you make of this? What do you get out of it?"

"The big question I get from all this is how did the Micmac Native Americans and the Men-of-the East Native Americans learn to use Egyptian hieroglyphics? Sometimes, by coincidence, someone could make symbols similar to another culture's symbols. But the meanings would be different. In this case, the meaning of the symbols is the same for both the Native Americans and the Egyptians. That throws a large 'monkey wrench' in the accepted version that the Norse and Columbus were the first to arrive in the hemisphere."

"Also, along those lines, I wonder Jake, how long the Micmacs and the Wabanaki had been using those symbols."

"Exactly. That would tell a lot. However, it currently tells a lot in that hardly anyone is aware of this. It tells us that this type of information is being and has been suppressed. The 'experts' cannot explain it so they tend to deny its existence. It's a shame."

"Well," Mr. Le Couteau stated, "it is quite the mystery."

Jake thought, *He is certainly saying the obvious. But he is making conversation. He is leading up to something or he doesn't know what to say.* Out loud, Jake replied, "There are many mysteries of ancient origins here in Maine and throughout New England."

Mr. Le Couteau smiled and said, "Such as?"

"Ogham scripts. This ancient form of writing has been found throughout the United States. One form is almost identical to Ogham script found on the Iberian Peninsula. Now this doesn't mean it was written by early Spaniards or Portuguese but, more probably, by ancient Phoenicians. Another form of this script appears to have a strong Celtic influence. Both these writing systems prove that Europeans were here long before Columbus.

"And ancient coins. There have been dozens, if not hundreds, of ancient Roman coins found in the United States. One interesting type of coin that has been found in eight different states – one in each state – is a Phoenician coin from the city of Carthage that was minted in one forty-six B.C. And the Metcalf Stone. Do you know about the Metcalf Stone and the Yuchi Native Americans?"

"No. I have heard the term Metcalf Stone but have forgotten anything about it."

"The Yuchi tribe used to live in the area that is now Fort Benning near Columbus, Georgia. They practiced an agricultural ritual that was identical to one described in the Bible . . . Leviticus, I think. Anyway, their language was unique. The Metcalf Stone was found in the nineteen-sixties near what used to be a Yuchi village. On this stone were symbols that were used in the Mediterranean area around two thousand B.C.

"The Hearn Tablet is another mystery. It is a very small lead tablet that had Sumerian cuneiform script on it from two thousand, forty B.C. The reason for the exact date of two thousand, forty B.C. is that the lead tablet tells that a scribe arrived in a particular year of a king's reign. It is thought that a team of metallurgists from the city of Ur set out in search of a source of metals. For some unknown reason, the tablet, about the size of a matchbox, was brought along and either discarded or accidentally lost.

"Another mystery is the Bat Creek Stone."

"I've heard of this one also."

"It is fascinating. It was found in an Indian mound in Tennessee. It was excavated by the Smithsonian in the eighteen-nineties. The writing on it is Canaanite, an early form of Hebrew. It is at least over two thousand years old.

"New England has over a hundred stone chambers. They are of similar dry wall construction. They used no mortar at all. They used huge stones to cap the chambers. These structures are extremely close to stone structures that one can still see in Ireland, Wales, Scotland, England and northern France. Archaeological 'experts' say that they are colonial era root cellars or birthing pens for livestock. In one of these 'root cellars,' after a thorough cleaning by a group who was examining and measuring several of these stone structures, a slit in the roof was noticed. At sunset, a ray of sunshine came through the slit and lit a small chamber in the back of the main chamber. Later, it was revealed that this was designed to light a specific place in the small chamber on the spring equinox. Not likely in a root cellar. In another chamber, an obsidian knife was found inside – lodged in a crevice near the top. Now, Jean, obsidian is a volcanic glass and it can be dated. The design of the obsidian knife did not match the stone knives of Native Americans. Obsidian can be traced through its chemical makeup. This was done and the obsidian that was used to make this knife that was found in a stone structure in New York came from volcanic activity in Ireland. Obsidian also begins to absorb water as soon as it is exposed to the air. Since this knife was shaped from a piece of obsidian, tests revealed that it had been cut approximately four thousand years ago. Question: how did a four thousand-year-old Irish obsidian knife wind up in a New York state 'root cellar?' Another knife, a Bronze Age Celtic dagger was found in a Native American shell pile in

Massachusetts.

"There are standing megalithic stones all over New England and New York State. Many of these have markings and carvings cut into the stone. There are many stone circles in New England. And dolmens. Did you know that the largest dolmen in the world is located in New York State?"

"Yes, actually, I did know that."

"Do you know who built it and when?"

"No, I don't know that."

"No one else does either. However, I find it fascinating. The archaeological 'experts' say that the dolmens in the U. S. are the result of melting glaciers depositing rocks on top of other rocks. They say this despite the construction looking very similar to dolmens in Wales, for instance. They say this despite the American dolmens having astronomical alignments.

"And petroglyphs. They are all over the United States. Most are undoubtedly done by Native Americans. But many are not. One of the most fascinating petroglyphs that I remember reading about is one of a sailing ship and a Christian cross. It is located here in Maine, on the coast, at Machias. The ship's design is so clearly outlined that it is possible to determine the time period – approximately from thirteen hundred to fourteen fifty A.D. One of Sinclair's Templar ships, perhaps?"

"Don't laugh. You may be right."

"I'm not laughing. Somebody etched that ship and the cross into that rock. Most of the New England petroglyphs are much older than that one."

"Uh, Jake?"

"Yeah?"

"I truly do think you've made your point. There are a lot of mysteries here in Maine . . . and the surrounding area. Wonder why there is not much information 'out there' about these mysteries?"

"Jean, I tell you, I think it is because the 'experts' are not willing to acknowledge what their common sense tells them. They were so locked into the concept that Columbus was the first that it took decades after the Viking settlement was discovered in Newfoundland and dated to around one thousand A.D. for the experts to accept it. But that is it! There can be no additional people, from anywhere else, having visited or, heaven forbid, settled in the Western Hemisphere. They are, of course, totally and completely wrong. Eventually, they will have to accept the obvious as science keeps revealing more and more evidence. I mean, these things, these astronomically aligned stone chambers, the carvings in stone, the written languages in stone, the aligned stone circles and standing megaliths are all there. People can go and see them, touch them and photograph them. They are real. They simply cannot be explained away as root cellars. I mean, really, who goes to all the trouble to align their root cellars with the rising or setting sun on a solstice. Real root cellars are down in the ground – not aligned up on the ground. What the experts say makes no common sense at all."

Mr. Le Couteau simply said, "I agree."

CHAPTER SEVENTEEN

"Every human soul needs to be aware of its existence."

– Byron Edwards

Early 21st Century A.D.

Jake got up and asked Mr. Le Couteau, "May I freshen your mug?"

"Yes, please."

Jake walked over to the coffee maker and re-filled their mugs. He returned and placed Mr. Le Couteau's mug on the wooden table next to his chair. Jake set his mug on the glass table and sat down.

Mr. Le Couteau picked up his mug and said, "Thank you."

Jake nodded and replied, "You're welcome." He reached for his mug and took a sip. The coffee was good. Jake was wondering what it was that Jean really wanted to discuss.

"Jake, I am wondering something. Are you happy with what you are doing for a living?"

Jake smiled. He replied, "I am a happy person. Primarily, I think, because I choose to be happy. I am a Christian. I think that all Christians should be happy just because they are Christians. Just knowing that Jesus died for us is enough, I think, to make one happy. I don't think my vocation of employment really has much impact on my happiness. I have had numerous different jobs throughout my life and I have been happy in all of them. Actually, I just sort-of stumbled, almost by accident, into the work I am now doing."

"I understand. I think that happens to a lot of people. They wind up doing something for a living that they never imagined they would be doing. I think I phrased my question incorrectly. Let me ask it again. Do you like what you are currently doing for a living?"

Without hesitation, Jake replied, "No, I do not."

"Ahhh. How long, then, do you plan to keep it?"

"Actually, I plan to resign from my current position before the end of the year. I am grateful for the position. It has made me financially secure and given me the opportunity to do almost whatever I wish with the rest of my life."

"Have you decided what that might be?"

"No, not yet."

"Any leanings? Any ideas?"

"Not really. I'm still trying to figure things out."

"Yes, I can understand that."

"My opportunity to become a major league baseball pitcher has probably gone."

"Yes, I suspect that is an accurate assessment of the situation."

They both laughed.

"Jean, you and your group of people here have somewhat withdrawn from the world. You are involved and participate but you live away from the world. I, however, do physically live in the current world of the twenty-first century. All around me, I can see anger, hate, selfishness, arrogance, intolerance and greed. And that is not just politicians."

Mr. Le Couteau laughed.

Jake smiled and continued, "I also see love, kindness, compassion, honor and brotherhood. There is much stupidity in the world but there is also much kindness. I do believe that the world is in the beginning process of undergoing a dramatic spiritual shift. Some have referred to it as an awakening. Prior to this spiritual change, I believe there will be a time – and I believe we are currently at the beginning of that time – of uncertainly and chaos. It will be a time of unrest and extreme questioning. People will ask, how can these things be happening? What has happened to basic beliefs of morality? Why has honesty and honor fallen out of favor? What fifty years ago was considered moral and right is today scorned and ridiculed. What fifty years ago was considered immoral and wrong is today praised and accepted as normal. God is even despised by some. And those that do not despise God, ignore him. Our culture ridicules talk about one's soul. Atheism is on the rise. However, despite all this wickedness, I do sincerely believe that it is the will of God that good will ultimately prevail over evil. I think that now we are beginning this time of confusion and upheaval. However, I believe humanity will get through this time and then there will be a strong spiritual shift in the world."

"The Age of Aquarius, perhaps?" Mr. Le Couteau smiled at Jake.

"Perhaps. I am hopeful that this time of confusion will not last real long before things begin to turn around. You know, Jean, this is not the first time our culture has degenerated into a horrible and unhealthy state. There have been many times in recorded history where this has happened. And always, when it does, there are a minority of people who continue to prefer light to darkness. It is true today as well. It will most likely get worse prior to getting better. However, people of the light will always exist. They will be the ones to lead the others out of their darkness."

"How will this happen, do you think?"

"I really have no idea. I am sure it will happen; but, what will be the spark that will ignite a spiritual revival? I don't know. Perhaps your organization here will play a role in that process."

"I hope so. I do want you to know that I do not disagree with your assessment and analysis of our current cultural decline. As you mentioned, from a historical perspective, I have often thought of it as a pendulum swinging back and forth. I'm sure you've previously heard this analogy."

"Yes," Jake replied. "But doesn't it seem a shame that so many people have to go through all this – most of them blissfully unaware that, instead of living in darkness, it is actually quite easy to move into the light and live a life in the light."

"True. You know, Jake, I think that many people are unaware that they are living in the dark. Many people today have no moral compass at all. They have no shame. They cannot be embarrassed. I saw an interview on TV with a guy who had robbed a convenience store."

Jake interrupted, "That is, I have always thought, one of the dumbest crimes ever committed. First of all, the thief is going to be on camera. His crime will be recorded. He usually uses a gun to threaten the person behind the cash register. That makes it a serious felony crime. And the thief's haul? Usually less than two hundred dollars. He ought to rob a jewelry store."

Mr. Le Couteau laughed. "I agree with you. But the point I wanted to make is that, when asked why he robbed the convenience store, his reply was that he didn't think he would get caught. He didn't see anything wrong with robbing the convenience store. His only concern was whether he was likely to get caught or not. He has no moral compass to tell him that stealing is not the right thing to do. I'm afraid we now have an entire generation of young adults who have reached their early twenties without a real education and without any real moral teachings."

"I disagree with you, Jean, when you say, 'an entire generation.' I think that what you have said applies to many, if not most, of that generation. However, among that group are some excellent students and some believers in God. Many of them are serving in the military."

"You are right. I painted a picture with too wide a brush. There are, thankfully, exceptions to my 'entire generation' statement."

"I tell you, Jean, something I really believe is that, through God, we are all connected. I believe that there is a part of the Divine in every human soul. That part connects us all to each other. That convenience store thief you mentioned is connected to you and to me. You and I are connected. A terrorist who straps a bomb on himself and detonates it in a crowded place murdering innocent people is connected to the people he murdered and to us. Obviously, he is not a follower of Christ and consequently his soul will spend eternity in darkness, in hell. It is such a terrible shame that some people never activate that spark of Divinity within. Now this may seem weird, but, in some ways, I think that everything is connected to everything else. I think that we humans are connected to the trees in the forest, to all the animals on the planet, to flowers that bloom in the wild, to rainbows in the sky, to water that flows throughout the earth, to stones that form mountains and hills, to everything . . . everything in the universe."

"I don't know, Jake. Humans, I get. Rocks, I don't get."

"There is a difference. The human to human connection is Divine. It is soul to soul. It is directly of God. The other connection is more of a spiritual nature."

Mr. Le Couteau looked at Jake with a funny expression on his face.

"Of course, they are both spiritual. What I mean is that as God is everywhere, his love, his connection is everywhere and in everything – trees, flowers, water, rocks. We are, I believe, all spiritual beings living in a flesh and blood body. Spirituality, I think, allows our spiritual being to connect . . . as God connects. Imagine that you are standing on a very small meteor in deep outer space. In this fantasy, you have no need of an astronaut's space suit. It is just you and the universe. You stand on this rock. You see the vastness and the beauty of the universe. You see galaxies spinning in space. You see infinity. You hold your arms up and you pray to God. And, at that moment, you can feel the connection with every single thing in the universe. There is an energy that passes out from your body and connects with everything. It doesn't make you special. It doesn't make you powerful. Every single human being who has learned how to love can do the same thing. The energy that connects you to everything . . . is love. There is no more powerful force in the universe than love.

"One way to express that love is to acknowledge the connections. It is only through God that one can do this. One definition of God is love. Try walking through a forest and admiring the beauty of the trees. Watch the leaves moving in the wind and appreciate the breeze on your face. Enjoy the songs of the birds. Smell the fragrances of the forest. Pick up a small stone and feel the texture. If it is in season, taste a wild blackberry. Connect with nature. Connect with love."

Mr. Le Couteau smiled. He said, "Okay, I get it. You actually had me feeling like I was in space. And then, I could easily visualize myself in that forest you described. I do understand what you are saying."

"It's basically viewing things with a different perspective. The only real requirement is that one has learned to love."

"Listen, Jake, after lunch, I'd like to introduce you to some of the people who have lived here the longest."

"Thank you. I look forward to meeting them."

Jake enjoyed a pleasant lunch with Laura. They talked primarily about megalithic stone structures.

Mr. Le Couteau came and collected Jake. He led Jake down a corridor to a door like all the others. Opening the door, he waited for Jake to enter. It was a small conference room with three elderly men sitting on one side of a small conference table. Jake and Mr. Le Couteau approached the table and Mr. Le Couteau said, "Jake Fleming, this is Edward Nesbitt, Howard Millar and Cyril Kent."

Jake reached across the table and shook hands with each of the men. He and Mr. Le Couteau then sat down opposite the three men.

Mr. Nesbitt looked at Jake and asked, "How are you finding things here at our little place?"

Jake smiled. "Fascinating. Your library is extraordinary. The food is delicious. And, the conversations and the company is exceptional."

Mr. Nesbitt looked at Mr. Le Couteau. Mr. Le Couteau

said, "He had breakfast and lunch today with Laura."

Everyone, including Jake, smiled or laughed.

Mr. Millar said, "I'm glad you like it here. We would like to ask you a few questions. Is that all right with you?"

"Yes. Fine," Jake replied. "First, though, if you gentlemen don't mind, would you tell me a little about yourselves?"

They looked at each other, a little confused.

Jake said, "Your history. How long you've been here. Your family. Your education. Anything."

"Oh, I see," Mr. Nesbitt stated. "Okay, I'll start. I am eighty-four years old. Born in nineteen twenty-one. I met Hugh Sinclair, Charles' father, when I was a college student in nineteen forty-one. After Pearl Harbor, I dropped out of college and joined the army in nineteen forty-two. In nineteen forty-five, I returned to college and was graduated in nineteen forty-seven with a degree in history. I married in nineteen forty-eight and we were together until she died two years ago. That was fifty-five years we were together. We moved here in nineteen fifty; and, I have been working in that library of which you have spoken so highly, ever since. That's now also fifty-five years."

Mr. Millar said, "My turn, I expect. Young man, you may find this difficult to believe but I was born in nineteen twelve. I am ninety-three years old. I was graduated from college in nineteen thirty-four. The Depression was a terrible thing. But we got through it. I also joined the service, the Navy, in nineteen forty-two. Never married. Joined up here in nineteen forty-seven. That's fifty-eight years for me. I've worked here as an accountant. Kept the books balanced all this time."

Mr. Kent smiled and said, "All right. I'm eighty-eight. Born in nineteen seventeen. Got my bachelor's degree in thirty-nine and my master's degree in forty-one. Joined the Marines in forty-two. They made me an officer. Got married in forty and we had three children. All three of them and their families are living right here. My wife passed in two thousand and one. She never thought she'd make it to the twenty-first century but she did. I've been here since forty-nine. Done enough research here to have earned several doctorates but they don't give out degrees here. Been at it now for fifty-six years. You see, son, this place doesn't believe in people retiring. We just stay at it until we either physically or mentally are unable to continue."

Jake was genuinely impressed by their brief accounts. He said, "Thank you for sharing that. I totally agree with your retirement policy. After someone has accumulated forty years of knowledge and experience, why turn them out and start all over with someone new? Like you said, if a person is able and wants to continue, it doesn't make sense to force them to quit. I hope to keep working as long as I am productive – regardless of my age."

All three men smiled and nodded their heads.

Jake thought it looked a little "spooky" to see all three elderly men smiling and nodding like bobbleheads – all at the same time. He just smiled back.

Mr. Kent said, "We would like to ask you a few questions."

"Of course."

Mr. Kent asked, "Who would you say built the great Giza pyramids of ancient Egypt?"

Jake was surprised and dumbfounded. He wasn't a hundred percent sure he had heard the question correctly. He looked at Jean but Mr. Le Couteau was looking directly at Mr. Kent.

Jake smiled and said, "Okay. I actually do have an answer for that question. I do not think that either they or the Sphinx were constructed by pharaohs or historic Egyptians. Rather, I think they were built much earlier than the 'experts' say by an advanced civilization that has been lost to history."

Mr. Kent replied, "Uh-huh. You base that on what? A hunch? A guess? How did you arrive at such a conclusion which is totally in disagreement with expert archaeologists?"

Jake smiled and answered, "Evidence. I base it on evidence and the lack of evidence. I'll explain. First of all, there is absolutely no evidence that the Egyptians of two thousand, five hundred B. C. had the ability to build either the Sphinx or the pyramids. The Sphinx complex or temple itself would be extraordinarily difficult, if not impossible, to construct today. We simply do not have the technical expertise to duplicate its construction. We don't have the machinery to lift the weight of many of the blocks of stone in the limited confines of the space in which they exist. Neither did the historic Egyptians. Nor do we know how the pyramids were built. It is a mystery. Why is it a mystery? It is a mystery because the civilization that history tells us built it did not have the means with which *to* build it. Conclusion. They did not build it. Further conclusion. Someone else . . . did build it. It is also interesting to note that, in all of the ancient hieroglyphics, there is not one mention of the construction of the pyramids. There exist, right now, today, stones on the ground in front of the Great Pyramid that were cut by sharp stone-cutting machines. You can go there, touch these stones, examine them, take photographs of them and see that they were machine cut. The stone box inside the King's Chamber of the Great Pyramid was machine cut. The inside corners are all perfect ninety-degree angles. Under magnification, the grooves of the cutting saw can be determined. The idea that the pyramids were tombs for pharaohs is utter nonsense. All under the Giza Plateau are dozens, if not hundreds, of ancient tunnels. These are smoothly cut tunnels. They are a mystery. Of course, in the last twenty years, it has been conclusively proven that the erosion to the Sphinx and its enclosure was caused by water, not wind. The two types of erosion are distinct and completely different. While I was in college, I had two courses in geology and learned enough to be able to tell the difference. There is no question today that water caused the erosion at the Sphinx and its enclosure. Due to the amount of rainfall needed to cause that erosion, the constructions of the Sphinx has to be moved from approximately two thousand, five hundred B. C. to approximately ten thousand B. C. It could have been, of course, much earlier than that."

Mr. Kent replied, "I see. So you think that all the professional archaeologists and those who study Egyptology are wrong?"

"I don't think it; I know it. They are totally wrong." Jake wasn't being arrogant, just sure of his facts.

"Why is it, do you think, that they cannot see what you see?" Mr. Kent asked but Jake thought he already knew the answer.

"I think the reason is that they have no answer for what civilization was around prior to ten thousand B. C. If they admit what the evidence shows, where do they go? Who could have cut those stones with machines? What was their power source? Where did they come from? Atlantis? Outer space? . . . Worldwide, there are numerous examples of things that were produced with advanced technologies. Ruins at Puma Pumku and Tiawanaku, in Bolivia, are extraordinary. They most definitely were not made with chisels but rather, machines. As are the huge stones nearby at Aramu Muru, all of these sites are close to Lake Titicaca. In Columbia, small models, made from gold, have been discovered that look amazingly like modern jet planes. One 'expert' said that their provenance was so poor that they were probably made in the nineteen sixties. However, most were discovered in the nineteen-thirties, and one was proven to have been in a museum since eighteen ninety-five. Archaeologists say that they are ritual items or religious artifacts. If you or I saw them, we'd say they look like jet planes. But we aren't experts. I know this sounds like I've gotten away from your question. But I haven't. It is the same as with the Sphinx and the pyramids. They cannot admit what their eyes show them because to do so would upset their entire paradigm of the progress of civilization."

Mr. Kent said, "Thank you."

Mr. Millar said, "My turn? Okay. Mr. Fleming, you have just said, in your explanation in response to Mr. Kent, that there must have been an advanced civilization prior to our recorded history. Would you give me one other example of where we have forgotten technology or science?"

"I could give you dozens. There . . ."

"Just one will do, Mr. Fleming."

Jake was amazed that Mr. Millar was 93 and had followed

his explanation to Mr. Kent's question so well.

"Sure. Around five hundred B. C., the Greeks were totally aware that the earth was a sphere and that it revolved around the sun. Two thousand years later, people thought the earth was flat and that the sun revolved around the earth."

Mr. Millar said, "Thank you."

Mr. Nesbitt cleared his throat to prepare for his question. He asked, "What are you doing here?"

Jake looked at Mr. Le Couteau but he was looking directly ahead at Mr. Nesbitt.

Jake replied, "I don't know."

Mr. Nesbitt responded, "Let me re-phrase the question. Why did you leave New York and travel to this remote corner of Maine?"

Jake answered, "I'm not sure."

"What do you think was the reason?"

"I can't exactly explain it. I felt . . . an urge – to travel up here."

"An urge, Mr. Fleming?"

"Yes. I just felt a need, an urge, a pull . . . to come to this area. I thought I'd know I had arrived when I saw it."

"Did you?"

"Yes. When I saw the lake and the little cove with the sand beach, I thought that it was the place I was supposed to be."

Mr. Nesbitt responded, "That all seems truly vague. It is difficult to imagine that someone would make such a journey based on a feeling."

"I know. You should hear how crazy my friend, Ted, thinks I am for coming up here."

"Do you often do major things based upon a feeling?" Mr. Nesbitt sounded serious.

"I'm not sure I've ever previously experienced a feeling like this one. It was like I was suddenly attracted to this area. I really cannot explain it."

"I think I understand," Mr. Nesbitt replied, "Thank you."

Mr. Le Couteau stood from the table. He said, "Thank

you, gentlemen."

Jake stood. He was confused. He said, "It was nice to meet each of you. I hope we get an opportunity to talk again sometime."

They all nodded in reply.

Outside the conference room, Jake turned to Mr. Le Couteau and said, "Jean, I don't understand what just happened. I mean, is that it? It seems slightly weird."

"No, not at all. They each asked a question and you answered."

"But what questions. I don't . . ."

"Sometimes," Mr. Le Couteau interrupted, "it is not the questions that are important but rather the meeting itself."

"I see," Jake replied. And he did. These were the people who had been at this underground facility the longest. They knew things. They were probably good at assessing people. In order to do that, in order to get a 'feel' for people, there had to be interaction.

"Jake, I've got a meeting in Montreal tomorrow. I'm leaving," Mr. Le Couteau looked at his watch, "in about an hour. You have the rest of today and all of tomorrow to yourself. Enjoy."

Jake smiled. "Thank you. Could you leave me directions from my guest room to the library?"

"Of course."

Once they arrived at Jake's assigned apartment, Mr. Le Couteau drew a map showing Jake where to turn, how many doors to pass and which one was the library door.

After Mr. Le Couteau had left, Jake took his shoes off and walked on the navy blue carpet from the living room to the bathroom. He returned to the kitchen, got a bottle of water from the fridge and sat down on the couch. He wanted to think. Puzzles and mysteries were enjoyable to read, however, being in the middle of one was not quite so enjoyable. What was this all about? Founded in eighteen sixty-five. That means it has been functioning for one hundred and forty years. Was he somehow "brought" here? Why did he feel compelled to travel to this remote area of Maine? Did God lead him here? Was he being "interviewed" in preparation for being invited to stay here? How did they even know he existed? Jake knew he could spend years in that library. Is that what God wanted him to do with the rest of his life? Jake prayed. He asked God to direct him. He asked God to show him the path to take. He asked for the Holy Spirit to guide him.

Jake thought about getting up and leaving. He could spend the night in his tent and, the next day, paddle back the way he had come. One night in his tent and the next night, in a motel in Fort Kent. The next night he could be in his condo in New York. Two days paddling. One day driving. He'd be back in the city. He'd just forget all about this place. He wouldn't tell anyone about it. He'd just forget it. As Jake continued to think about his options, he decided he was going to see it through. He had felt a genuine urge to get here. He would see what was going to happen. Indeed, they may decide not to invite him to stay. That would be okay. He would not tell anyone, even Ted, about them. He'd just say he spent his time fishing.

Just then, Jake heard a brief knock on his door. He got up from the couch and answered it. Laura was standing there. She was wearing tight jeans and a baby blue sweater. Jake thought she looked beautiful. Laura was surprised that Jake had not said anything.

She said, "Hello?"

Jake jolted himself back into reality. He replied, "I'm sorry. Come in. I was in the middle of daydreaming. What time is it? I've lost . . ."

"It's suppertime. I've come to see if you need a guide to the cafeteria."

"That would be great. Yes, I do need a guide."

Jake felt like a nervous fifteen-year-old boy. He picked up Jean's instructions to the library and placed them in his pants pocket.

Jake headed for the door, but Laura said, "You might want to wear some shoes."

Jake pointed his index finger at her and replied, "Good idea." They both laughed.

At the cafeteria, Laura and Jake seated themselves at a table for four. Jake hoped that no one else would join them.

"Laura, I met three extraordinary men this afternoon. All three have been here for over fifty years."

"Yes, there are some people here who are quite old."

"One of these men was ninety-three."

"We have some people here who are over a hundred."

"Really? I was under the impression that these men had been here the longest – except for Mr. Sinclair, I suppose."

"They have been here the longest but that doesn't mean they are the oldest. We have some people here over a hundred years old but they didn't join us until their fifties, sixties, or seventies."

"I understand. My fault. Laura, tell me about yourself. How long have you been here?"

Laura tossed her head so that her hair swung back in place. She answered, "I've been here since the fall of nineteen ninety-nine. Six years."

"All the way back to the twentieth century, huh?"

Laura smiled what Jake thought was a completely beautiful smile. She said, "Yes, I was here during the big Y-two-K scare."

Jake smiled. "Looking back, it sure seems silly how scared some people got."

"Not you?"

"No, not me. I actually spent New Year's Eve at the ocean in Destin, Florida. I didn't think anything was going to happen and, of course, it didn't."

"Well here, many were concerned about whether or not our computers would continue to operate. Has Jean told you about our computer system?"

146

"No, he hasn't."

"Well . . . Mr. Sinclair doesn't trust the security of the Internet."

"That's probably wise."

"He thinks that the government might use the Internet to keep track of people. Consequently, we have a network within our facility, with its own server, that is run through the Christmas tree farm business. We tap into that. That is how we have television and Internet access. It is through a satellite system."

"I understand."

"It works for our needs. We actually don't use the Internet all that much."

Jake nodded his head. "I think, in the future, it will grow and more and more people will become dependent upon it. But tell me, how did Laura Middleton come to be here?"

She smiled again and replied, "Many people here have amazing stories of weird coincidences concerning how they wound up being here. Mine is rather ordinary. I was teaching history at a private school in Springfield, Virginia."

Jake was nodding his head.

"You know Springfield?"

"Just where it is – right outside DC. By the way, I love to study history. But continue. How did you get from Springfield, Virginia to Nowhere, Maine?"

"Nowhere. I like it. It's not complicated. The history teacher they had here retired. They needed someone to replace him. They picked me."

"Hmmm. I think it may be more complicated than that. Why you? How you?"

"Why not me?"

"I certainly didn't mean to imply that you aren't qualified to teach history but there are literally thousands of history teachers across the United States. How did they choose you?"

"I've obviously asked myself that question many times. I did apply for it. I did have to go through an extensive interview process. At first, they just told me it was for a private school in

Maine. I liked the school I was at okay but did not like living in the greater DC area. It reminded me of Atlanta. I was ready for a change."

Jake had been looking deeply into her sparkling green eyes. With her lush red hair and fine facial features, she had a distinct Celtic appearance. To Jake, she looked intelligent and beautiful.

Jake asked, "Do you have Scottish ancestors?"

"Yes. Why?"

"I'm not sure. Did they inquire about your Scottish roots when they interviewed you?"

"No. . . . I don't think so. I don't really remember. They may have. It was six years ago. We have talked about it since I've been here. Most everyone here has done some genealogy research."

"Genealogy can be quite interesting."

"Yes, I find it fun. If you can go back far enough, you're bound to find some rouges, scoundrels and skeletons."

"I'm sure that's right. Are there a lot of people here with Scottish ancestry?"

"I haven't really thought about it. There may be. It's not a real diverse place. Everyone here is a Protestant Christian. Are you?"

"Yes." Jake smiled. "So tell me more about you. Where'd you go to college?"

"I went to a small college in north Georgia. I grew up in Savannah."

"A real Georgia peach."

Laura actually blushed. She said, "It was Breneau College." She looked at Jake but he shook his head.

"Most people have never heard of it either. It used to be a female only college. But, by the time I was there, they had allowed male students." Laura suddenly looked quite sad. She quickly added, "Anyway, that's where I got my teaching degree in history."

Jake sensed that something was now bothering Laura. The

tone in her voice had changed. She was upset. He didn't know what to say. Was she upset over male students? Was there a bad boyfriend experience? Or was she upset over teaching? Bad experience with a principal or another teacher? Thinking that the most likely scenario that had caused Laura to be upset was a bad boyfriend experience, Jake decided to talk about teaching.

Jake asked, "How long have you been teaching?"

She smiled and Jake presumed that he had guessed correctly. She answered, "Six years here. I was two years in Springfield. My first teaching job after graduation in ninety-three was in Morrow, Georgia – just south of Atlanta. It was a public school. I truly disliked almost everything about the school from the way the school system operated to the curriculum. And, I hated Atlanta. It is just too big. I only taught there one year. They wanted me to renew my contract but I said no. From there, I taught three years in Asheville, North Carolina. Loved the area. It is beautiful. Nice people there. But again, I just simply disagreed with the public school system. It was so political. What is in the best interests of students was not the primary concern of either the school board or the administration. As much as I liked the mountains and the people of the Asheville area, after three years, I left and took the private school position in Springfield. Private schools are so much better than public schools. Anyway, to answer your question, I have been teaching for eleven years."

Jake loved watching Laura as she spoke. He knew he was attracted to her. Using a little basic math, if Laura went straight from high school to college and was graduated in four years, depending upon exactly when her birthday is, Jake now knew that Laura was either thirty-three or thirty-four. Jake thought, *That's only eight or nine years difference. Was that too much?* It was, he thought, *right on the line.* Ten years would probably be too much. But why wasn't she married? Perhaps, like him, divorced? Perhaps widowed? Perhaps she simply hadn't yet met the right guy? *Could I be the right guy?* Slow down Fleming. You haven't even had a date with this woman yet. Or is this a date?

Jake asked, "What age students do you teach here?"

"As you might imagine, our school is rather small. Look around . . . there are maybe a total of a dozen school-age children in here right now. Consequently, I teach elementary, middle school and high school students. I really do enjoy it."

"You must enjoy being around children."

"Oh, I do. I like children. I used to be one."

Jake laughed. He said, "I bet you were just as cute as a button when you were a little girl."

Laura smiled. "Anyway, I like them so much, I'd like to have some of my own someday."

Again, Jake sensed sadness in Laura's voice. He replied, "I'm sure you will."

"I'm not. I was engaged to be married once. When I was in college. But, as we neared graduation, he changed. Or I grew...and he didn't. Some things...some principles are, I think, absolute. I don't think a woman should produce a child unless she is in love with the father of that child *and* is married to him. I just haven't fallen in love with the right man yet."

Jake tried to put on his most charming face as he said, "You will."

She quickly replied, "I'm not so sure."

Her tone almost sounded bitter. Jake decided to change the subject. He said, "I've always been fascinated by megalithic stones. How did you get so interested in them?"

Laura smiled. They had previously discussed specific stone structures in Great Britain, Ireland, France, Portugal, Spain and the United States. Neither of them had really mentioned why they found such structures to be so stimulating.

She replied, "They are truly fascinating, aren't they? As a history major, I am obviously interested in the past. Megalithic stones are certainly from our past. I guess what really turned me on to them is when I learned that there were actually hundreds of megalithic stone structures in America. Most are in New England and many are in Maine. New York also has a lot of them. I was already here when I learned this and was encouraged to use our library to research them. We have a rather large purchasing budget for books. My first order was for fourteen books. I devoured them. And ordered more."

Jake was nodding his head. He understood. He said, "I bet we've read several of the same books. I totally understand what you mean. When I was in college, I would often check out a dozen books on one subject – most often that subject had nothing to do with any of my courses. I would read all the books, return them and get more. I still do that – only now I buy the books and add them to my personal library."

"Yes. Once we've finished with any book we've purchased, it is added to the library's collection. We have a professional librarian on staff who catalogs all the new books."

"Jean introduced her to me. I like the library here."

"Most people do."

"It has a nice atmosphere. Jean and I were recently discussing some of the American megalithic sites. Why did that interest you so much?"

"First of all, I guess because I had been totally unaware that they existed. But they are there. Right now, they exist. We could go see them and touch them."

"You are aware, of course, that professional archaeologists deny that they are ancient man-made structures."

Laura gave Jake a sideways look that clearly demonstrated her disdain for professional archaeologists. She simply said, "Rubbish."

"I agree with you. It is total and utter nonsense. The reason they claim that the ancient stone structures, the dolmens and even the stone circles are either recent, as in colonial root cellars, or are the remnants of glaciers is that they have no explanation for who could have built them."

"Exactly right! That is the same conclusion I have arrived at. They cannot accept that this continent was visited, in ancient times, by people from the Mediterranean area and from what is now Europe. I have seen photographs of dolmens and stone structures, many of which are oriented to a solstice, that, if you showed the photographs to a professional archaeologist and told him that the image was from Wales or Scotland, he would nod his head and maybe ask how old it might be. But if you showed him the same image and told him it was from New York State, he would say it was created by glaciers and the structures were root cellars. It's crazy."

"Yes, it is. And it's frustrating because despite the evidence that these stone structures are ancient, the archaeologists seem to have the final say. However, I think the evidence is so overwhelming that the new crop of archaeologists will have to admit that America's ancient stone structures are man-made. The proof of the alignments makes a preponderant statement. Glaciers cannot lay out a perfect stone circle with an alignment stone that is pointed to a solstice."

"You are exactly right again."

"Thank you. I suppose if the stone circles in America consisted of huge stones like the Callanish stone circle on the Isle of Lewis in Scotland, they might more easily accept them."

"No, I doubt it. They'd say they were made by Native Americans. But you know what? I'd love to go to the Isle of Lewis and see those prehistoric stones."

"Me too. The photos I've seen from there are truly magnificent."

"Yes. Have you ever wondered why prehistoric man created stone circles?"

Jake laughed. He replied, "Frequently. I suppose everyone for the past two thousand years has wondered that. There are the usual guesses – like a circle has no beginning and no end. But so what? Why build a stone circle simply because a circle has neither a beginning nor an end? Of course, it is easy to make a solstice alignment with a circle. But again, a circle isn't needed – in order to do that. I've read that the stone circle represents either the sun or the moon . . . or both. I've read that they are fertility circles representing the womb. But none of those explanations make real sense to me."

"I've been toying with a possible explanation."

"Really? That's great. What is it?"

"It's still in the early stages of development but I may be able to do something with it eventually. Basically, I see the stone circles as representations of God. I think that those who built them considered them, once finished, as sacred places. The stones became special sacred stones that enclosed a special sacred space. I've read that some Native American tribes believed that God works in circles. I've also read that ancient Hebrews described God as a circle whose center is everywhere and whose circumference is nowhere."

"I've read that also. I like where you're going with this. Please continue."

"What I am thinking is that these prehistoric people wanted a special place to worship God. They built these stone circles with special stones and built the circles in special places. Places that 'felt' right – usually over an underground source of water. Anyway, once the circles were built, they could place an alignment stone outside the circle to point to a solstice. On the solstice, they would have a special worship service to thank God for spring or for an autumn harvest or for whatever. I don't think that they worshiped nature itself. But I think they might have seen the power of nature as a gift from God. To thank God or the Great Spirit for nature's blessings, they would have performed rituals that they considered sacred. What better place to perform these sacred rituals than their sacred space inside their sacred circles?"

"Laura, I truly think that you are on to something with this. That's the best explanation I've heard. You are one smart lady."

"Thank you. I've got more research to do. And I'd love to take an extended tour of many prehistoric megalithic sites. Of course, today, some people try to put the Druids into Stonehenge and other megalithic sites. But these sites were built long before the Druids came along. That's not to say that the Druids and others couldn't have used these sites for their own purposes but they certainly didn't build them."

"The more I think about it, the more I like it. You're right, of course, about the Druids. They had nothing to do with the construction of those megalithic sites. I really do like your idea of the stone circles being a sacred site for performing religious rituals."

"Thank you."

Looking around the cafeteria, Laura realized that they were the only people still sitting at a table. Jake followed her glance and noticed that the cafeteria staff were breaking down the buffet and cleaning up the room.

Jake nodded to a woman with a mop and bucket.

"I think that's our cue."

They took their dishes and trays to a large sink and left the cafeteria.

Laura asked, "Where to?"

"Jean took me on a tour – swimming pool, pub, bowling alley. This is your place. You decide."

"Okay. This way."

Laura led him down a hallway and past numerous doors. After several turns and twists, she approached a door, opened it and walked inside. Jake, of course, followed her. It looked somewhat like a club. There was a long bar along one whole side of the room. There were leather booths and wooden tables like a restaurant. There was a jukebox playing and a couple in their sixties was dancing. As Jake watched, another couple in their twenties got up and joined the other couple on the dance floor. There was a separate room full of video games. Through a large glass wall, Jake saw a guy who looked to be in his mid-fifties playing Pac-Man. The rest of the room was full of teens and pre-teens playing much more recent versions of video games. It was Saturday night and the children didn't have school the next day. Neither did Laura. In fact, it was a break between semesters this week and next week.

"What is this place?"

Laura smiled and led Jake to a booth.

"It's an activity center. The bar serves soft drinks, sandwiches, fries, ice cream, wine, beer and adult beverages. Do you drink wine?"

"Occasionally. And since this is an occasion, yes please."

"I'll get us some."

Laura went up to the bar, put in her order and returned to the booth with two wine glasses and a bottle of Pouilly-Fuisse, a very good French white wine. It had been opened at the bar. Laura poured them both a glass.

"Toast?" Laura said as she raised her glass.

Jake replied, as they clinked their wine glasses together, "To Nowhere."

Laura laughed and said, "To Nowhere."

They both sipped the wine. Jake thought it was smooth, dry and excellent. He took another sip and savored the taste.

"Nice choice."

"Thank you. I like this."

"Is this place like the cafeteria in that everything is free?"

"The cafeteria is not really free. It's included as part of one's wages. We get credits to use here and at the general store. The actual wages here are not real high but room and board are considered part of your total compensation. Now the children over there have to earn tokens. The machines take tokens rather than money. Once they run out of tokens, they can't play anymore. They earn tokens by doing chores, by achieving above-average scores in school and by participating in community projects."

"I get it. Tell me, today is Saturday. I arrived yesterday on a Friday. How is it that you, as a schoolteacher, were available to greet me?"

"We all take turns doing different jobs here. This term, I only have three classes. So I have some free time during the day. When you showed up, I just happened to be upfront with Peggy. Plus, and this is the main reason, we are currently on break."

"Okay. I understand."

"You look confused."

"I am. I still cannot get my mind to wrap around the concept that this place actually exists. I mean, I know it does. I'm sitting here in it with a beautiful woman. I know it's real but I just can't see how it has managed to escape notice all these years."

"I know. It is Mr. Sinclair's biggest fear – that the outside world will become aware of our existence. But you have to remember; they've been at this for over a hundred years. They've figured out a pretty good system for staying under the radar."

Laura thought, *He just called me a beautiful woman. I like that.*

"They must have. Whatever they've been doing, it has worked . . . If you wanted to go to Scotland, England, Wales, and Ireland, for example, could you?"

"Sure. There are two ways. One, I could go, on my own, on vacation. Two, I could apply for a research grant and, if accepted, go and do research on those megalithic stones using the resources of . . . Nowhere."

Jake smiled. "Does this place have a real name?"

Laura giggled and said, "You asked me that before."

"Yes, and you didn't give me a real name – you told me what some people call it but not what its real name is."

Laura poured herself another glass of wine. "That's right. I think I've actually forgotten its real name." Laura giggled and took another large swallow of wine. She said, "Ask Jean. He'll know."

Laura held up the bottle of wine to pour some in Jake's glass. He shook his head and she poured the remainder into her glass. She took another swallow and was really beginning to feel the wine.

Jake asked, "You don't drink wine often, do you?"

"Occasionally," Laura laughed. She finished the rest of her glass.

Jake laughed as well. He pointed his finger at Laura and said, "I like you."

"I like you too." Laura giggled.

"Would you like a sandwich . . . or some coffee?"

"No, I'm not hungry. And coffee might keep me awake. We've got chapel services in the morning. And you'll be the guest."

"I'll be the guest?"

"Yeah. You're the most recent new person to be here."

"Oh, I see. That's nice."

"Yeah. Jean will probably pick you up and take you to the service."

"No, Jean told me he would be gone tomorrow."

"Probably to Montreal. Well, I'll come get'cha then."

"Okay, thanks."

"You're welcome." She giggled again, louder.

Jake thought he ought to take Laura home. But he didn't know which door was hers. He didn't even know which door was his. He had no idea where he currently was or how to get back. About then, the "sixties" couple that had been dancing got up from a nearby booth and came over to Jake and Laura's booth.

The woman held out her hand and Jake shook it.

She said, "I'm Sherry and this is my husband, Bob."

Jake shook hands with Bob.

"Jake."

"Nice to meet you," Bob replied.

"You too," Jake said.

Sherry said, "Laura, how are you doing?"

"Fine. Fine. I'm fine."

Sherry turned to Jake and said, "You're the new visitor, aren't you?"

"Yes, I guess I am."

"Good. We were just leaving and we're wondering if we might be of use to you as guides."

"Absolutely. Thank you. Do you know where Laura lives?"

"Yes, of course. We pass your apartment on the way to Laura's."

When her name was mentioned, Laura asked, "What? I'm sorry, what did you ask?"

Looking at Bob, Jake asked, "You know where I'm staying?"

Sherry helped Laura up from the booth. Bob replied, "We presume you are staying in the guest apartment."

"I see. Lead on, please."

Holding Laura's arm, Sherry led the way from the club. When they got to the guest apartment, Jake opened the door, looked in and said, "Yes, this is where I'm at." He turned to Laura and said, "I'll see you in the morning."

She giggled yet again and said, "Okay."

Jake turned to Sherry and Bob and said, "Thank you for getting us back to where we belong."

Bob replied, "No problem. Glad to help. We'll see you at Chapel in the morning."

"Yes. Goodnight."

CHAPTER EIGHTEEN

"It does not require many words to speak the truth."

– Chief Joseph

Late 19th Century A.D.

After a shower, shave and cup of coffee, Jake decided he ought to wear a tie for Sunday worship service. His "outfit" would be the result of a somewhat limited number of choices available. There was one blazer – a navy blue one. Starting with that, Jake chose a traditional "look" with gray slacks, baby blue dress shirt and a striped light blue and navy tie. There was nothing wrong with his selections, he thought. Besides, he would sit in the back and blend in with everyone.

He got another cup of coffee and clicked on a morning news program. Just as he sat down, he heard a faint knock on his door.

Thinking it was Laura, he was greatly surprised to see Cyril Kent standing in his doorway.

"Good morning, Mr. Kent."

"Good morning. I've come to escort you to breakfast."

"Thank you. That's very kind."

"Not at all. My pleasure."

They began walking down the hall to the cafeteria.

Meanwhile, in Laura's apartment, she was feeling totally embarrassed for drinking more wine that she should have. She knew she had been nervous being with Jake. "But really," talking out loud, she told herself, *I know one glass is pretty much my limit. I bet I drank two-thirds or three-fourths of that bottle. What is wrong with me? I guess I made a fool of myself in front of Jake.*

He's probably written me off. And we were getting along nicely. He genuinely does like my idea regarding the purpose of stone circles. I need to pull myself together and go to chapel. I do want to hear Jake's talk. He'll be totally surprised to learn that he is to be the guest speaker this morning. It is always interesting to see how visitors react when they learn that they are expected to speak.

As a man of 88, Mr. Kent walked slowly but steadily. He said, "I enjoyed your responses to our questions yesterday."

"Thank you. The questions were rather . . . unexpected."

Mr. Kent smiled. He replied, "Sometimes things happen like that. Life throws us surprises. Things happen that are . . . totally unexpected."

"That's certainly true. Like me being here."

Mr. Kent nodded and smiled. They continued walking down hallways toward the cafeteria.

Jake broke the silence by saying, "You mentioned yesterday that your children and their families are living here. How many grandchildren do you have?"

Mr. Kent had a pleasant smile and he used it again. He responded, "I've now got a total of six grandchildren. It's nice being able to watch them grow into young adults."

"Yes, I imagine it is."

"You do not yet have children?"

"I appreciate the 'yet' but no, I do not."

"Well, you are *yet* a young man. You may have children someday."

"And I may not. Not everyone is cut out to be a parent."

"That's so. But you, however, would make an excellent father."

"Why do you say that, Mr. Kent?"

"Because you possess kindness and compassion. But mostly, because you have learned to love. People who have these qualities can do most anything."

They turned left and the smell of eggs and bacon reached them both. The doors to the cafeteria were open. Entering the large room, Jake noticed Mr. Nesbitt and Mr. Millar sitting at a table for four. Mr. Kent pointed to it. They walked over and joined them. Mr. Nesbitt and Mr. Millar already had plates of food. Jake asked Mr. Kent if he could get his breakfast for him. He did so and brought it back to the table with his own tray.

After some small pleasantries, Jake said, "You know what? I am truly awed by the history that you three represent. I genuinely respect and honor your military service during World War Two. The stories you men could tell."

Mr. Nesbitt replied, "I'm not being modest but the fact is we did what millions of other men, from several nations, did. It was, at the time, the only way to stop Hitler and the Japanese. They were evil. They had to be stopped. It was the same with the Soviets. They were evil. They had to be stopped. Fortunately, Reagan figured out how to do it without going to war."

Mr. Millar said, "Yes. It is always best, I think, to make every effort to avoid war. Sometimes, however, the other side will insist on violence and war. I have been particularly interested in Israel's situation surrounded as it is by nations and people who want to destroy it. I believe that God was active on Israel's behalf during the six-day war in nineteen sixty-seven. I believe it is important for the United States to always stand firm on Israel's side. If we were to ever to turn our backs on Israel, I believe it would harm us more than Israel."

Jake responded by saying, "Surely that would never happen."

Mr. Millar replied, "I hope not. But young man, I am in my nineties. I have seen things I never thought I'd see."

"I'm sure that is so. What was something good that you've seen that you might never have expected to ever see?"

Without hesitation, Mr. Millar said, "I never thought I'd see men walking on the moon."

Mr. Nesbitt and Mr. Kent nodded in agreement.

After breakfast, the three elderly men agreed to guide Jake to the chapel sanctuary. On the way, they wanted to stop at a restroom. Jake straightened his tie and waited outside. He had hoped to see Laura in the cafeteria, but she wasn't there.

As they continued to slowly walk to the chapel, Mr. Kent told Jake that attendance at the Sunday service was totally voluntary. If someone did not show up for the service, their absence was neither noted nor mentioned. He went on to remark that they expected, due to the guest speaker, a full house. They were descending a winding ramp. At the end of the ramp, Jake saw two large wooden doors. These were the first doors he had seen that did not look like every other door.

Jake opened the right door and waved the three elderly men inside. He then stepped inside himself and, with his first step, he literally stopped breathing. It looked more like a medieval cathedral than the small chapel he was expecting.

Mr. Kent recognized the look of awe on Jake's face. He said, "This way, son."

Jake walked on into the sanctuary. A dark rich navy-blue carpet covered the entire floor. There was a wide aisle separating traditional rows of beautiful wooden pews. At the front was a stone platform two feet high. The choir was seated up toward the back of the platform. A simple but solid wooden podium was placed in the center near the edge of the stone platform. The ceiling was a work of art! It didn't have any paintings – not that type of art. The intricate spacing of huge wooden beams latticed the ceiling as they crossed the high vaulted interior. It had obviously been constructed by master carpenters. When this cathedral was built, there were undoubtedly virgin forests above ground or certainly nearby. They would have contained ancient trees that had to have been used for the overhead beams and the huge wooden columns at the entrance of the sanctuary. Jake thought that this underground cathedral was magnificent. It was simple and graceful.

The pews were about three-fourths full. Jake followed his three elderly guides to the front row pew on the right side of the aisle. They sat down as more people entered the sanctuary. Jake looked around and noticed a large wooden cross on the wall behind the choir. Being underground, there were no windows. The walls were made of the same stone as the platform.

Sitting next to Mr. Kent, Jake whispered, "It's amazing."

"Yes, it is," Mr. Kent whispered back.

People were still coming in and filling the remaining places in the pews. After a few more minutes, the choir director, a young man about 30 years old, stepped forward to the podium.

He said, "We are going to begin today's service with a new hymn written by our own choir member, Stella Perdue."

During the opening hymn, Laura had entered the sanctuary and found an empty place in a pew near the back left side. Jake exceedingly enjoyed the choir's new composition. The acoustics in the room were excellent. Of course, Jake thought, I'm sitting in the front row. After the hymn was finished, the choir then sang a more traditional hymn.

When the last note of the organ slowly ebbed away, people shuffled in the pews in anticipation of the speaker. Jake was also wondering when the speaker was going to appear.

Mr. Kent leaned over to Jake and whispered, "Listen, it is our tradition here to have our special visitors be our guest speakers." Jake immediately felt his stomach fill with butterflies. "We always do it this way so that our guest will not be nervous for days in advance."

Jake whispered back, "But I'm not a minister; I'm not a preacher; I'm not . . ."

"We know that, son. Everyone here knows that. Just speak from your heart. Now listen, after you've spoken briefly, sit in that chair over on the side and the choir will lead us all in singing a couple more hymns. Then you can say whatever else you want to say and the choir will close the service with a final song. Go ahead."

Mr. Kent nodded toward the podium.

"Now?"

"Yes," Mr. Kent placed his hand on Jake's shoulder and said, "Go on up."

Jake took a deep breath. Not noticing the steps at the side

of the platform, Jake just stepped directly up on the stone platform from the floor. He walked behind the platform, raised both arms toward the ceiling, bowed his head and said, "Let's pray."

Laura had watched as Jake walked up to the platform and stepped up from the floor. He had simply been so nervous, she thought, he hadn't seen the steps. She thought, *I should have told him. He could have prepared something. I will pray for him right now.*

Jake's voice sounded clear in the vastness of the high vaulted ceiling.

"Heavenly Father, we are gathered here today . . . to worship You. We are humbled to call ourselves Your children and yet, so proud to call You our Father. We do so through our faith in Your Son and our Lord, Jesus Christ. Now . . . here . . . we claim His promise that when two or more are gathered in His name, He will also be present. We feel that Presence now and thank You for It. We ask of You that each person here will leave this worship with that Presence in their heart. In the precious name of Your Son, Jesus, we ask this and we thank You. Amen."

Jake lowered his arms and looked over the sanctuary. He looked at the expectant faces of the congregation. He felt the presence of the Holy Spirit. He did not have any idea what to say next.

As he looked out across all the people, he smiled. He said, "I think I can honestly say no one is more surprised than I . . . that I am standing here, in this place, at this time."

Jake smiled and many in the congregation laughed.

He continued, "Just so you know, my name is Jake Fleming and I have no idea why I am here. Especially right here." He smiled and several people laughed and smiled with him.

"I want to ask each of you to take a moment and look up – look at the ceiling of this room. Look at those huge beams of solid wood. Imagine the ancient trees from which they were produced. Think of the tremendous effort that must have gone into harvesting those trees, hewing those very beams and constructing them as we see them today. Someone, perhaps an architect, had a master plan. He envisioned how this sanctuary would look before the first tree was felled. As the men worked on those large logs, crafting them and shaping them to the needed size for those beams, mistakes must have occurred. Some of the logs probably cracked or split and were ruined for use as beams. Those would have been put to other uses. So it is, I think, with humans. God shapes us to be used as He intends. He knows what the end result is to be. However, along the way, some humans, being human, don't follow the plan. They crack."

Jake smiled and many in the congregation laughed again.

"Others, with the help of the Holy Spirit, Who is with us now, continually try to do as God directs. They try to do what is correct and right. However, being human, we will always be a work in progress."

Jake paused again and smiled. More of the congregation laughed.

"But even though some of us crack, it is nice to know that God is always with us and can still use us. We are still His children. He will never throw us away. He grants us the guidance of the Holy Spirit and allows us to develop and grow. We all, each of us in this room, have different talents and gifts. All of those, regardless of what they are, are important and valuable. We all have different roles to play. And *all* of those roles are also important and valuable. What we need to do is allow the Holy Spirit to guide us in the right direction that God intends for each of us."

Jake paused and noticed the people were smiling and nodding their heads in agreement. He thought that this might be a good time to sit down and let the choir sing. He turned, looked at the choir director and nodded to him. The director stood in front of the Choir. Jake walked over to the empty chair on the far side of the platform. As he walked to the chair, the choir stood. Jake sat down and the choir began to sing.

The first hymn was, Jake thought, a beautiful song. He had not previously heard it. While they were singing, Jake looked out over the congregation. He was looking specifically for Laura but did not see her. He looked at his three elderly guides. They seemed absorbed with the music. When the first hymn was finished, the choir began a second song. This one sounded somewhat like a medieval monk's chant. It was also, Jake thought, beautifully done.

When the choir finished, the director turned to Jake and nodded. The choir sat down and the director returned to his seat. Jake walked back to the podium. During the two songs, Jake had desperately tried to think of what to say next – but wasn't successful.

He looked out over the congregation and said, "You certainly have a first-rate choir here. That was beautiful and inspiring. As a guest here, it is probably not proper for me to thank you for coming today. But I do want to thank you for allowing me to visit with you."

Jake paused and looked out over the congregation. They were wondering what he would say next – and so was he.

He spoke and said, "Being a visitor here, you folks do not know much about me. I think I should reveal something to you. I am immortal. Yes, I am immortal. My soul is immortal. My soul is inhabiting this flesh and blood body. My body is, of course, mortal. But I will live forever. And so will each of you. In the eleventh chapter of John, verse twenty-six, Jesus said, 'Whosoever liveth and believeth in me shall never die.' I believe that. That is God talking. Who would not believe that? Only someone who does not know Jesus. I believe that life is a spiritual journey. Each of our souls is here on earth for a purpose. Each of our souls seeks to return to God. We are spiritual beings inhabiting human bodies. When one achieves a real relationship with God, one becomes a real human being – free to live as God intended humans to live. When we reach that relationship, we have learned, as Proverbs teaches, to trust in the Lord with all our heart.

"Realizing that God is always with us feeds our soul and creates a genuine sense of joy. Joy is not based on circumstances...but rather, on the promises of God. Joy is knowing that we have been saved by the blood of Christ and that our souls will, in God's own time, return to be with God. Isn't that knowledge wonderful? Doesn't that knowledge cause joy? I think that all Christians should radiate a sense of joy. Depending upon one's human personality, it may be understated . . . but it should always be present. Once we have acknowledged and accepted Christ, His beauty, His light, His love is within us all. What joy! And you know we can create joy in our hearts by simply being kind. The two go hand-in-hand. Kindness creates joy. And, seeking joy, we are kind. Isn't it wonderful to be a Christian and experience joy in our souls?

"I have frequently heard some Christians complain that they do not know what it is that Jesus wants them to do. I've been told that the verse where Jesus says, 'If you love me, you will follow my commands,' is confusing. They say, 'I would love to follow commands of Jesus but I don't know what they are. How am I supposed to follow his commands when I don't know what they are?' I answer these people with one of my favorite Bible verses. It is John fifteen twelve. Jesus is speaking. He says, 'My command is this.' Listen now, Jesus is telling us exactly what his command is. He says, 'My command is this: Love each other as I have loved you.' That eliminates confusion.

"Before I leave, I want to talk about the most powerful force in the universe. That force is love. Love is so powerful . . . it almost seems magical. When we show love to others, we create love. And that love will connect with our hearts and our souls. We will feel it. God created us with a desire to love. Love comes in many forms. Have you ever seen a little boy and his dog? There is genuine love between the two. There is, within the souls of Christians, a real spiritual love for each other. We often refer to each other as brothers and sisters in Christ. We want good to happen to all our fellow Christians. This is love. All Christians are linked together through the love of Christ. Remember what else Jesus said were commandments – first, love God; second, love your neighbors. I know that many of you here have had long marriages. I think all humans want to find, as the saying goes, that special someone . . . so that we can love that person. You who have experienced long marriages found the person God intended to be your mate. When we fall in love with the right person, we experience joy. We want to do special things for that person. We want to share experiences with that person. We want to display acts of kindness to that person. And this romantic love is not possessive . . . it makes no demands. Love offers kindness and compassion without any requirements that they be returned. Many of you have experienced this love through your marriages. It is a wonderful thing and when God is the center of such a marriage, things go so much smoother than when God is not present. Why is this? God is, after all . . . love. Love exists on many levels. But love means very little unless it is put into practice. Please practice love. If we do not have love, we have nothing. Love is the universal force of God. Go always with God. Go always with love."

Jake put his hand over his heart and then, opening his hand, palm up, he moved it in front of his body, toward and across the entire congregation. It was a gesture of love to everyone.

Jake then said, "Let us leave with a prayer."

He raised his arms, bowed his head and prayed, "Father in Heaven, we praise You and thank You for allowing us to worship You. We thank You for sending the Holy Spirit into our lives. We thank You for Your love. We praise You and thank You for all Your blessings and we pray this in the name of our Savior and Lord, Jesus Christ. Amen."

Jake turned and walked over to the chair on the side of the platform and sat down. The choir director stood and the choir performed its final hymn. When it was finished, Jake walked over to the choir director, shook hands with him and congratulated him on the quality of the choir. Several of the choir members came up to Jake and thanked him for his message. The members of the congregation had stood and were talking with each other. Jake stepped down from the stone platform to the carpeted floor. He was immediately surrounded by people shaking his hand, smiling and saying nice things about his brief talk. Jake eventually made his way over to Mr. Kent, Mr. Millar and Mr. Nesbitt. They each shook his hand and told him that they appreciated his remarks.

Mr. Kent said, "Thank you for your words. I think they were much appreciated by everyone here." He looked at all the people milling about, smiling and talking. He added, "I think people are reluctant to leave."

Jake responded, "I'm sorry. I suppose I was too brief. I guess . . ."

"No. No, not at all. People want to stay and savor the experience. I think your words touched us all."

Jake didn't know what to say. He quietly replied, "Thank you."

Laura had been trying to work her way from the back of the sanctuary to the front. People were smiling and greeting her warmly, as she did with them. But she was in a hurry to see Jake. She was still embarrassed by her behavior the night before but she realized something important through something Jake had said. He said that people in love want the best for the person they love. She had truly wanted Jake to do well. She had even prayed for him to do well. She wanted the best for him. Was she in love with him already? Did he have feelings of love for her? She didn't know but she knew she wanted to congratulate him on his talk.

Jake was beginning to think that everyone there thought that they needed to shake his hand and tell him that his message had meant something to them. He truly appreciated the kind words people were saying. However, he was quickly realizing that he had no idea exactly what he had said and couldn't repeat it if it were required of him. His three elderly guides had explained that many people skipped breakfast on Sunday mornings. Since the cafeteria cooks and crew were in attendance at the service, Sunday lunch wasn't ever ready until about two hours after the service was completed. This, thought Jake, explained why no one was in a hurry to leave.

Laura saw Jake standing near his three elderly guides. He was talking with a woman who was going on and on about how much she appreciated him "preaching the gospel." Laura could tell that Jake was embarrassed by all the attention. She stood to Jake's right. If he turned at all, he would see her. Laura was wearing a light red dress. With his peripheral vision, Jake noticed the red dress. He presumed it was another woman wanting to talk with him. He didn't really mind; but, he wasn't used to all this attention and it made him feel a little uncomfortable. Jake shook hands with the woman and she turned away. Jake turned to the woman in red and was stunned to see Laura standing there. She looked, he thought, absolutely wonderful.

He smiled and said, "I am so glad to see you. You look great. That's a nice dress."

"Thank you. You looked, and sounded, pretty good yourself standing up there." Laura nodded toward the platform.

"Thank you. Would you mind being my guide through the maze of hallways out there?"

Laura smiled. She replied, "My pleasure."

"Thanks. Let me explain to my other guides. Don't go anywhere."

Laura smiled and nodded.

Jake stepped over to his three guides. He said, "I hope you gentlemen don't mind but I've found a much prettier guide to help me make it through the maze out there." He nodded over in Laura's direction. They all turned to look at Laura and then they all smiled. They shook hands with Jake and said their goodbyes.

It took some time but eventually Laura and Jake made it to the big wooden doors and started walking up the ramp.

Jake said, "I know now why this ramp is so long. They had to dig deep to build the chapel with such a high ceiling in the sanctuary."

"I guess so."

"I never could locate you in the congregation. Where were you sitting?"

Laura explained.

"I must say," Jake commented, "that is one tradition I could have done without. I usually like old traditions but that was too much of a surprise."

"What are you talking about? You did good. I was very proud of you. We've had some people who just froze up and could hardly say anything. I felt so sorry for them. We've even had people who refused to get up on the platform at all."

"I can see how it could turn into a mean trick for the unsuspecting guest."

"They don't do it for every visitor – just the ones they think will be all right with it and the ones that they want to see how they will respond. Of course, we really don't get all that many new visitors here. It's a special occasion when we do."

"So it's a bit of a test?"

"For some people."

"Me?"

"I don't know."

Laura led Jake down a hallway with several hallways that branched off from the one they were using. Laura stopped at a door, pushed it open and indicated Jake should enter. He did so.

"This looks familiar."

"Yes. It's the same activity center we were in last night."

Looking around, Jake said, "There's no one here."

"Just us," Laura smiled. "It's not unusual. Nearly everyone went to chapel. And from there, they'll go to the cafeteria. I wasn't expecting anyone to be here."

Laura walked behind the long bar.

"What'll it be, Mac?"

"Do you have any Perrier back there?"

"Original or lime?"

"Lime, thank you."

"Coming right up."

Jake sat in the same booth that they had sat in the night before. Laura came over with a bottle of Perrier for Jake and a tall glass of iced tea for herself. She set them on the table and slid in the booth opposite Jake.

Jake said, "I want to ask you something."

"Sure."

"How is it that, when you greeted me, you were wearing that long white gown thing?"

Laura laughed. She had had no idea what Jake was going to ask but she certainly wasn't expecting this. She was even afraid he was going to ask her about her wine drinking habits.

She answered, "It's what we always wear when we greet new guests. Most of the few guests we have come through the Christmas tree farm. They are expected. They are also greeted by a woman wearing a white gown. If I didn't happen to have been there, Peggy would have greeted you wearing the same type gown."

"Why?"

"I think Mr. Sinclair thinks it's expected. I think he thinks that it sets a tone of mysticism or spirituality or something."

"I see."

"Do you?"

"Yes, I suppose so. Yet, that tone quickly goes away. I mean, everyone seems so normal here."

Laura laughed. "Wait 'til you know people better."

Jake smiled. "The only strange thing here is . . . the here. The place itself. It shouldn't exist. But it does."

"Why shouldn't it exist?" Laura sounded defensive.

"Oh, I didn't mean that it shouldn't – that is has no right to exist. I meant that it is incredible that it does actually exist. It seems unreal and yet, it is real."

Laura smiled. "We've all gone through the experience of processing this place's existence in our own minds. I do understand what you are going through right now. I understand what you are saying."

"Alice's Wonderland."

"Yes. Exactly."

"But I didn't follow a white rabbit."

"What did you follow?"

"That is a good question. I don't know. I was *following* a compulsion, an urge . . . a somewhat vague notion that I was supposed to come up here."

"You were supposed to come *here*?"

"Not here to this place. I had absolutely no idea that this place existed. No, it was just a desire to travel to northwest Maine. I wanted to get away – to go somewhere away from people. To just be. To be one with nature, I guess."

Laura looked at him with an expression of skepticism.

"I know it doesn't sound reasonable. I really cannot explain it. I just saw this area on a map and felt compelled to come here."

"Most of us here are recruited, as I was. I have . . ."

Jake interrupted and asked, "Did you come across the lake and down that forest path, as I did?"

"No, not at all. I arrived in a company car that had picked me up in Québec City. It brought me to the caretaker's cottage. The front door to this place is located in the basement of the caretaker's cottage."

"Who comes by way of the lake and forest path?"

"You are the only one that I know of who has come that way."

"The only one . . ."

"I've heard that, long ago, there were one or two others…but I really don't know."

"But what about the red light? And that path has been maintained."

"What red light?"

"At night, from my campsite, I could see a small red light. It was apparently a guide to the path."

"I don't know about a red light but the path is probably maintained so that people can go fishing on the lake."

"Hmmmm. I suppose the light could be a guide back from the lake in case someone got lost or was out too late on the lake in the dark. They could see the red light and know their way back."

"I guess."

"So how come I was expected?"

"I don't know. Jean told Peggy and I that they were expecting a visitor, you, by way of the forest path. He was actually expecting you the day before you arrived."

"Really? He knew my name?"

"Yes. He told us a Mr. Jake Fleming . . . and he described you. We knew it was you as soon as we saw you on the monitors."

"Amazing."

"No one ever contacted you about coming here?"

"No. No one…But I was expected. I wasn't even sure I'd make the trip myself."

Laura said, "I've heard it said that God works in mysterious ways."

Jake smiled. "Yes, I've heard that. And in wondrous ways. This place is both mysterious and wondrous."

"Wonderland."

CHAPTER NINETEEN

"For by grace are ye saved through faith; and that not of yourselves: it is the gift of God: not of work, lest any man should boast."

– Ephesians 2:8-9

Mid 1st Century A.D.

"So tell me, Jake, what do you think about death?"

"Jean, I have become convinced that it is inevitable, inescapable and unavoidable."

Mr. Le Couteau smiled and laughed. Jake got up and walked over to the coffee maker.

Holding up the pot, Jake asked, "More?"

"Yes, please."

Jake filled Mr. Le Couteau's coffee mug. He filled his mug, took the pot back and sat down.

"Seriously, Jean," Jake answered, "I am, in some ways, truly looking forward to my death. I have absolutely no fear of it at all. It will answer many questions and totally re-unite me with God. I am looking forward to that."

Mr. Le Couteau replied, "Ahhh, yes. But death is so permanent."

"No, I see it as a new beginning. Of course, the human body dies and that is permanent. Now don't get me wrong – I'm not going to do anything to hurry my death along."

They both smiled.

"I do believe that each of us has an appointment, in God's good time, with death. When it is my time, I will rejoice that God has chosen to call me home."

"I see. That is, I think, an excellent attitude. It is one that both Mr. Sinclair and I share."

"How is Mr. Sinclair?"

"Oh…he's doing fine. He remains primarily in his study. But you, Jake, are still a young man. You…"

"I have just recently become a forty-two-year-old man. I think it is safe to say that I am in the middle-age category – not the young man category."

"Yes, well, I suppose that is so. You are also, as I understand, a relatively wealthy man."

Jake thought to himself, *Is that it? Is that what they are after? They want me to make a large donation to this effort.*

Jake didn't respond. Mr. Le Couteau continued, "What is it you plan to do with the rest of your life?"

"Funny you should ask that. Lately, I've been asking myself that very question. As I've already told you, I have decided to resign my position with Excalibur and move on with my life. But what does that mean? I'm not sure yet. I love nature. Someone said, 'To know Nature is to be at one with the universe.' I understand that. I have thought of purchasing a small piece of real estate out in the country – maybe twenty to fifty acres. I would like some woods – a forest. And, I'm thinking, perhaps a few chickens, a dog, a cat, a garden. I don't really know yet."

"What else, besides nature, is it that you love?"

"Books. I enjoy reading books. I have an insatiable appetite for reading and learning. As far as I have gone in my thinking up to now, my house in the country will become primarily a library. I think I could be content to spend the rest of my life living in a library in the country."

"Cicero, in the first century B.C, said that all a man needed to be happy was a garden and a library."

Jake laughed. "While I disagree with that, I certainly understand the sentiment."

"Why do you disagree?"

"Happiness, I think, is not circumstantial. It does not

depend upon varying situations. Rather, I think, it exists within a person and is usually evident by a sense of peacefulness and kindness. I could be happy with a garden and a library. But I would also be happy if I had neither. My happiness does not depend upon having material possessions."

Mr. Le Couteau nodded his head in agreement. He said, "Your happiness, I presume, comes from your faith in God?"

"Yes, exactly. Are you familiar with the story of Daniel and King Belshazzar?"

"Yes, Daniel interpreted the writing on the wall."

"Right. But that is not the part of the story from which I get my happiness. Rather, the reason for the writing. Belshazzar ignored the God of Daniel. And more than just ignoring God, he began to praise gods made of metals, of wood and of stone. Those gods, of course, could not see, hear or know. Those statues were not merely representations of gods, they were considered to be gods in their own right. People bowed to them and prayed to them. What makes me happy is realizing, without any doubt, that God sees everything, hears everything and knows everything. Doesn't that fill your soul with joy? When I pray to God, and it doesn't matter where I am, I know, with complete assurance, that He hears me. That is why, regardless of my circumstances, I am always happy."

Mr. Le Couteau nodded his head. "I understand," he said. He really did understand. "Tell me, Jake, are you a member of any church denomination?"

"I suppose my church membership is in inactive status at a Baptist Church back home in North Carolina. I guess I could claim that membership. I have attended several non-denominational churches and actually go fairly regularly to one in New York. I have found them to be interesting places of worship. However, if I absolutely had to put down on a form my religious affiliation, it would have to be Baptist. I do believe that they try to remain true to the gospel."

"By implication then, are you saying that other religions...don't measure up?"

"I was implying a comparison among protestant denominations. To me, Christ must be the center of my religion. He is, I believe, the purest representation of love that has ever walked on this planet. He showed that love for us when He went to the cross and shed his blood as a sacrifice for us. His death and resurrection, for me, have to be the foundation of any real religion."

"Again, you are implying that any religion without Christ is not a real religion."

"Bad choice of words on my part. Instead of real, I should have used 'true' or 'correct.' I mean there are some really bizarre religions out there. I suppose anyone could get together and form a religion. It has often been done. Some have been based on UFOs, on hate and revenge, on sex, on devil worship, on nature and dozens of other things. They are, I suppose, real religions. But they have been created by man rather than God. That is why they can be real religions but not true religions."

Mr. Le Couteau smiled and said, "I follow you."

"Speaking of true religion, we are now in our fifth year of the twenty-first century. Suddenly, what was previously known to be true, is considered by many religions to now be questionable or, in some cases, totally denied and reversed. Some protestant denominations, I am sad to say, have become so...politically correct that they have lost the fundamental teachings of the Bible."

"For example?" Mr. Le Couteau prompted.

"For example, same-sex marriage. Marriage, for five thousand years, has been a religious institution. There is a written description of marriage from three thousand BC. It tells that the man and the woman must go to the temple and present themselves to the priest so that he can prepare them for the marriage ritual. It has only been in the last few hundred years that governments have gotten themselves involved in marriages. What right does a government have to issue a marriage license? None. Marriage is a religious ceremony. Today, more and more, gay and lesbian activists are imposing their lifestyles on our culture. They tell us, if we oppose same-sex marriage, we are prejudiced, small-minded and backward. I absolutely refuse to accept that twenty-first century homosexual activists have the right to redefine what constitutes a marriage. I will never accept that redefinition. Now let me say this: because I will never accept a redefinition of marriage to include same-sex marriages does not mean that I will ever harbor hate for a gay or lesbian person. Nor will I ever condone violence against anyone. But neither will I be pressured into accepting a lifestyle that I know to be unnatural and wrong. Back in North Carolina, there were two men in my neighborhood who lived together as roommates. As far as I know, they still do. They are both homosexuals; and, they are both two of the nicest people I know. They are great neighbors and are welcomed at all neighborhood functions. If they needed help, no one would hesitate to give it. If someone in the neighborhood needed help, they would not hesitate to give it. While everyone in the neighborhood knows that they are homosexuals, the reason, I think, that they have been totally accepted is that they have never tried to insist that we accept homosexuality as 'just another alternative but normal lifestyle.' They have never publicly mentioned or announced their homosexuality to the neighborhood. Privately, they have told different people, myself included. To the neighborhood, they are just roommates. They have never caused any problems. They have always been friendly. They both have good jobs and pay their taxes. They, and all the neighbors, have a 'live and let live attitude.' I know them both and I like them both. Now Jean, I am fully aware that my views on this subject would not 'set well' with the current crop of homosexual activists 'out there.' They would accuse me of being discriminatory against them. But I am not discriminatory against anyone. I think that all gays and lesbians should have the same legal rights as everyone else. They already have all the God-given rights with which everyone is born. But they do not have the right to redefine a religious institution to fit their particular requirements. To me, some things are absolute. Not all religions but most religions teach that it is wrong to steal something that belongs to someone else. After centuries of being taught that theft is wrong, some group could pop up and claim that they think it is okay now to take things from one's neighbor and use them for yourself. If you disagree with that, why then you are just being backward – you haven't evolved. You are non-accepting. You discriminate against thieves."

Mr. Le Couteau laughed.

"Jean, I cannot predict the future. But I seriously can see a time, in this century, when people become afraid to say, 'this is wrong.' The trends I see do not look good for the future. I can see that religion, politics, entertainment, education and culture are all headed in a negative direction."

"You mentioned, just now, politics. How do you view our political situation?"

"I think most all politicians are liars and crooks."

"No, really, tell me what you really think."

Jake smiled. "Based upon their actions, I really do think that. They are liars and crooks. I am old-fashioned enough to believe that character counts. Let me tell you about a conversation I had with a United States Congressman. When I talked with him, he was finishing up his thirteenth year in the House of Representatives. He had been elected seven times and was running for an eighth term. He was a relative – some type of cousin, twice removed or something. On my dad's side. Anyway, he had been campaigning all day, was worn out and in the mood to talk. It was just the two of us. This was in the early nineties. For about fifteen or twenty minutes, we talked about family and just general small talk. He then looked at me and asked me if he could talk 'off the record' with me. He wanted to be sure I would not reveal what he was about to say to any form of media. I assured him I would not and I never have told any media anything he said. The reason he was campaigning so early was that he had a serious opponent for the first time in several elections. He did not win re-election. He died a couple of years ago. He had a nice retirement. What he told me has always remained strong in my memory. He told me that, if I repeated what he was about to say, he would deny it. And, he said, so would every member of the House. They would all deny it. What he said was this: everything a Congressman says, everything a Congressman does and every vote a Congressman makes is geared toward his re-election. Every Congressman says what he thinks will help him get re-elected, not what he believes. He does what he thinks will help him get re-elected, not what he thinks is the best thing for him to do. He told me that the primary goal of every Congressman is his own personal re-election. That re-election overrides everything else. He looked at me and said, 'We are all liars. Every one of us.' He said that an honest man would not last long in politics. I remember asking him what he was most proud of accomplishing during his years as a member of the House. He laughed and replied, 'getting re-elected.' He told me he had learned not to be controversial. He didn't do anything. He voted safe, he said. About as far out on a limb as he would go would be to support motherhood and apple pie. And that, I remember him joking, would cost him some votes. He said there would be some voters whose mothers had abused them and some voters who couldn't eat cooked fruit. He said he had learned not to make waves. He told me that, for years, Congressmen had nursed good relationships with journalists in order to get good press. But, he added, journalists themselves were no longer objective. Most journalists, he thought, were now strong democrats. He told me that he would like to win re-election but, if he did not, his retirement was set. He would not have to worry about finances during his retirement years. He told me that simply because he had been in the House as long as he had, people assumed he was an expert in several areas. He said that they were wrong. The only possible area in which he was close to being an expert was politics.

"Jean, I remember being somewhat disillusioned by his discussion of what actually takes place in the House of Representatives. Then again, I remember not being all that surprised and not all that disillusioned. He told me some specifics about individual members that were awful. I was more surprised that he told me what he told me than by what he told me."

Mr. Le Couteau laughed again. "I understand. I followed what you said."

"That was, what . . . fourteen years ago. It is much worse now than then and, I think, will be even worse fourteen years from now. He was so right about journalism. When Gore ran against Bush, the media, both television and print, totally supported Gore. What they reported and, often more importantly, what they didn't report, all favored Gore. But it didn't work. Somehow, enough people recognized that Gore was a shallow manufactured politician. Then, when Kerry ran four years later against Bush, the media not only supported Kerry but it defended and protected him. This was new...and it was awful – for journalism. Now journalism has reached the point where the network news organizations and the majority of daily newspapers are now, in practicality, arms of the Democrat political party. They no longer even pretend to be objective news organizations. They ignore news that reflects favorably on Republicans or they 'bury' it deep on page twenty-three. If it is news that favors Democrats, it is on page one. Where will this lead? I think, perhaps somewhat hopefully, that it may make these large news organizations less and less relevant as people seek other, more reliable, news sources such as searching the Internet."

"It could happen that way. I can see them becoming less of a factor in the future."

"I hope so. Or what I really hope for, but don't expect, is that they would return to being objective journalists. Too much to hope for, I guess. Too much to expect that they would just report the news. I have lately seen editorial comments in the headlines of front page newspaper stories. Those headlines would cause a journalism student to flunk Journalism one-oh-one."

"You're right about that. I've seen those headlines. I know what you're talking about. So, what is your assessment of the future of politics?"

Jake seemed to sense an underlying reason for this question . . . but wasn't sure what that might be.

He replied, "As I mentioned earlier, I think the trend is not favorable. I think that any person in a political position, certainly a person in a position of making decisions and establishing policies must have not only an excellent knowledge of history but also a clear understanding of history. That is basic. Then, a person in a political position of power must have at least an average degree of intellect. And, this person must be able to think – and to think critically. Then, I think, this person should have character. This person should have a set of beliefs and values that will guide him, or her, as decisions are reached. Without these basics, a person in a power position could be easily manipulated by more intellectual and cunning people with their own agenda. This political person would be in danger of becoming only a figurehead or even a puppet for those associates of his who have a real agenda and use him to achieve it. With the trend we are on, I can see this happening here in America with horrible effect. I mean, look, it is the middle of oh-five. We just got over oh-four and people, primarily pushed by the media, are already speculating about oh-eight. Apparently, according to the 'experts,' which, by the way, I have a total lack of respect for experts – but, according to them, Hillary Clinton is an 'automatic.' What has she ever accomplished? What has she been successful at doing? She wasn't even a good First Lady. She has been proven to be a liar. She is arrogant and has no moral character. What qualifies her to be President? Two things. One, she is a woman and two, she is a Democrat. Despite her obvious lack of qualifications, people will vote for her because of the historic nature of voting for the first female President. Personally, I don't think anyone should vote for a person simply because that person is a female. I also don't think anyone should vote against a person simply because that person is a female. There are several women 'out there' that I would support and vote for – for President, but Clinton certainly isn't one of them. I honestly think that she would be a disaster for our country. But as much as I wish it were not so, I do think that is the way we are headed."

"You may be completely right about that."

"I don't know. That's what the 'experts' say and I have never seen them be right."

Mr. Le Couteau smiled and said, "They rarely are."

"However, and I think this is important to say, despite vast political differences and huge disagreements regarding the leaning of our society, I do think that we are all linked together through our souls. Did you know that the ancient Egyptians believed that everyone in the world had what they called a Ka – a creative life force that came into existence in the womb? This life force was a spiritual double of each person and it lived on after the mortal body had died."

"No, I wasn't aware of that."

"Yes, it is like our soul. I think our souls contain a small spark of the divine. Now this may only apply to people who have accepted Christ as their Savior and Lord. Once a person does that, the Holy Spirit comes to that person. That may be the spark of divinity that I am describing. Without Christ, no Holy Spirit – no spark of divinity. If we all have this within, then it follows that we must look within to find it and to learn about it. We must, as the ancient Greeks said, know ourselves, in order to recognize our souls – to know who we truly are. I think the truth lies within oneself. Searching for the truth begins by looking within – *Know Thyself.* I think all of us should ask ourselves, when we look within, do we like what we see?"

Mr. Le Couteau smiled. He responded by saying, "That's deep. I want to ask you something else. If you had to describe today's society, here in the U. S., in one word, what would that word be?"

After a few seconds of thought, Jake replied, "Disconnected . . . or perhaps, imbalanced."

"Why do you use those words?"

"We have amazing technological developments and accomplishments. At the same time, we seem to have a propensity to destroy each other. Both of these areas have far outpaced our sluggish spiritual development. Even Christians, who should be connected through the Holy Spirit, are not connected. We, as a society, are disconnected from God. Our society has not looked within. We have not sought to grow spiritually. We are imbalanced."

Mr. Le Couteau nodded his head in agreement. He said, "I understand what you are saying and I agree with it."

"Yes, you see, I believe that the soul, that each of us possess, may lie deep within the mass of human flesh but it is always a clear, bright, shining and precious tiny orb of light. At least, that's how I choose to perceive it. That's not Biblical. That just gives me a way to imagine it. I have no idea what our souls really look like. For me, that light is extraordinarily small but there, nonetheless. Of course, Christians, in addition to a soul, have the presence of the Holy Spirit. However, a large majority of the people on this planet do not even accept or recognize this concept at all. Many people today even deny the existence of a soul. Jesus is extremely clear about this – that we all have souls. But many people think, when their human body dies, that's it. It's all over. There is nothing beyond the mortal death of the body. When you think about it, that is really sad. A sad way to live."

"I think you're right about that. I want to discuss, in more depth, your thinking regarding religion and politics."

"Okay. Sure. You know, if you mix the two together today, you will come up with some unsettling conclusions."

"I don't follow. What do you mean?"

"Jean, the trend I see happening with the Democrat political party is that the ideology is moving so far left that it is leaving God behind. At best, Democrats are ignoring God. Indeed, the more I look at what Democrats stand for today, I don't see how a real Christian can also be a Democrat. That is a trend that I find unsettling."

"Okay. I see now what you are talking about. However, in America, historically speaking, religion has always been incorporated into politics."

"Yes, Jean, absolutely. By both political parties. But how do you ask God to get involved when you treat minorities as if they are second-class citizens too stupid to make it on their own who need you to provide everything from food to shelter for them? How to ask God to get involved when you support the murder of unborn babies? How do you ask God to get involved when you support homosexuality as just an alternative lifestyle? See what I mean? All three of those things go against what the Bible teaches. I'm surprised at how many Catholics are Democrats. It doesn't equate. If they are strong practicing Catholics, they would have to be extremely weak Democrats. If they are strong Democrats, then they have to be weak, in name only, Catholics."

"It is perplexing, isn't it?"

"Not really, Jean. If one has a set of moral beliefs based upon one's religion, then, to me, it is simple. You always stand on your principles – no matter what line of work you are doing. Even if you are a politician."

"Even if you are a politician?" Mr. Le Couteau smiled.

"Remember what my cousin said – they are all liars. You may not always get re-elected standing firm, being guided by your principles and telling the truth. But, you know what? That's all right. At least you can look yourself in the mirror and know that you are following a path of righteousness. The reality is, I'm afraid, Jean, that too many people are members of a religious denomination without truly living a Christian life."

"It can be tough to do sometimes."

"That is most certainly true. It's that human body that surrounds our souls that causes all the difficulties."

Mr. Le Couteau looked at Jake and said, "I don't believe I've ever heard it put like that. But I like it. How do you manage to live a Christian life, Jake?"

"For me, it's trying to stay in touch with the Holy Spirit. Prior to making any big decision, like coming up here, for instance, I pray and ask for guidance from the Holy Spirit. If I stay quiet and listen, I usually get an answer. Not always. I don't hear voices or anything, Jean. However, I generally know what I should do. If it is something wrong, something I should not be doing, the Holy Spirit lets me know. It is just a feeling I get that this is something I need not be doing."

"What about at . . ."

"Jean, let me tell you the truth. I used to be a really strong what I call a 'Sunday only Christian.' I went to church on Sunday morning and that was pretty much the extent of my Christian life. I believed that Jesus was who He said He was but I didn't live like it. I understand people who live that way. I would never judge them or condemn them. I lived like that for years. I know exactly what it is like. I came out on the other side and, someday, they can also."

"What I wanted to ask you is how you live as a Christian at work?"

"I use the same process at work as in the rest of my life. I'm just more private with it. When I say I pray prior to making a big decision, I don't mean I get down on my knees and make a big production of it. I can close my eyes at my desk and ask for guidance. When one gets in the habit of asking God for help, it becomes almost second nature. Throughout the day, whether I am at work or at home, I quietly thank Jesus. I just say 'Thank you, Jesus' and He knows what I mean. When I started working for my financial firm, Excalibur, I told myself I was always going to play it straight. I was not going to cut any corners. I was not going to lie to my clients. It has worked out well for me. It is honest work. But Jean, I don't like it. I'm actually planning on resigning my position with Excalibur."

"Yes, you mentioned that. When do you think you'll resign?"

"I haven't set a definite date yet. I will need to tie up some 'loose ends,' as they say, with some of my clients. But soon. I'd like to do it within the next month. Perhaps it'll take two months. But soon."

"Then what will you do?"

Jake laughed and said, "I haven't the slightest idea."

"Really? That surprises me. I would have thought you would have figured it all out before quitting."

"Me too. I guess I just feel like it is time for me to move

on to . . . something else. Being a financial broker and helping wealthy people get wealthier is not my career choice. This is not what I want to do with my life. It is fine for some people but I have become uncomfortable with it. I truly think that it is the Holy Spirit within who is making me feel uncomfortable."

Mr. Le Couteau laughed. He simply stated, "I see. Are you searching for something? Peace? Contentment? Happiness?"

"No. I already have all of those. I have Christ. What more could I need? Now that is not just a platitude for me. I realize, because I now have enough finances to retire comfortably, that people would comment 'Easy for you to say. You're not living paycheck to paycheck.' But I have lived paycheck to paycheck. For many years. I know what that is like. There is an uncertainty hanging over your head. However, when you have Christ in your life, He takes that uncertainty away. You asked if I was seeking something. I think all Christians, because we all possess a tiny spark of divinity within, are seeking to return to God. Most people, both Christians and non-Christians, however, are unaware that they are searching; and, those that do feel the emptiness inside don't realize that it is God they are seeking. They try to fill their lives with adventures, with fame, with wealth, with good works . . . but none of that will quench the 'search.' Jesus is the only way to return to God. You see, Jean, the way I see it, we Christians were not made for life in this world. We do not belong here. Our souls belong in another world. We belong to God. That is one primary reason I think so many Christians feel frustrated living in this world. You know, that reminds me of something I have just learned in the last year or two. It's one way to determine if someone is a mature Christian. I'm sure there are exceptions to this but I've found that people who have matured in Christ and who are under the influence of the Holy Spirit generally do not complain."

"Don't complain? About what?"

"About anything. While the human aspects of our being may feel the frustration of living in this society, our spiritual side knows that God is ultimately in control. The real us, the spiritual us, realize that we are only visiting here on Earth for an extremely brief time. This is not our home. Our home is with God."

"So why complain?"

"Exactly. Why complain?"

Both Mr. Le Couteau and Jake got up, stretched, walked over to the coffee maker, got a fresh mug, popped a cinnamon roll in the microwave and returned to their respective chairs.

Mr. Le Couteau looked at Jake and said, "Tell me about your marriage."

"My marriage?"

"Yes."

"It didn't last very long. Four years. What do you want to know?"

"Was it a good marriage while it lasted? What caused the divorce? What was she like? If you don't want to talk about it, that's all right. We'll move on to something else."

"No, I don't mind. It seems like a long time ago now."

"How old were you when you married?"

"Twenty-five. I was twenty-nine when we divorced."

"And you are . . . what, forty-one now?"

"Forty-two."

"Thirteen years ago. Not such a long time ago."

"Seems like it. There's been a lot of water under the bridge since then."

"Are you still in touch with her?"

Jake smiled. "No, not at all. I don't even know where she is living now. I heard that she had remarried but I don't know his name. I was told she has three children now. I sincerely do wish her all the best and do hope she is happy."

"No hard feelings?"

"No. No hard feelings. More a sense of regret than anything."

"How so?"

"Oh, just regret that it didn't turn out as expected. That the marriage was a failure."

Softly, Mr. Le Couteau asked, "What happened?"

Jake looked at Mr. Le Couteau and realized that he felt comfortable talking with him.

Jake said, "Jean, this may surprise you, but I actually, while still on our honeymoon, wondered if I could get our marriage annulled."

"Not a good honeymoon, huh?"

"Awful. The worst. Like many couples, we went away for a week on our honeymoon. During that week, the only time we made love was on our wedding night and that is only because I insisted on it. She didn't want to but I thought how terrible it would be to look back on our wedding and know that we weren't intimate on our own wedding night. And the lovemaking was awful. I never knew that having sex could be awful. But it was. I told myself I would never ever insist on having sex again. I kept that promise. I told her that I was always 'in the mood.' Whenever, in the future, she was ready, to let me know. For the rest of our honeymoon, nothing. Absolutely nothing. She acted as though everything was normal. We went to all the sights and places. She wanted to hold hands. We laughed. We had a good time. But no sexual activity at all."

"Excuse me. But was it her time of the month?"

No. Not at all. Jean, we had been sexually active as an engaged couple. Back then, I was still a Sunday only Christian. Now, I think it would be better if couples waited until they are actually married. But anyway, I told you that to tell you this. We had more sexual activity during the year we were engaged than we did during the four years of our marriage. Way more. When we got back from our honeymoon and got settled in our apartment, we didn't make love until a month later. When I asked her what was wrong, she always said 'nothing, I'm just not in the mood.' During our first year of marriage, we made love probably eight or nine times. Once, when we were engaged, we went on a three-day trip together. We made love more often on that three-day trip than we did the entire first year of our marriage. I could not understand it. It made no sense to me. She never wanted to discuss it. I was thinking of divorce. But I was also thinking of 'for better or for worse.' When we got married, I was totally in love with her. But six months later, I had come to the conclusion that she did not love me. Or else, why would she treat me this way? I was confused. I was quickly falling out of love with her. A couple of people whom I told my situation to suggested that some good professional counseling might help. I didn't think it would have hurt. However, looking back, with hindsight, I really don't think it would have helped at all. She didn't seem to think that there was a problem. Anyway, we both had jobs and stayed busy. She was always on the pill and, thankfully, we didn't have children. For the last three years of our marriage, we were more like roommates than husband and wife. I decided that I did not want to live with her anymore. I no longer loved her. I filed for divorce. I had naively thought that we could just go our separate ways. There were no children. We owned no real estate. All I wanted was my books and my clothes. She could have everything else. But to my surprise, she didn't want a divorce. She tried to talk me into staying with her. Before I physically moved out, she even snuck into the guest room where I was sleeping. She wore a see-through sheer baby doll nightgown that I had never previously seen. She had an extremely nice womanly body. She was a pretty woman with a sexy body. She seemed to think that she could change my mind with one sexual act and that would make up for four years of almost no sex. I told her it was too late and she left the room. When she realized I was serious about the divorce and was not going to change my mind, she showed me a side of her I had never seen. She counter-filed and that is when things got nasty. She actually had a higher salary than me. But she wanted me to pay her alimony. She got mean. And she really wasn't a mean person. Most of the time, she was kind and caring. I had never seen her be overtly mean until the divorce. She wouldn't agree to terms. She wanted a trial. We both wasted money on attorneys. She spread rumors about me in the community. She got an order of protection against me. Once I moved out, I never saw her again except for the court proceedings. The order of protection was just another way, she thought, of embarrassing me. Anyway, it dragged on and on. In court, she actually lied under oath. Perjury. The judge denied her request for alimony. I got my books, clothes and my car. She got everything else. What a waste of time and money. All the attorney fees. All the time wasted dragging it out for so long. Anyway, once it was final, I knew it had been the right decision. I moved on with my life. She moved on with hers. I do hope she is treating her new husband better than she treated me. You know, Jean, in those four years, I had numerous opportunities to have sexual affairs. Frankly, I was surprised at how many married women, knowing that I was married, came on to me during those four years. I mean, they didn't know I wasn't having sex with my wife."

"Did you?"

Jake smiled. "No, I never did. There was this one woman. Single. Twenty. Beautiful. I came close. However, I just didn't think it would be right. It would have been understandable, but still, not right. I was married. I still do not know why my wife ignored me in the bedroom. Other than that, she acted like we were a happily married couple. I just didn't understand it. I still don't. Anyway, that is all in the past. We cannot change the past. We cannot go back and undo our mistakes. We learn from them and grow."

"Do you think you'll ever get married again?"

"I don't know. I've thought about it, of course. Since my divorce, I haven't dated anyone seriously. I've had a lot of first dates without a second date. I'm not opposed to getting married. Perhaps, I simply haven't met the right woman yet. To answer your question, if I had to say yes or no, I'd probably say no. I think it is unlikely that I'll marry again."

Mr. Le Couteau smiled. "You say that you haven't met the right woman yet. Perhaps you have but haven't yet had the opportunity to get to know each other."

"It's always a possibility. I've met several nice women at work. But I don't see it happening with any of them."

Mr. Le Couteau sighed loudly.

"What?"

"I was thinking of Laura."

"Laura?" Jake blushed. Mr. Le Couteau noticed but ignored it. It told him something, though.

"Yes, Laura. You two seemed, to me, to have really hit if off well."

"We have. Yes. I really like Laura. She seems like a truly kind person."

"She is. I've known her ever since she's been here. She's solid. She's intelligent. She is a woman of character."

"In the brief time I've known her, I would certainly agree with everything you've said. However, you left out something about her that I have certainly noticed."

Mr. Le Couteau looked concerned. He asked, "What's that?"

"She is exceedingly . . . easy on the eyes."

Mr. Le Couteau smiled and nodded.

"What about you, Jean? How long have you been married?"

"Thirty-seven years now."

"You just spent the weekend with her, didn't you?"

"Yes. In Montreal."

"That must be difficult, at times, to . . ."

"We are separated by geography. But that is all. We see each other as often as we can. She used to live here with me. After a few years, she just couldn't adapt to this lifestyle. She visits here a few times a year. I visit her on the weekends primarily – in Montreal, about twice a month. We raised three children before we even knew this place existed. She wants to be a normal grandmother. She can do that in Montreal but not here."

"I understand."

Mr. Le Couteau looked at Jake and said, "You know, Jake, I truly think you do understand."

Jake nodded.

Jake's host stood up and stretched. He asked Jake if he

would mind having lunch delivered. Jake replied that it would be fine. Mr. Le Couteau said he wanted to continue their discussion without the interruption of having to go to the cafeteria and back. He then pushed some buttons on the phone, reached the cafeteria and ordered two meals. The meals soon arrived and the two men continued their conversation.

"Jake, I think you have an innate ability to perceive things and where they are headed. I'm interested in how you view the state of churches in our society today."

"I don't know about an innate ability. However, I do think God endowed humans with the ability to reason, to think critically, to analyze and evaluate and arrive at logical conclusions. I look at trends in our culture and I see where those trends are leading. As far as how several protestant denominations are doing, it seems to me that the trend is not favorable. There are many reasons, as I see it, for this. One is the almost daily influx of news media and entertainment media expressing viewpoints that are opposed to traditional church teachings. I expect that will get worse in the years ahead. Perhaps, though, the main reason I see churches having a difficult time in the near future is the trend many churches have adopted of trying to adjust their doctrine to accommodate changing cultural mores. That never works. Jeremiah said that the people of his time had 'perverted the words of the living God.' Some churches today have done exactly the same. Instead of becoming more liberal like the entertainment community presents in movies and television, churches should hold firm to Biblical truths. The gospel is straightforward. When churches 'water it down' to make it easier to swallow, they lose the essence of excitement that the good news of Jesus Christ presents. Jean, you may be wondering what denominations I'm referring to here. I'll tell you. The churches I see that are trending toward liberalism include the Methodist, Episcopalian and Presbyterian. I'm afraid these liberal policies that these churches are implementing, rather than increasing membership, will result in a decrease in membership. Some of these churches have become more of a social club than a place of worship. I think all churches have many members in their congregations who have never genuinely experienced a true Biblical conversion to Jesus. Jesus said, 'By their fruits you will know them.' Among the fruit of the Holy Spirit are love, joy and peace. There are many regular churchgoers who do not exhibit such fruit. I have to conclude that they may not have yet truly accepted Christ as their Savior. Churches today should preach Christ, and Him crucified. They should preach about the Holy Spirit and how He will come into each believer's life and direct that life, if asked to do so. This is so important and I think many of today's churches are failing to do this.

"For example, I think the homosexual movement will grow in strength. I can see it becoming an 'in' thing. I can picture the 'celebrities' of the entertainment world, the political world and the media world all falling all over themselves to demonstrate not only their tolerance for the homosexual lifestyle but also their acceptance and support of that lifestyle. And, I'm afraid, I can even see churches doing the same. If I'm right about this, and only time will tell, then people like myself and churches that stand true to Biblical teachings will be reviled and scorned for being 'out-of-touch,' for being 'backward,' for not evolving and for being non-tolerant. I can see a time coming soon when individuals and churches that do not compromise their beliefs and their teachings will be considered hateful. Christians love all people. But they will be accused of being hateful because they do not accept homosexual behavior as being normal. I see the same hateful trend being expressed against those who think that murdering unborn babies is wrong. By some twisted logic, Christians and churches that think killing babies is wrong are the bad people. The evolved intelligent people who support unlimited abortions are the good people. Anyway, that's the way I see the church trends of today developing."

"I hope you're wrong."

"I hope so too."

Shaking his head, Mr. Le Couteau said, "I'm afraid you just might be right."

"How does good compromise with evil?"

"Exactly!"

"You know, Jean, the trends of today do not look promising for our society in the future. But you know what? We Christians know our future. We know where our souls will be spending eternity. That knowledge alone should bring a sense of pure joy to every believer in Christ. At the same time, it makes us want to do whatever we can to share the gospel with others."

"Yes, but we still have to live our human lives. Most people have to get up, get dressed and drive to work every day to earn a living for themselves and their families. We can't spend our days witnessing to others."

"You're right, of course, Jean. However, we can be a witness for Christ every day by the way we live our lives at home, at work and at play. Can people tell, by our actions and our words, that we are Christians? Do we behave and talk differently than non-Christians? Do we have empathy and compassion as we live our lives? I think there should be a discernible difference between Christians and non-Christians. That difference is a witness for Christ."

Mr. Le Couteau looked deep in thought. He said, "I see what you are saying. Yes. Yes, that makes good sense."

Jake asked Mr. Le Couteau about his children and grandchildren. While Mr. Le Couteau explained all about them, Jake ate his cold lunch. Jake was curious to know if Mr. Le Couteau's children knew about this underground facility where their Dad now worked. They did not.

The two men continued their conversation throughout the afternoon until it was time for supper. They decided to eat in the cafeteria. They had a wide-ranging talk that included subjects that Mr. Le Couteau had not planned on discussing. Jake was good at finding ways to segue into other topics.

CHAPTER TWENTY

"God is a spirit: and they that worship him must worship him in spirit and in truth."

– John 4:24

Late 1st Century A.D.

During their supper, Mr. Le Couteau asked Jake if he would mind continuing their conversation that evening. Jake replied that it would be fine. The two had been talking all day and now it appeared they may wind up talking all night.

As Mr. Le Couteau and Jake were talking, Laura and Peggy stopped at their table.

Laura asked, "Mr. Le Couteau, just where have you been hiding Jake?"

He smiled and replied, "I just now let him out of the dungeon to eat."

"I see," Laura responded. Turning to Jake she asked, "And what did you do to get sent to the dungeon?"

"I got caught. I thought I'd get away with it . . . but no, they caught me."

Peggy laughed.

Laura asked, "Can I see you later?"

Jake shook his head, "I'd like to but I think Jean and I will be busy until pretty late tonight."

Mr. Le Couteau said, "I'm afraid, Laura, I've already booked Jake for tonight."

Laura smiled. "I understand. See ya tomorrow."

Peggy smiled and waved her fingers like a child waving goodbye.

"Bye."

Mr. Le Couteau turned to Jake and said, "She likes you."

"You're talking about Laura?"

"Yes. Of course."

"I like her too. I wonder though. Perhaps I am too old for her."

"Nonsense. Not at all. I think you two make a nice couple."

The two men finished their meal and returned to the lounge they had been using.

After both sat down with their after supper cup of coffee, Mr. Le Couteau asked, "I'm really interested in your views about how you see the future of our society. What do you think of our future government situation? We, right here, do not have any evidence that either the Canadian or the American government is aware of our existence. We started our little project prior to when all the numerous governmental regulations were implemented. We've managed to quietly 'fly under the radar.'"

"Yes. And that is amazing. If I weren't sitting here talking with you in late May of 2005, I would not find it believable."

"We hope everyone would also not find it believable."

Jake smiled. He said, "I still don't see how you manage it."

"Actually, it's not as complicated as you might think. We all earn relatively small salaries. This is because our food and lodging is included. We also earn 'credits.' You've seen the stores?"

"Yes."

"We pay for clothes, toothpaste, shampoo, soap and things like that with our credits. This way, we don't have to use money. We are paid in cash. Most of us bank in Québec City. A few, such as myself, in Montreal. We deposit our cash salaries in, primarily, savings accounts. Some people use checking accounts also. In my case, I give my wife my cash and she deposits, from her salary, the same amount in our savings account. She then uses the cash for groceries, utility bills, purchasing gas for the cars and little everyday things. It's a little bit of a bother but it works out all right."

"I see."

"We've generally found a way around most governmental regulations. Which reminds me, we've gotten off the subject. I really think you have a knack for seeing trends. Tell me what you see for the future."

"I certainly make no claims to being a prophet. I can predict nothing. I do think I have some understanding of history. That helps me to see some trends for the future.

"Jean, what I think is that, in the States, our culture, our entire society, is being overwhelmed by a huge centralized federal government. Canada is moving in the same direction. This government is becoming more and more authoritarian. Our Democrat political party is leading the way with this. It is showing, to me, the beginnings of a tendency toward tyranny. All it would take is a President with a disregard for the people of this nation, a disregard for the traditions of our culture, a disregard for our Constitution and an arrogant ego to move our federal government into a place of control that could destroy the freedoms that Americans have enjoyed for over two centuries. For this to be really successful, the Democrat President doing all this would need to be followed by eight years of another Democrat President. After sixteen straight years of such rubbish, it would have a truly strong grip on American society."

"Jake, I'm sorry, but I can't really see that happening. How could such a person get elected?'

Jake smiled. "I'll tell you how. Politicians lie. If they told, up front, what they really want to do, they would never get elected. Also, these liberal progressive socialists have the full support and protection of the media. It is not difficult to see one of these truly liberal socialist democrats obtaining the power to do real damage, in a short time, to this nation. Add to that the simple fact that most adult Americans do not know how to think."

"That's a pretty strong statement."

"I know. However, I'm afraid the facts bear it out rather

well. Fortunately, many of these people who can't think very well also don't vote."

"That's good, I suppose."

"Yes, but many of them do. For forty years now, our growing federal government has been fighting a war on poverty. It is losing that war big time. There are more people in poverty and a higher percentage of people in poverty in 2005 than there was in 1965. And the unintended consequences of the war on poverty are horrible. So what does the enlightened federal government do? It doubles down. It keeps expanding the whole entitlement process. People now expect the federal government to provide housing, food, medical care, disability benefits, unemployment compensation and whatever else they can milk from the government for themselves and any children they produce. These programs are growing and growing. Even illegal aliens are now expecting to receive these benefits including free public education for all their children. I don't foresee these programs getting smaller but rather, larger. Yet, logic tells us that they cannot be sustained indefinitely. They have resulted in morality changes not intended. Most obvious, perhaps, is the lack of a father in many families seeking government relief. Additionally, these programs have resulted in a major change in attitude. Some people now expect government assistance and believe that they are entitled to it simply by existing. There is no shame in being on the government dole. I see this as a major trend that will only get worse in the future. Someone, down the road, is going to have to have a strong backbone and stop this mess. It simply cannot be sustained forever. When someone does what has to be done, it is going to cause major problems. People who are able to work are going to have to work. When the government tells them that the free stuff is over, it will result in much unrest. Politically, no one wants to be the one who does it. Eventually, though, it will have to be done. The alternative, and here history demonstrates this to be true, is a financial collapse of the economy."

"When do you see this happening, Jake?"

Jake laughed. "I told you, I'm not a prophet. My guess is that it'll reach a crisis situation in twenty-five to thirty years. Someone will have to stand up, be an adult and say 'Enough. We cannot continue down this path.' Perhaps that person will have to say that *after* being elected."

Mr. Le Couteau laughed and said, "And not expect to be re-elected."

"Another thing, Jean, is that at the same time all this entitlement mess is going on, our public education is being more and more controlled by the federal government. Guess what the results of that are? Our educational product is getting worse and worse. Not much of a surprise there, huh? I'm not sure we can even call it mediocre anymore. It's just headed in the wrong direction. Think of where it was forty years ago and how badly it has deteriorated since then. The trend is that it will continue to get even worse. There are some excellent teachers in the public schools but they are a minority. And they will tell you how bad it is. Many of them have placed their children in private schools. In some large cities, the percentage of public school teachers with their children in private schools is as high as forty percent. My recommendation, for years now, has been for parents to find a way to enroll their children in either a Christian school or a private school.

"Another trend I see that is going to result in major problems in the future is the illegal immigration situation. We are the only first tier nation in the world that doesn't enforce its immigration laws. We obviously are a nation of immigrants. We should and we do welcome legal immigrants. However, illegal immigration should not be tolerated at all.

"This makes me think of the nonsense of political correctness. It has gotten so bad, people are afraid to speak the truth. The truth may offend someone. The truth may make someone feel uncomfortable. It's crazy. But Jean, I can truly see this getting even worse."

"You know, you're right about that PC stuff. I heard, just recently, some woman's organization was offended when a prayer began with 'Heavenly Father.' They questioned, why not Heavenly Mother?"

"I must admit, Jean, I haven't heard of that one.

"Jean, it seems so silly to me that some women's group is offended by the term 'Heavenly Father.' I mean, it seems like they are looking for something to complain about or create a fuss over. If they wanted, they could pray, *God in Heaven*. However, God is everywhere. I think *Heavenly Father* is more a term of endearment than a statement that God resides in Heaven or that God is male. Peter referred to God as the Father of Jesus. Yet, Jesus was with God from the beginning. Jesus said he was the alpha and the omega. This is something I do not understand – the Trinity. We try to put human relationships on God the Father, God the Son and God the Holy Spirit. I can't do it. I accept it on faith but do not claim to understand exactly how it is."

"Like you said, to be offended by Heavenly Father is nonsense. What else do you see happening in the future?"

"I feel like I ought to have a crystal ball in front of me. Seriously, I think all Christians should be aware of Revelation. I think, as Christians, we should support and pray for Israel and all Jewish people around the world. If the earth had a target on it, Israel would be the bull's eye. I see much happening in the future that revolves around Israel. This is a combination of knowing some scripture and seeing trends in the world today.

"Israel and the Jewish people have a supernatural aura about them. In May of 1948, Israel was recognized as a free and independent nation. In Amos, Isaiah, Jeremiah and Ezekiel, God clearly states that he will return His chosen people, the Jews, to the land he promised them. The twentieth century regathering of the Jewish people back to the land of Israel was an act of God. It is the fulfillment of God's promise. That act was a supernatural event. Another supernatural aspect is the hatred that the world has for Jewish people, for the nation of Israel and for a Jewish Jerusalem. It is a real phenomenon without any rational explanation. The trend today is for an increase in antagonism for anything Jewish. The United Nations, many countries of the world and most news organizations treat Israel as if it were some horrible, awful and despicable nation. Israel is the only democracy in the Middle East. It is the only nation in the Middle East that allows freedom of religion to exist. It makes no sense but most people believe Israel is an evil place. I think that Satan is the cause of such widespread Jewish hatred. It is supernatural hatred. And it intensified when Israel made Jerusalem its capital. I thought that President Bush might recognize Jerusalem . . . and he might yet. Maybe toward the end of his term. A democrat president will never recognize Jerusalem. Perhaps the next republican President will recognize Jerusalem as the capital of Israel. That's what it is. But you know, Jean, this all gets into Revelation and the return of Jesus to Jerusalem. Jesus said, in Matthew, that he would not return to Jerusalem until He was welcomed by the Jewish leaders of Jerusalem as the Messiah. I see supernatural things happening with Jerusalem, Israel and the Jewish people. I think this will increase in the future."

Mr. Le Couteau nodded his head in agreement. He said, "What you said about the hatred of Jewish people – it has gone on for over two thousand years – is right. It is supernatural. I've not thought of it that way. But you're right. It has to be supernatural. There is no reason for such hatred otherwise."

"No, there really isn't. When I went to high school. There were several Jewish students in my classes. It never occurred to me to treat them any differently than anyone else."

"Me too. I mean I went to a high school where we had Jewish students. I didn't even realize that some of them were Jewish. It just wasn't a factor."

"I know what you mean. I first learned that some of my classmates were Jewish when there was a Jewish holiday and they were absent from classes. Right now, though, I can sense a growing anti-Semitic wave of opinion – especially in Europe. I'm afraid it will only get worse. However, I am comforted by the knowledge that Jerusalem and Israel and the Jewish people are all chosen by God. He will ultimately protect them. It's not going to be easy – especially during the Tribulation period – but we, as

Christians, know Who is in control. We know how it is all going to end."

"Yes. It is truly something to look forward to. Tell me, Jake, I am always interested in things that people who like to think come up with and explain. Do you have any thoughts on everyday 'facts' that you can explain?"

"I know not of what you speak."

Mr. Le Couteau laughed. "I knew I wasn't explaining that very well. What I mean is that I've learned that people who know how to think have examined the evidence and come up with real conclusions."

"Give me an example of what you're talking about."

"Okay. Sure. Uh, let's see. Oh, I know. UFOs. Real? Or not real?"

"All right. I understand now. I'm with ya. Unidentified Flying Objects are obviously real because anything flying in the sky that cannot be identified is, by definition, unidentified. But you are referring to extraterrestrial objects. The answer is that they are real. The Roswell case alone has been proven to have been a crashed extraterrestrial flying craft with humanoid bodies. The U.S. government recovered not only the craft but also the alien bodies. Another reason I know that they are real is because I've seen one myself."

"Really? What was it like?"

"It was a slowly moving luminous craft that didn't make a sound. It was about two hundred feet away from me and the person who was with me. We both saw it. It slowly maneuvered over a crop field and followed the curve of the field and glided silently over the top of the trees at the end of the field. We could see the light from the craft reflected on the treetops as it slowly moved out of sight. Without discussing it, the woman with me and I drew what we had seen on a piece of paper. We drew the same shape and described it pretty much exactly the same. It really was amazing to see. I've only seen that one. I'd like to see others."

"I've never seen one."

"If you ever do, you won't ever forget it. I do feel fortunate to have seen that craft. It certainly removed any doubt from my mind that they are real."

"I guess so. What else?"

"Oh. Okay. Let's see. Okay. Most people will swear that the U. S. Constitution guarantees the separation of Church and State. But it does not. When Thomas Jefferson was President, he used to attend church services that were held in the capitol building. That building was under construction and sometimes services were held in the White House. The idea that, somehow, a Christian nativity scene on the city square is a violation of the Constitution is absurd.

"Another thing not in the Constitution that everyone thinks is is the concept that a child born in the U. S. is automatically a U. S. citizen. This belief comes from the 14th Amendment. I have seen this amendment quoted by liberals in the press but without the entire amendment quoted. They leave out an important phrase. The amendment does say that all persons born in the U. S. are citizens of the U. S. and the state in which they were born. However, and this is important, there is a phrase between those two statements that says that they must be subject to the jurisdiction of the state and of the U. S. To me, this says that a woman here as a tourist from another country who delivers a baby cannot claim that that child is now a U. S. citizen. No, that baby is a citizen of the woman's home nation. Likewise, an illegal pregnant immigrant cannot slip across the border, deliver her baby and then claim that the baby is now a U. S. citizen. That baby was not under the jurisdiction of the state or the federal government. If she had legally entered the U. S., she would have paperwork to support her claim that her baby was under the jurisdiction of the government and was, therefore, a citizen. In that case, she would be correct in that her baby would be a citizen. Nonetheless, if the illegal immigrant woman went to court and claimed that her baby was indeed born in the U. S., some liberal judge would undoubtedly rule in her favor.

"Something that is controversial but should not be is

evolution. First of all, it is a hypothesis – not a theory. That is an important distinction. Secondly, the reason it should not be controversial is because there is absolutely not one single scientific piece of evidence to support Darwin's concept of evolution. To me, it is simply a nonsense idea. I base that assessment on common sense. But I have an understanding of genetics, of geology and of biology. There simply is no science available to support evolution. One of the funniest explanations for evolution I have ever read was an attempt to explain the process of caterpillars turning into butterflies. You'd have to have a low-functioning brain to buy that explanation. More?"

"Please."

"Another obvious one is the concept of man-made global warming. Again, there is absolutely no scientific evidence that man's influence is causing any change in the planet's weather. All those 'scientific' predictions of gloom and doom in the next ten years are based on computer models – not science. Junk in – junk out. Right now, in 2005, there are all kinds of predictions of rising oceans, of melting ice caps, of extinction of polar bears and numerous other stupid things. I wonder what these brilliant scientists are going to say in ten years. In 2015, what will they say when none of this happens? They'll have some explanation to weasel out of what they predicted and they'll have new predictions of impending doom. And some people are so unable to think that they'll buy the new predictions. However…"

"You don't think any of the predictions will come to pass in the next ten years?"

"Absolutely not."

"Why?"

"Why? Jean, it's all a hoax. A scam. It's nonsense. Now, media people are so dumb they actually believe it. They have repeated the lie so often, they probably buy it. But real science does tell us something about the temperature. During the last hundred years, the planets Mercury, Venus, Earth and Mars have all had an increase in planet-wide temperatures. Mercury the most. Mars the least. Scientifically, what do these four planets have in common? Answer – the Sun. The science of geology clearly demonstrates that our planet undergoes cycles of warming and cycles of cooling. Recorded history also tells us that this is true. Something ridiculous that I just heard a few weeks ago was a statement made by a Hollywood celebrity. He announced, on behalf of some 'save the planet' organization, that unless all commercial fishing is immediately stopped, we will fish out the oceans in ten years. Now this Hollywood genius was simply repeating what he had been told to say. When I heard this, I thought 'if we tried our best, we could not fish out the oceans in ten years.' That was one of the stupidest statements I have ever heard. But some people will believe it and probably stop buying fish. Jean, our culture has developed to the point where people generally do not think for themselves. If they hear it on television or if some celebrity says it, they accept it as being reliable."

"I'm afraid you are right about that. Tell me, Jake, are you familiar with Francis Bacon?"

Jake replied, "Not in any great detail."

"Have you read *New Atlantis*?"

"I have."

"You've read a lot."

"I have. *New Atlantis* was published posthumously. Bacon died before he could finish it."

"Right. How would you sum it up?"

"To me, the main point of his Utopian society was to create a community dedicated to the completely free and open pursuit of learning. Along with that, he also emphasized the importance of studying nature."

Mr. Le Couteau responded by saying, "Exactly. And we are trying to do both of those things right here. When Bacon was writing, the concept of free and open pursuit of learning was revolutionary. That was in the seventeenth century."

"Yes. When your founder, Mr. Sinclair, began this place, this library, with the idea of open learning, in the nineteenth century, it was still a revolutionary concept. It's still frowned on in many countries today. We seem to be trending away from that ideal."

"I agree."

"I do think that the study of nature that Bacon stressed is extremely important. I think that a study of nature can reveal the presence of the Creator of nature. I think that a walk through the forest can bring one closer to recognizing one's spiritual nature. I think one can find God in nature."

Mr. Le Couteau nodded his head and said, "I so agree with that. We often take walks, through the woods and around the lake. Many do it as a group activity but I much prefer to do it alone. I do feel as though I can commune more easily with God while I am doing that."

"Yes, I have experienced that also. It is a time to be silent and know that God sees all, hears all and knows all. It is humbling; but also, a time to listen, to be aware and to recognize the majesty of God."

"I think one has to experience it to understand what you are saying."

"Probably. But you know, Jean, what we have been talking about reminds me of all the places on our planet that are unexplained."

"What do you mean?"

"I'm talking about structures that exist but have no real scientific explanation. Archaeologists sometimes try to offer an explanation but they really are only guessing. In my view, they don't have enough understanding of human nature to guess correctly. If they examine an artifact and have no idea what it is, they almost always say it is a ritual object used in a religious ceremony. They really do not know."

"What places are you talking about Jake?"

"I've already mentioned some of them. There are literally dozens and dozens, probably hundreds, of sites scattered across the globe for which the 'experts' have no real rational scientific explanation for their existence. These are places that anyone, with the means, can visit. We can go to these places, see them, touch them and photograph them. But no one knows how they were built, when they were built, who built them or why they were built. There is a huge stone platform in Lebanon. It is made of the third largest quarried stones known to man. By the way, China and Russia both have larger quarried stones. But no one knows who built this platform, when it was built, how it was built or why it was built. With all our modern technology and machinery, we cannot move those size stones today. It is totally unexplained. This is even true of the Sphinx and the pyramids in Egypt. Some archaeologists today still cling to the silly notion that the pyramids were really designed as tombs for the pharaohs. Utter nonsense. Puma Punka and Tiwanaku, in Bolivia, are two more examples of totally unexplained sites."

"I am aware of them. I'd like to go there someday."

"Me too. You know, this reminds me of a trivia question. Do you know who Auroleus Phillipus Theostratus Bombastus von Hohenhim was?"

"No, do you?"

"I'm not sure if I pronounced that correctly but that is the real name of Paracelsus."

"He was an alchemist, wasn't he?"

"Yes, he lived in the early sixteenth century. One of his most famous quotes is 'Truly it has been said that there is nothing new under the sun, for knowledge is revealed and is submerged again, even as a nation rises and falls. Here is a system, tested throughout the ages, but lost again by ignorance or prejudice, in the same way that great nations have risen and fallen and been lost to history beneath the desert sands and in the ocean depths.' Pretty good for a sixteenth century medical doctor."

"Well, we do know that many cities were lost to the rise of the ocean levels about twelve to fourteen thousand years ago."

"Yes Jean, India has actually located some of those places miles off that nation's current coastline. Another of my favorite quotes is from Galileo Galilei. This is from the early seventeenth century. He said 'The authority of a thousand is not worth the humble reasoning of a single individual. I do not feel obligated to believe that the same God who has endowed us with sense, reason and intellect has intended us to forgo their use.' He is my idol for critical thinking skills. I think of this quote when I think of man-made global warming."

CHAPTER TWENTY-ONE

"Again, I tell you that if two of you on earth agree about anything you ask for, it will be done for you by my Father in heaven. For where two or three come together in my name, there am I with them."

– Matthew 18:19-20

Mid 1ˢᵗ Century A.D.

The conversation between Jean Le Couteau and Jake Fleming continued late into the night. The topics of discussion ran the full range from religion, science, politics, education, history, archaeology and culture. Jake was reminded of how Ted used to say that he never had any idea what the two of them would wind up talking about until all hours of the early morning. Now, Jake was doing the same with Mr. Le Couteau. He realized that he was the common denominator. It must be his fault.

Mr. Le Couteau said, "I watched the recording of your talk. Mr. Sinclair also watched it. I liked what you said. Tell me, how does one recognize a true follower of Christ? I have been fooled by people in the past."

"I think that probably we all have. I do think that a true believer can yield to his human nature and fail to live up to his own spiritual expectations. I think all humans stumble from time to time. I'm not sure that a 'stumble' means that that person is not a true follower of Jesus Christ."

"Have you 'stumbled' yourself lately?"

Jake smiled and looked at his watch. "What time is it now? The answer is 'yes.' My most common stumble is to get angry at myself. I don't usually get mad at others but I get mad at myself for doing stupid things. When I do, I have learned to stop and ask Jesus to be with me. The anger goes away."

"That interests me. What is something stupid you did that resulted in getting mad at yourself?"

"I could give you dozens of examples."

"Just one will do."

"Okay. About a month ago, I tried to pick up a box of books that must have weighed around a hundred and forty pounds. It was only for a short distance. As soon as I lifted it, I knew it was a stupid thing to do. I called myself an idiot. I told myself that I was so stupid I couldn't think to put half the books in another box. I was too stupid to take a few books at a time. I was too stupid to drag the box where I wanted it to go without lifting it. It took two weeks for the pain in my back to go away."

Mr. Le Couteau smiled. He said, "I understand."

"If anyone had seen me then, they wouldn't have thought I was much of a Christian."

"You probably wouldn't have expressed your anger at yourself if anyone had been around."

Jake thought about that. He responded, "You are probably right about that. I tend not to show my frustrations. Back to your question about knowing or recognizing a true follower of Christ, Jesus told us Himself how to know. In John, He said, 'By this shall all men know that ye are my disciples, if ye have love one to another.' The main focus of Jesus' ministry was love. 'And the greatest of these is love.' His sacrifice on the cross, for us, was the ultimate statement of love. Sometimes, when we hear of a Christian doing or saying something that he should probably not be doing or saying, we might begin to question the sincerity of his belief. But that, I think, is not the proper response. Rather, I think we have to remember that each of us is at a different spiritual level – each of us have traveled a different distance down the path of spirituality. Some people are just taking their first steps. Others have traveled longer and, consequently, are farther down the path. Whether a person has accepted Christ or not, that person today is not the same person he was twenty, thirty or forty years ago. If he has accepted Christ, then he is a totally different person. It takes time to understand spiritual knowledge. It takes time to always recognize the presence of the Holy Spirit. But the answer to your question is, I think, love. Does this person have genuine love for others – for everyone? As we travel down the path, opportunities to learn and grow will always appear. Do we step up to the next level? Or do we stumble? Love, I believe, will generally carry us to the next level."

"Jake, I like how you describe that process. I can visualize it happening."

"It truly is a simple process but one that we humans frequently fail to understand. We need to understand that love is supreme. It is, I believe with all my heart, the most powerful force in the universe. Love should and must rule. Love must govern our spirit. If we allow this, then the spirit will govern our minds and our flesh. Each of us, as individuals, should love God first. Then, and this is often difficult, we must love ourselves. Next, we are to love others as ourselves. If we fail to love ourselves, how can we love others as ourselves? We must acknowledge and know that there exist within us a spark of light, a touch of divinity, a soul, an essence of the love of Christ – however we choose to define it, we must know that it is there within us. If we know that that tiny spark of divinity, a soul, is within us, we also know that it is within all other human beings on this planet. Everyone has a soul. Consequently, we can love all others by recognizing that they too contain a spark of the divine within them. This applies to everyone. This applies to even the most evil terrorists and murderers in the world. One thing I try to remember, and it is not always easy to do . . . but I try – is to remember that even in the most evil, cruel and perverted person there exists a tiny spark of the divine – a soul. I try to think that someone or something may, one day in the future, lead that person to know Jesus and thereby cause that person's soul to ignite and that evil person will show love. It is important for Christians to show love for everyone. It doesn't matter what race they are, what religion they are, what sexual orientation they have, what gender they are, how young or old they are, what political philosophy they embrace – everybody needs love. Jesus taught love. He said that his followers should love everyone – and so we should.

"It is true that there are several stories of men in prison for committing horrible crimes who have had a genuine conversion by accepting the truth of Christ as savior. They experienced real repentance for their crimes. By accepting Christ's forgiveness, the spark of divinity within their souls became active."

"Yes," Mr. Le Couteau added, "I remember reading about such a man on death row. He even witnessed to his guards. He told them that he now, with Christ, no longer feared his death. He told them that he now believed that when our body dies, our spirit, our soul, slips away from the body and moves to a spiritual realm, Heaven, to be with Christ. Those souls without Christ leave the body and go to a realm of darkness, Hell. This is what he said he came to know as he studied scripture in prison."

Mr. Le Couteau continued the conversation by saying, "As we near bodily death, one's perspective changes. I have had the privilege of being with several people as they faced their imminent deaths. One thing I have noticed that seems to be common to all of them is that they seemed to have no interest for things of this world at all. Worldly things just no longer mattered to them. They all recognized that they would soon be in a much better place – a spiritual place."

"Yes, I can understand that. Jean, I haven't had much experience being with people as they approached their deaths. But I do remember an elderly man with whom I had the opportunity to talk with, for several hours, about a week prior to his death. One thing I will always remember him saying is that the body does not have a soul; rather, the soul has a body. He told me that when the soul ceases to need the physical body, the soul sheds the body and continues on its journey."

Mr. Le Couteau thought for a moment and responded,

"I've heard it said that we are spiritual beings inhabiting physical bodies."

"That statement you just made, Jean, is one of the greatest mysteries that science cannot solve. How can spirit and flesh co-exist? Because it cannot be easily explained, many scientists deny the existence of a soul. Other scientists have actually scientifically proved the existence of an immortal soul in every human being. I believe that God is the source of all spiritual existence. He created us as spiritual beings and somehow, no one knows how, meshed us with human forms. Each spiritual being was given the capacity to be self-aware, to have free will, to develop an individual personality, to have independent thought and to have infinite creativity. Self-awareness is the factor that provides spiritual beings the ability to imagine and create. It is also, I think, one of the keys to spiritual growth and development."

"I'm beginning to wish I had recorded this day long conversation we've been having. I want to remember these things."

"You will. We both will. What we've been saying is not new. It's not a secret. It's easy to find. I mean, look . . . God took Jesus, His Son, for lack of better terminology, part of the Trinity, who knew no sin, and had Him accept our sin for us. In this way, through Jesus, we could be made righteous to God. This is the Good News. It is not a secret. This is the grace of God. This is the love of God. No one merits such grace. No one merits such love. But there it is – God's Gift to every human. All we have to do is accept that Gift."

"I like how you make it sound so simple."

"It is. It really is. Jean, I think that it is not a mistake that you are here at this time. Nor is it a mistake that I am here at this time. In God's design, everything happens for a reason. Everything we experience, every person we meet, every event we attend, every difficulty and obstacles we encounter, every moment of our lives can be a lesson. We are supposed to experience things so that we can learn."

CHAPTER TWENTY-TWO

"There is therefore now no condemnation to them which are in Christ Jesus, who walk not after the flesh, but after the Spirit."

– Romans 8:1

Mid 1st Century A.D.

It was after midnight and the two men were still talking about anything and everything.

"I don't know, Jean, I've always been a bit of an optimist. However, as I look down the road, it is difficult to see good things happening for our nation. It seems to me, more and more, we, as a society, are losing the ability to use common sense."

Mr. Le Couteau smiled. He replied, "That, I am afraid, has become all too obvious."

"It seems to be getting worse. As I mentioned previously, political correctness is a term that I do not admire. We have created, in our culture, several groups of people that have been designated as protected."

"Protected?"

"Yes Jean, protected. By that, I mean, if a member of a protected group does something wrong, we don't call him out for it . . . because he is protected. For example, illegal aliens have, in the media, become a protected group. Minorities have been a protected group since the nineteen-seventies. Homosexuals are becoming such a protected group. If I were to say something negative about a member of a protected group . . . say someone, a minority, stole something . . . if I were to refer to that person as a thief, which he obviously would be, why I would be accused of being racist, insensitive, bigoted and prejudiced. It is simply not politically correct to call a criminal a criminal if he is a member of a protected group. To me, it's all nonsense. Of course, it is not politically correct to say that. I am not a politically correct person nor do I wish to ever become one. But this is, I think, the way our culture is headed and I expect it to get worse before it gets better."

"Jake, you may not have heard about this case – there was a big stink about it in Montreal not long ago . . . in the newspapers. It involved a situation where there was some looting in Chicago. A young black man was shot and killed. They showed a picture of him lying in the street. One arm was stretched out over his head. The photo was cropped at the end of his hand. Have you heard about this?"

"No."

"Well, what the papers did, in the name of political correctness, was to crop out what was just beyond his hand. What was just beyond his hand was a pistol and just beyond that was one of those new flat screen plasma television sets. The TV was smashed and broken on the street."

"I'm surprised they ran the photo at all."

"Yes, there was a lot of criticism about that too. But the criticism was that they did not want to show the pistol or the stolen television. He was, as you say, protected. I think, Jake, it may be worst in Canada now than in the States. However, the U. S. is certainly on track to catch up with Canada in this regard of political correctness."

"Along this line of reasoning, I think our members of Congress have yielded to the power of political correctness so much that they are literally afraid to stand up for their own principles. That's presuming that they have some."

Laughing, Mr. Le Couteau said, "Many don't."

"True. But even those who pretend to have some convictions are afraid to take a stand. Jean, we really have extremely mediocre politicians."

"Tell me what you really think."

Jake smiled. "I really do not like politicians. I especially do not like members of the House and the Senate. When they run for office, they are conservatives. When they get in office, they become liberals."

"Are you referring to republicans or democrats?"

"Both. They both disgust me. But you know, now that you mention it, I think that the Democrat Party should change their name to the Socialist Party. That's what they are becoming. And that takes me back to religion."

"How so?"

"I don't see how a member of Congress who is also a democrat can also be a Christian."

Mr. Le Couteau laughed and said, "That most certainly is not a politically correct statement."

Jake smiled and replied, "No, I suppose not. But seriously, I don't see how a practicing Christian could vote for the things that a socialist proposes. The Socialist philosophy and Christian principles are simply not compatible. It's the same concept as the Muslim Sharia law and the U. S. Constitution. They are simply not compatible. If those are politically incorrect statements, I'm sorry, but they both happen to be well-established facts. They just are not compatible."

"You're right about that. I've often wondered the same thing about Christians serving in Congress. I think that, perhaps, as you previously mentioned, we are all at different stages of spiritual growth. Some Christians may just be beginning to walk down the spiritual path. Others are farther along."

"Jean, that may explain some members' situation. However, my take is that many members are Christians in name only. They are not practicing Christians. Maybe they are like I once was – a Sunday only Christian. They haven't accepted or allowed the Holy Spirit to control their lives. 'In all thy ways acknowledge Him, and He shall direct thy paths.' Progressivism, socialism, Marxism, whatever one wishes to call it – it is not compatible with Christianity. Today, the democrat political party is calling itself 'progressive' and is becoming more and more socialistic. It just keeps getting worse and worse. One of the strange things about socialism is that it is a failed philosophy. It has never worked. Once people understand it, no one wants to live under socialism. Socialism can be implemented but it cannot be sustained. It lasted in the Soviet Union for less than seventy years. It simply cannot be sustained. So why ever go in that direction?"

"Why?"

"Well . . . obviously, it gives the federal government more control – more power. That is always enticing to politicians. Either they have no knowledge and understanding of history or they have no respect for history. History clearly tells us that the direction the democrat party is headed in is a direction that is doomed to ultimately fail. I suppose the current crop of progressives or socialists think that they will be the exception to the rule. But, of course, they won't."

"You really aren't politically correct, are you?"

"Not at all. I like to deal in reality."

"I see that. I'm glad you do. Mr. Sinclair does also. He says that he doesn't have time to ignore reality."

"I tell you what, Jean, for some people, ignorance is truly bliss. They can afford to ignore reality and live their lives unaware of what is actually happening all around them."

"Yes, these are the people Mr. Sinclair refers to as the non-thinkers."

"Non-thinkers. Yes, that fits. These aren't bad people. They are simply people who do not know how to think. They have never been taught how to think critically for themselves."

"Exactly."

"Of course, Jean, where all this leads is to less and less individual freedom. It leads to more and more governmental regulations. Even the current republicans are headed in this direction of a bigger and bigger federal government. You know, this once again, reminds me of Jefferson. He was such a genius. He said the government that governs least, governs best."

"Yes, Jake, I've always agreed with Jefferson."

"Always might be a bit of a stretch. Jefferson was a genius. No question. However, he did not accept the reality that Jesus was the Messiah, the Son of God, or that he died for our sins and was physically resurrected from death. He couldn't intellectually accept this. He did not have faith enough to accept it. He couldn't accept that Jesus was exactly who He said He was."

"You know, I knew that Jefferson cut out and pasted certain sections of the New Testament to fit his perception of how it should be. But I didn't know he rejected the divinity of Jesus."

"Yes, he eliminated all the scripture references to miracles that Jesus performed and any mention of the divinity of Jesus. I don't like saying that about Jefferson because I really do admire him . . . but copies of his document called *The Life and Morals of Jesus of Nazareth* still exist. It can be read today. It is embarrassing for someone like me to see it because I really do think highly of Jefferson. I have been surprised by the presumption of Jefferson that he would think that he could re-write the Bible. You know what, Jean? People are doing the same thing today. There is a movement beginning to grow that is called Progressive Christianity. It is in its infancy right now. However, it is growing and will continue to grow. The Bible teaches that God does not change. But this new progressive theology teaches that feelings are more important than absolutes. There are no absolutes. It is an attempt to make Christianity conform to the changes in our culture. It denies scripture. It denies the divinity of Jesus Christ. Once you've gone down that road, then you have nothing. It is a false theology that offers nothing of permanent value."

After more discussion on a variety of topics and, after solving all the world's problems, Jake and Mr. Le Couteau called it a night. As they left the room and walked toward Jake's apartment, it was 4:20 AM on the morning of Tuesday, May 31st.

CHAPTER TWENTY-THREE

"For God, who commanded the light to shine out of darkness, hath shined in our hearts, to give the light of the knowledge of the glory of God in the face of Jesus Christ."

– II Corinthians 4:6

Mid 1st Century A.D.

Jake was awakened by Mr. Le Couteau pounding on his door at 7:15 AM. On his way to open the door, Jake noticed the time and figured he had gotten about an hour and a half of sleep. Never needing much sleep, he shrugged it off and opened the door.

Mr. Le Couteau stepped in and said, "Are you awake?"

"Barely. Good morning. What . . .?"

Excitedly, Mr. Le Couteau said, "Mr. Sinclair wishes to see you."

"Okay."

"No, you don't understand. He rarely sees anyone anymore. I haven't talked with him in person in over six months."

"Is he ill?"

"No, I don't think so. He just stays in his study all the time. I've never known of him visiting with a newcomer so soon."

"I'm a newcomer?"

"You know what I mean. You've only been here a few days. People have worked here for years and never even seen Mr. Sinclair in person. This is something that has never previously happened."

"I'll be glad to meet with him. But I want to mention that

I probably need to leave soon. If I don't turn up with my canoe on Friday, that company will probably send out a distress call to the sheriff's office or some rescue organization to search for me. They'll think I fell in the river or got lost."

"Not to worry. We have a secure phone line from which you can call them and tell them you are okay and running a little late."

"All right. When am I to meet with Mr. Sinclair?"

"As soon as you can get dressed."

"Okay. Can you give me half an hour? I'd like to shower and shave."

"Sure. I'll be back to take you to his study."

While showering, Jake began to think to himself, *I've read Lost Horizon. This is where the guy in charge decides to offer the new guy the opportunity to take his place. Surely that is not going to happen here. No one has ever explained to me how they knew I was coming here. Nor how they knew my name. I like the people here – Laura, Jean, those old-timers, the people in the cafeteria and even Peggy. They are all nice. Even the children are well behaved. Guess I'll see what Mr. Sinclair wants to discuss.*

Leading Jake down another hallway, Mr. Le Couteau said, "Mr. Sinclair's study is right down here."

At the door, Mr. Le Couteau knocked and said, "Mr. Fleming is here."

From the study, Mr. Sinclair replied, "Come on in Jake."

Jake turned to Mr. Le Couteau and said, "Aren't you coming?"

"No, he wants to visit with you alone. It'll probably be a brief meeting. Maybe ten minutes."

"Oh. Okay. Thanks."

Jake opened the door and walked into what looked like a secretary's office or a receptionist area. There was no one there. The door to Mr. Sinclair's private study was open. From behind a desk, a man waved Jake in to the room. The study itself looked like something out of a Victorian novel. There was a large wooden desk, lots of leather, hundreds of books, several interesting mementos and photographs and one wall had several oil paintings. Two of those Jake presumed were of Mr. Sinclair's father and grandfather. The study looked old but was in perfect condition.

At seventy-five, Mr. Sinclair looked every bit the part of an academic researcher – not the CEO of a secret organization. He was wearing a wool cardigan sweater with leather elbow patches. Jake thought, *I don't think I've ever really seen anyone wearing one of those – just in movies that took place in the 1950's*. He was of slight frame with thinning gray hair. As he stood up to shake Jake's hand, Jake guessed his height to be about five–ten. He had bright eyes that displayed intelligence. He had a nice welcoming smile that Jake found pleasing and reassuring. With a smooth shaven face, his wrinkle lines gave his face a certain character. He wore glasses with extremely thin gold-colored frames.

Pointing at a large leather chair, Mr. Sinclair said, "Have a seat."

"Thank you."

"Pipe bother you?"

"No, not at all. I like the smell of pipe tobacco. I smoke a pipe myself."

"Guess we all have our vices."

Jake smiled. He replied, "I'm sure that's so."

"Mr. Le Couteau has told me that he has much enjoyed the conversations he has had with you."

"I also have enjoyed them. I like Mr. Le Couteau. I'm afraid we frequently swerved and wandered off topic. My fault."

Mr. Sinclair added, "He told me you were quite well aware of the history of the Knights Templar."

"No, not really. I'm aware of some of the basics."

"Because of my ancestors' purported connections with some Knights Templar, I have tried to conduct a serious research into what actually happened after the King of France colluded with the Pope and had the Order disbanded."

"Have you been successful?"

Mr. Sinclair looked at Jake with a serious, almost mean, glare. Slowly, he shook his head. He answered, "No, not much. There are a few hints and implications but no real evidence. It has been truly disappointing to me that I have not been able to locate much real historical evidence. In my family history, the story is told of Sir Henry St Clair's expedition to North America in the late fourteenth century and early fifteenth century. Prior to leaving, he had built Kirkwall Castle in Orkney. The castle, by the way, is no longer there. When he returned from North America, he told of the lands he had seen and the native people he encountered. This is all just family history that has been handed down. But actual physical evidence of his journey does not exist. This was almost a hundred years before Columbus. Sir Henry was assassinated by English mercenaries in Orkney. It was Sir Henry's grandson who built Rosslyn Chapel. Have you ever been to visit it?"

"No. I would love to; but, as yet, I have not been to Scotland."

"Oh, you should go. The Chapel has a certain mystique about it."

"I'll have to plan a trip."

"You should. Why haven't you already done so?"

Jake smiled. "I guess I feel a little awkward traveling by myself. Right now, I don't have anyone with whom to share the experience."

"People always think that because my name is Sinclair that I know all the secrets of the Templars. Of course, I know none of them – if there are any. It's amazing to me that people have written books stating that Sir Henry traveled to specific places in Nova Scotia and buried the Holy Grail there. Other books say he went to Rhode Island. Still other books say he is responsible for burying the Templars' treasure on Oak Island in Nova Scotia. It's all nonsense, of course. These authors have no evidence – no proof – of anything they say."

"It must be frustrating for you to want to know the truth but not to have access to it."

"Very much so. I keep hoping that I, or someone somewhere someday, will find, in a dusty old library perhaps, a journal or a diary from one of Sir Henry's men. The journal will tell details of the expedition to North America. What a find that would be! But…alas, thus far, it is not to be."

"Mr. Sinclair, I am truly amazed that this place exists. How you, your father and grandfather have been able to keep it a secret is also amazing."

"My grandfather was a man of great vision. Yet, he would not believe what his project has become. That's his painting right there."

Jake looked at an ornately framed oil painting of a clean-shaven, dark-haired man with a determined look on his face. He was wearing a black coat with a white shirt and black necktie that was tied at his neck like a modern bowtie. It was appropriate attire for the time. Jake thought, *during this time period, most men wore beards. In many ways, he was different.*

Mr. Sinclair stated, "That was painted in 1883."

"You favor him."

"I am trying to continue his legacy."

"You have. That library, by itself, is incredible."

"It, and most of all this underground space that we have today, was constructed by my father. That is his painting next to my grandfather's. Speaking of the library, over two thousand years ago, Cicero said, 'If you have a garden and a library, you have everything you need.'"

"I like that."

Without any transition, Mr. Sinclair stated, "I understand, from Jean, that you are worried about the future. That the trends you see developing…"

"No, that's not accurate. I'm not at all worried about the future. I do think that the trends are negative. I do think that most people are either unable or unwilling to think and use common sense. But I'm not worried because I know who is ultimately in control. I don't have any anxiety or worry because Christ is always with me. I have absolutely no interest in transient things or what I consider trivial unimportant things. Because I have no interest in such things, I don't waste any time fooling with them. There are serious conflicts and difficulties in everyone's life – certainly for Christians. However, having the Holy Spirit active in my life gives me a real sense of peace. Having that Presence in my life takes away any worries that a nonbeliever would have. The way I see it . . . worrying about something would be an insult to God."

"All right. I understand that. I follow you. Perhaps concern would be a better word than worry."

"Perhaps. As long as there is a clear distinction between the two words. I think one can be concerned about an issue or a situation without being worried about it."

"I agree. What concerns you about the next ten to twenty years?"

"The growth and spread of Islam. And China."

"Islam?"

"Yes sir. You see . . ."

"Please call me Charles."

"Okay." Jake nodded a 'thank you' with his head. He continued, "From my office window, down in New York City, I can see the empty spaces where the Twin Towers of the Trade Center used to be. That was almost four years ago; but, that view influences my perspective, I'm sure. But what really causes concern is the fact that I have read the Quran and the Hadith. Have you read them?"

Mr. Sinclair nodded his head and quietly replied, "Yes." He re-lit his pipe and blew out a strong stream of smoke.

Jake responded, "They are eye-opening reads. I think that most Americans simply believe that Islam is another religion like Buddhism or Hinduism. It may seem to have a few unusual characteristics about it but it is just another religion and we can all get along peacefully. But that complacency will ultimately lead to disaster. It is not just another religion. After reading the Quran and the Hadith, it is obvious to me that it is as much a political ideology as a religion.

"This reminds me of the time when Thomas Jefferson was Secretary of State under George Washington and the Barbary pirates kept attacking American commercial ships. These pirates captured the crews and held them for ransom. Jefferson couldn't understand why they were attacking us. We had done nothing to them. He actually sought out the only man living in New York City who was a Muslim. He got this man to translate the Quran into English and Jefferson read it. Jefferson then understood why these Islamists were attacking American ships. He decided that force was the ultimate answer in dealing with them.

"Today, many Americans are still asking 'why?' Why did those radical Islamists attack the Trade Center and kill all those people? They are asking that question because they do not understand Islam. Political Islam is inconsistent and incompatible with modern democratic societies. It is totally incompatible with the U.S. Constitution. It is so important to understand what Islam actually teaches. It is not a religion of love, peace, brotherhood, compassion or tolerance like most religions. In a nutshell, the way I read it, Islam teaches that a messiah, the Islamic Mahdi, is at the heart of their beliefs. One of the ways in which a follower of Islam may serve the Mahdi is to annihilate everyone who is not a follower. The elimination of the Judeo-Christian civilizations will prepare the way for the return of the Mahdi. By getting rid of all those who do not follow Muhammad, the caliphate or Allah's kingdom on earth will be established. This caliphate is the ultimate goal of Islam. Obviously, it is not compatible with western civilization or with any other religion in the world. Islamists know that their beliefs are not compatible with the rest of the world. However, right now, most of the rest of the world does not recognize this incompatibility. The rest of the world, including America, is welcoming mosques and Islamic education centers into their communities. Most people, simply because they do not understand what Islam is truly about, cannot recognize the potential threat that these mosques represent."

Mr. Sinclair did not immediately respond. After puffing on his pipe for about fifteen seconds, he said, "Having also read the Quran and the Hadith, I cannot disagree with anything you've just said. How do you think we, western democracies, I mean, can oppose this threat? They cannot hope to defeat us militarily."

"No. I think terrorism like 9-11 will continue. It is one tactic to cause unrest, chaos and fear. History also tells us that they try to outwardly assimilate into societies. They build education centers and participate in community activities. They contribute to worthy causes and non-profits. Their children play sports. Historically, after many years, two things happen – one, some of them actually turn away from Islam and find another path and two, their leaders remind them of who they really are and what their purpose is as followers of Islam. When they feel strong enough, they begin demanding that, because of their beliefs, they be given accommodations. This is the historical way that Islam infiltrates a civilization when they cannot do it by force. A true follower is to do whatever he can to hasten the appearance of their messiah.

"Understanding them, governments should not make any attempt at appeasement or accommodations. These efforts, even though they have good intentions and are done in good faith, will not be successful. Islamists see accommodations as a sign of weakness. They see it as proof that they are winning.

"I think one way of defeating them is education – exposing them for what they are. American newspapers, in the 1930's, wrote that stories coming out of Germany about atrocities against Jews were exaggerated and unfounded. They were denied by the German government. Today, the media is making the same mistake regarding Islam. Today, the media reports that stories about Islam supporting atrocities against homosexuals, women, Christians and, of course, Jews, are exaggerated and unfounded. They are denied by Mullahs and Islamic governments. It is somewhat surprising to me that, in the name of political correctness, many politicians, who should know better, still claim that Islam is a religion of peace and tolerance. This tells me that such people either have no knowledge of history or no critical thinking skills at all. Or, perhaps, they are aware of the truth but have no 'backbone' to speak the truth.

"Another mistake I see as a possibility is that of becoming like them. By definition, Islam is a religion of hatred. Islamists *must* hate Jews, Christians and really anyone who is not a follower of Muhammad. Hatred cannot be stopped by hating. Love is the most powerful force in the universe. Those who hate must be shown compassion and love. Love will ultimately conquer hate. Exposing Sharia for what it truly is should do much to help educate people about Islam. And it's not a secret. The media could easily expose Sharia and Islam for what it says it is. You wouldn't have to make anything up . . . just report what it actually is. Christians do not approve of a homosexual lifestyle but Christians do not hate homosexuals and would never do them harm. They would show them love and respect and they would pray for them. Islamists do not approve of a homosexual lifestyle and they hate homosexuals. They believe it is best to kill them all. That is a big difference. The media does not seem to see the problem they have here. They have made homosexuals a protected group and yet they support Islam as just being another religion. No common sense working here.

"Another thing I like to remember is that each person in the world has a soul. I believe it takes a belief in Jesus Christ and the power of the Holy Spirit to fully activate it. I don't think Muslims are bad people. I do think that they are horribly misguided people. I knew a woman in college, from Iran, who was brought up as a follower of Muhammad. But she was smart enough, after living in America for several years, to see Islam for what it is. She turned away from Islam completely. By doing so, she knew that she could never return home. I have heard of other stories of people who were raised as Islamists but who have repented and become believers in Jesus. In some cases, these people say that Jesus appeared to them in a vision. This seems to be something that is on the increase. Many Muslims have had a spiritual vision of Jesus and, as a result, have turned from Islam and become Christians. We can learn a lot from listening to these people who have converted from Islam to Christianity. While I pray that more and more people, of all faiths and of no faith, will come to know the redeeming power of Jesus, I am concerned, to answer your question, Charles, that the majority of Islamists, over the next ten to twenty years, will remain true to their system of theology."

Jake smiled. He shook his head. He said, "I'm not sure I answered your question."

"Yes, you did. I asked what concerns you have for the next ten to twenty years."

"In addition to Islam, I would add China and the growth of socialism here in the United States."

Mr. Sinclair replied, "After 9-11, I suppose most Americans are concerned about possible additional acts of Islamic terrorism. Communist China is always a threat to world stability. Socialism is taking over the democratic political party. That is a shame. Tell me something about yourself. Have you ever known real fear?"

"Interesting question. Since becoming an adult Christian, no, I have not known fear. I still get butterflies in my stomach when I have to give a public speech – but real fear, no. I have had several unforgettable experiences where I was totally aware of the presence of God. Once you have had one of those, I don't think you are capable of knowing fear. There is an awareness of His absolutely immeasurable love. His presence gives you a total sense of peace and security. You realize that, if you were to die at that moment, it would be a beginning, not an end. When you walk with Jesus, led by the Holy Spirit, how can you possibly be afraid? You cannot.

"But, Charles, there was a time when I experienced genuine evil and, as a result, was truly afraid and felt real fear. I have only told this story to a couple of people but, even though it happened many many years ago, it is still extremely vivid to me.

"I was about eight and a half years old and lying in my bed late at night. Everyone else in the house was asleep. My bedroom door was open. While lying in bed, I could see down the hall into the living room. I noticed, in the short space from one side of the hall to the other, a dark 'form' glide through the living room. It was totally dark in the house. We had no night lights. But this form was darker than the dark. A sudden sense of complete fear came over me. My legs were instinctively drawn up so that my knees were on my chest. I tried to shout for my mom and dad but no sound would come out of my mouth. I was so totally afraid. I did not see the form move down the hall but I knew that it was now in my room. Somehow, it reached down to touch my head with its 'hands.' I was aware that it was evil. Just before it 'touched' me, I kicked out with both my feet where its 'chest' would have been. For some reason, that did it. It was gone. I lay in my bed and felt my heart pounding in my chest. It had been awful and I was so so scared. But I felt a real sense of relief for I knew it was no longer in the house. I tried to convince myself that it was a bad dream. But it was not. It was real. I had been awake the entire time and it really happened."

Mr. Sinclair asked, "You must have been extremely frightened?"

"Yes. Very."

"Did it return?"

"No. I was afraid that it would. But as the days passed without another occurrence, the fear receded and I tried to pretend that I had imagined it all."

"But you knew that you had not imagined it?"

"Yes. I knew it had really happened."

"That is truly strange."

"Yes, Charles, I know. In one sense, it reminds me of the UFO I saw."

"How is that?"

"As the years pass, I begin to question whether or not either event actually happened. But with the UFO, I was not alone. Another person who was with me also saw it quite clearly, quite close-up and for about three full minutes. I have to remind myself that both the UFO and the evil dark form were real."

"I've never seen a UFO."

"Most people haven't. I've only seen the one."

"I'd like to see one."

"It is fascinating to observe one up-close and watch it slowly fly by. It was only about forty feet off the ground. Amazing technology. Didn't make a sound."

"Jake, you impress me as a young man who . . ."

"I'm forty-two now. I don't think I qualify as a young man anymore."

Mr. Sinclair laughed. He replied, "I'm seventy-five. Everyone is young to me. But what I meant was that I see you as someone who finds it natural to analyze situations. You appear to be an inquisitive young . . . an inquisitive person. I see you as someone who knows a lot about a lot of different things."

"I do read a lot."

"Yes. Tell me then, what is your take regarding the Kennedy assassination?"

Jake thought to himself, *These people sure do ask questions from out of nowhere.* He replied, "Actually, I have looked into it. It happened in 1963. That was the year I was born. So I've had a little extra interest in it."

Mr. Sinclair smiled. He dumped his pipe and re-filled it. Striking a match, he lit it and said, "I was thirty-three when it happened. I remember it well."

"I've looked at the films and the photographs that were taken that day. I've watched reports and television specials about it. I obviously do not have access to all the files and information. However, I do think that the Warren Commission report was exceedingly flawed. If I remember correctly, it was, with all the appendices, numerous. I think it was about seventeen thick volumes long. The summary, I remember was eight hundred and eighty-eight pages long. It calls to mind a quote from the Native American, Chief Joseph. Chief Joseph was quite an intelligent man. He said, 'It does not require many words to speak the truth.' I do not think the assassination was the work of one man. Other than by being a patsy, I do not think Oswald was involved. To me, it is extraordinarily important that, after the headshot was made, everyone turned to look at the grassy knoll. A railroad man said that he saw a police officer standing behind the wall of the grassy knoll. But no police officer was assigned to that place. There probably should have been. An ex-military man, standing in front of the wall, said that he heard a gun being fired and heard a bullet whine as it passed close to his head. If you've ever heard a bullet whine, you never forget it. You will always recognize it if you ever hear it again. My analysis of the entire event is simply that, as stated by the government, it does not add up. There are way way too many unexplained aspects. Even the autopsy results are highly questionable. Are you familiar with the Latin proverb, 'Truth is the daughter of time?'"

"Truth is the daughter of time. I like it. No, I haven't previously heard that. It means, I presume, that the truth will out."

"Yes. That is what I am hoping will happen during the fifty year anniversary of the assassination in twenty thirteen. After fifty years, the government is supposed to release the sealed records. Whether they do or not, I do believe that the truth will eventually work its way to the surface. I think it always does. Sometimes, it takes a long time. But, as you said, Charles, the truth will out."

"I hope so. I also agree with your assessment. It was not the work of one man. Tell me, Jake, do you have any regrets about your life?"

There was quite a pause, for almost a full minute, before Jake answered. Jake was surprised at the unrelated, at least to him, nature of Mr. Sinclair's questions. Jean often did the same thing. Was he, in fact, being interviewed? Jake thought of the song with the lyrics *Regrets, I've had a few. But then again, too few to mention.* Did he have regrets?"

In a soft voice, Jake responded, "Yes."

Mr. Sinclair didn't say anything.

Jake continued, "In some ways, it is more a matter of wondering than regret. By that, I mean, I wonder what would have happened if I had turned left instead of right."

Mr. Sinclair smiled and said, "I understand."

"I do, however, have real regrets. I regret that my marriage ended in divorce. If I had chosen more wisely, perhaps today I would have a wife and children. I regret that today I have no woman in my life that I love. I would love to be in love."

Jake seemed to be lost in his own thoughts.

Mr. Sinclair brought him out of his reverie by saying, "Yes."

Jake shook his head and smiled. "I'm sorry, I guess I was thinking of days that can never come again."

"More regrets?"

"No, not really. Just thinking of how it is when we are in our twenties and thirties. The newness of everything. The time we think we have. The friendships that we make. I have some truly good friends. But they are scattered all over the country. One lives in Georgia, one in Maine, one in Alabama, one in Florida, two in North Carolina, one in New York who works with me and one in Tennessee. I live in New York. We stay in touch through email, phone calls and Christmas cards but I rarely get to see them anymore. They all have families and their own lives. I've developed a very good and strong friendship with a colleague of mine at work. But I'm planning on leaving that position and moving away from New York. We'll become email friends."

Mr. Sinclair said, "You sound sad."

"No. I feel fortunate to have several good friends. I guess I'm somewhat disappointed in myself that I haven't been a better friend to them."

"Considering that they live all over the place, what could you do differently?"

"I could call more often. I could write more frequently. I could send greeting cards more regularly – you know, on their birthdays, on their anniversaries, things like that."

Mr. Sinclair simply said, "Yes, you could."

Jake smiled. He got the message. He said, "Another regret I guess I have is that I never went to graduate school. I would like to have at least gotten my master's degree."

"It's certainly not too late for you to do that."

Jake smiled. He knew, of course, that Mr. Sinclair was right. Jake changed the subject by saying, "You know, Charles, you've got me thinking. There is an old saying I haven't thought of in years. It is that 'all the flowers of all the tomorrows are in the seeds of today.' And another old saying that goes with that one is 'No seed ever sees the flower.' I like both of those. Sometimes, I think, we can plant a seed without ever knowing whether it will sprout, grow and bloom or not. But, sometimes, just planting the seed is all we can do."

"Yes, I agree." He drew on his pipe but it had gone out. With matches, he tried to re-light it.

"Charles, in a way, you are planting seeds here."

Mr. Sinclair shook his head and said, "In a small way, we support a little outreach program over in Montreal. But we see our work here more as preserving seeds for future use rather than planting them."

"Tell me, do you think we are in the Biblical 'Last Days?'"

Mr. Sinclair was in the process of refreshing his pipe. He paused and then continued. After he had packed the tobacco down, he struck a match and lit his pipe. He looked at Jake and said, "Yes."

Jake nodded and said, "Me too."

"But," Mr. Sinclair continued, "one must be cautious. People, for hundreds of years, have thought that they were living in the 'Last Days' of the Bible."

"I know. I know. I've thought of that. However, it does seem like most everything is in place for the Second Coming of Christ."

"Yes, it does. But I do think that a few more things will happen prior to His return."

"Like?" Jake asked.

"Like the lessening of the United States."

"Lessening? You mean weakening?"

"Like Great Britain. One hundred years ago, in 1905,

Great Britain was the most powerful nation in the world. Today, it is barely a second-rate country. I think the same thing will happen to the U. S. prior to Christ's return."

"Yes, Charles, I can see that."

"Can you?"

"Yes. It fits."

Mr. Sinclair puffed on his pipe. "People won't like it."

"That's for sure. How will it happen, do you think?"

"Great Britain couldn't recover from the two World Wars. But America, I think, will be brought down from within."

There was a pause in the conversation as Mr. Sinclair drew deeply on his pipe and Jake was thinking.

Jake finally broke the silence by saying, "I think that you are probably right. America has turned away from God. Americans no longer respect our founding fathers and our history. God was an integral part of both. But today, God has been pushed aside. A nation that celebrates sin cannot continue to be blessed by God. Proverbs says, 'Righteousness exalts a nation, but sin is a reproach to any people.' You know, Charles, as I think about it, all it would take is two or three consecutive terms of a liberal democrat President to do some real damage to our country. Clinton is already expecting to have a coronation party in two thousand and eight. She could do a lot of harm rather quickly. And yet, you know what's strange to me – I genuinely cannot understand how anyone could actually vote for her."

Mr. Sinclair replied, "There may be some supernatural intervention involved. We may even get someone worse than her that could weaken us even faster than her."

"Yes."

"And, in my view, there are many many non-thinkers out there who vote."

Jake laughed. He said, "Jean told me of your non-thinkers. I think that they are also a sign that we are in the last days."

Mr. Sinclair pointed his pipe stem at Jake and said, "Yes! Yes! Exactly right. These non-thinkers go about their lives without any thought about what is taking place in the world. They aren't stupid; but they are ignorant and uneducated. Religion, to them, is old-fashioned. They are beyond that. It is now the twenty-first century. It is the digital age. They have evolved."

"Charles, I know many of your non-thinkers who live like that. However, there are still many Christians who believe and who live in America. I believe there are some things a Christian will do and some things a Christian will not do. The reason for both these actions is that the Holy Spirit has activated that spark of divinity, the soul, which is within all humans. This can only happen, of course, after one has accepted Jesus Christ as one's own personal savior. The Holy Spirit will then direct Christians to do some things and not to do other things. A non-Christian doesn't have this guidance. It is, of course, available to all. But only after one has accepted the gift of Christ."

"You are correct, Jake, in saying that there are still many Christians in America. But, as we progress in the last days, it will be more and more difficult for Christians to live as they wish."

"Yes, I suspect you are right about that."

"Jake, have you ever experienced a supernatural event?"

"Several. Let me tell you one that really opened my eyes and taught me an important lesson. This happened many years ago. I was in my early twenties. I had a pet dog – a large malamute. She was a beautiful animal and we were very very close. She weighed over a hundred pounds; and, she thought she made the perfect lap dog. I had gotten her as a puppy and named her 'Bo.' She quickly learned her name. I was single and living in my first house. It was just my puppy dog, Bo, and me. This was down in North Carolina. As always, before I did anything else, I let Bo outside as soon as I got up from sleeping. This particular morning, I was running a little late getting ready for work. I filled Bo's food bowl and water bowl. We had been living in this house for about seven months. Bo was eating her food on the back porch. I petted her 'goodbye' and walked through the house, picking up whatever I would need for the day, locked the front door and got in my car – which was parked in the driveway. I didn't have a garage. On this morning, I cranked up my car and noticed Bo running around the house toward the driveway. She lay down in the driveway right behind my car. She had never ever previously done anything like this. I got out of the car to see about her. I called her over to the side of the driveway. She wouldn't come. She just lay there behind my car. I grabbed her collar and tugged on it. She became dead weight. Over a hundred pounds of dead weight. I coaxed her. I petted her. I talked sweetly to her. I yelled at her. But she simply would not move. I was already running late. I did not need this. I could not understand it. She was supposed to be eating her food. She had never done anything like this. What had brought this on? She was determined not to move. I got back in my car, honked the horn and started moving slowly in reverse. Surely, I thought, she would get up and move. But no, she did not. I got out again. I was frustrated with her. Finally, I said, 'Bo, please get up and let me go to work.' And she did. She got up and ran back around the house to the back porch to finish eating. I didn't question it. I got in my car, put it in reverse and headed down the driveway. About a mile down the road was an intersection. My street had the right-of-way and the other street had to stop. As I neared the intersection, I saw that a terrible accident had happened just minutes earlier. Someone had not stopped at the intersection and had plowed into a car traveling on my street – that had the right-of-way. It occurred to me that, if I had left my home as usual, it may well have been me who would have been hit by the car that failed to stop. Bo had kept me from leaving. How had she known? Bo died of old age and I still miss her. But she never got behind my car again. In her whole life, that was the only time she ever did that.

"What I learned from that experience is to accept things as they occur without getting mad or upset. For instance, if I'm running late and I get a red light, I accept it. I tell myself . . . it is for the best. If I had made the green light, I may have been involved in an accident down the road. I still don't understand how that big old malamute dog knew what she knew but I'm still grateful to her for the lesson learned."

The whole time Jake had been telling the story about his dog, Mr. Sinclair had been smoking his pipe and listening intently. When Jake finished, Mr. Sinclair put his pipe down in a glass ashtray and said, "That is an amazing story. Animals often know more than we give them credit for knowing."

"True."

"What are you thinking now?"

Jake shook his head.

Mr. Sinclair smiled. He said, "For a moment there, you looked lost in thought."

"Oh, I guess I was thinking of the weakening of America."

"Regretting what must happen?"

"No, not regretting it. Just recognizing and remembering that Earth is not a Christian's home. Romans tells us not to conform to the patterns of this world. I was talking with Jean about death. At the time one leaves one's physical body, I do think that there is not a sense of regret or remorse but rather of relief. One is now going home to be with God. Earth was only a temporary place to visit. It provides us with the opportunity to accept the sacrifice that Jesus made for our salvation. Except for the time when Christ returns to set up His kingdom, a Christian's future is not connected with this planet, but rather, with Heaven."

Mr. Sinclair stated, "I do think that there are some perilous times ahead – not just for Christians but for all of humanity."

"You have a real Christian community here, don't you?"

"Yes, pretty much. We hope to be able to maintain it through the chaos to come. That is why secrecy is so important."

"Yes. I can see that it would be totally necessary. You would not be able to survive without your secrecy." As soon as Jake said this, he felt a twinge in his body. He suddenly felt that what he had just said was not true – was not accurate. But he didn't comment on this feeling.

"No, we wouldn't."

"Your secret is safe with me."

"I know that. Jean tells me that you seem to have a knack for discerning trends. Is that so?"

"Not really. I do read a lot and I respect history. That, and a little common sense mixed with a little critical thinking provides me with the 'knack' that Jean sees . . . Just curious. How does Jean tell you all these things?"

"By email primarily. Sometimes by voicemail."

"I see."

"It's the twenty-first century. Tell me, what do you see for the future of this century?"

"Wow! That's rather a broad request. As I told Jean, I cannot predict the future. Right now, I feel a sense of spiritual darkness descending and spreading itself all across our planet. I choose to avoid that darkness and yield to the guidance of the Holy Spirit and live in the Light."

CHAPTER TWENTY-FOUR

"But the fruit of the Spirit is love, joy, peace, patience, kindness, goodness, faithfulness, gentleness and self-control."

– Galatians 5:22-23

Mid 1st Century A.D.

Mr. Sinclair knocked the cold ashes from his pipe and began refilling it.

He asked Jake, "Where's your pipe?"

"I left it in the tent."

"Ahh, yes, of course. Tell me, Jake, as we are now entering the Age of Aquarius, this is supposed to be the dawning of enlightenment. People are supposed to be operating at a higher level of consciousness. There is to be peace in the world. What do you think?"

"I think peace in the world is a fine sentiment. But I'm afraid it is not very realistic. The twentieth century was full of wars. I can see nothing ahead for the twenty-first century that is going to change that. I don't think that there will be peace on earth until Jesus returns. I think most world leaders are devoid of true spiritual awareness. Let me give you an example. Suppose, just suppose that the leaders of Israel said to the Palestinians and the leaders of the Muslim countries around Israel 'We are going to lay down all of our weapons. We are going to park our tanks and aircraft. We will not fight any longer. We want to live in peace with you.' What would happen? . . . In a week, there would be no Israel and millions of Jewish people would be dead. Now suppose, just suppose that the Palestinians and the leaders of the

Muslim countries around Israel said 'We are going to lay down all of our weapons. We are going to park our tanks and aircraft. We will not fight any longer. We want to live in peace with you.' What would happen? Within a week, there would be peace in the Middle East. That's never going to happen. However, I think that peace can lie within each individual – it is not going to be found out in the world. The world has rejected the Prince of Peace. The result of that rejection can only be chaos and war."

"Yes Jake, I agree. I also think that the twenty-first century will not be one of peace. I do, however, sincerely believe that Christ will return during the twenty-first century."

"Wouldn't that be wonderful? Obviously, a rhetorical question. Charles, why do you think so?"

"Oh, I don't have any formulas or numbers worked out showing the return date of Jesus Christ. I just have a feeling that He will return this century. Things are in place. And the trends I see make me suspect that His return is not too terribly far away. I expect the next ten to twenty years will be very instructive."

"Might I ask you an important question?" Jake was a little hesitant and he wanted to preface his question with an explanation.

Puffing on his pipe, Mr. Sinclair responded by simply saying, "Of course."

Jake smiled. He said, "You know the story of the man who climbs a mountain to ask the wise old man who lives in a cave on top of the mountain a question. The wise man listens and responds with an answer that is usually a punch line or else something so confusing, it makes no sense. Something like 'When the grasshopper flies upside down on a calm day, you must transverse the solar eclipse and be one with the ultimate essence.' It can sound profound but it means nothing. I want to ask you something and I would like to get a straight answer."

"You are putting me in the role of the old wise man?"

Jake smiled. "Perhaps you are not old enough to fit the role of old man. But, yes, I do put you in the role of wise man. Jean concurs with that assessment."

Mr. Sinclair smiled. "That's kind. Perhaps too kind. Nonetheless, if I know the answer to your question, I'll give it to you straight."

"Thank you. That man who climbs the mountain – he wants to know why he is here. He wants to know the meaning of life. People often feel as if they are on a quest to unravel the mystery of their existence. We are all here to do something. Why are we here? What is the purpose of life? What is it that we are all to do? What is it that we are to do with our lives?"

Jake left it like that. Mr. Sinclair did not respond right away. He looked at Jake but did not appear to be looking at him, but rather, at his soul. He watched the smoke slowly drift upwards from his pipe. After almost three minutes of silence, Mr. Sinclair looked right in Jake's eyes and said, "**Learn**."

"What?"

"Learn. Just . . . learn."

"That is the meaning of life?"

"Yes."

"That is what we are to do with our lives?"

"Yes."

"I love to learn."

"As you Southerners say, *there ya go*."

Jake smiled. "I like it. It's encompassing and it makes sense."

Mr. Sinclair responded by stating, "To know is my reason for existing."

CHAPTER TWENTY-FIVE

"Those who are led by the Spirit of God are the sons of God."

– Romans 8:14

Mid 1st Century A.D.

Jake noticed that Mr. Sinclair was getting tired. They had been talking for over four hours. Jake shook hands with Mr. Sinclair, told him how much he appreciated the conversation and excused himself.

Staring at the hallway, he tried to remember how Mr. Le Couteau had led him there. Jake soon realized he had not been paying attention. Hoping to run into someone, he walked down the hallway and turned left. Another hallway. He walked down it until he came to an intersection and turned right. Another hallway. Up ahead, he saw a couple walking down the hallway and decided to follow them. They led him to the cafeteria.

After getting his tray of food, Jake sat down at the same table he had previously used with Mr. Le Couteau, Laura and Peggy. Sitting by himself, Jake thought, *At least Mr. Sinclair didn't offer me his job. That's a good thing.*

Jake was just about to put his first forkful of mashed potatoes in his mouth when someone placed their hand on his shoulder and said, "You just met with Mr. Sinclair. How is he?"

A young couple in their mid-thirties moved from behind him and smiled big smiles at him. Jake put his fork down. They introduced themselves, shook hands with Jake and repeated their question.

Jake returned their smiles and said, "He's fine."

Having heard the conversation, a man in his late forties or early fifties walked up and said, "I've been here almost five years and I've only seen him once . . . from a distance. What was it like to visit in his study?"

Jake replied, "It was nice. Very nice. I enjoyed it."

The three of them just stood there looking at Jake as if they expected him to say more. Another couple, this one in the mid-twenties, joined the group and stared at Jake. Out of curiosity, others walked over until many people surrounded Jake's table. One man asked what he and Mr. Sinclair had discussed. A woman wanted to know if it was true that he had spent all morning with Mr. Sinclair. Jake wanted to be polite but was at a loss to know how to handle the situation. More people were walking toward his table.

All of a sudden, a loud woman's voice said, "Jake Fleming, you promised to meet me in the library. What are you doing here?" She pushed her way through the crowd, grabbed Jake by the arm and led him out of the cafeteria. It was Peggy.

Once in the hallway, she pulled him along and said, "Hurry up. They'll probably follow us. Hopefully, they'll go to the library. This way!"

"Thanks Peggy. Where are we going?"

"The English Pub rec room. I presume you are hungry?"

"Yes. I didn't get a single bite before that crowd arrived. I didn't have a chance to eat any breakfast – but that's all right. I frequently go without breakfast." Jake realized he was rambling. He shut up.

After a few more turns in the hallways, Jake asked, "Peggy, what was that all about?"

"You just spent all morning with Mr. Sinclair. In the last twenty years, no one has done that. That makes you sort-of a celebrity around here. They didn't mean any harm – they are just curious about Mr. Sinclair. Here we go – in here."

Jake walked through the door and it looked like the same club or sandwich bar that he had previously visited with Laura. There were seven or eight people already there. They were eating hamburgers and fries. Jake sat down at a booth.

"Scoot over." Jake scooted over and Peggy sat down next to Jake and asked, "What would you like?" She had a really cute smile.

Jake looked up at the menu on the wall behind the bar. He replied, "A turkey club." Peggy answered, "I'll be right back."

It took about fifteen minutes but Peggy returned with two trays – one with a turkey club with fries and a soft drink and the other with a hamburger with fries and a soft drink. While she was waiting on their orders, Jake had looked at the others who were in booths against the opposite wall. He was relieved to notice that they were not paying any attention at all to him. Peggy pushed his tray forward and sat down directly across from him in the booth.

Jake said, "Thanks. And thanks for rescuing me from the cafeteria. I appreciate it. I owe you one."

"You're welcome. It was almost funny. You looked lost in there."

"I was. I don't understand what they expected me to say."

"Jake, there is no reason for you to know – but Mr. Sinclair is looked upon as something as a mystic, a wise man full of the Holy Spirit. He is viewed with awe around here. People have tremendous respect for him."

"Yes, I could tell that from the way Jean talks about him. But I didn't know . . . okay, I guess I understand now. Thanks."

Jake took a bite of his sandwich. "Ummm, that's good." He put mustard on his French fries and started on them.

Looking over at Peggy, Jake said, "Peggy, I'd like to ask you a question. I . . ."

"Shoot."

"You're a woman. I . . ."

"What was your first clue?"

Jake laughed. "Now, that's funny."

Peggy smiled her cute little pixie smile.

"I want to ask you something serious."

"Okay."

"I am wondering how much of a problem it might be for…no, that's not right. What I mean is, well, first of all, I really do like Laura. But I'm concerned about trying to have a serious relationship with her."

"Why? What's wrong?"

"Two things. One, our age difference. I'm thinking I may be too old for her. What do you think?"

Peggy laughed. She replied, "I don't think you're too old for me."

Jake looked surprised.

Peggy said, "Seriously, you are not too old for Laura."

"Really?"

"Yes, really. What's the second thing?"

"The second thing? Oh. I was wondering how I could . . . date Laura – with her in here and me outside."

"I understand. I see what you're saying. To answer you on that one, I really don't know. I'm not aware of it ever being done. I guess you guys would just have to find a way to work it out."

"I guess. Of course, she may have no interest in working anything out with me. I guess I'm being presumptuous."

"The best thing you can do is to talk with her about it."

"Thank you, Peggy. That is good advice."

"Speaking of the devil."

Jake turned around to see Laura approaching their booth. Laura sat down next to Peggy. Jake told her how Peggy had rescued him from the cafeteria.

Laura laughed. She said, "That explains it."

"Explains what?" Peggy asked.

"The crowd of people in the library. They said that they were expecting you, Jake. When you didn't show up, I thought I'd take a peek in here to see if you found anything to eat."

"Thanks. Yeah, this is good." He nodded at Peggy and said, "Thanks to Peggy."

"Laura, Jake has a question, or two, to ask you." Peggy smiled.

Jake looked shocked. He didn't want to discuss it with

Laura with Peggy and all the people around. He said, "I need to make a phone call."

Under her breath but probably loud enough for both Laura and Jake to hear, Peggy said, "Chicken."

Laura said, "What?"

Peggy replied, "Jake, you can't get a signal here – even above ground."

"No, Mr. Le Couteau said there was a secure land line I could use."

Laura said, "There is. I can set it up for you but maybe it's something Mr. Le Couteau should handle."

"I don't know. Mr. Le Couteau invited me to stay on for a few more days. I need to call that canoe rental company and let them know that I'm all right. If I don't call, they'll think I fell in the river and lost their canoe."

Peggy giggled. Laura smiled and said she could handle that call. Jake said he'd have to paddle the canoe back to his tent to get the phone number and paddle back. Laura said that that would be fine. For something like this, they always used the phone in the Christmas tree company office. Once he had the number, they could go there and make the call. Laura was glad that Jake was staying longer. So was Jake.

Later that afternoon, Laura walked down the forest path with Jake to his canoe. His life jacket had been placed in the guest apartment he was using. They had stopped and picked it up for the journey to his campsite. Jake was carrying it.

Looking at the canoe and with a big smile on his face, Jake turned to Laura and asked, "You wanna ride?"

Laura replied, "I don't know if I should."

"Why?"

"I don't know how to swim."

"You can wear this life jacket. With it on, you can't sink."

"What about you?"

"I know how to swim."

"Okay, I guess."

"Just don't stand up in the canoe and we'll be fine."

"Okay."

Jake paddled the canoe across the lake to his campsite. On the way, he tried to bring up the thing about their age differences but could not think of a way to get it into the conversation without it sounding contrived or weird. So he didn't. On the way back, maybe, he thought.

Laura was on the front seat and enjoying the ride.

She turned to Jake and said, "This is fun."

"I think so too," Jake replied.

Almost to his campsite, Laura said, "Jake?"

"Yes?"

"There is a label here near the front of the canoe. It has the name of the rental company and their phone number."

"Really?"

"Yes, really. We didn't need to leave the shore."

"I'm glad we did. I enjoyed our ride together."

"Me too."

"I might as well check out the tent. It looks just like I left it. No bears or wolves, it appears."

"You'd have more problems with raccoons than bears or wolves."

"Yeah, I know."

Once on shore, Jake went to his tent, unzipped it and walked inside. He looked around. Nothing had been bothered. Other than his camera, he couldn't think of anything he wanted to take back with him.

"Wow! I had no idea it'd be so big inside." Laura had followed him in the tent.

"Laura, would they mind if I brought my camera back?"

"I don't know."

"What if I just took photos of people – no rooms, not the chapel or library or anything?"

"I don't know. Who do you want a photo of?"

"You."

"I've got photos of me. I'll be glad to give you one."

"Okay."

"Why do you want a photo of me?'

"So I can look at you every day."

Laura smiled. She thought, *I can think of a better way of doing that.* But she said, "That's nice."

Standing near his fire pit, with the small sandy cove and the lake in the background, Jake turned to face Laura. He opened his arms and she stepped closer. They hugged each other. Jake looked in her eyes and they kissed long and deeply. Still holding each other, Jake put his lips next to her ear and whispered, "That's nice." He kissed her ear and they parted from their hug.

Jake said, "I guess we'd better get back."

"I guess."

The ride back was thoughtful. Both of them were thinking *Where do we go from here?*

They both tried some "small talk" but it fell flat. It was a pretty sunny afternoon and they enjoyed the canoe ride on the lake.

Back on shore, Laura said, "Let's write the number down."

Jake said, "No need, let me see it." He read the number from the label and said, "Got it. Let's go."

They went to the Christmas tree office. From there, Jake made his call. While he was talking with the rental company, he said, "You want the number of the canoe?" Laura turned and looked at Jake with concern. Jake replied, "No, I've got it. It's zero five, three one, one nine four five. He finished his call and he and Laura returned to "Neverland."

Laura asked, "Hungry?"

"Yeah, a little bit."

"Cafeteria or Pub?"

"Pub. Let's get our booth."

And they did.

And they stayed in "their" booth for over four hours. They told each other about their families, about their childhoods, about their colleges, about their hobbies and interests and events that had happened in their lives. They simply spent the evening getting to know each other.

Toward the end of the evening, Laura asked Jake, "Tell me the truth. Did you know that that phone number was in the front of the canoe?"

Jake smiled. He said, "I'd like to say that I did and I pretended that I didn't just so we could spend some time together. But the truth is that I really was not aware of it. I had always packed my camping stuff there and it blocked my view. When I was out on the lake, I just didn't notice it. I was always in the back seat and couldn't read the label from there even if I had noticed it. I must say, the truth is that I am glad I wasn't aware of it. I really did enjoy our canoe trip. It made me realize that I like just being with you. We don't have to be having great discussions like we had tonight. We don't have to be doing anything. I like just being with you."

Laura smiled a cute coy smile. She said, "That's nice."

Jake laughed and said, "It is, isn't it?"

"That's nice" became a phrase with special meaning to both of them.

Just as they were getting ready to leave, Mr. Le Couteau walked over and said hello. He said to Jake, "I understand you made your phone call."

"Yes."

He looked at Laura and smiled. He said, "Good."

Jake asked Mr. Le Couteau if he could use the library. He told him that Mr. Sinclair has said something that gave him an idea and he'd like to do a little research on the subject.

Mr. Le Couteau responded by simply saying, "Of course."

Laura walked Jake back to the guest apartment. They both wanted for Laura to come in and stay awhile. However, they knew that people might get the wrong idea. At the door, they gave each other a long kiss and a tight hug.

Inside, Jake thought to himself that Laura had already answered his concern about their age differences. He was confused. Being around Laura made him feel like an awkward teenager. Why? He knew that he liked her – liked her a lot. He enjoyed being with her but being with her made him feel uneasy. When they were separated, like they were at that point, he missed her and thought about her. Was he falling in love? They had only known each other for such a short time, could one fall in love that quickly?

Jake said, "Jesus, be with me. Thank you, Jesus."

CHAPTER TWENTY-SIX

"Even so, when you see all these things, you know that it is near, right at the door. I tell you the truth, this generation will certainly not pass away until all these things have happened."

– Matthew 24:34

Mid 1st Century A.D.

After showering and shaving, Jake skipped breakfast and went straight to the library. He quickly found resources he wanted and began to conduct his research. The area of his interest was one that had been previously extensively researched and "experts" had arrived at a variety of explanations. Jake wanted to come to his own conclusions as clearly as he could.

For the next three days, Jake spent all his waking hours in the library. The result of his research is the following brief paper:

The Last Days?
A Brief Analysis by Jake Fleming

Are we living in the Last Days? More and more churches, and even entire denominations, have rejected the eternal truths given to us in the Holy Bible. They say we have progressed, we have evolved, beyond the need to obey God and, consequently, they have turned away from God's directions. The consequences of doing so are clearly explained in the Bible. However, people who have turned from God no longer believe His Word.

Some protestant denominations and even some "Christians" are questioning not only the divinity of Jesus Christ but also even whether He ever existed. Those who accept Jesus as a historical person say that He was a good teacher. Good teachers don't lie. He said He was the Son of God! He said He was the only way to God! He said He died on the cross so that those who believe in Him could have their sins forgiven! Those are extraordinarily strong statements to make. A large majority of people do not believe them to be true. I believe!

Jesus also made another extremely strong statement. He said He would return. In John 14:3, He clearly states that He will come back and take believers with Him to His Father's house. In Acts 1:11, two angels appeared to Jesus' disciples as they were watching Him ascend up into the sky among the clouds. The angels told the disciples that Jesus would come back in the same way that He left. Jesus told his disciples in Matthew 24:27 that His return would be like a bolt of lightning. In Matthew 24:42-44, Jesus said to keep watch and be prepared. In Matthew 24:32-33, Jesus uses the parable of the fig tree so that we can know the season of His return.

Over the past 20 centuries, people have been predicting exactly when Jesus will return. Obviously, they have all been wrong. In Matthew 24:36, Jesus clearly stated, referring to His return, "No man knows about that day or hour, not even the angels in heaven, nor the Son, but only the Father." No one will ever be able to say that Jesus will return on a specific day or even a specific year. However, Jesus did use the parable of the fig tree so that we can discern the season of His return.

What will the "season" of Jesus' return look like? Jesus told us. He said, in Matthew 24:37, "As it was in the days of Noah, so it will be at the coming of the Son of Man." In Luke 17:28-30, Jesus compares the days leading up to His return as the same as it was in Sodom. What was it like in Sodom and Gomorrah and in Noah's time? Only three people, Lot and his two daughters, survived the destruction of Sodom and Gomorrah. Only eight people were permitted to enter the Ark. In Genesis 18 and 19, we see that Sodom and Gomorrah's sin was "grievous." Homosexuality was rampant and accepted. The people had turned away from God. In Genesis 6, we find that people, prior to the flood, had become wicked, violent, corrupt and . . . had turned away from God. A summation of what people will be like in the Last Days is given in II Timothy 3:1-9. In part, it says, "There will be terrible times in the last days. People will be lovers of themselves, lovers of money, boastful, proud, abusive, disobedient to their parents, ungrateful, unholy, without love, unforgiving, slanderous, without self-control, brutal, not lovers of the good, treacherous, rash, conceited, lovers of pleasure rather than lovers of God – having a form of godliness but denying its power." This section of Timothy continues by stating that people will be "swayed by all kinds of evil desires, always learning but never able to acknowledge the truth."

For those of us now living in the 21st century, in what has been called the "Information Age" and the "Digital Age," that last phrase is particularly interesting. Today, with Internet access, anyone can punch in a few keys and obtain information on any subject. We can constantly be learning about anything that interests us. However, with all this available knowledge, wisdom often eludes us. We often still refuse to see the truth.

The above tells us what people will be like in the Last Days. What will the world be like in the Last Days?

In Matthew 24:4-8, Jesus told us what would be happening at the beginning of the Last Days. He said that there would be false prophets, people claiming to be doing the work of Christ, some even claiming to be Christ, and there would be wars and rumors of war, famines and earthquakes all over the globe. It is now 2005 and wars and rumors of war are the norm. There are hundreds of cults around the world pretending to be following the direction of God. Hundreds of people die every day from starvation. Seismologists today record approximately 12,000 separate earthquakes every single day. Most of these are small and do no damage. However, they are large enough to be measured and recorded. In Revelation 6:8, one of the signs of the

Last Days is plagues and pestilence. Look at some of the diseases currently causing serious problems – even death: the HIV epidemic, typhoid, Legionnaire's Disease, malaria, cholera, Hoof and Mouth, Mad Cow, West Nile, Dengue Fever, Tuberculosis, flesh-eating bacteria and a huge increase in sexually transmitted diseases. It seems that old diseases that we thought were gone keep popping back up and are more resistant to antibiotics. It seems that, almost every year, some new virus or disease arrives on the world scene.

Jesus followed all of these statements about the last days prior to his return by flatly stating, in Matthew 24:14, "And this gospel of the kingdom will be preached in the whole world as a testimony to all nations, *and then the end will come.*" The italics are mine. Jesus said the Good News of Himself as the Savior, as the only Way to Heaven, would be available to all the nations of the entire world. Once this had been accomplished, the end would come. He did not say that all people must hear the gospel but that all countries would be exposed to it. In the 20th century, most nations did hear the gospel preached in their countries. Today, with the Internet, the gospel is available to every single nation.

Recorded in Matthew 24 and 25, Mark 13 and Luke 21, in response to questions from His disciples, what has become known as the Olivet Discourse was presented by Jesus. These passages are called that because Jesus spoke them while He was on Mt. Olivet in Jerusalem. Sometimes, these passages are called the end times messages. Jesus' answers to His disciples' questions refer to the generation of people who will be living on earth when He returns. In Matthew 24:34, Jesus said, "I tell you the truth, this generation will certainly not pass away until all these things have happened." The fig tree refers to the nation of Israel. Consequently, with the parable of the fig tree, we can know the season of Christ's return – but not the exact date.

Perhaps the most intriguing and fascinating of all the prophesies is the one stated by Jesus given above in Matthew 24:34. The obvious questions from that statement are when does that generation begin and how long is a generation?

Looking into these questions, I have been amazed at the mathematical formulas used to determine the average length, in years, of a generation. One interesting such formula takes the generations from Adam to Noah, from Noah to David, from David to Jesus and divides them by the years involved and comes up with a generation figure of 49 years. This researcher then determined that the Jewish recapture of Jerusalem in 1967 was the beginning of the generation that Jesus mentioned in Matthew 24:34. This would mean that between 1967 (adding 49 years) and 2016, Jesus would return. There are numerous such formulas "out there." I don't think that averaging lifespans, beginning with Adam, has any real validity. Initially, it was normal, in pre-flood times, for people to live for hundreds of years. However, for the last three thousand years, from King David's time, people lived approximately 70 – 80 years. The Bible is actually straightforward about the length of a generation. In Psalm 90:10, it states, "The length of our days is seventy years – or eighty, if we have the strength." A generation could accurately be said to be between 70 and 80 years.

Now, just to make sure we are all on the same page, let's look at Christ's return. There are actually two. The first is referred to as the Rapture. This is when Christ returns in the clouds as He departed in view of His disciples. This is the event that begins the seven-year tribulation period. Jesus takes His believers back to heaven with Him. He does not set foot on the earth. Seven years later, Christ returns and establishes His Kingdom on earth. This return to earth is the return usually referred to in Biblical prophecy.

We know the length of a generation (70-80 years) and we know the final event (Christ's return to set up His Kingdom on earth). What we don't know for sure is exactly when the Last Days generation begins.

There are numerous explanations of what event heralds the beginning of the Last Days' generation. After examining most of these, my conclusion is that the fulfillment of the prophesy of Isaiah 66:8 is the most likely beginning event of the Last Days generation. This is the prophesy which states that the nation of Israel, in one day, will be reborn. On May 15, 1948, Israel was reborn as a new sovereign and independent nation. This prophesy was made approximately 2,500 years before it was fulfilled in 1948. We can infer from this that the Rapture will take place sometime between now and 2021. Not very far away. What a glorious day that will be! The math, which I freely admit may be totally wrong, I have figured this way: from 1948, add 80 years; this gives us the maximum year 2028; subtract seven years from 2028 (the tribulation period) and we have a maximum date of 2021. It could actually be any day between now and then. Of course, I fully recognize that the establishment of Israel in one day may not be the "trigger" for the beginning of the Last Days generation. That is only a logical guess. I am completely aware that it is a guess. The Roman Empire destroyed Israel as a nation. The last resistance took place in 73 A.D. From this date until 1948, Israel did not exist as a nation. As it was predicted in Isaiah, Israel was reborn in one day. I find that amazing! However, I must accept that it may have nothing to do with the Last Days generation. Some people think that 1967 is the trigger year. This is when, after two thousand years, Jerusalem once again became the capital of Israel. Of course, there may not be a trigger event at all.

However, if we are truly living in the Last Days, I began to wonder, "What is the role of the United States?" The United States, economically and militarily, is the most powerful nation in the world. Surely it must be highly involved in the events of the Last Days.

Over the past few days, as I have researched the Last Days, I began to realize that perhaps America would not be a leader in these events. How could that be? The answer, it seems to me, is that the power and importance of the United States will need to rapidly decline.

I love studying history. It is time, in this look at the Last Days, to look at history. My primary source for the following information is the Bible – specifically I and II Kings. It can seem a little confusing at times but I have tried to boil it down to its essence. About 750 B. C., there were two distinct countries – two separate kingdoms. One was called Israel and the other, Judah. This followed the split of the twelve tribes of ancient Israel. The nation of Judah consisted of the two tribes of Judah and Benjamin. The other ten tribes were joined together as the kingdom of Israel. Jeroboam was the king of Israel. He was concerned that the people of the ten tribes might wish to reunite with the kingdom of Judah. Judah's capital was Jerusalem and there was a strong tradition of worshiping in Jerusalem. Consequently, Jeroboam changed and created a new religious system for the people of Israel. He forced them to worship idols of gold and even the false god Baal. The Levites were among the most educated of the tribes and many of them left Israel and returned to live in Judah. Baal was the "sun god." His day of worship was the first day of the week. Not only did Israel ignore God's Sabbath but, according to II Kings 17:16, they ignored all of God's commands. As a result of this total turning away from God, Israel was defeated by the Assyrians and the people of Israel were deported to Assyria. This was a three-year war (721 B. C. - 718 B. C.) and the Israelites were taken into slavery. Assyria was located east of the Black Sea and south of the Caspian Sea. Not long after their captivity, the Assyrians migrated, taking the Israelites, as slaves, with them. They moved to the area that is now known as Germany. After several generations, the Israelites, who had forgotten the ways of their ancestors, assimilated and gained their independence. The migrated and settled in what is now known as Denmark, Belgium, Scandinavia, France, England and Scotland. This is how these ten tribes of Israel became lost to history.

However, they did not become lost to God. The word "British" actually comes from the Hebrew language. The Hebrew word "b'rith" translates as "covenant." The Hebrew word "ish" translates as "man." British means covenant man. God fulfilled his covenant with Abraham through the British people by means of their colonizing throughout the world. Briefly, we need to understand that God gave his birthright promise to the two sons of Josèph, Ephraim and Manasseh. It is through them that God's covenant with Abraham would be accomplished. Just to be sure we are all together with this, let's step back and look at a summary of God's covenant with Abraham. It is stated in Genesis 22:17 – 18 – "I will surely bless you and make your descendants as numerous as the stars in the sky and as the sand on the seashore. Your descendants will take possession of the cities of their enemies, and through your offspring all nations on earth will be blessed, because you have obeyed me." This is God's promise. It includes national wealth, prosperity and territorial expansion – all accomplished through the descendants of Jacob's grandsons – Ephraim and Manasseh.

Using the day-for-a-year concept, as clearly explained in Numbers 14:34, God punished the Israelites for refusing to obey Him by making them wander for 40 years before allowing them to inherit the Promised Land. By the same method, when Israel disobeyed God by rejecting His commandments, God allowed them to be taken into captivity. He said he would punish them seven times for their sins (Leviticus 26:18). One year equaled 360 days. Again, using the day-for-a-year principle, seven times 360 years equals 2,520 years. This is how long God would punish Israel, including the descendants of Ephraim and Manasseh, before granting them the promises of the birthright blessings. If we add 2,520 years to the time of Israel's defeat and captivity (721 B.C. - 718 B.C.), we arrive at the dates of 1800 A.D. - 1803 A.D.

Prior to 1800 A.D., both Great Britain and the United States were small and somewhat unimportant nations. Great Britain had just lost a war to its own upstart colonies. It had been at war with France for years and was financially drained. We are talking about the 1700s. Right after the turn of the 19th century, amazing things began to happen for both nations. Great Britain quickly became the county with the most powerful navy in the world. It used that power to expand and quickly built an empire (Canada, Australia, South Africa, India, etc.). Thomas Jefferson became President of the United States and, in 1803, purchased the Louisiana Territory. This more than doubled the size of the United States and led the way for additional expansion all the way to the Pacific Ocean. God keeps His promises. He now fulfilled His promise to the descendants of Ephraim and Manasseh.

Between 1800 and 1950, Great Britain and the United States controlled almost every single important resource on the globe. They had joined forces to defeat Germany, Japan and Italy in the Second World War. In 1950, the United States was the undisputed world leader economically, militarily, technologically and agriculturally. For example, in 1950, the U. S. produced the majority of the world's supply of oil, coal, steel, copper, tin, iron, lead, aluminum, zinc, nickel, food and many many more natural resources and products. Fifty years later – not so much. What happened?

Thomas Jefferson wrote, "How little do my countrymen know what precious blessings they are in possession of, and which no other people on earth enjoy. Can these liberties of a nation be thought secure when we have removed their only firm basis, a conviction in the minds of the people that these liberties are a gift of God? That they are not to be violated but with His wrath?" George Washington said, "It is the duty of all nations to acknowledge the Providence of Almighty God, to obey His will, to be grateful for benefits, and humbly to implore His protection, aid, and favor." Abraham Lincoln proclaimed a national day of fasting and prayer. In doing so, he said, "It is the duty of nations as well as men, to own their dependence upon the overruling of God. All should recognize the sublime truth that those nations only are blessed whose God is the Lord." Now, in the early part of the 21st century, we are clearly a nation in decline. Why? As the three U. S. Presidents quoted above said, we must acknowledge and obey God. We are no longer doing that. We have, instead, turned away from God. We, as a nation, are now ignoring God's laws and commandments. We have taken God out of our schools. We have removed God from the "public square."

We have "evolved" from all that "Biblical superstition." In return, God is removing his special blessings on us.

For the United States, the decline will accelerate. It has already happened to Great Britain. Great Britain never recovered from World War II and it has instituted socialist policies that have further weakened it. As a nation, it has turned away from God. It is no longer a major international power. America is also turning away from God. This will hasten the decline of America.

In the Last Days, most likely Russia will join Iran, several northern African countries and the Islamic nations in an alliance against Israel. There are some strong indications that China will join this alliance. I am hopeful that the United States will always side with Israel but I realize that that can change quickly.

Prophesies from over 2,000 years ago are now in the process of coming true. Since 1948, numerous ancient prophesies have happened. In 1967, after more than two thousand years, Jerusalem once again became the capital of the nation of Israel. As I write this in 2005, the United States has still not recognized Jerusalem as the capital of Israel. One day soon, it will. In God's own time. We can read about prophesies being fulfilled almost daily in our newspapers (and the newspaper journalists have no idea). The next fifteen to twenty-five years should be full of them. As the countdown gets closer and closer, it will become more and more apparent to Christians all over the world that the time is near for Christ's return. Christians will see the supernatural power of God directing world events. It will be a time of some horrible atrocities – both against Christians and non-Christians. Non-Christians won't have any idea why what is happening is happening. They won't even question it fully. They will accept the cultural decline of America and, for many of them, see it as a good thing.

One thing I must address is a statement that Jesus made in Matthew 23:39. He is talking about Jerusalem. He says he will not return until Jerusalem invites Him by saying, "Blessed is he who comes in the name of the Lord." This is what the people of Jerusalem were saying when Jesus rode into the city a week prior to his crucifixion. It was necessary for Israel to have Jerusalem as its capital in order that the people of Jerusalem, the Jewish leaders, could invite Jesus to return to Jerusalem. They haven't yet done this – but they will. In God's own time. Whether this will be done prior to the Rapture or prior to the Second Coming, no one knows. Jesus doesn't actually set foot on the ground during the Rapture but, of course, he does during the Second Coming seven years later.

If you have read this and are not now a Christian who has repented of your sins, accepted Jesus as Lord and Savior, know that He died on the cross for your sins and, on the third day, conquered death, it is time for you to do so. It is time for everyone to do so. I know that most people won't but, for those who do, it will change your life. The Holy Spirit will activate your soul and, when Jesus does return, you will be one of His.

I conclude this brief study by stating that I believe that Jesus is the Messiah, the Christ, the Son of the living God and my personal Savior. I also believe that the signs Jesus gave us indicate that we are truly in the Last Days.

– Jake Fleming

It was Saturday, June Fourth and, at seven o'clock in the morning, there was a knock on Jake's door. The knock awakened Jake. Usually an early riser, he had gone to bed at around five-thirty. He stayed up until he finished entering his brief essay on the Last Days into a computer. He printed out four copies – one for Mr. Le Couteau, one for Mr. Sinclair, one for Laura and one for himself.

Jake heard the knock again. He glanced at the clock. Seven? Morning? Or night? He literally stumbled to the bedroom door. Passing a mirror on the dresser, he noticed he was only wearing a pair of briefs. Looking in the closet, he heard the knock yet once again. He shouted to the living room, "Just a minute!"

He found a bathrobe and, while walking to the door, put it on. He was wrapping the sash around his waist as he opened the door.

It was Laura.

"Hi," she smiled.

Jake snapped out of his stupor. He returned her smile and said, "It's good to see you." He stood there staring at her.

She asked, "May I come in?"

"Yes. Yes, of course. Sorry. I'm afraid I'm not fully awake yet."

"I woke you up, didn't I?"

"Yes. But that's all right. It's always good to see you."

"I'm sorry. I'll come back later."

"No, no. I'm fine."

"You look like you've been up all night."

"Almost."

"I'll let you get back to sleep."

"No, don't go. I'm all right. I probably couldn't get back to sleep anyway. I'll put some coffee on."

"Let me. You go get dressed and wake up."

Jake handed Laura a copy of his Last Days research. "Here. This is what I've been working on for the last three days. I want you to have a copy. You can read it while I shave and get dressed."

Laura went into the kitchen and started a pot of coffee. She returned to the living room, sat on the couch and read Jake's paper.

Meanwhile, Jake showered, shaved and put on some clean clothes. He could smell fresh coffee.

He walked into the living room and saw Laura sitting on the sofa. She was sniffling and crying.

Jake walked over, sat down next to her and asked, "What's wrong?"

Pointing at Jake's paper on the coffee table, Laura asked, "Is that true?"

"It's truly my best guess. Only time will reveal whether or not it is truly accurate."

"But that's so soon."

"If Israel becoming a nation in one day is the trigger, so to speak, that means Jesus will be returning soon. But Jesus never mentioned a trigger. He gave signs and indications of things that will be occurring just prior to His return. But no one really knows."

"It's scary."

"I think it's wonderful. For Christ to actually be here on Earth as the Ruler of Earth. No more wars. No more murders or crime. No more sickness and ill health. Only peace, joy and love. We will actually physically be living in His light."

"But you said the Rapture would probably take place between now and 2021? That's only sixteen years. I thought . . . I thought I'd have more time."

"Laura, for Christians, it is nothing to worry about. It is a time to rejoice. Ancient prophesy is being fulfilled right in front of our eyes."

"Tell me something that is being fulfilled that you didn't put in your paper."

"Okay. In Isaiah, chapter forty-one, it says that when Israel is once again a nation, the desert land will bloom with several varieties of trees. It even names them. Since 1948 and continuing to our present time, Israel has reclaimed desert land and planted thousands and thousands of those trees. From the air, much of Israel looks green. This prophesy was made about two thousand and five hundred years ago – and it is coming true today."

"It takes some getting used to."

"I understand that. I also understand that the rebirth of Israel as a nation in one day may not be a trigger event. There may not even be a trigger event. Some people think that the results of the Six-Day War in which Israel captured the ancient old city part of Jerusalem in 1967 is the trigger event. As Christians, we are to keep watching for Jesus' return. There will be no warning. We won't have a week to prepare for His return. It happens in a flash. Two people will be standing together and one will suddenly disappear and one will be left behind."

"I don't know. I just thought there would be more time to . . . I don't know, I'm just surprised by the quickness of it all." Laura shook her head.

"Historically, there have been numerous people who thought they had figured out the exact date of Jesus' return. They convinced themselves and others to sell all their possessions. They gave the money to the poor. They then stood around and, on the predicted day, waited patiently for Jesus to appear. Laura, I think that we have to continue living our lives as humans but with the expectation that Jesus may return at any time. It may be next year, it may be in twenty years or it may be in a hundred years. No one really knows. Jesus said that."

Laura smiled.

"Realize Laura, if we are really in the Last Days, in the next ten to fifteen years, we are going to see things happening, on a global level, that are unprecedented. These unprecedented things will begin happening over and over all around the world. Things that today we think would never happen will happen in the next ten years."

"Give me an example."

Jake got up, filled two mugs with coffee and returned to the living room. He set the mugs on the coffee table and sat back down next to Laura.

"Okay. If we are now living in the Last Days, homosexuality will become an accepted lifestyle choice. In the media and the entertainment world, homosexuality will be promoted as an equal lifestyle choice to that of heterosexuality. Already, in some European countries, there is a push for gays and lesbians to be allowed to be married to same sex partners. If we are in the last days, that will probably happen and also happen here in America."

Laura replied, "I really can't see that happening. Marriage is a religious thing. It is has always been between a man and a woman. How can it suddenly be okay for two men or two women to marry each other?"

"Jesus said it would be like it was in the days of Noah. In Noah's time, homosexual activity was common and accepted. If we are in the last days, I think that homosexuality, in the near future, will become more and more mainstream and more and more accepted."

Laura said, "I don't know. I really can't imagine two men getting legally married."

"Another thing, Laura, is that, if we are in the last days, around the world and even here in the United States, the predominant culture will begin to ridicule and attack Christians and their beliefs. There will be open hostility toward people like us who believe that Jesus was who He said He was."

"What makes you say that? America was founded on Judeo-Christian principles. Why do you think it will suddenly change?"

"It actually is not a sudden change. It has been going on for many years. Certainly since the nineteen sixties. It has been a gradual thing. It will probably accelerate over the next ten to fifteen years. In John fifteen, Jesus said that the world would be against His followers. He said, 'If the world hates you, keep in mind that it hated me first. If you belonged to the world, it would love you as its own. As it is, you do not belong to the world, but I have chosen you out of the world.' Our home is with Jesus – not with the world."

Laura smiled. She said, "Hey now. If you're going to quote scripture, I can hardly argue with that."

"No. When we quote Jesus, that pretty much makes one's point."

"How do you know all these Bible verses?"

"I have a pretty good memory."

"Yeah, I noticed that a few days ago when you rattled off that canoe number to that guy on the phone."

Jake took another sip of coffee and nodded.

Laura asked, "Are you one of those guys who has a super memory and remembers everything?"

"No. Not at all. I still have a tough time remembering

people's names."

Laura pointed at herself and said, "Laura."

"I'll never forget your name."

"Breakfast?"

"Yes, I'm hungry. At the pub?"

"They don't do breakfast. We'll have to go to the cafeteria."

After breakfast, Laura said, "It's Saturday. There is a walk through the forest along the east side of the lake and back. And, there is a day trip to Québec City. Would you like either of those?"

"I think I'd really like to see Québec City."

"Okay. The group leaves at ten."

"My passport is in my tent."

"You won't need it."

"How come?"

"We don't use any checkpoints. The road from the Christmas tree farm has several rural back roads that, before you realize it, you're in Canada. Indeed, some people think that the Christmas tree farm is actually already in Canada. We are that close to the border. Returning on those same roads, before you know it, you're back in the U. S. No one asks to see your passport. None of us take ours."

"Okay. Great."

"You'll love Québec City. Everyone does. It's a beautiful city with lots of history."

"I don't know any French."

"I speak some. Most of the people here know some French. Mr. Le Couteau speaks it and reads it like a native."

"Neverland" had, naturally, an underground garage. Many of the people who worked there had their own vehicle. Mr. Le Couteau usually drove over to Montreal many Friday afternoons. Laura led Jake to a white van. In addition to the two of them, there were six others joining the "expedition."

Jake whispered to Laura, "What if we get pulled over for

speeding or a missing light?"

Laura pointed to a man and said, "Henri is driving. He has a Quebec driver's license. Don't worry. We do this all the time."

Once on the road, Henri said, "For Jake's benefit, let's all introduce ourselves again and tell Jake a little something about ourselves."

Henri began with himself and the rest of the passengers, Jo and her husband Paul, Bruce, Linda and her husband, Trevor, did the same. After everyone had done so, one of them, Jo, suggested they play a game. Jo had a smile on her pretty face that lit up the van. She told of a memory game about which she had recently heard. Everyone had to think real hard and try to remember something that they had not thought of in years. Each person would share that memory with everyone else.

Jo, who was in her mid-fifties, was with her husband, Paul. She said, "Since Paul and I have had some time to think on this, we'll begin. But first, everyone think back – think back many many years. Look around and see if you see something that might trigger a memory from long ago."

Everyone looked out the van windows as they passed the rural countryside. There were crop fields on one side and pastures with cattle grazing on the other. Jake was trying to think of something. Everyone looked at each other. Every now and then, someone would say, "Oh, I've got one." Jake did not have one.

Jo said, "Okay, I'll begin. I haven't thought of this memory for forty-eight years. Other than Paul and myself, none of you have been alive for forty-eight years. I was seven when this happened. I remember my dad bringing home our first television set. It was a square TV with a small black and white screen. It was snowing that evening and my dad slipped in the snow and fell. He twisted so that he took the fall and the TV set was not broken. When we plugged it in and the screen showed a picture, we were all amazed. We had seen television in other people's homes and in department store windows – but this television picture was in our living room. It was incredible. I haven't thought of that in forty-eight years and yet, I can vividly see it all in my mind."

Paul followed Jo with a memory from his childhood in the nineteen fifties. Henri and the others told memories. Jake noticed, as Bruce told his memory, he pulled on his ear. That gave Jake a memory he had not thought of since he was in the fifth grade.

Laura began to tell her memory by stating, "This happened when I was also seven years old, like Jo. That was twenty-six years ago. What happened was my mom was sick and I wanted to help. I went into the kitchen and found a box of cookie mix. It was simple. I just added an egg, some butter and some cooking oil to the mix. I beat that batter until my arms were so tired." Everyone laughed as they could imagine a seven-year-old little girl trying to stir a bowl of thick cookie batter. "Anyway, I followed the directions and put the spoonfuls of dough on the cookie sheet, preheated the oven and baked away. My dad was genuinely surprised at my large plate of cookies. He and mom pretended to like them. But I realized later that the mess I made in the kitchen actually caused more work cleaning it up than my plate of not-so-good cookies helped. I think my dad actually wound up having to clean the kitchen."

Laura's story confirmed to Jake that she was 33. That was a difference of nine years. Too much? He didn't know. Then he wondered if she intentionally revealed her age because maybe Peggy had said something. Was she letting him know that the age difference was all right or was she letting him know that she wanted him to realize that there was too large an age difference? Then he thought that she had told her age simply because the others had as a part of their story. Then he thought, *her kisses are full of electricity. If she weren't interested in me, she wouldn't have kissed me like that. I wonder . . .*

His thoughts were interrupted when Jo looked at Jake and said, "You got one?"

Jake replied, "Yes. This is a little odd compared to all of yours. But I haven't thought of this since I was ten or eleven. I was in the fifth grade. This would have been thirty-one or thirty-two years ago. There was a boy in my class – I don't remember his name (Jake looked at Laura and smiled.) but he could wiggle his ears. He could wiggle his left ear or his right ear but not both at the same time. I never knew anyone else who could wiggle his ears but I can still see this guy doing it. During recess, all the boys tried to learn how to do it but none of us ever could."

Jo said, "Anyone here wiggle their ears? No? Well, I do think that this little game shows that we do store away some memories that can find their way back to our conscious selves. I do thank everyone for playing."

Laura replied, "Thank you, Jo, for suggesting it. It was fun."

Everyone clapped – even Henri, who was driving.

By now, the cattle pastures had given way to subdivisions, gas stations, convenience stores, fast food restaurants and other businesses that were on the outskirts of every large city. The van was now on Canadian highway 20. This highway ran parallel to the St. Lawrence River. The old part of Québec City was on the west bank of the river and highway 20 was on the east side. This meant, obviously, that they had to cross a bridge. They went about two and half miles south of Québec City to Levis, picked up highway 73, crossed the St. Lawrence River there and headed north on highway 136 right into downtown Québec City. Just after they crossed the river and turned onto highway 136, Henri pointed out the Quebec Aquarium.

He said, "Jake, we'll save that for another trip."

"Great," Jake replied.

Laura said, "It is nice. Well worth seeing."

As Henri pulled into a parking garage, Jo asked Jake what he was thinking.

Jake responded, "It's beautiful. It reminds me of pictures I've seen of old European cities."

"Exactly," Jo said. "This is Old Quebec. It is the only walled city in either Canada or the United States."

After everyone had gotten out of the van, the small group began walking down a cobblestone street.

"It's amazing," Jake said. "It's like stepping back in

time."

Jo said, "It is, isn't it? We've all been here often. It's always nice to hear someone's perspective who has never visited Québec City."

Paul stated, "Now this little square we are coming up on is known a Place Royale. It's where Samuel de Champlain first built in 1608. That, right there, is the oldest stone church in North America. It is called Notre-Dame-des-Victoires and was built in 1688."

Jo said, "I've told Paul he could be a tour guide."

Paul replied, "I could."

Jake smiled and said, "Good."

After a nice lunch in a quaint bistro, the group kept walking.

Suddenly, Jake exclaimed, "Wow, is that real?"

He was pointing at a castle that had an almost fairytale appearance.

Paul answered, "Yes. This area is called Dufferin Terrance. That castle, which is real, and that hotel over there, the Chateau Frontenac, are among the most photographed buildings in the entire world."

Trevor spoke up and said, "Jake, the first time I saw this, I had the same reaction as you. It's hard to believe those buildings really exist. I'd never heard of them."

Jake said, "Yeah, me either."

As they climbed, with the St. Lawrence River in the background, the view became more and more impressive.

Although everyone in the group was kind and pleasant to be with, Jake wished that he and Laura were by themselves. Several times, he wanted to say something just to her. Instead, he smiled awkwardly at her.

He knew he was being silly. These people had all been to Québec City numerous times. They were doing this tour for his benefit. He did appreciate it.

Later, as evening approached, Henri suggested a restaurant. The others in the group all nodded in agreement. It was an informal restaurant with large windows overlooking the St. Lawrence River. The food was delicious.

As they were finishing their meal, Henri asked Jake, "What are you thinking? You look lost in thought."

Laura and Linda had been talking. They stopped to listen to Jake's response.

Jake smiled. "I'm actually feeling quite ignorant right now. This place, this city, is amazing. I am totally in love with it and ready to move here and live. It is breathtakingly beautiful, so historic – and I love history – and, until today, I knew practically nothing about it."

Several of the others laughed.

Bruce said, "Jake, I understand exactly what you are saying. When my wife and I first visited here, we had the same reaction. It is beautiful. And, when we retire, we are seriously considering moving here to live."

Jo added, "Isn't there a couple from . . . our place (She actually looked over her shoulder.) who did retire and move here?"

Henri answered, "Yes, you're thinking of Robert and Henrietta Wells."

"Yes, that's right. I never really knew them."

The return trip was made after the sun had set. Henri knew all the roads to take and they arrived back at the underground garage at almost eleven o'clock.

As it happened, after getting out of the van and thanking Henri and the group for showing him Québec City, Jake found himself leading their little party down the exit hallway. Realizing his position, he stopped, put his back against the hallway, waved the others ahead and said, "I haven't got a clue."

They laughed. Laura moved next to him and said, "I'll show you the way."

At his door, he turned to Laura and said, "Nightcap?"

"What are you offering?"

"I have a somewhat limited supply. There is one bottle of

wine. I know nothing about it. So, I guess I'm offering you wine."

"Sounds exquisite. Yes, please."

Sitting on the couch, sipping wine, Jake went on and on about how much he liked Québec City. He seriously thought it was wonderful.

Laura laughed and said, "I'd love to take you back – just the two of us."

Jake replied, "I'd absolutely love that."

Jake wanted to talk about the two of them. He wanted to ask Laura if he could date her and, if so, how would one go about that. He had decided not to bring up their age difference. If she saw it as a problem, she would say something. Last time, in this situation, Laura had been concerned about visiting with him in his apartment. She had been afraid that it might create some negative talk. Tonight, she didn't seem to mind.

After a pause in their conversation, Jake asked, "Could we go to chapel services in the morning?"

Laura looked surprised.

"Together, I mean," he stumbled.

She smiled and nodded. "Yes."

I guess you'd best come by and pick me up. I'm almost afraid to ask. There aren't any more surprise traditions coming my way, are there?"

Laura laughed. "No, not that I know of. And, of course I'll come by and pick you up." Placing her empty wine glass on the coffee table, Laura stood up and pulled Jake with her. She walked over to the door and stopped. She put both arms around Jake and gave him a long kiss. Jake hugged her tight and returned the kiss.

Laura opened the door, turned to Jake and simply said softly, "Goodnight."

"Goodnight."

CHAPTER TWENTY-SEVEN

"If anyone acknowledges that Jesus is the Son of God, God lives in them and they in God."

– 1 John 4:15

Late 1st Century A.D.

As Laura and Jake entered the chapel, Jake saw Mr. Nesbitt. Jake gave him a copy of his "Last Days" paper and asked him to see that Mr. Sinclair received it. Laura and Jake sat together near the back of the sanctuary. Jake was so glad that he was sitting with Laura and was not standing up there at the podium. It was a nice message by their regular minister and the choir was excellent.

After the chapel service, while waiting for the cafeteria staff to get lunch ready, Laura and Jake went to the library. Jake stood there and simply stared at everything. He was still in awe of it. There were a few other people there. They were probably killing time also waiting on the cafeteria.

Laura and Jake sat down together at a wooden table. Jake was trying to move the conversation to a discussion of them as a couple. He needed to leave tomorrow morning. He wanted to spend his last day there with Laura. He was thinking of how he would be able to see her in the future. They could always email. They wound up talking about a lot of different things. She told him more of her experiences growing up on Tybee Island near Savannah. He told her more about growing up on a small farm in North Carolina. Tomorrow would be Monday, June sixth. He really needed to get back. Suddenly, someone opened the door and said, "They're serving now!"

Laura and Jake sat at a table for four. As they were eating in the cafeteria, Jake decided he had to move this along. He couldn't wait any longer. It was time to be serious. Jake was just going to ask Laura if she would meet him in Québec City in three weeks when Mr. Nesbitt stopped at their table.

Mr. Nesbitt asked, "Jake, did you think you were going to have to speak again this morning?" He smiled.

Jake returned his smile and replied, "Yes, and I was so so disappointed when I wasn't called up to give this morning's talk."

Mr. Nesbitt laughed.

Jake said, "The guy who did speak did a good job."

Mr. Nesbitt responded, "Yes, he did. What I really wanted is to give you a message. After you've finished eating, Mr. Sinclair wants to see you."

Jake looked at Laura. She looked at him. They had both been looking forward to spending the afternoon together.

Jake asked, "Will it take long?"

"I have no idea," Mr. Nesbitt replied. After a brief pause, Mr. Nesbitt added, "This is a great honor. Mr. Sinclair rarely meets with anyone and certainly not the same person in the same week. I can't remember this ever happening previously."

"Okay. I'll be right there. In his office?"

"Yes."

After Mr. Nesbitt left, Jake turned to Laura and said, "I'm sorry. I guess I should see what he wants."

Laura responded, "Definitely. I'll see you after your visit. I'll wait for you at *our* booth."

After they finished their meals, Laura took Jake to Mr. Sinclair's office. She squeezed his hand and left.

Jake knocked on the door.

"Come in."

Jake opened the door and stepped inside. He smelled the aroma of pipe tobacco and Mr. Sinclair called him in to sit down.

After exchanging pleasantries, both men were sitting in the same chairs they had been in during the first meeting. As before, Jake felt like he had stepped back in time. He was pretty sure the office furniture was original to the office.

Mr. Sinclair picked up the folder that contained Jake's research about the Last Days. He said, "I just read this and found it fascinating. I want to discuss it with you."

"Sure. Just so you know, none of it is original information. I simply compiled what others have written and tried to put it all together in an easy to understand format."

"Yes, I understand. Tell me how you decided that the period, or the season, of the Last Days began with the birth of Israel as a nation."

Jake smiled. He replied, "Obviously, that is the most important aspect of the entire *Last Days* scenario. I say that, because if that is accurate, and I fully recognize that that is a big 'if,' it establishes the remaining timeline. Jesus spoke only of a season. He did not set a 'trigger' for when that season would actually begin. So obviously, it is a bit of a guessing game as to when the season begins. For us, we have specific times when each of our four seasons begin. Spring, for instance, always begins on March twenty-first or, sometimes, on March twenty-second. This is the beginning of the spring season. As we move into April and May, the spring season progresses and develops with all the signs of spring like new leaves on the trees, blooming flowers, warmer temperatures and so forth. However, our dates are not without exceptions. The worst blizzard in the history of North Carolina occurred in late March . . . technically in spring, not in winter. Of course, the seasons are reversed for the southern hemisphere. The folks in Australia, New Zealand, Brazil, Ecuador and all of South America have summer when we have winter. Jesus used the example of the fig tree to explain the 'season' of the *Last Days*. The fig tree represents the nation of Israel. Just as we may still have snow at the beginning of the spring season, the season that Jesus mentioned would start slowly and develop more rapidly as it neared its end. Since the fig tree represents Israel, it seems logical to use its re-birth in May of 1948 as the beginning of the season Jesus was discussing. The key here is, of course, that Jesus said that that generation would not pass away prior to His return. Psalm ninety tells us that a generation is between seventy and eighty years. People tend to begin with 1948 and add seventy or eighty years. However, that is taking the outside number; it could be less than that. And, of course, another variable is that, supposed someone born in 1948 lived until 2048. A few people undoubtedly will. Since they are alive twenty years beyond the eighty-year number, that generation has still not passed away."

Mr. Sinclair said, "I had not thought of that."

"There are just too many variables to nail this down. That's why we are supposed to always be watchful and prepared for Jesus' return. While it might appear logical to us that the season would begin with the re-birth of Israel, that may have nothing to do with it. I will be among the first to say that, while it seems logical, it may not be accurate at all. Only God in heaven knows for sure."

Mr. Sinclair nodded in agreement. His pipe had gone out and he was in the process of refilling the bowl when he said, "Thank you. I understand."

Jake said, "Others place the beginning of the *Last Days* nineteen years later when Israel gained control of the Old City and made Jerusalem its capital. If that is the beginning of the season Jesus was referring to, then obviously that would extend the *Last Days* season by nineteen years. Of course, there may not be any 'trigger' event at all. However, as Jesus described the end times, the *Last Days*, it does seem that we are in them. If Jesus doesn't return in the next ten to fifteen years, I expect that those years will provide convincing proof that we are, indeed, in the season of the *Last Days*."

"What do you expect will happen in the next ten to fifteen years?"

"An acceleration of what is going on now. The Bible actually tells us – if we are in the *Last Days*. As in the days of Noah. One of the predominate aspects of the days of Noah was an acceptance of homosexuality. It wasn't just an acceptance – it was an 'in-your-face' attitude by homosexuals that others must accept and approve of their lifestyle. I think that attitude is coming to cultures all over the world. The 'live and let live' attitude toward homosexuality will no longer be enough. Homosexuals will insist and force their lifestyles onto mainstream culture. Christians will be scorned by the media for their 'outdated' and backward beliefs that homosexuality is wrong and is an affront to God. In addition to the acceptance of homosexuality as just another alternative lifestyle, the Bible tells us that in Noah's time, the world was corrupt and full of violence. For the next ten to fifteen years, I can easily see an increase in the acceptance of homosexuality, of a spread of corruption and an increase in violence all over the world. This won't just be in the United States and Canada; it will be world-wide."

"You actually believe that this will take place in the next ten to fifteen years? Including this attack on Christian values?"

"If we are in the *Last Days*, absolutely."

"What else?"

"Again, the Bible tells us. There will be constant wars and constant rumors of war. Now, that is nothing new. Although, I wonder if constant wars means something like wars that don't end. You know, World War II ended. It had a definite end date. I am wondering if we will have wars that go on for decades – if maybe that is what constant wars means. Anyway, during the *Last Days*, wars and rumors of war will remain with us and grow in intensity. There will be an increase in famine. We wouldn't think that now in the twenty-first century, we would still have people starving to death. But we do; and, it will increase. Another thing that will increase is disease. Diseases and epidemics will increase. New plagues will appear. Currently, there is a major breakdown in the family unit. This will only get worse. Worldwide, the basic building block of any society has always been a strong family structure. Without that family structure, society falls apart. Divorce rates continue to increase. Many children are being born without the security and stability of married parents. Numerous television programs and movies today make fun of traditional family values. Instead, they openly endorse fornication and adultery – and even promote homosexual relationships. In the media and entertainment world, Christian family values are simply too politically incorrect and totally not progressive. For example, if a Christian is opposed to abortion on demand as a means of birth control, well then, that Christian simply hasn't evolved with the times. The concept of 'right or wrong' does not enter into the discussion. The Christian is just an uneducated backward rube. I can even see this leading to violence. Democrats claim that they are tolerant but, like Islam, the reality is that they are not. If someone has a different view, perhaps a view that they determine is politically incorrect, then they demonstrate violence, not tolerance. If I were to say that, in my opinion, it is wrong for a woman to be the minister of a protestant church. Or that, in my opinion, it is wrong for a woman to be living with another woman as a lesbian couple. Or that, in my opinion, abortion on demand is wrong. If I were to state any of this publicly, I would not be entitled to my opinions. People would yell obscenities at me and call me every evil name in the book. I would do no violence. I would simply state that these views, according to my faith, were wrong. I would be threatened with physical harm. Christian principles simply are not compatible with "progressive socialist" ideas. Today, heterosexual promiscuity and same-sex relationships are celebrated on television shows and movies as the norm. They are viewed by millions of young people all around the world. The Internet can be used to support this degenerate view of culture. This has been called the 'age of instant gratification' and has resulted in selfishness, greed, materialism and a major lack of empathy for others. Additionally, our society is seeing a tremendous increase in drug and alcohol abuse. Along with this is an increase in crime.

"Two major things that are headed in the wrong direction are education and religion. Through the forces of political correctness, both have been 'watered down' to the point that they are extremely weak. They both have abandoned their roots – their purpose for being. Thankfully, not all religions are in this boat but many are. The results are obvious as our culture continues to deteriorate."

Mr. Sinclair spoke softly. He said, "I cannot disagree with anything you've said."

"If we are, indeed, in the Last Days, it is exciting and thrilling for a Christian to realize that Jesus is returning soon."

"Yes, of course."

After about a minute of silence, Mr. Sinclair said, "I am wondering about our future here."

Jake simply stated, "You have a great . . . a tremendous repository of knowledge here."

Mr. Sinclair didn't respond. He "picked-up" on a tone in Jake's comment and that tone led to an introspective thought. He was having an epiphany and was aware of it as it was happening.

Jake watched him think. This silence was not awkward.

Finally, Mr. Sinclair spoke. He said, "Are you saying . . . are you thinking that we . . . do you think we should . . . abandon our purpose here?"

"As I understand it, the basic purpose of this place is to preserve knowledge. Is that right?"

"Yes, of course."

Your family has created an amazing library here. Now that you have preserved all this information, it seems that the purpose of this place may move in another direction. A library is designed to disseminate information. It may be time to . . ."

Jake quit talking. He thought, perhaps, he had said too much. Mr. Sinclair appeared to be lost in thought.

With a start, Mr. Sinclair jerked himself back and asked, "Where were we?"

"Talking about knowledge. In the second chapter of Colossians, it states that all the treasures of wisdom and knowledge . . . I love that phrase, by the way – all treasures of wisdom and knowledge . . . are hidden in Christ. Even though we are in Christ and Christ is in us, that doesn't mean we automatically receive those hidden treasures. Perhaps we have to wait until Christ returns."

"The Rapture."

"Yes, and then, seven years later, the earthly return. The Rapture will remove all Christians from the earth. The earth will be in chaos. Is then when you intend for your truly fabulous library to be used?"

"No. Yes. . . I don't know. Probably not. Hopefully, our staff will be raptured – leaving no one to run this facility. The library would be useless. The world would not ever realize that it exists."

"Another aspect, one that I also have discussed with Jean, is that of abortion. People don't like to mix religion and politics. I understand that. It is not comfortable. I wish more Christians would enter politics but I do understand the reluctance to do so. Politics is dirty and self-serving. It's not compatible with a Christian lifestyle. It would be difficult, but not impossible, to get re-elected as a Christian. There was a Senator from the mid-west somewhere, back in the seventies, I think, who served his six years in the Senate but then chose not to run for re-election. He said that he was so disgusted and appalled by what goes on in politics that he did not, as a Christian, want to be a part of it. I understand that – but it leaves politics open to those without a conscience. Catholics seems to thrive in politics. Many of the strongest supporters of abortion are Catholics. The Catholic religion does not endorse abortion. In fact, to its credit, the Catholic Church is totally opposed to abortion. But many members of the Supreme Court and of Congress are Catholics who support abortion. They go against their Pope and their church in order to be politically correct. I am one hundred percent sure that a real Christian cannot support abortion and the pro-choice movement. Abortion is the taking, the murder of the innocent life of an unborn baby. This baby was created in the womb by God, as a gift. This baby has a right to life. Only God has the right to end that life. I know that the pro-abortion people say that it is not a baby in the woman's womb. Rather, it is only a mass of cells. It is like removing an appendix. But everyone who has seen a sonogram of that mass of cells sees a baby. It is, quite simply and accurately, murder. No matter how one tries to word it, it is not something a Christian can possibly support."

Mr. Sinclair puffed on his pipe. He responded, "What you say is logical."

"It is based upon scripture."

"Yes, of course. I wonder . . ."

Jake did not interrupt Mr. Sinclair's thoughts. Jake watched as he sat in his chair, lost in thought, as smoke slowly swirled from his pipe and floated upward. Jake thought he knew the direction Mr. Sinclair's thoughts were going. It would not be an easy decision for him. But he was back where they had been previously.

Suddenly, Mr. Sinclair shook himself, stared at Jake and apologized.

He said, "I'm sorry. My thoughts are running their own course. What were we talking about?"

Jake replied, "Would you mind if I asked you a question?"

"Of course not. Ask away."

"You said that everyone's purpose in life is to learn, right?"

"Yes. Exactly."

"What? What, exactly, is it that every person is to learn?"

"Ahhh, you want the answer to the million dollar question. All right, I'll tell you."

Jake sat back in the big comfortable leather chair. He was prepared to hear this answer from Mr. Sinclair and to soak it all into his very being.

"First of all," Mr. Sinclair puffed on his pipe, "you should know that the answer to your question is fairly simply. But most people will not understand it. You will, but most will not."

Mr. Sinclair sat back and prepared to tell Jake what it is that each person should learn. Jake was full of anticipation. Mr. Sinclair took a long pull on his pipe, cleared his throat and began with a question.

"Are you familiar with the Gnostics?"

Jake was surprised by the question but chose not to show

it. He replied, "I know that gnosis is a Greek word meaning knowledge. I know that, in the early days of Christianity, Gnostic beliefs were appealing to many people. Their teachings were accepted and they grew in numbers. But they were not under the control of any organized government or church. They had to be suppressed and they were."

"All true, Jake. Do you know what one of their central beliefs was?"

"No, I guess not."

"Gnostics believed that each individual person should look within himself or herself for his or her spark of divinity. They believed that each individual person could have a personal relationship with God without the need for a church hierarchy to intercede between God and the individual. What became the Catholic Church condemned their beliefs and tried to totally remove those who believed that way. The Catholic Church was quite successful in their efforts to discredit Gnostics. However, a few survived and continued to believe in a personal relationship, through Jesus, with God. They continued, through the centuries, usually in small secretive groups, to believe that Divinity exists in everyone in order that everyone could know God. They believed that each person's soul had a connection with God.

"Now Jake, at first, these people were real Christians. They believed as you and I do. They believed that Jesus was exactly who He said He was – the Son of God who became human in order to sacrifice Himself for us. Later, they went off the rails and started believing things that weren't scriptural. They went a little weird and began inserting things into their religion that were simply not Biblical and, largely because of that, they lost membership and faded away.

"You have heard it said that God created us in His image. But this refers to our eternal souls – not our finite bodies. God is forever – eternal. Our human bodies are not. God does not have illnesses. Our human bodies do. Created in His image means that God created our souls in His image.

"Are you with me, Jake?"

"Yes. I understand what you are saying."

"Good."

Mr. Sinclair's pipe had gone out. He knocked out the burnt ashes, refilled the bowl and re-lit his pipe. He looked directly at Jake and said, "From the time of our birth until the time of our death, the only constant in our lives are our souls. Life has been called a 'school for our souls.'" He paused, puffed on his pipe and continued, "The very essence of our lives on this planet is to take a spiritual journey that will be difficult . . . and amazing . . . in an attempt to move our soul closer to God." Mr. Sinclair paused again, sucked on his pipe and stared at Jake. He continued, "God is perfection. God is love, grace and forgiveness. These human bodies we inhabit prevent us from obtaining perfection. But love, grace and forgiveness are qualities that will bloom in our souls and make our souls happy. Why? Because those qualities will aid our souls in their quest to get a little closer to God.

"We come into this life for the purpose of changing our souls in order that they may move closer to God. Once we accept Christ as our personal Savior, we are, through our souls, drawn inextricably to God. For each person, this journey, this process of moving one's soul closer to God will be different. Your journey will be different than mine. Each individual person must *learn* what it is their soul needs in order to move closer to God."

Jake softly said, "Know thyself."

Mr. Sinclair smiled, "Yes. In a way, yes."

"I always wondered what that meant."

"That Greek phrase actually predates Christianity but it does apply in this situation. Spiritual Christianity has changed the original meaning of it but it is appropriate – if one understands what we mean by it. Jake, many Christians – no, most Christians do this without being aware that they are doing it. They are trying to get closer to God. This is what we are here to learn. We have, of course, the help of the Holy Spirit in this process. You have probably prayed, I know I have, for assistance and guidance from the Holy Spirit in helping you to get closer to God."

"Yes."

"What are you thinking, Jake?"

"I was just concerned about all those millions of people out there who are not Christians. And there are many many what I call 'Sunday only Christians.' I used to be one. They, and the non-Christians, are living their lives without the Holy Spirit, without Jesus . . . and are not even trying to get closer to God."

"Jake, are you a happy person?"

"What?"

"Are you happy?"

"Yes, I am." Jake smiled.

"Why?"

"Because, Charles, I'm a Christian. I don't understand how any Christian, filled with the Holy Spirit, and knowing Jesus, could not be grateful and happy. I often have an awareness of pure joy."

"I agree. Most people, however, have no concept of what you just said. Most people chase after pleasure. Pleasure is temporary so it must be sought over and over again. Pleasure focuses on the flesh. Happiness, as you described, focuses on the spirit and lasts a lifetime. Now pleasure itself is not evil. It is not something to be avoided and run from. We have both been married. Spending intimate time with our wives, whom we love, can be extremely pleasurable for both husband and wife. It is like money. Money itself is not evil. It is the attitude toward money that can be evil. It is the attitude regarding pleasure that can be evil."

"Of course."

There was again a pause in their conversation. Mr. Sinclair smoked his pipe. Jake was curious about something but did not know how to bring it up without it sounding like idle curiosity – which it was.

Mr. Sinclair smiled at him and said, "Go ahead. Ask me."

Jake looked startled. He was. Surely this man could not read minds.

Mr. Sinclair laughed at Jake's confusion. He said, "I'm

not reading your mind, Jake, it's just experience that comes with age. What is it you want to ask me?"

Jake smiled. "I am wondering how long ago was it that your wife passed away?"

This was not a question Mr. Sinclair had anticipated. But he answered, "She died eleven years ago. She was in her mid-sixties. Cancer."

Jake nodded. "Sorry. That must have been a rough time."

Mr. Sinclair responded. "Not so bad. With cancer, you have an opportunity to prepare yourself. Both she and I knew when the end was coming. We had the chance to say our goodbyes. As Christians, it is easier to deal with things like that. Only because we know that our souls live on and are with Jesus. I do believe that God allows things to happen – and that things happen for a reason. But I have also come to believe that there are accidents – that simple chance plays a role in what happens to our human bodies. The thing is that, with accidents, there is always something that could have been done differently that would have prevented the accident. With hindsight, one can see what could have been done differently. I remember reading about a young man who was standing on the edge of a high cliff. He was looking down about two hundred feet below the top of the cliff. The earth or the rock upon which he was standing gave way . . . and he fell to his death. It was a horrible accident. However, with hindsight, if he had stayed three or four feet from the edge, he would still be alive. If he had laid down horizontally and looked over the edge, he would still be alive. I can't think of a single accident where, with hindsight, you can't see that something different would have eliminated the accident. I don't think we can say that God is responsible for them, but rather, that He allows them to happen. He doesn't always intervene to prevent accidents. He pretty much lets us humans find our own way. We make mistakes. He allows us to make mistakes. We have accidents. He allows us to have accidents. Most are not fatal . . . but some are. Hopefully, we learn from our accidents and our mistakes. You lost your wife to divorce. There are reasons for that. You both have probably learned a lot from going through that experience."

Jake laughed and replied, "Yes, for me . . . that is most certainly true."

"Life is a learning journey."

"And yet, so many people seem to be existing rather than living."

"Those people are in the dark. Many of them are unaware that they are in the dark. But some of them sense that something is wrong – that this existence is not the way life should be lived. Those people can find their way out of the dark. Sometimes, if they see a little light, they can move toward it. Christians can be that light."

CHAPTER TWENTY-EIGHT

"I am the way and the truth and the life. No one comes to the Father except through me."

– John 14:6

Late 1st Century A.D.

Mr. Sinclair re-lit his pipe, looked directly at Jake, smiled and said, "I wondered why you came to us."

Jake smiled and said, "Me too." He wanted to ask more about that but Mr. Sinclair kept talking.

"I knew there must be a reason – but I had no idea what it would be. I hoped that, if we conversed for a while, you would reveal why you are here. And . . . I think you have."

"The library?"

"Yes."

After a brief pause, Mr. Sinclair said, "I have no idea how to go about it. Obviously, it will change everything."

Jake responded by saying, "Charles, perhaps not."

Mr. Sinclair laughed and said, "I've never believed that one could 'have their cake and eat it too.'"

"No. What I mean is that it will depend on how you approach things regarding exactly what changes will need to be made. Everything may not need change."

"How could that be? What are you saying?"

"Charles, is this place in Maine or Quebec?"

"We probably straddle the line. I think the lake is in Maine but the Christmas tree farm is in Quebec."

"Do you own the lake?"

"Yes."

"The land all around it?"

"Yes. We have a little over seven hundred acres, including the lake, the forest surrounding it and the Christmas tree farm. We get our mail at the Christmas tree farm from Canada. Simply because we have road access to Quebec and we have no real road access to Maine, we frequently go to the nearby Canadian towns and, of course, to Québec City and Montreal."

"I understand. You are going to obviously need the services of an attorney to establish this organization as a non-profit. I have absolutely no details about doing this but I would suspect that the government regulations may be more favorable from the Canadian government than from the U. S. government. Wait. The seven hundred plus acres you have – do you have a deed to them?"

"I'm not sure. We have some legal papers from when the property was purchased in the eighteen sixties. Whether they count as a deed or not, I don't know. I also don't know if those papers say we are in Canada or Maine. It may be that some of the land is in Quebec and some in Maine. I don't think I've ever actually read them. My father told me about them and where they are filed. I can get them. I don't know how we'll go about getting incorporated."

"You will need an attorney to determine that."

"We have a lawyer here within our organization."

"Great. Can he practice in Canada?"

"She. Yes, she can."

"That's perfect. I think you'll need to get her to set up some type of non-profit religious retreat center for your organization. You could build a lodge or hotel right on the shore of your lake. You could build a separate public entrance directly to the library and the chapel. Your staff here could remain in their apartments and continue working as they have always done. You may need to add more staff to work in the lodge and in the library. Perhaps some recreational activities centered around the lake would be needed. Perhaps a nice restaurant in the lodge. This way, families could vacation here and could, at the same time, access the resources of the library. I can see this working."

"The way you put it, I can too. However, I have always been afraid that news of our existence would leak out and ruin everything. Now, to just announce our existence to the world seems wrong."

"Charles, it would be better for you to announce it than for it to leak out, wouldn't it?"

"Yes. But it's not an either or situation. We do not have to go public."

"True. But Charles, what is the purpose of a library? How long can you simply store information? You have some truly rare books, some unique diaries, antique maps and thousands of rare photographs. These should, I think, be shared."

"My father will turn over in his grave."

"You have to decide what is best for you, for your family's legacy and all the people who are working here."

"Yes."

"I will support whatever decision you make."

"Thank you. Tell me more about some of the possibilities you see that could develop here."

The two men talked for another hour and a half. The cafeteria was closed and Jake got directions to the pub where his and Laura's booth was located. To his surprise and pleasure, Laura was there.

They saw each other at about the same time. Laura waved him over and Jake sat down opposite her in the booth.

Laura said, "You're late."

Jake smiled and replied, "Tell me about it. When you get two guys together, both of who like to talk, it just goes on and on."

"People are talking about you."

"Me? What did I do?" He looked around the pub.

"You've spent all afternoon and evening with Mr. Sinclair."

"Oh, that again. We're just a couple of talkers talking."

"Jake, you really do not comprehend the level of awe, respect and even mystique that people here have for Mr. Sinclair. What you have done – twice now, has simply never happened. In the history of this place, it is unheard of . . . even the old-timers, some of whom knew Mr. Sinclair's father, say it just doesn't happen."

"Mr. Sinclair said it was the reason I came here."

Laura looked puzzled and thoughtful. She responded with a long "Hmmmmm."

"I'm starving. Have you eaten?"

"No. What would you like?"

"I feel a little awkward not paying for anything."

"Don't be silly. I have credits. You, as a guest, obviously do not. What will it be?"

"Hamburger, fries, coke."

"The classic."

"Yep. Thanks."

"Be right back."

While Laura was getting their food, two women, in their mid-thirties, came over to Jake, sat down in the booth where Laura had just been and began questioning him about Mr. Sinclair. They were nice – just curious. Others in the room overheard the conversation and came over to join in the discussion of Mr. Sinclair. All Jake could tell them was that Mr. Sinclair was in good health and that they had talked about a variety of subjects.

Laura looked over and saw the crowd of people surrounding "their" booth. She changed the order "to go." When it was ready, she brought it to Jake and said, "Let's go."

Jake got up and followed Laura out of the pub. She led him to his apartment and they ate there. Sitting at the small dining table, Laura and Jake were enjoying being alone together.

During a brief lull in the conversation, Jake said, "Thank you." He said it seriously.

Laura replied, "For what?" She seemed surprised by his sudden serious tone.

"For everything. For nice conversation. For getting me out of the pub and away from all those people. For this food. For your pleasant smile."

Laura smiled. She said, "That's nice. You're welcome."

"I need to leave in the morning."

"I know."

"I . . . uh, I would like to . . . uh, I would like to stay in touch with you."

"I'd like that."

"You would?"

"Yes, I would." Laura smiled.

"Okay then. Uh, how does one go about that?"

"Staying in touch, digitally speaking, is best done here by email."

"All right. Let's trade our emails."

After doing that, Jake asked, "How does one stay in touch in a non-digital manner?"

"Obviously, we're not allowed to have guests visit us here. What people, especially family members, do, is to arrange to meet, usually in Montreal or Québec City."

"Could we do that?"

"If you'd like."

"Yes, I'd like. Very much."

"Email me and we'll set a time and date."

"Absolutely. Will do."

Laura smiled. Again using their special phrase, she said, "That's nice." She was already looking forward to them getting together.

Jake was also looking forward to meeting Laura in Québec City, he thought. He really liked it there. To Jake, it had a good "feel."

After they finished eating, Jake made a pot of coffee and they each took a mug into the small living room and sat on the sofa. They continued their conversation there. Laura said, "I want to thank you for something and apologize for something." Jake didn't say anything and Laura continued. "I want to thank you for not ever saying anything about me getting sorta drunk on you. I apologize for that. I'm sorry it happened. I didn't realize I was drinking so much."

"Laura, you don't need to apologize. It's quite all right."

"No, it's not. That's really not like me. I guess I was kind-of nervous around you."

"Me? You certainly need not . . ."

"I know that now. But I didn't then. And you had to get someone else to show you back to the apartment and to take me home."

"Actually, they volunteered. Nice people."

"I am so embarrassed and sorry that happened. And you never said a word about it. You never brought it up – even as a joke or kidded me about it. Thank you."

Jake nodded and smiled. He didn't know what to say. He thought, *I can't believe I made her nervous. I feel like a high school kid around her. I can talk with Mr. Sinclair and Mr. Le Couteau without any hesitation about any topic in the world. With Laura, I feel tongue-tied half the time. Why? Am I falling in love with her?*

Jake leaned over close to Laura and said, "Please don't give it another thought. It's all right." He then quickly kissed her.

Laura smiled.

Jake asked Laura about her interest in standing stones. They spent over an hour talking about the variety of stones and the wide diversity of countries with ancient stone circles. They discussed the problems associated with dating stones and some of the newer techniques being developed. They both agreed that they would like to take a trip to Wales, Scotland and England and visit several sites of standing stones in each country.

After they had about talked themselves through the topic of monolithic monuments, there was an inevitable lull in the conversation. Jake filled this by asking Laura if she was aware of the largest man-made construction in the world. Laura replied that she guessed it was the Great Pyramid in Egypt.

Jake said, "Most people think that; but no, there are

actually several things larger. The largest is a man-made hill or small mountain actually. It is in Quito, Ecuador. It is called Panecillo. From the air, originally, going across the top, the hill had an earthen mound that looked like a huge sperm cell. Some of that is still visible. On top of this man-made mountain is a unique structure called La Olla. This stone structure is extremely old. It, and the construction of Panecillo, is not recorded in any history. No one knows who built these things, or when, or why. La Olla, which is Spanish for *oven*, looks like an upside down beehive. It is all stone with an opening at the top and several tunnels extending out from the bottom. It's really intriguing."

Laura said, "It certainly sounds like it. You said from the air, there was a mound that looked like a sperm cell. How would ancient people know what a sperm cell looks like?"

"Exactly. In Brazil, there are numerous carvings in caves that look just like sperm cells. Most experts call them snakes. However, they look more like sperm cells than snakes."

"Why sperm cells?"

"We can only guess. A sperm cell represents the absolute beginning of life. Some archaeologists think that the celebration of life is represented by a sperm cell."

"Again, how could ancient people know what a sperm cell looks like? And if it could only be viewed from the air, who could see it?"

"Exactly. Who could see it? And why put that shape on top of a man-made mountain? Even if it were representing a snake, why put it there?"

Laura asked, "Why build a mountain? Why not use an existing hill or mountain?"

"Excellent question. I've thought about that. The only thing I can come up with is that the stone structure on top had to be at an exact altitude and at an exact position on the planet. The longitude and latitude had to be exactly there. Now why, I have no idea. No one knows what the stone structure was designed to do. But, whatever it was, it apparently had to be located in that exact spot."

"And all this is still there in Ecuador?"

"Oh yes. People take tour buses up to the top of Panecillo to visit La Olla. However, most people today, take the tour buses to visit a huge statue of the Virgin Mary, with angel wings no less, that has been built on top of Panecillo. La Olla is most often an afterthought. The government has constructed a cement barrier around La Olla that greatly distracts from the site."

"You mean this man-made mountain is big enough to drive buses on?"

"Yes, there is a paved road that winds up to the top. It is an extremely large man-made construction. Most of the people in Ecuador are not aware that Panecillo is man-made nor that it has a huge sperm cell on the top. Most Ecuadorians have never even heard of La Olla let alone are aware of the extreme ancient age of it."

"That is truly amazing."

"Yes, it is. Have you ever heard of, I don't know how to pronounce it, but it's the major Sanskrit epic of India. It's the Mahabharata."

"I've heard of it. But I haven't read it."

"I have. It's somewhat long and disjointed. However, it describes, in some detail, ancient wars that are not recorded in history. The weapons used in these wars sound like the nuclear weapons of today. This book also describes flying vehicles. It goes into some detail in its description of these aerial vehicles."

Laura asked, "Is this book supposed to be true or is it another heroic mythical legend?"

"It's supposed to be based on real events and most people in India accept it as fact – as part of their ancient history."

"But how could that be?"

"Indeed, how? It is interesting to speculate. But no one really knows with a hundred percent accuracy."

Laura looked at Jake and simply stated, "You know a lot about these type of things, don't you?"

It wasn't really a question but Jake responded by saying, "Yes, I guess so. These ancient mysteries have always interested me – like the standing stones."

"Let me ask you a serious question."

"Shoot."

"Do you fear death?"

Surprised by the question, Jake quickly answered, "No, why should I?"

Softly, almost as a whisper, Laura said, "I watched my grandmother die. It wasn't easy. The whole process frightened her. She wasn't ready to go. She was only fifty-nine. I was a teenager and have vivid memories of her fear."

"Are you a Christian?"

"I am."

"As a Christian, one of the many results of allowing the Holy Spirit to direct one's life is joy. For me, this does not mean that one is bubbly, if that is a word, all the time. It does not mean that one is constantly grinning with happiness. To me, it is an awareness of the presence of Jesus. That is joy. It is an inner knowledge that, as a Christian, I know my future is with Jesus. I think that the more spiritually aware a person becomes, the less that person will fear death. I mean, really, for a Christian, what is death? The death of one's physical body simply means the transition of one's soul from one form of consciousness to another form. Our physical bodies become irrelevant."

Laura shook her head. "I was with you," she said, "until you said we are irrelevant. I don't understand how . . ."

"Laura, I didn't mean to imply that we should do anything to hasten the end of our physical bodies. That would be a terrible thing to do. God has us here for a certain amount of time so that we can learn what it is we are supposed to learn. When our bodies die, our souls leave our physical bodies behind and we continue on our journey. Our souls, as Christians, will live forever with God. Forever. Eternity. That is difficult to comprehend. Laura, do you know what eternity is?"

"I guess it means forever."

"Yes. This definition is not original to me but I have forgotten who said it but I've always remembered it – eternity is simply the absence of time."

"The absence of time."

"Yes. It makes you think, doesn't it?"

Laura nodded. "Uh-huh."

After a brief pause of silence, Jake said, "I'm sorry about your grandmother."

Laura smiled. "It was a long time ago." After another period of silence, Laura added, "But I still remember her fear."

Jake thought of mentioning that he and Mr. Le Couteau had had a long discussion about death but decided there was no point in mentioning it to Laura. He dropped the subject by asking her about her teaching assignment in the organization's private school. Laura told him about her students and how she truly enjoyed teaching. They didn't return to the subject of death.

After several hours of conversation, Laura suddenly said, "You need to get to sleep. You've got two full days of paddling ahead of you."

Jake laughed. "That's true but I'm okay."

"No, I'm keeping you up."

"It's all right. I'm okay."

"No, I should go."

"Will you see me off in the morning?'

"Absolutely. I'll come by and take you to breakfast."

"Great. Thank you."

At the door, Jake held out his arms. Laura stepped into them and they hugged tightly. They kissed tightly and long. When they broke from their kiss, they both said, at the same time, "That's nice." They both laughed.

CHAPTER TWENTY-NINE

"But our citizenship is in Heaven. And we eagerly await a Savior from there, the Lord Jesus Christ."

– Philippians 3:20

Late 1st Century A.D.

During his last night "underground," Jake did not sleep much. When Laura knocked on his door, he was showered, shaved and dressed in the same clothes he was wearing when he arrived. Laura took him to the cafeteria for breakfast.

Sitting at a table for four, they were both wondering when they would next be able to see each other.

Laura asked Jake, "Are you sure you know how to swim?" She smiled at him.

"Yes. I'm actually a pretty good swimmer. I even have a scuba diving license."

"Good. I wouldn't want you to fall in the river and get swept away."

Jake smiled at her. "Not gonna happen."

"I'm going to miss you."

"Me too. I mean I'm going to miss you . . . also."

Laura nodded, smiled and just slightly jerked her head – causing her hair to fall back into place.

Jake said, "I know we've just met but I really do feel as though we've been good friends for a long time. It just seems we've known each other longer than we have."

Laura smiled and replied, "Me too."

Jake laughed and was about to say something when Peggy

came over to their table.

She said, "There you guys are." Looking directly at Jake, she added, "I was afraid you were going to leave without saying goodbye. I have really enjoyed getting to know you."

"Thank you, Peggy. It's been nice getting to know you too. And thanks again for rescuing me."

Peggy laughed and looked at Laura. She said, "You know what, I have a feeling I'll be seeing you again soon."

Laura blushed.

Jake said, "I hope so."

"Bye. Have a safe trip."

"Thank you. Bye."

After Peggy had left, Laura leaned over the table toward Jake and asked, "What do you think of Peggy?"

"She seems nice enough. I like her."

"From a man's perspective, what do you think of her appearance?"

Jake turned to look but Peggy was already out of the cafeteria. He turned back to Laura. "For me, I don't see her as pretty but I do find her attractive. I've seen very pretty girls who were not attractive."

"She is worried that she will never find a man who will love her and who she will love."

"She will. I'm sure of it. She has a pleasing personality. And, like I said, she's attractive."

Just then, Mr. Le Couteau walked over to their table.

"Good morning," he said.

"How ya doing?" Jake replied.

"Hi," Laura smiled.

"Fine. Fine. I understand you had another long discussion with Mr. Sinclair yesterday."

"Yes, it was nice." To himself, Jake thought, *I think I'll try to save the word nice for Laura.*

"Good. Good. I expect you made some suggestions to Mr. Sinclair."

"We talked about a variety of things – the same way you

and I talk, Jean."

"Of course. Of course. Well . . . I just want to wish you well and have a safe trip back to New York."

"Thank you."

"I really enjoyed our talks."

"I did too, Jean. Thank you for taking the time with me."

"My pleasure." Mr. Le Couteau smiled and shook hands with Jake. He patted Jake on the shoulder and said, "Goodbye."

Jake turned to Laura and asked, "Did he seem nervous to you?"

"Very. That was unusual."

"He didn't seem himself at all. He seemed to be . . . asking what Mr. Sinclair and I discussed."

"Did you make suggestions to Mr. Sinclair?"

Jake smiled. "I might have. Apparently, that is why I came here."

"What?"

"To talk with Mr. Sinclair. That is why I came here."

Laura batted her eyelids and said, "I thought you came here to meet me."

"No, you are a wonderful bonus."

"I was teasing."

"I know. But you are a real bonus."

"That's nice."

They both laughed.

Looking over Jake's shoulder, Laura said, "You've got more company."

Jake turned around. Walking toward them were Mr. Nesbitt, Mr. Millar and Mr. Kent. Jake got up and stepped over to them. He shook hands with each man and exchanged morning pleasantries.

Mr. Kent said, "We want to say our goodbyes."

Mr. Millar nodded to Jake and said, "It was good meeting you. I enjoyed your chapel talk."

"Thank you." Jake still couldn't believe he was ninety-three.

He asked Jake, "Do you know what day this is?"

"Yes, it's the sixty-first anniversary of D-Day." Mr. Millar looked at the other two men and smiled. He said to them, "I told you he would remember."

Mr. Nesbitt said, "It is extraordinary that Mr. Sinclair would meet with you twice and for so long. I hope you had productive discussions."

"I think we did, yes." Jake added, "Mr. Nesbitt, you questioned me on why I came here. I didn't know then. Now, however, I think that talking with Mr. Sinclair is why."

Mr. Nesbitt smiled. "I think so too."

Mr. Kent said, "Have a safe trip. Good luck to you."

"Thank you," Jake replied.

The three men turned and walked out of the cafeteria. Jake sat back down with Laura.

Laura asked, "Do you really think that that is the reason you came here?"

"That . . . and to meet you."

"I'm serious."

"I am too."

Laura smiled. "Okay."

As Laura and Jake returned to their breakfast, a news program from a nearby television broke in with a story from Ft. Kent, Maine. With the mention of Ft. Kent, everyone got quiet. This was somewhat of a local story. The announcer told that a little ten-year-old girl, Victoria Perdue, was missing. They showed a school photo of her. It seems she ran away from home the night before. She left a note for her mother. Because of the content of the note, the police questioned and arrested the mother's boyfriend. Volunteers had already come out to help the local police and sheriff's department hunt for the runaway child. They were searching all around the greater Ft. Kent area.

When the broadcast about the missing girl was over, everyone resumed talking and continued eating their breakfasts.

Jake said to Laura, "That's a shame. Poor little girl."

Laura responded, "Yes, and scary. Imagine that little girl

having to avoid the advances of her mother's boyfriend. And then, running away at night. She must have been so scared."

"Where would a ten-year-old go?"

"What do you mean?"

"Think like a ten-year-old girl. You used to be one. She must have had a plan. Where would she go? Where would she head to?"

Laura said, "Oh, I see what you mean. I suppose she would head to a relative's house – a grandmother, perhaps. Or . . . maybe to a friend's house."

"I suppose law enforcement will check all that out."

"Yes. I imagine that is standard procedure. They are probably doing that now."

"Good thing the weather is nice now. June is not cold in Maine. Maybe a little at night," Jake added.

"Yes, but we do get a lot of bugs. Most little girls don't like bugs."

"Most grown-ups don't like bugs."

They continued to eat their breakfast.

As they finished their breakfast and got up to leave, several people, some of whom Jake had not even met or seen, waved to him and made comments such as "have a safe trip," "I enjoyed your talk," or "hope you can come back and see us."

Laura walked with Jake down the trail to the lake where his canoe was tied.

"As soon as I get back to my condo, I'll send you an email."

"That's nice. I'll look forward to it."

"This was not, at all, the vacation I had envisioned. But I am very glad it turned out as it did."

"Me too. You thought you'd just relax on this lake, catch a few fish and enjoy doing nothing."

"Yes. And that's what I will have to say I did. At the beginning, I did do that."

"Try not to fall in the river."

"That's good advice."

Jake opened his arms and Laura stepped into them. They hugged tightly, broke for a long kiss, hugged again and then stepped apart. Jake walked over and climbed into the canoe.

Picking up the paddle, he turned to Laura and said, "It's truly been nice."

She smiled and waved her fingers in a bye-bye gesture. She said, "Very nice."

Jake smiled, said, "Bye" and made his first stroke with the paddle and moved away from the shoreline.

Laura simply said, "Bye" and waved goodbye.

Jake paddled the canoe across the lake to his camping spot. Laura had watched him until he was about halfway across. Then, she turned and walked back up the trail to the secret entrance in the rock face.

Peggy greeted her. "Are you going to miss him?"

With moist eyes, Laura replied, "I already do."

Jake quickly broke down his tent and packed everything tightly so he could load the canoe for the return trip. He carried the canoe back over the strip of land that separated the lake from the branch of the river that he had used to get there. Once he had the canoe in the water, he went back and retrieved his tent and supplies. Just as when he arrived, it took four trips to get everything loaded. Jake figured he would paddle to the same place where he had spent the first night, sleep there and paddle back to Allagash. With an early start, and paddling with the current, Jake thought he could get there before dark. Having eaten breakfast with Laura, getting a bit of a late start but paddling with the current in this branch, just as it was getting dark, he arrived at the little "beach" area where he spent the first night. Jake quickly gathered some wood and set up his tent. He would get a real early start in the morning, soon connect with the main stream of the St. John River and then it would be a straight course to Allagash.

Jake thought it was an absolutely gorgeous sunrise. As he watched the clouds changing from pink to red, Jake ate some beef jerky, peanut butter crackers and a handful of almonds. What a balanced breakfast, he thought. He wondered what Laura would have for breakfast. He missed her. He packed the canoe and shoved off for his trip back. This time, he didn't get his feet wet.

After about three hours of paddling with the current, staying to his left, Jake reached the St. John River. The current was stronger than he remembered. It made his strokes much easier as he was paddling with the current. He thought he would reach Allagash before dark, turn in the canoe, pick up his rental car and spend the night in a Ft. Kent motel.

As Jake was completing his third hour of paddling on the St. John, he noticed a wide clearing on the right bank up ahead. It was like a small beach with several large rocks and some logs scattered about the area. There was also, on the left bank, a much smaller beach-like clearing. He was paddling near the left bank. The hills on the left side, the north side, were higher and steeper than those on the right side. It was a beautiful summer day. Jake was happy and content with his vacation time. He was excited about meeting Laura.

His paddling was almost automatic. His thoughts were on the mysterious center that the Sinclair family had developed.

Suddenly, at the same time, Jake heard a rifle shot and noticed water coming in the canoe on the left side just below the water line. Without thinking, he stuffed a waterproof jacket sleeve into the hole and paddled as hard as he could for the right bank where the large open area was located.

Near the top of a hill on Jake's left, a man with binoculars said to a man with a rifle, "He's going to the wrong place."

"What? Why would he go over there when the left area is so much closer?"

"I don't know. But he's paddling for all he's worth to the right bank. Good shot, by the way."

"Thanks. But this means we're gonna have to cross the river."

"Yeah. Wait until he pulls the canoe up on the shore and then, I guess you'll have to shoot him."

"Okay."

Through the scope on his rifle, the shooter watched Jake tug the loaded canoe up on the bank of the river. Just as Jake bent over to grab the prow of the canoe, a bullet wined as it passed over his back. Jake quickly reached in his backpack and removed his .38 caliber revolver. He scrambled down behind the canoe. He went all the way down to the very end of the canoe and waited. Another bullet tore through the top edge of the canoe right in the middle. Jake jumped up and ran toward a large boulder. Just as he dove for the ground behind the boulder, a bullet grazed his thigh.

Jake had absolutely no idea why this was happening. His leg was burning. He took off a sock and his belt. He placed the sock over the wound and wrapped his belt tightly against it to stop the bleeding. He whispered, "Jesus, be with me."

From the side of the boulder, Jake peeked out and looked at the hill. The sun was shining brightly and, as he glanced over the hill, he noticed three reflections. He presumed two were from binoculars and one was from a rifle scope. He was right. Jake pulled back the hammer on his revolver. He quickly swung his arm over the boulder and fired at the area where he had seen the reflections.

When Jake's bullet hit a tree near him, the man with the rifle was stunned. He looked at his partner and nodded at the tree.

His partner, with the binoculars, said, "That does complicate things."

"You think?"

"We've got him pinned down behind that big rock. If he makes a run for the trees, you can plug him easy."

"What if he just stays there 'til dark?"

"We'll have to flush him out into the open. You know, this is a pain. He should have gone to the left area."

"I know. All the others did. There may be some of those tourists people coming down the river."

"They don't usually come this far."

"Sometimes they do. And the overnighters do. Sometimes they camp right where he's at."

"Let's go down to the river."

The two men worked their way down the steep hill to the riverbank. They stayed back in the trees.

Jake was undecided about his course of action. If he stayed where he was, "they" whoever "they" were, would have to cross the river and the open ground between the river and his boulder. During that time, "they" would be vulnerable. When he peeked around the boulder, he was vulnerable. They could easily see him from the hill. However, if they came down the hill to cross the river, he could crawl to the trees and be gone. Jake was confident he could lose them in the forest. Were they "just" thieves who wanted to steal his stuff? If so, they could have it. Or, were they murderers who wanted to kill someone? Or, was he the specific target of someone? He thought they must just be thieves who decided he was "easy pickings."

Jake peeked out again. He saw no reflections. Just as he pulled his head back, a bullet whizzed by the boulder and struck the ground several feet beyond. Jake thought, *That guy is a good shot. But that came from the bottom of the hill. Much closer.* Jake figured the rifle must be a bolt action. As soon as the bullet struck the ground, Jake stood up and fired into the trees across the river. Crouching behind the boulder, Jake immediately started crawling for a pile of loose rocks between him and the woods. The woods were his goal. His shot into the trees had made his attackers duck behind trees. He figured that the shooter would probably go upstream or downstream and try to flank his position behind the boulder. When Jake reached the pile of rocks, he crawled around them and behind them rather than over them.

Once behind the rocks, Jake paused and tried to breathe normally. From where he was at now to the first tree was about forty feet away. He would be exposed during that forty feet. If he got up and ran for it, he could probably make it. But then they would know he was in the woods. Right now, they still thought he was behind the boulder. If he could get to the forest without them knowing it, he could get a big head start on getting far away.

Jake decided to crawl extremely slowly toward the trees. He would make no sudden movements at all. He would do nothing that would attract attention. He figured that they were working their way across the river and through the trees to get at an angle so that they could see behind the boulder. He started his crawl. He whispered, "Jesus, be with me."

The two men were each crouched behind a large tree. They were still directly across the river from Jake's canoe and the boulder. They were not in a position to see Jake's crawl.

The man with the binoculars said, "He hasn't looked from around that rock since your last shot."

The man with the rifle replied, "I don't blame him. How we gonna cross the river?"

"Looks like we're going swimming."

"I don't know if I can carry this thirty-thirty and swim at the same time."

"I think there's a spot downstream just a bit where we can walk across. It's only about three or four feet deep there."

"Okay, let's do that. Let's cross there and come up behind him from the woods. While he's sitting behind that rock, I could probably get a clean shot of him from behind a tree."

"Sounds like a plan. Let's go."

While the two men were staying in the woods and going downstream, Jake was slowly crawling toward the trees. Jake got behind that first tree about the same time his two attackers reached the point at which they were going to cross the river. They couldn't see Jake and Jake couldn't see them. He scanned the woods across the river for any sign of movement. He saw none. Bending over, Jake slowly moved through the undergrowth deeper into the forest. He stood up and listened. Hearing nothing, he moved quietly still deeper into the woods.

Jake was "at home" in a forest. He loved the woods and being "one" with Mother Nature. Not hearing anything, Jake broke into a run. His thigh was stinging but he ignored it. Using the sun as a guide, he stayed somewhat parallel to the river. Jake enjoyed running through woods. He felt like a deer. It came natural to him and he was good at it. As he was running, he was also thinking. *Who in the world would want to kill me?* Jake thought, *I have certainly left the unreal world of Neverland and returned to the real world.* He knew his revolver only had three bullets left in it. He always kept the hammer on one empty cylinder. He had fired twice. If those guys were just out to steal his stuff, they could have it. He certainly didn't want to shoot anyone. Of course, he'd rather not get shot again himself.

Jake slowed to a trot. Seeing a small hill up ahead, staying behind trees and undergrowth, Jake climbed the hill. He figured he was now about three miles from where he had left the canoe. In the distance, he could see the sun's reflection on the river. He sat down and listened for any pursuit. He whispered, "I trust you, Jesus. Thank you for always being with me."

While Jake had been running, the two men had crossed the river and had slowly and quietly been approaching the boulder where Jake had hidden from them. Slowly moving from tree to tree, they finally got close enough to see the clearing. They saw the boulder; they saw the canoe; they saw the pile of rocks; but, they did not see Jake. They looked at each other and one shrugged his shoulders.

The other one whispered, "Where could he be?"

"Perhaps he heard us coming and is on the other side of that big rock."

The one with the rifle nodded and moved sideways through the trees so that he could see the other side of the boulder. He looked back at his partner with the binoculars and shook his head. The man with the binoculars scanned the woods. He could see no sign of Jake.

Cautiously and slowly, the two men entered the clearing. After taking just a couple of steps into the clearing, they noticed a man in a canoe paddling downstream. They took a few more steps and the man noticed them. He waved to them and returned to his paddling. They looked at each other.

The man with the binoculars was looking at the man in the canoe. He said, "That guy doesn't have anything in his canoe.

Look at this canoe. It's loaded."

The man with the rifle said, "You think that guy is our guy?"

Looking through the binoculars, he replied, "Yeah."

"Well, where in the world did this guy come from?"

"Dunno."

"What now?"

Still looking through his binoculars, he answered, "It's too late to try and catch up with our guy. We'd never get 'em now. And, we've got another problem."

"What?"

"It looks like about seven or eight canoes heading our way."

The two men scrambled back into the woods.

Before they even reached the clearing, several people had noticed Jake's canoe beached in the clearing. They all paddled over to the clearing. Their guide suggested a break and they stopped at the clearing. The guide said that they should wait a few minutes. He thought that the person with the canoe had stopped for a potty break. One of the women noticed the hole in Jake's canoe with the jacket sleeve stuffed into it. She pointed it out to the others. A man saw the other hole at the top side of the canoe and showed it to their guide. The guide shouted toward the woods. He asked if anyone needed help. They all began to look around and moved to the edges of the forest. They shouted and tried to contact whoever had been paddling the damaged canoe. However, they got no response. The guide wrote down the canoe's number and divided the contents among the other canoes. He left a note in the canoe explaining what they had done. The group then ate their late lunch in the clearing. After that, with no sign of anyone, they headed back downstream toward Allagash.

After they were gone, the two men came out of the woods and back to the clearing.

The man with rifle said, "Did you see all that gear they removed?"

"Yeah. That wasn't our guy. That was just some

wilderness camper. Wonder where he is?"

"Probably still running."

"Don't blame him. Let's go."

"Boss man is gonna be angry. We let the drug carrier sail right past us. He even waved at us."

"Everyone makes mistakes. Let's go."

Jake felt comfortable in any forest. He had a keen sense of direction and wasn't afraid of getting lost. He would simply walk to Dickey, get a ride to Allagash and explain to Rod, at the rental company, that someone had shot his canoe out from under him. Rod would respond by saying, "Sure. That happens all the time." Anyway, he'd get it straightened out, get his rental and drive to Ft. Kent, get a motel room, take a hot shower, eat a big supper and head south the next day. Jake figured he could reach Dickey and Allagash sometime the following afternoon.

As the sun began its descent, Jake starting looking for a place to spend the night. He had been walking all afternoon but decided he should stop and begin fresh in the morning.

The only "tool" Jake had with him was a pocketknife that he always carried in his jeans' pocket. With that, Jake cut several small twigs and branches from trees. He intertwined them and made a lean-to for cover. He placed one end against the trunk of a large tree and the other end on the ground. Off to one side of the lean-to, using his pocketknife and his fingers, Jake dug a small fire pit. He found some dry rotten wood from a tree that had fallen over long ago. He mixed that with some dry grass and tried to start a fire by "sparking" two rocks. He made a lot of sparks but not much else. Jake didn't have a jacket and would like to have the warmth of a fire. It wasn't really cold. It was June. Trying to start a fire was, Jake thought, certainly keeping him warm. Jake looked at the pile of sticks and small logs he had gathered. Oh well, he thought, I can survive a cool night. But still, Jake bunched-up a small pile of dry grass and banged his rocks. The sparks flew. After many many attempts, Jake finally got the grass to catch. He gently blew on it and added more grass and a few very tiny dry twigs. He kept gradually adding larger and larger sticks to his fire. It felt good. Jake leaned back against the trunk of the large tree and watched the flames of his fire consume the small logs. It was peaceful. Jake was hungry and thirsty. However, he was okay with that. Tomorrow night he'd be in a motel in Ft. Kent.

Looking at the fire, Jake said out loud, "Jesus, I know things happen for a reason. I know you are in control. Thank you for being with me and taking care of me. I don't yet understand why this is happening. But I'm sure you have a reason. Help me to learn the reason someday. Thank you, Jesus."

Unknown to Jake, of course, were all the events of that afternoon involving his canoe and its contents. The guide had returned with the tourists and they had collected all the contents of Jake's canoe. With the number from the canoe, Rod quickly pulled out the paperwork and the name of Jake Fleming was reported to the police as a missing person. The guide explained to the sheriff's office that he thought a bullet had caused both holes in the canoe. He told how a jacket sleeve had been stuffed in one of the holes in an attempt to prevent water from filling the canoe. It was early evening as the guide and tourists returned to Allagash to report finding Jake's canoe. Still, a search party could not be organized until the next morning.

Just as the sun was rising on the horizon, Jake shook himself awake. It was the morning of Wednesday, June 8th. He had actually slept for a couple of hours. He stretched and stumbled around a bit. His leg was throbbing a little. He made sure his fire was completely out and covered his fire pit with the dirt he had removed to make it. Jake had found a limb on the ground that was about seven feet tall and a couple of inches in diameter. He used it as a walking stick and headed east. Staying about a half a mile from the bank, Jake was keeping the river on his left and was trying to walk a straight line. However, the river, of course, had many turns and bends. When the sun was almost directly overhead, Jake turned left and walked toward the river.

Monitoring police radio calls is standard procedure for the media. The day before, on the six o'clock news in Bangor, Augusta and Portland, in addition to an update regarding the missing ten-year-old girl, it was reported that a tourist from New York City, Jake Fleming, was missing. There weren't any real details – just that his canoe had been beached and there was no sign of him.

Bad news has a way of traveling quickly. At a little after eight o'clock, one of the women who worked at Excalibur with Jake and Ted, called Ted and told him the news. Ted said, "I knew it. He's been abducted by aliens." At around seven-thirty, Mr. Le Couteau knocked on Laura's apartment in "Neverland." Laura opened the door and invited Mr. Le Couteau inside. He told Laura what was on the news. She paused, put her hand over her heart and looked to be in deep thought. She replied to Mr. Le Couteau by saying, "I think he's all right. I don't feel that anything real bad has happened to him."

"I hope you're right. Anyway, I thought you would want to know."

"Yes. Yes, of course. Thank you." She thought to herself, *Surely he didn't fall into the river. He said he was a good swimmer. What could have happened?*

Law enforcement got the Air National Guard to fly over the area from the clearing east to see if they could spot anything. They did not see anyone or anything out of the ordinary. Jake heard the plane fly over but did not see it. They had been flying around the Ft. Kent area looking for the lost little girl. She had still not been found. Most all law enforcement personnel were involved in the hunt for her. Nonetheless, a search effort for Jake was begun. In a small boat, four men traveled down to the clearing where Jake's canoe was beached. From there, the men fanned out in several directions. Eventually, the muddy tracks of two men, apparently crossing the river, were located. This caused the search effort to move across the river and up and over the hills there. The conclusion now was that Jake had been kidnapped and forced, by the second set of footprints, to leave his canoe and go with this unknown man. One of the men had noticed blood next to the boulder. They kept looking for more drops but never found any additional blood. The searchers were, of course, all looking in the wrong place.

During the noon news update, it was reported that a search team looking for Jake Fleming, a tourist from New York City, found evidence that he had apparently been shot and kidnapped. The search effort was being increased.

Laura heard that report and was truly upset. She decided to go to the chapel and pray. As she left her apartment, Peggy walked around the corner. Laura asked her to join her in the chapel. They saw Mr. Le Couteau ahead of them in the hallway. When they went inside the chapel, Mr. Nesbitt, Mr. Millar and Mr. Kent were already there. Indeed, there were about a dozen other people there. Everyone just sat in a pew and silently prayed that Jake would be found and that he would be all right. While they were at it, they also prayed for the little Victoria girl from Fort Kent – that she would be found safe.

It was Jake's custom, as he traveled through woods, to stop every now and then . . . and listen. Being close to nature was often a spiritual experience for him. In this situation, he wanted to listen in case anyone was following him. Nearing the river, Jake stopped to listen. His leg was hurting and he took longer than usual to get a sense about what was happening.

While "listening," Jake heard "something" that didn't sound like a forest sound. He held his breath and listened intently. He heard it again. He took a few steps in the direction of the sound. He stopped to listen. There it was again. Again, being as quiet as he could be, Jake took a couple more steps and stopped. Moving from tree to tree, Jake continued toward the sound. Eventually, he was close enough to recognize the noise. Peeking around a large tree, Jake saw Victoria Perdue sitting on the ground, with her back against a tree, crying. Her face was shiny from her tears. How in the world, Jake thought, had she gotten from Fort Kent to these woods? Jake wondered, *how can I approach her without scaring her and causing her to run off into the woods?* Even with my hurt leg, Jake thought, she can't outrun me, but I'd hate to scare her by running her down.

Talking loudly, Jake stepped around the tree and said, "Man-oh-man, I don't think I can take another step. My leg is really hurting me." Jake plopped himself down with his back against a tree. He panted as if he was having a difficult time catching his breath.

The little girl was startled. She stood up, picked up her backpack and took a few steps away from Jake. She stared at him. She noticed the blood stain on his leg.

Pointing at his leg, she asked, "How did you hurt your leg?"

In a calm soothing voice, Jake replied, "Someone shot me."

She stepped back. "You mean with a gun?"

"Yes, I'm afraid so."

"Why? Are you a murderer?"

"No." Jake shook his head and laughed. "I don't know why I was shot. I was paddling in my canoe in the river and someone shot me."

"Hmmmmm. Are you going to die?"

Jake smiled, "I hope not. I don't think so."

The girl was dressed in typical little girl clothes. She was wearing tennis shoes, jeans and a pink sweatshirt that had butterflies all over it. They were about fifteen feet from each other. She did not know what she should do. She took a couple more steps away.

Jake smiled and said, "Victoria, I know that you ran away from home." She didn't respond. Jake said, "I want you to know that I will help you. I will not do anything to hurt you. I promise." She just stared at him. "Your mother is worried about you. She misses . . ."

"She doesn't miss me! She only cares about her boyfriend."

"No, I heard on the news that your mother's boyfriend is in jail."

"Really?"

"Yes, really." After a pause, Jake pointed at her tree and said, "Sit down and let's talk."

After a few moments, Victoria dropped her backpack and sat back down with her back against the tree. She looked at Jake and said, "He told me he was going to teach me grown-up games. I told him I was too young for those grown-up games. He scared me."

Jake waited a few seconds and softly said, "I'm sorry you had to deal with such a creepy jerk like that. No one should have to . . . be in that situation. But he is now where he belongs – in jail."

"Really?"

Jake nodded his head and replied, "Yes."

"Good."

"Yes. But Victoria," Jake smiled, "I want you to tell me something . . . how did you get from Fort Kent to here?"

For the first time, she smiled and laughed. Then, she got serious and explained her journey. She said, "My best friend lives in Allagash. She would let me live with her. We are in the same class at school. Her name is Becky. I packed some clothes in my backpack. I snuck out of the house. I got the raft from the swimming pool. Then, I put it in the river and headed to Allagash. Then . . ."

"Wait a minute. What kind of raft was this? Surely this wasn't one of those plastic swimming pool rafts?"

"We used it in the swimming pool. But it wasn't plastic. It was some kind-of rubber or canvas, I think."

"Okay. Victoria, you are one brave little girl."

She smiled.

"You are also a very strong little girl. You must have been kicking really hard to get the raft to go upstream."

"I stayed as close to the bank as I could. It wasn't too hard to make the raft go."

"I understand. Go on with your story."

"I thought, when I saw the lights from Allagash, I could

steer the raft into the shore. But I couldn't. I just went right on past Allagash and past Dickey."

"How did you get to shore?"

"I used my legs and feet and kicked and kicked the water until I bumped into the shore. I tore the raft on some rocks. I think it is ruined. So then, I started walking back to Allagash. But I think I must have got turned around and walked the wrong way. I think I'm lost."

"Don't worry about that now. I will take you back. I promise." Pointing at her backpack, Jake asked, "Did you bring food with you?"

"Yes. But I ate it all yesterday. I didn't sleep my first night. I was hungry. I ate a lot then. I slept a lot during the first day. I ate more then. That night, I slept some. I didn't have any food left. I thought I was going to Becky's house."

"I understand. Victoria, we ought to get going. I don't think we are all that far from Dickey. You know, a lot of people are out looking for you."

"Why?"

"Because they are worried about you. They don't know if you are all right or not."

"Oh, I see. Okay."

"Of course, they have been looking for you over around Fort Kent. They don't have any idea that you are way over here. But we'll get back later this afternoon and show them that you are all right."

"Okay."

Jake stayed with his original plan to go over near the river and just follow it back until it reached Dickey. After almost an hour, Jake noticed that Victoria was having a difficult time.

Jake announced, "I'm really tired. I could use a breather."

Victoria said, "Okay."

They sat down together with their backs, this time, against the same tree.

Jake told Victoria, "You know, when I think of you getting on that raft in the middle of the night, I realize what a brave girl you are."

"I thought I could steer it . . . but that didn't work."

"No. But you survived two nights, in these woods, by yourself. You are a smart girl and a brave girl."

"Does your bullet hole hurt much?"

Jake laughed. "No, not really."

Just then, a plane flew overhead.

"They are looking for you, Victoria."

Actually, they were searching for any sign of Jake.

"They can't see us, can they?"

"No, I'm afraid not."

"How much farther is it?"

"Not much. We'll get there before dark."

"Okay."

"You ready?"

"Yep."

Jake figured that they were only about an hour and a half from Dickey. As they were walking east, Jake kept up a conversation with Victoria. He asked about her school. He wanted to know her favorite subjects. Did she like her teacher? What was her friend Becky like? Once he got her talking, Victoria had a lot to say.

After about another hour, Jake called for another rest stop. Victoria was really beginning to feel the full impact of her ordeal.

As they sat down, Victoria said, "You know what?"

"What?"

"You don't talk to me like I'm a little kid. You talk to me like I'm a grown-up."

"You talk like a grown-up."

"Do I?"

"Yes."

"I don't have any brothers or sisters. I guess I'm mostly around grown-ups. Except at school. Do you have any kids?"

"No, I don't."

"Why not?"

"I'm not married."

"Oh, I see." Victoria seemed to be in deep thought. Then she said, "When I grow up and get old, you can marry me."

Jake smiled. "That's quite a compliment, Victoria. Thank you. But there is a problem with that plan."

"What?"

"As you grow older, I will also be growing older. When you get old enough to get married, I'll be a really really old man. You wouldn't want to marry a really really old man, would you?"

Victoria laughed. "I guess not."

"After you graduate from college, you'll find a nice man your own age and you two will fall in love and get married."

Victoria laughed again. She said, "Okay."

"I guess we'd better get going. We're almost there."

Victoria said, "I was thinking. I am really really tired. And hungry. Would it be all right if I stayed right here? You could go on to Dickey and tell everyone where I'm at. They could come get me."

Jake looked at her with surprise. He replied, "No, I don't think that is a good plan. I'm not sure I could tell everyone exactly where this spot is. They might have a hard time finding you. Then, it might get dark before they could find you. You don't want to spend another night out here in the woods by yourself. We'd best just go on together. It's not much farther."

"Okay."

Shortly, they came to a bend in the river. Across the bend, they could see part of the small village of Dickey.

Jake pointed, "There it is. We just need to walk around this curve and we'll be there."

"Okay."

It took them almost thirty minutes but they walked right in to the little town of Dickey. There was a car parked on the main street with two teenage boys inside.

Jake walked over to the car. Victoria reached up and grabbed Jake's left hand. Jake leaned down to the window and asked, "You guys doing anything for the next fifteen to twenty minutes?"

The driver looked at Jake and Victoria like they were crazy. He said, "What's up?"

"I was wondering if you guys could give us a lift over to Allagash?"

They looked at each other, shrugged their shoulders, rolled their eyes and the driver said, "I guess so. Hop in."

Jake and Victoria got in the back seat.

"Where did you want to go in Allagash?"

Jake replied, "Do you know the canoe rental place on the river?"

They rolled their eyes again.

"Sure."

"Could you drop us there?"

"Sure."

"What are your names?" Jake asked.

The driver answered, "Earl."

The passenger said, "Bruce."

"My name is Jake and this is Victoria."

The two teens looked at each other and Earl asked, "Are you the guy that was shot?"

Bruce asked, "Is this Victoria Perdue, the missing girl?"

Jake answered, "Yes."

Earl said, "Well, I'll be . . ."

Jake said, "I really do appreciate you guys helping us out. We've both been walking a lot today."

"No problem. Glad we can help."

"Thank you."

It was a short drive over to Allagash. Earl pulled up at the rental store. Jake and Victoria got out of the car. Jake reached through the car window pass Earl and shook hands with Bruce. He then shook hands with Earl.

"Thanks guys. We appreciate it."

Earl said, "You're welcome."

Jake and Victoria walked into the canoe rental store. Jake had his revolver in the back pocket of his jeans. He pulled his sweatshirt down to cover it. He put his finger to his lips and shook his head. Victoria nodded in return. No one appeared to be there.

Jake called, "Rod? Rod, you back there?"

Rod eventually came from some back room. He stopped and stared. He pointed at them and said, "Both of you?"

Jake nodded. Victoria grabbed Jake's hand again.

"How are you here? Everyone's looking for both of you. Where did you come from?"

"Rod, could you call Victoria's mom or the police?"

Jake looked at Victoria and said, "Your mom is probably out with the search teams looking for you."

Looking back at Rod, Jake said, "Who is in charge of the search efforts? The Sheriff's office?"

Rod said, "I can't believe you both are here. Uh, yeah, uh, I don't know who is in charge."

"Tell you what, Rod, let me get my rental car and I'll drive Victoria and myself over to Fort Kent. I'll settle up with you tomorrow. Is that okay?"

"I guess so."

"Where's the police station in Fort Kent?"

"Look here. I'll show you on this map. You can't miss it. See. Go back down this road, turn left here and it will be on your right."

"Got it. Thanks. Would you call them and let them know that we both are fine and are on our way? They can get in touch with Victoria's mom."

"Yes. Sure. You bet."

"Right. See you tomorrow then."

Jake and Victoria got in the rental car to head for Ft. Kent. It wouldn't take long. Jake placed his revolver under the driver's seat. He told Victoria not to mention it. She nodded in agreement.

"You buckled in? You don't use a car seat anymore, do you?"

Victoria gave him a look of disdain.

"Sorry. I guess not. I don't have one anyway. I'm sure they will be in touch with your mom and she will get to the police station as soon as she can."

"Okay."

"Our adventure in the forest is almost finished. I'm going to miss you, Victoria. You make an excellent hiking partner." Victoria smiled.

Rod had reached the police station. When Jake turned left, he could see a crowd of people gathered on the right. The officer who had talked with Rod had already told the crowd that Victoria was all right and the missing guy had found her. Jake pulled the car over and parked. As Jake walked around the car to the passenger side, the crowd began clapping. When he let Victoria out and started walking toward the police station with Victoria, the crowd continued clapping and began cheering.

Jake nodded, waved and smiled as he tried to steer Victoria to the police station. He saw an officer coming toward them. Jake stuck out his hand and said, "I'm glad to see you." They shook hands and the officer said, "You can't imagine how glad we are to see little Victoria here."

"Is her mother here?"

"On the way."

Jake nodded and they followed the officer inside.

Jake and Victoria sat in some chairs. The officer was not able to contain his excitement. All the other officers and sheriff deputies were out as part of the search teams. Now, both missing persons just walked right into the office. He looked at them and said, "Can I get you anything?"

Jake and Victoria looked at each other and mouthed the word "food" to each other.

Jake nodded to Victoria and replied to the officer, "A couple of sandwiches and something to drink would be nice."

The officer nodded and said, "Of course."

After the officer had left the room, Jake turned to Victoria and said, "I don't know about you but I'm starving."

She laughed and said, "I'm really really really starving."

Jake laughed. Then he said to Victoria, "Listen, I think we are supposed to drink real slow and eat real slow. Don't wolf it down. If we eat too fast, it can make us sick and we might barf it all back up."

"Eeuuww."

"Yeah. Let's try to eat slow slow slow."

"Okay."

The officer returned with two egg salad sandwiches and two orange juice bottles.

Jake and Victoria took one of each and both said, "Thank you."

Jake nodded to the officer and said, "This is perfect."

Jake and Victoria watched each other take a small sip of the juice and then a small bite of the sandwich. They smiled as they slowly ate the sandwiches and drank the orange juice.

Just as they finished, two officers came in with Victoria's mother. She ran over and hugged Victoria over and over. She kept asking if Victoria was all right. She squeezed her. She looked her all over, up and down, and made her turn around. Finally, she said, "I just can't believe that you are here. How are you here?" She turned to the officer and asked, "Who found her?"

The officer pointed at Jake.

Jake stood up and offered his hand. Victoria's mom ignored the hand and rushed toward Jake and gave him a big hug.

Jake disengaged himself from Victoria's mom and said, "Actually, we kind-of found each other."

Jake looked over at Victoria and winked.

"Thank you so much. I just cannot tell you how grateful I am that my Vicky is safe – that she is here."

"Let me tell you that you have a very special daughter. She is an extremely smart, and brave, girl. You should be proud of her."

Victoria's mom didn't know exactly how to respond to Jake's assessment of her daughter.

She replied, "Thank you. I'm just glad she is back. I was so worried that something awful might have happened."

Jake said, "I understand."

Jake turned to one of the new officers and asked, "What is

the procedure here? I was shot at, several times, by two men. I was hit once in the leg." Jake pointed to his leg. "I suppose you need a report."

"Yes, we will need to get a statement from you."

"Can we do that tomorrow? I think I need about twelve hours sleep right now. I bet Victoria does too."

Victoria smiled and said, "At least."

"Of course. One question: did you get a look at the two men?"

"I'm sorry, I did not. I can't even swear that they were men. Could have been women or one of each. I am just presuming that they were men."

"I understand."

Victoria's mother asked, "Can we leave now?"

"Yes, of course. You may want to run her by her doctor's office and have her checked out. She has been through an awful lot."

"Do you think that's necessary?"

"Wouldn't hurt."

"Vicky, do you want to go see Doctor Brown?"

"No. I'm just tired . . . and hungry. You know I hate it when you call me Vicky. Do you have to do it public?"

One of the other officers spoke up and said, "I should warn you that a television crew from Augusta is out there. They will probably want a comment from you."

"Oh for Pete's sake. I don't have anything to say. I'm just glad to get my daughter back safely."

Holding Victoria's hand, her mom started toward the door. Victoria turned back and ran over to Jake. Jake got down on his knees and said, "Give your old hiking buddy a goodbye hug." She whispered in his ear, "Thank you. For everything." Jake whispered in her ear, "I'm going to miss you. You be good and no more running away. I understand why you did. But, if that ever happens again, tell your mom, tell your teacher at school or come here and tell the police." She nodded and said, "Okay."

Outside, the television reporter stuck a microphone in

Victoria's mom's face and asked, "How do you feel now that your daughter has returned safely?"

"How do I feel? How would any mother feel? I feel wonderful. I feel relieved. I feel happy. I feel grateful. I am grateful for all the people who helped with the search. I am especially grateful to Mr. Fleming for bringing my daughter safely home."

She and Victoria walked across the street, got in their car and drove home.

Three more officers, two of them sheriff deputies, arrived at the station. Jake shook hands with all three of them.

Jake sat back down and said, "I've been thinking about those guys who shot me. The more I think about it, the more I think that it was a mistake. I think that they must have mistaken me for someone else. I cannot think of any other plausible scenario."

One of the officers replied, "You may very well be right. How do you know that there were two attackers?"

"It is possible that there were more than two. But I do know that there were at least two. You see, I saw the sun reflecting on a pair of binoculars and on a rifle scope – at the same time. Had to be two people. Could have been more; but, at least two."

"That makes sense."

The officer that suggested that Victoria's mother might want to run her by the doctor's office asked Jake if he wanted a doctor to look at his wound.

Jake said, "It's really just a scratch. I'll put something on it. What time should I come by tomorrow?"

One of the officers asked, "Would ten o'clock work for you?"

"Ten o'clock is perfect. I had hoped to leave early to get back to New York tomorrow evening. That's not going to happen. I'll just be a day later getting back. I need to go square things with Rod regarding the canoe. I don't suppose insurance covers bullet holes."

"Probably not."

"Do you think that camera crew has left?"

"Probably not."

Jake smiled. He walked over to a window and noticed that the crowd was much larger than when he arrived. He turned to the officers and asked, "Why are all those people still here?"

"Like the television crew, they want to see you."

"Me? Why?"

"You really don't get it, do you? You are a hero to these people. You found a missing little girl, a local little girl that these people know – and you brought her safely back to her home. If you had not done that, she might have died in those woods. We were not looking down there for her."

"But I only did what any adult would have done if they found a child crying in the woods. That doesn't make me a hero."

"It does to these people. It may be true that any adult would have done the same. But you are the one who did it."

"It seems to me that the story here is about Victoria. She is an incredible little girl. Has the mother's boyfriend made bail?"

"No, not yet."

"Victoria is very afraid of him."

"We'll keep an eye on her."

Jake nodded. "All I want to do now is drive over to my motel, get a little something to eat and then go to sleep for as long as I can sleep."

"I can understand that. But you're going to have to work your way through that crowd and the TV crew to get to your car."

"If you guys arrest me, don't you have to feed me and lock me up in a nice cell with a bed?"

One of the officers laughed. He said, "You would have to do something that would require an arrest."

"I could spit on your shoes. Or call you disrespectful names."

"I think both of those are covered by free speech."

"I wouldn't do that anyway. I have a lot of respect for law enforcement officers."

One of the officers nodded toward the door. He said, "You might as well suck it up and get it over with."

"All right. I'll see you tomorrow around ten."

Jake opened the door and walked out of the building. The crowd applauded and cheered. Jake nodded and waved. As he turned to go toward the rental car, the television reporter was there with her microphone and cameraman.

She said, "Mr. Fleming, would you care to comment on the events of your rescue of Victoria Perdue and of your escape from assassins?"

"Yes, let me tell you. You folks up here have some wonderful children. Victoria Perdue is an extremely intelligent young lady. You all should be proud of her. She is also exceptionally brave. I have just spent over a week admiring the beauty of this area. You folks should be proud to live in an area where God spent a little extra time making it more beautiful than most other places."

The crowd cheered and clapped as Jake walked away from the television crew. He got in his car and slowly backed away until he could turn around and leave.

The television reporter was angry. She turned to her cameraman and said, "He didn't say anything. He didn't answer my questions at all. He answered like a politician."

Inside, the officers were smiling.

That night, the safe return of both Victoria Perdue and Jake Fleming was the lead story on the local television news stations in Maine. Laura and the people at "Neverland" felt that their prayers had been answered. Laura listened as they reported that Jake had been shot but, in the brief clip they showed of him in Ft. Kent, he didn't appear to be shot. She didn't understand.

The next morning, June 9th, Jake filled out as complete a report as he could remember regarding what had happened to him. The police agreed with him that he must have been mistaken for someone else.

Jake also went to the canoe rental shop in Allagash. All his stuff, including his cell phone, was piled up in a corner. Rod helped him carry it out to the rental car. He settled everything with Rod. He also got the full names and addresses of Earl and Bruce. He wanted to send them a thank you note that included a fifty-dollar bill. Rod knew both boys and was glad to look up their addresses.

Jake had a late lunch in Ft. Kent and decided to drive south. He would spend the night in Bangor and head back to New York the next day.

CHAPTER THIRTY

"Come to me, all you who are weary and burdened, and I will give you rest. Take my yoke upon you and learn from me, for I am gentle and humble in heart, and you will find rest for your souls."

– Matthew 11:28 - 29

Mid 1st Century A.D.

Friday, June 10th found Jake Fleming driving south on I-95 out of Bangor and headed toward Portland. Jake would simply reverse his trip up from New York. The night before, Jake had called Tom Jennings, the President of Excalibur, and explained his situation and apologized for being late. Jennings was already aware of the "situation" and expressed his concern. Jake had also called his parents and told them that he was fine. Lastly, he had called Ted. Ted was disappointed that no aliens were involved in his story. He had told Jake that he was the only person he knew who had been shot. Jake explained that the bullet had just passed completely through the tissue on the edge of his thigh. He washed it, put some antiseptic on it and changed the bandage every night. It wasn't like a real shooting, he explained. Ted would have talked for hours but Jake told him that he was really tired and needed some sleep.

Jake made good time and arrived back in New York by mid-afternoon. By the time he had stored his tent and camping gear, returned the rental and caught a cab back to his condo, it was almost six o'clock. It was hot and humid but Jake was glad to be back home. He microwaved a TV dinner, took it out on his balcony and enjoyed the view that was so familiar to him.

While puffing on his pipe and sipping his wine, Jake reflected on the last three weeks. So much had happened. He met so many new people. He had had numerous long conversations. He had had a birthday. "Neverland." Jean Le Couteau. Charles Sinclair. Québec City. Victoria Perdue. Peggy. The three elderly gentlemen. That unreal library. The beautiful lake. Most of all, Laura. He couldn't stop thinking about her.

When his wine glass was empty and his pipe was finished, Jake decided to go in and send Laura a long email. Laura had already sent him an email. She was worried. The news said that he had been shot. When she saw the news clip of him in Ft. Kent, however, he looked fine. She said that she realized that the news frequently got things wrong – had he been shot? If so, where? How badly? She had signed the email "All the best, Laura." All the best? All the best? Really? What had he expected? Love? But did he really want the first time he told Laura or she told him "Love" to be in an email? No, the first time should be in person.

Jake sent Laura a long email and explained what had happened on the river and in the woods. He asked more about her and what she was doing than he talked about himself. He told her that his wound from being shot was superficial and was healing up nicely. He signed his email with "Looking forward to seeing you soon, Jake."

Jake had a difficult time sleeping. He tried on his back. He tried on his front. He then tried on his side. He gave up. He went into his library, got a book, sat in his easy chair and tried to read. He couldn't. He read the same page several times and still didn't know what he'd just read.

Jake had too much on his mind. Why did he feel an "urge" to travel into the wilderness of northwest Maine? How and why were the people in "Neverland" expecting him? Was his purpose for going there to convince Charles Sinclair to go public? Was his purpose for going there to meet Laura? What was the reason his canoe was shot? What was the reason he was shot at?

Was it to force him to go ashore so that he could be in the right place to find that little girl and take her safely back to her home?

Jake realized he had no answers for these questions. He stopped trying to read and prayed. He thanked Jesus for being with him on his vacation trip. He asked God for guidance to understand why all this had happened. He asked for peace and felt the Holy Spirit give it to him. He told God that he had faith that these events happened for a reason. He didn't yet understand the reason or reasons but was confident that God would reveal that information in His own time.

Jake woke up Saturday morning in his easy chair. He felt sleepy. He got up, went into his bedroom and crawled into bed. He slept until almost noon.

After showering and shaving, Jake walked to the small grocery in the next block down from his building. He frequently shopped there. He needed milk, eggs, bread and a few other things.

Back in his condo, he thought he'd watch a ball game on TV and relax. However, he couldn't relax. He wandered around his condo. He was restless. He went out on his balcony and tried to watch the world go by – but he just couldn't sit still. His mind kept going back to Laura. When he tried to think of something else, he discovered that he was soon thinking of Laura again.

On Thursday night, Ted had told him that he had tickets for a Broadway show on Saturday night. He was taking his wife, Stacy, to the show. Ted and Jake had made plans to meet at their favorite seafood restaurant for lunch on Sunday. The restaurant was on Long Island and Jake was looking forward to it.

Jake went to bed early and was sleeping well when his phone rang. It was a reporter calling to interview him. When the television news report regarding his rescue of little Victoria Perdue had aired, the reporter had been in Camden, Maine and had watched the local news. She now wanted to interview him for her newspaper. Jake politely told her that he had no interest in being interviewed. She seemed shocked. She told him that she had already interviewed a sheriff's deputy, the mother of Victoria and Victoria. To complete her story, she needed to interview Jake. Jake declined. She said, "Mr. Fleming, you are a hero. I want to let the people of New York be aware of what one of their fellow New Yorkers has done. I want everyone to . . ." Jake interrupted her and said, "I appreciate your situation but I'd rather not. Goodnight." Jake hung up the phone.

He had a difficult time getting back to sleep. He gave up and read for about an hour and a half. He sat out on his balcony. It was two-fifteen in the morning and there was still much activity in the harbor and on the streets below Jake's balcony. Jake had thought many times in the past as he was thinking now – New York City truly is the city that never sleeps.

Jake usually attended an early morning worship service but this Sunday morning, he decided not to go. He arrived at the restaurant on Long Island around eleven-thirty. He was meeting Ted at noon. Ted arrived at twelve-twenty. They both ordered their usual seafood dinners – lobster and scallops for Jake and halibut and crab for Ted.

After they ordered, Ted said, "So are you telling me that you didn't see a single UFO on your entire trip?"

Jake smiled. He replied, "Yes, not a single one."

"Hard to believe. Perhaps they programmed your mind to say that."

"Perhaps." Jake gave Ted a big smile. He said, "Ted, I'm afraid that I had absolutely no luck in the UFO area at all."

"There's a big story in *The Post* this morning about you."

Jake rolled his eyes.

Ted laughed and said, "I read it. It was very detailed. Told about you being shot. Told about you rescuing that little girl."

"We just walked out of the woods together."

"Uh-huh. The article quoted the little girl and her mother. It didn't quote you but it did quote from the police report."

"That reporter woke me up about nine o'clock last night. I hung up on her."

"Now was that nice?" Ted smiled.

"I tried to be polite. I just have no interest in participating in that news story."

"The TV stations will be after you next."

"You think so?"

"Absolutely. If they don't catch you at home today, they'll probably try at work tomorrow."

"Good grief. That's all I need."

"Hey, maybe you're looking at this all wrong. This may be your chance for your fifteen minutes of fame."

"Ted, I don't want any fame."

"But it might help you at work. More people may want you to invest their money because you are a celebrity. You've been recognized as a hero and have been on TV. You could milk this for . . ."

"Ted, there's going to be no milking. I'm currently doing rather well financially. Besides, I have decided to resign from Excalibur."

Ted didn't say anything for about thirty seconds.

Then he asked, "What are you going to do?"

"I'm not sure. I still like the idea of getting a few acres in the country."

"Raising chickens?"

"Why not? I like chickens."

"You'll probably want a dog."

"Probably. Why not? I like dogs."

"You'll probably want to raise a garden."

"Why not? I like fresh vegetables."

"You'll probably want a wife and some children."

Jake didn't reply for about fifteen seconds. He actually blushed. Jake laughed and said, "Why not? I would love to have a wife and children."

Ted had noticed Jake's reaction and jumped on it. He said, "You met someone. On your vacation, you met someone."

As he thought of Laura, Jake smiled.

Ted said, "You didn't answer."

Jake said, "You didn't ask a question. You made a statement."

"Was it true?"

"Yes."

"Tell me about her."

"She's wonderful."

Ted had just taken a swallow of iced tea and indicated with a hand motion for Jake to tell him more.

"She has a natural kindness that I love."

"Okay, she sweet. What's she look like?"

"She's beautiful."

"Details."

"She's five-seven, trim with all the standard curves, dark red hair that looks beautiful. She has a way of tilting her head and all her hair just falls into place. She has a smile that lights up a room and it makes me happy just to see it. Her name is Laura and she teaches school."

"And you have already fallen for her, haven't you?"

"Yes, I guess I have."

"Amazing. So what's the down side?"

"Down side?"

"Yeah, you know. She's got two ex-husbands and three kids. She walks with a limp and has one glass eye. I'm just joking about the limp and glass eye. But there must be some negatives."

"Only one. And it is my fault. I am too old for her."

"Ahhh. I see. She's too young for you."

"She says it's not a problem."

Ted looked concerned. He responded by saying, "She's not still a teenager, is she?"

Jake rolled his eyes again. "Of course not. She's thirty-three."

"Thirty-three? Listen son, thirty-three is a grown woman. What are you now? You just had a birthday, didn't you?"

"Yeah, on my trip. I turned forty-two. That's nine years."

"Jake, you're not too old for her."

"You don't think so?"

"No, not at all. I absolutely don't think so. Now, how many children does she have?"

"None. She's never been married."

"That doesn't stop people these days."

"I know. But no, no ex-husbands and no children."

"How did you guys meet?"

"Schools are on summer vacation. She was vacationing in Maine and, of course, so was I. Actually, we almost literally bumped into each other. We were in 'Mother Nature' and I was walking around these rocks. She was coming from the other direction and there we were. We spent some time together and I asked her out for dinner. She accepted and we spent a lot of time getting to know each other. She is a Christian and we have that in common." To himself, Jake said, *forgive me, Jesus, for stretching the truth there.*

"Amazing. Where do . . ."

The waiter brought their meals. They both began to eat.

Ted picked up from where he had left off, "Where do you guys go from here?"

"I'm not sure. We've emailed each other. I'd like to see her again soon. Maybe we could get together for an extended weekend or something."

"Sounds like you've got it bad for her."

"I do and I like it."

"Jake, I truly hope it works out for you."

Jake nodded and replied, "Thank you."

"So you're leaving Excalibur?"

"Yes, I plan to tell Mr. Jennings tomorrow. I'll give him a month's notice."

"But you don't have another job and you don't even know what you're going to do or where you're going to live."

"True." Jake smiled.

"You do realize that it doesn't make sense?"

"Depends upon one's perspective."

Ted sighed. "Okay, from what perspective does what you are doing make sense?"

Jake replied, "From a Christian perspective. We are now five years into the twenty-first century. The world is in worst shape than it's been for a long time and it'll probably get much worse before it gets any better."

"Yeah, I've heard that."

"So . . . for me . . . and for many other Christians, the question becomes how does a Christian remain positive in a negative world?"

"I'll bite. How?"

"For me, I ignore the world's agenda and focus on the things that Jesus taught. Christians will never fit in with the ways of the world. They should not even try. In the book of Mark in the New Testament, Jesus said, 'What good is it for a man to gain the whole world, yet forfeit his soul?' Suppose you had billions of dollars, but you didn't know Jesus as your personal savior? Suppose you were elected President of the United States but you didn't know Jesus as your personal savior? Suppose you were a big Hollywood celebrity and you won the Oscar for best actor or actress but you didn't know Jesus as your personal savior? Christians should not want to be seen as acceptable to the ways of the world; but rather, as people who live separate from those ways. Now Ted, don't misunderstand. I am not saying that Christians should go live in some compound in the mountains as part of some cult. We have to work, shop and live our lives among the world. We just don't have to adopt the culture of the world. It is not compatible with a Christian lifestyle. The ways of the world are not the ways of Christians. By ignoring the ways of the world as much as possible, I can remain true to my Christian beliefs and stay positive."

"I guess I understand what you are saying. But now, unless I'm much mistaken, you're thinking of getting married."

"Yes. You know, when I married my 'practice' wife, I was deeply in love with her. But, over the four years we were married, she showed no interest in me. That lack of interest caused me to eventually lose the love I had felt for her. I think of how different the love that Christ has for us is. No matter how little interest we show in Him, He still loves us and will never leave us. That is supernatural love – total love.

"I have changed much since my divorce. Separation from my wife brought me closer to Jesus. When I was married, I was more of a 'Sunday only Christian.' I was saved but I didn't appreciate what all that meant. Today, I am trying to be a twenty-four seven Christian. I am so grateful to Jesus for the Resurrection and for the Holy Spirit. I am now much more aware of the daily presence of the Holy Spirit. Jesus offers non-ending and complete love. That has daily brought joy and peace into my life. Joy and peace are not the ways of the world.

"I am, as I mentioned, now forty-two years old. I would like to fall in love, get married and have a family. If it happens, wonderful. If not, I'll still be happy. I'll still have joy and peace in my life. I think all Christians should be happy people. I mean, Jesus saved our souls. Our souls are eternal. We have no reason not to be happy."

Ted asked, "What if one's parents, or anyone that was loved, died? Would a Christian be happy then?"

"First of all, happiness, I believe is not conditional upon outward things. It is an inner, almost spiritual, state of being. You asked about an exception to the normal course of life. Death is, of course, a normal part of life. It will happen to each of us. Everyone grieves in their own way. I think the manner in which a loved one dies also impacts the way a person will feel. If it is a gradual death of someone in their nineties, the surviving person has time to come to an understanding that this loved one is dying. They have the opportunity to say 'goodbye.' However, if the death is sudden and not at all expected, the surviving person may have a much more difficult time accepting the loss. Suppose a loved one, at the age of thirty-five, had a heart attack and died. The surviving person might have a much much harder time dealing with the death than if the person had died of a disease that took two years to take the loved one. If the person who died were a Christian, then the person who was still living would know that their loved one's soul was with Jesus. There would still be a period of sadness, of grief, because one's loved one was no longer in their human body and they could no longer interact with each other. But a Christian has the comfort of knowing that they will, one day soon, be reunited with their deceased loved one.

"Facing the death of a loved one or some other tragedy is an exception to the everyday rule. Our modern culture is trending toward more and more hostility to Christians. Our culture is rapidly changing. It is so concerned these days with wealth, status and political correctness. These are things that Christians have no interest in pursuing. Our culture has become so sexualized and politically correct that it is destroying the traditional family. Of course, Christians support the traditional family. This puts them at odds with our current culture. As I mentioned, Christians cannot go live in caves. We have to live in the world but we do not have to compromise our beliefs and become of the world. Of course, the world won't like us. However, we are not here to please the world; but rather, Jesus. I've preached enough, Ted."

"No, I follow what you are saying."

"Have you been practicing your office putting skills?"

Ted laughed. "No, I haven't even been in your office."

After they had finished eating, over several cups of coffee, they continued talking. Eventually, they both caught separate cabs and went to their respective homes.

When Jake got back, he turned on his computer and found a long email from Laura. She had written how glad she was to learn that his gunshot wound was not serious. She told him that, since he had left, "Neverland" seemed different to her. She told him about some of her students. She said she missed having a full summer off from teaching. School classes at "Neverland" took place year-round. They were on a semester schedule like a college rather than the typical public school. Laura had explained all this one time when they were eating at "their" booth. She must have forgotten that she had already told him. She said that Peggy said "Hi." She ended her email by saying that she also hoped they could see each other soon.

Jake wrote her back and told her that he was going to resign from his job the following day. He would give a month's notice. Looking at a calendar, he mentioned he would probably stay until July 15th. He asked her if she could get off for a few days after that. He told her that he could meet her in Québec City. He said that he would make reservations for separate rooms at the hotel Le Chateau Frontenac. Jake was a little concerned about his invitation to meet her in Québec City. Would she be put off by it? Would she think he was being too forward? However, given her living arrangements, Jake was at a loss to come up with a different idea for getting together. He signed off with a simple, "See you soon."

Again, Jake was restless all afternoon. He had trouble sleeping; but, Monday morning found him in a cab on his way to Excalibur. As he had done many times, he walked through the lobby of the office building and caught an elevator to his floor.

After responding to the most important emails and opening much of his regular mail or as Ted was now calling it "snail mail," Jake went to Mr. Jennings' office and gave his notice. He said he would stay on until Friday, July 15th and make that his last day.

Back in his office, Jake finished opening both his regular mail and his email. He had just about finished when he heard Ted pounding on his wall. Jake knocked back in return. It was lunchtime and Ted soon entered his office. Jake was at his desk. Ted lined up a putt, stroked it smoothly and . . . it went in the hole.

"Yes! Did you see that? A perfect putt."

Jake looked up. "No, I wasn't watching. Do it again."

Ted started grumbling. "Wasn't watching. Wasn't watching. A perfect putt and he wasn't watching. All right, Redfire will do it again."

Ted lined up his putt. He stroked the putter smoothly and…the ball went wide of the hole."

Jake said, "Yeah, sure you did."

Ted started to say something but then he noticed Jake was

grinning. Jake said, "I have great peripheral vision. I saw your first putt. Good shot."

Ted pointed his index finger at Jake and pretended he was firing a pistol at him.

Ted asked, "You ready to get some lunch?"

"Yeah, sure. You know, you shouldn't pretend to shoot a guy who just got shot with a real gun."

"I forgot. How's it going?"

"It's all right. I'm just teasing. I don't mind pretend guns at all."

"Where you want to eat?"

"A sandwich is fine with me."

"Tony's?"

"Sure. In fact, in honor of such a magnificent putt by Redfire, I will pick up the tab."

Ted bowed his appreciation.

In the elevator, when it was just the two of them, Ted asked, "Did you have a chance to talk with Jennings?"

"Sure did."

"How'd it go?"

"Okay, I guess. I told him that I'd stay on to wrap everything up by July 15th."

"Really?"

"Yeah. He asked me to reconsider. I said no. He asked me to stay on 'til fall. I said no."

The elevator stopped and several people entered. Ted and Jake stopped talking. Tony's was in the next block from their building. They frequently ate there.

Sitting in a booth, with a wave of his hand, Ted said, "If you really leave, you're gonna miss all this."

"I know. I will miss our rambling conversations."

"Me too. So tell me more about this wonderful woman with the hair trick."

Jake laughed. "I don't know what else to tell ya. I think I told you everything yesterday." To himself, Jake thought, *Yeah, everything. Everything except that she lives underground in a place that no one ever heard even exists.*

"Well," Ted replied, "She does sound nice. I truly hope it works out for you."

"Thanks."

"Hey, have you heard of *Myspace*?"

"That computer site where people go to connect?"

"That's it. I was thinking that you and your new girlfriend could communicate with each other on it."

Jake said, "Maybe. Are you on it?"

"Not yet, but I probably will be soon. I've been looking into it. It's still fairly new but, in a few years, it'll probably be really big. They say that people will still be using it twenty-five years from now. I'm wondering if I can use it, in some way, for business purposes. I know it's supposed to be a social network but why wouldn't it work for businesses?"

Jake shrugged his shoulders and took another bite of his sandwich.

Later that night, Jake was sitting in his comfortable easy chair, in his library, reading from the Bible – Matthew. It brought him real peace to read the Bible. It was real to him. The Holy Spirit used it, he felt, to make him more aware of his spirituality. Jake always read at least one chapter from the Bible every day. It resulted in a true sense of appreciation for what God had done by agreeing to let Jesus come, in human form, into the world as a sacrifice for anyone who would believe in Him and follow Him.

Over the next month, Jake was busy at work getting things in order and in place for whoever took his place. Jake began removing personal items, primarily paintings, from his office. He would take one home with him almost every day. He had more mementos than he realized – several personalized coffee mugs. By his last week, all his clients had been transferred to others in the company. Jake saw that Ted received several of his "plum" accounts. During his last week, Jake really had little to do. On the 15th, his last day, the office had a nice "retirement party" for him. It was at lunch and consisted of sandwiches, chips and a retirement cake. Jake truly appreciated the gesture, the kind words from Mr. Jennings and his colleagues, the cards and gifts from them and the office staff. After the party, Ted and Jake were in Jake's office.

Ted was lining up a putt and said, "I'm gonna sink this last one."

Jake replied, "No, that's not your last one. I want you to take the putting green and put it, with the putter and the balls, in your office."

"I can't take your putting green."

"Of course you can. You're not taking it; I'm giving it to you. Every time you use it, it will remind you to stay in touch with me."

"I'd be honored. How are things going with you and Laura?"

"We've been emailing each other fairly regularly. She still has dial-up where she lives so it isn't as easy for her as it is for me. The big news is that she is going to take the last week off and we are going to get together."

"That's great! The last week of . . .?"

"July. This month. I'm meeting her on Saturday, July twenty-third."

"I'm happy for you. I really hope it works out for you."

"Appreciate it."

Jake was looking out his window one last time. It was always difficult when he looked where the twin towers used to be.

He walked over to Ted and gave him a hug. They shook hands and Jake said, "I'll be in touch."

"You better."

They both smiled and Jake walked out of his office and headed for the elevator.

CHAPTER THIRTY-ONE

"Everyone should be quick to listen, slow to speak and slow to become angry."

– James 1:19

Mid 1st Century A.D.

Jake's plane touched down in Québec City, according to travel brochures, the most European city in North America, almost exactly at 11:30 AM. It was actually a fairly short flight from La Guardia Airport. It was Saturday, July 23rd and Jake took a cab to the Chateau Frontenac. As he checked in, he asked about Laura. They told him it was against hotel policy to answer whether or not she had arrived. He went to his room and found it to be very nice – luxurious even. The view was simply magnificent. It included a wonderful view of the St. Lawrence River. The St. Lawrence River flowed between the two sides of the city. He was on the Old City side where most of the attractions were located.

Jake had not eaten any breakfast and was getting hungry. He would like to wait on Laura but she had warned him that she didn't know when she would arrive. Henri had, weeks ago, agreed to drive her over and pick her up the following Saturday. However, she knew his schedule could change at any minute. Jake decided to go down to the lobby and wait on Laura. If she didn't show by one o'clock, he would grab a sandwich and they could eat a nice dinner together.

Laura did not arrive by one o'clock. After eating a sandwich, Jake returned to his room.

He called the front desk. "Has Laura Middleton checked in yet?" Again, they would not reveal that information.

"Can you tell me which room she will be in?"

"Non, monsieur. The lady will have to do that herself."

"I understand. When she does arrive, can you tell me that?"

"Non, monsieur. It is the policy of the Chateau Frontenac to respect the privacy of all our guests."

"Okay. I understand. Surely you can give her a note from me, a message?"

"Oui, of course monsieur."

"Good. Please tell Miss Middleton, are you writing this down?"

"Oui, monsieur."

"Good. Just say 'After you get settled in your room, call me at my room number.' And add my room number at the bottom and my name, Jake. Thank you very much."

"Bon, monsieur."

Jake thanked the clerk, placed the phone down and began to pace about his room. He would stop and enjoy the view. Then he would turn the television on, get quickly bored, turn it off and walk around some more. He was restless and anxious. He talked with himself. He told himself that Jesus was with him and that everything would proceed as it should. To help pass the time, Jake read about the history of Québec City. For Jake, it was fascinating. As one who enjoyed reading history, Jake was again surprised at how much had gone on in this city and how little he had known about it. Jake was reading about something of which he actually had some knowledge – the Battle of the Plains of Abraham. Jake had remembered that both the British General Wolfe and the French General Montcalm had been killed during the battle. As he read about what was now on the Plains of Abraham, his room phone rang and startled him. It was Laura.

It was almost four o'clock and Laura had just checked in and made it to her room. After talking for a couple of minutes, they agreed to meet in the lobby. She needed to go tell Henri that Jake had arrived and it was okay for him to leave and to pick her up the following Saturday. After doing that, she would be in the lobby.

Jake was waiting in the lobby and saw Laura as she returned from the front of the building. Jake thought she looked like a true vision of loveliness. She was wearing a cream-colored skirt that ended a couple of inches above her knees and accentuated her small waist. Her blouse was a crisp navy and cream striped top that matched her skirt and fit her well. Her shoulder-length red hair looked luminous and reflected the lights from the lobby.

Laura walked directly over to Jake and gave him a tight hug and a long kiss. He gladly returned both. When they broke from their kiss, Jake whispered in her ear, "That's nice." She smiled and nodded her head.

"Hi!" With enthusiasm, Jake said.

"Hi." Laura smiled her beautiful coy smile.

"I can't believe we are here."

"I know."

They headed for the door and went outside.

Jake said, "Where to?"

"Oh, we have to do as the locals do. We have to take a leisurely promenade along the Terrasse Dufferin."

"Leisurely?"

"Oh yes, to do it correctly, it must be leisurely."

Laura reached down and grasped Jake's hand in hers and said, "Come on."

The Terrasse Dufferin was a wide terrace that was part of the Chateau Frontenac. The views of the St. Lawrence River were outstanding. Jake had a camera and Laura became his model.

"You see, Jake, in Québec City, one does a lot of strolling and promenading."

"Leisurely?"

"Always."

Jake said, "So, tell me what's new in 'Neverland.' How is everyone?"

"Everyone told me to tell you 'hello.' Hello. And Peggy is shocked about my coming to spend a week with you."

"Peggy? That surprises me."

"You don't know why she is shocked. She is shocked that we are staying in separate rooms."

"I see."

"Yes, she said that she is going to have to give you boyfriend lessons."

Jake laughed. "Now that sounds like Peggy."

The Chateau Frontenac is on top of an elevated site. It was the original place that Fort St. Louis was constructed. Under the Terrasse Dufferin was a way to visit the historic ruins of that fort. Laura and Jake went down to that. Laura told Jake that she had never previously visited it. From there, they walked, or strolled leisurely, over to the Jardins du Gouverneur. This was a site in honor of both General Montcalm and General Wolfe.

Laura and Jake strolled through the Upper Town. There were quite a few street performers. There were also many shops and restaurants. Several of the restaurants had outdoor seating. Laura was reading the menus. She was looking for something specific.

She found it. She said to Jake, "Let's eat here."

"Sure. Inside or out?"

Laura asked, "Did you pack any sweaters?"

"Yes, a couple."

"Good. At night, if often gets down into the fifties here. Let's eat inside. I want you, on your first night, to eat a Québec City specialty. It's like going to Scotland. You have to eat haggis."

"I see. What's it called?"

"Poutine."

"Is it as gross as haggis?"

"No. It's actually not bad. But it's different. It is required, by law I think," and Laura winked at Jake, "to consume poutine at least once during your first visit to Québec City."

"I'll try anything once."

Inside, Laura ordered a seafood salad and Jake ordered the poutine. Poutine, it turns out, consisted of a plate of French fries with cheese curds and topped with lots of gravy.

When the waiter brought their food out, Jake thought that Laura's salad looked delicious. His plate however looked like someone had previously eaten it and barfed it back onto the plate. Laura started laughing.

"What?" Jake asked.

"The look on your face. Go ahead. Try it."

"It looks disgusting."

"Try it."

Jake did. "You're right. It's not so bad. It sure tastes better than it looks."

When they walked out of the restaurant, they were both surprised at how cool it had gotten.

Jake said, "Wow, you were right about needing a sweater."

Laura moved over closer to Jake and put her arm around his waist. Jake put an arm around her shoulder. Looking up and over to the east, Jake saw that, in the distance, the Chateau Frontenac was highly illuminated. He said, "I guess we go this way."

It was quite a little walk. Neither of them minded. They both enjoyed being with each other as they strolled back to the hotel. In the lobby, Jake said, "You know, I wouldn't mind attending a local church service in the morning."

"That would be nice."

Jake smiled. "In the tourist stuff, they mention two churches – the Sainte-Anne-de-Beaupre Shrine and the one we saw in the Place Royale when your group brought me here, Notre-Dame des Victoires. I don't even know if either of them still have church services. Do you?"

"No, I really don't."

"Why don't we just attend the nearest protestant church?"

"Okay by me."

They agreed to meet at the hotel restaurant at nine for breakfast.

Laura's room was one floor below Jake's. They were

alone in the elevator and Jake kissed her all the way up to her floor.

He said, "I should have booked us in a high-rise hotel with lots and lots of floors."

Laura laughed and stepped out of the elevator. Jake followed her to her room. At the door, he kissed her goodnight. He turned and walked back to the elevator. When it arrived, he rode up one flight. In his room, the night view of the St. Lawrence was magnificent. Jake looked out at the view and thought, *I am in love with Laura.*

After church and lunch, Laura and Jake went to Parc de la Chute-Montmorency. The waterfall there is higher than that of Niagara Falls. They chose to climb a stairway which gave them numerous scenic opportunities to take photographs. Later, they decided, since they were there, to go ahead and walk across the suspension bridge that went right over the top of the falls. They took more photos. They dined that evening at a very nice restaurant and then attended a play. It was a long day but they both enjoyed just being together.

Over the next four days, Laura and Jake, were typical tourists. They rented bicycles and toured the Promenade Samuel-De Champlain. This took them right along the bank of the St. Lawrence River. They picked up some seafood at Marche du Vieux-Port and took it next door to Bassin Louise for an outdoor lunch. They thought that lle d'Orleans was like stepping back in time. It is still somewhat rural with buildings that are several centuries old. There were many craftsmen and artisans on the island. Both Laura and Jake made purchases of small local art pieces that would make great souvenirs. They spent several hours one day at the Aquarium du Quebec. Walking through the Grand Ocean tunnel was an experience that no one ever forgets. They rode a double decker throughout Old Quebec. They enjoyed the view from the top deck. They also went to the Observatoire de la Capitale. This was the highest point in the city. Many more photographs were taken. Laura was in the foreground of most of the pictures that Jake took. The couple took a sightseeing cruise on the St. Lawrence River and was amazed at the perspective of Québec City from the river. They visited the Sainte-Anne-de-Beaupre Shrine. Both of them thought it was magnificent. It is the oldest Catholic pilgrimage site in North America. One place that particularly interested Jake was their visit to the Huron-Wendat Museum. This explained the heritage and traditions of the Huron-Wendat Native American nation. Jake had never heard of these people. To him, it was fascinating to learn about them.

On Friday morning, after seeing Parliament Hill, Laura and Jake walked over to the nearby Grand Allee. This was an area of many restaurants, gift shops and entertainment venues. The Grand Allee Drill Hall, a huge military building, was now a tourist attraction. Again, walking down a street in Grand Allee where all the homes and buildings had been constructed in the 1800s made Jake feel as if he were time-traveling. During the week together, Laura and Jake had become extremely close. They had fallen in love.

After lunch, Laura and Jake were walking among the Plains of Abraham. This was the site of a major battle in 1759 between the British and the French. Part of Québec City is built on a high plateau called the promontory of Quebec. This is why there is an upper town and a lower town. The Plains of Abraham is near the edge of this promontory. Today, the Joan of Arc Garden has been cultivated on part of the Plains of Abraham.

While sitting on a bench in this garden, Jake turned to his left, took Laura's right hand in his, looked into her eyes and said, "I love you."

She replied, "I know. I love you too."

Jake was briefly disconcerted by this. How had she known? He hadn't known that she loved him. However, that quickly passed and Jake realized that her comment lifted his heart.

Still holding her hand, Jake thought, *I had this all figured out in my mind but now I've forgotten exactly what I was going to say.*

He said, "Laura, I'd like for you to become . . ." *That's not right*, he thought.

Jake tried again. Laura was smiling at his discomfort. She thought she knew what he was trying to ask and was happy about it.

He said, "Would you be my wife?"

Laura answered, "Are you asking me to marry you?"

"Yes."

"Yes."

It took a couple of seconds for Jake to realize that she had accepted his awkward proposal.

He smiled and said, "I love you."

He put his arm around her shoulder and pulled her toward him and they kissed.

"I don't have a ring yet. But I know where a jewelry store is and you can pick out any ring you like. I was afraid I might get one that you didn't like. I was also not sure you would say yes."

Laura smiled and kissed him again.

He said, "Now that's nice."

She squeezed his hand. They got up from the garden bench and started walking back toward the Chateau Frontenac.

Jake said, "I realize that we have dozens of things to decide."

Laura asked, "Dozens?"

"I expect so. Where to live, for one. I've got my condo up for sale. I expect it will go pretty fast."

"I understand."

"You wouldn't want to live in New York City, would you?"

"Only if you are there."

Jake squeezed her hand and replied, "I really am ready to move far away from New York."

Laura smiled and said, "Glad to hear it." She added, "You could always move to Neverland. We could get a couples' apartment. They're bigger."

At first, Jake couldn't tell if Laura was being serious or

teasing him. He decided she was teasing.

He smiled and then, very seriously, said, "We could."

Now Laura didn't know whether he had taken her seriously or was just playing around.

She replied, "Okay, enough of this. We are not going to begin our married life by living in Neverland."

Jake laughed. He repeated what she had said about New York, "Glad to hear it."

Laura laughed.

"And where are we going to go on our honeymoon," Jake asked?

"Except for not sharing the same room, this week has seemed like a honeymoon to me."

Jake smiled and said, "Me too. I've felt that way. I promise, I mean, I really really promise that, on our real honeymoon, we will share the same room."

Laura squeezed his hand.

Jake added, "Another of the dozens of things to decide is exactly when we will be married."

Laura said, "Yes, I guess we do have a lot of decisions to make."

"And . . . that's nice."

They squeezed each other's hand.

Jake said, "I'm beginning to learn my way around this city. The jewelry store I was talking about should be around the corner here and down that street."

Jake told Laura, "Now look, if you don't find the ring you want, don't just settle. You're going to be wearing this ring for the rest of your life. I want it to be the ring you want. If it's not in this store, we'll go to another one."

Laura nodded and replied, "Okay." That reminded Jake of little Victoria.

After about an hour of looking at and trying on several different rings, Laura decided on one. It was a diamond ring just a tad over one caret in a gold setting.

Jake looked at it and said, "It's beautiful."

"You like it?"

"Very much. I love how it sparkles. Let's get it."

Jake gave the salesman a credit card and the purchase was made. Jake put the ring, which was inside a ring box, in his pocket. As they were walking out, Jake suddenly stopped and said to Laura, "As long as we are in a jewelry store, why don't we get our wedding bands?"

Laura bought a gold ring for Jake and Jake bought a gold ring for Laura.

After they left the store, Jake said, "We can get both wedding bands inscribed later, if we wish."

"All right. I think I'd like that."

"Let's eat at our hotel tonight."

"Okay."

After they had placed their meal orders, Jake said, "Laura Middleton, I have something for you." He took out the ring box, removed the engagement ring and slipped it on Laura's ring finger.

She moved it about so that the light would catch it and it would sparkle.

Laura said, "It's beautiful."

"That's what I was just thinking about you."

"Thank you." Looking at her ring, she said, "I'm glad you like it. You have excellent taste."

They leaned over and kissed.

Jake said, "Hmmmm, you taste good, like a fiancée should."

Laura looked surprised. "That's right. I'm a fiancée now. So are you."

After dinner, Laura said, "It's still early. Mind if your fiancée comes up for a glass of wine?"

"Not at all."

On the way up, Laura asked Jake, "Did you know that both Winston Churchill and Franklin Roosevelt stayed in this very hotel?"

"And now us."

Smiling, Laura said, "I love you."

"That's nice because I'm in love with you."

Once in Jake's room, Laura walked over to the window. "Your view is the same as the one from my room."

Jake was opening a bottle of wine.

He replied, "It's really nice. It's much better than my New York view."

"I'd like to see it."

"I'd like for you to see it. However, as you know, my condo is for sale and I expect it will go pretty quickly. But now that we are engaged, we need to think about where we want to live. I've never been to Savannah. What's it like?"

"It's okay."

"Your folks live on Tybee Island, isn't that right?"

"Yeah, I do love a warm ocean. But Maine is a lot prettier."

Jake brought a glass of wine over to Laura. After clinking their glasses, Jake gave a toast "to our marriage." Laura took a sip and so did Jake. They sat together on a sofa. Before long, they were kissing quite heavily.

Laura whispered in Jake's ear, "I wouldn't mind staying the night."

"I can think of nothing I would like better."

"But?"

"But let's do it right. Let's wait until our wedding night."

"All right."

"Are you upset with me?"

"No. Actually, I agree with you. I admire your restraint. It's just that . . ."

"I understand. You make me so very horny. Every time I saw you in Neverland, I wanted to hug you. Even the first time when you were wearing that white gown by the rocks. Right now, I would love to stay up all night with you. I promise, on our honeymoon, we will . . . have some sleepless nights."

Laura laughed. "Okay. It's a deal."

They finished off the bottle of wine. They talked about the

past week and all the things they had seen together.

Jake said, "Laura, I have thanked God for you. I want our marriage to be blessed by God. If we have any children, I want to bring them up with the knowledge that they are loved not only by us but also by Jesus. Laura, I promise I will always love you."

Tears started rolling down Laura's face. She found a tissue and wiped her face.

Laura replied to Jake, "I have thanked God for you, I am so grateful to have fallen in love with you and for you to return that love. I . . . uh . . . ."

Jake gave her a tight hug and they cuddled together.

A little after midnight, Jake walked Laura back to her room. At her door, Jake said, "I'll meet you in the restaurant at seven."

"That's right. Your flight leaves at ten-thirty."

"Yes." They kissed again.

Jake said, "You really do taste good like a fiancée should."

Laura smiled and they said "goodnight" to each other.

The next morning was Saturday, July 30th. After breakfast, they were a little awkward with each other. Neither wanted to say goodbye.

Laura said, "I've been thinking."

"Uh-oh."

"What?"

"Nothing."

"No, I've been thinking. Maybe we should just elope. What do you think?"

"I like it."

"But?"

"Laura, I didn't sleep much last night. I was also thinking. I came up with several options of things we could do and places we could live. I also thought of eloping but decided against it. I thought of . . ."

"I'm serious. I am ready to tell Henri, when he arrives to

pick me up, that I'm not going back. That we are going to find a minister and get married. I don't care where we live as long as we are together. We could get married here in Québec City, go on our honeymoon wherever you want and I could go live with you in your condo until it sells. Then we could find a house somewhere and turn it into a home."

"You have been thinking."

"I have. I have decided I don't want to wait. I want to be your wife as soon as we can get married."

Jake hugged her tightly. They were standing at the edge of the lobby just outside of the restaurant. He whispered in her ear, "I love you."

They sat on a small settee next to each other. Jake said, "I really like the impetuousness of the whole idea of eloping." Jake paused.

Laura said, "But?"

"But we have responsibilities. You will need to finish out your teaching term and resign. You need to leave Wonderland with good feelings. And what about all those people there? Won't they feel hurt if they aren't invited to our wedding? And your family? Wouldn't your parents be hurt? Mine probably would a little. My mom would. But she'd get over it. If we eloped right now, went on our honeymoon and came back to New York, we'd probably hurt a lot of family and friends. And don't women plan their wedding day years in advance? I've heard tales of girls as young as ten and twelve planning their weddings. They've got it all figured out except for the guy they are going to marry."

"Excuses. Excuses." Laura smiled. "I know you're right."

Jake hugged Laura. He said, "Let's not have a long engagement at all."

Laura replied, "I absolutely agree with that. I'm looking forward to your promise of sleepless nights on our honeymoon."

Jake smiled. He responded, "Me too. Let's make it a real short engagement."

Laura laughed.

Jake said, "I'm all packed. I need to get going. When you

get all packed and ready to check out, just give them your key. Everything is taken care of with your room. You might have to wait a little while here in the lobby until Henri arrives."

"Yes."

They walked over to the elevators. They weren't alone on the ride up to Laura's floor. Jake got off with her and walked Laura to her room. At her door, they hugged and kissed.

Jake said, "I'm already missing you."

Tears had started to form and roll down Laura's cheeks. She said, "Me too. I don't want you to leave me. I want us to always be together."

"We will be. We just need to go through the process, I guess."

Laura nodded her head. "I guess. But don't be too surprised if I show up at your condo."

"I won't. I love you."

"I love you."

They kissed and hugged again.

Jake turned and walked toward the elevators. Just before he walked around a corner, he turned around to look at Laura's room. She was standing in the doorway.

Jake waved to her and shouted, "I love you!"

Then he was gone. He got a bellboy to take his suitcase and packages down to the lobby. The Chateau Frontenac had a van service to the airport. Jake was thinking if his flight was on time, he might get back to his condo in New York before Laura got back to her apartment in Neverland. He missed her. He prayed that Jesus would be with her and give her a safe trip home. She had said the same prayer for him. Jake was already planning a honeymoon to Scotland, Wales and England. He was thinking of a tour of megalithic standing stones, circles and dolmen.

All the way back, Jake felt empty and alone. He had quickly gotten used to being with Laura. He truly was missing her.

CHAPTER THIRTY-TWO

"The Lord is my shepherd, I shall not be in want. He makes me lie down in green pastures, He leads me beside quiet waters, He restores my soul, He guides me in paths of righteousness for His name's sake. Even though I walk through the valley of the shadows of death, I will fear no evil, for you are with me. . . And, I will dwell in the house of the Lord forever."

– Psalm 23

Mid 11th Century B. C.

Without any warning, the car crossed the middle line of the highway and crashed directly into another car. The impact was so sudden and so severe that all the occupants of both vehicles were immediately killed.

After everything was sorted out, the police officers determined that both cars were traveling, in opposite directions, between 60 – 70 miles per hour. Neither car had any time to apply brakes.

Determining the identities of the five victims took some time. All five bodies were mangled and bloody. The police had to search through the men's pockets for wallets and the ladies' purses for identification. Eventually, they learned the identity of all five persons. The driver of the car that had caused the crash was a 17-year-old girl who had just gotten her first flip phone. They were quite a novelty and she had apparently been trying to use her new phone and drive at the same time. She obviously had not been successful in doing that. She was alone in her car.

In the car that was struck were two men and two women. They were identified as a married couple, Paul and Jo Morrison from Montreal, Henri Taine from Québec City and Laura

Middleton from Savannah, Georgia USA.

The date was Sunday, September 11, 2005. Laura had gotten her final fitting for her wedding dress on Saturday, the 10th. She had purchased a wedding dress in Québec City. It would be ready on the 17th. They had decided to stay over Saturday night and had attended a play together. Over Sunday lunch, while dining at a restaurant overlooking the river, Laura had taken a lot of kidding from the others about her upcoming change from a Miss to a Mrs. Jo had filled her in about all the things she was now going to have to put up with when she had a husband in the house. Laura laughed and had a good time with good friends.

During the month of August, Laura and Jake had been emailing each other almost every day. They had had a couple of phone conversations as Laura had received permission to use the landline. She had resigned her teaching position effective at the end of the summer term, August 26th. Jake had sold his condo but didn't have to move out until the end of September.

Laura and Jake had decided to get married on Saturday, October 8th. The wedding was to be at her parents' church in Savannah, Georgia on Tybee Island.

Early in the morning of Monday, September 12th, as the sun was just rising above the horizon, Jake's phone rang. It woke him. It was Peggy.

By the tone of her voice, as she had told Jake who it was, Jake knew that something was wrong.

He asked, "Peggy, what's wrong?"

"I uh, I don't know . . ."

"Is Laura ill?"

"No. . . . Jake, I have very bad news."

Jake did not respond.

"Are you there?"

"Yes."

"Jake, I don't know how to say this." She paused. Then, she said, "Laura was killed in a car wreck late yesterday afternoon."

Jake did not respond. His body and mind went numb.

Peggy whispered, "Are you there?"

Jake said nothing. He could not process her statement that Laura had died in a car wreck.

Peggy said, "Jake? Jake, can you hear me?"

"Yes. Surely there has been some mistake. Is Laura in the hospital? Maybe she will recover."

Peggy hesitated. "No Jake. Henri was also killed. And Paul and Jo."

Silence. Jake did not respond.

"Jake, Laura loved you so. She was happier than I've ever seen her. She was so excited about the wedding." Peggy was crying.

Tears rolled down Jake's face.

Peggy continued talking. "They were returning from Québec City. Laura told me that the week she spent with you there was the best week of her life. She was there getting her wedding dress ready."

"Noooooo! Don't say that! Ohhh noo. Oh No! It was my fault. Are you sure she's . . . she's gone?"

"Yes Jake. I am so sorry. What do you mean it's your fault? It was . . ."

"She wanted to elope. I talked her into having a traditional church wedding service with her family. If we had eloped, this wouldn't have happened. So, you see, it's my fault."

"No. No, it's not."

"I can't believe this. I just can't accept that this has happened. It just can't be. It must be some mistake."

Peggy softly said, "I wish it were."

They were both crying.

"Oh Peggy, this just hurts so much. I can't believe it."

"I know. I know."

Peggy paused. "Perhaps the funeral will give you some closure."

"Funeral! There's a funeral?"

"Yes, of course. Laura's body is being flown down to Savannah today. I don't know when the funeral will be. I don't know which funeral home will be handling the arrangements."

"Not a funeral. Laura is supposed to be having a wedding, not a funeral."

"I know Jake. I know. I am so sorry."

Jake did not respond.

"I don't know what else to . . ."

"How did it happen?"

"Some teenage girl was not paying attention. Her car crossed over and slammed into Henri's car. All five were killed instantly. There was no suffering."

"I see. I just . . . I just don't . . . I just don't know if I can handle this."

"It's hard."

More silence.

Peggy said, "I'm going to the funeral. I guess I'll see you there."

Jake did not respond.

"I hope you will attend."

"I don't know. I don't want to accept it. I want to go back in time and elope with her."

"I understand. I'm sure you can locate the funeral home on the Internet. There will probably be an obit in the Savannah paper."

"Good grief. Not an obituary. I don't want to read it. I don't know what I'm going to do. I don't know if I can . . . I don't know if I can handle this." Tears were rolling down Jake's face and dripping onto his bed sheets. "I just don't know. I feel lost and empty. I just can't believe it."

"I am so sorry, Jake. But . . . it is real. I will have four funerals to attend this week. Paul's, Jo's, Henri's and . . . Laura's. That seems very real to me."

"How can this be? I just can't believe it."

"I know. I know."

Silence.

Peggy said, "Mr. Sinclair said that he was going to call you. He wants to offer his condolences."

"I don't want to talk with anyone."

"Okay. I do hope you'll make it to the funeral. Bye."

"Bye."

Jake was quite literally in a daze. He had been sitting on his bed as he had talked with Peggy. He stood up and looked around the room. There were a lot of cardboard boxes. He walked out and over toward the balcony. Looking through the glass doors, he watched the sun rise in the sky. He wanted to share that experience with Laura. He began to cry again. He touched the glass with his fingers.

Out loud, Jake said, "Help me, Jesus."

Several hours later, Jake was sitting in his comfortable old easy chair. Most of his books were packed in boxes. He stared at the empty bookcases and empty shelves. He felt empty and sad.

Laura had been killed on Sunday and it was the fourth anniversary of the Islamic terrorists' attacks that killed so many innocent people. However, although on Sunday Jake had remembered the horrible event, now Jake did not connect the September 11th anniversary with Laura's crash. It just didn't occur to him. Grief and guilt were consuming him.

By mid-afternoon, Jake, still sitting in his favorite chair, had come to the conclusion that he was responsible for Laura's death. If only he had agreed with her suggestion to elope, they would now be married. They would have had their honeymoon with those sleepless nights. She would be with him right now. He thought of them living in a country farmhouse somewhere near a small town. They would have a dog, some cats, some chickens, maybe a couple of horses and, perhaps, a couple of children. Laura would make an excellent mother. They would be active in their church and in the small community in which they lived. If only he had agreed to elope. If only. Tears dropped from his eyes onto his bare legs. Since getting up that morning, he had never dressed. He had not shaved or eaten anything. As Jake sat there with tears falling, the phone rang. He slowly looked over at it and then looked back at the empty shelves. He wasn't actually crying but tears were falling from his face. He felt utterly alone. No one else knew that Laura was gone.

Jake whispered, "Jesus, help me."

Still sitting in his chair, still wearing only his briefs (his usual sleeping attire), Jake woke with a jerk. It was 2:20 AM on Tuesday, September 13th. Jake got up and went to the bathroom. He came back out and went out on to his balcony. As he watched a tugboat tow a mid-sized freighter out of the harbor, Jake thought to himself, *What now?* He stared at the ground far below. For the first time in his life, he could understand why some people, in this situation, would jump. Jake was not tempted to jump but he understood why some people would.

Jake sat back down in his library chair. He felt the anger within himself. He recognized that he was angry with himself. If only he had agreed to elope. He also felt an overwhelming sense of sadness. The loss of what was to be. In less than a month, he and Laura were to be married. Now, that wasn't going to happen. Instead, there would be a funeral this week. Jake felt so empty.

Sometime, a little after 5:00 AM, still sitting in his chair, Jake went back to sleep. He slept until almost ten o'clock. This time, Jake gradually woke from his sleep. For just half a second, he didn't know where he was nor that Laura was gone. Then, it quickly hit him – hard. He slumped back in his chair and recognized that his grief was overtaking him. But he didn't care. His mind was mostly numb and he was okay with that. He tried to pray – but could not. God had allowed this to happen. He could have easily prevented it. If Henri's car had been ten seconds ahead or behind where it was, the other car would have missed them. Laura would still be alive.

For about two hours, Jake just sat in his chair and tried not to think of what had happened. He tried not to think about what would have happened if they had eloped. Laura would still be alive. He tried to make his mind go completely blank. He wasn't particularly successful at this. After a couple of hours, he quickly got out of his chair and stood in the room. *What now?*

Jake thought. He decided he was thirsty, went to the fridge and got a bottle of water. He took it out on to the balcony and sat there for several hours. In another week, it would be autumn. The days were noticeably shorter than just a month ago. As dusk went to night, Jake stood up and went inside. He got another bottle of water and returned to the room that had been his library. Instead of sitting in his chair, he sat at his desk.

Jake's parents and two sisters were planning on attending the wedding on the eighth. He had decided to call his parents and let them know that there would not be a wedding.

His mom answered the phone. He quickly told her what had happened. As they talked, his mom kept repeating, "I am so sorry." He asked her to call his sisters and tell them that there would not be a wedding.

His mother asked, "How are you holding up?"

"I'm okay."

"Don't lie to your mother."

For the first time since Peggy had called, Jake smiled. It actually made him feel better.

His mother continued by saying, "Really now?"

"Really? I feel sad, empty, mad, angry and alone."

"Of course you do."

"And I am having a difficult time realizing that she is really gone. I mean . . . it's so permanent. I'll never see her again."

"I cannot imagine how hard this is for you."

"It truly hurts."

"I guess that proves you're human."

"I wasn't aware there was doubt."

"I know you're grieving but don't get snide with me. Here's your dad."

While she was handing the phone to his father, Jake overheard his mother say, "Laura was killed in a car wreck."

Those words hit Jake hard. He actually pushed his chair back from the desk to recover.

He heard his dad reply, "Oh no. No. That's terrible."

Then his dad spoke into the phone, "Hi son."

"Hi Dad."

"I am so sorry about Laura."

"Why Dad? Why? She was such a nice . . . sweet person."

After a brief pause, Jake's dad said, "I don't think that has anything to do with accidents."

"What?"

"Son, I have learned, over the years, that sometimes accidents are simply accidents. No one wants them to happen. But they do. Usually, they are due to negligence. When I am nailing a nail into a board and I hit my thumb with the hammer, that is an accident. I probably wasn't focusing as well as I should have been. It was an accident."

Jake did not reply.

"Are you there?"

"Yes."

"You are understandably hurting. Your heart is broken."

His dad paused and said, "There are a couple of Bible verses that have given me some comfort over the years. Psalm 34 says, "The Lord is close to the brokenhearted and saves those who are crushed in spirit." The other one I like is from Psalm 147. It says, "The Lord God heals the brokenhearted and binds up their wounds."

"Thanks Dad."

His mom came back on the phone. She said, "Jake, have you ever cut yourself shaving?"

"Mom, I really don't . . ."

"Humor me."

"Yes."

"Did you go to a doctor to heal it?"

"Of course not."

"Depending upon the cut, it healed up in a day or two."

"What's your point, Mom?"

"Time."

"Time?"

"Time heals physical wounds . . . and . . . and emotional

wounds. Time will heal your broken heart."

Jake did not reply.

"Jake, trust me on this."

Jake knew his mother was trying to help. But her words weren't really helping.

He said, "It just hurts so much."

"I know. I know. You know Jesus said that He would be with us always. He is with you now. Stay close to Jesus. Call on Him. If you will allow Him, He will comfort you."

Jake did not reply.

His mom asked, "When is the funeral?"

"I don't know."

"You should go."

"I don't know if I can."

"You can and you should. It will help you heal."

Jake did not reply.

His mom said, "You may feel, right now, like you don't want to heal. You may want to stay in your sorrow. You may think that it would be disrespectful to Laura's memory for you to get over it, to heal. But Jake, that is the wrong direction to go. You should go to her funeral. It would show respect for Laura. It would show that you truly cared for her. It would honor her."

Jake had begun to cry.

His mom continued, "You only have one opportunity to attend Laura's funeral. If you don't go, I think you will always wish that you had gone."

"It's just too hard. It's too painful. I don't think I can face her family."

For almost a minute, his mom didn't say anything. Then she softly asked, "Jake, are you feeling guilty about Laura's death?"

In a whisper, Jake replied, "Yes."

"I see. But why? She was killed in a car accident. How are you . . ?"

"Mom, you don't understand."

"No. I don't."

"Laura had been to Québec City to do something, a final fitting or something, with her wedding dress. On the way back, she was . . . the accident . . . happened."

"Yes?"

"Mom, when we were in Québec City together, Laura wanted to elope. I convinced her to have a church wedding with our families and friends. Don't you see? If I had agreed to an elopement, Laura would not have gone to Québec City about a wedding dress and this . . . accident would never have happened."

"I see."

"We would be married now." Tears were rolling down Jake's face. "We would be happy. Laura would be alive." Jake whispered, "It's my fault."

"I understand."

"And," Jake continued, "there was a nice married couple, Paul and Jo . . . and a real nice man, Henri, who was driving -- they were all also killed. They probably wouldn't have gone to Québec City except to help Laura. If we had eloped, they would all be alive."

"Oh Jake. Jake. The pain you must be feeling."

His mom didn't know what else to say.

Breaking the silence, she said, "Jake, I don't know what to say." After a pause, she added, "I do know that 'if' can be a tiny word with extremely large consequences. You know what Monday morning quarterbacking is?"

"Yes."

"Okay. On Monday morning, a guy whose team lost at the last minute may say 'if only he hadn't thrown that pass and if that pass hadn't been intercepted and if that defender had not run it into the end zone for a touchdown, we would have won.' The quarterback who threw the pass was trying to do something good for his team. If only the pass hadn't been deflected off the receiver's hand, it wouldn't have been intercepted. If only. But the pass was thrown and the team lost."

Jake softly said, "But it was the quarterback's fault."

"Maybe. Maybe it was the receiver's fault. But, in either

case, they were both trying to help their team. These things are going to happen. Interceptions happen. Accidents happen. That's why they call them accidents."

Jake didn't say anything.

His mom continued, "Jake, if I come to an intersection, I may have the choice of going straight, turning left or turning right. Whatever choice I make will determine what I see and what I encounter. If I turn left and am in an accident, I could always say 'if I had turned right, this wouldn't have happened.' But where does that get me? Nowhere. Most of us, when we make decisions, try to make the best decision we can at the moment we are making it. But none of us knows what the future is. If we could look into the future, we would sometimes make different decisions. But we cannot look into the future. So, we make the best decision we can at the time we make it. Second-guessing does not do any good. We simply cannot go back and change the past."

"I sure wish we could."

"But we can't."

"I know." Jake paused and said, "Mom, the bottom line is my decision not to elope put Laura in that car."

"Did Laura agree with your decision?"

"Yes, but that's not the point."

"Only by knowing what we know now can anyone say that you should have eloped. At the time you and Laura agreed to wait and have a church wedding, that was the absolute best decision to make. If you had asked her parents, if you had asked us, if you had asked any of your friends, if she had asked any of her friends, all of them, all of us . . . would have advised you both to wait and have a church wedding. It was the right decision. You cannot blame yourself for this accident."

Jake did not reply.

His mom sighed and said, "Now, you have to make several decisions. One important decision is whether or not you are going to attend her funeral. I truly think that you should go."

"Yes," Jake whispered.

"Now, *if* you are killed in a plane crash going to Laura's funeral, I may say '*If* only I had not advised him to go and instead, convinced him not to go.' You see what I mean? You must make the best decision you can make at the time you make it. It does often help to pray about any decision you make. Pray about attending Laura's funeral. Follow the guidance of the Holy Spirit."

"Okay."

When Jake's mom hung up the phone, she turned to Jake's dad and asked, "Do you know the name of Jake's friend up there in New York?"

"No, he's got several friends around the country but I don't know their names."

"We need this guy's phone number. Jake hasn't called anyone . . . wait! This is the guy Jake asked to be his Best Man. Didn't you get something from him about a bachelor party?"

"Yes, it was to be in Savannah."

"Find it. I want to call him."

Jake had put on a pair of shorts over his briefs and was standing on his balcony with his hands in his pockets. It was after nine o'clock on Tuesday night. Jake tried praying but was having a difficult time of it.

His doorbell rang and startled him. It was extremely unusual for his doorbell to ring. He slowly walked over and heard someone knocking on the door.

He opened the door and Ted walked inside.

Ted was carrying a pizza and a laptop. He said, "I've brought food."

Jake smiled and closed the door. They stood staring at each other.

Ted said, "I am so sorry, Jake."

Jake nodded and tears began to roll down his face.

Ted walked over to the kitchen and set the pizza box and his laptop on a kitchen counter. The counter had stools on one side.

Jake wiped his face with the sleeves of his t-shirt and

followed Ted into the kitchen.

Jake said, "My mom called you?"

"Yes . . . she told me what happened." Ted opened the fridge and pulled out plastic bottles of soft drinks. He put them on the counter with the pizza. He looked at Jake and said, "You look like crud."

"I feel like crud."

"You have every right to feel that way. Let's take these out on the balcony." Ted took the pizza and his laptop and carried them out and sat them on the small table on the balcony. Jake brought the drinks.

Ted asked, "When's the last time you ate anything?"

"I'm not hungry."

"I know. But when was the last time you ate?"

"I dunno. Sunday evening, I suppose."

Ted opened his drink and said, "I'm hungry. I'm going to have a slice." He opened the box, took out a slice.

Jake opened his bottle, took a sip and said, "Ted, I do appreciate your coming over but I'm not in much of a sociable mood."

"I didn't expect that you would be. But it wouldn't hurt you to eat a slice of pizza, would it?"

Jake smiled, "No, it wouldn't hurt."

"Go ahead, have some."

Jake took a slice and began eating it. Nodding at the laptop, he asked, "What's with that?"

Ted replied, "Knowing that you wouldn't be in a sociable mood, I brought some quotes I want to read to you."

"Ted, I really . . ."

"I know. But I do think they may help." While Ted opened his laptop and turned it on, Jake took another sip and another bite.

Ted said, "Okay, now listen to this one."

"'Death is simply a change of address. We all have souls that are eternal. Eternity is the absence of time. A hundred years from now, our souls will be somewhere. A thousand years from now. Ten thousand. A million years. We will all be somewhere. This brief time in these human bodies will seem like a very brief moment.' Do you know who said that?"

"No."

"You did."

Jake didn't respond.

"Those are your words."

"Just words."

"No. Those are good words, Jake. They are true words. And you know what? Science has proven them to be true."

"What?"

"Yes, science has proven that every human being has an immortal soul. This has nothing to do with faith or religion. This is just science. Listen."

Ted scrolled down on his laptop.

He said, "This is a quote from Dr. Becker Mertens of Dresden, Germany. He was part of a team of scientists who conducted experiments trying to determine if the soul is real. He said, 'The inescapable conclusion is that we have now confirmed the existence of the human soul and determined that it weighs one three thousandth of an ounce.'"

"That's awfully light." Jake took another slice of pizza.

"Of course. It's a spirit. Here's another from a physicist. Professor Dr. Han-Peter Diur, who was the head of the Max Planck Institute for Physics, said, 'The wave-particle dualism between the body and the soul is real. The information that I have stored in my physical brain I have also transferred onto the spiritual quantum field. I could say that when I die, I do not lose this information, this consciousness. The body dies but the spiritual quantum field continues. In this way, I am immortal.'"

Jake didn't say anything.

Ted said, "There are numerous international physicists who now state publicly that science has determined the existence of an immortal human soul. But the last thing I want to tell you about this is not scientific nor is it religious. It is more common sense. There exists in our world material things like cars and furniture. We can see them and touch them. There also exist immaterial things like justice, brotherhood, bravery, kindness and so forth. These are not things of the material world. Rather, they are spiritual in nature. A person may say, 'Today, I will build a chair.' This is a material thing. If this person has not already built a chair, he can get a book that will tell him how to do it. He can probably reverse engineer it by looking at a chair. Where does the knowledge come from to form ideas of immaterial things? These are realities but they are spiritual. The common sense answer is that in order for a human to will into existence an abstraction like kindness there must be a spiritual reality or an immortal principle, a soul, within every human."

Jake got another slice of pizza and said, "I follow that. It makes sense."

Ted smiled. He said, "One more. Who said, 'Love lasts forever. Love survives death?"

Jake shook his head.

Ted answered his own question by saying, "You did."

Jake did not respond.

Ted said, "Love is obviously another of those immaterial things. Love is real but it is an abstraction. It exists but not in the material world. It is spiritual. God is love. The results of love can be material and be seen. But love itself is spiritual." Ted paused and then continued by saying, "And love survives death."

"Ted, I do appreciate all this. You are telling me that Laura's soul currently exists."

"Of course. You already knew that."

"Yes, but it is nice to be reminded. Thank you. And thank you for the pizza."

"You're welcome. Your mom said that you probably had not eaten anything since you heard the news. Is your microwave still functioning?"

"Yes. Why?"

"I thought you might have packed it."

"No, that would be the last thing to go."

"I want to warm up this pizza."

Ted got up and went into the kitchen. He warmed the remaining pizza and returned to the balcony.

As he sat down, Jake said, "You're a good friend. Thanks for coming over."

"You would have done the same for me."

Jake nodded. He said, "I've been thinking. I guess I will go to Laura's funeral. You know, even saying that, it is hard for me to believe that she is really gone."

Ted took a bite of pizza. After swallowing, he asked, "When is her funeral?"

"I don't know. Probably Thursday or Friday."

"More likely Thursday. You better check."

Jake said, "I'll do it now." He went back into his library and fired up his computer. He found *The Savannah Morning News* site and located Laura's obituary in that day's paper. He didn't want to read it. He called Ted.

"Ted, I found it. But I don't want to read it. Would you mind?"

"Of course not."

"Look for the funeral home."

"Okay."

Ted read the obituary.

Jake pointed at a pad on his desk and said, "Write down the funeral home and phone number."

Ted did so. He said, "Visitation is tomorrow and the funeral is Thursday."

"Thanks. I'd better call and see about getting plane tickets."

"I think most airlines have some special way of getting seats for people going to funerals."

"Yes, I think so."

"It's a real nice obituary. You are mentioned as a surviving fiancé."

"I don't . . ."

As tears formed in his eyes, Jake turned away.

Ted pretended not to notice. He said, "If you'd like some

support, I'll go with you."

With red and watery eyes, Jake turned around and said, "Thank you. I do appreciate that but I think I'll be okay."

"Good. If you change your mind, just call." They walked to the door.

Jake said, "Thanks for coming. It helped."

"You're welcome."

They gave each other an awkward hug and Ted said, "You're gonna be all right."

Jake nodded and closed the door behind Ted.

Jake called, explained his situation and got a round-trip ticket to Atlanta with a two-hour layover and then a connecting flight to Savannah for the following day, September 14th. His return trip would be on Friday, the 16th. He called a hotel in Tybee and got a reservation for two nights. He packed a suitcase, set his alarm and went to bed. It was late.

Jake arrived at the Savannah airport at about 4:15 PM. He got a rental car and drove to his hotel on Tybee Island. His room had a balcony, which looked out at the ocean. It was a nice view – palm trees, seagulls, the beach and, of course, the ocean itself.

It was a quarter until six. The visitation at the funeral home was scheduled to be over at eight. He could change clothes and get there by seven. However, Jake didn't want to go. On his flight to Atlanta, he decided that he would not attend the visitation. Now that he was here on Tybee Island, he was even more convinced that he did not want to go to the visitation.

Although Jake had maneuvered through the airports in New York, Atlanta and Savannah, rented a car, found his way to Tybee Island and checked himself into a hotel, he was functioning on automatic. He still felt numb and thought he was in a mental daze. Jake had not eaten all day and found, surprisingly, that he was hungry. The hotel had a nice restaurant and Jake decided to use it.

It was almost 7:30 when Jake returned to his room. He had lingered over his seafood meal. The restaurant had a nice huge glass wall with a great view of the ocean. He had bought a local paper and tried to read it while he ate. As long as he had something to read, it never bothered Jake to eat alone.

With a soft drink in his hand, Jake sat down out on the balcony and listened to the waves as they rushed to shore. It was almost dark outside but there were still people walking along the shoreline. He saw a couple walking along holding hands. Jake immediately got a lump in his throat and his eyes began to water. There was a little metal table and two metal chairs on the balcony. He sat his drink on the table and looked at the empty chair. He quickly looked away. But it was too late. Overwhelming grief just consumed his being.

Looking out over the ocean, with his face wet with tears, Jake whispered to Laura. He said, "Laura, I love you. I am so sorry. I wish so hard . . . I wish, more than anything, that we had eloped. I am so very sorry. I miss you more than you will ever know. I love you, Laura."

A gust of wind blew by the balcony. As it passed, Jake thought he heard it say, "That's nice." Jake shook his head and told himself that he was imaging things – he was wishful thinking. He wanted so much to believe it was real but . . . his room was on the 4th floor and the wind felt pleasant. Jake sat out there on the balcony for another couple of hours. He knew it was silly but he refused to look over at the empty chair. He was missing Laura so intensely it hurt. She should be sitting in that empty chair. They should be sharing this great view of the ocean. He began to think that maybe he wouldn't go to the funeral.

So that he could hear the waves on the shore, Jake left the door to the balcony open. He stripped down and crawled under the covers. Despite the salt air, the gentle ocean breeze and the rhythmic sound of the waves as they broke against the shore, Jake got very little sleep that night.

Jake watched the sun rise against the ocean. It was a beautiful beginning to a beautiful day. It was also September 15th, the day that Laura would be buried. The thought of Laura being buried in the ground made his whole body go numb again.

Jake showered and shaved. In his underwear, he sat on the corner of the bed. He said, "Jesus, be with me. Jesus, help me make it through this day. I know that this is a day that you have made and I thank you for it. Please Jesus, stay with me this day. I don't think I can make it without You being with me. You promised that You would always be with us. Thank You for that. I need to feel Your presence today. I thank You for that. Thank You, Jesus."

Jake got up and walked around the room. He felt a little better. He tried to remember Laura's family. She has a younger sister and even younger brother. Both her parents were still alive as were three of her grandparents. One of her grandmothers had died when she was in high school. He forgot how many aunts and uncles Laura has . . . Jake stopped in his thinking to correct himself. He was using "has" in his thoughts when he should be using "had." The thought made him even more sad. He sat back down on the bed and began to cry. He quickly stood up, wiped his face and thought *Jesus, be with me*.

He thought that all of Laura's relatives would be there today. He looked through the sliding glass doors and stared at the ocean. Tears began to trickle down his cheeks. He took a deep breath and returned to the room.

Additional viewing and visitation was scheduled from noon to two o'clock. The funeral service was to begin at two o'clock with burial to follow at Bonaventure Cemetery.

It was too early for Jake to dress in the clothes he was going to wear to Laura's funeral. He put on some jeans and a t-shirt. He wasn't hungry. He looked at the balcony and saw the table and two chairs. Jake took another deep breath, said, "Jesus, be with me." He walked out and sat down. The view was really nice. Jake wished so hard that he could share it with Laura.

Jake shook the feeling of grief, stood up and went back inside. He put on some shoes, took the elevator and walked out on the beach. When he got to the water's edge, he took his shoes off and waded in the surf. It suddenly occurred to Jake that Laura had probably walked along this beach many times. That thought made Jake stop walking. It felt nice to be where Laura had been. However, at the same time Jake felt sad being where Laura had been – knowing that he would never see her again. Still carrying his shoes, Jake headed back up the beach and returned to his hotel room. He took another shower and got ready to attend Laura's funeral.

The rental car had a new device that directed the driver to a specific address. It had brought him from the airport through the city of Savannah to the hotel on Tybee Island. Now it was taking Jake to the funeral home. Jake thought that the woman's voice sounded like it had a touch of a British accent.

Jake pulled into the funeral home parking lot, parked the car, got out, removed his suit coat from the back, put it on and walked to the funeral home. It was a few minutes after one o'clock. Before opening the door, Jake whispered, "Thank You, Jesus, for being with me."

Jake signed the guest register and walked down a hall that led to the front of the funeral home chapel. He saw the closed casket and his stomach lurched. A woman walked over to Jake and asked, "Mr. Fleming?" Jake turned toward her and replied, "Yes." She said, "I'm Laura's mother." She gave him a hug. Then she said, "Just a minute." She turned and went to the front pew of a separate section of the chapel that was reserved for the family. She reached in her purse, pulled out an envelope, brought it back to Jake and said, "This is for you." Jake simply said, "Thank you" and put it in his coat pocket. Mrs. Middleton introduced Laura's father to Jake. Laura's brother, Bill, who was still in college, walked over and shook hands with Jake. Standing near the casket, talking with one of her friends, was Laura's sister, Anne. Mrs. Middleton pointed her out to Jake. At about the same time, Anne had just whispered to her friend, "He's even more handsome in person than in the photos Laura sent."

Jake walked over to the casket. He placed his right hand on it and tears began to roll down his face. He turned and walked to the main chapel seating that faced the front of the chapel where Laura's casket was displayed. He walked to the back and sat down in the last pew on the right side of the chapel. He had stuffed his side coat pockets with tissues and he pulled some out to wipe his face, dab his eyes and blow his nose. He took a deep breath and said to himself, "Be with me, Jesus."

Jake heard a familiar voice say "Hello, Jake." It was Peggy. He stood up and they hugged each other.
Peggy quickly whispered, "I'm a teacher who taught with Laura and we were good friends."

Mr. Sinclair stepped over and shook Jake's hand. He said, "I am Laura's principal."

Anne said to her friend, "Now who are those people?"

Anne walked over to her mother and said, "I'd like to meet Jake. He's sitting at the back of the chapel. I thought you wanted him to sit with us."

"I do. Let's go fetch him."

Mrs. Middleton and Anne walked to where Jake, Peggy and Mr. Sinclair were talking.

As they approached, Jake turned to Mrs. Middleton and said, "Mrs. Middleton, this is a fellow teacher and very very good friend of Laura's, Peggy Curtis. And this is her principal, Mr. Charles Sinclair."

They exchanged pleasantries and Mr. Sinclair and Peggy offered their condolences.

Mrs. Middleton suddenly said, "Oh, I'm sorry. This is Laura's sister, Anne."

Again, pleasantries and condolences were offered.

Mrs. Middleton said, "Mr. Fleming, I'd . . ."

"Please call me Jake."

"All right, Jake, we'd really like for you to join us and sit with the family during the service."

Before Jake could decline, Anne put her arm between Jake's arm and his body and pulled him with her toward the front.

Peggy and Mr. Sinclair sat down in the pew where Jake had been sitting.

There were eight pews that were reserved for the family. They were separate from those facing the front. They also faced the front but from the side of the chapel. Anne pulled Jake with her and led him to the front pew. Still with her arm wrapped around his, Anne sat down on that pew and Jake was obliged to also sit down next to her. As the visiting period wasn't over, Mr. and Mrs. Middleton were still receiving visitors. Anne turned to Jake and gave him a very pleasant smile. She asked about his trip from New York down to Savannah.

Jake thought it was a weird question. He knew that people grieve in their own way. She probably didn't know what to say and was just trying to make conversation. He replied by saying that the trip had been fine.

Bill came over and sat down next to his sister. Anne scooted over closer to Jake and Jake scooted further down the pew.

Jake asked Anne, "How are you and Bill holding up?"

Anne smiled and replied, "Pretty good. Of course, Bill was just a child when Laura left for college. I am only a couple of years behind Laura so we were real close."

"Of course. How are your parents doing?"

"Better than I expected. How about you?"

"Not very good. It's still difficult for me to realize that she's gone."

Jake turned his head away from Anne. His eyes had begun to water again. He dabbed them with a tissue.

Anne didn't know what to say. Bill pretended not to notice that Jake was crying. All the aunts, uncles, grandparents and cousins were now sitting in the family pews. Mr. and Mrs. Middleton came over and sat down next to Bill. Jake wished he were sitting on the back pew with Peggy and Mr. Sinclair.

One of Laura's cousins got up and sang two songs. Then the minister stood up and walked behind the podium. He was in his sixties, short, bald and pudgy. He had a nice smile. He used it as he told how he had known Laura ever since she was a little girl. The minister then said a prayer. It was similar to several other prayers that Jake had heard at funerals. The minister followed that by telling a couple of cute stories about Laura when she was a little girl in Sunday School. Jake tried to smile. He whispered for Jesus to stay with him. Laura's sister Anne heard Jake whispering but didn't understand. The minister read a very nice and touching poem. It made Jake cry again. Jake used his tissues.

Tears were still escaping from Jake's eyes as the minister finished his talk. He said it was okay to feel sad. Sorrow was real. He said everything happens for a reason and that Laura was in a better place now.

Those last two comments made Jake feel worse, not better. He really needed his tissues. Anne was not even misty-eyed. Jake thought that she must have already cried herself out so that she had no more tears. Jake's tears surprised Anne. He tried to hide them but it was obvious. She thought, *He must have truly been in love with Laura.*

The minister asked if anyone wanted to say anything. Did anyone have a story they wanted to tell about Laura? No one said anything. From where the family was sitting, they could not see the main chapel seating nor could those in the main chapel seating see the family. Jake felt several of Laura's family looking at him. The minister looked at him. Jake shook his head. He knew he wasn't capable of speaking without choking up and losing it.

Suddenly, a man in the back of the chapel spoke. It broke the silence of the chapel and startled some. He said, "My name is Charles Sinclair. I was Laura's principal where she taught school. She was an excellent teacher . . . but she was more than that. She was a wonderful and kind person. I never heard any of the other teachers or anyone ever say a bad word about Laura. Laura was one of those special people who come along all too rarely. She had a bright future ahead of her. I know that she had found genuine love with Jake Fleming. They were scheduled to be married in about three weeks . . . Laura died much too young."

Jake could not control his tears. His tissues had almost reached their total absorption rate. He was a mess and he knew it.

Peggy then commented, "I was a good friend of Laura's. We taught school together. I honestly can say that all her students loved her. She never had any problems because all her children loved her. She was a special person with a good sense of humor. I am going to miss her more than anyone will ever know. I...uh...I loved her as a sister and a friend." Peggy was crying and had a lump in her throat. Still sniffling, Peggy continued, "Laura found love with Jake. Jake, you made her so happy. The last weeks of...the last weeks of her life...were the happiest weeks of her life. That was because of you, Jake."

Jake could not see Peggy but he certainly heard her. He was sobbing as he tried to hold back his grief. Three or four other people spoke and said nice things as they remembered incidents that happened with them and Laura. Jake didn't really hear the stories.

When it was over, people stood as the pallbearers carried Laura's casket out to the hearse. Jake wanted to drive his rental to the cemetery. However, Anne pulled and pushed him to a limousine. Jake composed himself and told himself that, with the help of Jesus, he was going to get it together and do better at the cemetery. Mr. Sinclair and Peggy rode together, in Mr. Sinclair's rental, in the line of cars heading to the cemetery.

Laura would be buried in a family plot in Bonaventure Cemetery. Jake was surprised by the cemetery. It was one of the oldest cemeteries in Savannah. There were many large beautiful trees with Spanish moss hanging from them. The cemetery was so old that there were no more available places for burials unless your family already had a plot that still had room.

The limousine followed the hearse to the Middleton family plot. Jake got out, took a deep breath and walked around. He noticed a river running along one side of the large cemetery. The river flowed through a marsh. As he walked, Jake noticed that the Middleton plot was next to a Cannady family plot. He was reading grave markers when Anne pulled him to a small covered area with chairs. This was primarily reserved for family members. Mr. and Mrs. Middleton, the three grandparents, aunts and uncles were already sitting. Anne sat in a chair in the next to last row. She indicated for Jake to join her. He sat next to her and admired the surroundings. Jake could not look directly at Laura's casket. It was too painful and he was trying to hold himself together.

The minister spoke directly to the family. He told another story about Laura. He told them that they were going to miss Laura and it was all right to grieve. He spoke of the future and said that they had to go on living their lives. The minister said that they would be reunited with Laura in Heaven. He continued with a brief prayer and finished by quoting Philippians 4:7. "And the peace of God, which transcends all understanding, will guard your hearts and your minds in Christ Jesus."

Jake looked away as Laura's casket was lowered into the ground. He thought of how beautiful she had looked when they were together in Québec City. He cherished the memories of them together for that week up in Canada. Then, the thought that they would never be together again caused the tears to roll down his face. Finally, he realized that the people under the cover were standing. Others were starting to walk back to their cars. Jake quickly stood and looked for Mr. Sinclair and Peggy. He saw them looking at him. With a hand gesture, he asked them to wait. He wanted to talk with them.

Anne grabbed Jake's arm and said, "We're having a celebration of Laura's life tonight. It's at my parents' house. We really do want you to be there."

Jake looked at Anne. She had a nice smile. Laura had a wonderful special smile that sparkled. He was just starting to tell her that he didn't feel like attending a celebration of Laura's life when Mrs. Middleton walked up and gave Jake a hug. She said, "Now, I really expect you to be at our house tonight. We have a lot of photographs of Laura we want to show you. We also want to hear all about your week in Canada with Laura."

Jake tried to smile. He paused and said, "I took a lot of pictures. I can send them to you."

Mrs. Middleton quickly replied, "I'd love to see them. Thank you. You will stay and come tonight?"

"No, I don't think I am up to it."

Anne said, "No one will blame you for feeling sad. We would just like to get to know you better."

Jake said, "Thank you. But I'd really rather not."

Anne responded, "But surely . . ."

"I'm afraid I would truly be poor company. I simply don't feel like I'm to the place where I can celebrate Laura's life. Hopefully, I will be able to do so someday. But not today. The sense of loss . . . I'm still grieving too . . . I'm sorry." Jake's eyes got misty.

Anne asked, "Will we see you tomorrow?"

"My flight back to New York leaves tomorrow morning."

"Listen, here is my email. Stay in touch."

Anne gave him a hug and kissed him on the cheek.

Mrs. Middleton gave him a hug and said, "We really would like to know you better. Please do stay in contact. You made Laura so happy and I thank you for that. Our address and phone number is in that envelope I gave you earlier."

"Okay. Thank you."

Jake shook hands with Mr. Middleton and Bill.

Anne asked, "Aren't you going to ride back to the funeral home with us?"

"No, I'll catch a ride with Laura's principal and friend."

Jake walked away from the covered area and toward Mr. Sinclair and Peggy. The roads in the cemetery were dirt roads and the three of them walked down one of those roads to the rental car. They didn't say anything. They walked in silence to the car. Jake sat in the back seat. Mr. Sinclair was driving and Peggy sat up front in the passenger's seat. Other cars were leaving the cemetery but they stayed. Jake was crying.

Mr. Sinclair asked, "Where to?"

Jake tried to control his sobbing. He answered by saying, "My rental is at the funeral home."

Mr. Sinclair cranked up the car and slowly drove out of Bonaventure Cemetery.

Peggy turned around and asked Jake, "Are you planning on going to the Middleton's tonight?"

Jake felt like screaming. Not at Peggy but at the idea that the Middletons were hosting a party that night. Instead, he just shook his head.

Then, he asked, "How did you know about that?"

Peggy replied, "Mr. Middleton invited us."

"I see. What did you say?"

Mr. Sinclair answered, "No."

He then said, "Jake, if you feel like it, I would really like to talk with you tonight."

Jake responded, "I don't know. I really don't feel much like talking."

"How about listening? I've decided to follow your suggestions. We're going to go public. We're going to build a large lodge on the lake. I want to tell you all about it."

Peggy said, "How about over dinner? You are going to eat, aren't you?"

"I'm not so sure. I haven't eaten anything today. There is a restaurant at my hotel. We could meet there."

Mr. Sinclair said, "Good. How about seven?"

"Okay."

Jake had stopped crying. They rode in silence back to the funeral home.

After about ten minutes of total silence, Jake suddenly said, "I just can't believe . . . it is so hard for me to accept that it is all over . . . that Laura was in that casket."

His eyes started watering again. Peggy and Mr. Sinclair didn't respond. They drove on in silence.

At the funeral home, Jake pointed out his rental. There were only a few cars in the parking lot. Mr. Sinclair stopped right in front of Jake's rental car. Jake got out and started walking toward the car.

Mr. Sinclair said, "We'll see you at seven."

Jake nodded and waved. He got in the rental and drove back to his motel. Mr. Sinclair and Peggy drove back to theirs.

Peggy asked, "Do you think he'll show up?"

Mr. Sinclair replied, "I don't know."

"He is truly brokenhearted."

"Yes. It is understandable."

"He really loved Laura."

"Yes. It's a real shame. A real loss."

They continued in silence.

Jake drove back to his hotel. He changed into jeans and a t-shirt. He was restless. He walked around the room. He looked at the balcony with the two chairs. He walked out, picked up the chair on the left side of the table, brought it inside and set it down in a corner of the room. He went out on the balcony, sat down and watched the seagulls and the ocean. Jake felt totally empty and alone. He sat and stared at the waves. With a jerk, he realized it was getting late. He went back in his room, looked at the clock and noticed that it was 6:45 PM. He put on some shoes and went to the restaurant.

Mr. Sinclair and Peggy were already there. Jake was led to their table. They had ordered drinks and the waiter came over and asked Jake what he wanted to drink.

Jake replied, "Water."

The waiter asked, "With lemon?"

"No, thank you."

Jake turned to Mr. Sinclair and Peggy and said, "I truly appreciate what you both said about Laura. That was kind of you."

Mr. Sinclair said, "It was the truth."

Jake tried to smile as he said, "It made me cry like a baby."

Tears began to form in Jake's eyes. He shook his head and dabbed his eyes with his napkin.

He said, "So when are you announcing that Neverland exists?"

The waiter showed up and took their orders.

Mr. Sinclair answered, "We're going to announce the construction of the lodge first. But Jake, we've got some excellent architects onboard and a lot of plans for expansion. I think you'll like them."

"I'm sure I will."

"Jake, one of the things I wanted to discuss with you is your future."

"Charles, I have absolutely no idea what I'm going to do now."

Peggy inadvertently jerked back. She was in awe that she had traveled down with Mr. Sinclair, was riding in a car with him and was eating with him. However, when she heard Jake call him Charles, she was totally surprised.

Mr. Sinclair responded, "I have a suggestion. Jake, this new direction that we are now headed in is going to take a lot of effort on my part. I am no longer a young man. I am going to need help. I am hoping that, perhaps, you would consider becoming my assistant."

Jake started shaking his head.

Mr. Sinclair continued, "Before you say no, let me explain. I am going to have to have some official title. You know, like Manager or Director. I want you to be the Assistant Director. When I retire, I want you to take my place as the Director."

Peggy was smiling. She thought this was a great idea.

"It would give us continuity. It would give us stability. Will you consider it?"

Jake shook his head and said, "I don't think I'm ready for something like that."

Mr. Sinclair replied, "I don't mean for you to start tomorrow. But when you are ready, we would like for you to join us."

Jake looked at Mr. Sinclair. Then he looked over at Peggy. Tears started to form in his eyes.

He said, "Charles, I do sincerely appreciate the offer but I don't know if I could ever go back there. I'm afraid it would be too . . . too painful. Peggy, you remember that booth Laura and I used to sit in and talk for hours?"

"Yes, of course."

"I don't think I could stand to see that booth again."

Tears rolled down his face. Jake quickly wiped them

away.

He said, "I'm sorry. I'm really a mess."

Mr. Sinclair said, "Jake, don't make up your mind right now. You need to grieve. It is a process you must go through. Peggy and I are also grieving, not just for Laura but for Henri, Paul and Jo. We have to go through the same process. Somehow, I think, with four people to grieve over, it is less intense. That may seem strange. I guess the grief is spread out over four different people instead of being concentrated on one person."

Jake looked up. He replied, "I'm sorry. I didn't mean to overlook their loss. I didn't get to know them well but, from what I knew, they were all extremely nice people."

Peggy said, "Yes. Yes, they were. I'm going to miss them a lot." Tears started rolling down her face.

"Speaking of grieving, what is it with having a party on the night of someone's funeral?"

Mr. Sinclair responded, "Don't be too critical. It's like a wake. It's a time to remember the . . . deceased. It's a time to honor the deceased. It gives some people a healthy closure."

Peggy said, "I'm with Jake on this one. It seems a little morbid."

Mr. Sinclair replied, "No, it's not morbid. Everyone grieves in their own way. What works for some does not work for others. I'm sure that there were others besides us who chose not to attend tonight. That is fine. But don't criticize the ones who wanted to attend. Some people grieve by going off and being alone. Others like to grieve with others. Neither is right or wrong. Each individual must grieve in their own way."

Jake said, "I understand that. It just seems like a celebration of life would be better if it were a month or two after the funeral – not on the night of the actual funeral."

Mr. Sinclair said, "Like I said, grieving is different for everyone. Some would prefer the day of the funeral and others, like you, would prefer to wait. However, being practical, how many people would show up for a celebration if it were a month or two later? Would you fly back down here in a month or two to attend a party in Laura's memory?"

"I certainly see what you mean. I might."

"And you might not. Most people would not. We shouldn't criticize others."

Peggy said, "Okay. But can I criticize Laura's sister for hitting on Jake?"

Jake jerked back. He said, "What?"

Peggy answered, "Laura's sister was hitting on you at Laura's funeral."

"Surely not."

"You men are so blind. You can never tell when a woman is hitting on you unless she comes out and says, 'I'm hitting on you.' And then you will think she is joking."

Mr. Sinclair laughed. He said, "Really, Peggy. What could she possibly hope to gain by hitting on Jake in such circumstances?"

"She wants to take Laura's place in Jake's affections."

Jake said, "Peggy, that's silly. I thought she was trying to be nice."

"Jake . . . Mr. Sinclair, I promise you – that woman was hitting on Jake."

Mr. Sinclair responded, "Well, whatever. It doesn't matter now."

Jake said, "I don't expect I'll ever see any of those people ever again."

Mr. Sinclair asked, "What is it you plan to do now?"

Jake said, "I haven't any plan. I don't know. My condo has sold and I have to be out by the end of the month. I might rent a house or an apartment somewhere."

"In New York?" Peggy asked.

"No, definitely not in New York. I honestly do not like the city of New York at all. Upstate New York is nice. It is a lot like New England. I don't know where I'm going. I do know it won't be in New York City."

The waiter brought their orders. They sat in silence for a few minutes, as they tasted their food.

Jake said, "Yesterday, just as I was leaving to catch my flight, I got a phone call from one of my sisters. It upset me quite a bit. I have tried to ignore it. I know she meant well...but I..."

Mr. Sinclair asked, "What did she say?"

"She said that I had plans to marry Laura and raise a family. However, she said, God has a different plan for me."

"And that upset you?"

"Very much."

"Why?"

"The implication is that God killed Laura . . . and Henri and Paul and Jo so that we would not get married and interfere with God's plan for me."

Peggy interjected, "And there was a teenage girl killed in the wreck."

"Yes, right. All those people died so that I could carry on with God's plan?"

Mr. Sinclair said, "I don't expect . . ."

"I mean, really, if God did not want us to get married, He could have had Laura tell me that she had thought it over and did not want to get married to me. He would not have to kill her. Laura could have told me that it was over . . . that she didn't love me. Whatever. I would have been confused and sad but that would have been the end of it. If God has other plans for me, Laura did not have to die."

Mr. Sinclair said, very gently, "Jake, some things are just accidents."

"That's what my dad said."

Mr. Sinclair responded, "Jake, I do believe every human being has an immortal soul. One day, in the distant future, I hope...your soul will leave your body and go be with Jesus. That's where Laura's soul is now. You will be reunited with her. I don't really know but I don't think that there will be couples in heaven. I think our souls will love one another with a spiritual love that we cannot fully comprehend now. I expect that we will have some memories of our brief time on earth in our human bodies but I doubt those memories will mean much in heaven."

Jake didn't respond.

After about twenty seconds of silence, Peggy said, "This crab soup is delicious."

Jake smiled.

Mr. Sinclair took a bite of his flounder.

After they had finished their dinner, Jake walked with them out to their rental car. Mr. Sinclair had explained that Peggy and he were flying to Montreal the following day. Paul and Jo's funerals were scheduled there the following afternoon. Their flight left at 7:30 AM. Henri's funeral was on Saturday. Jake's flight back to New York didn't leave until 11:30 AM. This was goodbye. With tears in his eyes, Jake hugged Peggy. She started crying. He shook Mr. Sinclair's hand.

Sitting in the car, Mr. Sinclair rolled the window down and said, "Think about it."

As they drove away, Peggy asked Mr. Sinclair, "Do you think we'll ever see him again?"

Mr. Sinclair thought about it and replied, "Yes. Yes, I do. All these changes were his ideas. I think it is his destiny to join us and continue the work."

Jake returned to his hotel room, got a bottle of water and sat out on the balcony for several hours. He thought, *So . . . this is the day that Laura was buried. It's over. She's gone. Forever. It's still so hard to believe. But here I am. Alone. I fly back to New York tomorrow. And then what? What do I do? Where do I go?*

Jake talked to Jesus. He asked Jesus to never leave him. He thanked Jesus for that. Jake talked with Laura. He told her how sorry he was that they didn't elope. He told her how much he missed her. He told her that he loved her. He told her that he would always love her. He cried.

After an hour or more of just staring at the ocean, Jake realized he was feeling sorry for himself. He didn't like that feeling. However, it was real and, right now, was a part of him.

Walking back into his room, Jake noticed his suit jacket on the bed where he had thrown it after returning from

Bonaventure Cemetery. He suddenly remembered the envelope that Laura's mom had given him. She had said, "This is for you."

Jake opened the envelope. There was a smaller envelope and a sheet of paper inside. Inside the paper was Laura's engagement ring. Jake felt like screaming. He felt like throwing the ring into the ocean. He had not thought about Laura's ring – or what would become of it. It just had not occurred to him. He calmed down and asked Jesus to be with him. He looked at the ring. It *was* a very beautiful ring. And, Laura had picked it out from among hundreds of others. Jake looked around the room. He went into the bathroom and looked around. He went back to the room, noticed a package of stationary, envelopes, information about the hotel and a restaurant menu. The entire package was on top of a dresser and it was held together by a blue ribbon. The ribbon was wrapped around the package and tied with a big bow. Jake quickly untied the ribbon. He put one end through Laura's ring and tied it around his neck. He put it inside his shirt and decided that he would wear Laura's ring next to his heart for the rest of his life.

For some reason, having Laura's ring around his neck made Jake feel better than he had felt since learning of her death. Through his shirt, Jake took his index finger and his thumb and squeezed Laura's ring. As he felt it, he felt better.

CHAPTER THIRTY-THREE

"The Lord will be your everlasting light, and your days of sorrow will end."

– Isaiah 60:20

Early 7th Century B. C.

It was Friday, September 23rd and Jake had been back from Savannah for a week. He had finished all his packing. The movers were coming on Monday, the 26th. Ted was coming over to say goodbye in person.

Jake was sitting out on his balcony watching ships in the harbor. He looked over at the second chair. It was empty. He remembered how Laura had once said that she'd like to see the view from his condo. He shook his head and told himself he needed to stop thinking like that. He asked Jesus to be with him. Through his shirt, he touched Laura's ring.

A little before 7:00 PM, Jake heard a knock on his door. As he was walking to the door, he heard the doorbell ring and Ted shout, "Pizza delivery!" Jake smiled, opened the door and his friend stepped in with a large good smelling pizza. The last time Ted had come over with pizza, he had had a tough time getting by the lobby guard. Jake had given permission for Ted to be allowed to come straight up without the intercom system.

After taking a big bite of pizza, Ted asked, "So, how you holding up?"

"Pretty good."

"Really?"

"No, not really. It's just so hard. I still have a difficult time realizing that she's . . . gone. It hurts."

Ted nodded. "How was the funeral?"

"It was okay. I mean how good can any funeral be? I was a total mess. I mean, I'm glad I went. Not that it matters – but the cemetery was beautiful. People said a lot of nice things about Laura." Jake realized that he was rambling. He stopped talking and took a bite of pizza.

Ted nodded. "So, you all packed?"

"Yes. Except for some clothes and a few things I'm going to carry with me in a rental car."

"So . . . it's North Carolina, huh?"

"I'm going to put all my books and the rest of my stuff in storage down there. Did you know that they have climate controlled storage units now?"

"Yes, I think I read that somewhere."

"I wasn't aware of that. Anyway, the movers are going to put all my stuff in two of those units. Books in one and furniture and kitchen stuff in the other. Then, I'll spend a few days with my parents."

"Then what?"

"Ted, I have absolutely no idea."

"No plans at all?"

"Nope. Nothing."

"You would be welcome back at Excalibur. But I'm keeping the putting green. I'm actually making some shots now."

Jake smiled. "Old Redfire is hot now, huh?"

"That's right."

"I suppose I could look at buying a house somewhere."

"Where?"

"Now Ted, that is the problem. I have no idea."

"I can see where that might be a problem."

"Yeah. I've thought of Maine. It is so beautiful up there. But they have a terrible tax system. It seems to be totally unfair. They want to tax money that you have saved and already paid taxes on once. They want to tax it again. Doesn't seem right to me."

"Me either. But there are a lot of other pretty states."

"True. I don't know. I don't know what I want to do."

Ted went back inside and got another slice of pizza. He called back to Jake, "Microwave packed?"

"Yes, afraid so."

"It's still warm. Can I get you another slice?"

"No, I'm good."

Ted sat back down. "What kind of job would you like to do?"

"I don't know. I guess I'd like to do something that helps people. I don't have to worry about a salary and paying my bills."

"You cleaned up with this condo, didn't you?"

"Yeah, pretty much."

"You thinking about something like teaching?"

"Yeah. Something like that. But not that."

"I hear ya."

"You know, Ted, I really liked the idea of getting a few acres. Raising some chickens. Having a garden. Maybe a couple of horses. A dog. Maybe even a cat or two. Finding a job in a small town. Maybe working for a charity or something. I don't know."

"But now?"

"But now, without Laura . . . I just don't know." Jake paused for a few seconds and then said, "I've even toyed with the idea of going back to college and getting another degree – this one, in archaeology."

"Really?"

"Yeah, people my age are often going back and getting a degree."

"That's true. They say it's never too late. Why archaeology? Why not get your master's?"

"In my situation, a master's wouldn't mean anything. If I were looking for a job in business, yes. That would be a natural thing to do. But I have no desire nor any need to go back into a business position. I am interested in archaeology. Always have been. I decided against going back and studying it because, and I don't think it's an exaggeration to say that I've probably read more archaeology books than most archaeology professors with their doctorates. With many of those books that I've read, I think the authors often come up with conclusions that are pure nonsense. From what I can tell, most professors have a closed mind on examining artifacts and ancient sites that don't support the accepted archaeological positions. I find that attitude to be unacceptable. Right now, I can go to a specific site in Ecuador and touch it. But archaeologists cannot explain what it is, who built it, when it was built or why it was built. Their reaction to it, therefore, is to ignore it and pretend it doesn't exist. I wouldn't fit into a classroom with a professor like that."

"No you wouldn't. That's for sure."

"So, I just don't know what to do."

After about twenty seconds of silence, Ted responded by saying, "You'll find something that will be perfect for you. You'll figure it out."

Ted and Jake talked for about two more hours. As usual, their conversation covered a wide variety of topics. Ted noticed that Jake would frequently reach down and feel Laura's ring through his shirt. He never said anything about it to Jake.

Wherever he went and whatever he wound up doing, Jake promised to stay in touch with Ted. They gave each other a hug and said goodnight. Neither knew how long it would be before they would see each other again.

Jake spent another three hours sitting on the balcony. He was thinking of everything. He was thinking of the balcony on Tybee. He was thinking of Laura's funeral and Bonaventure Cemetery. The woman he was supposed to marry in two weeks was buried there. He was thinking of his future. He could live in North Carolina. Maybe along the Outer Banks? Maybe in the Asheville area? Maybe he could find a small town, join a local church, get active in the community and raise a few chickens? He smiled at the thought. He really didn't know anything about raising chickens. When he was a child, his parents had had a few. All he ever did was collect eggs. However, Jake knew he could learn. Jake thought about Neverland and what they were planning. It would be interesting to be a part of that new venture.

He touched Laura's ring. He felt a pang of grief sweep across his being. Jake didn't feel that he was ready now to return to Neverland. Maybe someday. But not now.

In a couple of hours, Jake realized, the sun would be rising. He went to bed and tried to sleep. Out loud, he said, "Jesus, help me. Help me to know what to do now."

It was Thursday, October 6th. Jake had been staying at his parents' house for a little over a week. Sitting on a patio at the back of the house, Jake thought, *I've been here long enough. I need to leave.* His sister, Lucy, was arriving in the afternoon. He thought he might leave the next day. But he didn't know where he would go. He thought that it wasn't that far to Savannah. It might be nice to visit Laura's grave on the eighth. That was the day they were to be married. He wanted to be alone on the eighth.

Jake got his dad to drive him into town to a car rental place. After getting the car, Jake drove around town. He drove past his old high school. He smiled at some of the memories and cringed at some of the others.

When he got back to his parents' house, Jake noticed Lucy's car in the driveway. He parked behind her and walked inside. She gave him a big hug and told him how sorry she was for his loss. Jake touched Laura's ring and smiled at his sister.

Later that afternoon, while sitting out on the patio, Jake reminisced with Lucy. She was graduated from the same high school as Jake. Her 25th reunion had been last year. Jake's was coming up next year.

Jake asked, "Did you attend your twenty-fifth reunion?"

Lucy's face brightened. She answered, "Of course. It was good to see all those people again. I went to our tenth, fifteenth and twentieth. It was natural for me to go to the twenty-fifth. Aren't you planning on going to your twenty-fifth?"

Jake replied, "I haven't really given it any thought. Probably not. I haven't been to any of them."

"Why not?"

"You enjoyed your high school years. You were popular

and part of the 'in' crowd. I was not. I didn't particularly like most of the people in my graduating class back then. I don't see any reason to get together with them now and pretend that I did."

"That's kind of cynical, isn't it?"

"Yes, I suppose so. I know that they have changed since high school. We all have. They are probably nice people now. But I have no desire to get together with them and talk about high school."

"Well, at my twenty-fifth, after remembering high school things, we mostly sat around and talked about our children and, in some cases, grandchildren. We talked about our current jobs. That sort-of thing."

"Yes, I understand that. But you were talking with people that you like . . . and that you liked in high school. You were talking with people, some of whom you have stayed in touch with through the years. My friend, Russell, who lives in Florida now, is the only high school friend I've stayed in contact with all these years."

"How is he?"

"He's good. His youngest is now in high school. We talk on the phone every now and then and, just lately, have started emailing each other."

"Soooo, what are your plans? Mom said you quit your job and sold your condo."

"Yes. I don't really have any plans." Jake reached down and touched Laura's ring.

"You must have some idea of what you want to do next?"

"No, not really. Not now."

"Well, I simply don't understand that. Where do you want to live?"

"I don't know. I can't decide. I need to know what I want to do before I decide where to live."

"Yes, I can see that. But surely you must have some idea. What are you leaning toward doing?"

"I'm really not leaning toward anything."

"What? Are you just going to hang out here until you

think of something?"

"No. Actually, I'm leaving tomorrow."

"Tomorrow? Where are you going?"

"I'm not sure. I'm thinking of going over to the coast."

"The Outer Banks?"

"Yes."

"Why?"

"I don't know. Guess I'm hoping that something will come to me during the drive or while I'm there. I've always liked the ocean."

"Okay, but why are you leaving tomorrow? I just got here today. I'd like to visit with you some."

"This has nothing to do with you. I've been here for over a week now. That's long enough. And, I want to be alone on the eighth."

"What's the eighth? Oh, sorry. I forgot. Wouldn't you rather be with your family?"

"No, I don't want to be with anyone. I don't want anyone to remind me of what I was supposed to be doing on the eighth. I don't want anyone telling me how sad it is and how sorry they are."

Lucy didn't say anything. She was remembering what it was like when she lost her daughter, Katherine.

Jake added, "I just want to be alone."

Before sunset on the next day, Friday, October 7th, Jake was settled in a rental cottage, right on the beach, in Avon, North Carolina. In order to get the cottage, he had to take it for a week. He thought that this might actually be a good thing.

Jake had taken the scenic route over to the Outer Banks. Once on Highway 64, he just drove east until he ran out of road. That drive had given Jake a lot of time to think. He examined his relationship with God and was thankful for that relationship. Jesus promised that He would never leave anyone who believed on Him. As Jake looked back over the past three weeks, as low as he had felt, he knew that Jesus was always with him. He had not handled Laura's death well. But knowing that Jesus was always with him had given Jake, in the back of his mind, a sense of peace. Laura's death had been such a shock that he knew he didn't hold up with any dignity. He realized that he had been a complete wreck at Laura's funeral and burial. He cringed when he thought of them both. Poor Charles and Peggy, in one week, had been to four funerals.

Jake had never previously been to the Outer Banks. The actual strip of land was extremely narrow. Jake was surprised by that and by how small everything was. From highway 64, Jake had turned south on highway 12. He had driven along the Cape Hatteras National Seashore and then ran out of road. He had had to catch a ferry to reconnect with highway 12. He had passed the Pea Island Wildlife Refuge, then more of the Cape Hatteras National Seashore and then several small towns. He had driven through Rodanthe, Waves and Salvo before arriving in Avon. These were all tiny towns. Jake had thought that, perhaps having come from New York City, any place would seem small. He didn't have a reservation and had actually never heard of Avon. He noticed a sign advertising the cottages, stopped at the office and rented one for the week. October was obviously not a peak season.

Jake had previously stopped and bought groceries. After putting them away in the kitchen and putting his clothes in the bedroom, Jake walked out of the cottage and onto the beach. As Jake stood on the beach and looked out at the ocean, the sun was setting behind his back. It made the ocean look almost golden. It was a beautiful sight. Jake felt a pang of loneliness as he realized such a beautiful sight should be shared.

While walking back to the cottage, Jake noticed a young couple, three cottages down from him, getting a suitcase out of a SUV. Jake waved and the man waved back. Jake went inside, fixed himself a sandwich and brought that, with some chips and a soft drink in a glass with ice cubes, outside on the front porch of the small cottage. He placed his food on a small table, sat down in a wicker chair and admired the view of the ocean. Jake felt the presence of Jesus with him and he thanked Him for that.

The next morning, Jake took a bag of small, powdered donuts and a mug of hot coffee and sat back down on the porch. He watched the waves. It was Saturday, October eighth – his and Laura's wedding day. He touched Laura's ring and felt truly sad and alone. Once again, tears rolled down his cheeks.

Suddenly, Jake realized that he was crying for himself. Initially, he had been crying for Laura. However today, now, he was crying for himself. He was crying because he was alone. He was crying because he was not marrying the woman he loved, on this very day, as he should have been doing.

Jake had reached the conclusion that sometimes accidents are just accidents. God was a spirit who could exist everywhere at the same time. The Bible tells how God is aware when a sparrow dies. If a sparrow flew into a glass door and died, God would be aware of it. It was an accident. The sparrow didn't mean to fly into a glass door and kill himself. God could have sent an angel to prevent that sparrow from flying into a glass door . . . but He did not. He let the accident happen. When that seventeen-year-old girl crossed the centerline and slammed into the car Laura was riding in, God could have sent an angel to prevent it. But He did not. He let the accident happen. Jake realized that that girl's parents must be grieving for the loss of their daughter. She had most of her life ahead of her. Henri, Paul and Jo also have people grieving for them. He was still grieving for Laura. Although he still felt some guilt for not eloping with Laura, her death was the result of an accident. He loved her more than he had ever loved anyone. He was to marry her this very day.

Could he, Jake Fleming, question God? Of course not. God is . . . God. He, a mere human, is in no position to question God. God knows the souls of those five people who died in that wreck. Jake decided that he has to accept it as an accident that God allowed to happen. It isn't easy to accept that. Jake thought, *I'm trying.*

Over 200 hundred times, angels are mentioned in the

Bible. Jake knew, from personal experience, that angels were real. Once, when Jake was about eight or nine, he had been running through the woods behind his parents' home. He came upon a fallen tree and, in his most deer-like fashion, jumped over the tree. As he was coming down, Jake remembered being pushed on his back. He jumped much farther down the path and, when he landed, he stumbled and fell forward. He should have hit the ground but he did not. Instead, he felt a push on his chest. He righted himself and turned to look back at the tree he had just jumped. On the ground where he should have landed, if not for an angel's push, was a coiled-up rattlesnake. Jake had felt the push on his back and the push on his chest. He always believed those pushes were the result of an angel. If that angel had not pushed him, Jake would have had a serious accident with a rattlesnake.

Jake sat staring at the ocean. He did not know what to do with himself. He could sit on the porch and watch the waves. He could do some beachcombing. He could visit the Cape Hatteras Lighthouse. The next little town south of Avon was Buxton. The lighthouse was there. Jake got his camera and decided to go see the lighthouse. He took some photos but declined to take a tour. The next town south of Buxton was Frisco. Frisco was home to a Native American Museum. It reminded him of an island in the middle of the St. Lawrence River that Laura and he had visited. Without being conscious that he was doing so, Jake reached down and felt Laura's ring. It was interesting to realize that Native Americans had lived on this narrow strip of land hundreds of years ago.

Jake returned to the cottage, ate a late lunch and waded in the surf. He took some pictures. He was lonely. He felt that, in all the world, he was the only person who realized the significance of this day and was mourning because the wedding could not take place. He asked Jesus to help him. Jesus did. Jesus made His presence known to Jake. Jake thanked Him and felt better. There were several college football games on television. Jake figured he could pass several hours watching them. He wanted to get through the day. However, after about half an hour, Jake gave up on the football games and sat out on the porch and watched the ocean.

The next day, after a mostly sleepless night during which Jake simply could not turn his mind off, Jake sat out on the porch with a hot mug of coffee and watched the sun rise above the ocean. He thanked Jesus for allowing him to witness this view. It was Sunday, October ninth. The eighth was over. Although he had shed a few tears, he had gotten through it without completely losing it. He thanked Jesus for that.

Jake had thought about attending a local church service but decided against it. He felt like it would be the thing to do but he didn't feel like going. Instead, he went back to bed. He slept until almost noon.

There were several attractions in the area. However, Jake thought he had all week to visit some of those. He microwaved a frozen TV dinner and sat in front of the television watching a pro football game. He found it boring to watch when he didn't care which team won. He tried his old game of calling the plays before they happened. When he saw a handoff to the running back go for two yards up the middle, he said, "You should have tried the quick slant pass I called." But he really wasn't interested.

Jake got his camera, went out and walked along the edge of where the water came to shore. He passed a few people, nodded and said, "hello." There weren't many people around. With school in session and the autumn weather in the air, this just wasn't a good time for visitors with children. Jake saw an elderly couple walking towards him. They were probably in their late seventies and they were holding hands. As they passed, Jake gave them a big smile and said, "hello." They both smiled back and said, "hello." Jake and Laura had held hands all throughout Québec City. Jake touched Laura's ring and felt sad.

Walking back to the cottage, Jake saw a nice shell on the beach. He picked it up, rinsed it off in the surf, carried it with him back to the cottage and sat it on the glass-topped coffee table. He "nuked" another TV dinner. They had been on sale; ten for ten dollars and Jake had bought ten of them. He switched the television on and there was another football game showing. Flipping through the channels, he found an old *Dick Van Dyke Show* playing. It was one of his favorites – the haunted cabin one – he had already seen it several times. But he enjoyed watching it again. Even though it was all "make believe," Jake found himself being envious of the relationship between "Rob and Laura." That was the first time he had associated his Laura with Rob's Laura.

The next morning was Monday, October 10th and Jake had decided to do some sightseeing. He took his camera and drove north, caught the ferry and drove to Nags Head. There was a state park in Nags Head. It was called Jackeye Ridge. Jake had already come to the conclusion that many of the towns that made up the Outer Banks had been named by people who were drunk at the time. However, there was a nice historic district in Nags Head. Jake had always admired old houses. For one thing, they were better constructed than new houses. Jake was intrigued by the histories of the families who had once lived in them. Jake took photographs of the old homes that particularly impressed him. Nags Head also had a nice art section. There were numerous paintings of the Cape Hatteras Lighthouse, of the ocean, of seagulls and some of the old houses. Jake bought a copy of the Charlotte newspaper, sat outside at a local restaurant, ate his lunch and enjoyed a warm breeze while getting caught up with the news. For the past three weeks, he had not paid any attention to what was happening in the world.

That evening, as Jake was sitting on the porch eating another TV dinner, he noticed a man fishing in the ocean right from the shore. He watched as the man cast his line pretty far out into the water. He seemed to be using an artificial lure. After finishing his meal, Jake walked out on the seashore. He walked up to the fisherman and asked, "Any luck?"

"Not so far. But I've just got started."

"What are you using?"

"It's a green lure I've had luck with before."

"Well, hope it works for you again."

"Thank you."

The two men nodded at each other and Jake continued his walk down the beach. He thought, *It takes patience to be a good fisherman.*

During the next three days, Jake visited the Wright Brothers National Memorial near a town called Duck, the North Carolina Aquarium on Roanoke Island, the towns of Kill Devil Hills, Kitty Hawk, Rodanthe, Waves and Hatteras. He was in no hurry and made a leisurely visit to each place he went. One thing he noticed was that several of the local people and occasionally some of the other tourists would give him an odd look. At first, Jake thought that they might be thinking that he was someone they recognized or were wondering if he were someone else. Then Jake realized that people were questioning or wondering why he was alone. Why was he visiting the Pea Island Wildlife Refuge by himself? As he thought about this, he began to notice that he was the only person by himself. He would touch Laura's ring and think to himself, *I would love to be sharing these experiences with someone else.*

On Friday morning, October 14th, as Jake watched a beautiful sunrise, he felt tears in his eyes. He felt Laura's ring and wished so much that he could share this glorious view with her. He took some photographs but his heart wasn't in it.

He ate another TV dinner for breakfast. He packed up and loaded everything into the rental car. He checked out at the small office and headed west back to his parents' home.

He left the seashell on the coffee table.

CHAPTER THIRTY-FOUR

"The heavens declare the glory of God; the skies proclaim the works of His hands. Day after day they pour forth speech; night after night they display knowledge."

– Psalm 19:1-2

Mid 10th Century B. C.

It was dark when Jake pulled into his parents' driveway. Jake noticed a strange car parked there. When he walked inside, his oldest sister, Donna, gave him a big smile and a big hug.

His mom came over and asked how he was. She looked concerned.

Jake answered by saying, "Good. I'm okay."

"How was your trip?"

"Good, Mom. The Outer Banks are worth a visit. Driving back today, the leaves were just beautiful."

His mom said, "Okay." She clearly was not satisfied with Jake's answers.

His sister took his arm and pulled Jake outside on the patio. She said, "Let's talk."

Jake said, "All right. But do you mind if I go to the bathroom first? Maybe get something to drink?"

Donna replied, "Of course not. Go ahead."

There was a pretty strong breeze blowing. This would keep the mosquitoes away. Jake hated mosquitoes. Jake considered Donna to be his favorite sister. He liked them both in their own ways. Lucy was a little absent-minded but she had a good heart and Jake was fond of her. She was strong after the death of her daughter, Katherine. Her son, Steve, needed that.

Jake admired her for that. Donna was more practical, down-to-earth and direct. She was five years older than Jake. When they were children, that made a lot of difference. Lucy was two years older than Jake. He often felt sorry for his parents, especially his mom, with three children so close to the same age. As adults, of course, the age differences didn't matter at all. Jake felt comfortable talking with Donna.

With a soft drink in his hand, Jake sat down with Donna on the patio.

Jake asked, "How's Bob, Junior and Gloria doing?"

"Bob is fine. Both Junior and Gloria are in college now. They seem to be doing well. But the question is how are you doing?"

"I'm okay."

"Really?"

"Okay is a relative term. I'm much better now than I was a few weeks ago."

"Mom said you were having a real tough time dealing with it."

"I was."

Donna didn't respond.

Jake added, "I was a total mess at her funeral."

"I don't understand. She was a Christian?"

"Yes."

"And you are a Christian?"

"Yes."

"Don't you believe that her soul is now in heaven?"

"Of course."

"What's the problem then? As a Christian, I would think that you would accept things and move on with your life."

Jake didn't immediately respond. When he did, he said, "Donna, I am a Christian but I am also human. I am not perfect nor do I pretend to be. Becoming a Christian doesn't automatically make one perfect. Our souls are living in human containers. I do believe that when the container dies, the soul of a Christian goes to heaven."

Donna did not say anything.

Jake continued, "Donna, I love Laura more than anyone I have ever loved. We were scheduled to be married a week ago. It is still difficult for me, sometimes, to realize that she is gone. I mean, mentally, I know she is gone but emotionally, for a brief moment or two, I still can't believe it. Mom told me that it takes time to recover from such a shock. I think she is right." Jake's eyes were misty.

"But . . . as a Christian, I would think . . ."

"Donna, when I first heard the news, my human body went numb. That is something you cannot control. I just went numb. I couldn't think straight. I just shut down. I knew that Jesus was with me but I couldn't process things. That is the human aspect kicking in and causing problems."

Donna didn't say anything.

"Are you familiar with the shortest verse in the Bible?"

"Yes, of course. 'Jesus wept.'"

"Do you remember why he cried?"

"No."

"Jesus loved Martha, Mary and their brother, Lazarus. Jesus knew that Lazarus had died and He knew that He was going to raise Lazarus from the dead. However, when He saw Mary and the others crying, He was moved and He also cried."

Donna didn't respond.

Jake continued, "Jesus is the Son of God. He lived a perfect life in a human body. I think he may have shed tears then partially to show the rest of us that it is all right to grieve. If it was all right for Jesus to cry, then I feel no guilt for crying over the loss of Laura."

Jake wiped his eyes.

Donna softly said, "I guess you have to go through it to understand it."

"I don't know. I think everyone reacts and grieves in their own way. Suppose Bob suddenly had a heart attack and died. Do you think you know how you would handle it?"

"I would like to think I would handle it as a mature

Christian. I would be sorry but I would accept it and move on."

"That's what your brain is telling you now. And, maybe you would. But your human body and your human emotions may react differently."

"Maybe."

"And what you are saying about accepting it and moving on is probably correct. But, I think, it takes people different amounts of time to process things and come to that conclusion. I mean, what other choice is there? Suicide? No, of course not. Not for a Christian. Eventually, we all have to accept it and move on. But there are real emotions of grief, sadness and sorrow. Everyone may react to those emotions differently. But I do think it takes people different amounts of time to mourn and process the shock. One person's way of mourning is not right or wrong for someone else. Each person, I think, must mourn in whatever way works for them."

"Okay, I guess I can see that."

"It's only been a little over a month since Laura . . . Laura has only been gone for a little over a month. I'm doing much better now than I was at her funeral." Jake touched Laura's ring.

"I noticed that you cannot bring yourself to say 'dead' or 'died.' You always say 'gone.'"

"It's easier for me to say gone than died."

"All right. Well. Now what? What are you planning on doing now?"

"I don't know."

"Mom said you quit your job up in New York City."

"Yes."

"I never have understood exactly what it was you did up there."

"It doesn't matter."

"Mom said you made a lot of money."

"It costs a lot to live in New York."

"I imagine it does. So what type of work do you want to do now?"

"I'm not sure. I had an idea come to me when I was

visiting different places on the Outer Banks."

"Yeah, what was that?"

"I'm thinking about writing a book."

"You? Write a book? Come on. You can't write a book."

"Not, perhaps, a typical novel type book. I'm thinking, rather, about a book of photographs."

"That's been done. Many times. And you aren't a professional photographer anyway."

"I know. But what I am thinking of doing is this. You know how I've always been interested in ancient sites and monuments? Especially those that cannot be explained."

"Yes. So?"

"I am thinking of going to those places, all over the world, taking photographs of them and writing a brief explanation of each one. You see, on the left page of the book would be a description of the image. On the right page would be the image."

"Do you honestly think that enough people would buy this book so that you could even break even with your expenses?"

"No, of course not. But that's not the reason for doing it. I want to let people be aware – to know that these things exist. Additionally, I think it could be a fascinating journey for me to take. I think I would love doing it."

"How long do you expect this to take?"

"I haven't figured that out yet. I've just started toying with the idea of doing it."

"Guess."

"I expect I could do it in about two years."

"Two years! For a project that will cost money rather than make money." Donna paused and then said, "Jake, why don't you settle down and raise a family?"

Jake looked at Donna with total disgust. He replied, "A month ago, that was my plan."

"It's still a good plan. You just need to find a new . . . I mean, you are still young enough. There are plenty of women out there who would like to marry you."

Jake sighed and waited a moment to respond. He said, "Donna, I know you mean well. After my divorce, it took me twelve years to find Laura. Even if I were interested in doing that, which, right now, I am not, if it took me twelve years to find someone, I'd be fifty-four years old."

"I didn't mean for you to take twelve years."

"Right now, I am not at all interested in that plan."

"Okay. It was just a suggestion. But traveling all over the world? By yourself? For two years?"

"Yes. Yes. And yes."

"Really?"

"I don't know. I just said I'm thinking about it. It is something I would like to do. Whether or not I actually do it is another question."

Donna and Jake continued to sit on their parents' patio and talk. They reminisced about things that had happened when they were children. They shared memories of events that had taken place when they were in school. Even though it began poorly, it did Jake good to talk with his big sister.

CHAPTER THIRTY-FIVE

"Surely God is my salvation; I will trust and not be afraid. The Lord, the Lord, is my strength and my song; he has become my salvation."

– Isaiah 12:2

Early 7th Century B. C.

Just about nine weeks later, on Thursday, November 17, 2005, Jake found himself standing west of the Bolivian Altiplano in the Titicaca Basin at an altitude of 13,300 feet. Jake wanted to begin his journey of exploring unexplained sites by visiting one of the, if not the, most mysterious places in the world – Tiwanaku / Puma Punku. It was late spring and summer was on the way but, at this altitude, it was still cold. Jake was simply wandering about the site on his own. In the morning, he was scheduled to meet the guide he had hired.

Jake had done his homework. He had read numerous articles about this place. Puma Punku was actually a part of Tiwanaku. Even though Jake had read about the site and studied photographs, he was still surprised by how large Tiwanaku was. It was huge.

Jake was amazed by what he was seeing. One of the reasons the site was so mysterious was that there were numerous megalithic stones that had been cut with machines. Jake noticed one huge block of granite that had a cut about half an inch deep in a straight line all the way across its surface. The cut was about a quarter of an inch wide. Both sides and the bottom of the cut were as smooth as glass. There is simply no way it could have been cut by hand with chisels. Nonetheless, according to what

Jake had read, that's what professional archaeologists claim. Nonsense, thought Jake.

Jake saw the somewhat famous "H" blocks at Puma Punku. No one needed to be an "expert" to immediately tell that these huge stones had not been chiseled. Rather, they had been worked by machines. However, the "experts" say that these ruins had been constructed around 1,500 – 2,000 years earlier. The technology, the machines and the energy for such machines, to produce such cuts and such surfaces simply did not exist during that time period. Consequently, they had to have been made using the available technology – chisels.

After taking several photographs, Jake decided to return to his hotel. He was looking forward to meeting with his guide in the morning. Perhaps he would have some insights about the things that Jake had seen.

The next morning, while sitting in the lobby of his hotel, Jake noticed a short thin man in his mid-fifties. He was wearing the traditional clothing of the native people who lived along the shore of Lake Titicaca. The man seemed to be looking for someone and Jake presumed that this was his guide. When he looked Jake's way, Jake stood up and smiled. He nodded at the man. The man walked over to Jake and asked, "Mr. Fleming?"

Jake smiled, replied that he was and they shook hands.

His guide introduced himself as Josè Nunez. Jake asked Mr. Nunez to call him Jake. The man smiled and said, "Call me Nunez." He spoke excellent English.

Mr. Nunez had a small backpack for water and lunch. Jake had the same. The two men spent all day roaming around the ruins of Tiwanaku. Mr. Nunez explained that the largest pyramid in Tiwanaku, the Akapana, was originally thought to be a hill. When archaeologists eventually excavated the "hill," they were surprised to find a massive pyramid under all the soil. The Akapana is a step pyramid with an unusual feature on the top. There is a large sunken area, cut in twenty right angles, for which no one knows the purpose.

After exploring the Kalasasaya, a large "courtyard" over 300 feet long and with huge megalithic "gateways," Jake asked Mr. Nunez, "What was this?"

Mr. Nunez replied, "No one really knows. They call it a courtyard . . . but really." He shrugged his shoulders. This was the answer that Jake frequently got from Mr. Nunez.

Jake took photos of the Gateway of the Sun. This was probably the most recognized item from Tiwanaku. It was cut from a single 10-ton stone. Jake had asked Mr. Nunez to tell him the real story about this site, not the legends that tourists expect to hear. Jake had questioned the practicality of roaming through these ruins in his native outfit. Mr. Nunez had smiled and said, "The tourists expect it." Jake had told him to wear more comfortable clothes tomorrow.

Looking at the Gateway of the Sun, Mr. Nunez said that there were carvings that had been interpreted by archaeologists over a hundred years ago. These carvings told that the people were aware that the earth rotated on its axis and around the sun. They also showed that the people were able to calculate eclipses.

Mr. Nunez said, "That's rather sophisticated stuff. Then other archaeologists have found pottery on site and dated it to around 250 A.D. They think some of the images on the pottery indicate a religious belief in a sun god. As a consequence of that pottery, the archaeologists say that this site is approximately two thousand years old."

Jake replied, "I'm afraid I will have to disagree with that estimate. I can stand here and *feel* that this place is ancient – way beyond two thousand years. The answer is obvious. There were two groups of people – those who originally built this place and those people who moved here much much later. They would have had no knowledge of who had built this. There would have been no connection. The people who built this were too scientifically advanced to believe in a sun god. The people from two thousand years ago would not know that the earth rotated around the sun and would believe in a sun god."

Mr. Nunez said that the "experts" say that Viracocha is

carved on the Gateway to the Sun." Then he looked at Jake, winked and added, "No one really knows for sure. It could be Viracocha. It could be something else."

Jake placed his hand on the Gateway of the Sun and said, "You know, I've seen images of this all my life. I've often wondered about these two horizontal slits on this side. It almost looks like they were designed for some big forklift to come along and move it."

They spent the rest of the day walking over the ruins of Tiwanaku. Jake took a lot of photographs. That evening, back at the hotel, Jake invited Mr. Nunez to join him for supper. He declined – saying that he needed to get home, as his wife would be expecting him.

In the morning, Jake saw Mr. Nunez in the lobby. He was wearing jeans, a sweatshirt and a jacket. This was the day they were to go out on Lake Titicaca.

On the way to the lake, Mr. Nunez began to tell Jake things about Lake Titicaca.

"Lake Titicaca is at the highest altitude, twelve thousand, five hundred feet of any nav-ba-til, nav-ga-bull . . ."

He looked embarrassed.

Jake quickly said, "Don't worry about it. Everyone gets tongue-tied over words they know well and have often used. It happens even to professional speakers. You have used navigable many times, I'm sure. It just happens sometimes to all of us. No problem." He smiled at Mr. Nunez who nodded back with a smile.

"Anyway," Mr. Nunez stated, "to avoid all the tourist stuff that you have already read, let me tell you about a somewhat recent mystery that has been unveiled regarding this lake."

Jake replied, "Please do. I am truly interested."

Mr. Nunez said, "You may be aware that most archaeologists think that Tiwanaku used to be a port city on Lake Titicaca."

Jake nodded and said, "Yes."

Mr. Nunez continued, "If so, that would mean that the

lake has receded almost twelve miles and either dropped eight hundred feet or Tiwanaku has risen eight hundred feet. The archaeologists think that the lake has dropped and receded. There is no question that the lake, due to evaporation, has slowly been getting smaller and smaller. There are no rivers nearby. The lake is evaporating faster than the rainfall replenishes it. However, it is a very slow and gradual process."

"I understand," Jake said.

"Okay. Remember that. For centuries, the locals have had legends that an ancient stone city is located beneath the waters of Lake Titicaca. In 1968, the French underwater explorer, Jacques Cousteau and his team explored the lake looking for any sign of underwater buildings or any man-made structures. They primarily looked around the two islands where people have been living for centuries – the Island of the Moon and Island of the Sun. Cousteau and his team found absolutely nothing. This fact . . . that he found nothing . . . gave much support to the concept that all the legends were mythical."

Jake nodded.

"However, and here is where it gets really interesting and mysterious. You have probably never heard of him but in Bolivia and among those who study pre-Columbian structures, the name of Hugo Rojo is well respected. What he did was to go to the village of Puerto Acosta, which is on the northeast corner of the lake. There, he asked a man who was a hundred and one years old, and had lived there all his life, about the legend of an underwater city. The man explained that he had been told this from his father who had been told from his father and on and on. This elderly man told Rojo where to look. His divers did so and they found huge megalithic man-made structures. They filmed them and made a documentary about them. There are very large temples and buildings. There are steps and stone roads. It is a very large site. So, the myths, the legends become facts. However, and this may not surprise you, Jake, but even though the documentary clearly shows these buildings built with huge blocks of stone, the archaeologists pretend that the underwater site does not exist."

Jake asked, "When was this?"

"1980."

"Wow, twenty-five years ago." Jake paused. Mr. Nunez stared at him. Jake said, "I think I see why the 'experts' ignore this finding."

Mr. Nunez nodded. "Yes, it creates a major mystery. All the archaeologists agree that Tiwanaku is around two thousand years old. They also agree that, for the past three to four thousand years, Lake Titicaca has slowly been getting smaller. If both these things are accurate, then how can one possibly explain the existence of this underwater site? The site undoubtedly exists exactly as the locals have always said. We have film to prove its existence. People can dive down and touch it. If the lake has been getting smaller for thousands of years, how can this site be underwater? The only obvious answer is that the site was built before the lake existed."

Jake responded, "Wow. This truly upsets the chronology of the experts."

Mr. Nunez smiled, "There is something else that supports this. Archaeologists have found many artifacts from Tiawanaku six feet below the surface. These are different from the pottery dated to 250 A.D. These experts cannot explain where the six feet of soil came from. Wind erosion won't explain it. At this height, there are no mountains high enough or near enough to produce water runoff that would reach here. So, where did six feet of soil come from? It is deposited on top of the Tiawanaku structures. To the experts, it remains a mystery. They cannot explain it."

"Yes, so they ignore it." Jake paused and then said, as much to himself as to Mr. Nunez, "They all three must have existed at the same time."

Mr. Nunez asked, "Three?"

"Yes, Tiawanaku, Puma Punku and the underwater site."

Mr. Nunez nodded, "Yes."

"This would make them far older than what the "experts" say."

Mr. Nunez replied, "The first archaeologist who really examined and studied Tiawanaku thought that it had been constructed around 17,000 B.C."

"I've read that. Due to the alignment with the stars. He may have been completely accurate."

"So, if these three places were in existence around twenty thousand years ago, what could have destroyed them, tossed huge blocks of stone around, deposited six feet of silt and created Lake Titicaca?"

Jake smiled, "A flood."

Mr. Nunez responded by saying, "That's exactly what the locals say. They have a strong legend about a worldwide flood. The Peruvians do also."

Jake responded, "I do too. I believe that there was a worldwide flood."

"It would explain this site. Wonder when it happened?"

"Nunez, a flood would explain the current condition of this site, wouldn't it? I don't know when the flood actually happened. Maybe five thousand years ago?"

"Also, Jake, you might be interested to know that Tiawanaku is over four hundred acres in size. That is a lot of stone cutting and construction. What is truly surprising is that, as of today, only about forty acres of Tiawanaku has been excavated. That's only ten percent of the total. There is no telling what is yet to be found."

"Wow, wonder why some archaeologists haven't been down here doing research?"

Mr. Nunez looked at Jake and said, "There is no telling what is yet to be found." He let that sink in for Jake.

Jake said, "You're saying that they are afraid of what they will find. If they find evidence that this place is thousands and thousands of years older than the accepted date, the question would arise 'who was around then who would have been capable of building this site?'"

Mr. Nunez nodded his head.

Jake asked, "Who do the locals say built Tiawanaku,

Puma Punku and the underwater site?"

"The ancient ones."

"The ancient ones? Wonder who they were?"

By ferry, the two men visited the islands of the moon and sun. Some local traditions say that those ancients who built Tiawanaku first lived on the Island of the Sun. Back on shore; they drove to the small village of Puerto Acosta. Jake would have loved to have the opportunity to speak with that 101-year-old man. However, since he would now have to be 126 years old, it didn't seem likely. At the village, Jake bought a small souvenir. It was designed by the locals for any tourists who made it to their little town.

Back at the hotel, Jake shook hands with Mr. Nunez. He said, "It's been a fascinating day, Nunez. Thank you."

Mr. Nunez replied, "Tomorrow is Puma Punku."

The next morning, Jake was sitting in the lobby but Nunez did not arrive at their scheduled time. After waiting about 40 minutes, Jake decided, that for some reason, he wasn't going to show. Jake started out for Puma Punku on his own. He'd only taken a few dozen steps down the road when Mr. Nunez arrived.

Mr. Nunez began apologizing. He looked ashamed and embarrassed. Jake smiled at him and told him to forget it – that it was nothing to worry about at all.

"You are not angry?" Mr. Nunez asked.

"No. We're good." Jake replied.

"I thought you'd be mad at me."

On the way to Puma Punku, Jake told Mr. Nunez the story about his big malamute dog, Bo.

At Puma Punku, Mr. Nunez stated, "What makes Puma Punku so mysterious is the absolute precision of the structures here. They are also very complex."

Jake replied, "I see that. How in the world were they cut?"

Mr. Nunez smiled, "That is the mystery. No one knows. There are no chisel marks. It's like they were cut with extremely sharp high-powered machines."

"Do you tell the tourists that?"

"Not most of them. Some of them, however, figure it out for themselves. Some of those cuts are so narrow and so perfect, they almost have to have been done with machines." He smiled a big smile.

"Which is oldest – Puma Punku or Tiawanaku?"

Mr. Nunez shrugged his shoulders. "Most of the experts think that Puma Punku was built after Tiawanaku. Again, no one really knows. The famous "H" blocks are extremely sophisticated. No one knows their purpose. Much material from both sites has been removed. Over the years, the stones have been quarried from both sites and used as building stone for homes, commercial buildings and even as bedrock for the railroad. Speaking of quarrying, the original quarry for most of these stones has been located about twelve miles from here. Some of these huge blocks of stone are estimated to weigh between one hundred and one hundred and thirty tons. The quarry is at a lower elevation than these sites. No one knows how those huge stones were lifted and moved to be used here."

"Yes, Nunez, I've read about that. One article said that they were dragged here using llama-skin ropes."

Mr. Nunez grinned. He said, "I too have heard that. Look at this massive piece of rock. It is thirty-six feet long, sixteen feet wide and six feet thick. That would have to be some mighty tough llamas."

Jake laughed. Overlooking several huge stones, Jake and Mr. Nunez sat down and ate their lunches. As they were eating, Mr. Nunez pointed at an "I" shaped clamp hole that had originally been filled with hot molten metal.

He said, "How they had the ability to melt and pour metal is still unknown."

Jake smiled, "Maybe the llamas helped."

Mr. Nunez said, "The people who say things like 'llama ropes' have never actually been here on site and looked at the size of these structures."

Looking around, Jake said, "I can see why so many people call this place the most mysterious place on the planet."

Mr. Nunez cleared his throat.

"May I ask you some personal questions?"

"Sure."

"You remember I spent two years in London?"

"Yes, I remember you told me that. I thought what an amazing difference there is between this place and London."

Mr. Nunez laughed, "That's for sure. What I want to ask you is about Jesus."

Jake was surprised but didn't show it. He said, "Sure."

"You frequently touch your chest and whisper the name Jesus. Why do you do that?"

Jake smiled, "It is my way of reminding me that Jesus is always with me. I thank Him for His presence – for being with me."

Mr. Nunez looked like he was in deep thought. Indeed, he was. He said, "Today is Sunday. You are here, not in church."

Jake replied, "Yes. However, Jesus is still with me. I don't need to be in a church building to feel the presence of Jesus. I usually do go to church on Sundays but this trip makes that difficult to do. I do not speak nor understand Spanish."

Mr. Nunez said, "In London, many people went to the Church of England on Sundays. But the rest of the week, they didn't seem any different from anyone else."

Jake smiled. "It happens. Sunday only Christians."

"You are different from the tourists I usually see. You do not get angry."

"Do the tourists get angry?"

"Yes. They are angry that there are dirt roads. They are angry about having to walk so much. They are angry that there are not signs explaining what each block of stone is called. They are angry that there are not more amenities. They even get angry that everything is in ruin. I've had some who complained that the altitude was too high."

Jake laughed.

"But you never complain. You never get angry. You smile a lot. You laugh a lot. Why?"

"When you are a Christian, when you believe in Jesus, there is no reason to get angry. As humans, we sometimes do. I get angry at myself – for getting angry. Being a believer in Jesus makes a person happy."

Mr. Nunez paused. He was thinking.

Finally, he said, "Around here, we all go to the Catholic Church. We are all Catholics. We try to do right but we are missing something."

"Perhaps it is a personal relationship with Jesus?"

"Perhaps. We do pray to Mary to intercede on our behalf to Jesus."

"Have you read the New Testament?"

"No. We don't read the Bible much at our church. How does one . . . can anyone have a personal relationship with Jesus?"

"Yes, anyone and everyone. Jesus loves everyone and He teaches us to love everyone."

"How do you go about . . . I mean, someone like me. Do I need to talk with our priest? How can I . . . Jake, I've done some bad things in my life."

"We all have." Jake smiled. He said, "God accepts everyone if they sincerely come to Him with a true belief in His Son, Jesus."

Mr. Nunez smiled, "I believe in Jesus."

"The Bible says, 'To all who received Him, to those who believed in His name, He gave the right to become children of God.'"

Jake continued, "Do you remember the story of the thief who was also being crucified on a cross next to Jesus?"

Mr. Nunez replied, "Yes, because he recognized Jesus as the Son of God, Jesus saved him right there. How can I do that?"

"It is actually quite easy. Since you already believe Jesus is who He said He was, you can do it here, right now."

"What do I need to do?"

"What everyone who wants to be saved by Jesus must do. The first thing is to admit that you are a sinner and that you need Jesus. Next, you need to repent. This means that you are willing to turn away from sin and live a different life following Jesus. Next, you must believe, with all your heart, that Jesus died for you, for you personally, on the cross and then rose from His grave."

"That's it?"

"That's it. The Bible says, 'If you confess with your mouth, *Jesus is Lord*, and believe in your heart that God raised Him from the dead, you will be saved.'"

Mr. Nunez smiled. He said, "I do believe that."

Jake smiled. He responded, "I do too. One of my favorite verses in the Bible is when Jesus asks Peter whom Peter thinks He is. Peter responds by saying, 'Thou are the Christ, the Son of the living God.' When people ask me about Jesus and who He is, this is my response also."

"I can say that too."

"You must believe it."

"I do. I really do."

Jake replied, "Let's pray together. Will you repeat after me?"

Mr. Nunez nodded.

Jake began, "Dear heavenly Father."

"Dear heavenly Father."

"I know that I have sinned."

"I know that I have sinned."

"I am sorry for my sins and ask You, in Your Son's Holy name, for forgiveness."

"I am sorry for my sins and ask You, in Your Son's Holy name, for forgiveness."

"I do believe that Jesus died on the cross for my sins."

"I do believe that Jesus died on the cross for my sins."

"I do believe that You raised Him from the dead to life."

"I do believe that You raised Him from the dead to life."

"I want to turn away from my sins and trust in Jesus as

my personal Savior."

"I want to turn away from my sins and trust in Jesus as my personal Savior."

"I know that Jesus died for me and I want to follow Him for the rest of my life."

"I know that Jesus died for me and I want to follow Him for the rest of my life."

"From this day forward, I want to trust Jesus as my Lord and my Savior."

"From this day forward, I want to trust Jesus as my Lord and my Savior."

"I ask that You send the Holy Spirit into my life and have Him direct my life."

"I ask that You send the Holy Spirit into my life and have Him direct my life."

"Heavenly Father, I thank You for sending Your Son to cleanse my sins."

"Heavenly Father, I thank You for sending Your Son to cleanse my sins."

"Heavenly Father, I thank you for sending the Holy Spirit to guide me."

"Heavenly Father, I thank you for sending the Holy Spirit to guide me."

"I pray this in Jesus' precious name, amen."

"I pray this in Jesus' precious name, amen."

Jake said, "That's it. You should now pray directly to God, in Jesus' name, frequently. It will bless you to do so."

"Thank you."

"This is the beginning of a whole new you. A new way of living. You will begin to feel the presence of the Holy Spirit in your life. Take time, every day, to be alone with God. Start reading the Bible."

"Okay."

"Let me warn you. Sometimes new Christians expect to suddenly feel totally different – joyful all the time. They can become disappointed when that doesn't happen. You have just taken the first steps on a new path. Don't expect to experience everything immediately."

Mr. Nunez nodded.

"Remember this, 'For it is by grace you have been saved, through faith – and this not from yourselves, it is the gift of God – not by works, so that no one can boast.' Of course, being a Christian now, you are going to want to do the works that the Holy Spirit is going to guide you to do. Some people seem to think that they can get to heaven by doing good works – supporting a church, donating to good organizations, helping young children, teaching in Sunday School and those type of things. Those are good things to do. However, in the Bible, Jesus said, 'I am the way and the truth and the life. *No one* comes to the Father except by me.' We cannot be good and get to heaven. The only way is the way that you have just done – to accept Jesus as your personal Savior."

Mr. Nunez replied, "There's that word personal again."

"Yes," Jake responded, "when Jesus died on that cross, He was dying for your sins and for my sins. He wasn't dying for the world's sins but for the sins of each individual person who would acknowledge Jesus as the Son of God, who would repent of their sins and follow Jesus. In the Bible, Paul said that the resurrection of Jesus was proof that Jesus is the Son of God. With the resurrection of Jesus, God was saying that He accepted Jesus's death on the cross as payment for our sins. The blood of Jesus is what cleans us from sin. Without the resurrection of Jesus, there is nothing. With the resurrection of Jesus, there is everything."

"This is what communion is about."

"Yes, but it is more than that. When we repent and accept Christ by faith, this also means that we intend to obey Him. He becomes our Lord. If, as Christians, we follow the teachings of Jesus, we will obey Jesus. Remember, He is with us always. That's why I touch my chest and say, 'Thank you Jesus' or 'I trust you, Jesus.'"

"There is so much to learn."

"That is true. However, you have the rest of your life to

learn. I am certainly still learning every day."

Mr. Nunez looked confused. He said, "I'm not sure I understand it all."

Jake smiled and replied, "No one does. There are things in the Bible I absolutely do not understand. However, I accept them on faith. You are a brand-new Christian now – a baby Christian. Like a child, you will learn a little more each day. Don't worry. The Holy Spirit will guide you. As John was finishing one of his books in the Bible, he wrote, "I write these things to you who believe in the name of the Son of God so that you may know that you have eternal life.'"

Mr. Nunez said, "I have neglected my duty to show you the rest of Puma Punku."

"Tell you what, José, I've seen enough. I've got enough photographs. Let's head on back to the hotel."

As they were walking, Jake said, "Listen, do you have Internet access at home?"

"Yes, we do."

"Good. There are several Christian organizations with websites. Some of them provide the means for new Christians such as you to ask questions. They can also provide you with guides to help you grow in your faith and as a Christian. When we get back, I'll write some of them down for you."

Thank you. Where do you go from here?"

"Cusco."

"That should be interesting."

"Yes, I expect so."

Back at the hotel, Jake handed Mr. Nunez an envelope with his fee for being a tour guide for three days. Jake included a generous tip.

Jake said, "José, you and I are now brothers in Christ. You now have millions of brothers and sisters in Christ all around the world. I would like to stay in touch with my new brother. Would you write your email address for me?"

"Yes, of course. That would be nice."

"Due to my travels, I am not going to have constant

access to a computer. I won't have a mailing address. But give me your mail address and I'll write to you."

Nunez did. The two men shook hands and then hugged.

As José walked away, Jake said, "I will be praying for you."

CHAPTER THIRTY-SIX

"For the wages of sin is death, but the gift of God is eternal life in Christ Jesus our Lord."

– Romans 6:23

Mid 1st Century A.D.

Late in the afternoon, on Monday, November 21, 2005, Jake's plane touched down in Cusco, Peru. Jake checked into a nice hotel with a restaurant and gift shop. He needed the gift shop for more film. His camera was a 35 mm. He had looked into a new type of camera – digital. Jake had taken a small digital camera with him when he traveled to Neverland. However, Jake had determined that digital cameras would not work for his purposes. They had to be constantly downloaded to a computer. He knew he was probably taking way too many photos – he was planning on using only one for each site for his book. However, Jake thought, he would most likely only visit these places once in his life and he would enjoy all the other photographs himself.

Jake spent the next day touring the most famous site in Cusco – Sacsayhuaman. In its prime, it would have been an astonishing place. Today, the remains consist primarily of those huge perfectly fitted stones. Like in Tiawanaku, many stones were removed and used in other buildings.

Jake took a day trip to Ollantaytambo. At this huge construction, one can easily see that there are huge megalithic stones at the bottom and more recent and much smaller Inca stones toward the top. The massive walls were built with granite stones thousands of years before the Inca came along. The Inca reconstructed and repaired pathways and walls that were ancient.

The Inca work was well done but was still inferior to that of the ancient builders.

The next day, Jake took a train ride to Machu Picchu. Because both Cusco and Machu Picchu are located in the Andes Mountains, the views from the train were often both beautiful and breathtaking. Since Jake had previously studied Machu Picchu, he thought he knew what to expect. However, what he found was that this site was not originally built by the Inca. The bottom stones were huge like those at Ollantaytambo. The upper stones and the repair stones were much smaller and were the work of the Inca. Like Tiawanaku, Puma Punku and Ollantaytambo, no one really knows who the original builders of these places were. After they had fallen into disuse, other people arrived and used them.

Jake couldn't get a flight to Quito, Ecuador until Monday, the 28th. It was a fairly short flight and he arrived before noon. While Quito has many interesting historical sites, the site Jake was most interested in seeing was located on a hill in the middle of the city. It separated north Quito from south Quito. Jake's hotel was in north Quito and he could see the hill from the hotel. The Spanish had named the hill El Panecillo meaning bread loaf hill. The Inca had called it Shungoloma, which translates, to hill of the heart.

Through the hotel, Jake got a tour guide for the next day. Jake met his guide the next morning and they drove to the hill. One of the books Jake had read claimed that it was the largest man-made structure on the planet. Excavations have shown that the hill, which is huge, has no layers of soil. It also has no rocks. It is as though the soil that makes the hill was all laid down at one time. There are homes and roads on this hill. The local people, even those living on the hill, have no idea that it is considered to be man-made. There are no other hills nearby. It sits by itself – now in the middle of Quito. When it was built, it would have been by itself - all alone in the middle of nowhere.

At the very top of the hill, Ecuador constructed, in 1976, a large aluminum statue of the Virgin Mary. It is the only known statue of Mary with wings. This is what the guide wanted to take Jake to see. Jake was not interested in touring the statue. Instead, also located at the top of this hill, is an extremely ancient construction. Today, it is called the Olla del Panecillo. That translates to pot of bread. Currently, the Ecuadorian government has released tourist information about it and they call it a rain catcher built in the early 1800s to irrigate crops. Jake read that and said to himself, "What utter nonsense." Jake had seen numerous images, both inside and outside of the structure. The government had built the ugly concrete that now surrounds the structure and put up a fence that is there to keep tourists from exploring the structure. At the bottom, it has tunnels running from the interior to the outside. The government's viewing area for tourists hides those tunnels. The shape of it looks slightly like an inverted wasp nest – and was the same color as a wasp nest. Jake was intrigued by the ring around the very top. The top of the structure curved upward until, at the very top, a small opening had been placed. The purpose of this opening or ring is without explanation. Indeed, the entire structure made no sense. Who had built it and for what purpose was totally unknown. Its real age was also unknown. Jake was fascinated by it. His guide was bored by it. Jake had read a book about this structure that had been written in the 1960s. The photographs in that book had clearly shown the interior and the tunnels from which one could access the interior. Jake was disappointed by the way the Ecuadorian government had treated this ancient site. He took many photographs from all around it. To Jake, it looked like the structure was designed for something to fit into the opening at the top. His mind began to explore possibilities. A crystal? A communication relay device? A light? Could this man-made hill have been constructed so that this structure could be built at a certain altitude at a certain longitude and latitude? He had discussed this with both Mr. Le Couteau and with Laura.

The hill itself was a favorite place for muggers and thieves. All the brochures warned people not to walk alone. They even warned about using taxi cabs. Jake noticed that almost everyone was in a group or with a guide. His guide drove him back to his hotel. Other than that it existed, the guide had not known anything about the ancient structure on El Panecillo.

Even in Old Quito, Jake noticed that the lower layers of stone structures were of better quality construction than the upper layers. Jake concluded that there had been people living in South America long before the people of recorded history.

Jake decided to pass on the stone balls in Costa Rica and the gold models of jet planes in Columbia. They were certainly of unknown origin but he knew he couldn't cover everything. He decided to travel next to Teotihuacan just north of Mexico City.

Arriving in Mexico City on December 1, 2005, Jake took a taxi to a motel within walking distance of Teotihuacan. The next day, Jake began his exploration of this ancient city. He climbed the Pyramid of the Sun. It was a huge magnificent structure. It was also mysterious. No one knows who actually built it or exactly when. At one time, in its past, it had apparently been covered with mica. There are also tunnels running under the pyramid itself. No one knows what the tunnels were for or the purpose of the mica. More mysteries for Jake to solve, he thought. Jake loved the view from the top. Some archaeologists had determined that there was a representation of the nine planets in our solar system built into the layout of Teotihuacan. Jake wondered, if that were accurate, how did these ancient people become aware that there were nine planets revolving around the sun? Jake walked down the massive monument and started walking down the 'Street of the Dead.' It was a long wide avenue that went straight from the Pyramid of the Sun through the entire city for over a mile. Teotihuacan had been a very large city. According to the most recent research, it had been built around 900 B. C. Around 500 A.D., it had a population of 175,000 people. However, by 700 A.D., they were all gone. The city was deserted. No one knows why.

Jake decided to stay at Teotihuacan. He climbed the Pyramid of the Moon and many of the other structures. He took many photographs. Jake found a guide with a car and made a day trip to Cuicuilco, which is now a suburb just south of Mexico City. It is on the southern shore of Lake Texcoco. Archaeologists say that it is one of the oldest structures built in Mexico and Central America. It is a round pyramid. It has been dated to sometime around 800 B. C. There is a lava flow from Xitle, a nearby volcano, that for years had been misdated. With modern dating techniques, the lava flow, which covered part of Cuicuilco, has been dated to 250 B. C. The entire place was abandoned during the 2nd Century A.D. No one knows why.

That evening, back in his hotel room, after a week at Teotihuacan, Jake decided he would stay one more day and then fly out the following day. The next day, December 9, 2005 Jake got up before the sun. He walked over to the Pyramid of the Sun. He climbed to the summit, which was the fifth level, got out his camera and waited on the sun to rise. He got some nice shots but it was not what he had hoped to see.

Jake sat at the very top of this huge massive pyramid. He let his legs dangle over the edge. This place felt spiritual. He prayed a long prayer of thanks to God. He stood, held out his arms to the sky and said, "Thank you, Jesus."

On the 10th, Jake flew from Mexico City to Los Angeles. Jake did not like Los Angeles. He thought it had bad "vibes." The next day, December 11th, Jake flew from Los Angeles to Rapa Nui -- Easter Island -- by way of Hawaii. He arrived at dusk and decided to stay at his hotel until sunrise. There was one place he was eager to see.

Most visitors to Easter Island expressed surprise that the moai were facing the inside of the island – not out toward the ocean. Jake had done his homework and knew much about the moai and their punkao hats. However, no one, not even the "experts" knew exactly how they had been moved from the volcano's crater to the different places on the island. The volcano, Rano Kau, had not been active for thousands and thousands of years. It's crater, Rano Raraku, which contains a small fresh water lake, was the source, the quarry for all of the moai.

That morning, on his way to the cliffs, Jake visited the crater and took several photographs. There were numerous moai there. Indeed, Rapa Nui had almost a thousand moai located throughout the island. There was a place on the cliff trail where the "experts" said a moai once stood. It was a spot on the trail right at the center of a curve. The ocean was a long drop down from the trail. Since this individual statue was no longer in its niche, people speculated that, when several moai had been toppled over, this one had been moved so that it fell into the ocean right below the trail. Divers had, in fact, found the pieces of a moai right there below the cliff. The trail made a curve as it approached where the moai had once stood and a curve as the trail proceeded away from the spot. As Jake examined this spot, he realized that the idea of the "experts" that the moai had been moved by men pulling ropes and rocking it would not have worked for this location. Where would the men stand? There was no room for them. How could the moai have rocked up the trail and moved into the niche that had been carved into the cliff face? There was simply no place for the men to stand. No, Jake concluded, there had to be another explanation for how the moai were moved.

Jake stayed a few more days on Rapa Nui. It was certainly an interesting place to visit. On Friday, December 16th, he flew from Easter Island to Ponape Island in Micronesia.

One of the mysteries of Ponape is the large megalithic temple of Nan Douwas. The temple stands above the canals of the "city" of Nan Madol. It was constructed out of basalt. Some of the writings that Jake had read claimed that there was no basalt rock within a thousand miles of Ponape. It was supposed to be a big mystery as to how all these structures on Ponape had been built with basalt. However, Jake quickly learned that there was a huge natural outcropping of basalt on the island. This was the source for all the temples and structures that were built both above ground and beneath the ocean. This is a primary mystery of Ponape – there is a large "city" with numerous columns and structures down in the ocean. All this construction was done using basalt stones. Many of the current temples of Nan Madol appear to be built on top of some form of substructure that is now deep in the ocean.

Jake did quite a bit of scuba diving for the next week. He got several nice photographs showing the underwater temples at Nan Madol. The questions without answers are when were they built? By whom? How? Why? If they were originally above ground, how long ago was that? When did the ocean level rise above the temples and structures that are underwater today? Some scientists have speculated that there was a huge rise is the oceans about 14,000 years ago. That would coincide with the end of the ice age and many other worldwide events that happened around 12,500 B. C. Jake had always thought that questions without answers, while interesting, were frustrating.

On Friday evening, December 23rd, Jake landed in Tokyo, Japan. While Japan has some unexplained megalithic stone structures, Jake wasn't planning on visiting them. He was planning to stay for about 10 days in Japan to relax, rest and plan the next places he wanted to examine.

The International Date Line had messed up his timeline. Jake decided to continue to keep his journal according to his calendar. On Christmas Eve, he called his parents and both of his sisters. He enjoyed talking with them. He sent a Christmas greetings email to Ted, several of his other friends in the States and one to Josè Nunez. In Japan, Christmas is not the holiday it is in the United States. However, there are some Christians in Tokyo. Jake found a church that was holding a Christmas morning service. Jake took a cab and attended that church. He didn't understand anything that was said but he thoroughly enjoyed it.

There were several other tourists in attendance. After the service, he met and talked with a couple from Canada. They were from Calgary. Jake told them how much he loved Québec City. They had a brief, but nice, visit.

On his cab ride back to his hotel, Jake thought about the

expression on their faces when they realized he was traveling alone. He touched his chest and said, "Thank you, Jesus. I trust you, Jesus. With you Jesus, I am never alone."

Jake spent the next week visiting museums and historic sites. It was fun for Jake to just be a tourist. On New Year's Eve, Jake watched some of the celebrations on television in his hotel room. He didn't feel like mingling with the crowds in Tokyo. The Japanese did New Year's very well.

At midnight, when, traditionally, everyone brings in the New Year with a kiss, a total feeling of being alone swept over Jake. He thought of Laura and missed her so much. He thought of all the things that they would not get to experience together. A tear rolled down his cheek. Suddenly, Jake shook his head and said out loud, "No, I'm feeling sorry for myself. I need to stop this. Jesus, be with me." Jake felt the peace and comfort of Jesus sweep over his being. He smiled and said, "Thank you, Jesus."

On Monday, January 2, 2006, Jake flew to Manila in the Philippines. He changed planes there and flew to Kolkata, which he had always known as Calcutta, India. While there, one of the museums Jake visited had large copies of old maps. The Reinal map of 1510 A.D. showed India as its coastline looked in 11,500 B. C. The Pizzagano map of 1424 A.D. shows Japan and Taiwan as they looked around 12,600 B.C. Several maps show Antarctica as it would look without an ice cap. On a map dated 1513 A.D., there is an island located in the Atlantic Ocean off the coast of Ireland. On this map, the island is named Hy-Brazil. Modern underwater surveys have revealed that there is a landmass where this map shows the island. However, this land mass had not been above water since approximately 10,000 B.C. The map was dated 1513 A.D. Jake concluded that these maps were copied from much older maps. What people had been around who could make maps of ancient India, Japan, Taiwan, Antarctica and Hy-Brazil? Indian archaeologists have located several underwater cities, in some cases, many miles off the current coast of India. Jake recalled that Plato had written of a vast continent on the other side of the ocean. How, in ancient Greece, had Plato known that? This was a fascinating museum tour for Jake.

There were many mysteries and unexplained places in India that Jake planned to visit. At that time, in early January, Jake did not know that he would spend the next seven and half months in India. He flew to Delhi. There were museums there he wanted to visit.

One such museum was dedicated to explaining the Indian epic Mahabharata. Several years earlier, Jake had read an English translation. It seems to be a history of Indian people from years prior to recorded history. In addition to this epic, there are numerous other writings that had been passed down from generation to generation. These include some fascinating Vedas – there are four primary Vedas that are considered to be quite ancient and sacred to the Hindus. They were written in early Sanskrit and have been translated into English. One Veda provides accurate descriptions of how to build 109 different machines. In the Mahabharata and the Vedas, there are explanations that show the ancient people of India were aware of electricity, radium, the speed of light, higher mathematics, surgical procedures, of how to construct airships, of the principles of gravity and of firearms. They tell of extremely destructive weapons that they built and used. The Ramayana is another ancient book from India. It describes the sun as a star. It accurately tells the distance between the earth and the sun and the distance between the earth and the moon. These ancient writings are said to have originated more than 12,000 years earlier. Because of their age and what they describe, archaeologists tend to ignore them. Historians tend to ignore them. Jake knew why. It was because they had no answer to the question of who could have possibly had all this information. What civilization existed that could have calculated the distances between the earth and the sun and the moon? What civilization, what people, could have built airships, firearms, machines? How could they know of electricity? The "experts" simply have no answer to these ancient books of India.

Jake hired a guide and, over the next several months, he explored temples all over India. The Kailasa Temple, at the caves of Ellora, Jake found to be so awesome – it defies explanation. The entire temple, which is massive, was carved from the top down out of rock. There are no building blocks. It is just one huge temple carved directly from solid rock. That this was done with nothing but chisels and picks seemed very unlikely, if not impossible. Jake thought that, since the ancient people of India knew how to construct machinery, that was the answer as to how the temple had been built.

Jake also visited the Padmanabhaswamy Temple, the Veerabhadra Temple, the Brihadeesware Temple and the Konark Sun Temple. Jake had planned to visit the ancient cities of Mohenjo-Daro and Harappa but things were not settled in Pakistan and Jake decided that he did not want to travel there.

Throughout India, Jake met some very fascinating people. In Mumbai (Bombay to Jake), he met a man who claimed to be 127 years old, although he didn't appear to be that old. However, since Jake had never seen anyone that old, how could he say with certainty that he was not.

Jake realized that he could spend another year in India and still not do it justice. It was a fascinating country with an ancient history that had been lost in time.

After convincing the Chinese (his passport helped) that he was taking photos of ancient sites for inclusion in a book, Jake was granted a seven-day visa to visit in China. On Thursday, August 10th, Jake flew from Delhi to Beijing. Jake was actually assigned a guide. Jake knew he was working for the Chinese government but that didn't matter to him. He wanted to get to the Longyou Caves. These were ancient man-made caves carved into solid rock. Located underground, the people had carved a huge city out of solid rock. Jake took many photographs. It was an amazing site.

In Yangshan, there are huge worked stones larger than those at Baalbeck. Jake would have liked to visit that site but did not have time to do so. Jake knew that, in the Ural Mountains of

Russia, there are even larger worked stones than those in China. Perhaps he could visit those. There was a pyramid that Jake wanted to visit but was told that it was not accessible at that time.

From Beijing, on Wednesday, August 16th, Jake flew back to Delhi. He had to wait until Sunday, the 20th, to get a flight from Delhi to Jerusalem. While Israel, of course, has many ancient sites; they are not unexplained or mysterious. Jake had always wanted to visit Israel and Jerusalem. This visit was to be like his stay in Japan. He was a tourist without having to be concerned over getting "the perfect shot."

Jake settled down in his hotel in Tel Aviv. It was right on the Mediterranean Sea. He had a balcony that looked out on the sea. It was truly nice. The balcony and the view reminded Jake of his experience in Savannah when he attended Laura's funeral. The view of the second empty chair on the balcony caused Jake to, once again, feel the pain of Laura's lost. Laura's ring was in a safe deposit box back in North Carolina. Over concerns for its safety, he had not brought it with him. However, Jake had gotten in the habit of touching his heart, where her ring used to be, and thanking Jesus. Mr. Nunez had noticed it. He still did it. It brought Jake comfort and he knew that Jesus was with him.

The next day, August 21st, Jake joined a tour called "Walk where Jesus Walked." It was, of course, in Jerusalem. Jake found it exciting and, as the tour ended, painful. Jake thought that they should have shown some of the places Jesus walked after He had risen from death.

After the tour, Jake ate a late lunch at an outdoor cafe in Jerusalem. As he sat there and watched people going about their daily lives, Jake was amazed at where he was. He was sitting in old Jerusalem. This ancient city was now the capital of the nation of Israel. Jake had read so much about both places in the Bible. Now, here he was – sitting at a cafe eating his lunch – in Jerusalem. He found it somewhat surreal.

Suddenly, an elderly lady that Jake recognized from the morning's tour, approached his table with a tray of food and asked if he minded if she sat down. He had noticed that she was by herself on the tour and they had smiled at each other.

She introduced herself as Mrs. Lorna Brown from Nashville, Tennessee. Jake introduced himself. Jake thought she must be in her early eighties.

She asked, "How did you like the tour?"

"It was all right. It was special to realize that Jesus had walked along those same streets."

"Yes, I agree. That was what made it worthwhile."

As they both continued to eat their lunches, Jake said, "I've never been to Nashville. I've always heard good things about it – friendly people."

Mrs. Brown replied, "Yes, for the most part. It's changed quite a bit since I was your age. Most of the changes, I'm afraid, have not been an improvement."

Jake laughed, "I have seen that situation all over the world."

"But we both know who is in control and what the ultimate outcome will be."

Jake smiled at her and responded, "Yes, of course."

"Are you here alone?"

Jake answered, "Yes. I'm traveling about, taking photographs for a book."

"That must be exciting."

"Yes, it is. And educational."

"I suspect so."

"Are you also here by yourself?"

Mrs. Brown sighed and said, "Yes. This was a trip that my husband and I had always planned on taking. We kept putting it off until later. Then, he had a heart attack and died. I am just trying to bring his memory, the memory of him, with me and, I don't know, share the experience with his memory."

Jake smiled and nodded.

She said, "I guess that sounds silly . . . but I just wanted to take this trip alone – with the memory of him."

"No, not silly at all. I understand."

She looked at Jake. She asked, "Do you?"

Jake answered, "Yes, I really do."

After a pause, she asked, "Have you lost someone recently?"

Softly, Jake said, "Yes."

"I see." After a few moments, she said, "It's nice we both have Jesus in our lives, isn't it?"

Jake's face brightened. He responded, "Yes. Absolutely. I truly feel sorry for people who do not know Jesus."

Mrs. Brown and Jake continued to talk long after they had finished their lunch. They talked primarily about Jerusalem and Israel. They both enjoyed their conversation.

The next day, Jake visited a museum in Tel Aviv. The day after that, he visited several churches and museums in Jerusalem. Following that, he visited Bethlehem.

Jake spent all day on August 25th trying to book a flight to Egypt. Doing so from Israel seemed to complicate matters. Finally, he got a flight to Cairo for Monday, August 28th. There wasn't a direct flight but arrangements were made. He had to fly to Jordan and from there to Cairo. Once there, he had to apply for a temporary tourist visa. Throughout all his travels, Jake had always obeyed the laws and customs of each country he visited.

Jake enjoyed the two days left to him in Israel. He went swimming, briefly, in the Mediterranean Sea – just so he would always know that he had done so.

On the afternoon of the 28th, Jake's plane touched down in Cairo. The Egyptians were very used to dealing with tourists. Jake explained what he was doing and applied for the maximum time for a tourist visa – 90 days. After looking long at his passport, he was granted a 90-day visa. It could be renewed once for an additional 90 days. After that, he had to leave the country.

Jake began where most tourists begin – at the Giza Plateau. He took the tour of the Pyramids. Although he had seen numerous photos and videos of the Great Pyramid, he was not prepared for just how huge the structure actually was. It was so massive it was difficult to believe it was there.

Having read numerous books about the pyramids and the Sphinx complex, once he was back outside the Great Pyramid, Jake began to look for certain rocks. Sure enough, right where one book had said it would be was a large rock with obvious machining having been done to it. As Jake was taking photographs of this rock, he realized he was on his last roll of film. He would need to go back and purchase more at his hotel in Cairo. Before he left Tel Aviv, he had mailed his last bunch of about four dozen rolls of film to his parents.

The next morning, with fresh rolls of film, Jake headed for the Sphinx complex. The Sphinx itself, although heavily eroded, was awesome. Jake was actually more interested in the Sphinx Temple complex than the Sphinx. Jake had taken two courses in geology in college. Even with that little bit of knowledge, it was clear that the erosion on the Sphinx and especially on the enclosure walls was caused by water, not wind.

Jake was truly amazed by the size of the blocks of stone that were used to build the Sphinx Temple. Two obvious questions occurred to Jake. How in the world had they placed such huge blocks into such a confined area? Where would one place the machinery needed to handle such enormous blocks of stone? Secondly, Jake wondered why. Why use large and obviously very heavy blocks of stone when smaller stones would have done the same job? Or, thought Jake, would they? It was a currently unexplained mystery. Jake had read that, even with modern cranes, those blocks could not be lifted and placed where they were. There simply is no room for the cranes to operate. How was it done? The stones are perfectly quarried with smooth finishes. After thousands of years, they still fit together tightly without any need for mortar.

An extensive tunnel system deep under the Sphinx and the Sphinx Temple Complex was discovered in 1837. It was described in detail in a book from that time. Other tunnels have since been located under the pyramids. Jake took a photograph of a grate that blocked the entrance to such a tunnel. For some reason, the Egyptian government has totally downplayed this system of tunnels. Some officials even deny they exist. Other officials say that they are too dangerous to allow tourists to visit. Jake reluctantly knew that he would not be allowed to explore the tunnels.

Having received permission to take photographs from the top of the Great Pyramid for his book, the next day, August 31st, Jake climbed the Great Pyramid. It was not as bad a climb as Jake thought it might be. Jake was 43 now; however, thanks to all his climbing and walking during his recent travels, he was in excellent physical condition. From the top, Jake took many photographs from several angles. While there, he prayed to God a prayer of thanksgiving. The climb down was more tricky than the climb up had been. Once on the ground, Jake looked back up the pyramid and thought *I still can't believe this thing exists*.

Jake traveled down to Saqqara to visit the Serapeum there. Inside this underground chamber are 25 stone boxes that weigh between 70 and 100 tons. They are cleanly and smoothly machined. What makes this site so mysterious is that, like so many things in Egypt, it should not exist. How those huge stone boxes, complete with heavy large stone lids, were placed inside a small confined space is unexplained.

From Saqqara, Jake traveled up to Alexandria. Like Tel Aviv, Alexandria is located on the Mediterranean Sea. Jake's hotel did not have a view of the sea but rather was located in downtown Alexandria. As Jake toured this city, he found himself wondering what ancient things existed underneath the ground he was walking upon.

On Monday, September 11th, Jake stayed all day in his hotel room in Alexandria. It was exactly one year ago that Laura had been killed in that horrible horrible car wreck. Jake reflected on all that had happened since that awful day. He thought of her funeral. He thought of his visit to the Outer Banks. He thought of all the places he had been and all the people he had met. He felt utterly alone. He felt his eyes begin to water. Jake put his head in his hands, looked at the floor and just let the tears come. After a few minutes, Jake wondered to himself, *Am I crying for Laura or for myself? Probably both,* he thought. He had asked himself this question on several previous occasions. Jake simply did not feel like seeing anyone or talking with anyone. He crawled back under his sheet and went to sleep.

Jake went back to Cairo to visit all the museums. He questioned the accuracy of some of the exhibits but, of course, he never said anything about his concerns to anyone.

After a week in Cairo, Jake spent the next six weeks visiting many lesser known sites in Egypt. On Sunday, October 8th, Jake was in Luxor. He was determined not to mope around all day. This was the one-year anniversary of something that never happened – his wedding to Laura. He spent most of the day in a museum.

There were many places that Jake wanted to see. Often, one of the guides would suggest a site about which he had never heard a thing. By mid-November, Jake realized that his visa would run out in a couple of weeks. He returned to Cairo and requested another 90 days. He was asked where else he wanted to go. Jake replied, "Abydos." The clerk smiled and gave Jake his extension.

From Cairo, Jake arrived in Abydos on Friday, November 24th. Prior to visiting the site, Jake wanted to tour the local museum. It was closed on Saturday, the 25th but would be open on the 26th. Jake decided to stay in his hotel and read.

After visiting the museum on Sunday, on Monday the 27th Jake toured the Great Temple of Abydos. On Tuesday, he toured the Temple of Seti I. Wednesday, November 29th was the big day for Jake. This was why he was in Abydos. He toured the Osirion.

The Osirion is one of the most mysterious sites in all of Egypt. In the early 20th Century, archaeologists were excavating the Temple of Seti I when, totally by accident, they discovered the Osirion. It had been completely covered by sand and lost to history. Traditional Egyptologists consider the Temple of Seti I and the Osirion to have been built at approximately the same time. After an initial tour, it was obvious to Jake that this was not the case.

What impressed Jake right away was that the construction of the Osirion was far superior to that of Seti's Temple. The Osirion was built almost exactly the same as the Sphinx Temple Complex. Huge blocks of stone, which were quarried over 200 miles away in Aswan, have the same stark megalithic construction style as those at the Sphinx Temple. Some of the massive stone blocks weigh over 100 tons. Like those at the Sphinx, they are fitted together with precision that require no mortar. Jake would visit the site several times over the next few weeks. He eventually came to the conclusion that dynastic Egyptians had definitely not constructed the Osirion. Like the Sphinx Temple, historic Egyptians simply did not have the technology to build the Osirion. The more Jake studied the site, the more amazed he was with it. He thought it to be incredible.

By Christmas, Jake was finished in Abydos. Rather than go back to Cairo, he decided to stay in Abydos until the new year arrived. On Christmas Eve, using a computer in the hotel lobby, he sent out Christmas greetings to his family and friends. He realized that he had not contacted some of his friends since the previous Christmas. His friend, Russell, down in Florida was one of them. He explained his situation of constant travel.

Like in Japan, Christmas was not celebrated in Egypt. Nonetheless, Japan had some acknowledgment of Christmas. Egypt did not. On Christmas Day, as Jake was eating in the hotel restaurant, he thought about the Egyptian government tracing and copying his emails. He had written, in his emails to his family, that every single Egyptian he had met had been extremely kind, nice and helpful – even the governmental officials. That was, in fact, true. He hoped that that comment would go over well with the governmental officials.

There was very little New Year's Eve celebration in Abydos on Sunday, December 31, 2006. Jake went back to Cairo on Tuesday, January 2, 2007.

The next day, Jake was back at the Sphinx Temple. He asked one of the guards, who spoke English quite well, if he had ever been to Abydos. The guard said that he had not. Jake explained that he had just returned and thought that the Osirion and the Sphinx Temple had been constructed by the same people probably about the same time. The guard thought a moment and replied that it was certainly possible. He pointed at the Great Pyramid and said, "If they could build that, then they could build anything." Jake looked at the Great Pyramid. The guard had been referring to dynastic Egyptians. Jake thought that his response was probably true but applied to a much older civilization than the dynastic Egyptians.

From Cairo, Jake flew to London and from London, he flew to New York. He arrived on January 7th and it was bitter cold – freezing. Jake checked into a hotel near where he used to live. He knew he wasn't finished exploring sites that could not be explained. There were several in the United States he wanted to visit – many in New England.

The next day, Jake called Ted at work and they made plans to meet that night at the seafood restaurant they both liked on Long Island.

Jake arrived at the restaurant a little before their scheduled meeting time. Jake took a booth and told the waitress he was waiting on a friend to join him. When Ted showed up, Jake stood, shook hands and hugged Ted.

"Man, it's good to see you," Ted smiled. "You look like you've lost a little weight."

"A few pounds."

"Not to worry. I found them." Ted patted his stomach.

"How are Stacy and the little ones, Christy and Mark?"

"She's doing well. Gone back to college. Taking night classes twice a week."

"That's great."

"Yeah, it gives me two nights a week alone with the 'little ones,' as you call them."

Jake laughed. "You love it."

"Yeah, I suppose I do."

"Ted, I know I've expressed my condolences in an email but I want to tell you how sorry I am about your dad's passing. I know that has been tough for you . . . and for Stacy. How are you guys all holding up with his death? I imagine the children miss their grandpa."

"Thanks Jake. We're doing all right. Christy and Mark are resilient. They have accepted it. Of course, we had plenty of time to prepare for things. It wasn't a sudden shock or anything. I think those books you loaned me really helped. I'll get those back to you."

Jake waved his hand and said, "No hurry at all. My books are all in storage."

Ted nodded. "You know, we all knew, as the time drew near, that he was going to die. I thought I was prepared. But, when it happened, it still hurt a lot. I miss him."

Jake slowly nodded his head up and down. "Ted, I'm sure you do. Cherish the memories you have of him."

After a 30-second pause in the conversation, Jake asked, "Is Redfire getting any of his putts to fall in at work?"

Ted smiled. "You know, I certainly am. I think of you every time one drops and wonder where you are at – South America, Japan, India. I can't keep up with you."

"I have been getting around."

"That's an understatement. What's the most fascinating place you've visited?"

"Puma Punku and Tiawanaku in Bolivia."

"Really? I wasn't expecting that."

"Most people wouldn't."

"Why? What makes that place so special?"

"Numerous things. When I stand there . . . among the ruins . . . it feels . . . different. It feels ancient. It was once a truly special place. It has not yet been accurately defined."

"Why not?"

"One reason, I believe, is that it is much much older than archaeologists want to admit."

Their waitress came and took their orders. They both

ordered the same thing they had ordered over a year earlier – lobster and scallops for Jake and halibut and crab for Ted.

Ted asked, how do you know it's older than they say?"

"One example is this: there are carved reliefs of a toxodon and an elephant. I saw them. I took pictures of them."

"What's a toxodon?"

"It's a hippo-like animal. It went extinct around ten thousand B. C. That's twelve thousand years ago. Elephants also became extinct in South America around the same time. How would anyone, say two thousand years ago, have known what a toxodon and an elephant looked like? No, the site is much older than that. There are also many many stone blocks that were obviously machined."

"What do you mean?"

"I mean they were cut using machines. They were not chiseled. There is simply no way that anyone could do what was done there by hand. There are some very narrow cuts that are perfectly smooth on both sides and on the bottom."

"Yes, I understand what you are saying."

"The alignment of some of the buildings show a knowledge of precession."

"Now that is amazing."

"Yes. You know what, Ted? What I've found everywhere I've gone – from Bolivia, Peru, Ecuador, India and Egypt . . . the older construction is vastly, and I mean vastly, superior to the latter, more recent, construction. For example, at Machu Picchu, the bottom layer of stonework is of a much better quality than that of the Inca. At Ollantaytambo . . ."

"What? Say again."

"Most people have never heard of it. It's an ancient site in Peru. It has megalithic construction thousands of years old with massive walls made from granite. You've probably heard of amazing stone roads and paths that the Inca constructed in a short period of time."

"Yeah. Sure."

"I am now convinced that what the Inca did was repair

already existing roads. The Inca did not construct Ollantaytambo. It was built thousands of years before the Inca ever existed."

Their food arrived and, while it was hot, they began to eat.

Ted asked, "So what was Egypt like? I've always wanted to see the pyramids."

Jake smiled and nodded. "They are worth the trip. However, I am totally convinced that they are much older than archaeologists say. They, like the Sphinx and the Osirion were definitely built by pre-dynastic people . . . not by historic Egyptians. In museums, I saw stone vases that were worked on lathes. Again, if the stone vase was found in a tomb, the experts date the vase to the time when the person in the tomb died. However, the vase could have been handed down in the family for generations. The vase could have been found under the sands of the desert somewhere sometime. The outside of the vase could possibly have been carved by hand. The experts say that they were polished by rubbing sand against them for several months. However, these are stone vases. How was the inside done? No one really knows. Some have a small opening at the top and the entire inside has been hollowed out. This is solid rock. Even for the outside, it's hard for me to believe that someone would spend months polishing a vase with sand."

"That does seem like an awful lot of time to spend on a flower vase."

"Yes, really. Another thing, like at Puma Punku, there are examples of stone, in Egypt, that has been machined. Under microscopes, that has been proven. But, on some of the stone structures, if you look at them from an angle, you can see the machine marks. The historic Egyptians certainly didn't have machines."

"So what do you conclude?"

"Several things, Ted, several things. One is that our current crop of archaeologists refuse to accept facts that are right in front of their faces. For example, they refuse to admit, despite overwhelming evidence, that there was transatlantic contact prior to the Vikings in Canada and the Columbus trips. Egyptian mummies, thousands of years old have been proven to contain traces of cocaine and tobacco. This residue is there. Either there was transatlantic contact with this hemisphere or else there was cocaine and tobacco growing over there somewhere. Thus far, there is no evidence to support cocaine and tobacco growing anywhere other than this hemisphere. So how do archaeologists explain it? They don't. They ignore it and pretend it doesn't exist. They do the same with all the machined stone works around the world. They ignore the water erosion at the Sphinx Temple. They ignore the astronomically aligned stone sites here in the U. S. They ignore all the ancient Ogham script carved into stone, also here in the U. S. I mean, you can go to these sites and touch them but archaeologists don't want anything to do with them."

Ted asked, "Why? Why not examine them?"

"The truth doesn't fit their concept of civilization. If the historic Egyptians did not construct the Sphinx or the Osirion, then who did? Both of these sites in Egypt are much older than archaeologists say. However, they have no explanation for who existed that could have built such amazing things. You see, Ted, they have a concept that humans and civilizations progress and evolve in a steady forward movement. For example, in one lifetime, man went from the awkward plane built by the Wright brothers to landing men on the moon. That is the way they believe all civilizations have done. Yet, we can see, during historical times, that that is not true. The Roman Empire is a prime example. The Sumerians are another good example. Egypt certainly falls into this category. If, as the 'experts' say, the Sphinx Temple Complex, the pyramids and the Osirion were built by dynastic Egyptians, that would have been the pinnacle of Egyptian civilization. According to the 'experts,' that civilization should have progressed for the past four thousand years. Instead, it has gone backward. It didn't evolve into something better and greater – it went the other direction until today it has become a pathetic third-world nation. Can you imagine Egypt today trying to build the Great Pyramid? No nation on Earth could do it. We still don't know how it was done. All over the world are huge, massive stone blocks that have been quarried and moved. Despite this staring them in the face, archaeologists ignore it and pretend it's not there."

Ted had about finished his meal. Jake had been doing all the talking.

Jake said, "So, tell me all about what's going on at Excalibur."

While Ted did, Jake ate his meal. When he had finished, he asked the waitress to bring them a pot of coffee. As they drank their coffee, they continued to talk.

Ted said, "This is really interesting stuff. You've done a lot of research."

"I think someone could spend a lifetime in India and still not discover all the mysteries over there. That is an amazing place. And again, India today is not nearly as accomplished as it was in the distant past."

Ted nodded and asked, "What is the one thing you have found that most people have never heard about at all?"

Jake immediately replied with one word, "Tunnels."

Ted was taken back. "What about tunnels?"

Jake smiled, "They are everywhere. Just as there are amazing similarities among ancient megaliths all around the world, there are massive underground tunnels, and, in some cases, underground cities, throughout most of South America, Egypt, Europe, China and even in Scotland. The underground tunnel system in Scotland has been dated to around twelve thousand B. C. That same date is given to most of the tunnel systems in the world. These are quite sophisticated and extensive. What people existed in China, South America and Europe fourteen thousand years ago who could have built such a large tunnel system? And why?"

"I've never heard of them."

"Most people haven't. They cannot be explained so they are primarily ignored."

"Are there any here in the United States?"

"Good question. The only underground structure of any size, of which I am currently aware, is in Death Valley. Native Americans used to live there. But that doesn't mean that they built it. I am going to take a look at it."

"Oh, you are not finished with your . . . research?"

"No. I'm going to look at some sites here in the U. S. There are quite a few in New England."

"Speaking of which. Have you heard about this project going on in Maine up around the Canadian border?"

Jake was surprised. He replied, "Yes, I think I've read a little about it in the news." He knew that they have revealed themselves and were working on a lakeside lodge.

Ted said, "It's got quite a story. Apparently, there has been an *underground city* existing there, totally unknown to anyone for a hundred and fifty years. Isn't that amazing?"

"Yes. Absolutely."

"They had a big article in the paper about it several months ago."

"What are they planning to do?" Jake was curious.

"I'm not sure. I think that they are going to create some type of research center. I'm just awe-struck that they could keep their existence a secret all this time. If they hadn't announced that they existed, we still wouldn't know anything about it."

Jake started to respond but thought better of it.

Ted asked, "So, what are your plans now?"

"I guess I'll go down to North Carolina for a few days and see my parents. Then, I'm going to look at several sites here in the U. S. Then, I'm planning on going to England, Wales and Scotland. That might finish it up for me. I don't know for sure."

"I envy you for having the freedom to travel the world as you do."

"I envy you for having a wife and children."

There was an extended period of silence.

Ted stated, "You are still missing Laura."

"Everyday. It still hurts."

"You may yet find someone to love."

"I don't know. I'm like everyone else – I'm not getting younger."

"You're like me. We're still young men."

Jake smiled. "At forty-three, be forty-four in May, I don't think I can still be called a young man. I'm pretty sure I'm in that middle-age category."

"There are still plenty of women 'out there' who are also looking for love. When I thought of you traveling all over, I was reminded of that old song about a traveling man who had a girl in every port."

"I travel by plane, train and car. No ports." Jake smiled.

They had finished their pot of coffee.

Ted said, "It's my turn to pay." He picked up the check.

Standing in the foyer, they hugged goodbye.

Ted asked, "When will I see you next?"

"I don't know. I'm sure my flights will take me through New York. When they do, I'd like to call and talk with you. I enjoyed this evening."

"Me too. Anytime you're in New York, please do call and let's get together. We can always eat seafood."

"Will do."

Back at his hotel, Jake accessed his email account from a computer in a room by the front desk that was available to hotel guests. He had several emails from friends who had responded to his Christmas greetings while he was in Egypt. He also had one from Peggy. It was really long.

Jake opened hers first. She was extremely excited. She was engaged to be married. A man, Arthur Habersham, she has been dating for almost a year proposed to her on New Year's Eve. She calls him Art. He teaches at the Neverland school. That's how she met him. Peggy went on and on about what a wonderful guy Art was. She said that they haven't set a date yet but definitely wanted Jake to attend. She did mention that construction of the lodge had begun and that everyone seemed relieved that they had gone public.

Jake sent an email back to Peggy. He told her that he was

truly happy for her and wished her all the best. He thanked her for the invitation and the news about Neverland.

Jake wondered if Art had taken Laura's place at the school. Either way, it wouldn't matter or make any difference to Jake.

Jake replied to all of the emails. He was glad to receive a nice one from Josè Nunez in Bolivia. He let everyone know that he was still traveling.

A few days later, on Friday, January 12, 2007, Jake arrived at his parents' house in North Carolina. He had spent a few days in New York planning his U. S. schedule.

Over supper, Jake mentioned to his parents something interesting that he had come across. He said, "You might be interested in this. I find it fascinating. I recently read a translation of a Spanish report from 1526. A Spanish explorer, his name was Ayllon, landed on the coast of what is now South Carolina. He came across a tribe of white Indians living in what they called Dunhare. In his journal, Ayllon said these people kept herds of deer and that they milked the deer. They drank it but also made cheese from it. He logged in his journal that these people had ducks, geese and chickens. Ducks and geese are native to North America. However, chickens are not. Where did the chickens come from? The supposition is that they were brought over by the original white settlers. Ayllon's account was confirmed several years later by another Spaniard. I don't remember how to say his name. However, his report said almost exactly the same things that Ayllon's journal had documented. They both noted that the chief of the white tribe lived in a stone house."

Jake's mom asked, "Are you planning to go investigate this?"

"Oh no," Jake said, "I am only interested in documenting things that can be seen and can be touched – but cannot be explained. I just thought that was an interested tidbit. There is no way to learn anything about those people now. They have vanished from history."

Jake's dad asked, "Where do you think they came from?"

"I really have no idea. Some of the people who have seriously looked into it think that they probably were descendants from some of Modoc's Irish immigrants from the twelfth century. One of the biggest surprises for me about this story is the idea of milking deer. How does one go about that?'

Jake's dad laughed. He replied, "Good point. Where are you headed next?"

"California. From there, I will work my way back east until I finish in New England."

"And will that be the end of this . . . trip?" Jake's mom really didn't think much of what Jake was doing.

He answered, "No. When I finish in the States, I'm going to Great Britain. That may wind it up for me. There are a couple of places in Russia I would like to see but I probably won't go there."

"I hope that England will be the end," his mom stated.

Jake just stayed for the weekend. After church on Sunday morning, Jake's mom made a special effort to introduce him to a "single young lady." When they all got back in the car, Jake's mom turned around in her seat and asked Jake what he thought of her.

"She's very nice, very pretty and very young. Mom, she must be half my age."

"She might look it but she's not."

"Close to it then."

His mom turned back around.

"I leave for California tomorrow."

With only one plane swap, Jake arrived in Las Vegas, Nevada in the evening of January 15th. The next morning, he got a rental and headed for Death Valley, California. The site he was looking for was beneath the Inyo Mountains in the northern section of Death Valley. By the time he had located it, it was too late to do it justice. He turned around and headed back to a small town he had passed through that had a motel.

The next morning, Jake headed back to the site of the

underground "city." This was part of the Death Valley National Park and a ranger gave a tour. She explained how the Native Americans had lived underground at this place during the winter. During spring, summer and fall, they lived on the slopes of the mountains.

Someone asked how long it had taken for the Indians to dig all this out and where had the dirt and rocks gone. The ranger replied that no one really knew how long it had taken. She also said that archaeologists presumed that, over hundreds of years, the dirt and rock had been washed away.

Jake was skeptical of her explanation. To him, this just did not look like the work of Native Americans. It was somewhat similar to the man-made caves he had seen in China. Jake thought that this place had been carved out long before the Native Americans came along and began to use it during the severe winters. He took photographs of the interior. It was interesting to him that the ranger never questioned that the underground complex was man-made – not a natural formation. Her talk just made the presumption that Native Americans had constructed it. The only questions Jake had were who actually made it, how, when and why.

Ogham script is an ancient, primarily Irish, writing system that was an effective form of communication. It was used as early as 1,000 B. C. There are numerous examples of this script in New England. Jake was on his way to examine some of these examples. On the way, however, he stopped in Nebraska, of all places, and photographed Ogham on the rockface of a small cliff. It shouldn't be there . . . but there it was.

Jake originally thought he would stop at the Serpent's Mound in Ohio. It was astronomically aligned to the summer solstice and the "experts" said it was a representation of a snake about to consume an egg. Jake had seen many photos of this site and read about the alignments. Still, there was something about the snake and egg interpretation that had always bothered him. The "tail" of the snake doesn't look right. The "head" of the snake doesn't look anything like a snake's head. The "egg" doesn't look like a chicken's egg. When the serpent mound was constructed, there weren't any chickens in the western hemisphere. Some say it is a snake about to swallow the sun. It really doesn't look like an egg or the sun. For Jake, it just never made sense. There was something about the whole image that was missing. Why go to all the trouble of building this huge mound with astronomical alignments of a snake and an egg? It could just as easily be interpreted as a stylized sperm cell about to fertilize a human egg. The only problem with that is it brings up the question of how anyone hundreds or thousands of years ago would know what a sperm cell and a human egg looked like. Of course, if whoever built it was aware of astronomical alignments, might they also be aware of microscopes? Perhaps not. And yet, sperm cell imagery, as the absolute beginning of life, was somewhat common among ancient peoples. The top of that man-made hill in Ecuador had a sperm cell image running across the entire surface. In Brazil, there are many examples of sperm cells carved into cave walls. Jake decided to skip the Serpent Mound and go on to New England.

On Friday, January 19th, Jake arrived in Boston. There are so many ancient sites in New England; Jake did not know where to begin. His research showed that there are exactly 275 astronomically aligned chambers in New England. There are several more in New York state. There are 105 in Massachusetts, 51 in New Hampshire, 41 in Vermont, 62 in Connecticut, 12 in Rhode Island and 4 in Maine. These are the ones that have been surveyed and proven to be astronomically aligned. There are several others that have not yet been surveyed.

In his rental car, Jake set out on the 20th and headed to western Massachusetts. He found Burnt Hill. At the very top of Burnt Hill is a circle of standing stones. If someone were shown a photograph of this site, that person would automatically say it was in England, Wales or Scotland. No one would guess it is in Massachusetts. Jake was very impressed with it and took numerous photos. A few of the standing stones had fallen over but this was true for many such sites in Great Britain also. He thought that he would like to return to this site when there wasn't any snow on the ground. Nonetheless, one of the photos he took showed the site, with snow on the tops of the stones and on the ground, as a place of isolation. It gave the impression of loneliness.

For the next several weeks, Jake crisscrossed New England. He visited the Upton Chamber, dated to 710 A.D., in Upton, Massachusetts. He took several photographs of Gungywamp in Connecticut. Most people think that Gungywamp is a Native American word. It is not. It is an ancient Gaelic word meaning "Church of the People." It has a double circle of stones and two stone chambers. One of the chambers was designed to capture the rays of the setting sun only on the spring and fall equinox. There are over 200 dolmens in New England. Jake visited one in Salem, Massachusetts. Dolmens are huge rocks balanced on three or four smaller rocks. This is a common megalithic structure associated with Great Britain.

Jake spent several days at the Mystery Hill site in New Hampshire. It has been renamed "America's Stonehenge." A fire pit that was recently uncovered when a stone was moved gave a charcoal date of approximately 2,000 B.C. The exact alignment of the monolith stones give a similar date of anywhere between 1,900 B.C. and 2,500 B.C. The "experts" simply cannot accept this. In addition to the date, America's Stonehenge has several features that cause excitement. There is a complicated underground "oracle" room. There is a large four to five-ton "sacrificial" stone. No one really knows for what purpose this stone was used. The entire site covers about 30 acres. There are numerous stones that match up with solar and lunar alignments. When Jake was there, tour guides had been out with brooms to sweep away some of the snow. This made it easier for Jake to see how the stones lined up to indicate exact directions.

All of these megalithic sites in the U. S. are inexplicable to archaeologists. According to them, they should not exist. However, they do. Jake was documenting their existence with his photographs. The fact that they exist and that there are numerous examples of Ogham on cliff walls, rocks and boulders throughout New England has implications that the "experts" do not want to face. It's the same paradox as with the Sphinx. If geology tells us that it was built at least around 10,000 B.C., who was around then to build it? If these ancient sites in New England were built between 2,500 B.C. and 700 A.D., who built them?

Sitting in a motel room in Manchester, New Hampshire, Jake faced a dilemma. He looked at a map. As the crow flies, he wasn't all that far from *The Library*. Mr. Sinclair had decided to name their new public venture "The Library." There would be no Neverland, or Wonderland or Shangri La. From their new website, Jake saw many changes – some of which Peggy had already informed him by email. Access was from the Canadian side. Roads already existed there whereas there were none on the Maine side. The Christmas tree farm had been turned into a parking lot. A new door took visitors into a reception area and then directly into the huge library. This new entrance was located at the bottom of a gradual slope from the parking lot. The doors to the library that Jake had used now required an electronic key for employees to use. This way, none of the visitors had access to the residential apartments, pubs, cafeteria, chapel or game rooms. They were in the process of making the chapel accessible to the public through a new separate entrance. A large lodge, complete with a restaurant and snack bar, was almost finished on the eastern side of the lake. A paved heated walkway was being constructed between The Library and the lodge.

Jake could take a few days and drive up there. He would like to wish Peggy well with her upcoming marriage. He would like to have a cup of coffee with Mr. Le Couteau. He would enjoy visiting with Mr. Sinclair. He would like to see the three men who referred to themselves as "the three old-timers."

The other place Jake would now like to visit was Great Britain. However, this is where he had planned to honeymoon with Laura. Both *The Library* and Great Britain had attractions but both brought up memories of Laura.

Jake got his notes out and wanted to see if he had missed anything major that he had intended to visit. He noticed that there was a pyramid, Cholule, in Mexico that was being billed as the world's largest pyramid. It had been constructed by the Olmecs and had accurate alignments for celestial events like the equinoxes, the solstices and lunar appearances across the horizon.

Jake also found notes on the Danta pyramid in Guatemala. It was built by the Maya and has a base that is half a mile long. It is much larger than the Great Pyramid in Egypt.

However, for both these pyramids, there was no great mystery about their construction. They are both huge. However, they were built with small stones. The only real mystery about them is exactly who built them and why they were built and why they are so large. They were truly interesting but Jake decided he couldn't cover everything.

There were some quarried stone blocks in Russia that are supposed to be the largest stones ever quarried. Again though, there they were. No one knows who quarried them, how they were moved or why they were quarried so large. Jake thought that he would really like to photograph them but decided to skip them.

Jake next looked at some of the information he had gathered regarding dozens of different tribes of Native Americans living in the New England area. The Eastern Algonquins had a culture hero named Ksiwhambeh. The Penobscots' culture hero was called Kuloscap. The culture hero of the Passamaquodds went by Glooscop. The Mi'kmaq and the Abenaki believed that a great teacher named Kloskurbeh had visited them in "ancient" times. Jake wondered if this could have been the same person who visited all these different tribes. He noticed, in his notes, that several of the coastal Native American tribes' religious beliefs centered around Manitou. Manitou was a spiritual power who encompassed the entire world. Jake thought, *sounds like God.*

Jake read on and remembered several of the strange events recorded by early trappers and visitors to these native peoples. At least two tribes had a written language with which they communicated with each other. He had told Mr. Le Couteau about them. One tribe's clothes resembled the clothes of Chinese people. These kinds of stories were fascinating to Jake but he saw no way of proving or disproving them now. He concluded that there was nothing he could photograph. He decided to skip these legends of the Native Americans. It did not mean that Jake did not give them credence. However, at this time, there was nothing he could do with them – especially with his proposed book.

It was Tuesday, March 20, 2007 and Jake had put off his decision long enough. The next day would be the first day of spring. Jake would certainly be glad to see the end of all the recent snow. On the 21st, he sat in a "root cellar" in New York and photographed sunshine on the back of the stone enclosure as it shone through an opening on the top of the structure. Archaeologists had determined that this stone structure was a colonial period root cellar. However, it was quite accurately aligned with solar solstices and equinoxes. Jake truly wondered, 'who built this, when and why?'

Back in Boston, Jake thought about what was now being called *The Library*. Even though it had been a year and a half since Laura's accident, Jake felt that he was not ready to walk the halls that he and Laura had walked together. He knew he didn't want to see "their" booth in the pub or "their" table in the cafeteria. Jake decided it was time to go to Great Britain. He knew it would be hard to visit the megalithic sites that Laura and he had discussed. He knew the trip would involve experiences that he had wanted to share with Laura. He had planned on them taking their honeymoon in Great Britain. In one way, he told himself, each site he visited would be in honor of Laura. However, that really didn't help much and he wasn't convinced it was even true.

Jake prayed and asked Jesus to stay with him on this trip and to help him deal with the emotions that were sure to arise. Jake booked a flight from Boston to London.

After doing some sightseeing in London, on Monday, March 26th, Jake got a rental car and headed west. He found he really had to concentrate on driving on the left side of the road. He tried to keep the passenger side of the car close to the left edge of each road.

West of London, there are numerous megalithic sites along the southern coast of England. Jake spent three days in the Stonehenge area. He visited the West Kennet Long Barrow, the largest in England. Jake climbed Silbury Hill, the largest man-made hill in England. He spent a full day at Avebury, located 20 miles north of Stonehenge and considered by many to be both the largest and grandest site in all of England. Stanton Drew is the second largest stone circle in England and Jake enjoyed seeing it. He, of course, visited Stonehenge and took photographs of all these sites. Jake was somewhat disappointed with Stonehenge. It was much smaller than he had thought.

Jake was anxious to visit Ballowall Barrow on the ocean at the most southwesterly tip of England at Land's End. Jake spent the weekend there. It is a unique structure with a totally unknown reason for its existence. It was constructed about 5,000 years earlier. Jake was fascinated by it. He also enjoyed the scenery at Land's End.

On April 2nd, Jake drove to Men-an-Tol, a round stone with the center completely carved out. If one looked through the circle, from either side, one would see a standing stone.

Through a pouring rain, Jake drove over to Dartmoor. Here were around 60 stone rows. A stone row consisted of two parallel rows of stones. It is presumed that one would walk between the two rows of stones. Jake managed, from inside his rental car, to get a few photographs of one of the stone rows. He used a telephoto lens but because of the rain, he didn't get the image he wanted. Also in Dartmoor, there are stone circles with multiple rows of stones. One site has four concentric stone circles. Another has two concentric stone circles. Jake remembered a small similar site with two concentric stone circles in Connecticut.

In Oxfordshire, Jake took photos of the Rollright Stones. They are dated to 3,000 B.C. Again, what was the purpose, what was the reason for making such a circle?

In Wales, Jake visited the largest capstone in Great Britain at Tinkinswood. This capstone is 30 feet long and weighs 50 tons. No one knows how it was moved and used in the construction of this site. In Pembrokeshire, Jake saw the mountains where the blue stones for Stonehenge were quarried. In Wales, there are numerous dolmans. In Pembrokeshire, there is a famous one, Pentre Ifan, that Laura and he had discussed. He had planned to take her there on their honeymoon. He remembered that, after they had talked about Pentre Ifan, she had expressed a very reasonable hypothesis regarding stone circles. She hypothesized that the stone circle represents God. Several cultures do represent God as a circle. She thought that, once the circle had been completed in a special place, then the interior of the circle became a sacred place in which to conduct rituals to worship God. It became a special play to pray.

Jake was torn and confused about whether or not he wanted to visit Pentre Ifan. For Laura, he wanted to see it in person. He wanted to photograph it. However, because he had planned to visit it with Laura, he did not want to go. He thought it over and decided to go. He took several photos of it.

From there, Jake went to Ysbytty Cynfyn. As he stood looking at the solid stone circle, he thought to himself, *easy for you to pronounce.* The stone circle was different in that there are no gaps or spaces between the standing stones. He next went to Bryn Celli Ddu, a barrow with a petrified wooden column inside. Just how old was this site?

Ireland has hundreds of prehistoric sites. Many of them are quite amazing. However, Jake decided to pass on Ireland.

Back in England, Jake shot photos of the Nine Ladies of Stanton Moor. Nearly all of the megalithic sites had myths and legends surrounding them. The nine standing stones of Stanton Moor were once nine women who had been turned to stone. Long

Meg and her daughters was another such site. This one had originally consisted of three stone circles with about 70 stones.

Jake took some unusual shots of Rudston Monolith. This standing stone, at 26 feet tall, is the tallest standing stone in Britain. It is estimated that there must be at least another 9-10 feet of stone in the ground. It had been moved 10 miles from the place it had been quarried.

In southwest Scotland, at Cairnholy, ring markings are quite pronounced on the stones. These ring markings are also found in Ireland, Wales and England. Jake touched some of the rings as he realized that, most likely, for thousands of years, many people had done the same thing. They reached out and touched the stones. Driving his rental, Jake approached a huge complex, Kilmartin Glen, that had apparently been used for thousands of years. It has cup and ring markings throughout the site. It also has several lunar alignments.

On May 3rd, Jake arrived on the Isle of Lewis. The Isle of Lewis is located on the outermost Hebrides off the coast of northwestern Scotland. Approximately 4,000 years ago, unknown people picked out special stones, filled with quartz, and somehow moved the huge monolithic stones to a hilltop. They aligned these stones with the moon's cycles. This circle is called Callanish and has been named the grandest circle in Britain.

Jake found Callanish to be a beautiful place. The stones are shaped differently than those of other stone circles. He spent the evening of the third among the stones. The views from the hilltop, Jake thought, were amazing. There is a view of Loch Roag and toward the south, mountains. However, what Jake truly enjoyed was touching the standing stones. Each stone seemed to have its own "personality." The next two days rained. However, every now and then, a beam of sunlight would break through the clouds and the stones would sparkle. Jake got some excellent shots of this happening. On the 6th, Jake was standing among the stones and realized that they had been standing there for four thousand years. He reflected on all the people, throughout those years, who had come and stood exactly where he was standing and touched the same stones he was touching. Jake thought, *Unless Jesus returns soon, these stones will be standing long after I'm dead.* He thought again of Laura's hypothesis that the circles represented God and the space within was sacred. He thought, *If I do publish this book, I'm going to mention Laura's idea and put it in with the information about the Callanish stone circle.*

CHAPTER THIRTY-SEVEN

"But if we walk in the light, as he is in the light, we have fellowship with one another, and the blood of Jesus, his Son, purifies us from all sin."

– 1 John 1:7

Late 1st Century A.D.

Jake had arrived on the Isle of Lewis by ferry. Now, on Monday, May 7, 2007, he arrived, by a commuter plane, on the Mainland of the Orkneys. The Orkneys are located almost directly north of Scotland. Although there are well over several dozens of prehistoric sites on the island of Mainland in the Orkneys, it is perhaps best known for the Ring of Brodgar. This is a huge site that has been dated to 3,100 B.C. It is a massive stone circle with a large rock-cut ditch that surrounds the circle. It is also the center of the Neolithic Orkney World Heritage Site.

By the time Jake had filled out the paperwork for his new rental, a tiny car, and driven it from the airport to Kirkwall, the main town in the Orkneys, and registered at his hotel, it was too late to visit the stones. Early the next morning, Jake was standing among the stones of the Ring of Brodgar. He immediately felt himself immersed in a spiritual atmosphere. Jake felt as though he were in a holy cathedral. He thought, *this is a special place.* He raised his arms and prayed to God. As he was praying, a breeze blew across his face. When he began praying, there had been no breeze. When he finished praying, the breeze went away.

The stones that make up this circle are unique and enigmatic. Some of them are narrow and shaped like rectangles. Some have odd cuts and slanted tops. Some are actually smaller at the bottom and larger at the top. Jake had never seen a standing stone circle like this one. He had read that the intricate architecture was due to precise solar alignments. Although many of the original stones are no longer present, it is still the third largest stone circle in Britain. The island across the water, with its gentle hills, made a nice backdrop for the Ring. Jake was totally enthralled by his experience among these stones.

After his spiritual experience among the Ring of Brodgar stones, Jake was curious to see what the other sites in the Orkneys would bring. Just a few miles from the Ring were the Wedgecup Standing Stones of Stenness. Jake drove over to look at them. One had the diagonal sliced top like some of those at the Brodgar site. Others had been cut horizontally across the top. These stones were all of an unusual appearance. They had been extensively worked to specific shapes. They were tall stones – taller than those at the Brodgar circle. This site had been dated to the same time period as the Ring. Jake did not feel the spiritual connection with this site as he did with the Ring site. However, both sites have been determined to be the most technologically advanced stone circles in all of Britain.

The next day, Jake visited cairns and Neolithic tombs. Some of the relics, tools and jewelry from these sites were on display in a museum located near the Ring of Brodgar. Jake photographed the Maeshowe Chambered Cairn, the Wideford Hill Chambered Cairn, the Cuween Hill Chambered Cairn and the Rennibister Earth House. This Rennibister Earth House was an underground stone-lined passage with a chamber in the earth. Jake recognized that some of these cairns and the earth house had similar construction techniques to those chambers he had seen in New England and, with the Earth House, similar to construction he had seen in Egypt.

Jake went back to his hotel. He was tired and hungry. It had been a very long day and he had skipped lunch. He slept in late on the 10th but spent the rest of the day at the Skara Brae Prehistoric Village. This was a 5,000-year-old stone village located right next to the ocean. He walked among the ruins. They were actually in pretty good shape. The roofs were missing but the rest of the stone houses and other structures there were almost as if the people had just left. He stood in a house where those ancient people had stood and lived their lives. Jake took a lot of photographs of this site. He sat on a hill overlooking the site and thought about how it must have been five thousand years earlier. Jake got an excellent shot of the Neolithic village with the ocean in the background.

On his way back, Jake thought he'd stop at the Ring of Brodgar and watch the sunset, such as it was. It didn't actually get real dark at night that far north. However, when he got there, there were dozens of tourists roaming all over the site. He turned around and went back to his hotel.

At sunrise on the 11th, Jake was standing, once again, among the unusual stones that made the Ring of Brodgar. He was alone. He took more photos including some of the sun rising from the horizon. He again began to feel the "atmosphere" of the site. He used the occasion to, once again, pray to God.

Unknown to Jake, on both that morning and the morning of the eighth, through the large windows of the museum, a woman had observed him in the Ring. She was a volunteer at the museum who came in early to prepare the building before the staff arrived. Plus, she also enjoyed being at the Ring at sunrise.

As he stood in the Ring, for some reason, it suddenly occurred to Jake that, in less than two weeks, he would be forty-four years old. He shrugged it off and looked around. He saw that the museum lights were on and walked over to it. It was early but the door was not locked. Jake walked inside.

The museum was welcoming. It had a nice "feel" to it. Unlike several museums he had visited around the globe, this museum was extremely clean. It had a small cafe with windows that had a view of the stones. The displays were well lit, clean and with good signage that explained what was contained in each of the display cases.

The first display case that Jake examined was one with miniatures of the Ring of Brodgar as it looked today and as it is thought to have looked 5,000 years earlier. As Jake was looking at this display, he noticed a woman looking at a display of rocks. She was tall and thin with long auburn hair. Her intelligent face was crowned with a pair of glasses. Jake thought, *Perhaps she only needs them to read?* He was noticing her with his peripheral vision and trying not to stare. He thought she was probably in her early thirties. He liked the way she looked.

Suddenly, she turned and walked over to Jake. She held out her hand and said, "Hi, I'm a Christian."

Surprised, Jake smiled and shook her hand. He replied, "Hi, me too."

"I thought you were."

Smiling, Jake asked, "What gave me away?"

"I saw you among the stones. You can sense the energy coming from the Ring. Most people cannot. I thought you might even be praying."

"I was. Yes, I can feel the energy. Can you?"

"Oh yes. I could even as a little girl."

"You're a native?"

She smiled. "Yes. Although I haven't always lived here, this island has always been my home."

Jake said, "I'm Jake Fleming."

"Rebekah West."

"It's nice to meet you."

"You also. What is a Christian from America doing on Orkney this early in the morning?"

"I understand how you knew I was a Christian but how did you know I'm from America?"

Rebekah laughed. "With that accent? Come on."

"Okay. You don't seem to have the heavy Scottish accent that I've heard from others."

"American television shows."

"I understand. Do you work here at the museum?"

"Volunteer. You didn't answer my question."

Jake told her about his efforts to photograph unexplained things that could be seen and touched for a possible book. Rebekah walked over to the display case she had been looking at and waved Jake over.

When he got there, Rebekah pointed down and said, "You should add these to your unexplained mysterious collection."

Jake looked down and saw three carved rocks about the size of a baseball. They were carved with channels that left the rocks with knobs protruding all around.

"What are they?"

"Scottish stone spheres. Some people call them the carved stone balls from Scotland. These three were found at Skara Brae. Have you been there yet?"

"Yes. That would make these stone spheres around five thousand years old."

"Give or take five hundred years."

"What were they used for?"

"Ahhh, that is what makes them mysterious. No one knows."

"Tell me about them."

She said, "Thus far, about four hundred in total have been found. Most of them come from Aberdeenshire. Sometimes, an isolated sphere will be found somewhere in Scotland. Some have been found in the vicinity of stone circles. A few have been found in northern England and in Ireland. Different explanations have been given for their purpose. Most involve them being a weapon. If one was somehow hurled at an opponent and struck him in the head, it would crack his skull and probably be fatal. Some have even suggested they were used as assault weapons with a catapult. That, of course, makes no sense. The thing is, none of the spheres has even been found with damage. No scars, no dents, no broken knobs, no cracks. They all seem to be in prime condition. If they were used as a weapon, it seems likely that there would be some damage to some of them. Now here's a real mystery for you – one was found in Tiwanaku in Bolivia. It looks exactly like the ones found here in Scotland. Do you know about Tiwanaku?"

Jake smiled. He responded, "It was the first place I went to on this journey of mine. Orkney will be the last place I visit.

Odd that a Scottish stone sphere would be in Tiwanaku."

"Yes, it is. How did it get there?"

"Exactly. Is it possible that someone from the twentieth century could have carried one there and lost it?"

"Possible, I suppose. Not likely. My understanding is that it was found several feet in the ground. But who knows? Perhaps it was lying right on top of the ground."

"Tiwanaku is a fascinating and mysterious place."

"So I've heard. Would you like a cup of tea? My treat."

"Thank you. Yes, that would be nice."

Rebekah led Jake over to the cafe. Like Rebekah, the waitress and cook always arrived early to handle the tourists who visit the ring. As Jake and Rebekah sat down, the waitress brought them a pot of tea.

When she had left, Jake said, "Mind reader?"

"No, everyone begins with a pot of tea."

"Oh, okay."

Jake sipped his cup of tea, set it back in its saucer and added some cream to it.

Rebekah asked, "Why did you sip it and then add your cream?"

"By tasting it first, I then know how much cream I want to add."

Rebekah nodded.

Jake said, "They have breakfast. Would you like some? My treat."

She smiled and said, "Breakfast here is usually fish and beans."

Jake smiled, "Okay. When in Rome . . ."

They ordered two breakfasts and continued to talk.

"So," Jake asked, "What do you do here in the Isles of Orkney?"

With a pleasant smile, Rebekah answered, "Two things. One, I'm an artist and . . ."

"An artist?"

"Yes."

"What do you paint?"

"Mostly landscapes and seascapes. Prints of some of my work are in the gift shop."

"Great. I look forward to seeing them."

The waitress brought their food. She asked, "More tea?"

Rebekah said, "Yes, please. Thank you, Victoria."

Jake leaned over and said, "I guess, since you volunteer here, you know everyone."

"Yes. It's a small staff."

Jake asked, "What is the second thing you do here?"

Rebekah replied, "I teach school."

Jake recoiled in his chair as if he had been pushed. Rebekah was concerned. She asked, "What's wrong? Are you all right?"

Just then, their waitress returned with a fresh pot of tea. She sat it on the table. She noticed Rebekah staring at Jake. Jake began to smile. He nodded his head and said, "I'm all right."

Rebekah said, "Thank you, Victoria."

She turned to Jake and asked, "What was that all about? Do you have seizures?"

"No. . . . no. I'm sorry for that reaction. It's . . . I've been going through . . . it's a little difficult to explain."

"But you're all right?"

"Yes. Fine."

"Okay. Tell me about this world-wide journey of yours."

"I have photographed and touched things all over the world that archaeologists cannot explain. In most cases, they really do not know who built or how . . ."

"Give me an example."

"Sure. The Ring of Brodgar."

They both looked over at it.

Jake said, "No one knows for certain who placed those stones there . . . or why."

Rebekah smiled. "Another."

"The Sphinx and the pyramids in Egypt."

Rebekah did not respond. She looked over and saw that

Victoria had sat down on the other side of the room. She was busy wrapping forks, knives and spoons in napkins.

Jake continued. "And they certainly do not know how they were built, when they were built or why they were built."

"You must have met a lot of people."

"Yes. Most of the people I've met have been extremely nice and helpful. However, I've seen some horrible places with horrible poverty. India was among the worst. Some of the people there are living in deplorable conditions. And yet, India has an ancient culture going back thousands of years. I'm convinced that India had an ancient civilization that was way more advanced that what is there today."

"Why so?"

"Because we are unable to duplicate today what was built in the past. We simply do not have the technology today to accomplish what was done thousands and thousands of years ago."

"Hmmmm. All right. As a Christian, how do you explain civilizations existing before Adam and Eve?"

Jake smiled. He said, "You know, I've thought about this for many years – long before I began this current journey. Modern human skeletons have been found that are over half a million years old. The concept that we evolved from apes in a steady continuous line of improvement is total nonsense."

"How do you explain it?"

"I'm not sure I can."

CHAPTER THIRTY-EIGHT

"That if you confess with your mouth, 'Jesus is Lord,' and believe in your heart that God raised him from the dead, you will be saved."

– Romans 10:9

Mid 1st Century A.D.

Sitting in the small restaurant of the Orkney Museum, Rebekah and Jake were sipping their tea.

Jake said, "I've prayed and prayed about this. I have asked for an explanation. Science, archaeology and common sense tells us that there were dinosaurs millions of years ago. Also, they tell us that there were modern human beings here hundreds of thousands and maybe even millions of years ago. However, the Bible tells us that God created Adam and Eve, as the first couple, about six thousand years ago. The Sphinx, in Egypt, is older than that. How do we reconcile this?

"One day, when I was standing in Tiwanaku and realized that there had been a six-foot-deep layer of silt throughout the site, I had an inclination of how this could be reconciled. At the bottom of the six feet of silt were pottery pieces and artifacts. However, there were no human bones – no skeletons. The massive structure had obviously already been built but had been deserted by the time of the flood.

"People often question who Cain married. Some automatically presume it must have been a sister. However, I think Genesis provides another answer. After Cain killed his brother Abel, God banished him. Cain complained that his punishment was too severe. Cain told God that he would be a restless wanderer and that whoever found him would kill him.

471

God replied with a 'no.' God put a mark on Cain so that whoever found him would not kill him. Now," Jake continued, "the obvious question becomes who are these 'whoever' people that both God and Cain discuss? To me, this truly does imply that there were other humans 'out there' and that Cain was afraid of them.

"The Bible says that Cain moved to the land of Nod. The very next verse states that Cain lay with his wife and she, in due time, gave birth to Enoch. It seems to me that Cain found a wife among the people of Nod.

"Now the Bible gives the chronology from Adam to Noah and then from Noah to Abraham and from Abraham to David and from David to Jesus. Both Mary and Joseph were of the House of David. Now here's where I am going with all this in order to reconcile the two timelines. Both, I believe are accurate. The Jewish people are God's chosen people. Throughout history, including up until today and including the future, Israel and the Jewish people have been, are and will be . . . God's chosen. He set them aside as special. I believe, by creating Adam and Eve, he made a special foundation for His chosen people.

"In Genesis, after God began the development of the earth by saying 'let there be light,' and finishing with the land animals, He created man in His own image – male and female. This is Genesis 1:27. In Genesis 1:28, God blessed the male and female. He told them to be fruitful and increase in number. He told them to fill the earth and subdue it.

"Then later, in Genesis 2, God placed Adam in the Garden of Eden. From Adam's rib, He created Eve. God had told Adam that he could eat of any tree in the garden except for the fruit from the tree of the knowledge of good and evil.

"I am certainly no Bible scholar, but to me this seems like two different creations of mankind. The first was much earlier than the second. The second, of Adam and Eve, was specifically to found and establish His chosen people.

"What do you think?"

Rebekah had listened intently to Jake's long explanation.

She replied, "I have never heard that. It seems to be logical."

"I hope so."

"I had always heard that Cain must have married one of his sisters."

"Yes, me too. But God had banished him from the area of Eden where his parents had lived. He moved to Nod."

"I understand what you are saying. It does make sense to me."

"If accurate, it would certainly explain all these ancient structures that are certainly more than six thousand years old."

Rebekah turned to Victoria, who had been listening to Jake's explanation, and asked, "Victoria, could we get more tea?"

Victoria came over to their table, picked up the pot and went into the kitchen. She quickly returned with a fresh pot, sat it on the table and returned to her napkins.

Jake said, "Thank you."

Victoria smiled.

Rebekah said, "I want to ask you a question."

"Shoot."

Rebekah looked confused.

"I mean, go ahead and ask."

"All right. In the Bible, there is an instance where Jesus is talking with His disciples. He asked them who the people said that He was. The disciples responded and told Jesus that some people thought He was John the Baptist, Elijah, Jeremiah or one of the prophets. Then Jesus said, 'Who do you say I am?' Jake, that is my question. How was Jesus answered?"

Jake smiled. This was one of his favorite Bible verses – Matthew 16:16.

Jake replied, "Peter said, 'You are the Christ, the Son of the living God.'"

Rebekah smiled. "Just testing."

Jake smiled, "Let me ask you one."

"All right." She grinned.

"According to the Bible, how long does one generation

live?"

"I know this. It is in Psalms."

"Yes."

"It is seventy years but, if one is in good health, as much as eighty years."

"Right."

During all this time, no one else had come into the little cafe. Other than Rebekah and Jake, there was not a single customer.

Victoria came over and stood by their table.

Rebekah said, "We're fine. Thank you, Victoria."

She just stood there.

Jake asked, "Did you want to ask us something?"

Victoria smiled and nodded. She said, "I heard what you both were talking about. How do you . . . I was wondering, how do you two know about those things?"

Jake smiled at her. He replied, "Sit down, join us and I'll tell you."

Victoria looked around the empty restaurant, pulled out a chair and sat down between Rebekah and Jake.

Jake asked, "Victoria, do you go to church?"

"No, not really. I went to a funeral once at a church."

"Okay. Have you heard of Jesus?"

"I just heard you say that He was the Son of God."

"Yes, that's right."

Rebekah stated, "Victoria, to answer your questions, we learned about those things from reading the Bible."

Victoria replied, "Uh-huh."

Jake smiled. He looked at Victoria and said, "You can learn those things too by reading the Bible."

"I don't know. My parents said there wasn't much to all this religion stuff."

"How about science?"

Rebekah looked oddly at Jake but didn't say anything.

Victoria answered, "I like science. What about it?"

"Scientists have proven, through science, that every

human being – you, Rebekah, myself and everyone in the whole world has an immortal soul. Do you know what that means?"

"No, what is immortal?'

"It means that we all have a soul within our bodies that never dies. One day, our bodies are going to die. However, our souls, inside our bodies, never die."

At first, Victoria didn't respond but then said, "I understand."

"All right. That is the science part. What science cannot answer is what happens to the soul when the body dies. Where does everyone's soul go?"

"Where?"

"That is where . . . the answer to that involves a belief in God. Do you believe in God?"

"I guess so. I don't know."

"When you stand on a hill here in the Orkneys and look out at the ocean, see birds flying overhead and observe the beautiful blue sky with the shining sun, do you think that that just happened by chance? Or, as Rebekah and I believe, do you think that maybe it was created by God?"

"What is God?"

Jake smiled and answered, "Love."

Rebekah was surprised by Jake's response but she agreed with it.

"Love? I don't . . ."

"Victoria, there are many types of love. There is the romantic love between a man and a woman. There is the love that one has for a pet – say a favorite dog or a horse. There is the love that one has for one's parents and siblings. There is the love one has for one's children. There is the love that one has for one's friends. There is the love that one may have for one's home or one's country. I'm sure some people love Orkney. Others may not. Victoria, love is the most powerful force in the universe and God is love."

Victoria didn't respond.

Jake continued, "God is a spirit Who exists everywhere.

He is, right now, in this very room. He is out there at the Ring. Everywhere. God is love. God loves everyone. God loves you."

Victoria seemed taken back by that. "How could God love me? He doesn't know me. I've not gone to church. I've not prayed."

Jake said, "God knows everything about you, Victoria. God is love. He loves everyone. He loves your soul and He wants your soul to be with Him when your body dies."

"And how does that happen?"

"It's fairly easy. In fact, in the next few minutes, you can guarantee that your soul will go to Him."

Victoria looked doubtful.

"Rebekah and I are sure that our souls are going to be with God when our bodies die. You can also be sure."

"Where else can my soul go?"

"There are only two options – one is to be with God forever and the other option is to be separated from God forever. With God, you will be with love. Without God, there is no love."

Rebekah said, "Heaven or Hell, Victoria."

"Oh, I see." After thinking for a few moments, Victoria asked, "So how do I guarantee, as you said, that I will be with God?"

"Believe. There are several things that you must believe to be true. Some of them you will have to accept as true on faith. That's what Rebekah and I did."

"I don't know."

"Let me explain it to you and then you can decide. You can say, 'Yes, I believe' or you can say, 'No, I don't believe that.'"

Victoria nodded.

"First, you have to believe that there is a God. Remember that scientists have proven, scientifically, that all humans have a soul. That soul will live forever. God created us with souls. Jesus spoke about our souls. Anyway, God, because He loves us, wants everyone's soul to be with Him forever. However, God is pure and cannot have sin around Him. He can't have any sin in

Heaven. You, Rebekah and I are sinners. Everyone is a sinner. The Bible says that we all have sinned – that we all have fallen short of the glory of God. Jesus was the only person to ever walk on the earth without sin."

"And He was, you said, the Son of God."

"Right. Jesus said He was the Son of God. Another thing then that we have to believe is that we are sinners."

"I believe that. I know I'm a sinner."

"The Bible says that the result of sin is spiritual separation from God. In other words, because we are all sinners, our souls should spend eternity away from God. But he didn't want that to happen. Consequently, He provided a way for us sinners to be forgiven for our sins so that our souls could be with God forever.

"God sent His Son, Jesus, to die as a sacrifice for our sins. Jesus died on the cross for our sins in order that we could have a permanent relationship with God. In the Bible, the book of Romans, it says God showed His *love* for us, in that while we were still sinners, Jesus died for us. This is another one of those things you need to believe. However, Jesus didn't just die on the cross for us. He was buried but, on the third day, He overcame death. His body was dead but He came back alive. This is what Easter is all about. If you, or anyone, believe that Jesus Christ died and rose from the dead for your sins, then your soul will go to be with God when your body dies. Jesus said, in the book of John, 'I am the way and the truth and the life. No one comes to the Father except through me.' If you believe what Jesus said and truly repent, be sorry, for your sins, then you can guarantee that your soul will be with God forever.

"Because we are all sinners, none of us deserve to be with God. However, we are saved from separation from God by God's grace and love - Jesus. If we admit that we are sinners and turn away from sin in the future and believe that Jesus was exactly Who He said He was – the Son of God – then Jesus will be our savior. He will intercede on our behalf before God. Now Victoria, this takes some faith to believe. You should know that God knows your heart. He knows whether or not you are sincere."

"You said He is in this room?"

"Yes."

"So if I accept what you have told me as being true, God will know."

"Absolutely. However, I should tell you this. If you accept Jesus as your personal Savior – that He died for you – you will not automatically become some type of angel. Being a Christian is often difficult. But, once you accept Christ, He sends the Holy Spirit to live within you and help you live as a Christian. That doesn't mean you won't ever commit a sin. But when you do, you can recognize it as a sin and ask God to forgive you and try not to do it again. This is important. When you tell God that you are sorry for the sins you have done, you also are telling God that you are going to try not to do them ever again. Suppose you were a thief. You stole small things. Maybe you were a shoplifter. Everyone knows that it is not right to take something that does not belong to them. If you become a Christian, this means that you will no longer steal anything. You know that it is wrong. It is a sin. So you don't do it anymore. If a family wanted you to come babysit in their house and they knew that you were a Christian, they would feel comfortable hiring you. Why? Because they know that Christians don't steal. They know that Christians are loving and would take excellent care of their baby and their small children."

Victoria wanted to say something but hesitated. Rebekah and Jake looked at one another.

Victoria said, "I think I've followed what you have said but I don't know if I'm good enough to have Jesus accept me."

Jake smiled and said, "I know if you are good enough. The answer is no. You are not good enough. Neither am I. No one is. But, if a person truly is sorry for their sins, has faith in Jesus, God will accept everyone. Have you ever murdered someone?"

"No, of course not."

"Even murderers have repented, accepted Jesus and been forgiven."

Victoria looked confused.

Jake added, "Victoria, God, through His grace and love, will forgive all sins if a person believes that Jesus is His Son, that Jesus died to cleanse us from our sins and rose from death to be our Savior and our Lord."

"Even me? I don't know."

Jake replied, "I understand. However, you should know that God wants everyone, including you, to believe in His Son Jesus so that their souls can be with Him forever. It is that belief in Jesus that saves our souls. We cannot get to God by being good or doing good things. I mean, we should be kind and do good things but that will not save our souls. Only having the faith to believe in Jesus can do that."

Victoria hesitated. After a few moments, she said, "I believe in all that you just said. What do I do now?"

Jake smiled and said, "First, I think that Rebekah and I would like to give you a hug and welcome you as a fellow Christian."

Rebekah hugged Victoria and Jake followed with a hug. They sat back down at the table.

Jake asked Victoria, "Would you mind repeating a prayer right now?"

Softly, she answered, "No."

"Let's hold hands."

Jake, Rebekah, and Victoria held hands in a circle around the table.

Jake said, "Victoria, repeat after me."

"All right."

"Heavenly Father,"

"Heavenly Father," In a soft voice, Victoria repeated what Jake said.

"I know that I am a sinner."

"I know that I am a sinner."

"Please forgive me for my sins."

"Please forgive me for my sins."

"I truly do believe that Jesus Christ is your Son."

"I truly do believe that Jesus Christ is your Son."

"I believe that Jesus died on the cross for my sins."

"I believe that Jesus died on the cross for my sins."

"I believe that Jesus overcame death and rose from the grave to life."

"I believe that Jesus overcame death and rose from the grave to life."

"From this day on, I want to put my faith and trust in Jesus as my Savior."

"From this day on, I want to put my faith and trust in Jesus as my Savior."

"Please guide my life and help me to do whatever You want me to do."

"Please guide my life and help me to do whatever You want me to do."

"I pray this to You Heavenly Father in the holy name of Your Son, Jesus."

"I pray this to You Heavenly Father in the holy name of Your Son, Jesus."

"Amen."

"Amen."

Tears were rolling down Victoria's cheeks. She looked embarrassed.

Jake said, "Now, if you start crying, you're going to make me cry also."

Victoria laughed. Jake handed her one of the napkins that was wrapped around silverware. She wiped her face. She stood up.

"I guess I'd better get back to work. Thank you both so much."

Jake smiled at her. He said, "You may want to go to church on the thirteenth. They will probably have some information there that you can take home to read. It will help you to grow as a Christian. You will probably want to start reading the Bible. And listen, when you do, read it as though God is speaking to you. Because He is. You may want to begin with the book of John."

Victoria smiled and nodded. She returned to the kitchen.

Rebekah took Jake's hands in hers and said, "Thank you for what you said. I'm not sure I've ever previously heard that approach to explaining the plan of salvation."

"Me either. But she seemed to understand."

"Yes."

"I've got a friend name Victoria. I don't know when her birthday is but she's either eleven or twelve years old."

Rebekah smiled. "She your niece?"

Jake smiled, "No, just a little girl I met in the woods a couple of years ago."

Rebekah looked puzzled.

Jake said, "Remind me to tell you about it sometime."

Rebekah replied, "All right. Listen, the reason I'm not in my classroom right now is that we are on break for this week and the next two weeks."

Jake nodded and said, "I understand."

"If you'd like, I'd be glad to give you a personal tour of our island here . . . and surrounding areas."

Jake's face lit up with a big smile. He said, "I'd love that. I appreciate it."

"It's nice for me to see places I am so familiar with through the eyes of someone else. Your perspective will be refreshing to me."

Rebekah and Jake spent the next day, Saturday, May 12th visiting some of the sites Jake had already seen. However, Rebekah's local knowledge added an entire new layer of interest for Jake. She knew things that the tour guides didn't.

They both enjoyed their day together. Rebekah had been driving his rental all day. Jake invited her to dinner at the restaurant that was located in his hotel. After dinner, Jake asked Rebekah if he could attend church with her in the morning. As he drove her back to the museum where her car was parked, Rebekah showed Jake where the church was located. She told him she would meet him there.

In the gift shop at his hotel, Jake bought a Bible to give to Victoria. He didn't know whether or not she would attend Rebekah's church but he decided to take it with him. He wrote inside, "To Victoria, from Rebekah and Jake. May 2007."

The next morning, while standing outside the church waiting on Rebekah, Victoria walked up to Jake with a big smile. Jake returned her smile with one of his own.

She said, "I was hoping that you and Rebekah would be here. I'm not sure I know anyone else here."

"Oh, I bet you'll know lots of these people. Other than me, they are all locals."

"Would you mind if I sit with you and Rebekah? You are waiting on her?"

"Yes. No, we would be glad for you to sit with us. In fact, I've got something for you."

Jake handed her a box with the Bible in it.

"What is it?"

"Open and see."

She did. She hugged the Bible. She hugged Jake and said, "Thank you. Thank you. This is so nice of you."

"You are very welcome. Maybe you can use it during the service."

Rebekah had parked and was walking up to join them. Victoria had looked in the Bible and saw that it was from both Rebekah and Jake. She greeted Rebekah with a hug and said, "Thank you. I really like it." She showed the Bible to Rebekah. Rebekah was confused. With his hands, Jake quickly pointed at her and then back to himself and then used a "giving" motion to indicate that they had both given Victoria the Bible.

Inside the church sanctuary, while sitting together prior to the beginning of the service, Rebekah looked at Victoria's Bible and noticed the inscription that read "from Rebekah and Jake." Then she fully understood Victoria's hug and comments.

During the service, Jake could not understand very much of what was said. The minister's Scottish brogue was so thick that he couldn't follow it. Everyone in the congregation knew Rebekah and most of them knew who Victoria was. They knew not, however, who the man sitting between Rebekah and Victoria was. They also did not know why Victoria was attending. She had never previously been in the church.

After the service, numerous people came up to Rebekah and, of course, she had to introduce them all to Jake. Several of them talked with Victoria and said that they were glad to see her. One young man, who had been a year ahead of her in school, came over and talked with her.

As they walked to their different vehicles, Victoria mentioned that she needed to get back home. Jake invited Rebekah to lunch at the hotel restaurant. She accepted and they drove separate cars to the hotel.

After lunch, Rebekah said, "I want to show you something." She drove Jake's rental and took him to the base of a small hill. They got out and walked to the top of the hill. Looking out over the ocean, Jake commented,

"It's absolutely beautiful."

"It is, isn't it? I think it may be my favorite spot on all of Mainland. When you described that ocean scene with the birds, blue sky and everything to Victoria, I thought of this place."

"It does look like what I described to her as the handiwork of God. It's beautiful."

Still wearing heels, Rebekah led Jake back down the hill to a small beach. There was a bench there and they sat on it and talked.

Jake learned that Rebekah had just celebrated her 38th birthday on May 7th. Rather than being in her early thirties, she was in her late thirties. He told her that he would be forty-four soon – on May 24th. Rebekah shared with Jake that she had never been married. Her father died almost ten years prior. She had one younger sister who was married and was living in Edinburgh with her husband and two children. She still lived with her mother on the family's croft. She loved working with children as their teacher. She had a dog, a rescue mutt, that she loved and with whom she had bonded. Her name was Ellie. They sat in the sunshine on that bench and watched the tide go out. It was a pleasant afternoon and they both enjoyed each other's company.

Beginning with the next day, Monday, May 14th and continuing the entire week through Saturday, May 19th, Rebekah gave Jake a thorough tour of Mainland, the largest island in the Orkneys. One particularly sunny day, on Thursday, May 17th, they went back to Rebekah's favorite spot. Jake had picked her up at her home. She had packed a picnic lunch and they spent the day there at her spot. They still needed sweaters and jackets like the first time but it was a day of bright sunshine.

Sitting on the bench, Jake asked Rebekah if anyone actually came to this beach and swam. She laughed and answered by telling Jake that the water was much too cold for swimming. She told him that, for about three or four days every year, it was warm enough that teenage girls would wear their bikinis and lay out in the sun. However, she said with a smile, they primarily were wearing them to impress their boyfriends.

Still sitting on the bench, Rebekah leaned over and laid her head on Jake's shoulder. While spending the week together, they had become close. Jake did not mind at all having Rebekah leaning against him. However, it did cause him to think, for the hundredth time, what could the future of this relationship be? If he had not met Rebekah, he would have already returned to North Carolina.

She interrupted his thoughts by snuggling more against him and saying, "This is nice."

Jake immediately thought of Laura. But he did not move and replied, "Yes, it sure is."

"I could sit here like this, next to you, with the sunshine…the waves gently coming in against the beach…the gulls flying about…the birds walking along the shoreline…the fluffy clouds against the bright blue sky…I could stay like this for hours."

Jake thought that Rebekah might be falling asleep. He replied by simply saying, "Me too."

This was the first overt romantic gesture that either of them had made. Jake didn't mind it but did not know where it could lead. He really liked Rebekah. However, he also knew that there was an ocean between them. He whispered, "Help me, Jesus."

After a few minutes, Jake put his arm around Rebekah's shoulder and, with his hand on her arm, pulled her in tighter. She snuggled against him and murmured, "Mmmmm."

It reminded Jake of a kitten purring.

They sat that way for about another 15 minutes. Jake was losing the feeling in his arm. Rebekah sighed and sat up on the bench.

She said, "This is very enjoyable but I suppose we ought to be getting back. When the sun begins to set, it quickly gets cool."

They loaded the picnic basket and other things into the car and headed back. On the way, neither said anything about their "close" time on the beach.

Rebekah asked, "Do you know of the man who had Rosslyn Chapel built down in Edinburgh?"

"Yes, I actually do. It was Sir William Sinclair."

"Right. One of his titles was Lord of Orkney. He built a castle here on the island. Tomorrow, I'll take you to see the ruins. There is actually very little of it left. But it has a nice view."

"That would be nice. I'd like to see it."

"It's a beautiful spot. There are also the ruins of another castle. There is much more of it left to see."

"All right. Tomorrow is castle day."

Jake drove Rebekah home. He walked her to her door. At the door, Rebekah turned and quickly gave Jake a kiss on his cheek.

She said, "You're a sweet man."

On the drive back to his hotel, Jake wondered about the kiss. *It was nice but it was a kiss that either of his sisters could have given him. 'You're a sweet man.' That was also something one of his sisters might say.* Jake thought that this relationship was almost like they were in middle school. Jake thought, *where do I want this to go? Am I falling in love? Does she have feelings for me? Or does she see me as a friend only? A sweet man? I suppose that is a compliment. But it doesn't sound like one.* What did he expect her to say? *Goodnight? See you tomorrow?* Jake continued thinking, *Am I over Laura enough to fall in love with someone else? In four months, it will be two years. And I still miss her. And it still hurts. I haven't told Rebekah about Laura. Why not? Why should I? I told her about my ex-wife, my practice wife. Of course, if we actually do fall in love with each other, that will change everything. Are you afraid, Jake, to fall in love again? I don't think falling in love is something you get to choose. It either happens or it doesn't. She may not have any romantic feelings for me at all. Perhaps she is just being nice to a fellow Christian. No, that's not all. There's more Jake. Now I'm talking to myself in my thoughts. If we don't fall in love, it will make my life simpler. If we do fall in love, how can we make it work? There's that ocean thing in the way. All this deep thought Jake and you haven't solved a thing.*

Jake ate in the hotel restaurant by himself. He suddenly realized that he missed Rebekah. He quickly became lost in his thoughts again.

Meanwhile, Rebekah had prepared supper for her mom and herself. As they ate, Rebekah's mom asked about Jake. Rebekah replied by telling her mom that they were just friends.

Her mom said, "Really? You appear happier than I've seen you in years."

"Mom, you know I'm always a happy person. I'm a Christian and that makes me happy."

"I realize that. Nonetheless, you seem to be even happier this past week than usual."

Softly, Rebekah said, "I guess I'm falling in love with him."

"No. There's no guessing. Love is either there or it's not. Do you love this man?"

Rebekah didn't answer. Ellie ran and jumped up in her lap. Rebekah petted her.

Her mom said, "Listen to your heart. Your heart will tell you the answer. Then, follow your heart."

Rebekah replied, "Yes."

"I thought so. Good. It's about time you gave me some grandchildren like your sister has done."

Rebekah blushed. Then she said, "He probably doesn't care about me like that. He probably thinks of me as a friendly tour guide."

"No, there's more there than that. You said he had finished his photographs for his book. Well, why is he still here? You. You're the reason he is still here."

"I don't know, Mum. He's really rich."

"Well, don't hold that against him."

Rebekah laughed. "No, what I mean is he could have anyone. Why would he want me?"

"For love, Rebekah, for love. If he loves you and you love him, love will find a way."

"I just don't see how. He lives in America. I live in Orkney. There is an awful lot of space between us."

"If it's meant to be, love will find a way. Pray about it."

Rebekah smiled.

CHAPTER THIRTY-NINE

"The soul that sees beauty may sometimes walk alone."

– John von Goethe

Late 18th Century A.D.

"It's beautiful!" Jake exclaimed.

Rebekah was driving Jake's rental. The road was right next to the water as it curved around the island. The gently sloping hills were covered in bright green grass. Every now and then there would be bursts of color as flowers bloomed in all their glory.

Jake said, "I really appreciate you driving. If I were driving and trying to take in all this beauty, I'd drive off the road. This entire island is almost all open spaces of grass. I love it. I also love how the road hugs the water."

"Before going to the ruins, let me drive you all around the coastal road."

"Do it!"

They continued to go around the island. They saw the Pentland Firth, St. Margaret's Hope, the Kirk Sound and, on an island across some water, Rebekah pointed out the Old Man of Hoy. It was a natural rock formation that, from the side, looked like a man's face. Jake pointed at a bunch of seals in the water. Rebekah informed him that that was Birsay and seals were common there. There were rock walls separating the road from pastures. It reminded Jake of all the rock walls in New England. They had passed a sign indicating the Marwick Head Nature Preserve and now were coming up on one called the Mull Head Nature Preserve.

Jake asked Rebekah to pull over so that they could see

this one. She did and it had a footpath that they took. As they were walking along, Jake reached down and took Rebekah's hand in his. She squeezed his hand and they continued walking together holding hands. It was a beautiful walk. Jake noticed a total absence of trees. The climate in the Orkneys just didn't allow trees to grow. Jake took several photos. He took several of Rebekah and thought that she improved the scenery.

Back in the car, Rebekah continued on their tour. She pulled over and said, "I think you might find this interesting."

There were dozens, almost a hundred people, milling about a small structure. It was a church.

Rebekah said, "Bad timing. One of the cruise ships has unloaded at Kirkwall Harbour. This is The Italian Chapel. It was built in World War II by Italian POWs."

Jake responded, "I noticed the Italian flag flying and was wondering what that was about."

Waiting until the crowd got back on their buses, Rebekah and Jake visited the small chapel. It was beautifully done. It had curved ceilings with paintings that looked professionally done.

Jake said, "This is amazing. How did they get the materials in the middle of the war? How did it happen that they had prisoners who knew how to do this and how to paint such nice images?"

"I don't know. You are right, though, it is amazing. You might be interested to know that Churchill came up here during World War II. German submarines were able to move between islands. He had causeways built connecting different islands. The real purpose was to prevent the subs from being able to travel among the islands."

Continuing with the tour around the island, Rebekah stopped to show Jake one of the "stone forts" that Scotland was famous for having. The stones had "melted" and formed glass as they merged together. No one knows how that had happened. The heat that had to be involved was tremendous. Jake took some photos. Rebekah also showed him the remains of a broch. Like the "forts," no one really knew what the real purpose of them was. Jake got more shots for possible inclusion in his book.

Driving down a rise and around a curve, Jake noticed a sign that told them they were entering the "City and Royal Burgh of Kirkwall."

Jake said, "I didn't realize my hotel was in a Royal Burgh. I've been staying in a Royal Burgh and didn't even know it."

Rebekah smiled. She said, "Lunch?"

"Yes, I'm starving. I noticed a restaurant here in Kirkwall we could try." He pointed it out to her. She nodded. It was almost two o'clock in the afternoon. They were both hungry. Rebekah found a parking lot and they walked to the restaurant from there.

After a nice lunch, they were walking in downtown Kirkwall when Rebekah grasped Jake's hand and pulled him along. She said, "I want to show you something I'm sure you will appreciate."

Holding hands, they approached a large brick church. It was St. Magnus Cathedral. The interior was majestic. It had beautiful stained-glass windows and huge round brick columns. Rebekah had been right. Jake did appreciate seeing this church. He pulled Rebekah over to the end of a pew and sat down. He bowed his head and said a prayer. Rebekah did the same. Jake prayed that God would direct him in his relationship with Rebekah. Rebekah was praying for the same thing. Neither knew what the other was praying but, when they finished, they both smiled at each other.

Outside, as they were walking back to the car lot, Jake saw a huge cruise ship. He said, "I had no idea that the Orkneys received those cruise ships."

"Yes, they've been coming here to Kirkwall Harbour for many years. They'll be more in June, July and August. It's a little early for them now. Those tourists are a big help to the local economy. If they quit coming here, it would hurt. People have gotten used to all the business they bring."

"Yes, I can understand that. I'm sure they enjoy visiting here. It's beautiful."

Rebekah drove to the ruins of Sir William Sinclair's

castle. They walked around and Jake took a few pictures. He mentioned that he thought it was a shame that these ruins were all that was left of so many once magnificent structures. Rebekah explained that, even when they were originally built, the cost of construction and maintenance of a castle was enormous. Today, she told Jake, the expense of maintaining a castle was so high that it was prohibitive. Most family castles, like Drum castle of the Irvine clan, near Aberdeen, have been donated to the National Trust of Scotland. Tourist money and public pounds are used to maintain it. She told Jake that, no matter how wealthy a person was, unless you were the Queen, it just didn't make sense to live in a castle as a private residence.

"There are several more castle ruins. Would you like to visit them?"

"Not really. If you don't mind, I'd just as soon go back to your little beach spot and watch the ocean."

"I don't mind at all. She drove them over to it."

They got out and walked toward the ocean. However, it was way too windy to sit on the bench so they returned to the car. They made small talk until it became uncomfortable.

Jake decided it was probably past time for him to say something serious. In his mind, he said to himself, *help me, Jesus.*

He said, "Rebekah, I want you to know that I truly have…feelings for you."

Rebekah thought to herself, *Uh-oh, I expect a big 'but' to follow that sentence.*

Jake continued, "Meeting you and getting to spend time with you has been wonderful."

She smiled and replied, "For me too." She thought, *But.*

Jake smiled and said, "I am really at a loss to know what to say or do. If it . . ."

"Kiss me."

"What?"

"You said you didn't know what to do. Kiss me."

Jake smiled, leaned over in the car and gave her a long

and passionate kiss. They both felt that special kind of electricity go through their bodies.

Rebekah thought, *he sure passes the kissing test.*

Jake thought, *Wow! I could spend the rest of my life kissing this woman.*

They smiled at each other. Jake put his arm around her shoulder and pulled her close. The small rental car made that easy. Rebekah, still on the driver's side, scooted over on the bench seat until her left leg brushed up against Jake's right leg. Jake was thankful that some European cars still had bench seats in the front. They sat together in pleasant silence and watched the waves roll in on the beach.

Jake thought, *Rebekah is the first woman I have kissed since Laura.* He felt a little guilty . . . but not much. Thinking of her, Jake said to himself, *I am, however, falling for her. She is an extremely nice person. She is a Christian. She is intelligent. She is amazingly attractive. But, where do we go from here?*

Rebekah was also thinking. *Is this really happening? I just turned thirty-eight and now I'm falling in love again. The first time, I was devastated when he left me. What will Jake do? Will he leave me too? Does he love me? I've got one more week of break and then I go back to the classroom. He is nice. He is a Christian. I do like the way he looks and I love the way he kisses. What now?*

They looked at each other and smiled. Jake pulled her even closer and kissed her again. She returned the kiss with passion. They broke the kiss and stared in each other's eyes. It was difficult to hug in the small car but they tried. It got awkward and they both laughed.

Rebekah said, "You were telling me that you are developing feelings for me. I'm sorry, but I interrupted you."

"You can interrupt me with a kiss like that anytime."

"Good to know."

"I can add kissing to the things I like about you."

"Really." Rebekah smiled coyly. "What else do you like about me?"

"I love your accent."

"My accent! You think *I* have an accent?"

Jake nodded. "Seriously Rebekah, I think you are a beautiful, naturally kind Christian woman. What's not to like?"

"Naturally kind. Hmmmm. I'm not so sure you know me well enough."

"I think so. I feel it. You are a kind woman and it is natural, not forced. It is part of your character and I love it."

"That's kind of you to say."

"And that's kind of you to mention." They both laughed. "I'm just stating what I see to be the truth."

"Thank you. Listen, I'd like you to come over to my house for supper tomorrow evening. I want you to meet my Mum."

"I'd love to. Thank you. What's your mother like?"

"She's nice. You'll like her."

Jake thought, *I hope she likes me.*

It was getting dark. They had spent the day together and, for Jake, it had been a wonderful day. It was a "break-through" day. Holding hands, kissing, hugging. Rebekah stayed in the driver's seat and drove back to her home. Jake got out and walked her to the door. They had a passionate kiss goodnight.

Jake drove back to Kirkwall and his hotel. On the drive back, he was thinking. *The mother meeting. This is early for the mother meeting. I know I am falling for Rebekah. How can we date? She is teaching school in Scotland. I don't even have a house to live in and, if I did, it would be in the United States. Could I live in Scotland? Could she move to America? Where do we go from here?* The easiest thing to do would be to tell Rebekah that he truly enjoyed her company and he truly did like her but he needed to return to America. However, his heart was telling him to stay. His mind was telling him to go. Should he follow his heart or his mind? He put his hand over his heart and said, "Jesus, help me. Help me know what to do."

Jake spent a leisurely Saturday. He read a lot of local history. Not only did he read about the islands around Mainland but he also read extensively about the Shetland Islands. He thought it would be a good place to spend a few days. He wondered if Rebekah would like to go there with him. Then he thought about the week he had spent with Laura in Québec City. That had been a wonderful time and he had fallen totally in love with her. He was in love before they went. Was he in love with Rebekah now? He thought that he was.

The hotel gift shop had a large cooler full of flowers. He bought two bouquets and two vases – one for Rebekah and one for Rebekah's mother. He considered getting a bottle of wine but decided against it. Her mother may be just a tea drinker.

Now, thought Jake, *what does one wear to meet the mother of the woman with whom one is falling in love?* Jake decided on black dress shoes, with black socks, dress slacks and a baby blue dress shirt. He decided to top it off with a natural beige wool sweater that he had previously bought in Kirkwall.

At her mother's, Rebekah was trying to decide what to wear. She thought maybe some pants with a nice top. Her mother said, "No, you should wear a nice dress." She wore a blue dress that looked somewhat casual but fit her, as her mother said, "just right." Her long auburn hair cascaded over and around her shoulders.

While Rebekah was putting the finishing touches to her meal, her mom came into the kitchen and started talking.

She said, "You want to know if this man loves you or not, right?"

"Of course."

"Okay, I'm going to tell you how to tell. First, if he shows up in jeans and a sweatshirt, he does not love you. If he shows up in a suit, he is too insecure and will cause you problems. If he arrives wearing nice clothes, is clean shaven and has his hair combed, then he is in love with you."

"Oh, Mum, you can't tell by that. He may wear a suit to impress you."

"You mind what I say."

Jake drove up and got out of his rental. Inside, they heard

the car door slam. Jake walked up and used the knocker. Rebekah opened the door. Her mother was behind her. They saw Jake standing there holding two vases of flowers. Her mother whispered in her ear, "Perfection."

Rebekah turned to her mother and said, "Oh Mum." She turned back to Jake and said, "Come on in." As they exchanged pleasantries, Jake handed them each a vase. They both thanked him and asked him to sit.

Jake sat and looked about the room. It was a somewhat typical croft house from the 19th century. The room was cozy with candles burning on the mantle.

Jake said, "I really like this room. It is perfect."

Rebekah's mom, who had asked Jake to call her Wendy, replied, "This house was built, we think, sometime in the eighteen-eighties."

About this time, Ellie came in. She stared at Jake. Jake said, "Hi Ellie, I've heard about you and what a wonderful girl you are." Ellie wagged her tail and walked over to Jake. He reached down and petted her. She put her front paws up on his leg. He rubbed her head and she enjoyed the attention. He talked "baby dog talk" to her. Rebekah looked around the corner from the kitchen. She couldn't believe that Ellie was letting Jake pet her.

Getting back to Wendy, Jake asked, "Has this house been in your family all that time?"

"Yes, actually."

"I think that is so nice."

Wendy looked at Jake and pointed at his chest. She said, "Your sweater."

Jake looked down at his sweater.

"I recognize it as one that Mrs. Morrison made."

She turned and spoke to Rebekah. Rebekah appeared at the kitchen doorway. Her mother asked, "You remember Mrs. Morrison?"

Rebekah replied, "Of course."

Wendy turned back to Jake. "She makes some of the best

sweaters on the island. I'll have to tell her that Rebekah's fellow bought one of her sweaters."

Both Rebekah and Jake were surprised by the term "Rebekah's fellow." However, on second thought, they both liked it.

Rebekah said, "Everything's ready. Let's eat."

Wendy and Jake stood and went into the kitchen. Wendy turned to Jake and said, "Rebekah cooked this entire meal without any help from me. She wanted to."

In a little nook near the back door, a small wooden table was set for three. There was a candle burning in the center. Jake remembered that he had told Rebekah that he really liked candles. He didn't know if this was normal for them or if she had done this for him. Rebekah brought steaming bowls of vegetables and placed them on the table. Then, she took a roast from the oven, put it on a platter and brought it over to the table.

They had an extremely pleasant meal together. Everything was delicious and Jake complimented Rebekah on her cooking skills. He offered to help her clean up but she would not "hear of it." Instead, she wanted him to visit with her mum.

Sitting back in the living room, Wendy said, "Thank you again for the flowers. They are beautiful."

"You're welcome."

"Rebekah has told me about your recent travels. Photographing different sites for a book?"

"Yes."

"You don't sound sure."

"I'm not. I don't know if I'll actually go through with the book idea. I'm beginning to think the whole thing was just a way for me to escape from . . . I'm sorry, I don't know why I'm telling you this."

Wendy smiled. "It's all right," she said. "I've got more years 'going around the block' than you. I might be able to help."

Jake smiled and said, "That's nice of you. You see, I'm usually a fairly decisive . . . fellow." Jake paused and then continued, "I really do like your daughter. But . . ."

"No, I think it's more than 'like.'"

Jake didn't respond.

Wendy said, "I think your feelings for Rebekah are deeper than 'like.'"

Jake laughed, "What gave me away?"

"I can tell these things. It's a knack I have." She thought to herself, *it's so blatantly obvious that these two are in love with each other that a child could see it.*

Jake nodded as though he understood about her "knack."

Wendy leaned over and whispered, "Can I give you advice?"

"Sure, I wish you would."

"You're confused right now."

"Yes. And that is not like me. I normally . . ."

"You don't know what to do."

Jake nodded and quietly replied, "Yes."

Wendy leaned in even closer and whispered, "Follow your heart." Just as Rebekah returned, she sat back up in her chair.

Rebekah asked, "What are you two talking about?"

Her mom answered, "This and that."

"Oh, this and that. I know a little about this but not so much about that."

Jake laughed.

Wendy stood up and said, "I'm going to leave you two alone. I've got a book I want to finish." She started to leave but turned back and said, "Jake, come here for a moment."

Jake walked over and she led him into the kitchen.

She said, "For now, this is just between you and me. Before you leave here tonight, kiss that girl."

Jake looked surprised.

"Trust me." And Wendy winked.

Jake walked back in and sat down next to Rebekah.

Rebekah said, "I want you to forget and ignore whatever my Mum said to you."

"No, I don't think I'll do that. I know I won't."

Rebekah smiled her little coy smile. Jake had been

admiring that smile for several days now and he loved seeing it again.

"All right. I'm not even going to ask."

"Earlier, your mother gave me some advice."

Rebekah didn't say anything. She was almost afraid. She thought maybe her mum had told him to go back to America and forget her.

"She told me to follow my heart."

Rebekah still didn't respond.

"My heart is leading me to you."

In a soft voice, Rebekah said, "She told me the same thing and my heart is leading me to you."

Jake put his arm around Rebekah and, for at least a full minute, they kissed.

Jake said, "My heart isn't wrong."

Rebekah smiled and said, "Mine isn't wrong either."

They hugged.

Jake took her hands in his and said, "Rebekah, this has all happened so quickly. I would never have expected . . . things to develop this fast. I mean, we met on the eleventh and today is the nineteenth. That's only eight days and our hearts are talking with each other. It seems like we've been friends for a long time."

Rebekah nodded. Jake noticed her hair glistened as it reflected the candlelight from the mantel.

Still holding her hands, Jake said, "I want to ask you something."

Rebekah thought, *my goodness, is he going to ask me to marry him?*

"What I am wondering is this: would you truly pray about our relationship tonight? I'll do the same. I'll see you in church tomorrow morning. After church, we'll get some lunch in Kirkwall and then go to your spot by the ocean and talk."

Rebekah nodded and replied, "Yes." With her coy smile, she asked, "Just talk?"

"Well . . ."

Outside the door, as Jake was leaving, he and Rebekah

had another long kiss.

Jake said, "With kisses like that, you're going to make it difficult for me to pray tonight."

Rebekah laughed and slapped him on the arm. She said, "Goodnight."

As soon as she closed the door, her mother asked, "Did that boy kiss you?"

Rebekah was startled. She smiled and said, "Yes."

"Good. You do know he really loves you."

"How could you tell?"

"You're kidding? Did you see the way he was dressed? It couldn't have been any better."

"Oh, you and your clothes thing."

"Do you deny that he loves you?"

"He hasn't said that he does."

"Do you love him?"

"Mum, I've already told you I do."

"Have you told him?"

"No."

"All right then. Don't doubt me on this. I know that he is in love with you. And, I like him."

"Oh?"

"He brought me flowers, didn't he?"

The next day as Rebekah and Wendy pulled up to park at the church, they saw Jake standing outside talking with Victoria. Just then, Victoria's new boyfriend, Eric Morrison, walked up and joined them. Victoria introduced them. Jake shook hands with Eric. Victoria and Eric walked into the church. Rebekah and Wendy walked over to Jake and they entered the sanctuary together.

After church, Wendy drove back to her house and Rebekah joined Jake. They drove to a restaurant in Kirkwall. After lunch, they drove to Rebekah's favorite place in Orkney.

CHAPTER FORTY

"You are the light of the world."

– Matthew 5:14

Mid 1st Century A.D.

Sitting "leg to leg" in Jake's small rental car, as soon as they parked in front of the ocean, Jake turned to Rebekah and they kissed.

Jake said, "Now that's the way to begin a discussion."

Rebekah smiled and replied, "I agree."

"Did you have a chance to pray about us last night?"

"Yes."

"And?"

"I don't really feel any different today than I did before I prayed."

"Me too. I don't know what I was expecting. Maybe a sign in the sky that said, 'She's the one.'"

Laughing, she replied, "I know what you mean. That would be nice."

"I don't feel like I'm supposed to *not* see you anymore. I don't feel anything negative about . . . us. I only feel good things when I think of . . . us. I want to keep seeing you and being with you."

"Me too. I mean, I feel the same way about *us*."

"I've heard it said that God works in ways that are mysterious."

"I'm sure that's true."

"Rebekah, I guess one of the problems I am having is that this has all happened so quickly. I think I had feelings for you when I first saw you standing by that display case – before you even introduced yourself. By the way, I still love that introduction."

Rebekah smiled, "What you are describing is 'love at first sight.'"

"Exactly! I guess that is what bothers me a bit."

"It bothers you?"

"Perhaps bothers is not the right word. It seems almost too good to be true. I mean, this has all just happened . . . so fast. I mean, I will be forty-four next Thursday. I never expected to . . . fall in love again. Then, all of a sudden, out of nowhere, I meet you. . . . And, here we are."

"And here we are."

Rebekah looked directly out at the ocean. In a soft voice, she asked, "Jake, have you fallen in love with me?"

Jake reached up with his hand and turned Rebekah's face toward him. Looking in her eyes, he answered and said, "Yes. I never thought I would. But I feel real love for you. I . . ."

Rebekah leaned over and kissed Jake. They separated and she kissed him again. Then she said, "I love you Jake. I don't understand how it has happened so fast but I do believe it is real."

They hugged each other as best as they could while sitting in the front seat of the little car. They kissed deeply. Passion was overwhelming both of them.

They separated a little and looked at the ocean.

Jake said, "This really is a beautiful spot."

Rebekah laughed. "You're trying to change the subject."

"What's the subject?"

"Us."

"Right. I guess I should tell you about some of the baggage I carry around."

"You already told me about your marriage."

"That's not baggage. To me, it's like it never happened. I have no idea where she is living now, what she is doing now or whom she is with now. And, I don't care at all. I wish her well and hope that she is happy. But she is not a part of my life at all."

"Not baggage." Smiling, Rebekah asked, "So what is your

baggage?"

"Two years ago, I was completely in love with a woman to whom I was engaged. We had set our wedding date for October 2005. . . . in September, she was killed in a car crash."

Rebekah whispered, "How awful."

"Yes."

"You must have been . . ."

"Devastated. Yes. . . ."

"That's why . . . is that why you went on your worldwide trip?"

"Partly."

"To heal?"

"Yes. Some."

"Did it work?"

"Yes. Some."

"I see."

"Do you?"

"Yes, I think so. I understand."

"That is why I never expected to fall in love again. I just didn't think it would happen for me again. Then, I met you. Everything changed."

Rebekah whispered, "Love does that. It changes everything."

"Yes." Jake smiled at Rebekah.

"While we are exposing our baggage, I should tell you about mine." Jake didn't say anything. Rebekah continued, "I too was once engaged to be married. This was back right after I graduated from college. We dated for about a year before he asked me to marry him. He wasn't a Christian and kept pressuring me to have sex with him. I told him I wanted to wait until we were married. Anyway, I was living in Aberdeen then. I was teaching there. One day, out of the blue, I got a letter, a note really, from him. He said he had decided to move to London and had already done so. He said that he had decided that he didn't want to be with me anymore. I thought, after all the time we had spent together that a 'Dear John letter' was a cowardly way to break up with someone. My friends told me that I was lucky to have avoided marrying such a jerk. But, even though he was obviously a jerk, I didn't immediately stop loving him. I don't think you can turn love on and off like that. But it caused me, over the years, to distrust men in general. They often say one thing and do another."

"Sometimes. Politicians always do."

Rebekah smiled. "Like you, I neither know nor care where he is now or what he is doing. But the way he treated me has caused me to be apprehensive around men. I thought I would never have love for anyone again. I had reconciled myself to that." Using Jake's words, she added, "Then, I met you. Everything changed."

"Yes."

After a brief pause, Rebekah asked, "What was your fiancée's name?"

"Laura."

"Laura?"

"Yes."

"You are feeling guilty for falling in love with me?"

"Some."

"I understand."

"You do?"

"Yes, I think so."

"I don't. I mean, I totally loved Laura. But, she is . . . gone. There is no reason for me to feel guilty."

"Maybe not. But it's like I said earlier, emotions can't be turned on and off like a light switch."

"You're right about that."

Jake looked at Rebekah and said to her, "I do love you."

He kissed her and they hugged.

"Would you like to walk along the beach?"

"I'm wearing heels."

"I was just looking for an excuse to hold your hand."

Laughing, Rebekah said, "You don't ever need an excuse. Here."

For the next several hours, they sat together, hugged each other a lot and confirmed their love for each other. Just before they left to get some supper, Jake took Rebekah's hand again and asked her to pray with him. He asked God to bless them as a couple and be with them as they tried to figure out their future.

For the next week, they spent every day together. Rebekah took him all over the island. She informed him, that, according to her mother, they had become an "item" on the island. One morning, at sunrise, they met inside the Ring of Brodgar. They were alone and, as the sun rose in the sky, they kissed. They both felt the electricity of the Ring and it enhanced their kiss. They tightly hugged each other and felt the power of the Ring.

When Jake first saw Rebekah in the museum, she had a pair of glasses on her head. Since then, he had only seen them one other time. That time, they were also on her head. She had taken him all over the island and he had never actually seen her wearing her glasses. Jake was curious about how she looked with glasses. He thought that maybe she was self-conscious about her appearance with glasses. Jake thought she was beautiful and wearing glasses wouldn't change that at all. He decided not to bring it up and let her, in her own good time, wear her glasses in front of him.

Thursday, May 24th was Jake's 44th birthday. Rebekah gave him one of her paintings. It was of "their spot." She was now calling it "our" spot. Jake thought it was beautiful. He loved it.

Rebekah had to go back to her teaching job on Monday, May 28th. Jake knew he should probably return to the States. If not for Rebekah, he would have already done so. He did not want to leave Rebekah.

After church on the 27th, at "their" spot, Jake told Rebekah that he had been offered the job of Assistant Director of *The Library* with the promise that, when Mr. Sinclair retired, he would become the Director. Rebekah immediately felt the pain she had experienced when her fiancé had left her and moved to

London.

In an almost angry voice, she asked, "Are you going to take it?"

Ignoring her tone, Jake answered, "Not anytime soon. It was offered to me almost two years ago. I haven't decided. Honestly, I don't know what to do with the rest of my life. I don't want to leave you but I don't know if I can even stay here much longer. Most countries have some sort of limit on how long a tourist can stay as a tourist."

Rebekah was relieved by Jake's answer about *The Library*. However, she also knew that a tourist could not become a resident. She knew this conversation was inevitable but now that it was here, she did not like it.

"You have to go back to your school tomorrow."

"Yes, I know."

"I'm going to miss you. I already do. It's been so nice spending this week together with you."

"I agree. I do love you, Jake."

"I love you too."

They hugged.

Jake said, "I am thinking of going up to Shetland."

"Shetland? Whatever for?"

"To see the ponies?"

"Right."

"I am thinking that the trip might re-establish my credentials as a tourist. And, I am interested in seeing some of the attractions on the islands."

"How long would you be gone?"

"Until the weekend. I'll be back to see you on Saturday."

"I'll miss you."

They hugged and Jake whispered in her ear, "I will miss you very much. Save a kiss for me for when I get back."

"Will do."

On Monday, Rebekah went back to her classroom and Jake caught a flight from Orkney to Shetland. Jake had considered taking a ferry, just for the experience, but that trip took between 12 and 14 hours. The flight from Kirkwall to Sunburgh airport, at the southern tip of the island, south of Lerwick, the capital of the Shetland Islands, was usually less than an hour.

At the airport, Jake rented a car (they called it a car hire) and drove to a hotel in Lerwick, checked in and stored his luggage. He then went out and began a walking tour of the town.

Jake walked down to the old waterfront. The variety of boats was amazing. He took photos of warehouses (lodberries) that were built in the 1700s and whose foundations are still in the ocean. Most of the buildings along the waterfront, Jake learned, dated back to the 1700s. The French had burned the town in 1702. That obviously destroyed most of the structures and consequently, what was built after that is what remains. From the lodberries, Jake walked north on Commercial Street to the Shetland Museum and Archives. It was a modern building right on the water. As someone always interested in history, Jake found the museum to be fascinating. While there, he got the same impression that he had first perceived on the Outer Banks two years previously. People seemed to look at him suspiciously because he was by himself. In fact, an attractive employee of the museum approached Jake and asked if she could help him find anything specific. Jake knew that the last time an attractive woman approached him in a museum he had fallen in love with her. The museum also had an art gallery. Jake looked for any of Rebekah's paintings but didn't see any. He found out later that there were prints of some of her paintings in the gift shop.

Jake got some lunch at a downtown Lerwick cafe. In his rental, he drove to Fort Charlotte. It had really strong-looking walls that were built, beginning in 1665, to protect the Sound of Bressay from the Dutch. According to a sign, it was rebuilt during "The War of American Independence." About a mile from Fort Charlotte was an ancient site called Clickimin Broch. It was a round stone structure dating to 1,000 B. C. The broch tower was impressive and Jake got some good shots of it. Jake drove from there about seven miles to Scalloway Castle. The castle is in ruins but Jake thought it was still worth seeing. It was built in the very late 1500s and is still three stories high. It was built by the Earl of Orkney and Shetland, Patrick Stewart. He was apparently extremely cruel to his tenants. However, that didn't cause his downfall. That happened because he crossed some of his fellow earls and lords. He was executed in 1615. Jake found these tidbits of historical information interesting. He took a photograph of an inscription on a panel over the primary door of the castle. It read, "Patrick Stewart Earl of Orkney and Shetland. That house whose foundation is on a rock will stand but if on sand it will fall. AD 1600." Jake recognized that this was a direct reference to the words of Jesus in the 7th chapter of Matthew.

Jake drove back to his hotel. On the way, while admiring the scenery, he thanked Jesus for being with him. He knew, that no matter where he went, from South America to India, from Egypt to America and from America to Shetland, Jesus would always be with him. It was an extremely comforting feeling for Jake. He looked at the empty car seat and wished that Rebekah were with him. He missed her.

That evening, he called Rebekah and they talked for about an hour. She told him about her students and he told her about the things he had seen. They ended the phone conversation by telling each other that they loved each other.

When they had finished their call, Jake said out loud in his hotel room, "I do love her." He seemed surprised. However, the realization swept over him and he knew that it was true. He had been questioning himself, because it had all happened so quickly. Now, for some reason, he knew that he really was in love with Rebekah. He just knew it! He thanked God for revealing it to him once and for all.

In the back of his mind, Jake had been thinking that the easiest thing for him to do was to tell Rebekah that he just couldn't see any way that their relationship could work. He had to return to America. She was teaching in Scotland. It would be best if they just said goodbye to each other and got on with their lives. Now, that thought was gone for good. Jake knew that being in love with Rebekah, as he was, meant that they should be together for the rest of their lives. It was a wonderful feeling. He again thanked God and asked God to provide an answer to the problem of an ocean that separated he and Rebekah.

The next morning, still walking in Lerwick, Jake visited the Lerwick Town Hall. It was a huge old building with turrets. However, the stained-glass windows were the main attraction. From there, Jake went to the Shetland Library. It looked like a church. Jake loved libraries and this one was no exception. He enjoyed the look and smell of this library.

Jake, of course, thought of *The Library*. He thought of Mr. Le Couteau, Mr. Sinclair, Peggy, the "old gentlemen" and the pub where he and Laura had sat so often. That led him to think of Québec City and the week he had spent with Laura. For the first time, Jake realized that those memories were pleasant rather than sad. They were of another time when he had been happy and in love. They were good memories. He said, "Thank you, Jesus."

Once a year, Shetland held a weird, unusual and unique Fire Festival called Up Helly Aa. There was a permanent exhibition at the Heritage Centre. Jake walked over and took a look at that. Many of the men marched in a parade wearing long fake beards, pointed hats and carrying torches. It was weird. *But probably fun*, thought Jake.

After lunch, Jake drove down to the Sumburgh Head Lighthouse which also included a visitor's center and nature reserve. It was right on the ocean in a beautiful setting. Jake spent several hours there and took plenty of photographs.

Jake ate supper at the hotel. Back in his room, he watched a local news broadcast and plotted out the places he wanted to visit on Wednesday and the rest of the week. He planned to visit Jarlshof, first settled almost 3,000 years ago and in use until the 1600s. He wanted to see the Fair Isle Bird Observatory and the Waterston Memorial Centre and Museum, also on Fair Isle. He had planned to visit Unst but decided to skip it. He wanted to go to the Bronze Age Bressay site and the Iron Age Broch and

Village at Old Scatness. He definitely had the huge Iron Age Mousa Broch on his schedule. Jake thought he would like to see the Quendale Water Mill and Britain's northernmost castle – Muness Castle.

Jake called Rebekah again that evening. They talked for an hour and a half. He truly enjoyed his conversation with her. Again, they closed their talk by saying, "I love you" to each other.

Jake looked at his list of all the places he wanted to see. He thought of Rebekah. He picked up the phone and bought a ticket back to Orkney for the following day. He had to pay extra because the ticket he had already purchased was for Friday.

On Wednesday morning, May 30th, Jake checked out of his hotel. He had an afternoon flight. He drove his rental to a jewelry store he had seen advertised as carrying locally made jewelry. He found a necklace that was inspired by the Shetland seascape. He thought it looked somewhat like their spot. It wasn't large and Jake thought it would look good with Rebekah's long auburn hair. He had it gift-wrapped and then he placed it in his luggage. Jake ate a nice lunch at a small local restaurant and drove back to the airport. He turned his car for hire in and waited for his flight to board.

An hour later, Jake was back in Kirkwall. He got another rental and went back to the same hotel where he had previously been. They recognized him and welcomed him back.

Jake waited until he was pretty sure Rebekah would be home from school and drove over to her house. He knocked on the door. She looked out the window but didn't recognize the rental car. When she opened the door, Jake smiled at her. She rushed into his arms and gave him a tight hug.

Rebekah stepped back and said, "What are you doing here?"

Jake thought of saying, *they kicked me out*. Instead, he told the truth and said, "I missed you."

Rebekah gave him another hug.

Jake asked, "Have you eaten?"

"No, we were just about to begin."

"Can you come with me? I'd love to talk with you."

"Sure. Let me get a jacket."

Wendy had come to the door. "Hello Jake."

"Hi. I'm sorry about this but I'd really like to talk with Rebekah."

"Don't apologize. No need. I'm not surprised to see you. You know I have a knack about these things."

Rebekah came by just as her mother had told Jake about her knack again. Rebekah said, "Oh, Mum. You and your knack. Bye."

In a nice restaurant in Kirkwall, after they had ordered, Jake gave Rebekah the small gift-wrapped box. She thought, *surely he hasn't bought me a ring*. When she opened it and looked at the necklace, she whispered, "It's beautiful." She put it on and said, "Perhaps I'm not dressed to be wearing this now but I do like it. Thank you."

Jake smiled. "You are welcome."

"What's the occasion?"

"Not one. I just wanted to bring something back to you from Shetland."

Rebekah smiled.

CHAPTER FORTY-ONE

"Do everything without complaining or arguing, so that you may become blameless and pure, children of God without fault in a crooked and depraved generation, in which you shine like stars in the universe ..."

– Philippians 2:14-15

Mid 1st Century A.D.

After the waitress brought their orders, Rebekah said, "So, what did you want to talk about?"

"You."

"Me?"

"Yes, you. You are causing me all kinds of problems."

Rebekah didn't know whether he was teasing or whether he was serious.

She smiled at him with her coy smile that he loved so much and asked, "How?"

"Just by being you."

"I don't . . ."

"There I was – touring the Shetland Islands. I was visiting ancient sites, castles and seeing beautiful landscapes – and all I could think of was you. I was wishing you were with me. I was missing you so much. It got so bad, I had to give up on my visit and come see you."

Rebekah smiled.

"Ahh, so you think it's funny. I'll have you know, young lady, I had an entire itinerary all scheduled out for Wednesday and Thursday. Because of you, I had to give it all up and return here."

Softly, Rebekah said, "I'm sorry."

"No you're not. I see that smile. And you know what? I'm not sorry either. While I was up there, after I talked with you yesterday, I realized that I am truly in love with you. When we finished talking, we both said, 'I love you' to each other."

"I meant it."

"Me too. But God revealed something to me then. He showed me that I was absolutely, for real, without any hesitation, in love with you. When two people are in love with each other...they belong together. Rebekah, I don't understand how this has happened so fast, but it is, I am convinced, real."

"Yes, it is."

"When I don't understand something, I try to put my trust in Jesus and let him handle things. He is first in my life and, I believe, first in your life also."

"Yes."

"Rebekah, I don't understand how this will work out but Jesus does. If you will have me, I'd like for you to be my wife. Will you marry me?"

With her coy smile, Rebekah answered with a soft "Yes."

Jake took her hand in his and said, "I will always love you."

Tears started rolling down Rebekah's face. Jake was surprised by that. He was happy she had said yes. She was crying. He gave her his napkin and she blotted it on her face.

The waitress came over. She saw Rebekah crying and asked, "Is anything wrong?"

Rebekah shook her head.

Jake said, "We just became engaged. She started crying."

To Rebekah, the waitress said, "Congratulations."

Rebekah nodded. Jake said, "She just suddenly started crying."

The waitress turned from Jake and asked, "Would you like me to take you to the ladies room to freshen up some?"

"No. . . . No, I'm all right."

As she left, the waitress turned to Jake, "You men are so

silly. You don't understand anything."

Jake ignored her and asked Rebekah, "Are you okay? What's wrong? I thought we just got . . ."

"Nothing's wrong." Rebekah had stopped crying. "Have you never heard of 'tears of joy?'"

"Sure."

"That's what you just saw."

Jake smiled. "Okay. I'm with you now."

The manager came out with a bottle of wine. He knew Rebekah. He said, "Rebekah, I just heard about your engagement. I want you two to share this."

Rebekah nodded.

Jake said, "Thank you."

The manager opened the bottle and poured them each a glass of wine. This was different than the procedure in the States where the man was given a taste prior to pouring the wine – but, Jake thought, *this was a gift not a purchase.*

They both sipped the wine and smiled. It was good.

"I wish you both the best," the manager said.

"Thank you," Jake replied.

He turned to Rebekah. "I certainly didn't mean to upset you. I had planned to ask you at your spot but . . ."

"Our spot."

"Our spot. But I couldn't wait. I love you."

"The waitress was right. I'm not upset you silly man. I am simply so happy . . . that the man I love . . . wants to spend the rest of our lives together."

"Rebekah, I've been thinking about this all day. I was hoping you would say yes. You have only had a few minutes to think about it so . . ."

"You silly man. I've . . ."

Smiling, Jake said, "If you keep calling me that, I'm going to begin to take offense."

Rebekah smiled. "None intended. It's not personal. All men can be silly at times. You said I've only had a few minutes to think about us getting engaged. I've been thinking about this since we had that breakfast at the museum."

Jake didn't know what to say so he said, "I love you."

Rebekah smiled and said, "I love you."

"I've checked the flights and we could fly down to Aberdeen and back on Saturday."

"We could. Why?"

"You silly woman. To get you an engagement ring."

Rebekah's face lit up in a happy smile. She nodded at Jake.

"I'll get the tickets tomorrow."

They ate a little of their cold meal and drank some of the wine. They both were smiling and both were happy. Neither knew how it was going to work out but they were both leaving it up to Jesus.

After they finished eating, they drove over to their spot. They sat on the bench and watched the waves come to shore. They snuggled and kissed and hugged and held hands and realized that they were actually engaged to be married.

On Saturday, June 2nd, Rebekah and Jake were sitting next to each other on a flight to Aberdeen. It was a fairly short trip.

Rebekah was looking out the window and Jake asked, "You used to live in Aberdeen, didn't you?"

"Yes. I taught there for several years."

"From what I've read, it sounds like a neat city with a lot of history."

"Yes, it's quite historical but also a very modern city." She took a magazine out of the pocket on the back of the seat in front of them, lowered her glasses, found what she was looking for and showed Jake a photo of a modern mall with glass, neon and chrome.

"I prefer candles and wood."

"I know what you mean."

"Look at me."

Rebekah turned her head and faced Jake. She asked, "What?"

"I just wanted to see you with your glasses on."

Rebekah gave Jake her coy smile and said, "What's the verdict?"

"Sexy."

Rebekah pushed Jake's arm. But she was pleased with his assessment and verdict.

"You know, I thought your mother wanted to come with us."

"She probably did."

"Should we ha . . ?"

"No. No, absolutely not. She means well . . . and I love her completely."

"She does have a certain knack."

"She likes to think she really does. That all started as a joke years ago. But now, I'm beginning to think she really believes it."

"I like your mom."

"I'm glad. She's a genuine person. Very nice."

"Your sister lives in Edinburgh, doesn't she?"

"Yes, with her husband and my nephew and niece."

"Edinburgh isn't far from Aberdeen, is it?"

"Not too far. They aren't real close. They are both on the east coast. Edinburgh is south of Aberdeen."

Rebekah reached over and took Jake's hand in hers. In response, he squeezed hers. It made him think of Laura. After their first time together in the small museum restaurant, Jake had told himself that he was definitely not going to compare Rebekah with Laura. He loved Rebekah. He was going to marry Rebekah. He did not want to think about the time he and Laura had gone shopping for an engagement ring in Québec City, Canada. Now, he was doing the same thing with Rebekah in Aberdeen, Scotland. He was determined not to make comparisons.

Jake looked over at Rebekah. He said, "You know what?"

"What?"

"I really like you."

Rebekah looked confused. She said, "I'm glad."

"No, listen. Some guys love their wives but they don't really like them. I like your personality. I like your female perspective on things. I like your kindness. I like being with you. I like talking with you. I like the way you look. I like you. Even if we weren't getting married, I would like you. Even if I didn't love you, I would like you."

"Okay, I understand now."

"It's like I have two sisters. I love them both but I like one of them better than the other."

Rebekah squeezed his hand.

After the plane landed, they got a taxi to Union Square. It was next to the railway station and had almost a hundred different stores.

Jake had told Rebekah to select a ring that she truly liked. He told her not to be concerned over the cost. He wanted her to have a ring that she would enjoy wearing for the rest of her life.

They went to two jewelry stores and Rebekah couldn't find a ring that she wanted. She suggested they go to Union Street. She told Jake that, when she lived in Aberdeen, the locals called it the "Granite Mile." She told him he would see why when they got there. He did. Most of the buildings were built of granite and were well over a hundred years old.

Rebekah said, "When I see my ring, I'll know it."

Jake smiled. He replied, "I completely understand that. That's what I want you to do – wait until you see it."

They went into a jewelry store that seemed to Jake as if he had stepped into the past. It had well-worn wooden floors, wooden walls and a wooden ceiling. He loved it. Rebekah looked at numerous rings but didn't see "the" ring. Jake looked over and saw her talking with a man who appeared to be in his eighties. He left and came back with a box. Jake walked over and joined them. The old man opened the box and the rings sparkled.

Rebekah said, "That one." She pointed at a specific ring. The man handed it to her and she put it on her ring finger. It almost fit but not quite. She turned it over and looked at it from many different angles. She handed it to Jake. He turned it around and noticed how it sparkled. It was clear and about one and one-fourth carets in size. Jake looked at it through the jeweler's magnifying glass and could not find any blemishes.

To Rebekah he asked, "Is this the one you want?"

Rebekah nodded and answered, "Yes."

"Okay." He turned to the man and said, "We'll take this one. Can you re-size the band today?"

He measured Rebekah's finger and answered by saying it would only take about an hour. Jake paid for the ring and joined Rebekah as she was looking out the front door.

She pointed across the street.

"There's a restaurant."

"Good idea. That should take an hour."

They walked across the street.

Sitting at their table, Rebekah asked, "Have you had any haggis yet?"

Jake laughed and said, "No. And . . . I don't plan to have any soon. Have you had it?"

"Once."

"There ya go. I imagine most people only have it once."

"Actually, some people like it and have it over and over."

"If you say so. To each his own. I think I'll have fish and chips."

Moving her glasses back down and looking at the menu, Rebekah said, "That's pretty safe."

"That's why I'm having it. Did you like living here in Aberdeen?"

"Yes, it was nice. I had a small apartment. I enjoyed teaching. Of course, I was in my early twenties then. I used to enjoy sitting on the harbor wall while watching all the marine activity. There were two friends of mine who used to join me. We got kidded about three girls sitting on the wall watching the men in the harbor. I actually enjoyed watching the marine life. I've stayed in contact with one of those friends. I'd like her to be in our wedding. That all seems like such a long time ago."

"When I first saw you in the museum, I thought you were

about thirty years old."

Rebekah smiled.

They enjoyed their lunch and returned to the jewelry store. Rebekah's ring was ready. She tried it on and it fit perfectly. Jake asked for the ring to be gift-wrapped. He took it and put it in his pocket. They caught a taxi back to the airport. They had to wait a couple of hours for their flight.

By the time they got back to Kirkwall, it was starting to become dark. Jake took Rebekah to the same restaurant where he had proposed. They had the same waitress. After they ordered, Jake said, "Rebekah West, I love you and want to spend the rest of my life with you. I have something for you."

Jake handed her the small gift box. She smiled and opened it. There was her engagement ring sparkling in the ring box. She turned to Jake and said, "You put it on my finger."

"With pleasure."

Jake slipped it on Rebekah's ring finger and it sparkled as it reflected the candlelight from the candle on their table.

When the waitress returned, Rebekah showed her the ring. The waitress made a fuss over it. After she returned to the kitchen, Rebekah said to Jake, "That's what women do."

The manager came out with another bottle of wine. He said, "Rebekah, let me see this ring."

Rebeka showed him the ring as it glistened on her finger. He said, "That's really nice, Rebekah. Now that you two have made it official, I want you to have this celebration wine."

Jake and Rebekah thanked him.

The next morning was Sunday, June 3rd. Jake met Rebekah and Wendy in front of the church. Several of Rebekah's friends, neighbors and members of the congregation had already heard that she had an engagement ring. The women all wanted to see it.

After church, Rebekah went to her car and exchanged her heels from a pair of comfortable walking shoes. She and Jake then went to a fast-food place, got some take-out (grab and go) and drove to "their" spot. They walked down to "their" bench and ate lunch.

After watching the waves and enjoying the breeze, Jake said, "I guess it's time we addressed the elephant in the room."

"What elephant? I don't see no stinkin' elephant."

Shaking his head and grinning, Jake responded, "Waaay waaay too much American television."

Rebekah smiled and said, "Actually, I like elephants."

"Me too . . . but not this one."

Seriously, Rebekah replied, "Obviously, I've been thinking about this ever since I fell in love with you. I didn't know if you felt the same about me. My mum told me that you did. I was hoping you did and I was hoping you would ask me to marry you. So, I have given this a lot of thought and have prayed about it."

"And?"

"And I've decided that I will go wherever you want to go. I . . ."

"But that's . . ."

"No, let me finish. I want to be with you. I will live wherever you want to live. As long as we are together, that is the main thing. You said that when two people love each other, they should be together. I love you. Wherever you want to live, I will go. I want to be your wife. For me, a wife supports her husband. I will always support you. You decide where we should live and I'll be happy with wherever it is."

"That is so sweet. It's no wonder I love you. I do appreciate you saying that."

"It's the way I feel."

Jake smiled. He said, "That's wonderful. But there are many factors to consider."

"I know."

"I think of marriage as a partnership. I think we should make important decisions together."

"I agree. However, I believe it is Biblical for the husband to be the predominate partner in that partnership. The husband should have the final . . . say. So, whatever you say, I will follow."

"I love you."

"I know. That is why I believe it is best for me to follow the Bible's instructions. Because you love me, I know that you will take care of me, protect me, support me and do what is in my best interests."

"A husband is to love his wife as Jesus loves those who believe in Him."

"Exactly." Rebekah smiled her coy smile.

Jake leaned over and kissed her.

"All right. However, as partners, we should both be involved in the process of making decisions. We've known each other for less than a month. I don't know, for example, if you would like to continue teaching or not."

Rebekah looked surprised. She said, "I haven't even thought about that."

"I don't know what would be involved in me becoming a citizen of Scotland. I have absolutely nothing in the world against Scotland but I'm not sure I want to live here for the rest of my life. I don't know what's involved with you becoming an American citizen or whether you would want to live in the States."

"How are you able to afford to travel all over the world? Did you inherit a fortune?"

"Gracious no. I grew up in a middle-class home. The last job I had in New York City proved to be . . . extremely profitable for me. I made really good commissions which I used to make really good investments. I bought a condo which I sold for several times what I paid for it. We could live off the interest and income from that money and never have to work again."

"Is that what you want to do?"

"No, I think I'd like to be working."

"What is it that you want to do?"

"That's the problem. I don't know. I know several jobs that I don't want to do. I've told you about the job offer with *The*

Library. That won't stay open for me forever. Mr. Sinclair is around seventy-eight. He wants someone to take over for him. He seems to think that I am to be that someone."

"Do you want to?"

"I don't know. And that bothers me. I am usually somewhat decisive. However, with this, I can't seem to decide one way or the other. I've prayed about it but it's not clear to me."

"What were you going to do when you had planned to marry Laura?"

"I didn't know then either. We had talked about getting a few acres, having a garden, raising some chickens and being a part of the community. I still like that idea."

"Was Laura planning on continuing to teach?"

"She wasn't sure. We thought we might have children and she didn't want to teach if that happened."

Rebekah paused and said, "Do you still want to have children?"

"If you do, yes."

"I would love to have children. Well, maybe two at the most."

"Yes, two would be plenty."

Still sitting on the bench, they kissed again.

Rebekah looked out at the ocean. She asked, "Jake, can I ask you a real personal question?"

"Yes, of course."

"If it makes you uncomfortable, you don't have to answer."

"You're to be my wife. I want us to always be open and honest with each other. What is your question?"

Still looking out at the ocean, Rebekah asked, "Did you and Laura ever have . . . make love?"

Jake smiled. "No, we never did. We decided to wait until our wedding night. We thought about it though." Jake laughed.

"Have you thought about it with me?"

"Often."

"Often?"

"Since the first day I met you."

In a playful gesture, Rebekah pushed Jake.

"Jake, when I was engaged, I didn't have sex either. I wanted to wait until we were married."

"I understand. I believe that is the way it should be. I think it means more if a couple waits until they are married."

Rebekah said, "Today, nearly all engaged couples have sex before the wedding."

Jake didn't know where this was headed. He said, "Yes, I've read that somewhere."

"In fact, I read that today most people, including high school age teens, are having sex on their second or third date. Some on the first date. They haven't even thought of getting engaged."

Jake responded, "Yes, I suppose that is true. I guess only real Christians are waiting. And many young people are not real Christians. I wasn't."

"Did you and your ex-wife have sex before you were married?"

"Yes. Actually, we had more sex before we were married than after we were married. At the time, I was what has been described as a 'Sunday Christian.' I believed Jesus was who He said He was but I was not living the life of a Christian. I mean, I wasn't doing anything mean – but I wasn't following Jesus on a daily basis as a part of my life. That happened after the divorce."

"You may be disappointed with me."

"What do you mean?"

"I never . . . I haven't ever had sex."

"Please don't be concerned over that. I don't want to sound sexist but I think that sex comes more naturally to women than men."

"I don't know."

"Rebekah, we're far from being teenagers. Please don't worry about that. Love will overcome any . . . apprehension. Let me tell you a story. Back in the *Middle Ages*, there was a Prince who married a beautiful woman. In those days, it was expected that every woman was a virgin until her wedding day. As the Prince and his bride made love on their wedding night, he was surprised by how . . . loving his new wife was. Later, in the middle of the night, she woke him up and wanted to make love again. Then, just before sunrise, she woke him again to make love. Although the Prince very much enjoyed his wedding night, he thought that his bride could not have been a virgin. She was just too good at making love. He went to his wife's mother to complain and accused his wife, in front of her mother, of not being a virgin. He explained that she was simply too good and too eager to be a virgin. The mother took the Prince over to a shed where baby ducks had just hatched out of their eggs. The mother took several of the hatchlings into her hands and carried them down to a pond. As she started to put them in the water, the Prince said, 'Stop, they are only babies – they will drown.' His new wife's mother put them in the water and they immediately began to swim around. They even seemed to enjoy being in the water. The mother turned to the Prince and said, 'Some things come naturally.' The Prince and his wife enjoyed a long happy marriage together."

Rebekah smiled. "That's a cute story."

"Our wedding night should be the least of your worries. I love you. I promise you I will never do anything to hurt you. We will let Mother Nature guide us."

Rebekah gave Jake her coy smile. "Don't misunderstand, I am not afraid. I am truly looking forward to our wedding night. I just don't want to disappoint you."

"I don't think that that is possible. Later, let's get back to our decision of where we are going to live. For now, let's set a date for our wedding."

"I've been thinking about that."

"After our most recent talk, how about tomorrow?"

Rebekah playfully pushed Jake again and laughed.

Rebekah asked, "You want to do it as soon as possible or do you want a long engagement?"

"As soon as possible."

"Me too. I think July would be too early. It wouldn't give me enough time to get everything ready. So, I was thinking of early August. Now, you may not understand this, but my family has been living on Orkney for well over two hundred years. If I don't invite just about everyone on the island, feelings will be hurt. So, what I was thinking is this – we could have our wedding right after a Sunday service and invite everyone to stay for the wedding. What do you think?"

"I'm good with that. What about lunch or the reception?"

"I've thought of that. We could have the ceremony at 12:30 p.m. The reception could be outside or, if it's raining, inside the church's fellowship hall. And, we would have to leave earlier than normal – normal wedding receptions can last for hours and hours here in the Orkneys – because of our flight to go on our honeymoon."

"Works for me."

"Looking at a calendar, I am thinking of Sunday, August 5th."

"Sounds good. Reserve the church."

Rebekah smiled. "I will."

"One thing."

"Yes?"

"During the wedding service, you may need to poke me."

"Poke you?"

"Yes. I can't begin to understand what your minister is saying. When it's time for me to say, 'I do,' poke me."

"If necessary, I most certainly will."

"Speaking of honeymoons, you've got me excited about ours."

Rebekah pushed him again.

"What I was saying, do you have a preference for where you would like to go on our honeymoon?"

"I have been thinking about this."

"And?"

"And, my preference is for somewhere warm. I'd like to

go to an ocean where the water is warm enough to swim."

"We can definitely do that."

"You pick the exact place and surprise me."

"All right. Consider it done. Is your passport in order?"

"Yes."

"What do I need to do to help with the wedding?"

"Just give me a list of people you'd like to invite."

"That will be a short list. My parents, my sisters – they probably won't come – and a few friends that won't come but will want to be invited. My friend Ted, that I've told you about, he and his wife will come. That's about it."

"I'll need names and addresses."

Jake smiled. He stood up, took Rebekah's hand and pulled her to the surf. He said, "Let's try out those walking shoes." Holding hands, they walked along the beach just at the edge of the surf.

Back at his hotel, Jake read up on the island of Rousay. It was just two miles north of their island of Mainland. Jake read that there were about 70 islands in the Orkneys. Many of them had several archaeological sites. Rousay was a small island but had so many archaeological sites that it is known as the "Egypt of the North." There are over 160 such sites on this small island. On the island is the Westness Heritage Walk. It is a mile long path along the coast that presents ruins of *Stone Age* people from approximately 5,500 years ago. From those people, the path presents *Iron Age* sites, Viking ruins, the time of the Earls and the crofting clearances. Jake thought it sounded like an amazing place and wanted to visit. It was an easy day trip. He thought he could go one day during the week while Rebekah was in school.

Tuesday night, after Rebekah got home, Jake called her. He told he had been looking at all the things on Rousay.

"Yes, it is fascinating that people wanted to live on these islands so long ago."

"I was thinking of a day trip."

"Why don't we go on Saturday? I've been there dozens of times and can give you a professional tour."

Jake responded, "That would be great."

After they finished talking, Jake realized that, from now on, he was going to need to include his fiancée and later, his wife, in all his activities. Rebekah, he now knew, would have been hurt if he had gone alone to Rousay. He did not want to hurt the woman he loved. Over the past year and a half, he had gotten used to just picking up and going where he wanted, whenever he wanted. He had gotten used to traveling alone and the stares that that sometimes generated. It would be much more pleasant to have Rebekah with him.

He spent the rest of the week emailing his family and friends. He told them all about Rebekah and gave them the date of August 5th. Jake asked Ted to be his best man. He wrote Peggy and told her about his engagement and wedding plans. That was difficult for him to do. He didn't know how she would respond to the news that he was getting married. He asked her to tell Mr. Le Couteau and Mr. Sinclair. He figured she would anyway but he wanted to give her permission to tell them.

On Saturday, June 9th, Rebekah and Jake caught the ferry over to Rousay. While leaning over the rail, looking at the view, Jake said, "Just think, in less than two months, we'll be married." Rebekah looked surprised. She replied, "That's not long. I've got so much to do. I don't know if . . ." Squeezing her hand, Jake interrupted and said, "You'll do fine. Everything will work out as it should. You'll see. I believe that God is going to bless our marriage." He kissed her on the cheek and said, "I love you."

After getting off the ferry, they walked everywhere they went. They visited the Midhowe Cairn, the Midhowe Broch, the Brough Farm, the Wirk and St. Mary's Church – all part of the Westness Heritage Walk. Then they visited the Knowe of Swandro, the Westness Farm and a Viking site. The island was a beautiful green with small hills.

On the short ferry ride back, Jake asked Rebekah if she,

as a West, was related to the Westness people. She replied that they were but that her people had dropped the "ness" back in the 1800s.

Back on Mainland, Jake took Rebekah to their "wine" restaurant in Kirkwall and they enjoyed a nice dinner.

Rebekah said, "Jake, we barely scratched the surface of all the sites worth seeing on Rousay. We better save those for another time."

"Okay."

"I gave notice yesterday."

"You did?"

"Yes, I told them I would not be back next term. They seemed to expect it. Everyone on the island knows that we are engaged."

Jake smiled, "I see."

"No secrets here."

"I'm sure that's true."

"You seem a little different tonight. Is anything wrong?"

Jake smiled, "You know me better than I would have thought you could."

"It's been over a whole month since I first saw you," Rebekah said with a smile.

"Oh. Well then. I guess that explains it."

"So, what's wrong?"

Jake paused. He looked down at his plate and then back up directly at Rebekah. He said, "I guess it's . . . I guess I need to get back to the States and take care of things. I've been away for some time now."

"I understand."

"But I don't want to leave you."

Rebekah smiled. "We'll have the rest of our lives together."

"I know. But I'm just going to miss you so much."

"Me too."

The next day was June 10th. After church, they got a "grab

and go" lunch and drove out to their spot. Jake reached behind the front seat and brought up a vase of red roses.

As he gave them to Rebekah, he said, "To celebrate one month together. I met you in the museum on May 11th. Tomorrow will be one full month."

"That's true but I saw you on May 8th. You were in the Ring. So I've known you longer than you've known me."

She smelled the flowers and said, "Thank you." Still in the confines of the little car, she tried to give Jake a hug. "Thank you, this is so sweet of you. You know, I kept thinking I was smelling roses but didn't know where it could be coming from at all."

"I wanted to celebrate our one-month anniversary."

Rebekah responded, "You know what? I really truly do love you."

They walked over to their bench and, as they watched the tide come in, ate their lunch.

Finished with lunch, they sat together with Jake's arm around Rebekah as she snuggled in close with him. As they watched the ocean, Jake said, "This is truly nice."

"Ummm-huh," Rebekah replied.

They sat snug against each other and just enjoyed being together. It was a beautiful place. Jake was already missing it and, even though he had her tight against him, he was missing Rebekah. Suddenly, he had a horrible thought. What if Rebekah was killed in a car wreck before they got married? He said a quick prayer and asked God to watch over her and protect her.

"What are you thinking about?" Rebekah was wearing her coy smile that Jake loved.

He replied, "You. The future. Us."

"Are you worried?"

"No, I'm upset with myself for not being able to figure out what I should do with the rest of my life."

"Let's take it a day at a time. That's what my mum always says when things look bleak or undecided."

"Wendy is a smart lady."

"I think so. But don't forget her "knack.""

Jake smiled. He said, "We're getting married in two months. We've got to live somewhere."

"It will work out. God will lead us to where He wants us to go."

Jake nodded in agreement. He looked at Rebekah and said, "I love you."

"I love you too."

They kissed, got up and, holding hands, walked along the shore.

CHAPTER FORTY-TWO

". . . *clothe yourselves with compassion, kindness, humility, gentleness and patience. Bear with each other and forgive whatever grievances you may have against one another. Forgive as the Lord forgave you. And over all these virtues put on love, which binds them all together in perfect unity. Let the peace of Christ rule in your hearts.*"

– Colossians 3:12 - 15

Mid 1st Century A.D.

On Monday, June 11, 2007, Rebekah returned to her classroom and Jake flew to London. The next day, he flew from London to Atlanta. From Atlanta, he caught a short flight to Charlotte. Jake spent the night in Charlotte. From there, he called Rebekah and they talked for about half an hour. The time difference was not favorable, but she said she didn't mind.

The next morning, Jake got a rental and drove to his parents' home. Jake had called them the night before and "warned" them that he would be there the next day. Both his parents were in their early seventies but, as far as Jake knew, in pretty good health. They both greeted him with hugs. His mom was extremely excited about his engagement to Rebekah. They brought him up-to-date with all the latest neighborhood, church and family news. The worst news, his mom stated, was that his sister, Lucy, was going through a divorce. Jake reflected on his divorce and knew, from personal experience, that divorces were never pleasant. However, depending upon the reasons, it may not be bad news at all. Lucy may be much happier after the divorce. He didn't know any details.

Sitting in the living room, Jake's dad asked, "So, tell us

about Rebekah."

Jake smiled. He replied, "Dad, she's beautiful."

His mom asked, "How old is she?"

"She just turned thirty-eight."

His mom smiled. She was thinking of more grandchildren.

Jake continued, "She's very smart. She's a Christian. She's kind. She teaches school."

His mom wondered, "Does she have any children?"

"She's never been married."

His dad and mom looked at each other.

Jake said, "I told you, she's a Christian. She doesn't have any children."

His mom asked, "Where are you going to live?"

"I don't know yet."

His dad asked, "Where are you going to work? That will determine where you live."

"I know. But the only job offer I have is with *The Library*."

His mom replied, "That place up in Maine?"

"Yes. But I don't think I want to take it. At least, not now."

His dad said, "Son, you may not have noticed but you aren't getting any younger. You . . ."

"I've noticed."

"I'm just saying . . . it's probably time for you to settle in one place, make a home for your wife and any children you may be blessed with. Become a part of the community."

"I know."

"That all takes time."

"I know. I just don't know what I want to do with the rest of my life."

His mom said, "You could do so many things. You just need to pick one and do it."

"I know. I may see if I can find a publisher for my book of photographs."

His dad responded, "You could live anywhere and do that."

Jake smiled and replied, "I know."

His dad nodded and said, "Speaking of photographs – you've been out of the country for a while. Have you heard about these new cameras? They don't use film. They got some kind of computer inside of them or something."

"Yes, I have heard. They're called digital cameras. A couple of years ago, I bought one."

"You think they will catch on?"

"Yes dad, I expect they will. They will have to improve them some and make them more user friendly and bring the price down. But I suspect all that will happen in the next few years. And then, they will completely take over the camera market. Film will become obsolete."

"You really think they will catch on that much?

"Yes, I do."

"What's next?" his mom asked.

"I suspect that you and dad will be getting your own computer and be emailing everyone instead of writing them."

His mom smiled and replied, "I don't know about that. I can't see us having our own computer."

"They are really common now. Every home will have one soon. Most already do. They are like television was. People were fine with their radios. But once television caught on, every home had to have one. The same thing is happening with computers."

His dad said, "We've talked about it but just don't see the need for one."

Jake smiled, "You will."

His mom asked, "What do you and Rebekah want in the way of wedding gifts?"

Jake shook his head and answered, "That is a problem. Rebekah and I have talked about it. We know that her family and friends want to get her something but we don't need anything. I've got all my stuff in storage. She won't be able to move things like toasters and stuff over here. It would cost more to mail a toaster than to buy a new one here. She is thinking of putting a note in with the invitation like 'No Gifts, please.'"

His mom replied, "So y'all are definitely not going to live over there?"

"I don't think so. I like Scotland but Britain is moving toward becoming a socialist nation. That never works. I wouldn't want to live in a socialist or even a semi-socialist country. I guess we'll live here . . . somewhere."

His dad stated, "We've got a few of them socialists up in congress. They claim to be democrats but they might as well just come out and tell the truth that they are socialists."

"I hope it remains just 'a few.'"

"Me too, son."

The next day, Jake spent several hours at the local library. It had three computers that patrons could use. When Jake got there, no one was using any one of the three. He went to numerous websites looking for a place for their honeymoon. He decided on a small town on the Gulf of Mexico in Florida called Port St. Joe. It is on "The Forgotten Coast" and Jake was able to rent an old house about a mile and half west of the town right on the Gulf. There is a large barrier island, St. Joseph Peninsula that protects St. Joseph Bay. Port St. Joe is on the Bay. Jake wanted to be on the Gulf. He rented the house for August 7th to August 14th.

It had taken Jake a little over two hours to decide on Port St. Joe. He spent almost three more hours searching small towns. Many that he thought about did not have a website. However, he had already decided that, for financial and environmental restrictions, he did not want to live in Maine. In New England, he narrowed it down to New Hampshire. In the South, he pretty much decided on either North Carolina or Georgia. His parents lived in North Carolina. The Asheville area was beautiful. He also liked the Outer Banks. Jake had previously eliminated the west coast states and, really, all the states west of the Mississippi River. He couldn't stand Atlanta but thought that some of the small towns near Savannah and along the coast might be a possibility. While Jake had not decided on a place for them to live, he was satisfied with what he had done. He was now thinking that he and Rebekah could take trips to several places and then decide together.

Jake checked to learn about applying for citizenship. It turned out that, if someone were married to a U. S. citizen, it wasn't all that difficult.

On Friday evening, June 15th, Rebekah and Wendy were sitting at their table just off from the kitchen. They were eating their supper.

Rebekah asked her mom, "Do you think I'm doing the right thing?"

"Why do you ask that?"

"I don't know. I've only known Jake for about a month."

"Are you getting cold feet?"

"No. I know I love him. I know he loves me."

"But?"

Rebekah smiled. "But, it all seems like it has happened so fast."

Wendy replied, "That's because it has all happened so fast. Think how Jake must be feeling."

Nervously, Rebekah asked, "What do you mean?"

"Jake came here to photograph the Ring. After he did that, he planned to fly home. Instead, he met you and fell in love. I imagine he wakes up in the morning and thinks to himself, 'What happened? How did I end up engaged to be married?'"

"Mum, do you really think so?"

"I wouldn't be surprised. You feel the same way."

"No, I really do love him."

"I know. I think he really does love you."

"Yes, I know he does."

"Didn't you tell me that Jake said that when two people are in love with each other, they ought to get married?"

"Yes." Rebekah smiled at the memory.

"Okay then. Listen, grown daughter of mine, I did not like

that man you were engaged to right out of college. The main thing was that he was not a Christian. You and Jake both are. You are sure that Jake is?"

Rebekah laughed and said, "Yes, I tested him and he tested me. We both passed."

Wendy smiled and replied, "My 'knack' agrees. I think he is a real Christian. Now listen to me, real Christian men make excellent husbands. I don't mean men who go to church on Sunday and live like they never heard of Jesus for the rest of the week. I mean real Christian men, like Jake. They love their wives and would never do anything to hurt them. If you and Jake make Jesus the center of your marriage, you both will be happy."

Rebekah nodded. "That's true."

"Besides, I like Jake. If you don't marry him, I just might."

Rebekah laughed and said, "Oh, I'm going to marry him. I was just . . . concerned about how fast it is happening."

"I know. However, you must consider this: I want more grandchildren. If you two were to have a two or three-year engagement, there might not be any grandchildren."

"Oh Mum."

"I'm just saying."

Early Saturday morning, Jake got up and called Rebekah. It was a little after ten in the morning on the Orkney Islands. They were seven hours ahead of North Carolina. They talked for about an hour. Jake told her that he had found a warm place by the ocean for their honeymoon. He told her to pack her bikini. She laughed and told him that she hadn't worn one since she was a teenager. She guessed that she might still have that one somewhere but didn't think it would fit anymore. Jake told her "the smaller, the better." He told her that she had to get one and bring it. He told her that it was a law in the U. S. that every bride must have a bikini on her honeymoon. Rebekah laughed and promised that she would bring one.

Later that afternoon, Jake was sitting at his parents'

kitchen table by the sliding glass doors that opened to the patio and the backyard. He was drinking a mug of coffee and reading the newspaper.

His mom came in and sat down.

She said, "You do realize that August fifth is less than two months away."

"Yes, I'm aware."

"I've been thinking about your . . . indecision about what to do with the rest of your life."

"Yes?"

"I think you should quit trying to decide. You should pray about it and follow the leading of the Lord. If you are receptive to it, He will make His will for you known. Quit fretting. Instead, pray."

"I have been praying."

"I know. But now, do it with this request. He will answer such a prayer. Ask what He wants you to do."

"Okay. Thanks."

"You have described Rebekah as a real Christian."

"Yes, she tested me and I tested her. We both passed."

Jake's mom looked confused. She replied, "Good. A real Christian woman makes a good wife. That first wife of yours was not a real Christian."

"I wasn't either, mom."

That evening, Jake called both his sisters. Donna, his oldest, was full of questions about Rebekah and about his book of photographs. Lucy, who was two years older than Jake, still lived in her house. Her husband had moved out and into an apartment. They talked about divorce and how awful it was to go through. Lucy asked for details about Rebekah. She, like Donna, said that she wouldn't be able to attend the wedding in Scotland. They both wished him all the best.

That night, the 16th of June, Jake decided that, rather than stay at his parents' any longer, he would visit some of the towns he had found on the Internet. After reconsidering, he had decided against any towns in the Savannah area. He thought that being near Laura's grave would not be a good thing. Her death still hurt him. Rebekah, however, was helping him to heal.

The next day, Jake went to church with his parents. The following day, he got a rental car for a month and went shopping for some new clothes. Then, on Tuesday, Jake drove over to the Outer Banks area. He visited some of the same little towns he had visited almost two years previously. He took photos of each so that he could show them to Rebekah. He also visited towns a few miles inland from the ocean. Jake decided against looking in Florida. He thought he would wait until Rebekah was over and, after their honeymoon, they could look at some small towns there.

From North Carolina, Jake drove south. He passed through a few small towns near Charleston that were nice. He liked to visit Charleston but didn't think he wanted to live in that area. As it was just beginning to get dark, Jake drove over the Savannah River from South Carolina into Savannah, Georgia. He got a room in downtown and stayed there for the night.

The next morning, he drove out to Bonaventure Cemetery. He found Laura's grave and put some flowers on it. He stood there and admired the scenery with all the ancient trees and Spanish moss. With misty eyes, he spoke to Laura. He said, "Laura, I still love you. I miss you more than you can know. I am so sorry that we didn't elope. If I could go back in time, I would certainly elope with you." Jake looked around to see that he was still alone. He thought how awful it would be if he ran into any of Laura's family. He turned back to the family plot and said, "Laura, I've fallen in love with a wonderful woman. She is from Scotland. Her name is Rebekah. I love her and have asked her to marry me. She has accepted my proposal and we are to be married in August. I wanted to tell you this. I don't know why . . . but I wanted to. I wanted to let you know. I guess I will always love you. I absolutely cherish my memories of us together in Québec City. I guess I am here to tell you goodbye. It hurts for me to say that but I need to . . . I need to say goodbye. I am moving on with my life. I truly believe that God put Rebekah in my life. She is a wonderful woman and I love her completely. I think you two would have been friends. Now I'm getting silly. I'm crying and I don't know why. I just wanted to come down, tell you about Rebekah and say goodbye. I love you, Laura. Bye."

With tears running down his face, Jake turned and walked back to his rental car. He wiped his face with his sleeves. It was June in Savannah and it was hot and humid. He sat in the car for a few minutes and composed himself. He turned the air conditioner on high. He had been eating primarily fast food and had several napkins in the car. He used those to blow his nose and wipe his eyes.

Jake drove back to Savannah, found the entrance to the bridge and drove back over to South Carolina. As he had headed back to Savannah, he had said out loud to himself, "Whew, that was a lot harder than I had expected. I don't want to still be holding a . . . I want my feelings for Laura to be . . . over. She is gone. Actually . . . Laura has . . . died." His eyes got misty again and his nose started running. Still talking to himself, Jake said, "This is silly. I know I am totally in love with Rebekah." He smiled. Out loud, he said, "Rebekah does make me smile. She makes me happy. So did Laura. But Laura is . . . dead. I am marrying Rebekah and I don't want to ever compare them. That is not fair to Rebekah."

Jake kept driving north and by mid-afternoon he was back in North Carolina. He had not eaten anything all day and decided to stop at the first fast food place he saw. After consuming a double cheeseburger with a large order of fries and a large drink, he headed over to Wilmington, North Carolina. It had a nice feel to it and he spent the night there. The next morning, he traveled north. He stopped at a few small towns in Virginia but decided against them. He had been following his mom's advice about praying for Jesus to let him know when he found the right place for Rebekah and he to settle down. He had faith that when he saw the right place, he would know it. It was like when he was paddling the canoe in Maine.

Jake drove on up to New York City. After checking in, he called Ted and they agreed to meet the next night at their seafood restaurant on Long Island. Jake caught a cab there and back – it was just too much trouble trying to drive. He and Ted had a nice visit. Ted agreed to be his Best Man at the wedding.

From New York, Jake drove to Boston. He was near many of the places he had visited earlier that year when there was snow on the ground. He went to some of them again and took new photographs.

Jake knew that most people now had an email address. However, without a computer, it was somewhat difficult to stay current. He was still calling Rebekah but now he could do it on his new mobile phone. International calls were tricky and extremely expensive. Jake often just called from the motel where he was staying. That was also very expensive. To get Rebekah in the evenings, he need to call in the late mornings. This made him get a late start for his daily trips. However, Jake wasn't in a hurry and the New England states were very close to each other.

On Wednesday, July 18th, Jake drove into Concord, New Hampshire. To Jake, it had a nice "feel." At the same time, Jake knew that this was not "the place." He thought, *maybe nearby*.

Jake spent the night in Concord. He did a lot of research about the surrounding areas. He became interested in the town of Hopkinton. The town actually consists of three villages – Hopkinton, West Hopkinton and Contoocook.

Hopkinton was about ten miles west of Concord and the next morning Jake drove over to "feel it out." While there were settlers in the area in the early 1730s, the town wasn't incorporated until 1765. What excited Jake about that was that homes from that time were still standing and being lived in by families. He drove around through all three villages. Jake was surprised to see that Contookcook had a river running right through the center of town.

Jake drove back to Boston, spent the night there and started driving south the next morning. He had already arranged his and Rebekah's honeymoon flights and overnight stays. He had reserved rooms for his parents, Ted and Ted's wife, Stacy, and himself at the hotel he had stayed at in Kirkwall. He had tickets for his parents and himself for the flight over to Scotland. Even though he had those arrangements all made, he still thought it was time to get back to North Carolina. He thought his tux probably needed to be cleaned.

Jake made a leisurely drive of his trip back south and arrived at his parents' on Sunday, July 22nd. He thought, *I'll be marrying Rebekah in two weeks.*

Sunday, August 5th:

A half-hour after the church service, Jake, Ted, one of Rebekah's male cousins and the minister were standing at the front of a full church sanctuary. Wendy served as hostess to Jake's parents that morning. Jake's parents had never attended a Presbyterian church. Jake had assured them that it was not that much different from their Baptist church.

Music began and Rebekah's little niece, who was serving as a flower girl, started to walk down the aisle of the church sanctuary. She was followed by a bridesmaid and a Maid of Honor. Then the wedding march began and Rebekah was standing at the back of the aisle. Jake was stunned. Rebekah looked more beautiful than he had ever seen her. As she walked slowly down the aisle, Jake smiled, stood up straight and continued to be amazed at how wonderful she looked. He thought she was an absolute beautiful vision of loveliness in white.

They all took their places facing the minister. He said a few words of welcome. He then turned to Jake and said, "Jake, wilt thou have this woman to be thy wife, and wilt thou pledge thy faith to her, in all love and honor, in all duty and service, in all faith and tenderness, to live with her, and cherish her, according to the ordinance of God, in the holy bond of marriage?"

"I will."

The minister turned to Rebekah and said, "Rebekah, wilt thou have this man to be thy husband, and wilt thou pledge thy faith to him, in all love and honor, in all duty and service, in all faith and tenderness, to live with him, and cherish him, according to the ordinance of God, in the holy bond of marriage?"

"I will." Rebekah gave Jake one of her "special" smiles that he loved.

Placing a ring halfway down on Rebekah's finger, Jake then repeated the vow that the minister announced. "I, Jake, take you, Rebekah, to be my wedded wife, and I do promise and covenant, before God and these witnesses, to be your loving and faithful husband, in plenty and want, in joy and in sorrow, in sickness and in health, as long as we both shall live." Jake pushed the ring all the way down on Rebekah's finger.

Placing a ring halfway down on Jake's finger, Rebekah then repeated the same vow. "I, Rebekah, take you, Jake, to be my wedded husband, and I do promise and covenant, before God and these witnesses, to be your loving and faithful wife, in plenty and want, in joy and in sorrow, in sickness and in health, as long as we both shall live." Rebekah then pushed the ring all the way down on Jake's finger.

The minister then proclaimed that Jake and Rebekah were now husband and wife. He turned to Jake and said, "You may now kiss your wife."

They then walked down the aisle and outside for the reception. During the reception, the minister brought out a large book. Under the date of August 5, 2007, Jake and Rebekah signed their names next to groom and bride. Rebekah signed as Rebekah Fleming. In parentheses, she put West. Everyone posed for the traditional photos. They also had a man shooting a video of the wedding and the reception. Jake met with all of Rebekah's relatives and numerous people from the church. Victoria and her boyfriend, Eric, were there. Jake whispered in Victoria's ear that he bet that the two of them would be getting married soon.

After cutting the cake and listening to toasts from the Best

Man and Maid of Honor, Jake and Rebekah had the first dance – a waltz. After the reception, Ted drove the newlyweds to Wendy's home where Jake and Rebekah changed clothes. Ted then drove them to the airport. They caught a flight to Edinburgh and from there to London, where they would spend their first night together as man and wife.

After being carried across the threshold, Rebekah walked around the extremely luxurious honeymoon suite. She said, "I've never before stayed at such a nice hotel."

Jake responded, "Me either."

They did not get much sleep at all.

The next morning, they took a flight to Atlanta, Georgia and spent the second night of their honeymoon there. The following morning, driving a rental, Jake and Rebekah traveled south toward Florida. Their destination was Port St. Joe. It was a lot longer trip than Jake had expected. They arrived in Port St. Joe about 45 minutes after the sun had gone down. The place that they were to register and get their keys to the house on the Gulf was closed. They had to spend the night in a motel. Jake was embarrassed that he had misjudged the amount of time it would take to get there. Rebekah assured him that it was all right.

The next morning, they got their keys and went to their rental house on the beach. Most people went to the beaches in the St. Joseph Peninsula State Park. It was advertised as having the best beach in the United States. Jake and Rebekah were happy with the beach in front of their rental. That first morning in the house, after a honeymoon activity of lovemaking, Jake and Rebekah put on swim suits for their first trip to the Gulf waters. When Jake saw Rebekah in her bikini, he said, "Wow. I don't think you are allowed to go out in public looking like that."

She gave him one of her coy smiles and asked, "Why not?"

He hugged her and whispered in her ear, "You just look too sexy."

They stayed inside for another lovemaking session.

Eventually, holding hands, they waded in the waves as the small waves broke on shore.

Jake asked, "What do you think of Florida?"

"It's beautiful. But it's really warm. I didn't realize anyplace in America actually got this hot."

"August in Florida will do that."

Jake was concerned about Rebekah's fair skin. He was afraid, despite the sunscreen, that she might get sunburned. She agreed and wore a cover-up most of the time. During their week there, they went to the St. Joseph State Park, they ate fresh scallops from the bay, they went deep sea fishing and grilled some of their catch, they went shopping in downtown Port St. Joe, kayaking in the bay, dining in Apalachicola and Carrabelle, they bought an original watercolor in an art gallery and they attended a performance at the Dixie Theater in Carrabelle (the theater was built in 1912 but had been completed renovated).

One of their favorite activities was sitting on the front porch and watching the waves and the beach. It rained really heavy one day. However, the newly-weds didn't mind staying indoors. While sitting on the front porch, they enjoyed the thunderstorm. Tropical Storm Edouard passed by in the Gulf before making landfall in Texas on August 5th. Rebekah and Jake were, of course, getting married in Scotland on August 5th. The week after they left, Hurricane Fay hit Florida and caused considerable damage. Looking back on it, the two honeymooners felt lucky to only have had one day of rain.

Because they hadn't been able to use the house on the 7th, and because it wasn't rented until Friday the 17th, the landlord let them stay another day. They enjoyed it!

On August 16th, driving the rental car, Jake looked over at Rebekah and asked, "Where to?"

She smiled and said, "After this week in Florida with you, I'll go anywhere you take me."

"Okay. I think we are going to have one very very long honeymoon."

"That's great by me!"

Jake drove over to Jacksonville and they spent the night there. From there, they went up the Georgia coast. They toured Cumberland Island and spent the night on Jekyll Island. From there, Jake got on Interstate 95 and headed north. He skipped stopping in Savannah and drove on into South Carolina. They spent the night on an old plantation, near Charleston, that had built a guest house hotel right on the grounds. The next day, they toured several of the old plantations. Rebekah had been unaware of such a lifestyle in the 1800s in America. That night, they stayed in Charleston and the next morning, toured some of the downtown attractions. From Charleston, Jake drove north again and they drove over to Wilmington. It still "felt good" to Jake. Rebekah liked Wilmington also. They spent the night there and put it on their list of possible places to live. The next day, they drove up to the Outer Banks. After spending the night in a motel, they checked in at a cabin rental place that let them have it for three days. The ones Jake had previously stayed in only rented by the week. Jake showed Rebekah some of the same sights he had seen almost two years earlier. It was so much nicer, he thought, having Rebekah with him than being alone. They used the cabin as their "headquarters" as they visited several small towns inland a few miles. They even looked at some houses and properties. Jake had decided that he really wanted to get a few acres. That wasn't available right on the ocean in the Outer Banks.

After three days there, Jake asked Rebekah if she was tired of living out of a suitcase and wearing the same clothes over and over. She replied that she was having fun and enjoyed getting to see so much of America.

In the Orkneys, Rebekah had been Jake's tour guide. Jake decided to be Rebekah's tour guide. They went to Washington, D. C., walked the mall, saw all the museums, went up the Washington Monument and toured the Capitol building. After a few days there, they went to Philadelphia to see the historic sights there. They went to New York where they had dinner with Ted and his wife, Stacy. Jake took Rebekah shopping. From New York, they went to Boston. From Boston, Jake drove to Concord,

New Hampshire. Hopkinton was his goal. He wanted to see how Rebekah would feel about that area.

After spending the night in Concord, Rebekah and Jake woke on the morning of Wednesday, September 5th. Without the other knowing, they had both purchased anniversary cards.

Upon waking and with a quick kiss, Rebekah said, "Happy Anniversary!"

Jake smiled and replied, "Happy Anniversary!"

This led to another kiss, a real kiss this time and that led to another lovemaking session. Afterwards, Rebekah got up and went to her suitcase. She retrieved her anniversary card for Jake. When he saw it, he got up and got his anniversary card for Rebekah. They exchanged cards and kissed again.

After breakfast, they drove over to Hopkinton. It was a short but pretty drive with nice scenery.

On the way, Jake said, "I want you to use your woman's intuition. I want to know what you 'feel' about this area. I want to know whether or not the Holy Spirit is telling you anything or not."

Rebekah smiled, "Okay."

They drove through Hopkinton, West Hopkinton and Contoocook.

Jake turned to Rebekah, "Well?"

"It feels like home."

Jake smiled. "It does, doesn't it? I had the same impression."

"We could live here?"

"If you want to. Right now, everything is green. Soon, it will be autumn and the leaves will turn. It'll be beautiful. However, that will be followed by cold and snow. Lots of it."

"Have you forgotten where I'm from?"

Jake laughed. "No, but I was thinking that, perhaps, you've had enough snow in your life. Maybe you'd like a place without any snow."

"This place feels right."

Jake nodded. "Okay, let's drive around and see if we can

find a house that feels right."

Rebekah smiled. "Let's."

"You don't mind spending our first anniversary looking at houses?"

"Not at all. I will enjoy it."

"One of the things I like about this area is that they have preserved their history. They have saved covered bridges, old homes, railroad depots and historic sites. Of course, compared to the Orkney Islands, these historic places are brand new. However, like Orkney, the natural beauty of this area speaks for itself."

Rebekah laughed, "I guess the Ring of Brodgar does have a few years on these . . . sites."

They drove around in Hopkinton, West Hopkinton and Contoocook.

Looking at a road sign, Rebekah read, "Little Tooky Road." Not familiar with all American expressions, she asked, "What's a tooky?"

Jake replied, "Tooky is a nickname or short cut word for Contoocook."

"Yes, I see."

They saw several "for sale" signs. Most didn't reveal how many acres were included. Rebekah wrote down the names and phone numbers of the real estate companies and agents along with the addresses of the houses in which they had some interest.

Driving back to Concord, they checked into a hotel, had a nice dinner and, in their room, began searching through numerous newspapers and brochures listing houses for sale. They had seen a big Victorian house in West Hopkinton but it only had one acre of land with it. They both wanted a few more acres than that.

The next morning, having narrowed their list down to five possibilities, they called real estate companies and made three appointments for that afternoon. They eliminated two that afternoon and were still interested in one with six acres in Hopkinton. Tomorrow, they wanted to look at the other two.

As they walked through one house in Contoocook,

Rebekah and Jake both felt good about it. They looked at each other, smiled and nodded. The original part of the house had been built in the 1780s. It still had seven acres of land surrounding it. It was a large house and had been renovated and modernized most recently in 2002.

"Let's go back to the hotel and pray about this. If we both still feel good about it, we can meet with the agent again on Monday morning and make a bid on the property."

Rebekah responded, "I'm really excited about it. I can see us living there."

"Me too."

"Of course, that is a really large house. We don't need that much room."

"We'll fill it up."

"Just how many babies do you think I'm going to have?" Rebekah laughed.

"I didn't mean that. But that's one way. What I really meant was that, from what I've seen, no matter how large a house people have, they always seem to fill it up with "stuff.""

"Stuff?"

"Yeah, good old stuff. It starts with furniture and, before you know it, you don't have room for everything."

"I don't know."

"Let's pray about it."

On Saturday, September 8th, they drove up to the White Mountains. They rode the cog railroad to the top of Mount Washington and took photographs from the summit.

Rebekah said, "I do think you've got enough photos of me for our honeymoon scrapbook."

"But our honeymoon is far from over."

Rebekah smiled and said, "I hope it never ends."

"Me too."

"These are beautiful views but it's really cold up here." Rebekah shivered.

"That sounds like an excuse for someone who wants a

hug."

Rebekah smiled, "Give me one." As they hugged, Rebekah whispered, "Just for the record, you will never need an excuse to hug me."

On Monday morning, Jake called the real estate agent and asked for another tour of the house and grounds. They made an appointment for ten.

There were some nice old maple trees behind the house and some along the driveway at the entrance to the property. Walking among the trees, Rebekah asked, "Can we afford this?"

"Yes, but one never pays the asking price. Do you want it?"

"Yes, I think I do. I know I do. I have prayed and prayed about it and I feel really good about it."

"Same here. Okay, let's make an offer."

Rebekah said, "It's a big decision. Are you sure?"

"Yes. I've prayed about it also. The Holy Spirit hasn't nudged me away from it. So, I'm good with it. You're good with it. We are making this decision together. If it doesn't work out, we can blame each other."

The real estate agent had been standing back at the house as they were discussing buying it. They had walked from the maple grove to the barn. They turned and walked back to the house. Jake told the real estate agent that they wanted to make an offer. He told them that the owner was pretty set on his price. They followed the agent back to his office to draw up the offer paperwork. Jake offered $25,000 less than the asking price.

The agent said, "I really don't think the owner will accept your offer."

Jake smiled and replied, "Then, we'll just have to look at other properties. You've got our mobile number. When you have an answer, give us a call."

The next morning, the agent called and told Jake that the owner made a counter-offer. He said that the owner would take $10,000 off his asking price. Jake told the agent that his offer for

$25,000 less than the asking price was as high as he was willing to go. He told the agent that this would be a cash transaction. There would be no financing involved. He said that he would pay for an independent inspection of the house and for the title search. His offer to purchase the property was contingent upon the outcome of both of those. Unless there had been a recent survey of the seven acres, he would expect the owner to pay for half of that. Jake told the agent that that was his final offer.

Rebekah said, "I don't think I've ever seen you so tough. Do you think he'll accept it?"

"Yes. Two things. One, I really feel good about this place. I think it is meant to be for us in this house in this town. Two, remember, the agent told us that the house had been on the market for three and half months. He wants to sell. He is still making good money. It's a very fair price. I think he'll take it but, if he doesn't, we'll keep looking. Of course, the entire sale is contingent on the inspector's report."

"Oh. If he finds something bad, the sale will be off?"

"Not necessarily. If the owner will pay to have it fixed, we can proceed. It depends upon what he finds."

Jake was sitting on the corner of their bed. He was still holding his phone. He sat there for a couple of minutes without saying anything.

Rebekah asked, "Is something wrong?"

Jake turned to look at her. She was sitting in a chair in the corner of the room – reading a local newspaper.

Jake smiled. He said, "Rebekah, this is the anniversary of two horrible events in my life. I try not to dwell on them . . . but every now and then . . . it's . . . difficult."

Tears formed in Jake's eyes.

Rebekah said, "Tell me."

"This is the two-year anniversary of the day that Laura was in that awful crash."

Rebekah got up and sat down next to Jake. She took his hand in hers. She softly said, "Jake, I am so sorry. I know she was a wonderful person."

Jake nodded. "She was." Tears slowly rolled down his cheeks.

Rebekah took a deep breath and asked, "What else happened on this day?"

"September eleventh is the anniversary of the destruction of the Twin Towers in New York City. This is the sixth anniversary of that horrible event. From my office window, I could see the Twin Towers. After the terrorists destroyed them, I could see the empty spaces."

"Did you know anyone killed in that attack?"

"I didn't have any close friends or family. I did, however, know two people who died. They were work associates. Almost three thousand people killed. Why? The families and friends of those three thousand are grieving today."

Rebekah was thinking, *And you are grieving for Laura today. If she had not been killed, you would be married to her today. She and you might be living here in Contoocook. What does that make me?*

Jake continued, "That attack did nothing to advance the cause of Islam. Indeed, it only made the international community despise Islam even more. It made us Christians realize that all the followers of Islam are not evil or bad people. They are misguided and need to be prayed for like anyone else. However, it also made us realize that there were some followers of Islam who were evil and so misguided that they think killing everyone who is not a follower of Islam is a good thing. That attack changed a lot."

Jake looked at Rebekah. She looked lost in thought. She looked sad. Jake said, "Both of those events are in my past. My mom told me that time heals. She was right. Jesus said that He would be with the broken-hearted. He has been with me. When Laura died, I thought I would never love again. Then this beautiful woman walked up to me with the best opening line I've ever heard, 'Hi, I'm a Christian.' And . . . and I fell in love with her . . . almost immediately. And the Holy Spirit was so good to me. He blurred her vision and numbed her brain – and she returned my love."

Rebekah pushed Jake back on the bed.

"It's true. Ever since I heard, 'Hi, I'm a Christian,' I've been more in love than I've ever been in my entire life. I feel so blessed that that beautiful woman, with that beautiful long auburn hair, agreed to be my wife."

Rebekah crawled up and lay on top of Jake. She said, "You're being silly."

"No, not at all. In remembrance, this is a sad day. However, with you here, lying on top of me with that beautiful hair in my face, I am happier than I've ever been. And, I thank you for that and I thank Jesus for that. I am more in love now that I have ever been. I'm in love with you."

Rebekah gave Jake a long hard kiss on his lips. He held her tight and kissed her back.

Rebekah gave Jake that smile he loved.

Jake asked, "Mrs. Fleming, just what are your intentions?"

"You'll soon see."

Later that evening, the real estate agent called and told Jake that the owner had agreed to the terms of his offer.

Jake turned his phone off, turned to Rebekah and said, "I believe we have just bought a house."

CHAPTER FORTY-THREE

"There are different kinds of gifts, but the same Spirit. There are different kinds of service, but the same Lord. There are different kinds of working, but the same God works all of them in all men.

– 1 Corinthians 12:4 - 6

Mid 1st Century A.D.

During the next three weeks, the inspection and all the paperwork was completed. The inspection had not revealed anything of any consequence. The owner supplied a copy of a survey of the property that had been completed three years earlier. Jake and Rebekah closed on the house on Tuesday, October 9th.

For most of those three weeks, the honeymoon continued in Maine. They visited Old Orchard Beach, spent several days in and around Portland, walked the Rockland breakwater to the lighthouse at the end, drank some blueberry soda (not a hit with either of them), drove to the top of Mt. Battie and marveled at the views from there. They spent several days in Camden and then drove up to Bar Harbour and Acadia National Park. Jake and Rebekah stayed almost a week in that area. Everywhere they went, the autumn leaves were beautiful. They celebrated their second month anniversary, on October 5th, at a motel with stunning views of Frenchman Bay. They thought about driving up to Baxter State Park and seeing Mount Katahdin. However, they decided to stay along the coast and eat as much lobster as they could.

Jake told Rebekah more about his canoe trip in northwest

Maine, and about meeting Victoria in the woods on his return. He had previously mentioned some of this when she had noticed the bullet scar on his thigh. The fact that he had been shot had concerned her. He shared more about *The Library* with Rebekah. He told her that, since he was there, they have made a lot of changes.

On October 8th, they were back in Concord, New Hampshire. They drove over to Contoocook and looked at their home-to-be. The leaves on the maples were gorgeous.

Jake turned to Rebekah and said, "You've got a lot of shopping to do, Mrs. Fleming."

"Me?!"

"The house *is* empty. We will need to fill it up – furniture and stuff, you know."

"Actually, I do have some ideas for some of the rooms."

Jake smiled. "I thought you might. Tomorrow, this will be our house. We need to turn it into our home."

Rebekah squeezed Jake's hand and said, "We will."

The next day, Rebekah and Jake Fleming signed their names several times as they completed the closing. That afternoon, they went shopping for bathroom supplies. They had to get the electricity and water changed into their names. They opened a checking and savings account at a local bank. All the repetition required them to learn their new address and it had helped Rebekah to remember to sign her new last name.

There were, Jake said, at least a hundred and one things they needed to do. With cold weather headed their way, they decided not to get any animals until spring. Jake reminded Rebekah that he had some furniture, some "stuff" but mostly books in storage in North Carolina.

By their third-month anniversary, November 5th, they were settled in their home. Jake had purchased a new car and a used pickup truck. By shopping locally, they were getting to know some of their neighbors. They still had plenty of finishing touches to do and some rooms in the house were completely empty but they were happy in the old eighteenth century home.

Each Sunday, they had attended a different church. The Presbyterian church was not like Rebekah's Presbyterian church in the Orkneys. This one had a woman minister and Rebekah had found that odd. She didn't like it. They attended two Baptist churches and felt more comfortable at one of them.

Thanksgiving 2007 was coming up and they both felt that they had much for which to be extremely thankful. Sometimes, they prayed together. They always thanked God for Jesus and the Holy Spirit. They always thanked God for each other. They thanked God for always being with them.

Jake's parents had invited them to come down for Thanksgiving and they decided to make the trip. They had an ulterior motive. Jake wanted to get his "stuff" and his books out of storage. He had had a local carpenter come in and turn one of the extra bedrooms, one with a fireplace, into a library. He had built shelves all around the room. Those empty shelves needed books and Jake knew where to get them. They flew down to North Carolina and rented a car to drive over to his parents' home.

His sister, Lucy and her son, Steve, were staying at his parents for Thanksgiving. Donna and her family were not there. They liked to have their own Thanksgiving traditions. Steve was a senior now at Duke University. Jake had always liked Steve and thought he had now turned into a nice young man. He had, of course, lost his sister, Katherine, years ago, to a terrible accident when she was just a very young girl. His mom had just gone through a divorce and his dad was now "out of the picture." Jake thought he was "solid" and would be all right. He thought finishing college would help him grow and mature. Lucy and Rebekah seemed to hit it off and talked with each other as if they had been friends for a long time.

Jake got his dad to drive Steve and himself to a truck rental place. He rented a truck for a one-way trip to Concord, New Hampshire. From there, Jake and Steve drove the truck to the storage units that Jake had rented over two years earlier. With

Steve's help, they unloaded the units and loaded the truck. Jake drove the truck back to his parents' house. His parents had a large box full of rolls of film. Jake packed them tightly in the box and put it in the truck. On his first visit back, they had given him another box of film. He had gotten those developed and discovered that he did have some usable shots. As he had had no place to take them, he had left those prints with his parents. Now he was getting all those prints and all the undeveloped rolls of film and taking them back to Contoocook.

Both his parents really liked Rebekah. Once, while standing out in the back yard, Jake's dad said, "I tell you what. Rebekah is so much of an improvement over that first one you married, I can't tell you how much better I like her."

Jake replied, "I'm glad you do. I consider myself to be a very lucky man."

Jake's dad laughed and responded, "You should. You are lucky."

Rebekah and Jake were staying in a motel. They drove the rental over on Thanksgiving Day and everyone enjoyed a nice meal and they acknowledged that they were all thankful. Lucy was especially thankful that her divorce was final.

The next day, Rebekah and Jake drove over from the motel to his parents, put their suitcases in the truck, got his dad to follow him to the car rental place, turned in the rental, came back with his dad, told his mom and dad, Lucy and Steve, goodbye, got in the truck and headed north. They arrived at their home on Sunday afternoon. Most everything in the truck was in a box so it wasn't that difficult for Jake to unload the truck by himself. However, Rebekah insisted on helping. This is how they spent most of Monday – unloading the truck and carrying everything inside the house. Most of the boxes went to the library. Some of the others were kitchen items. Jake then moved a chair into the library, much to the chagrin of Rebekah.

Once their work was completed, Jake and Rebekah turned the truck in and then stopped for dinner at a local restaurant.

While eating, Jake said, "I'm sure glad that's done. Thank

you for all your help."

"Glad to. About that chair . . ."

"It's really really comfortable. I enjoy sitting in it while I'm reading."

"It won't fit the décor of the room."

"What décor? It will be the décor. Everything else is just shelves of books."

"Hmmmm."

Jake took a big bite and didn't say anything. He had a feeling that the "chair discussion" wasn't over yet. But he really liked that chair.

Christmas was like a fairy tale for the Flemings. Rebekah decorated the house with wreaths outside and, inside, with garlands, many candles and a beautiful tree that sparkled. They had neighbors over, took a sleigh ride and sang Christmas carols with a church group. After a Christmas Eve service at their church, Rebekah and Jake sat in front of a fireplace. They were enjoying watching the flames, smelling the wood smoke and snuggling together.

Jake said, "Well . . . I guess we might as well go on up to bed. He's not going to come."

Rebekah looked startled. "Who's not going to come?"

"Santa Claus."

She threw a small sofa pillow at him.

On Monday, December 31, 2007, Rebekah and Jake were sitting in front of a different fireplace. This room had a television on and the ball was about to drop in Times Square. They were actually spending much more time watching the fireplace than the TV.

Rebekah looked over at the television and asked, "Do you think your friend Ted is there?"

Jake laughed. "I'm sure he is not. There's no way he would want to get involved in all that. He's probably watching it on TV. He and Stacy are probably letting Christy and Mark stay up late and see the New Year in with the ball drop."

As the seconds were counting down, Jake pulled Rebekah to her feet. He hugged her and when it was the New Year, they kissed.

Jake said, "Happy New Year!"

"Happy 2008!"

Sitting in front of the fire, they sipped some wine.

Rebekah asked, "Resolutions?"

"Actually, yes. I am going to do a better job of staying in touch with my friends. With almost everyone having email these days, it shouldn't be hard to do. You?"

"I have been thinking that I might like to go back to teaching. I want to find out what I need to do to get a teaching certificate in this country."

"First of all, this country does not issue teaching certificates. You have to get a teaching license for the state in which you are planning to teach."

"From New Hampshire?"

"Yes. There is a state department of education that issues teaching licenses. We also need to proceed with your citizenship process."

"What happens if I get a certificate from New Hampshire but want to teach in Maine or another state?"

"You have to get a new license from whatever state in which you plan to teach. It's crazy . . . but you have to start all over with each state. They won't accept anything from another state. One state does a background check, gets your college transcripts, gets letters of recommendation and checks on your previous employment but the new different state makes you start all over. It will do its own background check, ask for new letters of recommendation, ask that your college transcripts be sent to them. The fact that you went through all this previously and were issued a license has absolutely no bearing with the new state. I knew of a teacher from North Carolina who had been teaching there successfully for seven years. Her husband got transferred to Kentucky. When she looked into getting a Kentucky teaching license, they treated her as if she was fresh out of college. They even wanted her to write an essay. She said it wasn't worth the hassle."

"What did she do?"

She applied at a private school and they took her based upon her North Carolina license. You might be happier at a private school. They would probably be more likely to accept all your teaching experience in Scotland. I can't believe we're talking about you becoming a local school teacher."

"I'm not one hundred percent sure I want to do it. But I want to look into it and see what it will involve."

Sipping his wine, Jake said, "When I look back at where I was last New Year's and where I am today, I realize how much has happened and how much Jesus has blessed me."

"Me too."

"You know, if we were both right out of college, we'd probably be living in a small apartment somewhere. You did that in Edinburgh. I also did it with my first job. I know what it is like to live paycheck to paycheck. It's not easy. It's not easy to save any money for emergencies. I don't know about you but for me, I remember getting my paycheck, paying my rent, utilities and bills. Whatever I had left was for groceries that had to last me until my next paycheck. I ate a lot of soup and noodles. I feel so blessed to have had the opportunities I had in New York. I have no regrets about leaving that position. The financial rewards were large. But we have enough to live on comfortably. This is the beginning of a new year. I am so grateful that we have each other and that we have the opportunity to live here."

Rebekah snuggled in close with Jake and they continued to watch the flames.

For their first April in New Hampshire, it was still cool. However, the leaves came out on the trees and everything looked green. Jake, the non-handyman but proficient with a hammer and a saw, built a chicken coop. He hired someone to put fencing up, not so much to keep chickens in as to keep predators out and away from the chickens. While he was at it, Jake also got the handyman to fence in three acres for possible livestock use.

Rebekah and Jake ordered 50-day-old Rhode Island Red chickens. With a heat lamp and lots of luck, they didn't lose any of the chicks. It turned out that they had exactly 30 roosters and 20 hens. When they were seven weeks old, Jake spent an entire day turning 28 of those roosters into fryers for the freezer.

After a lot of discussion, Rebekah and Jake bought a four-month-old male Highland calf from a farm in Vermont and a five-month-old female Highland calf from a farm in upstate New Hampshire. These were the shaggy cattle famous for being from Scotland.

They almost bought a couple of Morgan horses but decided to wait on that. They had a local man come out to plow and disk an area for a small vegetable garden. Rebekah was anxious to get some seeds in the ground.

From an animal shelter, they adopted both a puppy and a kitten. Rebekah had left Ellie with her mom. Their puppy was some type of mix with a terrier and border collie. The kitten was a beautiful calico. Rebekah said that they were really becoming "countryfied."

Sitting on their back porch in the evening of Wednesday, April 30th, Rebekah and Jake enjoyed the view of the three-acre "forest" and the three-acre pasture. There was a nice steady breeze that felt good to both of them.

Jake said, "You know, I do thank the Lord for this. For you, for this view, for this breeze."

"It is nice."

"Yes. If Ted and those other New York City folks could see me now, they would never understand why I would trade New York for this."

"My friends in Orkney would not believe we are living in the country near Contoocook, New Hampshire. Sometimes, I don't believe it." She laughed.

"I know what you mean. And, our neighbors are truly nice

people. I like them. I like the people at our church. You like the people in your reading club at the library."

"Yes, I agree. Everyone we've met has seemed friendly. I was talking with Sandra, at the post office, and she was telling me about her son, who is in college. He is studying to be a veterinarian and she is so proud of him. She said that when he was growing up, she was worried about him because he wouldn't take anything seriously."

"You got all that from buying stamps?"

Rebekah gave Jake one of her smiles. "Yes, I guess so."

"I think that your accent has been a great help to us in fitting in in this community."

"*My* accent? What accent?"

"Your beautiful Scottish accent – that's what accent."

"Oh, that?"

"Yes. People are curious where you are from . . . and that kind-of opens a door."

"Maybe. You do realize that you haven't completely gotten rid of your southern accent. Living in New York City may have taken the edge off but, every now and then, that magnolia accent comes out and says 'Howdy y'all.'"

Jake laughed. "Not to change the subject but to change the subject, we've already been to most of the local attractions but I would like to visit soon in the Hawthorne Town Forest. It really does sound interesting and it has a walking trail. Maybe one day next month."

Rebekah teased, "Perhaps we should both just skip next month and pick things back up in June."

Jake had no idea. He replied, "Okay . . . but I haven't yet figured out how to do that."

She smiled. "It's easy."

"All right. Why do we want to skip May?"

"Because we both become a year older in May."

"Oowwwwwe. That's right. Okay. I'm with you. We'll skip it."

"I'll be thirty-nine on the seventh. You'll be forty-five on the twenty-fourth."

"Okay. Okay. You've convinced me. Forty-five. Mercy. That does seem old. Five years and I'll be fifty. Wow. I'm afraid, Mrs. Fleming, you have married an old man."

Rebekah laughed. "What about me. In one year, I'll be forty. I'm afraid, Mr. Fleming, that you have married an old woman."

"You sure don't look like you are thirty-nine. I would definitely put you at thirty or thirty-one. Barely in your thirties."

"Thank you. However, I do have access to a mirror."

As they were talking on the back porch, a doe, with her tiny spotted fawn, stepped out of the woods. Jake and Rebekah became silent and didn't move. The doe looked around and went back into their small stand of trees.

Jake said, "We need to bring a camera with us when we sit out here."

Rebekah looked at their puppy. He slept through the deer sighting.

Later, as they were getting ready to go to bed, Jake said, "It's going to be difficult for me to forget my birthday with that hanging on the wall."

"What? My painting of our spot?"

"Yes. You gave that to me on my last birthday. Every time I look at it, I love it and remember that it was a special birthday gift from you. I also remember a special kiss I got in that spot."

"I remember several special kisses while we were there. I guess it's not so easy to skip birthdays."

"I have heard it said that, if no one wishes you happy birthday on your birthday, it doesn't count."

"Wishful thinking, I'm afraid."

"When are you going to get back to your painting?"

"Actually, I have been thinking of that lately."

"I think you could do some excellent paintings of these mountains."

"I'm going to try."

"Good."

Snuggled together, under their bed sheet, Rebekah said, "I've been thinking."

With some hesitation, Jake responded, "Okay."

"My prescription for birth control pills runs out soon. What do you think about not renewing them? I can just stop taking the pills I have and not renew the prescription."

"We were just talking about how old we are. You . . ."

"I know. That's why we need to hurry."

"Most likely, you would be, at best, forty when a baby would be due. Will you be all right at that age?"

"Sure, some women are having babies in their mid-forties."

"I'm not concerned about those women; I'm concerned about you."

"I'm healthy. I don't think there should be any complications."

"If we did have a baby that soon, I'd be sixty-four when he . . . or she . . . graduated from high school."

"So? You said you would love to have children."

"I'm not arguing against it. I'm not arguing at all. I'm just pointing out some facts."

"Yes. Obvious facts. We're old . . . and getting older."

"If you are all right with it, I'm certainly okay with it. I have prayed about it a lot. I haven't felt the Holy Spirit leading one way or the other. You're right, I do love the idea of us being parents."

Rebekah turned over and kissed Jake.

"Thank you. Yes, I'm fine with it. I've always wanted children."

"I know. It'll change everything."

"There you go with the obvious again."

"Guilty. I just want us to go into this with our eyes open."

"We've talked about this."

"I thought we were going to wait until we had been married for a year."

"We were. We're only two months away. It'll take around

a month to get the pills out of my system. I may not even be able to conceive. It may take a year or more for me to get pregnant."

"That's true."

"I was expecting some comment from you about how you were willing to try often."

"Now who is stating the obvious?"

Rebekah laughed and pushed him.

Despite their best efforts, they both had birthdays in May and turned a year older. During the week of August 5th, they spent their first anniversary in Maine. They had a real nice neighbor lady who came over and fed their animals and watered their plants. Rebekah and Jake had previously done the same for her.

In mid-September, Rebekah and Jake visited Wendy. The Orkney Islands looked the same. Ellie remembered them both and was so glad to see them – especially Rebekah. They drove out to their spot. It was still beautiful and they still kissed passionately there. One evening, they took Wendy with them to their special restaurant in Kirkwall. When the manager learned that they had recently celebrated their 1st wedding anniversary, he brought them a complimentary bottle of wine.

The evening before they were to fly back to London, sitting in her croft house, Wendy asked Rebekah to come into the kitchen with her. Wendy turned to her daughter and asked, "Are you expecting?"

Rebekah looked away. She said, "I'm not sure. I may be."

"I think so."

"Why?"

"It shows in your eyes."

"Really? I did miss my monthlies last time."

"I knew it. That's wonderful! Does Jake know?"

"No, I haven't said anything yet. I want to wait until I'm sure."

"When you're sure, let me know. But, I'm pretty sure right now."

"I hope so. We've both prayed about it a lot."

"Jake wants a child?"

"Yes, very much. He's a little concerned because of my age, but yes, he does want a child."

"Good. You two will make wonderful parents. And that child will have an absolutely wonderful grandmother."

"That's true, Mum."

"I'm so happy for both of you."

"Thanks Mum."

Jake walked into the kitchen and said, "You aren't talking about me, are you?"

Both Rebekah and Wendy laughed.

Rebekah answered, "Indirectly."

And they both laughed again.

Jake was confused. They all went back to the living room. Rebekah began explaining how one could travel between Scotland and New Hampshire.

Wendy said, "I'd really like to come in May."

Jake didn't have any idea why she wanted to wait so long. Rebekah did the math, smiled at her mother and said, "That would be perfect. I hope it works out so that you can stay for a long time."

Wendy replied, "We'll see."

After picking up their car from the airport parking lot, as they drove from Boston to New Hampshire, they noticed that the leaves were just beginning to turn. When they drove up their driveway, Jake stopped about halfway up, looked at the big old eighteenth-century house, and said, "This truly does feel like home."

Rebekah responded, "It does. It really does. I'm happy we waited until we found a place that felt right."

"Me too. I think it was the Holy Spirit directing us here."

"Yes."

CHAPTER FORTY-FOUR

"Woe to those who call evil good and good evil."

– Isaiah 5:20

Early 6th Century B. C.

Jake had been absolutely elated when Rebekah told him that she was pregnant. She had waited until the first week of October. She was now sure. She made an appointment with her doctor and she had referred her to an obstetrician.

By the end of October, the leaves were mostly gone from the trees. The pines and other evergreens were still green and still beautiful. The previous year, they had learned that New Englanders really celebrate Halloween. This year, they had some Jack 'o lanterns on their front porch along with some corn shucks, a couple bales of hay and some Halloween decorations. They had quite a bit of candy for the trick-or-treaters.

November brought much cooler weather. Jake asked Rebekah how they had kept chickens through the winters in Orkney. She told Jake that chickens were actually quite hardy. It turned out that keeping water available for the chickens was the most difficult task. Water had a tendency to freeze during the winter. Although they didn't need to, their entire cattle herd got in the habit of going into the old barn at night. They both had become pets. Jake had got in the routine of closing the chickens up for the night and then going to the barn to say "goodnight" to their two Highland pets. He actually petted them both and they came to expect it every night.

By New Year's Eve, Rebekah had a healthy little baby bump. They celebrated by sitting in front of a fireplace sipping grape juice from wine glasses.

January 2009 was cold. Jake had adapted to all the snow. He had experienced snow in New York and considered that he was not a novice. Their neighbors had been great help with advice about the weather.

At the Bible study group, in the first week of February, one of the men, Steven, asked Jake if they could talk privately after the meeting. Jake agreed. When they were alone, Steven said, "Jake, I've noticed something about you that is different from the other men in our group."

Jake smiled and said, "My accent?"

Steven smiled and replied, "No. I am talking about being a Christian – your Christianity. I have seen how you handle things in our meetings. You let others do all the talking and then, when you do speak, what you say usually straightens everything out."

"I'm not sure I know exactly what you mean."

"I mean you always get us back on track. You make things clear. You ask good questions. Although I suspect you already know the answers to the questions you ask. You ask them to make a point. You ask them to allow others to follow the correct path."

"I promise, I'm not planning this out. I just try to contribute to our meetings when it seems appropriate. Some meetings, I may not say anything. Others, I will say more."

"But when you do, it adds something positive to the meetings."

"Thank you, but I just say what seems to me to be helpful."

"Exactly. And I think it is coming to you what to say from the Holy Spirit."

"I don't know. I suppose it could be."

Steven said, "It is. And here's the thing. I'm not like that.

I don't have the Holy Spirit in my life."

"All Christians do."

"Yes, see. That comment came from the Holy Spirit. I am questioning whether or not I am truly a Christian."

"Who do you believe Jesus is?"

"Jesus is the Son of God."

"That sounds like a response that a Christian, under the direction of the Holy Spirit, would give. Do you truly believe that Jesus died for you and rose from the dead?"

"Yes."

Jake pointed at Steven and said, "Christian."

"Sometimes, because I've been in church, I think that I just know the right words to say. But I question if I am sincere."

"Because?"

Steven sighed, paused and replied, "Because I don't think the Holy Spirit is working in me."

"Have you admitted to God that you are a sinner and asked God for forgiveness?"

"Yes."

"Doing that, and meaning it, could be, I think, an act that comes from the Holy Spirit. When someone genuinely admits they are a sinner, repents of sin and accepts the saving grace of Jesus – for a person to do that, I think the urge, the call, the desire to do that comes from the Holy Spirit. It is instantaneous. The Holy Spirit directs one to accept Jesus as his Savior and, at the same time, enters the soul of that brand-new believer."

"You think so?"

"I do. I pray almost every day for the Holy Spirit to lead me, to direct me, to be more of an influence on me. I pray that I will be more receptive to the Holy Spirit. I have learned that I cannot direct the Holy Spirit. I often want the Holy Spirit to lead me in a specific direction. Usually, he does not. I can only follow the Holy Spirit. Sometimes, I strongly feel His presence. Other times, not so much."

"I'm just not sure I have ever experienced that presence of the Holy Spirit in my life."

"When you accepted Christ, did you not feel almost a push to do so?"

"I haven't thought of that. Yes. Yes, I did."

"That was the Holy Spirit."

Jake opened his Bible and read out loud first Corinthians, chapter twelve.

Jake said, "See how it works. The Holy Spirit will determine what gifts He will give."

Steven repeated, "Jesus is Lord."

"Exactly. No one can say that and truly believe it except through the Holy Spirit."

"You have a calmness and peace about you that I wish the Holy Spirit would give to me."

"Ask Him for it."

"You have heard how upset some of the men in our group are with the results of the election. I didn't see that in you."

"I don't like the results. I think our new president is not a very intelligent person. I do think he is extremely deceitful. I doubt that he is going to be a very good president. However, his republican opponent was not a very strong candidate either. He is also not a very intelligent person. His vice-presidential candidate was, I think, the best person of the four running. I would vote for her for president."

"But you didn't get upset like some."

"No. What good would it do to get upset over the results of an election? It wouldn't change anything. I think getting upset is a sign of a weak mind. God is in control. Jesus is with me. All this election mess is secondary. If the country moves too far left, the pendulum will swing back to the right. Meanwhile, I take comfort in knowing my future home and my real home is with Jesus. These political things seem almost petty. So no, I don't get upset; I don't worry about them. I think for a Christian to worry is offensive to Jesus. It's like saying, 'I don't trust you, Jesus.' I do trust Jesus. This new president will probably weaken our country. He will do things that are not in this nation's best interest. God probably has a reason to allow this to happen. I will pray for the new elected leaders, including this new president. I hope they will do a good job. However, I don't expect much positive from this new bunch."

"See, that is the kind of attitude I want to have – to know that Jesus is in control and trust Him. I don't have that."

"Steven, I think that all of us Christians are on a spiritual path. Some of us are further down the path than others. A brand-new Christian is just beginning to walk that path. We all have to begin at the beginning and grow spiritually as Christians."

"That's what I want to do."

"That is the Holy Spirit working in you."

"You said that you would pray for this new president we have. That thought never occurred to me. It should have. I know that that is the right thing to do. But I never thought of it. The things he stands for just seem so wrong to me."

"They are wrong. But he is still a human being who needs the guidance of Jesus. He doesn't have that now. But we all need that. I will pray for him first, because he is a person who needs the love of God; second, because he is now our nation's president."

There was a pause in their conversation.

Then Jake said, "You just said that you want to grow spiritually."

"Yes, very much."

"I do too. I think all Christians should strive for spiritual growth. But that desire that you have to grow spiritually is, I think, another example of the Holy Spirit working with you. It certainly isn't coming from the devil."

Steven's face lit up and he smiled.

"Pray, Steven, for your spiritual growth. It will come. With it, peace and joy also comes. That calmness you mentioned is a result of the peace and joy of the Holy Spirit."

"Thank you, Jake."

Jake asked Steven to pray with him. Jake prayed for the Holy Spirit to be more active in both of their lives and to be more receptive to its direction.

When Jake finished praying, he asked Steven, "What was it, Steven, that actually caused you to begin questioning your relationship with the Holy Spirit?"

Steven replied, "It is somewhat embarrassing. I didn't know what to say. I was talking with this man at work. We started talking about church. He said that he didn't believe that there was a God. Then he said, 'But if there is a God, I cannot believe he would send a good person to Hell.' He said that he had always been faithful to his wife, he had supported his children, he donated to charities, he had never intentionally harmed anyone – he could not see a loving God sending someone like him to Hell. I did not know how to respond. I didn't know exactly what to say."

"I understand. You expected the Holy Spirit to guide you to know what to say."

"Yes, exactly. And I had nothing."

Jake paused and replied, "Remember, Paul said that all Christians 'worship by the Spirit of God.' In Mark 13:11, Jesus says, 'do not worry beforehand about what to say, just say whatever is given you at the time, for it is not you speaking, but the Holy Spirit.' Let me tell you, this is good advice. This happened to me about four years ago. Literally, without any warning, I was asked to get up in front of a congregation and give a talk, a message, a sermon, I guess. I did not know what to say. I prayed for guidance. I started talking and I said something. It seemed to go over rather well with the people there – but I thought it was too short. The point is though, Steven, that the Holy Spirit will, if you allow Him, direct your words. Call on Him. Ask Him to help you, to guide you. He may not want you to say anything. If He does want you to talk, He will lead you to say what He knows will be effective. You must have faith in Him and just begin talking."

Steven responded by saying, "Okay, I get that now. But what should I have said to him?"

Jake paused and replied, "Steven, every situation is going to be at least slightly different because each time you speak with someone, it is a different person. You are familiar with the verse where Jesus says that no one comes to the Father except through Jesus?"

"Yes, of course. But this guy doesn't believe . . ."

"Jesus also said, in John 3:5-6, 'I tell you the truth, no one can enter the kingdom of God unless he is born of water and the Spirit. Flesh gives birth to flesh, but the Spirit gives birth to spirit.' We worship God in spirit with the help of the Holy Spirit. Jesus called Him 'another Helper.' Knowing these things, as a Christian, how do we respond to your colleague at work? What I might say, led by the Holy Spirit, might be totally different from what you might say. Neither would be wrong." Jake paused again and continued, "I think I might have told this guy a story. A story about rules. God has rules. He wants everyone to be with Him in Heaven. He has laid out some rules that apply to anyone and everyone. He cannot abide having sin in Heaven. Heaven is a place without *any* sin. That is God's rule. He is God. He gets to make the rules. He sent His Son, Jesus, to die as a sacrifice for our sin. If we accept that Sacrifice, we can go to Heaven without sin. If we refuse to accept Jesus, then we cannot go to Heaven."

Steven said, "I know all that is true but how do I relate that to someone who does not believe that God would be so demanding of a good person?"

"First of all, everyone, even a really really good person like this colleague of yours, is also a sinner. We have all sinned against God. I would simply point out that these are God's rules. Then I would tell a story about human rules. Let's say that there is a law enforcement officer. This person is a family person with a spouse and children. A good person. Let's say that there is a prosecutor who is also a good person. Let's say that there is a judge who is also a good person. Now, let's say there is a person who has never done anything wrong and has lived a good responsible life. Suddenly, for some reason, this good person murders someone – maybe a spouse. Murder is against not only God's rules but also man's rules. Because this person broke one of man's rules, the good law enforcement officer arrested the murderer. Because the evidence of guilt was overwhelming, the prosecutor was successful in convincing a jury of twelve good people that this person was guilty of murder. Because of the conviction by the jury, the good judge sentenced the murderer to death. How could all these good people send this person to death? In our society, we call this justice. This person did not obey the rules of our society. The consequence of not obeying the rules, in this case, was death. In other cases, it may be prison. Breaking the rules, the laws, has consequences. The same is true for good people who do not obey God's rules for salvation. God is a just God. One of His rules is that He cannot allow *any* sin in Heaven. That is how a good and loving God can allow a good person's soul to go to Hell."

Steven said, "I like that explanation. I will remember that."

By the middle of April 2009, Rebekah's baby bump had become huge. Every time Jake saw it, he could not understand how that baby wasn't being born at that moment. Rebekah and Jake knew that the baby was a boy. They had discussed numerous names and decided to name him after Rebekah's father, Scott.

Rebekah's mother, Wendy, was scheduled to arrive at Boston on Friday, May 1st. Jake was worried that, while he was gone to pick Wendy up, the baby would arrive. If he did, they arranged for a neighbor to be the backup. She had had three children and now had two grandchildren.

While driving Wendy back to Contoocook, Wendy, knowing of Jake's interest in the unusual, told him of the strange May Day rituals that used to be fairly common in the Orkney Islands and in all of Scotland. Jumping over fire was, she thought, still being practiced in some of the more remote areas of both the Orkneys and in Scotland itself. The May Day Pole was a ritual that traced its beginnings back hundreds of years. Wendy told Jake that, when she was a little girl in early grade school, they performed a May Day dance around a pole with streamers from the top. It was the custom to do that every May Day at the school. She said that it has stopped being done and has completely been phased out of school activities. For some reason, someone had determined that it was politically incorrect.

Jake found the stories to be interesting. He appreciated Wendy telling them to him. It took his mind off of Rebekah. He wasn't, he decided really worried about Rebekah. He knew that Jesus was with her. He decided he would have faith that everything would be all right.

As they were approaching Concord, Jake turned to Wendy and asked, "When we were visiting you last year, you said that you would like to come visit us in May. How in the world did you know then that the baby would be born in May?"

Wendy smiled. She said, "A grandmother knows these things."

Jake was highly skeptical of her answer. He said, "At that time, I didn't even know that Rebekah was pregnant."

"I told you before, I have a knack for these things. Oh, speaking of which, you might be interested to know that Victoria and Eric have gotten engaged."

"Really? That's great. I think they will be a good couple together."

"Yes, I agree."

"Rebekah will be glad to hear that. You may not know this, but Victoria joined Rebekah and I during our first meal together – a breakfast at the museum."

"Is that right?" Wendy knew about it and knew that Rebekah had been jealous over it. She had also been jealous when she saw Jake talking with Victoria outside the church. However, Wendy knew, Rebekah had quickly gotten over it.

"Yes. I'm glad she and Eric hit if off all right."

While driving up to the house, Wendy expressed her admiration for the house and the trees in the yard. As they pulled up to the driveway, Wendy quickly gathered her things and was out of the car walking briskly up to the front door. Rebekah opened the front door and, as Wendy stepped inside, she tried to hug her daughter. It wasn't easy. Jake walked up with a couple of suitcases. To Wendy, he said, "I'll take these up to your room. Rebekah, can you show your mom, your mum, around?"

"Yes, I can still walk . . . waddle maybe."

Jake returned and found mother and daughter sitting at the kitchen table. He joined them. When there was a break in the conversation, he asked Wendy, with her "knack," could she say when the baby was going to be born.

Wendy made a big show of examining Rebekah's eyes. She turned to Jake and replied, "Soon. Very soon."

Jake laughed. "Alright. I could have said that."

Baby Scott Fleming was born the next day, Saturday, May 2nd. Both baby and mother were in excellent health. Jake had been in the delivery room and about ten minutes after the birth, was holding his son in his arms. Emotion overtook Jake and tears rolled down his cheeks. He carried Scott over and laid him next to Rebekah. He leaned over Rebekah, gave her a quick kiss and said, "I love you."

Jake left the room to tell Wendy. He had wiped his face but Wendy could tell he had been crying.

She said, "It's emotional to witness a miracle."

"Tears of joy," Jake smiled. He remembered Rebekah's tears of joy when he had asked her to marry him.

He said, "Thank you, Jesus."

Five days later, on May 7th, Rebekah turned 40 and on May 24th it was Jake's 46th birthday.

On May 4th, 2011, Sarah Fleming was born to Rebekah and Jake. Two days earlier, on May 2nd, Scott Fleming reached the age of two. Three days later, on May 7th, Rebekah became 42 and on May 24th, Jake turned 48. May was most definitely the birthday month for the Fleming family.

Jake's mom came up from North Carolina to help out for a couple of weeks with baby Sarah. Sitting at the dining room table, Jake and his mother were talking.

His mother said, "Lucy is engaged to be married. Sometime in July, I think."

"I thought she would remarry."

"Yes. Oh, they had a story about your book in the local paper. You know, local boy does good type of thing."

"There's no danger of it becoming a best-seller but I'm glad I found a publisher. They think there is enough interest in the topic to find a reasonable audience."

"Well, your dad and I like it. I hope it does well for you."

"It might create some discussion."

After a pause, Jake's mom asked, "Are you hunting for a job? Do you plan to go back to work?"

"Putting that book together was a lot of work."

"You know what I mean."

"Yes, I do. Yes. I would like to go back to work. However, doing what . . . I don't know."

After another pause, Jake continued, "It's strange; but, last year, when Rebekah was granted her citizenship, I was so proud of her . . . but during the ceremony, I started thinking, 'I'd like to get a job.' Then we found out that we were going to have another baby and I just put the job thing on the back burner."

"I understand that."

"Rebekah was interested in getting her teaching license and getting back in the classroom."

"Really?"

"Yes, but Scott put an end to that for the time being. Now, Sarah will delay it again for a while."

"I can see that also."

"As you know, she is really an accomplished artist. She has been creating some new paintings and may do more of that."

"I'm sure she enjoys that."

"Yes. Mom, we really do appreciate you coming up and helping out with everything."

"Wendy came when Scott was born. I figured it was my turn."

"You know that you and dad are welcome here anytime."

"I know. Thank you. Now listen, Scott and Sarah only have two grandmothers. If you have a third child, who would come for that one?"

"We're not planning on a third."

"I'm glad to hear that. You do realize, don't you, that you are getting old."

"Mom."

"You may not look as old as you are . . . but I was there when you were born. I know how old you are. You are pushing fifty. You're pushing it hard."

"Okay. I know how old you and dad were when I was born. If you want me to add fifty years to that, then . . . ."

"All right, end of the discussion about ages."

They both laughed.

On Tuesday, May 31, 2011, Jake drove his mother to Boston to catch a flight to Atlanta. They took Scott with them on the trip. This was the first time Rebekah was home alone with Sarah.

"Mom, do you think she'll be all right?"

"Who? Rebekah or Sarah?"

"Both."

"You meant Rebekah. Of course she will. So will Sarah. It's been almost a month. There are no complications. She is fine. She's already lost most of her baby fat. That's amazing. Took me a year to lose mine. Don't worry."

"Okay."

On the way back, Scott, in his car seat in the back, kept up a conversation with Jake. He was just beginning to be able to read on his own. Jake was proud of him for that. An unexpected but welcomed consequence of that was that his vocabulary increased. He liked to use some of the new words he had learned and, sometimes, he used them out of sequence. Jake at times had difficulty keeping up with what he was actually saying. Nonetheless, it was fascinating to Jake to be having such interactions with his two-year old son.

A couple of months after they had moved to Contoocook, Rebekah had joined a ladies reading club at the local library. They met once a month and discussed a book that they all had read since the last meeting. Rebekah had always enjoyed reading; and, she enjoyed their monthly book discussions. She had missed the April, May and June meetings but was back at the July meeting. Jake was babysitting so she could attend.

The July book was an Agatha Christie mystery. Rebekah always liked reading Agatha Christie's books. As the meeting was breaking up and the ladies were leaving, a woman, Melinda, who had always been friendly with Rebekah, asked if she could talk for a few minutes. Rebekah liked Melinda. They were both slightly introverted – Melinda more so than Rebekah but they had always connected. Rebekah had invited her to a July 4th barbecue get-together back in 2010. Melinda had attended and seemed to have a nice time. She was a single mom with two children in middle school. She had divorced her husband three years prior and Rebekah had tried to comfort her some then as she was going through the process.

After everyone else had left the room, the two women sat back down at the large conference table.

Melinda said, "I feel like I can talk with you."

Rebekah replied, "Of course you can."

"How is your new baby doing?"

"We've been lucky with this one – she sleeps right through the night."

Melinda laughed. "What's her name?"

"Sarah."

"That's nice."

"How are Madison and Harry doing?"

Melinda's smiled. She said, "They're all right. I think they both are bored with summer. Harry plays games online all the time. I think he enjoys it. Madison does the same. They both communicate with people in Europe. Different people. I've read some of their texts and I am convinced that they are really talking with children about their same ages. They both know more about news events than I do. They even know what is taking place overseas. I do wish that they would get out more. I tried to get Harry to join a baseball team this summer but he has no interest in sports at all. From what I can tell, that seems to be fairly normal for kids his age these days. But they seem to be doing okay."

After a brief pause, Melinda said, "I want to talk with you . . . or ask you . . . you see, for some time now, I have been feeling really sad."

"I'm sorry."

"I guess I'm probably depressed. I've had some really negative thoughts lately."

"What do you think has caused this feeling of sadness?'

"I guess I'm feeling all alone in the world. I'm lonely. I really do look forward to these book meetings. I get to be around adults."

Rebekah replied, "I know what you mean. I love both my children completely but it is good to get away for a few hours every now and then."

Melinda smiled. "Yes, but you have a husband to go home to. You can talk with him. When I get home from work, the kids are involved in their activities and I have no one to talk with."

"Do you not have any family nearby?"

"No, I don't. My ex got transferred to Concord and we moved up here for that. I've thought of moving back home but..."

"Where is home?"

"Kansas."

"That's a lot different than New Hampshire, isn't it?"

"Yes. Although both have severe winters. But, you see, the economy has gotten so bad. I don't know if I could find a job back home. And, I hate to pull the kids out of school and make them start all over at a new school."

"At their age, they would make new friends."

"I suppose so."

After another pause, Melinda said, "I'm thirty-four. That's

not old."

"Definitely not."

"I could stand to lose a few pounds but I am a mother of two."

"I know what you mean."

"I don't know if you do. Look at you. Your baby was born only two months ago and you've already lost all your extra weight."

"Thank you. It wasn't easy."

"You don't even look like you've ever had a baby."

"You're being kind."

"Anyway, what I'm trying to say is that I would think a thirty-four year-old woman could find someone to date. But I can't. I just don't know. I don't feel like putting forth the effort. I guess I've given up on the idea of ever re-marrying."

"Please don't do that. I got married, for the first time, at thirty-eight."

"Thirty-eight? Really?"

"Yes." Rebekah nodded.

"How. I mean, didn't you . . .? I've been single for three years. Guess how many dates I've had?"

"I have no idea."

"One. And he wanted to sleep with me on the first date. There wasn't a second date."

Rebekah said, "I do understand your situation. However, I do think that you may be relying too much on having a man in your life to make you happy."

"I really miss holding a man. I miss hugging a man and having him hug me. Is that so wrong? To want that?"

"No, of course not."

"I mean, I just feel all alone. I feel sad and depressed. Lonely. I don't see much future for me."

"Melinda, let me ask you something."

"Okay."

"How old were you when you accepted Jesus as your Savior and Lord?"

"That's a question I did not expect. I don't know. It was when I was in elementary school. I had been attending a vacation Bible school."

"I understand. Listen...sometimes...when someone becomes a Christian that young...sometimes they don't grow...spiritually. Sometimes, they are just too young to understand how to...develop a spiritual path – a spiritual life. Jake told me that, for years, he was a Sunday only Christian. He was a Christian in that he believed Jesus was who He said He was. He believed that Jesus died on the cross for his sins and that He rose from the dead. Believing all that, he still wasn't living a Christian life. He wasn't allowing the Holy Spirit into his life. Jake told me that, for many years, he was just standing at the very beginning of his spiritual path. For years, he just stood there. He never took that first step down that path."

Rebekah paused. Melinda was in deep thought.

Rebekah continued. "Many regular church-goers are living that way. They are not bad people but they simply haven't started walking down their spiritual path."

With a very soft voice, Melinda asked, "How does one begin walking their spiritual path?"

"I think it begins with faith. Faith in God. Faith in Jesus. Faith in the Holy Spirit. If you have even a little faith, you can pray and ask the Holy Spirit to become active in your life. Then, in faith, start walking down your path. Trust that Jesus always loves you and is always with you. The Holy Spirit is not going to hit you with a lightning bolt or write a message in the clouds for you, but you will begin to notice his presence. In small ways, as you go about your day, you will feel the Holy Spirit guiding you. Should I do this? Should I do that? The Holy Spirit will let you know."

"I don't know. How would I know it was really the Holy Spirit?"

"You just know. And you know He isn't going to tell you to do something evil. Sometimes, the devil may put evil crazy thoughts in your mind. He'll try to convince you that it is not real. That the Holy Spirit is not real. When that happens, just turn to Jesus and he will get rid of those doubts. This is the way mature Christians live. It involves reading the Bible. It involves prayer. It involves attending a church."

"I still don't understand how I would know . . ."

"You are a Christian now, right?"

"Yes."

"Then the Holy Spirit is already within you. You just haven't allowed Him to be active in your life. You haven't been following Him."

"But . . ."

"Let me ask you a question. Should you go home tonight and, after you have the children in bed, should you read a chapter from a book in the Bible?"

"I haven't been doing that."

"Should you?"

"Yes. I suppose so."

"Who told you to say 'yes' just now?"

"I don't understand."

"You could have answered my question with either a 'yes' or a 'no.' Who told you to say 'yes?'"

"I don't know. I guess it just seems like the right thing to do."

"How would you know that?"

"I don't . . ."

"A Christian would know that because the Holy Spirit would lead a Christian to that answer. The Holy Spirit told you to say 'yes.'"

"The Holy Spirit told me?"

"It sure wasn't the devil. The devil doesn't want people reading the Bible. It's a nice feeling when you know that the Holy Spirit is guiding you, isn't it? If you ask Him to, He will direct you down your spiritual path."

Melinda smiled. "It does feel good."

Rebekah responded, "You said earlier that you didn't see much future for you."

"Yes."

"One of my favorite passages in the Bible is in Matthew. It's at the end of chapter six. Jesus is talking. He says do not worry about tomorrow. I have always liked that. I think that if a Christian worries all the time, it probably offends Jesus. I told you that I didn't marry Jake until I was thirty-eight. When I was in my twenties, I was worried that I would never fall in love. I kept meeting different guys but, usually after one date, I knew that I didn't want a future with that guy. When I turned thirty, I began to live as a real spiritual Christian. I stopped worrying about everything. I prayed. I read the Bible. I went to church and joined a Bible study group. That all helped me to follow the guidance of the Holy Spirit. I still wanted a husband. I wanted a Christian husband. I prayed about it. I reconciled myself to never marrying. I talked to Jesus one day and told him I would like to have a family but that I was willing to do whatever He thought was best for me to do. I volunteered in this small museum back in Scotland. I had been there hundreds of times. One morning, in the museum, I looked up and there was this man that I had previously noticed outside among an ancient stone circle. I walked over and introduced myself. About five minutes after I met Jake, I knew he was the one for me. He was the man I had been waiting on for so long."

"What did you do?"

"Honestly? I started worrying again. I'm embarrassed to admit it but I was worried that he wouldn't return my feelings for him. We had several obstacles. I was a citizen of Scotland. He was a citizen of America. There was an ocean between us. I prayed and prayed. I finally quit worrying and thought 'if it's God's will, it'll happen.' And it did. I didn't know it at the time but Jake told me later that, for him, it was love at first sight."

"Okay. But why didn't God put you two together when you both were in your twenties? You could have had all those years together."

"I am not going to question the wisdom of God. When we were both in our twenties, we were both just Sunday Christians.

If we had met then, it probably wouldn't have worked out. I have learned to trust God. God knows best. I know you know that."

"Yes."

"We just have to have faith. Remember that children's Sunday School song – *Jesus Loves You*? He does. He really does. He loves you, Melinda."

Melinda smiled.

"And He loves your children. Don't you imagine that Jesus wants you to be a Christian role-model for your children?"

"Yes, I guess He does."

"The Holy Spirit is talking with you again. Follow the Holy Spirit. He will talk to your heart. You might want to begin reading a chapter in the Bible every day. Lots of people begin with the book of John."

"What was that passage you mentioned before?"

"Matthew. Chapter Six."

"I think I'll begin with Matthew."

"That's probably the Holy Spirit leading you to that book. Read it expecting to get a message from the Holy Spirit."

"Okay."

"Melinda, anytime you want to talk, just call. Here, let me give you my number. If you don't have a church home, you are certainly welcome to attend where Jake and I go. We'd love to have you check it out. Again though, the Holy Spirit will lead you to the right church for you and your children."

That evening, Rebekah told Jake about her conversation with Melinda.

Jake said, "It sounds like you were able to give her some good advice and steer her in the right direction."

"I hope so. I want you to pray for her."

"I will."

"She seems so sad. So lonely."

"I think that is true of many people today. Apparently, many high school boys are spending most of their time away from school playing computer games. When they graduate, they don't have any real friends."

"That's sad."

"Yes, and, in the future, as computer games get even more sophisticated, it will probably get worse."

"To go through school without at least one good friend seems . . . it would be difficult and lonely."

"Your bridesmaid at our wedding that you had known for so long – what was her name?"

"Moyra."

"Yes, Moyra. You and her have been friends . . ."

"Since we were eleven."

"Yes. That's amazing. All through school together. And now, you're emailing each other and still sending Christmas cards to each other."

"I was in her wedding."

"She in yours."

Rebekah smiled. "Of course."

CHAPTER FORTY-FIVE

"I pray that out of his glorious riches he may strengthen you with power through his Spirit in your inner being, so that Christ may dwell in your hearts through faith, . . ."

– Ephesians 3:16-17

Mid 1st Century A.D.

Late one evening toward the end of August 2011, Rebekah and Jake were sitting on their now screened-in back porch. They had baby monitors for both Scott's and Sarah's rooms. Both babies were asleep. Even though it was late and the fan was on, it was still warm. They were working on a bottle of wine but it didn't look like they were going to finish it. They had their dog, the ferocious Ruffles, on the porch with them. As she had matured from the little puppy they had found in the shelter, her Border Collie background showed itself. She was a collie/terrier mix and had a friendly disposition. She loved the children and they loved her. She had made herself a welcomed part of the Fleming family. In the day, the old maple trees provided shade. At night, if there was a breeze, they could hear the leaves rustling in the wind. Also, in the day, from this back porch, they could watch their Highland herd (three now) of cattle grazing in the pasture. Often, they would catch glimpses of real wildlife. They enjoyed that. The back porch was a pleasant and peaceful place for both Rebekah and Jake.

As they were enjoying each other's company, the phone rang. The caller ID indicated "Le Couteau."

"It's *The Library*," Jake said to Rebekah.

"Hi Jean."

"Hi Jake. How are you folks doing?"

"Great. Great. Enjoying small town life."

"A little different from New York City, huh?"

"A little. How are things up there?"

"We keep changing. You wouldn't believe all the new things."

"I noticed that you have a personal phone now."

"Yes, that's one little change that going public has made possible."

"Are all the changes for the good?"

"Yes, I think so. Opening up to the public has been truly good. Mr. Sinclair gives you credit for that idea."

"How is he doing?"

"He's eighty-one now and as sharp as ever. Actually, that's why I'm calling."

"Oh?"

"Yes, Mr. Sinclair was asking about you. He wanted me to invite you to come up for a visit." After a brief pause in which neither man spoke, Mr. Le Couteau said, "So consider yourself invited."

"Thanks Jean, but I've got two babies now."

"Bring them along. We're very family friendly here."

"I don't know. It's not easy to just pick up and leave. We have animals that have to be fed and taken care . . ."

"You can arrange for that. Mr. Sinclair really wants to talk with you."

"We are really happy here."

"Come up and talk about the possibilities. It's a different place than when you were last here. And you don't have to paddle your way here in a canoe."

Jake laughed.

"You do have to get here from the Canadian side."

"Let me discuss it with Rebekah. Let me pray about it."

"Of course. When you decide on a time, let me know. I want you to be our guests at *The Lodge*. That's what we call it . . . *The Lodge*. Like we call the entire organization *The Library*."

"I will think about it . . . and pray about it."

"Let me know."

"Yes, of course. How are the 'old men' doing?"

"They keep getting younger."

Jake smiled. "Good. How's Peggy?"

"Actually, she's expecting."

"That's great. I'm happy for her."

"I really hope you can make it. It's been six years. You do realize that your coming here was not an accident. I can think of three strong reasons God led you here. There are probably more than three."

"I promise I will pray about it."

"Good enough. I miss our long talks."

Jake laughed, "Me too. We did have some long ones, didn't we?"

"Sure did. You know, people up here are still reading that paper you wrote about the last days."

"No, I didn't know."

"Yes. Listen, I hope to see you soon."

"I'll let you know. Goodnight."

"Goodnight."

Rebekah said, "What was that all about?"

Jake had previously told Rebekah about his strange experiences at *The Library*. Now, he told her what Jean Le Couteau had said and about the invitation.

Rebekah replied to Jake's explanation, "This is a little odd. I've been thinking that I'd like to take a little trip. You know, our first family outing – with all four of us."

"Let's both pray about it. Let's see where the Holy Spirit leads us."

About a week later, in early September 2011, they had both decided to make the trip. A few days later, Rebekah and Jake were sitting together on a sofa in the family room. Scott and Sarah were on the floor in front of them. Ruffles was sleeping over by the fireplace. Scott had a book that Jake had read to him numerous times. He was trying to "read" the book to his baby sister. Sarah, at four months, was trying to crawl across the carpet. She wasn't making much progress and she wasn't paying her big brother very much attention at all.

Rebekah noticed that Jake was also not paying any attention to their children. He looked far away. She asked him the question husbands hate for their wives to ask.

"What are you thinking?"

Jake turned to look at her. He said, "Remembering."

"About?"

"The 11th."

"Oh. Sorry." Rebekah knew that, for Jake, the 11th meant two things – the destruction of the Twin Towers and the death of his fiancée, Laura.

Jake said, "It's been ten years. Doesn't seem that long."

"What do you most remember about it?"

"Standing in my office window. It was one of those windows that went from the ceiling to the floor. I remember standing there . . . looking at all the smoke and dust. Someone came in and said that they were evacuating the building. But I didn't go. I just stood there. And then, one building collapsed. A little later, the second one also collapsed. Eventually, the smoke and everything cleared and there was just empty space where the towers had been. It was so sad. At that time, I didn't know how many people had been killed. I knew it had to be a lot."

Rebekah didn't know what to say. After a few moments, she said, "I guess that is a memory you will never forget."

"I suppose you are right."

"You also lost Laura on the 11th."

"Yes. That was a tough time."

"I imagine so."

"But I have also been blessed – blessed with a wonderful wife whom I love more than anything . . . and two healthy children."

After discussing it with their neighbor and animal caretaker, Mrs. Teal, they decided that they could go to *The Library* for about ten days in early October.

Just after sunrise on Sunday morning, October 2nd, with Scott and Sarah strapped into their car seats, Jake and Rebekah backed out of their driveway. The big old maple trees were just beginning to show a slight tinge of color. Jake put his hand over his heart and said, "Be with us, Jesus."

On the way north, Jake told Rebekah all he could remember about his time at *The Library* six years earlier. He told her how no one seemed to know what to call it then. He got in the habit of calling it *Neverland*. He told her of his shock when he learned of its existence. He told her of his conversations with Mr. Le Couteau, Mr. Sinclair, the "old gentlemen," Peggy and Laura. He told her about their "trick" in having him speak at a worship service. He told her about paddling back, getting shot and finding little Victoria.

The drive north through the mountains was full of beautiful scenery. It would be even more magnificent on the drive back with the leaves in full color. With Rebekah still nursing Sarah, they were not in any great hurry.

As the crow flies, it wasn't a long trip. Their destination for the night was the town of Pohenegamook, a town in Quebec. It was just west of the U. S. border with Maine. There was also a very small town just east of the border between Maine and Quebec called Estcourt Station. Both towns were right on the border –Pohenegamook is located on both sides of a large lake – Lake Pohenegamook.

They spent the night in a motel in Pohenegamook and drove down to *The Library* the next morning. There was a nice professional-looking sign, *The Library*, at the entrance. Jake immediately noticed that part of the Christmas tree farm had been turned into a parking lot. After getting both of their children into strollers, they began walking down a sidewalk. Straight ahead, the sidewalk led through some trees. That way led to The Lodge. The sidewalk also branched off to the left. This led to a downward sloping broad walkway. It turned out that this led to the main entrance of *The Library* – to the front door. For Jake, this was all new. Inside, there was a nice lobby. There was a large curved receptionist desk at the back wall of the lobby. To the right was a large bronze plaque. At the top, it read "In Admiration and Memory of four wonderful members of *The Library's* family who were tragically killed in an automobile accident on September 11, 2005." Under that, the four names, in alphabetical order, were listed: *LAURA MIDDLETON, JO MORRISON, PAUL MORRISON, HENRI TAINE.*

Rebekah said to Jake, "that's very similar to your dedication in the front of your book."

Jake nodded.

"Did you know that they had done this?"

"No. . . . It's nice." Jake reached out and ran his index finger across Laura's name.

A young woman had entered the lobby. She looked at the receptionist's desk and then at the people standing at the plaque. She saw Jake rub his finger on it. She walked over and asked, "Did you know them?"

Rebekah was slightly startled. Jake turned to the young woman and answered, "Yes, I did."

The woman said, "Oh, I recognize you. You're Jake."

"Yes."

The woman turned toward the desk, then turned back and looked at Jake and then back at the desk. She seemed confused about the situation.

Jake asked, "What is your name?"

"Pamela. Pamela McDowell."

Jake put out his hand and shook hers. He said, "Pamela, it's good to meet you. This is my wife, Rebekah." They shook hands. "This is my son, Scott, and daughter, Sarah."

Pamela said, "Hello" and waved the fingers on one hand up and down.

Scott, from inside his stroller, said, "How do you do?"

Pamela, surprised, responded, "Very well, thank you. And you?"

Scott replied, "Fine. Thank you."

Pamela said, "Oh, I'm sorry. I'm supposed to call Mr. Le

Couteau as soon as you arrive."

She went over to the desk, pushed an intercom button and told Mr. Le Couteau that they were in the lobby.

On the left side of the lobby was a large photograph of the grounds. It was taken from the air. It showed the lake, the new lodge, the parking lot and all the trees.

Looking at it, Jake pointed at the small beach area on the other side of the lake from *The Lodge*. "This is where I camped when I first came here," Jake told Rebekah.

"Jake!"

With his hand stretched out in front of him, Mr. Le Couteau approached Jake. Jake ignored the hand and embraced Mr. Le Couteau with a hug. They patted each other on the back. After introductions were made, Mr. Le Couteau led them back outside.

"Jake, I want you and Rebekah to get settled in, take care of Scott and Sarah, get freshened up and join me, all of you, for lunch at the employee cafeteria. I've reserved the best suite at *The Lodge* for you. Just come back to the lobby and I'll get someone to bring you to the cafeteria."

"Thank you, Jean."

"My pleasure. After lunch, maybe we could have another long talk."

"Sounds good."

Mr. Le Couteau and Jake went to the car, retrieved all of their luggage, joined Rebekah, who was now pushing two strollers, and headed down the sidewalk to *The Lodge*.

Mr. Le Couteau said, "We actually have a luggage service that will transport guests, with their luggage, in golf carts from the parking lot to *The Lodge* by the back route. However, I want you to see the scenic route next to the lake."

Rebekah said, "I love these trees."

"Yes," Mr. Le Couteau responded, "We avoided cutting down as many of the large ones as we could. That's one reason this walkway is so curved. It's heated, you know."

Jake said, "No, I wasn't aware."

"Yes, it keeps the snow and ice from accumulating. Each year, we've had more and more winter guests."

Inside, the lobby of *The Lodge* had a huge fireplace. It was beautiful and Jake could easily imagine how it would look in the winter. *The Lodge* itself had been constructed with massive logs – logs from trees that had been cut down to make room for the building. *The Lodge* had replaced the trees that were used to build it. Their suite was truly nice – even luxurious. It had two bedrooms, a common area, a small kitchen and a great view of the lake. It was on the top floor of *The Lodge* – the third floor. A baby crib had already been set-up in the smaller bedroom. While Rebekah nursed Sarah, Scott and Jake unpacked the luggage.

Mr. Le Couteau had asked them to meet him at 1:00 PM for lunch. About 12:30 PM, the Fleming family rode the elevator down to the lobby. Using the strollers, they took a leisurely walk back to the main entrance.

Pamela was still there. She said, "Hi! I'll buzz Mr. Le Couteau."

As they were looking at the aerial view of *The Library*, they heard, "Jake!"

They all turned. A pregnant Peggy Habersham came running toward Jake. They embraced in a tight hug.

"It's so good to see you!" Peggy grasped Jake's arm with her hand and held it.

"Peggy, this is Rebekah. Rebekah, Peggy." They shook hands.

Rebekah said, "It's nice to meet you. I've heard a lot of good things about you."

Peggy replied, "Jake has told you about his adventure here six years ago?"

"Oh yes."

"Good. I'm sure we will be great friends."

Jake said, "Peggy, I want you to meet the younger members of the Fleming clan. This is Scott."

"Hi," Peggy said.

"How do you do?" Scott responded.

"And this is Sarah."

"Oh, what a darling. How old?"

Rebekah answered, "Five months tomorrow. Do you know what you're having?"

Peggy smiled, "A boy. Let me take you to the cafeteria. You know, Rebekah, when Jake was here before, he never could figure out our underground maze."

The three girls walked on ahead. Scott, still in his stroller, and Jake followed behind. As they got to the entrance of the cafeteria, Jake heard Peggy tell Rebekah, "I absolutely love your accent." Mr. Le Couteau waved them over to a large table. Sitting with him was Peggy's husband, Arthur Habersham. After introductions were made, a highchair was brought over to their table. As he put Scott into the highchair, Jake said to Arthur, "Soon, you're going to need one of these." Jake smiled. Arthur smiled, "I think you're right."

While they were in line to choose their food selections, Peggy whispered to Jake, "I want you to know that, before we knew what sex our baby was going to be, we picked out Larry for the boy's name and Laura for the girl's name."

"That was really sweet of you."

"Laura meant a lot to me. She was a good friend."

After lunch, Rebekah said, "Peggy has agreed to give me a tour of everything down here. I'm curious to see the chapel and the library." Turning to Jake, Rebekah said, "Why don't you and Jean have your talk and I'll take the tour? I'll see you back at *The Lodge*."

Peggy announced, "When those two get to talking, you may not see Jake for several days."

Both Mr. Le Couteau and Jake laughed. Jake said, "That's true."

Mr. Le Couteau led Jake down halls with twists and turns just like he remembered. Mr. Le Couteau opened a door and followed Jake into the room. It was the same room where Jake and Mr. Le Couteau had initially met. It looked exactly the same.

Jake said, "Nothing's changed."

"I think the coffee pot is new."

The two men sat in the same places they had sat six years earlier.

Meanwhile, Arthur needed to return to school. He had a class to teach. Peggy took Rebekah and the children on a grand tour. She always mentioned the connection that Jake had with each room she showed Rebekah. Rebekah was truly awed by what she was seeing. The actual library was huge and unbelievable. Peggy told her that they have had researchers come to the library from over twenty different countries. She showed her the chapel and told Scott that his daddy had stood on the stone stage and spoke to a full room of people. Peggy showed Rebekah one of the game rooms where children were playing electronic games.

Peggy said, "If we had more time and hadn't just eaten lunch, I'd take you to a new venture. It is above ground, over on the eastern side. It is an English tearoom. You being from Scotland, you would probably enjoy it."

"I'm sure I would. Maybe later in the week."

"Of course. Let's do it."

"Okay."

"Most of the rest of the things here are apartments and offices. Arthur and I live down here in one of the apartments. Since we've gone public, several people have moved up to Pohenegamook."

"Yes, I understand. We stayed in Pohenegamook last night."

Peggy nodded. "Okay. Let me walk you back to *The Lodge*."

"Jake told me that there are some nice informal pubs down here. Are they still here?"

Peggy seemed embarrassed. She said, "Yes, there are two."

"Jake said that he and Laura used to sit in a booth and talk for hours."

"Yes. Yes, they did."

"Could you show me?"

"Of course."

"Both Scott and Sarah are asleep. Is it real noisy?"

"At this time of day, I doubt if anyone will be there."

Walking into the pub, Rebekah said, "This is nice. I like it. I can see why Jake would like it too."

Peggy smiled. "One time, while Jake was trying to eat in the cafeteria, he was literally mobbed by people wanting to talk with him. He had just spent several hours talking with Mr. Sinclair. Back then, that just didn't happen. No one spent that kind of time with Mr. Sinclair. At that time, some people had worked here for years and never even seen him. That made Jake something of a celebrity around here. He had spoken at our chapel service so everyone knew what he looked like. They swarmed around his table all asking questions at the same time. Anyway, I rescued him."

"Rescued him?"

"Yeah. I said that he was supposed to be meeting someone in the library. I took him by the arm and dragged him here. The mob went looking for him in the library. We ate in here instead of in the cafeteria."

Rebekah smiled. "What was she like?"

Peggy paused. "She was my friend. I still miss her. She was sweet. She had a sense of humor. She was older than me but we got along great. We used to kid each other. Her students really loved her. . . . I went to her funeral in Savannah. I traveled with Mr. Sinclair. That was such an experience. I found out he is just like us, like everyone . . . That was the last time I saw Jake. That was six years ago. I honestly didn't think I'd ever see Jake again."

"Why?"

"I didn't think he'd ever come back here. But Mr. Sinclair did. I don't think he thought it would take six years but he always said that Jake would come someday."

Rebekah smiled and said, "Thank you."

Peggy took Rebekah back to *The Lodge*.

Sitting across from each other, Jake and Mr. Le Couteau each sipped a mug of coffee. Mr. Le Couteau said, "Jake, you sure have traveled a lot since you were last here."

Jake nodded at the obvious.

"We've got your book in the library."

Jake laughed. "You're the one. . . . That book does kind-of show where I've been. I think, Jean, that I have also traveled some as a person – spiritually, I mean."

Mr. Le Couteau looked at Jake's face and studied his eyes. He responded, "Yes. Yes, I think you most definitely have. We all either stand still, go back or go forward down the spiritual path. I do think you've been going forward."

"Maybe a few steps."

"Mr. Sinclair will be glad to hear that."

"How is he really doing?"

"Physically, he probably should retire. Mentally, he's as good as ever."

"Is he ill?"

"No. No, just age, I suppose. I doubt that he will ever retire. If he did, he would probably go downhill rather rapidly."

"I understand that."

After a pause, Mr. Le Couteau said, "The world, including very much the United States, has changed a lot since you and I sat in this room six years ago."

"That certainly is so. Technology alone has grown at a tremendous pace."

"Yes. However, I was referring to a major decline in our culture. Personally, Jake, I don't see that most changes have been positive. Politically, our nation is a mess. Real journalism no longer exists. Newspapers, television and radio news no longer even makes a pretense of being objective. Religion even has succumbed to pressures of political correctness. I don't know, it just all seems a shame."

Jake replied, "Perhaps, it's a sign of the times. If we are nearing the end times, then I suppose what you have just described could be a sign of the coming of the last days."

"I guess."

"If we are nearing the last days, these things are to be expected."

"It's like people have forgotten how to think. No one seems to think for themselves anymore."

"Again, sign of the times."

"It doesn't bother you?"

"Not really, no. I know how it's all going to end. That keeps me positive."

"That is, I suppose, the best way to look at it."

"I am concerned about the world Scott and Sarah are going to grow up in. Of course, if we are truly near the last days, they won't grow up in this world. But we don't really know when Jesus will return. As long as we can, Rebekah and I want to provide them with an excellent education – a good understanding of history – and a saving knowledge of Jesus."

"Yes, of course. That is exactly one of the purposes of *The Library* now. We have here a great collection of original documents that can be used to provide an accurate account of what truly took place in our history. For political purposes, people often distort or ignore parts of history. Our library contains documents which can present the facts of what actually happened in the past."

"That's good, I'm glad to hear that. Are the librarians here in the process of transposing those historical documents to a digital format?"

"No, I don't think so. That's a good idea. Listen Jake, I realize you just got here but I want to ask you if you might have a suggestion or two for some things we could do to improve the place."

"Yes, actually. As we were walking from the parking lot to *The Lodge*, I was wondering what it would be like if it were raining or snowing."

"Raining? Snowing?"

"Yes. I know it rains up here. I once got caught in a

thunderstorm out on the lake. My suggestion would be to build a roof or a cover of some type to keep rain and snow off of your guests as they walk back and forth from *The Lodge* to the library or to the parking lot."

"But a roof over the sidewalk would block the view of the trees."

"Make the roof out of clear unbreakable glass or plastic. Just something to keep the rain and snow off of everyone."

"Hmmmmm. I like it. That's another good idea. I'll pass that on to Mr. Sinclair."

The two men reminisced and discussed the deterioration of politics, culture, the status of the U.S. and the economy of the past few years.

After a couple of hours, Jake said, "Jean, I know it's not midnight but I think I'm ready to call it a day. I didn't sleep much last night."

"Of course, I understand."

"I'd like to visit with the 'old gentlemen' if they wouldn't mind."

"They will be delighted to see you again."

"Will I have the opportunity to see Mr. Sinclair?"

"Most definitely. He is anxious to see you."

"Good."

"He doesn't stay secluded like he used to do. He even eats in the cafeteria some and at the restaurant in *The Lodge*."

"That's good."

"Jake, let me give you a heads-up."

"Sure." Jake thought that Mr. Le Couteau was going to pass on some important information.

"Try the trout tonight. They were caught this morning."

Jake smiled. "Thanks, I'll do that."

CHAPTER FORTY-SIX

"If you believe, you will receive whatever you ask for in prayer."

– Matthew 21:22

Mid 1st Century A.D.

The next morning, Jake was to meet Jean at around 9 a.m. Rebekah was going to take the children to a playground/park on the left side of *The Lodge*. Sarah would be in her stroller but Scott would be walking like a "big boy."

As Jake was leaving, Rebekah, nursing Sarah, asked, "Don't you want some breakfast?"

"No, I'll grab a donut, or two, and a mug of coffee with Jean."

"What do you guys talk about anyway?"

"Everything."

"Everything?"

"Just about. Yesterday, I gave him a brilliant idea for a roof over the sidewalk," Jake grinned.

"A roof over the sidewalk? That's brilliant?"

"Yes. To keep rain and snow off of people walking on it. The brilliant part is to make the roof out of a clear substance that won't break."

"Okay."

"But we talk mostly about science, religion, history, politics, literature . . . you know, we even sometimes solve all the world's problems."

"I bet." Rebekah gave Jake one of her smiles that he loved.

"Really, we do. The only problem we haven't solved is how to get anyone to listen to our solutions."

Rebekah laughed. Sarah didn't appreciate the interruption.

Jake opened the door, turned and said, "I love you."

Rebekah replied, "I love you too."

As Jake was walking through the trees from *The Lodge* to the entrance to *The Library*, he noticed the sun sparkling on the water of the lake. Several tourists had stopped to take pictures. Jake approached the group and saw a tall grey-haired elderly man looking over the people who were standing there looking out at the lake. Jake nodded to him and said, "Good morning."

The man responded, "Good morning. This sure is a beautiful setting for so many books."

Jake replied, "Yes. Yes, it is."

Jake continued on down the walkway. To the right, he noticed the small rock cliff that contained the secret door through which Laura had first taken him inside the underground "Neverland." Jake stopped and backed up a little to look at the rocks from a different angle. Even knowing it was there, Jake couldn't see the door.

"What are you looking at?" The elderly man Jake had just spoken with asked.

Jake answered, "Those rocks there. They don't quite look like they belong there, do they?"

"I hadn't noticed. Now that you mention it, they do look a little out of place."

"I guess that's Mother Nature for you."

The old man smiled and said, "I guess." He shook his head and continued to look at the small outcropping of rocks.

The rest of the photographers had caught up with them. Jake noticed that they were not all together as a group. They were separate families and couples and singles that made up the group. As they made the turn toward the front entrance to *The Library*, Jake noticed Peggy and Arthur standing in the walkway.

Before he could greet them, he heard Peggy say, "What's wrong? Are you sick?"

Arthur replied, "I don't know. I feel funny."

Two things then happened at almost the same time. Arthur grabbed at his chest and crumpled to the pavement and Peggy screamed – loudly. Immediately, the group of people crowded around Arthur. Jake stepped over to Peggy. She was standing over Arthur with her hands over her face. She looked to be in shock. Jake walked to her, placed his hands on her shoulders, looked her in the eyes and said, "It's going to be all right."

Peggy wailed, "You don't know that."

Jake said, "Yes, I do. Have faith in Jesus."

Jake turned to all the people standing around. He said, "Please make a circle and hold hands. Please pray for this man. His name is Arthur."

One man said, "I'm Jewish."

Jake answered him, "We pray to the same God. Pray."

This all had taken less than a minute. Jake knelt down beside Arthur, placed both his hands on Arthur's chest and prayed out loud. He prayed, "Holy Spirit, I am asking you in the name of Jesus to heal this man, Arthur Habersham, right now. In Jesus' name, I am praying that whatever is wrong will be healed immediately. Thank you, Jesus. Thank you, Holy Spirit."

Still kneeling next to Arthur, Jake backed away. Arthur opened his eyes. He looked around at everyone. He saw Peggy crying. He smiled at her. He looked at Jake and asked, "What happened?"

Peggy knelt down and answered, "You grabbed your chest and collapsed. That's what happened. How are you feeling?"

"Fine. I feel fine."

The people in the circle were still holding hands. A few of them still had their heads bowed in prayer. They all began to smile. They stopped holding hands, looked at each other, and some of them grinned.

Arthur tried to get up but Peggy pushed him back.

She said, "No, you've just had a heart attack. We need to have you examined."

"I really feel fine," Arthur said. "Maybe I just fainted."

Peggy said, "You had a horrible look of pain on your face, you grabbed your heart and you fell down. When a person faints, they don't have pain and they don't grab their heart." She turned to Jake, "What do you think?"

"Arthur, I can't see what harm it will do to have a doctor look you over and see what's what."

"I think I hurt my knee when I fell."

Jake asked, "Peggy, do you guys still have a doctor on staff here?"

"Yes. I was thinking of a hospital."

"Take him to see the doctor here first."

"You mean just walk him down to the doctor's office?"

"Yes."

Jake stood up. He reached down and helped Arthur to stand.

"Which knee is it?" Jake asked.

"My left. I guess I hit it hard when I fell."

"I guess so. Explain that to the doctor."

"Excuse me. Am I the only one who thinks that my husband just suffered a heart attack?"

Jake replied, "Whatever Arthur suffered, Jesus just healed him."

"Jake, I truly appreciate you praying for Arthur but you don't know that he is healed."

"Yes, I do."

"How?"

"Faith."

Jake leaned over to Arthur and said, "No matter how strong our faith is, I think we tend to worry about the ones we love. Your wife is worried about you. You had best go get that knee looked at by the doctor."

Arthur smiled and nodded as he walked down the ramp with Peggy.

The group of people, who were smiling, began commenting. One lady said, "I think he was dead. I couldn't see him breathing."

A man said, "He (pointing at Jake) saved his life."

Another said, "He healed him all right."

From watching Arthur and Peggy walk down the ramp, Jake turned and faced the people. He said, "I thank you all for holding hands and praying. God obviously heard all of our prayers and healed Arthur."

"It was you. I saw you place your hands over his chest and pray. He was almost instantly healed."

"No. Please don't start saying that I healed him. It . . ."

"You did. I saw it."

"No. What you saw was someone praying. What you saw was Jesus answering that prayer. Jesus healed Arthur. Not me. Not me at all. We all prayed. We were all part of the prayer that Jesus heard and answered. Please . . . if you tell your friends about this, please make sure that you tell them that Jesus healed this man."

"It wouldn't have happened without you. You . . ."

"Listen, any Christian, with faith, could have prayed as I did. Jesus said that, if we have faith and believe that our prayers will come to pass, they will, indeed, come to pass. The catch is that you have to believe it will happen. See, I believed. Before I prayed that Arthur would be healed, I knew he would be healed. Any Christian who believes in Jesus could pray the same. What you just saw was Jesus performing another miracle. You and I were a small part of that miracle in that we all prayed for it to happen."

"What about me?" It was the man who had announced that he was Jewish.

"Are you familiar with the name Yeshua?"

"Yes, of course."

"You will need to accept Yeshua as the Messiah."

After a pause with everyone else listening, the man said, "That would be . . . difficult."

"Actually, it is quite easy. It may be difficult, after the fact, trying to explain it to your family and Jewish friends."

"Yes, that would be very hard."

Jake smiled. "I know, without any doubt, that Jesus is the Christ, the Messiah. He saved my soul and is my Lord. Every Christian . . . every believer . . . must come to the same realization. The fact that you are a Jewish person with Jewish heritage will never change. However, I think one of the most logical and reasonable things to happen to a Jewish person is for that person to accept Yeshua to be exactly who He said He was."

"The Messiah?"

"Yes. However, on a personal one-on-one level. He is also our personal savior. He died for our sins. That death on the cross is what cleanses a believer from all his sins."

Jake had not intended to have this discussion. He had not, of course, intended to stop and pray for Arthur. However, none of the group of people had left. There was a little five-year old boy standing with his mother and father. He was listening to the conversation between Jake and the Jewish man.

Jake walked over to the little boy and said, "Thank you for praying for that man."

The boy just smiled. He didn't say anything. Jake shook his hand and then the hands of everyone there. Then Jake said, "Listen, each of you have been a part of a miracle. You witnessed a miracle today. You participated in a miracle today. That is a wondrous thing. Look, they've got a chapel here. It's Tuesday and I doubt that anyone is using it. If any of you would like to continue this discussion, let's meet up there in the chapel at . . . say, two o'clock this afternoon. I hope to see you there. Just ask for directions and someone will take you there."

Jake walked over to the Jewish man and introduced himself. "I'm Jake Fleming."

"Rosen. David Rosen."

"I hope we can continue our talk."

Mr. Rosen nodded.

Jake went inside *The Library* and got Pamela to take him to the room where Mr. Le Couteau was waiting.

"Thanks Pamela. Hi Jean. I apologize for being late. Arthur had a situation and I helped Peggy a little with that. Are there any donuts?"

"Cinnamon rolls."

"Good." Jake got a mug of coffee and cinnamon roll.

"Jake, I want to talk with you about a conversation I had with one of our neighbors."

"Sure. First though, let me ask you. Are you still scoping me out for Mr. Sinclair?"

Mr. Le Couteau laughed. "No, not at all. That was over when you left six years ago."

"Okay." Jake nodded.

"You might remember that my wife and I have a condo in Montreal. She works there and I try to make it over most weekends."

"Yes, I remember. That's a long drive."

Mr. Le Couteau nodded. "As I was saying, I had a conversation with a neighbor of ours. This . . ."

"Just to be clear, you are talking about a neighbor in your condominium complex, not a neighbor of *The Library*?"

"Yes. Our conversation involved both religion and politics."

"Dangerous topics for casual conversation."

"Yes, you're right. It didn't turn out well. You might be aware that Canada is moving more and more toward socialism."

"Yes, I've heard that. So is the United States. Our current administration doesn't seem to think much of our Constitution or our Declaration of Independence."

Mr. Le Couteau laughed. "I've noticed that. This neighbor of mine claims to be a devout Catholic and a strong supporter of socialism."

"The two are not compatible."

"Exactly! That's what I told him. He got all offended. I said to him that socialism does not accept a role for religion in its philosophy."

"What did he say to that?"

"He said that that may be true for pure socialism but not for an adapted form that is designed specifically for one country.

In this case, Canada. I asked him what was the positive of socialism for Canada. He said that, with socialism, the government treats everyone the same. I immediately pointed out that that concept has never been put into practice anywhere socialism has been implemented."

"Socialism is for the masses, not for the socialists."

"Exactly right! I told him that. I said that the people running a socialistic government usually become extremely wealthy and live lives of luxury. The peons, the masses . . . usually barely have enough to survive. When the government officials need medical treatments, they do not want to be treated like everyone else. They travel to other countries for their medical care. The masses must wait months to see a doctor. I told him that people in Canada are already seeing this problem with their medical care. They frequently have to wait a long time to see a doctor. I asked him if he hadn't found that to be true."

"What did he say?"

"He admitted that sometimes the wait time was way too long. He said that they didn't have enough doctors in Canada."

"Perhaps that is because of the medical system that the government has imposed."

"Yes, I suggested the same thing. Then I asked him how, as a devout Catholic, he could support a policy that encourages abortion, that is in favor of same-sex marriage, that limits personal freedom and liberty and that wants to eliminate religious freedom."

"How could he possibly respond to that?"

"He had an answer. He said that would never happen in Canada."

Jake said, "It's already happening in Canada. That, what you just stated, is the policy of socialism.

"Jean, this whole thing about Catholics applies to the Congress in America. The democrats in Congress have numerous members who are Catholic. Yet, they support legislation that is not compatible with their religious teachings."

"They probably aren't aware of their religious teachings."

"Probably not. The democrat political party is now proudly calling themselves liberal progressives."

Mr. Le Couteau said, "Another name for socialism."

"Absolutely. Now they are even trying to control what we eat and what we drink."

"Control is the key word. That is what socialism is about – control and power."

After another hour of talking and solving problems on a variety of topics, Mr. Le Cousteau and Jake went to lunch in the cafeteria. When they walked in, there was a big round of applause.

Jake said, "Jean, did you win some award?"

"No, did you?"

"No." They both laughed, went through the cafeteria line and sat down. People immediately surrounded their table. People were patting Jake on his back and shoulders. Jake finally realized what it was about – the incident with Arthur.

Mr. Le Couteau asked, "What happened?"

"Jean, I told you I was late because of a situation with Arthur . . ."

"Situation!" One man shouted. "He saved Arthur's life. He healed him from a heart attack."

People started clapping again. There were so many people talking at the same time that Mr. Le Couteau and Jake could not hear each other speak. Jake made a couple of attempts to explain what had really happened but could not be heard. Someone said that the entire incident had been recorded on the security tapes. It was impossible for either Jake or Mr. Le Couteau to eat their lunch. They got up and left the cafeteria. In Mr. Le Couteau's apartment, Jake explained what had happened. He also told Mr. Le Couteau that he had promised to meet with whoever wanted to talk about it in the chapel at 2 p.m.

Later at 2 p.m., Jake walked into the chapel through the big wooden doors. He looked up and was still impressed with the craftsmanship that went into building the ceiling system with the huge logs. There were about twenty-five people sitting in the front pews. Jake walked up to the front, got a chair from the side near where the stairs go up to the stone platform, brought it to the front and sat down facing the people gathered there. Jake made small talk with everyone. Jake asked one couple where they called home. The woman said they were Sheila and Terry from Tennessee. Jake told them that he loved all types of music and wanted to visit Nashville and Memphis sometime. As Jake continued to talk, more people drifted in to the chapel. By 2 p.m., there were thirty-five people present. Those in the circle had obviously told others but Jake was fine with that.

Jake remained sitting in the chair. He asked, "How many of you were in our prayer circle this morning?"

Eight people raised their hands, including the five-year old boy and his parents. Mr. Rosen was also one of the eight.

"Right. Okay. Listen, I don't expect this will take very long. It better not because my wife is probably already wondering what has happened to me."

Several people laughed at that.

Jake continued, "I know that you are curious about what happened this morning. . . . A miracle happened this morning. Those of you who were there, you witnessed a miracle. God performed a miracle."

A man spoke up and said, "Hi, my name is Ron. I wasn't there, but I heard that you cured or healed a man who fell down from a heart attack."

Jake responded, "No, Ron, that is not accurate. What happened was that I prayed, with the help of all those who were there, and Jesus heard and answered our prayer and *He* healed Mr. Habersham. Jesus performed another miracle."

A woman, who identified herself as Sandy, had been there that morning. She said, "I saw you place both your hands over his heart."

"Yes. I probably didn't need to do that. Listen, this is really simple. Jesus said that His followers, if they truly believed

. . . had faith . . . they could, through the power of the Holy Spirit, do the things that He had done. See, I am a Christian. I am a follower of Jesus Christ. Since I believe Jesus to be Who He said He was, I believe that His death on the cross and His resurrection from the dead cleanses me of all my sins. Consequently, through the grace of God, because of my belief and acceptance of Christ, my soul is saved from the eternal damnation I deserve. . . . Jesus Christ lives in me through the Holy Spirit. When anyone, anyone at all, accepts Jesus, the Holy Spirit becomes a part of that person and guides that person on their spiritual path. . . . So, you see, I did not heal Mr. Habersham. Jesus did."

Jake stood up and carried the chair back to where he had gotten it. People stood and began to leave.

One man asked, "Is that it?"

Jake said, "Do you have any questions?"

"No, I guess not. I thought . . . I guess I was expecting . . . I don't know what I was expecting."

"God performed a miracle this morning. That's pretty exciting."

"Yes. Yes, you're right."

Jake asked everyone, most who were still standing, "Are you all Christians? If not, would you like to become a Christian?"

Several people smiled and said that they were Christians and started to walk down the aisle to the back of the chapel to the door that led outside. The parents of the five-year old boy took a few steps toward Jake. A man by himself did also. Jake motioned them over to the other side of the chapel and they all sat together on the front pew. Mr. Rosen continued to sit in the pew he had been in all along. Speaking to the couple and the man, Jake explained what they needed to do to accept Jesus as their savior and their Lord. They agreed to repent and ask Jesus to come into their lives. Jake led them in a prayer. He told them that their lives would be different from this moment forward. He encouraged them to begin reading the Bible daily and to find a church home that preached the gospel of Jesus Christ. Jake hugged each of them as new fellow Christians.

The five-year old boy said, "What about me?"

Jake smiled at him, got down on one knee and said, "In a few years, you will be old enough to decide for yourself that you want to become a Christian. Your parents will help you. You will probably be going to a Sunday School soon where you can learn more about Jesus. I have a little boy like you – only he is younger than you. I tell him that Jesus loves him. Jesus loves you too."

Jake stood up and said to the three new Christians, "Never forget that Jesus always loves you and will always be with you."

Jake noticed that Mr. Rosen was still sitting in the same place. Jake walked over and sat next to him.

Jake said, "I'm glad you came."

"Thank you. It was a nice explanation of what happened this morning."

"However . . . you are having a problem accepting it."

Mr. Rosen smiled. "You could say that."

"You know that the Torah has numerous prophesies regarding the Messiah?"

"Of course."

"Yeshua fulfilled them."

"Except for ruling the earth as King."

"Ahhh, but He will return and do that. That is in the future."

"I don't know."

"Do you honestly think that someone, yet to come, will be born of a virgin in Bethlehem, will enter Jerusalem riding on a donkey, be crucified on a cross, conquer death and rule the earth as King? There are dozens and dozens more prophesies from the Torah that Jesus Christ fulfilled. Do you think that someone is yet to come who will fulfill all of those? Yeshua is the Messiah."

"Well . . . "

"There is no well. From my perspective, it seems like the most natural thing in the world for Jews to be followers of Jesus."

"Not from my perspective. How can a Jew become a Christian?"

"Many have. Anyone can become a Christian. Gentiles

were not born Christians. Jews are born Jewish. You do know that Christians consider Jews to be the chosen people of God. The history of the Jewish people has been a history of supernatural events. Jesus was a supernatural event. As gentiles mature, some become Christians and others, perhaps most, do not. For a Jew to become a follower of Yeshua does not mean that that person ceases to be Jewish. More and more Jewish people are accepting Yeshua as their personal savior . . . as their Lord . . . as the Messiah."

After a few moments, Mr. Rosen said, "You said, this morning, that any Christian could do what you did. Is that true?"

Jake thought for a brief while and answered, "Perhaps not. Perhaps yes. I think some new Christians, like those three that just left, or some Sunday only Christians may not yet have the faith to do that publicly. They may not yet be spiritually mature. Jesus said that any of His followers, if they believed, could do what I did this morning. When you get down to it, all I did was ask Jesus to heal Arthur. I felt comfortable that He would. I believed that He would. And Jesus did. He might have decided not to heal him. It is His decision. I don't question God's decisions. I may not understand them. But it certainly isn't my place to question them."

"What is your place then? I mean in relation with the decisions of God?"

"Accept them. I acknowledge that He knows best."

"Well, yes."

"Through Jesus, God answers my prayers. It is nice to have that personal relationship."

"I can see that."

"Have you ever read any of the New Testament?"

"No, I have not."

"Try it. You might want to begin with the Book of John."

"John?"

"Yes. Read a chapter a day until you finish it. Before you begin reading a chapter, pray to God and ask Him to help you understand what He wants you to understand."

"I don't know."

Jake said, "You owe it to yourself to find out what God might be saying to you. You can do this."

"Yes. Yes, I can. . . . But . . ."

"What do you have to lose? At the very least, you will gain some understanding of what makes Christians tick."

Mr. Rosen laughed. He said, "Okay, I can do that."

"Of course you can."

The two men stood. They walked out the chapel doors and back outside to the parking lot. Mr. Rosen said he was staying in Pohenegamook with friends. They shook hands.

Jake said, "I'll be praying for you."

Mr. Rosen smiled and nodded his head. He walked toward his car and Jake walked down the sidewalk toward *The Lodge*.

Reaching their suite, Jake found that Rebekah had just finished nursing Sarah. They took Scott and Sarah downstairs to a daycare facility. Sarah would sleep and Scott would play on one of the children's computers.

Jake and Rebekah took the opportunity for a little diversion. They both put on life vests and paddled out on the lake in a canoe. As they were smoothly slicing through the water, Rebekah said, "I understand you've become some kind of a hero."

"No, you understand incorrectly. Where did you hear that?"

"I heard people talking in the restaurant. They didn't know I am your wife."

"The reality is that Jesus performed a miracle this morning and I am getting credit for it. It's absurd. I've tried to explain what really happened."

"What really did happen?"

"Arthur, Arthur Habersham had a heart attack. I prayed and asked Jesus to heal him and Jesus did. Some people seem to think that I healed him. I can't heal anyone."

Rebekah, in the front seat of the canoe, turned, smiled and

said, "That does explain what I overheard in the restaurant."

Paddling across the lake, Jake was steering them to the area where he had camped six years earlier. On the way, he commented, "The trees sure look beautiful from out here on the lake."

"Yes, this is really nice."

"They'll probably be at peak in a week. It is simply pretty – so peaceful."

Rebekah replied, "I've always felt closer to God when I'm surrounded by nature. Back home, in the Orkneys, I would go to our spot by the ocean and feel the presence of God."

"I know exactly what you mean."

Jake directed the canoe to the little cove and let it drift slowly to the shore. They got out and walked around. Jake showed Rebekah where he had put his tent. Some remains of his firepit were still there. It was just a shallow hole in the ground. He walked over to the stream that connects with the St. John River and told Rebekah that the stream leads to Fort Kent, Maine.

Rebekah asked, "Have you ever figured out what drew you to travel from New York City to this isolated spot?"

"No, not really. Somehow though, the people over there seemed to know I was coming. They were expecting me."

Jake had pointed in the direction of *The Library*. He told Rebekah about the red light at night.

Standing on "Jake's spot," Rebekah said, "It is beautiful here."

Jake responded, "You're beautiful here." He hugged her and they shared a long passionate kiss.

That evening, while eating in the restaurant at *The Lodge*, Jake received a message delivered by one of the "bell boys." Mr. Le Couteau had called and been unable to get either Jake or Rebekah. He left a message at the front desk. Taking the written message, Jake said to Rebekah, "I thought they only did this in movies from the forties."

Reading the message, Jake told Rebekah that the three

"old gentlemen" would like to talk with him tomorrow afternoon at 2 p.m. Jake had hoped that he would have an opportunity to visit with them. He explained to Rebekah that they all had to be in their nineties now. He had felt an almost immediate connection with all three of them.

After lunch the next day, Jake changed clothes and walked over to the lobby. Pamela guided him to a room where the three men were waiting on him. Jake added six years to their ages from when he first met them. Edward Nesbitt was now 90. Howard Millar was now 99. Cyril Kent was now 94. Jake remembered them as being intelligent and kind. He also recalled that all three had served in some branch of the armed forces during World War II.

Jake sat down at a table across from the three men. After they exchanged small talk, Mr. Kent asked about Jake's travels. Mr. Millar then asked about his marriage and home in New Hampshire. Jake had thought that they might ask about the incident with Arthur or that they might mention Laura but they never did.

Mr. Nesbitt asked Jake if Jake remembered what he had asked Jake six years earlier.

Jake replied, "Actually, yes I do. You asked me what I was doing here."

Mr. Nesbitt responded, "That's right. And you didn't know. Do you know now?"

Jake said, "I know why I'm here this time. At least, I think I do. However, I still do not know exactly what compelled me to show up here six years ago."

Mr. Nesbitt smiled. They all three smiled.

Jake continued, "Do you know what it was that caused me to come up here six years ago?"

All three men just smiled.

Jake asked, "I don't suppose you would mind telling me what you know about it, would you?"

Mr. Nesbitt replied, "Do you believe in the power of

prayer?"

"Most certainly."

"You may not remember . . . but sometime in the spring of 2005, you gave a community talk on money management."

"Yes, I remember those. I did two of them. My company, Excalibur, was sponsoring them."

Mr. Nesbitt continued, "All three of us and Charles Sinclair were at one of them. We heard your talk and your Q and A session."

"Wow, I had no idea. All four of you traveled down to New York City."

Mr. Nesbitt said, "We didn't travel there specifically to hear your talk. We had business there and met with Charles' son. But we enjoyed your question and answer time."

"Did any of you ask me a question?"

Mr. Kent answered, "No. Nonetheless, we were impressed. Charles decided to invite you here."

"I never received anything."

"Yes, you did. What happened is this. All four of us prayed that you would show up here. If you did, then we hoped to establish . . . a relationship . . . with you. If you did not, then Charles felt it was not to be."

Softly, Jake said, "And I came here."

Mr. Nesbitt said, "Yes, in answer to prayer."

Jake looked at each of the elderly gentlemen and asked, "What's next?"

Mr. Kent responded, "Charles wants to discuss that with you."

That evening, the Fleming family ate their supper in their room. Jake explained his meeting to Rebekah.

Rebekah asked, "About what . . . does Mr. Sinclair want to talk with you?"

"I don't really know. I suspect he wants to offer me that job as Assistant Director of this place."

"My . . . What will you say?"

"If he does, I'll say I have to pray about it, discuss it with you and think about it."

"It is beautiful up here."

Jake stared at Rebekah. Finally, he replied, "Yes. Yes, it is. Of course, we haven't seen it in winter."

Thursday, October 6th, 2011 was a day of heavy rain and thunderstorms. The Flemings spent the day inside *The Lodge*. In the afternoon, a note from Mr. Sinclair arrived asking Jake if he would meet with him on Friday at 1 p.m. Jake responded to the note by saying that he would be delighted to meet with Charles at the designated time.

The following day, Pamela guided Jake to Mr. Sinclair's office. It was exactly the same as Jake remembered it. It still smelled like pipe tobacco and Mr. Sinclair was smoking his pipe. They shook hands across the desk and Jake sat down.

Mr. Sinclair asked, "The pipe bother you?"

"No, not at all. I've given it up but I certainly don't mind others smoking one."

"Why'd you stop smoking your pipe?"

"Several reasons. Mostly because I have a wife and children now."

Mr. Sinclair nodded his head. "Being married does change one's habits."

Jake laughed. "That's a blunt but truthful way of acknowledging things."

Mr. Sinclair smiled. "I certainly remember being married. I wish she were still alive and still with me."

Jake didn't know what to say in response. He asked, "How is your son, John, doing?"

"Oh, he's fine. He thinks it's good that we have gone public with everything." Mr. Sinclair smiled. He looked at Jake and said, "He doesn't know everything about our little operation...or program here. We still have a secret or two with which we haven't gone public."

Again, Jake didn't know what to say. He said, "Charles, I think that you have done a wonderful job with *The Lodge* and with *The Library*. I've heard that you've had several serious academic researchers up here."

Mr. Sinclair nodded, "Yes, that's true. It has been nice to be able to share our library with others. Everyone is welcome. I know this is not an easy place to get to for most people. I know that they have to make an extra effort. When they find that effort to have been worthwhile, I'm glad."

Mr. Sinclair puffed on his pipe but it had gone out. He used a match to relight it. After a few puffs, he pointed the end of his pipe at Jake and said, "You know, when we said goodbye to you in Savannah, Peggy didn't think we'd ever see you again. I told her we would."

"Here I am. It is beautiful up here. Pohenegamook is a beautiful little village on a very nice lake."

"Yes, several of our employees live there. There is no problem with the Canadians but, for the Americans, they can't live there year-round. Pohenegamook has a little less than three thousand year-round residents. Many more live there in the summer. We are trying to see if we can get an exemption or an exception for our American employees so that they could buy a house in Pohenegamook and live there year-round without having to become Canadian citizens."

"If Canada won't make an exception, have you thought of building a subdivision of homes here on the Maine side of the border?"

Mr. Sinclair looked totally surprised.

"No, I actually have not thought of that," he puffed on his pipe.

"You've got a lot of flat land where the rest of the Christmas tree farm is. Or, you could sell lots on the opposite side of the lake and let people build their own type of home. Some may want a traditional brick home, others a log home. They are doing some really good things with underground homes these days. Considering the history of this place, you might want to look into building an underground subdivision. It would certainly cut down on one's heating expenses in the winter."

"Jake, you might really be on to something."

"Perhaps the Canadian government will make an exception and you won't need to do anything. People can live in Pohenegamook."

Mr. Sinclair puffed on his pipe. He said, "Even if they do, it still might be a good idea to develop some homes over here."

"Might be something to consider."

"Yes, listen Jake, how are you doing?"

"Never better. I live closer to God now than I ever have."

Mr. Sinclair smiled. "That's good. That's good." With some hesitation, Mr. Sinclair asked, "How are you doing with Laura's death?"

Jake didn't respond.

Mr. Sinclair continued, "We miss her here. She was a wonderful person."

Very softly, Jake said, "Yes, yes she was."

"When I saw you at her funeral, I felt so sad for you."

"I was a total mess then."

"That would not be unexpected."

"I have come to peace with Laura's loss. . . . At the time, I never thought I'd ever be in love again. The first time I saw Rebekah, that little Cupid guy shot me with one of his arrows."

Mr. Sinclair grinned a big smile.

Jake added, "I had no choice. With that arrow in my heart, I had to fall in love with Rebekah. I would never have thought it could happen so fast. But it did."

"Any concerns, Jake?"

"No. Well . . . maybe one."

"Tell me about it."

Jake paused. He replied, "Sometimes, I wonder if Rebekah feels like a 'second choice.' I have thought of looking up information on how widowers handle their second marriages. But I haven't done that. I don't know why. I promised myself that I would never compare them. And I haven't. But I know, and Rebekah knows, that if Laura had not been killed in that wreck...Rebekah and I would not now be married. Our children would not be hers. I don't know how Rebekah feels about that. She is not my second choice. I just met Laura before I met Rebekah. If I had met Rebekah first, I would have fallen in love with her first. Actually, Charles, my coming here six years ago resulted, in a roundabout way, in me meeting Rebekah in Scotland. We've been married for four years now and it's been wonderful."

"Jake, your coming here six years ago resulted in several positive things. However, before I get to that, you mentioned that you don't know how Rebekah feels about the situation of you marrying her after Laura died. You should simply ask her. Clear the air."

Mr. Sinclair blew out a strong steady stream of smoke.

Jake laughed and said, "Clear the air." He waved his hands and arms as if to clear away the smoke.

Mr. Sinclair smiled and responded, "Bad timing."

"But good advice. I'll take it. I'll ask her."

"I do think it is good for any marriage to keep things, including feelings, out in the open between husband and wife. Rebekah may completely understand and accept the situation without any negative feelings. On the other hand, she may be harboring some negative feelings that you may be able to alleviate."

"I really don't think she is. But you are right. We should discuss it."

"Jake, you know that I once offered you a position here as the Assistant Director. I have been hoping that John would reconsider and take that post with the intent of becoming Director when . . . I retire."

Jake quickly replied, "I think that would be best."

"Yes, well, that is not going to happen. He is even less interested in being a part of this than ever."

Jake didn't say anything.

Mr. Sinclair continued, "Anyway, I want you to consider accepting the offer. I am confident that you would do an excellent job here. And, when I retire, I am sure that *The Library* and my family's heritage would be in good hands."

"Thank you, Charles. I will consider it. I will pray about it."

"Of course."

"I will discuss it with Rebekah."

"Of course. You should. Say, would you and Rebekah be my guests for dinner tonight?"

"That would be nice. Yes, we'd be honored."

"It'll give me a chance to meet Rebekah."

"I've told her a lot about you and the history of this place. She would love to meet you."

"I have a special dining room in *The Lodge*."

"You get out more frequently, I understand, now than in the past?'

"Yes, I've lost some of my aura of mysticism or spirituality. People no longer are in awe of me. Just a regular Joe."

Jake laughed. "Somehow, I don't see that ever happening."

"Let's say 8 p.m.? Ask for my private room."

"Okay. See you tonight."

Rebekah was concerned about what to wear. Jake told her that Mr. Sinclair had said that he was a "regular Joe" now. Rebekah didn't know what that expression meant. While she was deciding what to wear, Jake called and got a babysitter for the evening. *The Lodge* kept several on call.

As Jake began to tell the Maître d' that they were there to dine with Mr. Sinclair, he interrupted and said, "I know who you are, Mr. Fleming. Unfortunately, the cleaning crew was working in Mr. Sinclair's private room this evening. When he called, it was too late to get it ready. The chairs have been turned over on top of the tables and the carpet is wet. We have a special table for you over here."

He led Rebekah and Jake to a table in the corner. Almost as soon as they were seated, Mr. Sinclair arrived. Jake pointed him out to Rebekah. They could see the Maître d' explaining the situation to him.

After Jake introduced Rebekah to Mr. Sinclair, he began apologizing for the situation. He said it was his fault that he waited until the last minute to call and reserve his room.

"Think nothing of it. Wet carpet. That's all. This table is fine. Perhaps, with your back to the room, you will go unnoticed and not be bothered. If anyone does recognize you, they'll just think you're a 'regular Joe.'"

Mr. Sinclair smiled and replied, "Perhaps. Jake, you failed to tell me what a beautiful woman you married." Looking at Rebekah, he continued, "It is a pleasure for me to meet such a lovely and charming lady."

Rebekah smiled and simply said, "Thank you."

"Tell me," Mr. Sinclair asked, "what do you think of our little place?"

"It's beautiful. However, I imagine your grandfather selected this site for its isolation rather than the scenery."

Mr. Sinclair seemed surprised. He looked at Jake and said, "Jake, your wife is not only outstandingly attractive; she is intelligent."

Jake laughed. He replied, "I knew both of those things to be true about Rebekah five minutes after I met her."

"And now, I can say the same thing," Mr. Sinclair smiled.

Laughing, Rebekah said, "Will you two quit talking about me like I'm not here?"

Mr. Sinclair said, "Sorry. My fault. Did you get a tour of all the underground facilities?"

"Yes, Peggy gave me a complete tour. It's an amazing place. The chapel and the actual library are both unbelievable."

"Thank you. I think so too. I've been trying to talk your husband here," Mr. Sinclair jerked his head in Jake's direction, "into joining our little group."

Jake was about to say something when their waiter arrived. After they had all placed their orders, and the waiter left, a young couple with their daughter came over to the table. Jake had seen them walking over and said, "Charles, I think you've been recognized."

They came and stood by the table. Mr. Sinclair smiled and asked, "Are you enjoying your stay?"

The man replied with a quick "Yes."

Looking at Jake, the woman asked, "Are you the man who can heal people?"

Before Jake could respond, she stated, "Our daughter, Wendy, was born with a speech impediment. She has had an operation but it was not successful. Can you heal her?"

Jake was taken back by the situation. He didn't know what to do or say. Mr. Sinclair and Rebekah looked at each other.

Jake placed his hand over his heart and silently, to himself, asked the Holy Spirit to guide him.

He looked at the parents and answered, "No, I'm sorry I cannot heal your daughter . . . or anyone." All three looked totally defeated. The little girl looked like she was going to cry.

Jake looked at her and asked, "Wendy, how old are you?"

She held up both hands with her fingers spread wide.

Jake smiled and said, "You are two hands old. You are growing up."

Wendy smiled.

"Wendy, I cannot heal you. However, I know someone who can heal you."

Wendy and both parents smiled big happy smiles.

"Wendy, the person I know who can heal you is Jesus."

Wendy kept smiling but her parents looked dejected. The mother said, "We have been praying for her since she was born. Our church has been praying for her."

Jake said, "Jesus gets to decide who He heals and who He does not heal. Jesus gets to decide when a person will be healed and when he will not. If you don't mind, I would like to pray for Wendy and ask Jesus to heal her."

The mother and father looked at each other. The father said, "It can't do any harm to try. Thank you."

Jake got up and walked over to the two solid wood doors

that led to Mr. Sinclair's private room. He propped one of them wide open. He walked back and held out his hand to Wendy. She took it and they walked into the private dining room together. Her mother and father stood at the door and watched. Ignoring the damp carpet, Jake walked over to the middle of the room, removed a chair from the large table and sat in it. Wendy was standing in front of him. Jake smiled at Wendy and asked, "Wendy, do you know who Jesus is?"

Wendy nodded her head.

"Good. He is the Son of God. He is God. He can do anything. He can heal you. Do you believe that?"

Again, Wendy nodded her head. She spoke a yes but it sounded like "sasss."

Jake said, "I believe He can heal you too. Now Wendy, there is nothing to be afraid of at all. This will not hurt. I am going to put my hands on your throat and pray. Okay?"

"Sasss." She nodded.

Jake smiled at her and gently placed his hands on her throat.

He prayed, "Holy Spirit, I am asking you to use your immense power. I am asking in the precious name of Jesus. In His holy name, I am asking that you heal this child, Wendy, from all speech impediments. Heal whatever is causing the problem. I am praying that whatever is wrong will be healed immediately. Jesus, please heal her right now. Thank you, Jesus. Thank you, Holy Spirit."

Jake removed his hands from Wendy's throat. He smiled at her and said, "I believe Jesus has healed you."

Wendy looked confused.

Jake asked, "How do you feel? Would you say something?"

"Yes," she replied.

Wendy was startled at her pronunciation of the word "Yes."

Jake smiled. He said "Thank you, Jesus. Thank you, Holy Spirit. Thank you, God."

Wendy ran over to her parents and told them, in a clear voice, that she was all better. The parents had not heard Jake's conversation with Wendy or his prayer. However, they could certainly hear that their daughter had been healed.

After putting the chair back on top of the table, Jake came out of the room, closed the door and sat back down.

Rebekah asked, "How did it go?'

Jake replied, "Jesus healed her."

"That's wonderful!"

"Yes. It is."

Wendy and her parents, after many hugs all around, came over to the table and were full of appreciation for Jake. They thanked him. Over and over, they thanked him. He kept telling them to thank Jesus. Jesus, he said, is the One who healed Wendy. They should be thanking Jesus.

Wendy walked over to Jake, gave him a hug and said, "Thank you for praying for me. I will thank Jesus for healing me."

As they left, their waiter brought their dinners. Mr. Sinclair had been silent throughout this entire event. After the waiter walked away, he asked, "What just happened here?"

Jake smiled and said, "Jesus just performed another miracle."

"But how . . . how did you . . . when did you receive the ability to heal people?"

"I didn't. I don't have the ability to heal. However, Jesus gave all of his followers the authority to do things in His name. In Mark 16:16-18, just before He ascends into Heaven, Jesus says that whoever believes on Him and, as a sign of that belief, is baptized . . . that person will be saved. Then Jesus says that those who believe, in His name, they will be able to do several things. Some of them will be able to drive out demons, speak in different languages and they will be able to place their hands on sick people and, in His name, those sick people will get well. They will be healed."

Mr. Sinclair was silent for a few minutes. They began to

eat their food.

Jake smiled and turned to Rebekah. He softly said to her, "Her name was Wendy."

"I know."

Mr. Sinclair asked, "What's that? What's the child's name have to do with anything?"

Jake said, "Rebekah's mother is named Wendy."

"Is that why you agreed to pray for her?"

"No. The reason I agreed to pray for her is because I felt the Holy Spirit telling me to do so."

"So, if you had not felt the Holy Spirit telling you to, you wouldn't have prayed for her?"

"Yes, I suppose that's right."

"Jake, why doesn't . . . why don't . . . I mean, how come every Christian doesn't do this?"

"I've thought about it. I think it is due to a lack of faith. When I was in my twenties, I would never have prayed for someone to be healed. I mean, like this. By placing my hands on them and asked for a healing. I would pray, in my normal prayers, for someone to be healed. Wendy's mother said the whole church had been praying for Wendy. I would have prayed like that in my twenties and thirties."

Mr. Sinclair responded, "I guess I'm beginning to understand."

"All Christians are not as far down the spiritual path as others. We all have to make that journey. Someone who is farther along than others is not any better than others – just farther down the path. We all start at the beginning. We all have to take the first step."

"Yes, that makes sense."

Pointing at her plate, Rebekah said, "This is really good."

Mr. Sinclair smiled. "I'm glad. We were talking about something when we were interrupted."

Rebekah said, "Yes, the waiter arrived as you were telling me that you want Jake to join you here."

"Yes. This afternoon, when I again asked him, do you

know what he said?"

"What?"

"That he would have to discuss it with you."

"That seems like a logical response," Rebekah smiled. "I'm listening. Convince me."

Mr. Sinclair turned to Jake and said, "I like her."

Jake replied, "Me too."

Later that night, when Rebekah and Jake were lying together in bed, Jake asked, "Did Charles convince you?"

"Not yet."

"He thought he had found a weakness when he learned that you used to teach school. I thought his suggestion that you teach one or two courses instead of full-time was a good tease. He knew, with the children, you wouldn't want a full-time teaching position."

"That was a good suggestion."

"So?"

"I'm thinking about it. Like I said earlier, ultimately the decision is yours."

"I hope the Holy Spirit will make it for me."

"You want to see it written in the clouds?"

"That would be nice."

CHAPTER FORTY-SEVEN

"You are my lamp, O Lord; the Lord turns my darkness into light."

– 2 Samuel 22:29

Mid 7th Century B. C.

On Friday, October 11th, 2013, Rebekah and Jake drove down to Boston on a date. They attended a symphony presentation of Beethoven's Ninth. A neighbor, Mrs. Plaisted, was babysitting. Rebekah and Jake got back about 12:45 AM. Their dog, Ruffles, announced their arrival. Mrs. Plaisted had fallen asleep in a chair. The barking woke her but not the children. Jake walked Mrs. Plaisted home and paid her for babysitting.

After checking on both children, Rebekah changed clothes. As soon as he got back, Jake also changed. They took a glass of wine and sat outside on the back porch.

Rebekah took a sip and said, "Thank you for a lovely evening."

Jake smiled, "You're welcome . . . but it's not over yet."

"Oh?"

"No . . . Rebekah, I don't want us to ever stop going on dates."

"Okay. What brought that up?"

"I read an article somewhere that said only about a third of married couples still went on dates. Let's promise each other that we will, even when we're real old, still date."

"All you have to do is ask. My answer will always be yes."

They clicked their wine glasses together.

Jake said, "I can't believe I am fifty years old."

Rebekah replied, "I'm heading that way."

"You're forty-four but you look to be about thirty-two. People are going to start thinking that I am out with my daughter."

Rebekah laughed. "You are flattering me."

"No, I'm proud of you. I enjoy saying, 'Meet my wife, Rebekah.' People probably say, 'What does that beautiful young woman see in that old man?'"

"Stop it. You're not an old man."

"Okay. If you say so, I'll buy it."

"I say so."

"Good. More wine?"

"Maybe half a glass."

Jake returned with the wine. They sat in silence and enjoyed the cool night air. The leaves were at their peak fall colors. In any direction one looked, it was simply beautiful.

Jake asked, "You know what?"

"What?"

"It smells like autumn."

"How much have you had to drink?"

Jake laughed. "No more than you. No, really. There are probably only two or three weeks in a year when it smells like this. It smells like autumn."

"Okay."

"Do the Orkney islands have a special autumn smell?"

"I've never thought about it. Of course, we don't have the trees there like here."

"It's nice. I like it."

After a few minutes of silence, Jake said, "We need to talk about something serious."

Rebekah was startled. She said, "All right. What?"

"Our finances."

Relieved, Rebekah asked, "Are we having financial problems?"

"No, not at all. I would have told you that as soon as

something like that happened."

"What's wrong with our finances?"

"The Bible says that much is expected from he who has been given much. We have been given much."

"We donate a lot to several charities."

"We do and we should. However, I'm thinking more long-term."

Rebekah didn't like the direction this conversation was headed. She reminded Jake of the playground incident. She said, "Remember, soon after we moved here, they had a community fund drive to purchase more playground equipment for the park. Do you remember what you donated? A hundred dollars. They were trying to raise forty thousand. You could have written a check for the whole forty thousand. But only a hundred. I thought you were being petty or cheap. I thought you should have sent at least ten thousand. Remember?"

"Yes."

"That's when you started including me on all charity donations. I have always appreciated that. You told me it wasn't your money. It was our money. That's when you explained why you donated only a hundred dollars. It was a community event.

"We should participate. However, we should not take away the opportunity for others to participate. This way, everyone in the community could be a part of the effort to raise those funds. Someone may give twenty dollars. Someone else may give fifty. A child may give five or ten dollars. Everyone would feel that they were a part of the new playground equipment. I understood that. You were right."

"Rebekah, I am talking about something else. We do contribute to several organizations that are working to bring the gospel to Jewish people . . . all around the world but especially to those in Israel. We've talked about this. It really is important. I think all Christians should do what they can to help spread the truth that Jesus was the Messiah and that He came initially and specifically for the Jewish people. Their rejection was predicted. However, their acceptance is also predicted. When Jesus rode into Jerusalem on a donkey on what we now call Palm Sunday, the people, the crowds shouted, 'Blessed is He who comes in the name of the Lord.' That is Matthew 21:9. Then, in Matthew 23:39, Jesus tells the city of Jerusalem that it will not see Him again until the city says, 'Blessed is He who comes in the name of the Lord.' Jesus is telling us all that He will not return until the Jewish leadership in Jerusalem admits that Jesus, Yeshua, is, in fact, the Messiah, the Son of God. Obviously then, it is important to spread the message of the gospel to Jewish people everywhere – but especially in Israel."

Rebekah replied, "Yes, I agree with all that. I agree we should continue to support and pray for those groups who are witnessing to Jewish folks. So, what is it with our finances?"

"It is important that we be good stewards of the money we have been given."

"I agree."

"I want to set up college funds for both Scott and Sarah."

"Of course."

"I think it would be best for them to attend Christian schools. Scott can begin kindergarten next year. We ought to begin checking out all the Christian schools in our area."

"Yes, of course."

"No one knows the future. I am fifty. You are forty-four. The odds are that you will outlive me and . . ."

"No! Let's not talk about this now."

"I think . . ."

"I'm not ready to discuss this . . . It's too upsetting for me . . . right now. Let's talk about it later . . . another time."

"All right."

"Are you mad?"

"No."

"What are you doing?"

"Smelling autumn."

Halloween came and went. Scott had wanted to go trick-or-treating. Jake had told him no. He told him "There is a rule that you have to be at least five years old to go trick-or-treating."

Scott thought this over for about 20 seconds and replied, "Who made this rule?"

Jake answered, "I did."

"Okay."

"Next year, you will be five. Next year, you can go trick-or-treating."

Scott smiled. "Okay."

During the first week of November, Rebekah and Jake seemed to be in touch with almost everyone they knew. Both moms wanted them to visit for Christmas. Jake heard from both his sisters. Rebekah heard from her sister. Jake heard from Peggy and Arthur at *The Library*. Jake and Ted talked for over an hour on the phone. After that, Jake called several of his other friends that he had not talked with in months. Over the past three years, Rebekah had become good friends with a woman from their church. Her name was Vivian. On Saturday, November 9th, she and Rebekah went on a fall shopping trip to Boston. Jake stayed home and played with Scott and Sarah. That afternoon, Mr. Le Couteau called. He told Jake that Mr. Sinclair was in a hospital in Québec City. He also told Jake that Mr. Sinclair had asked that Jake come see him. Jake said that he would.

Early on the morning of Sunday, November 10, 2013, Jake was driving north. He had decided, based on the flights, that he could get to Québec City almost as quickly by driving as he could by flying.

The drive gave Jake a lot of time to think. He could feel the Holy Spirit with him and he said out loud, as he frequently did, "Thank you, Jesus." Jake knew that simply seeing some of the sights he had seen with Laura would bring happy . . . and sad . . . memories. Of course, he had not been back to Québec City since his week there with Laura. That seemed so long ago now.

At the border, the Canadian custom officials could not have been nicer. Jake always appreciated politeness. Just as it was getting dark, he arrived at Québec City. With GPS, he drove to the hospital. Visiting hours were still active. As he approached Mr. Sinclair's room, Mr. Le Couteau was standing in the hall with Peggy. A nurse was just leaving them. Seeing Jake, Peggy ran over and gave him a hug. Since traveling with Mr. Sinclair to Laura's funeral in Savannah, to the funerals of the others and to Chicago, Peggy had become close to Mr. Sinclair. She was obviously concerned. Jake shook hands with Mr. Le Couteau.

"Jean, what is his status?"

"As I mentioned on the phone, it is his heart. The nurse we were, just now, talking with said that the doctor had prescribed a pill that would keep his asleep until morning."

"Is he sleeping now?"

"Yes."

"I understand." Turning to Peggy, he asked, "How are Arthur and baby Larry?"

Peggy smiled, "They're fine. Arthur is babysitting Larry. Rebekah?"

"She's home taking care of Scott and Sarah."

Mr. Le Couteau asked Jake, "Have you eaten?"

"No."

"Neither have we. Let's go find some supper."

"Is there a motel near here?"

"Yes. We've got rooms at one a couple of blocks down the street."

"Great. Do they have a restaurant?"

Mr. Le Couteau looked at Peggy. She said, "Yes, they do."

"Good."

They had walked from the motel to the hospital. Jake drove them back and they gave him directions.

As Jake parked, he said, "Let me get checked in and I'll meet you both in the restaurant . . . in half an hour?"

Mr. Le Couteau replied, "That's fine."

Jake checked in, went to his room, dropped his suitcase on the bed and called Rebekah. He wanted to let her know that he had arrived all right and bring her up-to-date regarding Mr. Sinclair. As he had to go meet with Peggy and Jean, they only talked briefly. Rebekah told Jake that while he had been driving up to Québec City, her mom had called and that they had had a nice talk. Jake was glad to hear that Wendy was doing all right. He told Rebekah that he loved her and would let her know, as soon as he knew anything, how Charles was doing.

He met Mr. Le Couteau and Peggy in the restaurant.

Rebekah's conversation with her mom that afternoon was good for both of them.

Rebekah said, "Mum, I'm glad you called. I was thinking of calling you."

"What's wrong?"

"Nothing really. Jake said a couple of things a few days ago and it's been bothering me."

"What?"

"First, he said, 'I want to talk with you about something serious.'"

"Yes?"

"Just that. My first thought was that he was thinking of divorcing me."

"Why would you think that?"

"I don't know."

"Has he done anything to make you think he was unhappy?"

"No, nothing. That's not it. It's me."

"Has he started arguments with you?"

"No, never. It's me, Mum."

"What does that mean?"

"I'm not sure. You know, years ago, when I was engaged…he just suddenly left me."

"You were lucky he did."

Rebekah smiled. "I know. Nonetheless, I think that does something to a person. If Jake were to leave me, I don't think I could . . . handle it. I love him so much."

"First of all, Rebekah, Jake is not going to leave you. He loves you . . . totally and completely. I know about these things. I could tell that the very first time he came over to visit."

"You and your clothes thing."

Wendy laughed. "No, it's much more than that. Believe me, Jake loves you."

"I know he does."

"You've got absolutely no reason to worry."

"I know."

"Then what?"

"I told you, Mum, it's me. That was the first thing I thought of when he said he wanted to talk seriously. I know he and I are both Christians . . . and I know he loves me. I know he would never do anything to hurt me. I know that. But that was the first thing I thought of. I'm ashamed of myself for thinking that. But there it is. That's what I thought about first."

"What did he want to talk about?"

"Our finances."

"Okay. That's good. You should talk about them."

"He said that he would probably die before me."

"That's most likely."

"Mum!"

"He's being honest with you."

"I think he wants to make wills."

"That's a good idea."

"I'm not ready for that. I don't want to talk about things like that."

"Is that the other thing he said that upset you?"

"Yes."

"I love you Rebekah but I have to side with Jake on both of those."

Rebekah laughed. "I side with Jake on them too. Still, they upset me. I know he's right. I know we should get our finances settled. I know he's thinking about what's best for the children and me. He said he wanted to set up a college fund account for both Scott and Sarah. I just don't want to talk about wills . . . and death."

"We all get to experience it."

"I know."

"Do you remember Mr. Stirling? From church?"

"Yes, I think so."

"He and I have been . . . keeping company."

"Dating?"

"I guess so."

"That's wonderful. I'm happy for you, Mum."

"Thank you. Your sister thinks I'm too old to start dating anyone."

"Nonsense."

"We're both in our sixties."

"That's nice. You'll have a lot to talk about with each other."

"We do. We really do. Let me say hello to Jake."

"Jake's on the way to Québec City."

"Oh?"

"Yes, a friend of his, Charles Sinclair, the head of *The Library*, is in hospital there. Something to do with his heart. I told you about meeting him a couple of years ago."

"I remember. I hope he'll be all right."

"Yes. I've been praying for him."

The next morning, after breakfast together, Mr. Le Couteau, Peggy and Jake were standing in the hall outside of Mr. Sinclair's hospital room. A doctor came out of the room.

The doctor asked, "Are you folks relatives?"

Mr. Le Couteau answered, "No, we're friends. I've contacted his son and expect him to arrive today."

"Uh-huh."

Jake asked, "Can we see him?"

"He is asking for someone named Jake."

"That's me."

"I guess it's all right. Perhaps one at a time would be best."

Jake asked, "How is he doing?"

"Perhaps I'd better wait for his son to arrive."

Peggy asked, "Is he going to be all right?"

After a brief pause, the doctor smiled and replied, "The

heart is a tricky thing."

Jake thought to himself, *Did this man have to go to medical school to learn that?* However, Jake didn't say anything. Jake entered the hospital room.

"Good morning, Charles."

"Is it?"

"Yes, it's a beautiful morning."

"They probably won't let us talk very long. I've wanted to tell you something."

"Sure."

"You are aware of the legend of Henry Sinclair?"

"Yes."

"He was an ancestor of mine. It has come down through the family that the story of his travels to North America is true. However, we have no physical evidence to support it. My grandfather, who began *The Library*, spent a lot of time, effort and money trying to find some proof. There are a few carvings in stone that could be from Henry's time. Henry could most certainly have constructed the stone tower in Rhode Island. Again, no proof. I believe it to be true . . . just because it came down through the family."

"I understand."

"John has no interest in this at all. I have told him about it; but, he doesn't care."

Jake didn't say anything.

"I wonder if you would look into it for me. I may have overlooked something. I also would like you to take over the . . . running of *The Library*. I'm not going to be able to continue much longer."

"Charles, let me tell you. I've been playing with an idea to set up a foundation. It might be good to connect it with *The Library*."

Mr. Sinclair's eyes looked brighter. He asked, "What type of a foundation?"

"Do you remember, when I first visited *The Library*, I asked you what the meaning of life was – what was our purpose here?"

Mr. Sinclair smiled and answered, "Yes, I remember."

"Do you remember what you told me we are to do with our lives?"

"Yes, of course. Learn."

"I am thinking of a foundation that will help people learn."

"Learn what?"

"Learn how to begin walking in the Light. Learn how to take the first steps on a spiritual path."

Mr. Sinclair didn't respond. He was obviously thinking. Finally, he replied, "I think this is why you first came to us."

"What?"

"This is the perfect addition, or next step, for *The Library*. I love this idea."

"I'm just thinking out loud. I haven't even discussed it with Rebekah yet."

"No, it's perfect. I knew you were supposed to come visit with us. I thought it was for you to replace me. Perhaps you will still do that. But this foundation . . . this is why. Yes, it all falls into place now. I see . . ."

There was a knock on the door. A nurse stepped in and said that Jake had used his visitation time.

Jake turned to Charles, "We'll talk more later."

Jake walked out and Peggy walked in.

Jake said, "Jean, he seems very clear. Not confused at all."

"Good. Good."

Mr. Sinclair said to Peggy, "Every single time I talk with Jake, something good happens. The Lord is with him."

Peggy replied, "I think a better way to say that is to say that he is with the Lord."

Mr. Sinclair smiled. He said, "Yes, that is better. You are right Peggy."

Mr. Le Couteau and Jake, while standing out in the hall waiting for Peggy, both felt uncomfortable. Not knowing what else to talk about, Mr. Le Couteau told Jake about the roof over the walkway and all the new houses around the lake. *The Library* had purchased three and rented them out to researchers for two weeks or more at a time. This way, they didn't have to drive back and forth from a motel or stay in *The Lodge*. They could use a kitchen and they could bring their families with them. There was now a paved path that encircled the lake. It did not yet have a roof. All around the lake, *The Library* had lots for sale. Some of their employees had purchased lots and were in the process of building houses on those lots.

When Peggy came out, Mr. Le Couteau headed inside to see Mr. Sinclair. Jake told him that Peggy and he were going to wait in the visitors' waiting room. They would wait on him there. He nodded in response.

Peggy asked, "What did you think?"

"He seemed to be pretty good to me."

"You haven't been around him much lately. He has gone downhill some since you and Rebekah visited a couple of years ago. At that time, he really thought you were going to move up and become the Assistant Director."

"Time wasn't right."

"Is it now?"

"I don't know."

"Can you go in his hospital room and pray for him to be all better and have him be healed?"

"Peggy, it doesn't work that way. If it did, we could keep praying for someone over and over and that person would never die."

"I didn't mean that, I just . . ."

"Of course, I have been praying for him. I've been praying for you, Arthur and Larry, for Mr. Le Couteau and his wife, for many people. I think to pray for a healing like you are suggesting, for me, I need to feel the direction of the Holy Spirit. That's not everyone. Just me. I don't understand it all yet. I'm still asking for guidance."

Mr. Le Couteau returned. He said, "He fell asleep on me."

Peggy asked, "Is that good or bad?"

"I don't know."

Jake asked, "When will John arrive?"

"When I talked with him, he said today. That's all I know."

Jake said, "I guess all three of us need to call our spouses."

Two days later, after running a series of tests, Mr. Sinclair was dismissed from the hospital. He left with four new prescriptions for his heart. His son, John, left on November 12th on a flight to New York. On Wednesday, November 13th, Mr. Le Couteau and Peggy took Mr. Sinclair back to *The Library*.

On the same day, Jake headed south. During his brief time in Québec City, Jake had not ventured out to see any of the city. He had stayed at his motel. He just didn't want to see anything that would remind him of Laura. As he made that decision, he told himself that he was being silly. The week with Laura in Québec City was one of the best weeks of his life. He should cherish those memories – not be afraid of them. Jake told himself that he did cherish them. However, he was afraid that he would "see" Laura at certain places and go through all the heartbreak all over again. Jake realized that, although he had learned to accept Laura's death, he was still grieving.

On the way back to *The Library*, Mr. Sinclair told Mr. Le Couteau and Peggy that he now knew why Jake had originally come to them back over eight years earlier. He told them that it was going to play out as it was supposed to do.

By the time Jake got back home, it was dark. As he drove up the driveway and saw the old house with the lights shining, he thought to himself, *This does feel like home*. Before he got out of the car, Jake said a little prayer. He said, "Thank you, Jesus. Thank you for getting me home safely. Thank you for being with Charles. Thank you for Rebekah. Thank you for Scott and Sarah. Thank you for this home. Thank you for all Your blessings. Help me to know what to do next. I think I'd rather stay here. However, Lord, if You want me to go . . . elsewhere, I will go. Thank you, Jesus. Amen."

CHAPTER FORTY-EIGHT

"Blessed are those who have learned to acclaim you, who walk in the light of your presence, O Lord."

– Psalm 89:15

Mid 8th Century B. C.

Disappointing both of their mothers, Rebekah and Jake decided to celebrate Christmas at home with Scott and Sarah. Christmas was on a Wednesday and it had been snowing since Saturday. Due to all the snow, the Christmas Eve service at their church had been canceled. They held their own service in front of the Christmas tree. The lights from the tree, the fireplace and several candles lit the room. Jake told the story of baby Jesus in Bethlehem. He read from the second chapter of Luke, verses 4 - 20. Even little Sarah seemed to understand that celebrating Christmas was something special.

The birthday month of May 2014 for the Flemings had come and gone. Jake was now 51. Rebekah was 45. Scott was 5 and Sarah was 3. Rebekah and Jake were, by far, the oldest parents of all the children in Scott's summer kindergarten class at a private Christian school.

It was Saturday, June 14th, 2014 and Jake was sitting in Mr. Sinclair's office at *The Library*. Mr. Sinclair, now 84, was puffing on his pipe.

He smiled and said, "Let's talk."

Jake replied, "Okay."

"I understand that you and Rebekah have decided how you want to establish a foundation here."

"Yes, we have."

"Would you explain it to me? Simply, so that I can understand."

"Sure. Connecting with the mission of *The Library* to provide the resources for people to learn, we want this foundation to provide the means by which people can become aware of their spirituality and learn how to develop that."

"That sounds wonderful. How would it manifest itself?"

"That is still, of course, in the planning stages. Rebekah and I have been praying about it. We are thinking that the foundation would provide a week of free instruction to teach Christians how to grow in their . . . spiritual life. We are thinking of providing also a week of free lodging – maybe even free meals."

"I don't know. I've always found it is good for people to have 'some skin in the game' when you do things like this. It makes them more committed."

"You're probably right about that, Charles."

"You are thinking in terms of a retreat?"

"Yes, I suppose so. We would need to get at least a couple of truly spiritual Christians to agree to come here and teach."

"You think that will be effective?"

"With the help of the Holy Spirit, with the right instruction, the right curriculum and people who truly want to learn . . . yes."

"I see." That was all Mr. Sinclair said.

Jake continued, "Life is for learning. That's something I learned from you. People today seem to think that they have no time to confront the real issues of living a spiritual life. I think that the most important thing for all humans to learn is a knowledge and an awareness of divinity – of God. Those who would be accepted to this one-week class would already have that awareness . . . as they would all be Christians. This class would provide practical instruction on how to begin living their lives in the light that is Jesus. Charles, I was once a 'Sunday only' Christian. I believed that Jesus was Who He said He was but I didn't live like I knew that it also involved living a Christian life in fellowship with Jesus. I didn't allow the Holy Spirit to influence me very much. I did things; I said things; I thought things . . . things that a Christian should not.

"Actually, one of the things I learned, as I began to grow spiritually, is that life's difficulties can be developed by a Christian to use as a source of strength. As I look back at times in my life, I can see, from today's perspective, that some of the toughest times led me to spiritual growth. My divorce, for example. I don't think anyone wants or expects that their marriage will end in divorce. I didn't want mine to end with a divorce. Nonetheless, it was best for both of us. It was the beginning of my spiritual awareness. I really don't know what has happened to her. Once the divorce was finalized, I never heard of her anymore. She obviously wasn't happy with me. I certainly wasn't happy with her. I presume she is better off now. I certainly hope so. Every now and then, I pray for her.

"Anyway, Charles, I think a class on learning how to understand that all of us physical human beings have a spiritual aspect to our lives . . . is extraordinarily important for a Christian to learn. I mean, we all have eternal souls. Where those souls go when our physical bodies die is of paramount importance, don't you think?"

Mr. Sinclair smiled and blew out a stream of pipe smoke. He answered, "As one who is near that physical death, I am extremely interested in the destination of my soul. As a Christian, I know what Jesus has said and I am happy and secure in that knowledge."

"For some Christians, understanding that can be the beginning of a walk in the light."

"Yes, Jake, I can see that."

"In 1 John 3:18, it says that we should not love with words but with actions. We often say that we love all of our fellow brothers and sisters in Christ. That is easy to say. This foundation, that we are thinking of creating, is one way of putting action to those words."

"Yes, I like that. So, Jake, how much money are you and Rebekah going to put toward this foundation?"

Jake replied, "Most of what we have – three and a half million."

Charles said, "That is strong. You know *The Library* has an endowment. I can match your amount from our endowment and that will give your foundation seven million. It should be able to operate off the interest of that."

"I would think so. Charles, this is an unexpected . . . I mean, I never thought that . . . thank you."

Mr. Sinclair smiled. "I believe in what you are trying to do – to get Christians to begin living like Christians should."

"Exactly. I don't want people to think that I think I am better than them. I am simply a little farther down the path than some of them are. I've certainly been at the beginning of the path. We all have. One's place on the path doesn't make anyone better than anyone else . . . perhaps maybe just a little older."

Charles laughed. He said, "I know what you mean. However, I've seen old Christians – some even older than me – who have yet to begin their walk down the spiritual path."

"True. I hope that we can accept all Christians who are ready to begin that walk."

Jake found Rebekah and the children in the park that had been built on the left side of *The Lodge*. Sarah and Rebekah were on swings. They were swinging in unison and Jake thought that they both looked beautiful. Scott was intensely watching something in the lake. He laid on the ground right next to the lake – staring at the water. When Sarah saw Jake, she jumped off the swing and ran straight to him. As he held her, he turned around and around. She squealed with delight. Rebekah walked over to join them. Together, all three of them walked over to Scott. Jake put Sarah down and all three of them lay down on the ground next to Scott.

Jake asked, "What are you looking at Scott?"

He answered, "A fish. He keeps swimming back and forth."

Sarah said, "I don't see him."

"Right there," Scott said, pointing at the water. "I wonder what he is thinking."

Jake said, "I don't think fish are big thinkers."

Scott responded, "After my examination of this fish, I must conclude that you are correct. Fish are not thinkers."

"I still don't see the fish," Sarah complained.

Rebekah said, "I don't see him either, Sweetie."

They got up and headed back to *The Lodge*.

Prior to driving up this time, after a lot of discussion and prayer, Rebekah and Jake had decided to make the move up to *The Library*. Jake had told Rebekah of Mr. Sinclair's generous addition to their monetary gift to set up the foundation. He had not discussed it with Mr. Sinclair but was certain that the offer to become the Assistant Director of *The Library* was still on the table. Now, Rebekah and Jake were trying to determine if they wanted to live in Pohenegamook or buy a house on *The Library's* lake.

After lunch, they drove over to the town of Pohenegamook. The Pohenegamook Lake was huge. There were houses built right on the lake. They peeked in the windows of two houses for sale. They liked neither. They drove up the driveway at one house that was for sale, however, they did not get out of their car. They simply didn't like the look of the house. Rebekah and Jake looked at each other and they both shook their head "no." Jake commented that the lake was nice. Rebekah countered by saying that the lake at *The Library* was also very nice. Before driving back to *The Library*, they ate at a fast food place.

Monday morning, Jake was back in Mr. Sinclair's office. The pipe tobacco smoke was thick.

Mr. Sinclair spoke, "Jake, let's get something out of the way."

"Okay."

"I am officially offering you the position of Assistant Director of *The Library*. Do you accept?"

Jake smiled. He nodded and answered, "Yes."

"Good. My plan, right now, is to work for another year until I am eighty-five and then retire. At that point, you will become the Director and your salary will double."

"My salary?"

"Yes, these are paid positions."

"That's nice. I guess I'll need a salary now."

"When can you begin?"

"Let's see, this is June 16th . . . sometime before school starts. Scott will be in first grade. I noticed that the developer is finishing up with more new houses down at the end of the lake. Do you know anything about them?"

"No, I really don't. You thinking of moving into one of those?"

"It's an option, I suppose."

"You do realize that your new position comes with a full apartment here?"

"No, I didn't realize that. What else comes with it?"

"Cafeteria privileges. Use of the company van. . . . Tuition paid for two children."

"Charles, you're making this up as you go along?"

They both smiled.

Mr. Sinclair said, "One of the perks of being the Director. Jake, I want you and Rebekah to be comfortable here."

"I do think that we'd be more comfortable in a separate house than living here underground."

Mr. Sinclair puffed on his pipe and said, "I expect you would. Will you have any trouble selling your house down in New Hampshire?"

"We're not sure, Charles, that we want to sell it. We may try to keep it and rent it out. We'll have to sell our cattle and chickens."

"Cattle?"

"Four head."

"I see."

"That will actually be hard on Rebekah. All four of them

are pets. She's given them names and frequently pets them."

"And you?"

"I pet them too."

Mr. Sinclair laughed.

"This afternoon, we might drive around to the end of the lake and take a look at those new houses."

"Please do that. You meeting with Jean tomorrow?"

"Yes, in the morning."

"Good, good."

That afternoon, Rebekah, Scott, Sarah and Jake drove around to the end of the lake. The developers had built a nice smooth road all the way around the lake. Instead of being on the shore side, it was behind all the properties. All of the houses faced the lake but their driveways connected to the road behind their houses. There was a paved walk all the way around the lake that was right next to the shoreline.

On the drive, Jake said to Rebekah, "If we keep our place in Contoocook and pay cash for one of these houses, it'll just about wipe out our savings. If we finance a house here, the interest we pay will be more than the interest we will get from the bank from our savings. We could sell our place in Contoocook and use that money to pay for a house here."

"You know, I'd really like to keep our current home."

"I know. Me too. It would be a great place to live when we retire."

"Yes. You know, before we came up here, we talked about all this. We decided to keep our home and rent it. Let's see what our options are here. It seems strange to me. I grew up in a cottage that was well over a hundred years old – built in the 19th century. We've been living in a house that was built in the 18th century. Now, we're thinking of living in a brand new house built in the 21st century."

"Remember Rebekah, when we both saw our current place, it felt right. It felt like home. Let's see if any of these feel that way."

"Okay."

When they got out of their car, Jake spoke to Scott and Sarah. He said, "Now listen, this is important. Your mom and I need your help. We are going to look at some houses. We may choose one to live in while we are up here. We want to know what each of you thinks about the houses. Okay?"

The both nodded yes and Scott said, "Absolutely."

"Good. Let us know if you like something or if you don't like something. Scott, you look after your little sister."

Scott replied, "Okay."

It turned out that there were three houses under construction. All three were almost finished. They parked behind the first one of the three. Then they all walked around to the path that went around the lake near the shore. Standing on the path, they looked at the first house. Rebekah and Jake looked at each other, shook their heads "no" and started walking to the next house. Jake picked up Sarah and carried her down the path to this house. This one, they toured. Scott had several comments.

As they left the house Rebekah whispered to Jake, "I'm not feeling it."

They continued on down the path to the third house. Looking at it, both Rebekah and Jake smiled. Rebekah said, "I think I'm going to like this one."

"It does feel nice," Jake responded.

To the left of the front door, which was not centered but over to the right side of the front of the house, was a huge glass wall. Inside, all four of them stood looking out through this glass at the lake. There was a large fireplace in the room.

Scott said, "I like this room."

Sarah echoed his sentiment by saying, "Me too."

Rebekah agreed, "Me too."

Jake smiled and said, "Me too. Let's see what the rest looks like."

Later, standing out on the path looking at the house, Rebekah said, "I like how they have done the garages here. They all open to the rear of course . . . because the road is behind each house, but I like how this one is connected to the house."

Scott said, "Mom, they are all connected to their houses."

"I know. But I like how this one is done."

Holding the description of the property in his hand, Jake asked Scott and Sarah, "Would you like to live in this house?"

Scott said, "Yes, I think it would be nice."

Sarah asked, "Can we bring Ruffles with us?"

Rebekah answered, "Yes, of course Ruffles will come with us and live here too."

Sarah said, "It feels like living in the woods. I like it."

Rebekah had her own copy of the property description that she too had gotten from the kitchen counter. As they were walking back to their car, she said, "I thought these were all one acre lots. This one is almost two acres."

"Yeah, I noticed that. Must be due to the lay of the land here at the curve of the lake where it begins to go back."

"Is that why it costs more than those others?"

"Maybe. I suspect that all that glass in the front room is expensive."

"I like that."

"It is nice." Jake picked Sarah up and they continued to walk back to where they had parked.

Driving back on the road through the trees, Jake said, "Sarah, you are right – living here would be like living in the woods. Is anyone hungry?"

Both children loudly admitted that they were hungry and that they wanted to eat at the fast food place at which they had eaten the day before.

Jake looked at Rebekah.

She said, "Okay by me."

Jake said, "I guess this is a special occasion."

"Yeah!"

Jake drove over to Pohenegamook. After paying for their meals, Jake said, "That's just about the last of my Canadian money.

CHAPTER FORTY-NINE

"Love is patient, love is kind. It does not envy, it does not boast, it is not proud. It is not rude, it is not self-seeking, it is not easily angered, it keeps no record of wrongs. Love does not delight in evil but rejoices with the truth. It always protects, always trusts, always hopes, always perseveres."

"And now these three remain: faith, hope and love. But the greatest of these is love."

– I Corinthians 13:4-7 and 13

Mid 1st Century A.D.

At 8 a.m. the next morning, Pamela was leading Jake through the hallways to the meeting room where Mr. Le Couteau was waiting.

Pamela said, "I understand you are joining us here."

"Yes."

"Congratulations!"

"Thank you. It doesn't take long for news to get around down here, does it?"

Pamela laughed. "Oh no, it travels fast. Not very many secrets either."

"I'll have to remember that."

"Here we are." Pamela knocked and opened the door.

Jake said, "Thank you."

Pamela replied, "God bless you."

Jake nodded his thanks and responded, "Thank you."

Mr. Le Couteau walked up and shook Jake's hand.

Both with mugs of coffee and paper plates with donuts, the two men sat down in their usual places.

Jake said, "Jean, it is difficult for me to think that it was nine years ago when I first sat here with you."

Mr. Le Couteau smiled. He said, "A lot of water under the bridge since then."

"A lot. I wonder. Little Victoria must be eighteen or nineteen by now. Guess she's in college somewhere."

"Probably. You've never heard anything from her?"

"No, I wouldn't expect to."

"You did save her life."

Jake took a bite of his donut.

Mr. Le Couteau asked, "Have you ever heard from any of Laura's relatives?"

Jake was a little surprised by the question but quickly answered, "No, not at all. . . . I've made no attempt either."

"Peggy said that she thought they were . . . unpleasant people – at the funeral."

"It was a funeral. People are, perhaps, not themselves."

Mr. Le Couteau changed the subject; "Anyway, I want to welcome you to our little group. I understand that you are going to join us later this summer."

"Yes. I'm looking forward to it."

"Good. I'm sure you will be a major asset to *The Library*."

"Thank you. I'll try to be. I will be leaning on you for guidance and help."

"Anytime."

Jake nodded, "Thank you. One of the first things I'm going to have to do is learn my way around these hallways. I can't have Pamela leading me around all the time."

Mr. Le Couteau laughed.

"You know, Jean, Mr. Sinclair first asked me directly to join you guys back in 2005. He brought it up at Laura's funeral."

"Yes, I remember him mentioning it. You know what, Jake? After our first lengthy talk together, I thought you would be a great addition to our organization."

"It was not the right time. I am a different person today

than I was nine years ago."

Touching his gray hair, Mr. Le Couteau said, "Aren't we all?"

"Charles and I were talking about something similar to this. I did things, went places in my teens, twenties and thirties that I would never say or do today. Over the years, people change. Most of us mature. Christians should develop spiritually. That is what we are going to try to do with the new foundation."

"Yes, that is going to be a great addition to *The Library*. Is Rebekah going to be . . . active with that?"

"We don't know. I think she would be a tremendous person to speak with groups of women. Of course, I'm prejudiced. She doesn't think so. She is thinking that we should probably use professional psychologists or sociologists who understand how to approach topics and address them. I think we need people speaking and sharing from their hearts."

"I can see both points. Perhaps, we can find both attributes in one person."

"Perhaps. Anyway, Rebekah is more interested, I think, in getting back in the classroom as a teacher."

"I'm sure we could use her with our private school."

"She will want to wait until Sarah is a little older."

"Sure."

"She could teach a class at the retreat or whatever develops with the foundation."

"Yes, that's an option. Jake, are you aware of the fruits of the Spirit?"

"Yes, I am so very grateful for them. What? Do you want me to name them? I'm not sure I can. How many are there? Nine?"

Mr. Le Couteau smiled. "Yes, nine. Do you know where they are given?"

Jake smiled. "This reminds me – before we were married, Rebekah 'tested' me to see if I was aware of something in the Bible. Luckily, I passed her test. I think the fruits of the Holy Spirit are in Galatians."

"Yes, you pass again."

"What about them?"

"You mentioned that you have changed since your teens, twenties and thirties. Are the fruits of the Holy Spirit what changed you?"

"Good question. Let's see, what are they all? Love, I know is always first."

"Yes, what else?"

"Self-control is probably the one with which I have the most trouble."

"I've never seen any evidence of that."

"Jean, I get mad at myself. I get frustrated with myself. When I do, I tell myself that I need more control of myself so that I don't get so frustrated when things don't go as I expect."

"I'm not following you."

"Oh, it's usually something silly. For instance, I remember recently I was trying to unlock the door in the dark. The light next to the door was out and I couldn't remember to replace the bulb during the day. I only remembered it at night. Anyway, I dropped my key and then I couldn't find it. I got frustrated and angry at myself. I do get over it quickly."

"That's just being human."

"Exactly. Self-control is a fruit of the Spirit. I should not allow myself to lose control over such small silly ridiculous things – but I still do. And then I get upset with myself for getting upset over some little stupid thing."

"Okay, but we have several fruits from the Holy Spirit."

"Yes, I know. And I truly appreciate them. There is joy and a sense of peace. Kindness, patience and goodness are three more. Uh, I don't know. Do you . . . wait, faithfulness is another."

"One more."

"One more. I can't think of it. What is it?"

"Gentleness."

"Gentleness, yes."

"Everyone who has accepted Jesus should live by the Holy Spirit. If we do, these are the fruits of living under the direction of the Spirit."

"Yes, you are right, Jean. Thank you. This is something of which we should definitely make Christians aware during our foundation classes."

"I would think so."

"Thank you."

Mr. Le Couteau smiled. He stated, "Self-control, huh?"

"Afraid so."

"Honestly, when you describe it like that, I could put myself in the same category."

Jake tilted his head to indicate he understood. Then he said, "When we see all the turmoil in our society today, we can see how many people do not have the fruits of the Spirit."

"You first have to have the Holy Spirit in order to receive those fruits."

"Of course. Jesus said that we had to be born twice. Once in the natural physical way from our mothers and secondly, be born again in spirit. In order to receive the birth of the Holy Spirit, one must acknowledge Jesus as one's personal savior and Lord. Then, that person will receive the Holy Spirit. From that comes love, joy, peace, kindness . . . gentleness and all the others. I suspect that those who come to our classes on spirituality will have already accepted Christ but have not allowed the Holy Spirit to guide them. I used to be that way. I understand it."

Mr. Le Couteau replied, "Me too. It takes time and prayer, I think, to grow in the Spirit."

"Not necessarily, Jean. I think that there are some individuals who receive a baptism of the Holy Spirit in which they almost immediately are aware of the presence and guidance of the Holy Spirit. Most will also be given the gift of speaking in tongues. Some will then be given other gifts – healing, for example. However, for most Christians, I think you are probably right – it is a gradual growth and development of learning to follow the Holy Spirit. As these Christians grow spiritually, the Holy Spirit can also give them gifts . . . including healing, wisdom, knowledge, prophecy and others."

"Yes, I agree. I have even met people who received that type of anointment of the Spirit. I am thinking of two and they were both very humble men. They always said that everything that happened through them was due to God, not them."

"Of course. Jesus still performs miracles. He does so in response to prayer that is offered through the guidance of the Holy Spirit."

"Yes. Are you planning, Jake, to teach in any of the classes that will be offered during the . . . retreats? What are you actually going to call the Foundation that you are starting?"

"I think I'm going to leave the name up to Rebekah. She has been working hard on it and I'm expecting that she will come up with a good name. As far as me teaching – no, I'm not planning on doing any of that. I expect helping Charles with *The Library* will be pretty much a full-time job. I guess I could be a guest speaker from time to time."

"Jake, you mentioned all the turmoil in our society today. You indicated that it is a result of people not knowing the Holy Spirit. Tell me what you mean."

"Sure. I can give you many examples. They are all around us. Look at those various groups who march in the streets yelling obscenities and carrying signs with obscenities written on them. When I see that, I think 'what do they expect to accomplish? Who is paying them?' I conclude that the objective of such demonstrations is to get on television. Journalism today is, of course, a complete total joke. Consequently, they will run shots of the people marching, yelling and carrying signs over and over. Their goal, as journalists, is to help make their audiences think that this is what most people think. Now obviously, neither the demonstrators nor the 'journalists' have the fruits of the Holy Spirit. There is no joy, no kindness, no gentleness in any of them. I feel sorry for them and find myself praying for them."

"What else?"

"There are so many. I recently saw the results of a study which indicated that a majority of people who identified themselves as 'practicing Christians' support having female pastors. An even higher majority of Catholics support female priests. Where does this view come from? Certainly not from the Bible. Numerous times, specifically in 1st Corinthians and also in 1st Timothy, the Bible states that women are not to be leaders in the church. I have even heard this explained away by saying that Jesus was a victim of the cultural norms of His day. Today, we are more enlightened, more progressive than those of Jesus' time. Women, according to the Bible, have important and necessary roles to perform in the church. However, they do not have the same roles as men. Imagine saying that Jesus was a victim of the times. Jesus is God. Jesus was not a victim. He came here as a human to save us from our sins. He is the total and complete representation of love.

"It is supposed that our society has progressed to a level where denying life to an unborn baby is an accepted and approved procedure. The fact that it is murder is ignored. Our culture has also evolved to the point where marriage can now take place between people of the same sex. Marriage is a religious institution. Up until a couple of hundred years ago, the government was not even a part of marriages. As long as no one is being hurt or children aren't involved, a court of law has no jurisdiction over religious beliefs. For over five thousand years, we have had a written definition that a marriage is between a man and a woman and the ceremony is performed by a religious leader. Yet, today, a court believes it has the authority to overturn God's laws. Can you see any of the fruits of the Holy Spirit in these people? Of course not.

"Jean, one of the latest things I have heard about is that now, gender is a choice. If a man chooses to identify as a woman, then our culture and our society must accept that choice and start calling him 'miss' instead of 'mister.'"

"Where do you see all this headed, Jake?"

"It's on a track to get worse. I do feel sorry for these people without any awareness of the Holy Spirit. I do pray that the day will come when they too will experience the love and joy that Christ gives. What bothers me is the Christians who think these types of things are acceptable. It's like they think God's Word is up for a vote and our society today has voted to change God's Word to fit our lifestyle. The opinion of man means absolutely nothing to God. God is unchanging. If one hundred percent of all humans on earth said that it is okay to murder babies, it would not change the mind of God. To say that Jesus was not enlightened is pure nonsense. This is Jesus Christ, the Son of God – God. And we are going to say that He was wrong. Incredible nonsense.

"You know, Jean, I can understand all this political correctness rubbish coming from people who do not know God. However, when people who say that they are Christians – followers of Christ – when they agree with things that are absolutely, according to the Bible, wrong . . . then it has to make one wonder. It reminds me of what Jesus said in Matthew 16:26."

Jean smiled. "Yes, I agree."

Jake said the verse out loud. "What good will it be for a man if he gains the whole world, yet forfeits his soul? Or what can a man give in exchange for his soul?"

"Jake, people today don't seem to understand that."

"I'm afraid not. Yet, it seems obvious. In Romans, chapter six, it says that 'the gift of God is eternal life in Christ Jesus our Lord.' How can someone not see the importance of accepting Jesus?"

"Jake, they simply don't believe what Jesus said."

"Suppose someone won the lottery and suddenly had two hundred million dollars to play with . . . that person could . . ."

"The government would take half."

"You're right, Jean. Okay, they have one hundred million dollars. They could still do almost anything here on earth. Suppose that they built a huge house, traveled in luxury all over the world, ate fine foods, bought expensive clothes and jewelry, whatever. Then, without knowing Jesus as Savior and Lord, that person died. What would happen to his soul? Jesus said he would lose it."

Jean said, "There are only two places a soul can go . . .

Heaven or Hell. Jesus is the only way for one's soul to get to Heaven."

Jake continued this thread of their talk. He said, "I learned from Mr. Sinclair that we are here on earth to learn. What we are talking about is something that everyone needs to learn – sometime during their life. Let's say a person lives to be eighty or ninety years old. During all those years, what is the single most important thing that person can do? Answer: learn how to prepare one's soul for eternity. When we die, our souls separate from our fleshly bodies. Those souls will go to one of two places – either to be with God or to be without God."

"I hadn't thought of it quite like that. But I do agree with what you just said. It is most certainly the most important thing that everyone needs to learn. Where is their soul going to spend eternity?"

Jake responded, "I know we have to live our lives as humans while we are in our human bodies here on earth. Nonetheless, for Christians, I don't understand the lack of awareness that this is all so very temporary."

"So true."

"I do understand being a Sunday Christian. I was one for years."

"What changed you?"

"Reading the Bible. Reading what Jesus actually said. It made me realize I was not experiencing the fruits of the Holy Spirit. It made me realize that I had not allowed the Holy Spirit to guide me. It changed my entire perspective on life."

"How? In what way?"

"In every way. For several years, when I was a Sunday Christian, I had pretty much dead-end jobs. I thought that if I had more income, I would be happy. Then, I allowed the Holy Spirit into my life. I mean, he was always there. I just wasn't paying attention. I didn't follow his direction and guidance. After I began listening to the Holy Spirit, I still had dead-end jobs with little income. I was still living paycheck to paycheck; but, major change, I was happy. The fruits of the Spirit were mine. Mine, without the money I thought I needed to be happy. I realized that living without a lot of money was okay. I had Jesus and the Holy Spirit in my life. As Isaiah 2:5 says *'let us walk in the light of the Lord.'* I was. And, I was happy. I didn't have much. I didn't have a woman in my life. I had several 'first dates.' But I never found anyone with whom I wanted to have a second date. But you know what, Jean? I wasn't lonely. I knew that Jesus was always with me."

"I understand that. I know what you are saying. One of my favorite verses along these lines is from John, 8:12."

As he recognized the verse, Jake smiled and said, "Yes."

Jean quoted it by saying, "Jesus said, 'I am the light of the world. Whoever follows me will never walk in darkness, but will have *the light of life.*'"

"Jean, a verse that I like along these lines explains how I was once a Sunday only Christian but the Holy Spirit changed that. It is from Ephesians 5:8-9. It says, 'For you (meaning me, Jean) were once in darkness, but now you are light in the Lord. *Live as children of light* for the fruit of the light consists in all goodness, righteousness and truth.'"

"Yes. I totally see that."

"You know, Jean, one of the things I have learned is that, as a Christian, we should . . . we need . . . to be constantly aware of Jesus throughout every day. It is not easy. I try. But I forget. I get involved in things and forget to acknowledge the presence of Jesus."

Mr. Le Couteau laughed, "I'm riding with you in that same boat."

"I have tried to say 'Thank you, Jesus' at least once every hour that I am awake. I haven't been successful yet."

"I know. You would think it would be easy. It just shows how involved we get. I'll be sitting in my office and two or three hours will have gone by and I never once thought of Jesus."

"I understand exactly how that goes. It happened to me all the time when I worked at Excalibur. I tried to alternate between 'Thank you, Jesus' and 'I trust you, Jesus.' I still would forget sometimes. And every time I acknowledge the presence of Jesus and the Holy Spirit, I feel a sense of joy."

"I think, Jake, it just shows how strong our humanity is. By that, I mean simply being human. I think that that sense of joy you feel is from just recognizing God. As I'm driving, sometimes I look at beautiful clouds and recognize the presence of God with me. It is a wonderful feeling."

"Joy."

"Exactly. Joy."

"Another thing I like to do is to sit quietly by myself, in a comfortable chair I've had for years, and 'know that He is God.' I used to do this for thirty minutes every morning. Now, with the children, sometimes I only do it for ten minutes. Nonetheless, the stillness . . . the quietness is a real blessing. For me, it is a wonderful way to begin each day."

"We were talking earlier about walking in the light. What does that phrase mean to you?"

Without hesitating, Jake answered, "For me, it means walking with love for others. One thing I have learned is that every single person is loved by God. Every single person's life has meaning and is important. It doesn't matter what a person has done; it doesn't matter what color a person's skin is; it doesn't matter what sexual orientation a person has; it doesn't matter what a person's political perspective is; it doesn't matter if a person is an atheist; all of those people have a soul, their lives have meaning and God loves them. So, for me, living in the light means loving other people as Jesus does. Jesus loves everyone. I think that, as Christians, as followers of Jesus, we should also love everyone. It is difficult sometimes."

Mr. Le Couteau smiled, "That is certainly true. What you say about love, though, is accurate. Christians should try to love everyone. We can disagree with people but still love them."

"Of course. When terrorists murder Christians and blow up their churches, they are removing people who pray for them. When homosexuals protest churches and businesses that disagree with their lifestyle, they are protesting against people who pray for them. When the liberal democrats try to eliminate any mention of God, they are distancing themselves from people who pray for them. Christians aren't going to harm terrorists, homosexuals or liberals. Instead, they will pray for them and love them. If we are living our lives in the light that is Jesus, that includes loving everyone – even those who say bad things about us. Terrorists, homosexuals and liberals will attack Christians but Christians won't attack them. We disagree with them but we won't harm them. We pray for them."

Mr. Le Couteau responded by saying, "Especially those. It is easy to love people you know – say, the people in your church or your neighbors. It is more difficult to love people who are hateful, who are prejudiced, who despise Christians, who tell lies about you and on and on. However, as Christians, we are to love even those people."

"Yes, I agree. Without love, there is nothing. Love is what separates a Sunday only Christian from a true follower of Christ. Love is what makes a Christian Christian."

CHAPTER FIFTY

"I am the light of the world. Whoever follows me will never walk in darkness, but will have the light of life."

– John 8:12

Late 1ˢᵗ Century A.D.

Disappointing both of their mothers again, Rebekah and Jake decided to celebrate Christmas at home with Scott and Sarah. It was their first Christmas in their new home. Rebekah had decorated with lots of greenery and candles. She even hung some mistletoe in their bedroom.

It had been an exciting and extremely busy five months. They had moved into their new home at the end of the lake in August 2014. Jake had begun his duties as Assistant Director of *The Library* and Scott had entered the first grade. Rebekah had done much of the work of getting the foundation established. They were expecting to begin the retreat classes in the summer of 2015. Rebekah had decided to call the foundation *Walking on Water*.

It was late on Christmas Eve. Snow was gently falling. As the lights twinkled, the Christmas tree was sparkling. Gifts, wrapped with Christmas-themed paper and tied with ribbons and bows, were under the tree – waiting to be opened early on Christmas morning. Instrumental Christmas carols were playing. Scott and Sarah were sleeping in their beds. Standing in front of the large glass window and holding hands, Jake and Rebekah looked out across Lake Laura. Ruffles was at their feet - also looking out the window at the snow coming down.

Even with all the lights on at *The Lodge*, Jake had made sure that one little bright red light, at the other end of the lake, remained on, to guide anyone who might see it, to *The Library*.

Books by Byron Edwards

Non-Fiction

How to Have a Happy Marriage
ISBN: 0-9623979-0-3
Bestseller

Fiction

Cherokee Adventure
ISBN: 978-0805925890

Secrets of Lost Atlantis
ISBN: 0-932349-29-3

Dawn
ISBN: 978-0595099887

The Mystery of Melissa's First Date
ISBN: 978-0595188369
Bestseller

Lips
ISBN: 978-0595673872

Living in the Light
ISBN: 978-1-64373-345-6

Author Byron Edwards' website: byronedwards.net

CPSIA information can be obtained
at www.ICGtesting.com
Printed in the USA
LVHW080953311022
731983LV00006B/16/J

9 781643 733487